"ANGEL EYES has what Lustbader fans are looking for—action, some glimmers of faraway cultures, some hope for heroes of tomorrow."
Palm Beach Post

"Here, we meet modern-day women who, although they are feminine, also happen to be competent, intelligent and brave. . . . The beauty of ANGEL EYES is that there is no waste—every character and each twist or turn of the plot is there for a purpose."
The Miami Herald

"Global in scope . . . [It] has all the hallmarks of this popular author's work: heroic women and men in a complicated plot that hurtles along like a high-speed Japanese train."
The Trenton Times

"Has all the elements of a bestseller—travel, romance, violence, conspiracy and betrayal in high places—and Lustbader's attentions to martial arts and Zen teachings again spice the mix."
Publishers Weekly

Also by Eric Lustbader
Published by Fawcett Books:

THE NINJA
SIRENS
BLACK HEART
THE MIKO
JIAN
SHAN
ZERO
FRENCH KISS
WHITE NINJA

The Sunset Warrior Cycle:

THE SUNSET WARRIOR
SHALLOWS OF THE NIGHT
DAI-SAN
BENEATH AN OPAL MOON

ANGEL EYES

Eric Lustbader

FAWCETT CREST • NEW YORK

A Fawcett Crest Book
Published by Ballantine Books
Copyright © 1991 by Eric Van Lustbader

All rights reserved under International and Pan-American Copyright Conventions. Published in the United States by Ballantine Books, a division of Random House, Inc., New York, and simultaneously in Canada by Random House of Canada Limited, Toronto.

Library of Congress Catalog Card Number: 90-82331

ISBN 0-449-21852-X

Manufactured in the United States of America

First Hardcover Edition: February 1991
First International Mass Market Edition: July 1991
First U.S. Mass Market Edition: February 1993

Design by Holly Johnson

ACKNOWLEDGMENTS

Thanks are due to the following for their invaluable assistance:

Jeff Arbital, for nuclear engineering and theory
Bob Immerman, Columbia University
Uri Lubin, Boston University Russian Research Center, for background on Soviet ethnic minorities
Roman Koropeckyi, Ukrainian Institute at Harvard University—Russian Research Center, for the specifics of the Ukranian ethnics inside the USSR
Constanza Collazos, for background on Colombia and specifics for Medellín and Cali
NASA personnel at the Johnson Space Center in Houston:
Bob Holkan, director, Astronaut Training Program
Theresa Gomez, assistant to the Astronaut Selection Board
Bob Kunikoff, for unlimited travel arrangements, and 727 scheduling
Richard Koerner, for Russian translations
My father, for proofing the galleys

Spiritual guidance on my South American tour: Jorge Luis Borges

Dolphin consultant: Mandy

*Who shall ascend the hill
of the Lord?
and who shall stand
in his holy place?
He that hath clean hands,
and a pure heart.*
—PSALMS 24:3–4

*Men must have corrupted nature
a little, for they were not
born wolves, and they have
become wolves.*
—VOLTAIRE

SANCTUARY

BUENOS AIRES/SAN FRANCISCO

Whenever Tori Nunn was bored, she went to Buenos Aires. Partly it was because Buenos Aires was a place she had never worked, so, essentially, no one knew her—what she had been. Partly, it was because in Buenos Aires, sitting beneath the natural awning of the jacarandas, their clattering shade striping her face, she could at last forget Greg. But perhaps more than anything else, she came to this incomplete city because here she could begin again to define herself, as if now even her own shadow had become unrecognizable.

Here, in Buenos Aires, inhabited by the *porteños*—the port dwellers, as the city's natives were known—controlled by the *alta sociedad*, there was a mix of stupendously beautiful, sensual people who were exhaustingly proud even as they were consumed by shame at being *South* Americans. They were, like college dropouts, inevitably embarrassed by themselves and their place in the world. When they went to New York, they always said, "I am flying to North America."

This is what made the *porteños* interesting to Tori: their inner hurt was protected by their cultural traits in the same way a tortoise is protected by its shell. The patrons of the Café la Biela and the nearby Café de la Paix proved this to her. They might smell of imported suntan oil, of perfumes by Calvin Klein and Jean Patou, just as their city might smell of auto fumes and *maté*, the local herb tea, but beneath it all, Tori knew, the *porteños* and their streets were redolent of cigar smoke and marzipan.

This was their history, as Jorge Luis Borges wrote it, as their forefathers had lived it, where illusion, like the rich smoke from rolled tobacco, had come to create the past even as it obscured the present. In the decade after the Second World War, the fathers of these exquisite *porteños* had amassed their wealth by selling their slaughtered cattle and the fruits of their Pampa to a starving Europe. But by the middle of the fifties the excesses of the Peróns had bankrupted the country, throwing Buenos Aires and, indeed, all Argentina into chaos. Escalating terrorism from the far right and left began to tear the country apart. The result was the coming to power of a succession of repressive military juntas.

But the country's frightening, two-year bout with hyperinflation—12,000 percent per year—riots, and civil unrest had toppled a succession of elected governments. Despair had gripped the nation until some months ago, when a coalition led by Las Dinámicas, the two most powerful women in Argentine politics, managed to win control of the government. Their party, the Union of the Democratic Center, had pledged to end Argentina's long history of authoritarianism by instituting reforms granting extensive individual liberty and an end to the crippling control of the government in business. "The beginning of a free market economy," went their successful campaign slogan, "is an end to hyperinflation." The first priority had been to convert the official currency into American dollars, which had the effect of immediately stabilizing the runaway Argentine inflation.

Through all this bloody history, the *porteños* survived and, perhaps, even flourished, for it is said that every Argentine heart beats most strongly for myth, and myth cannot exist save as a balm against pain and suffering.

But myth was too often illusion. And the truth of illusion— the truth that no *porteño* can truly face—is that no matter how dazzling its exterior may be, there is nothing inside.

Tori knew this, knew the *porteños* almost as well as they knew themselves. Thus she was comfortable here in their city, strolling down their wide boulevards, sunbathing amid cocoa flesh on their beaches, surrounded by their aura of failure and by their very real sensuality and sense of style.

These people carried their pain as she did—deep inside them—though often through the chic facade in which they had wrapped themselves she could discern the stench of their desperation.

Tori lifted her arm, ordered another hot chocolate, the richest, thickest in the world. With it, she knew, would come a silver tray of small sweets, an array as heady, as opulent as the smoldering stares of the *chantas* who came to the cafés with their mistresses to while away an hour or two between bouts under the sheets.

A small breeze, redolent of this city's peculiar perfume, stirred the long branches of the jacarandas, and Tori felt the caress of their tears patter across her shoulders, the excess water of these beautiful semi-succulent trees.

The *chantas*—Buenos Aires' wheeler-dealers—interested Tori most of all. She had even allowed one or two to seduce her now and again, but in the end they had found her too much even for them, disconcerted by her habit of watching them intently during the most intimate throes of sexual congress.

"What are you doing?" they would ask her at those moments. "This is a time for release, not concentration."

They did not understand—and she would not tell them—that for her sex with them was to be observed, that by doing so she could pierce their chic shells, feel the texture of their shame and hurt, comparing it with her own. This concentration that so puzzled them was to her as sweet and richly flavored as was her hot chocolate at the Café la Biela.

But this "strangeness," as the *chantas* called it, was hardly the only reason they held her in awe. They had heard stories that she had climbed barefoot the massive Iguazu Falls six hundred miles to the northeast, had, in fact, helped the male members of her party when their strength flagged or they were in trouble. They had heard she was courageous, indefatigable—which was, after all, why they sought to seduce her.

In her strangeness—the enigma of such brute strength and stamina in a female—the *chantas* sought answers to the mysteries that obsessed them: who were they, where did they come from, why were they such failures?

Tori sipped her chocolate, consumed a sweet in one voracious bite. Somewhere, along the Avenida Quintana, a man played a bandoneon, squeezing out a typical tango melody, infused with the bittersweet essences of Latin macho, unrequited love, and blood vengeance.

The Avenida Quintana, filled with swaggering *porteños* and

cliques of rabid Japanese tourists, was one of the main streets of the swank residential Recoleta district. The Recoleta had been born near the end of the last century due to a plague of yellow fever in the city's southern districts that caused the aristocracy to move north. Years ago, when the Recoleta was home to slaughterhouses, its streets ran red with the blood of cattle during the heavy winter rains. Now winter brought only melancholy, and a gathering sense of dissolution. Then, Buenos Aires was to be avoided.

By the time she had finished her second cup of hot chocolate, Tori decided it was time to go. The sun was low in the sky, turning the Recoleta's blocky white high rises the color of blood oranges. Blue shadows lay in the street like the dead, or unwanted reminders of "the disappeared"—those people taken by the military in its zeal to ferret out a group of young radical terrorists. In those days—the seventies—to be a teacher, a union member, or merely to be known as an intellectual, was to risk being drawn into *el proceso*, a trial without either lawyer or jury; it was to risk being "disappeared."

Her thoughts turning by moments more and more morbid, Tori gathered up her purse and small shopping bag. But before she could rise, she saw Estilo. He was a German-Argentine *chanta*, one of the few who had sought out her company but not her bed. He was different in other ways, as well. He was a square-jawed man in his early fifties with long steel-gray, slicked-back hair, a patrician mustache, and a sense of style no full-blooded German ever had. His manner was often brusque, but he told the truth more often than other *chantas*, and for this Tori forgave him everything.

Estilo made his way toward her table. He was smiling, surprised and happy to see her. He had with him a younger man, slim-hipped, wide-shouldered. The man, handsome, with the rugged outdoorsy face of an *estanciero*—a rancher—was most likely in his mid-thirties, roughly the same age as Tori. He was dressed in a pair of baggy silk trousers and a washed silk shirt, open at the neck, under a trim linen sport coat. He had the thick black hair, the heavy-lidded eyes of the Latin *porteño*.

Estilo caught her appraising look. "My darling Tori!" he exclaimed, clamping her in a fervent embrace. "Why didn't you tell me you were coming? I would have made preparations!"

"I didn't know myself until the last minute," Tori said. "You know how my life is."

Estilo gave her a rueful look. "Too chaotic for someone in

6

so early a retirement." He clucked his tongue against the roof of his mouth. "I keep telling you to find a line of work that interests you." He smiled, showing large, nicotine-stained teeth. "And if not, you have a permanent invitation to join my business."

"Just what is your business?" Tori asked.

Estilo threw his head back and laughed, then he grabbed at the sleeve of the younger man, pulled him down to a seat next to him at Tori's table. "Tori Nunn, I'd like you to meet a friend of mine, Ariel Solares. Ariel is a *norteamericano* who spends a majority of his time here. His most fervent desire is to become a *porteño*, no, Ariel?"

"My friend exaggerates, as usual," Ariel Solares said. "Actually, I wish to *understand* the *porteño*. I come to Buenos Aires to soak up the air of the mythical yesterday." He took a deep breath, let it out. "Can you not smell it, perfuming the air like a rose?" He shrugged. "My own past—my whole life up until now—could not be more prosaic, so I visit Buenos Aires to let this city touch me, perhaps in some way to change me."

"Nonsense," Estilo said. "You come here to do business." But Tori could see that he was impressed with what Ariel had said. Estilo, like all *porteños*, was drawn to myth and all its fascinating ramifications. For him, ancient gods dwelled in the rain forests and in the Pampa, and, because they had been written about, spirits inhabited his city, sitting like gargoyles upon the cornices of the modern buildings. This was the power of myth.

"You speak of Buenos Aires as if it were Lourdes," Tori said, suddenly wanting to draw Ariel out. "As if it had mystical healing powers." It did for her, why not for him?

Ariel Solares cocked his head. "Well, I never thought of it in just that way, but perhaps there is some truth in what you say. But 'healing,' I don't know whether that is quite the correct word. I am not sick, merely bored."

"But, my friend, surely boredom is a form of sickness," Estilo said, his gaze swinging from Ariel to Tori. "A person—all people—need a purpose. Without one, life becomes meaningless, and further sickness—of a deeper, more serious nature—will surely follow."

Now Tori knew that Estilo was speaking directly to her, and she averted her eyes. The tango music, drifting along the avenue, had turned bitter, introspective, a harbinger of the last burst of violence and fury that was, inevitably, to come.

7

"I'm quite all right," Tori said softly, not looking at either man, but rather into the heart of the dark tango.

"Of course you are, my darling," Estilo said, patting her hand affectionately. He had big hands, blunt and strong. "I did not mean to infer otherwise"—although Tori knew that was precisely what he had meant to do. "I merely assumed your boredom needed alleviating. In that event, I would be delighted if you joined me tonight at my home." His mustache arched as he smiled. "A very private party. If you aren't a friend of mine, you aren't coming." He paused a moment, then said, "Ariel will be there."

Tori turned her head, looked again at the younger man, his skin burnished by the sun and the wind. She could imagine him riding the infinite pampas or, bending slightly, his hair swept back by the wind and the speed of his mount, swinging a polo mallet at Palermo Fields. But there was something different about him; he was not a typical *porteño*, or even trying to be, and these things intrigued her.

"All right," Tori said.

"Wonderful!" Estilo beamed at her as he rose. "Until tonight, then!"

For a moment Ariel sat facing her, his coffee-colored eyes staring into hers. Then he took her hand, kissed it lightly, and was swept away by Estilo.

After the men were gone, Tori sat and sipped a brandy. It was, to her mind, a melancholy drink, invoking intimations of broken promises, lost dreams, the ashes of desire.

When at last she rose, the tango had finished its haunting tale, and only the unlovely noises of the restless city remained.

Estilo's home was an apartment that took up the entire top floor of an anonymous-looking high rise in the Recoleta. It was just a few blocks from the cemetery, the ne plus ultra address in all of Buenos Aires, which perhaps told you as much about the *porteños* as you needed to know: the dead possessed a presence that made them in some subtle, mystical sense less dead than the dead of other cultures.

The vast apartment which snaked from east to west was furnished in Italian high fashion, which was to say with equal amounts of chic and money. Each piece of furniture exhibited low, sleek lines and the distinctively patterned fabrics of Ungaro and Missoni.

The place had been designed by Estilo's current mistress,

8

Adona, a stunning black-haired Argentine woman from the *alta sociedad*—the cream of *porteño* society—who, in some ways, reminded Tori of herself. She had wanted more from her relationship with Estilo, and had insisted that he take her into the jungles of South America, where many of his dangerous business dealings took place. Adona was as good at dispelling distrust as she was at disarming Estilo's enemies.

She was an unusual hostess in this snobbish city, for she genuinely loved people, and attended to their individual wants. She and Tori embraced warmly, in the manner of sisters too long kept apart.

She drew Tori aside. In the kitchen uniformed servers were loading chased-silver platters, enormous chafing dishes, with food. Adona ignored these people.

"You look tired, Tori."

"Perhaps I am, a little. But if so, it's only the fatigue of inaction."

"Yes." Adona nodded. "I know you well. You need passion. Like with Estilo and me, there is a passion. But your passion is for what? This violence, living on the edge of the great abyss?" Her eyes were sad. "I think this is not healthy."

"Estilo said much the same thing to me this afternoon."

Adona smiled. "Estilo is very fond of you." She laughed, a beautiful musical sound. "Did you know that in the beginning I was quite jealous of you?"

"You had no reason to be," Tori said.

"Why not? Estilo is no angel. But then who is? Me? Are you?"

"No," Tori said, abruptly thinking of Greg, soaring like an angel above Earth's atmospheric envelope. And then, while crawling outside, along the skin of his vehicle, something had punctured his EVA suit, and all the oxygen had been sucked from his lungs. A matter of seconds, that's all it had taken. From heaven to hell, with only the brittle blue starlight for company. "Death by hypoxia," his death certificate had read, but that was so cold, so clinical. It had not described his iced body, blistered and bruised beyond recognition by the cruel vacuum of space.

"Tori." Adona was gripping her arm. "Here, take some brandy, you've gone white."

"I'm all right." But just the same, Tori downed the liquor.

Adona shook her head. "There was a time," she said, "when I longed for the life you lead: armed to the teeth, in the jungle, the enemy just ahead. It made me feel so . . . I don't know, alive." She took the empty glass from Tori's hand. "But times change, *I've* changed. The truth is that the only time I felt safe was when I had a MAC-10 in my hands and a knife on my hip. Then I knew I was the equal of any man—not sexually, and certainly not emotionally. But still I felt equal. A man could kill, and so could I. I was respected, even at times deferred to. Then, at last, there was no difference between us. You understand."

Tori looked at her. "What changed?"

Adona shrugged. "The world turns on its axis, the seasons change, day into night. Who really can say with certainty? But I suspect that I have found that whatever I was reaching for is nonexistent or, at least, illusory. I feel as though in trying to measure up to men's standards, I've been sucked whole into their world. And I've discovered I don't like it."

"What does Estilo say to all this? He met you in the jungle; that's where you fell in love."

"Estilo doesn't know."

"But you must tell him," Tori said. "Estilo loves you; he wants you to be happy."

Adona's liquid brown eyes locked with Tori's. "Yes, he loves me. But happiness, now that's another matter entirely. Estilo is the consummate businessman—he lives for the deal, it doesn't matter what the deal is. Because each deal is well-defined, and Estilo's world is well-defined. I have spent so much time and effort to become a part of that world, and now, as far as he's concerned, everything meshes perfectly. He couldn't let me go. My role is too well-defined. If I were to leave, a black hole would appear, an undefined gap he could not tolerate."

"But do you want to leave him?"

Adona gave off a little smile, like the glow of a tiny candle as darkness falls. "I don't know."

"Don't let him go," Tori said. "He's a good man."

"Well, at least he's a little good."

Adona suddenly leaned forward, kissed Tori on both cheeks. "Go enjoy the party. Too much gloomy talk is bad for the soul."

Tori squeezed Adona's hand, left her to monitor the coming food. The rooms were filled with people—Buenos Aires' most famous artists, models, *chantas*—and smoke, but somehow Estilo found Tori, pushed a Kir Royale into her hand, kissed her on the cheek, murmured an endearment in German. He used German infrequently, only when he was slightly drunk, and never in a place where he could be overheard. He was Argentine, after all, and had his own myth to foster.

"It is times like this," he said, linking his arm in hers, "when I miss Munich most." Tori knew he traveled to Germany several times a year. "Have you ever eaten in Die Aubergine?"

"I've never been to Munich," Tori said with a sense of déjà vu. They'd had this conversation many times.

"Ah, to look out on the Maximilianplatz and dine on such food!" Estilo shook his head. "Still, Buenos Aires is home. And, after all, Munich is not such a mysterious place. And the Germans—ach, the Germans never change. That is supposed to be their great strength. But I have never found much to admire in stone and concrete."

He guided her outside, onto the terrace that overlooked Buenos Aires. It faced west, and one could see the boundary, the end of the city's lights, the darkness along the wind-whipped plain where the Pampa—Argentina's great prairie, filled with cowboys, ranchers, people used to a hard, dusty existence—began.

Estilo pointed to the darkness. "There is where I was born, *schatzie*. Not in Germany, like my father. He married the daughter of an *estanciero*, and I like to think I was born atop a horse." He laughed abruptly. "But that may be just another myth. My analyst says I rely too heavily on myth. But she doesn't understand. I am half German; I, more than most *porteños*, need the sanctuary of myth in order to live with myself. I don't know what my father did during the war and, God help me, I don't want to know. Do you think I can tell my analyst this?" He shrugged. "It doesn't matter, really. The truth is, I'd rather take her to bed than talk to her." Estilo looked at Tori suddenly. "And you, *schatzie*. What is the truth about you?"

"I thought we had an agreement," Tori said.

"We do. Ask me no questions and I'll tell you no lies, yes? We have helped each other out in the past without being told precisely what the other did." He shrugged. "That does not mean we don't know, eh?" Estilo was very grave. "But I must tell you that sometimes you worry me. I never had children; I never thought I wanted them; I am far too self-indulgent. But I confess that often I feel as if you are my daughter. I feel the urge to protect you even though I know that is the last thing you want from anyone."

All at once, Tori understood that Estilo was afraid of offending her. She felt a corresponding rush of emotion that threatened

11

to strangle her: thinking of Greg, who had only wanted to protect her. She went immediately into *prana*, deep, controlled breathing that sent oxygen through her entire body.

"You're very kind," she said at last. The lights of the city shone through the night, illuminating the undersides of lowering clouds. The air had turned heavy; soon it would rain. "And you're very dear to me." She gave him a tiny smile that had about it an ironic edge. "But it is you *porteños* who are mad about analysts."

"In my many years on this planet," Estilo said, "I have come to realize that everyone can, at one time or another, benefit from introspection. You are an extraordinary human being, Tori, but in this, I think, you are no exception."

Tori smiled, kissed him on the cheek, embraced him briefly. "Thank you, Papa," she said in German.

Estilo looked into her eyes, and she was reminded of Ariel, of how the younger man also had looked her in the eyes this afternoon at the Café la Biela, of the different emotions the two men stirred in her.

"Ariel has been searching for you since he arrived," Estilo said. "I think he is smitten."

"He is very handsome," Tori admitted.

"I think he will be good for what ails you, *schatzie*," Estilo said.

Tori laughed. "You sound like a soothsayer. What does he do?"

"Oh, I think that depends," Estilo said. "His business is beef—very boring, as he said. It's perfectly legitimate. But I believe that he has another reason for being here: the disappeared. I think he is conducting a clandestine investigation into the atrocities committed here in the name of justice."

"Interesting."

"I was certain you'd think so," he said. Then he pushed her back into the milling throng of the party. "Go find him before he faints from anguish." Estilo was obliged to shout this last in order to be heard over the din of music and cacophonous conversation.

Ariel was dressed in black. In that first instant when Tori spotted him through the crowd, he looked like an angel she had once dreamed about. He had no halo, however, and when he saw her, he broke out in a smile, his white even teeth shining, and the image dissolved. Angels—at least as Tori conceived of them—never smiled.

"I thought you had changed your mind," Ariel said, coming up to her. "I was certain you weren't coming."

"Didn't you consult an *adivina*?" Tori's tone was deliberately sardonic.

"I will tell you a secret," Ariel said, coming close to her. "I put no stock in fortune-tellers. But don't tell my *porteño* friends. They would never understand." He grinned at her. "Fortune-tellers and analysts are sacred here, like cows in India."

Tori laughed, surprised at how comfortable she felt with this man. There was a danger in that, but only to her self-imposed exile from the human race. Perhaps, she thought, there was something to what Estilo had said. Perhaps she had come down with an illness for which there was as yet no name. She wondered if there was a cure.

Ariel said something but, in the din, she could not hear what it was. She shrugged at him, pointing to her ear, and shook her head.

He put his lips against her ear, said, "Let's go somewhere else."

Ten minutes later they were entering the Recoleta cemetery where the esteemed ancestors of the *alta sociedad* lay interred beneath flower-strewn earth and ornately carved marble. This was a city of the dead, a baroque necropolis from which many of the myths of the *porteños* were born. From death to life: there was a certain poetry to the notion, at least from an Argentine point of view.

The jacarandas dripped moisture, but rain was on the way. A low rumble filled the air, its echoes reluctant to fade away.

Ariel led the way as if he were a frequent visitor here. The oppressive darkness of marble and stone ornately carved in the French and Italian Renaissance styles gave way to a soft glow, increasing as they went forward.

Soon they had come upon a crypt. Around it were laid out wreaths woven of flowers, bouquets, bunches of wildflowers. Under the trees where the rain could not penetrate, the flames of perhaps a hundred candles flickered. Into the crypt's face was carved, simply, EVA DUARTE.

"Here is myth," Ariel said, pointing to the last resting place of Eva Perón. "More has been written—quite erroneously—about her than anyone in this country. Was she saint or demon?"

"Perhaps she was neither," Tori said. "Perhaps she was just a woman."

"Well, don't let the *descamisados*, the shirtless ones, hear

13

you say that." He was speaking of the workers who had slavishly followed their hope, the Peróns. "It would not be enough for them." Ariel turned to look at her. It had begun to rain, a fine pattering through the trees that made Tori think of airports and farewells. "You think it is not understandable? Everything else has been taken from them."

"Even their children," Tori said. "Their future."

"In a very real sense, yes. Those that disappeared in the night during Argentina's reign of terror will never be heard from again. The disappeared are now only mute witnesses to this country's savage history. Oppression stilled their voices forever." Ariel looked out across the sea of baroque headstones and crypts. "It's quite sad."

Stone angels surrounded Tori and Ariel, their tiny carved wings encrusted with the soot of the city. Rain rolled down their cheeks like tears as they remembered the dead. The polished marble of the necropolis was milky, eerily luminous in the aqueous light from the massed candles.

"Does this display mean that after all this time Perónism still lives?"

"Only in a sense," Ariel said. "It is like a dream, you see. The *descamisados* continue to hope, but now the new leaders of Perónism veer from one political platform to another instead of facing the truth: that the true essence of Perónism is today an anachronism."

Tori stared into the candles' flames. "Here the children paid for the sins of their fathers." She turned to look into his face. "Where is the justice in that?"

"We are in Argentina," Ariel said. "A place where justice is, at best, misunderstood."

The rain drowned the candles' flames, and darkness once again enwrapped the city of the dead. Tori had the abrupt feeling that she and Ariel both knew what the worst was: justice used as a weapon to destroy, and as a shield behind which to obscure culpability.

Ariel shivered as if the night had suddenly turned cold or a spirit had touched the back of his neck. "Perhaps it was a mistake to come here tonight," he said.

"Do you mean Estilo's party or the Recoleta cemetery?" Tori asked.

Ariel smiled, and Tori realized that she liked his face. In repose it was a formidable visage: stern, strong-willed, with an almost defiant edge—seemingly far from the bored businessman

14

he claimed to be. But when Ariel laughed, the forbidding cast disintegrated into a kind of boyish charm she found irresistible.

She felt this last odd and a bit discomfiting. It had been a long time since she had found anyone irresistible.

Ariel looked at her. "I believe you have the most extraordinary eyes I've ever seen," he said. "This afternoon they were turquoise, green, I thought. Now they are the color of cobalt."

Tori laughed. "My father used to call me Angel Eyes. My brother and I had the same eyes."

"Had?" Ariel had caught a tone as well as a tense.

Tori put her head down into darkness. "My brother's dead."

"I'm sorry."

Tori took a deep breath. "Well. He was a wonderful man. And he was blessed. Before he died, he flew like an angel. And like an angel, he saw the whole planet spread out before him." Ariel looked at her quizzically, and she smiled sadly. "My brother was an astronaut."

Ariel snapped his fingers. "Nunn. Wait a minute. Greg Nunn? The American who died in that joint mission to Mars with the Russians? What was that, last year?"

"Eighteen months."

"Greg Nunn was your brother?"

"Yes."

It was just a whisper, but it told the discerning listener volumes. Ariel wisely decided to change the subject. "Estilo mentioned that you are retired," he said. "From what?"

What to tell him? "Family business," Tori said. Not exactly a lie, but not the truth, either.

He grunted. "Me, too. Only I'm still in it." They began to walk. "It used to be fun when my father ran it. I could do pretty much what I wanted. I never realized how boring the meat business was until my father died and I was obliged to take it over. Responsibility seemed to drain all the fun out of the work."

They were at the cemetery's gate, and passing through into the street, Tori had the feeling that an oppressive weight had lifted from her. In there, it had seemed as if the very air she had been breathing was humid with the spirits of the dead. She took one last look at the sad-faced stone angels, as though she could hear their wings rustling in the windswept night.

"So running the business isn't enough," Tori said, giving him an opening to perhaps talk about why, as Estilo had said, he was really in Buenos Aires.

"I don't believe I'm in the mood to go back to Estilo's,"

Ariel said, as if he hadn't heard her question. "It's raining, and the climate is not conducive to a party."

Tori wondered whether by the climate he meant the weather or his state of mind. Either way, it was all right; she had no desire to wedge herself back into Estilo's ultratrendy crowd.

He took her to Café Tortoni, a well-known jazz bar on the Avenida de Mayo.

"Are you often up late at night?"

"Only when I'm traveling," Ariel said. He shrugged. "I don't know what it is, but all my business associates seem to be aficionados of *la vida nocturna*—night life."

Tori had been in love with the night life; twice. As an underage teenager she had used her beauty to hang out in Los Angeles' most dangerous night spots. Years later the clandestine late-night clubs of Tokyo, so far away from her native L.A., had held another form of danger. But by that time she was an entirely different person, wasn't she?

They drank cane brandy while a black saxophonist made noises in concert with a West Indian snare drummer and a blond, slick-fingered bassist. It didn't sound much like music, but everyone seemed content to listen to it.

When the set was through, Ariel looked at his watch. "It's after midnight. Are you tired?"

Tori shook her head.

"Good." He paid the check, then led her out of the restaurant. They picked up a taxi on the avenue, and Ariel told the driver, "La Manzana de las Luces." The driver shrugged, headed south into the downtown district.

The Square of Enlightenment, between Peru and Bolívar at the intersection of the Avenida Julio Roca, was a treasure trove of historical landmarks. But the only one Tori could remember offhand was the offices of *La Prensa*, Argentina's most famous newspaper.

The taxi let them off on Peru, and Ariel stopped in front of number 222. It had an Italian-designed facade typical of the mid-1880s, though Ariel informed her the building itself was more than a hundred years older than that.

"This place has belonged variously to two newspapers and the University of Buenos Aires," Ariel said. "But by far its most interesting tenant was the General Attorney of the Jesuits, for whom, apparently, it was built. King Charles the Third of Spain kicked the order out in 1767. But before then some fascinating goings-on occurred here."

16

"Like what?"

"Come on," Ariel said. "I'll show you."

He led her around to the side of the structure. Here the narrow alley was dimly lit. They went down a flight of ancient stone steps so worn they were concave in their centers. Tori saw that even in the gloom Ariel had no difficulty negotiating them.

A moment later she heard what she suspected was the grate of an old key in an even older lock. A stained wood-plank door creaked inward on iron hinges. A musty darkness loomed.

"Is this okay?" Tori asked.

"Do you like to take chances?"

She heard his voice as a disembodied whisper, and did not answer.

"Watch your step," Ariel said, reaching back and taking her hand. He pulled her inside, closed the door behind them.

He led her through absolute blackness. She heard the squeal of another door opening, Ariel's voice whispering, "Now duck your head."

There were more steps, and the chill mineral dampness that bred mold and lichen wafted over her. The steps were very steep and quite narrow. The rich scents of limestone and earth enveloped her. Tori thought, It's like smelling one's own grave, and for an instant she felt the hairs stirring at the base of her neck.

"These tunnels date back to the eighteenth century." Tori wondered why he was still whispering. After all, down in the bowels of the earth who could overhear their conversation?

"These tunnels are something of a tourist attraction nowadays," Ariel continued, his lips brushing her ear. "The tourists are told that these tunnels were built to aid in the defense of the city during wartime. But the truth is the Jesuits built them in order to smuggle in contraband. The king had decreed that Buenos Aires, like the other Spanish colonies, could trade only with Spain. But at the behest of the clever Jesuits, ships of other nationalities moored in the port, pretending to work on repairs while the priests off-loaded their cargo into these secret tunnels."

Ariel snapped on a flashlight, and Tori could see the arched ceilings, the branching corridors. Along the sides of the tunnels were modern lights within protective metal grills above the equally modern concrete walkway.

He led her around a turning, into a small chamber, down another steep flight of stone steps. Here the tunnels seemed older, cruder, or perhaps merely in a state of disrepair. The air

17

was closer, mustier, and there were no modern lights, no concrete walkway. Loose stones ground beneath their feet.

Ariel stopped them abruptly. He squeezed her hand as he played the beam of the flash over a heap of pale bones. With a start, Tori saw that she was staring at a grisly jumble of human skeletons.

"Here is all that's left of the disappeared," Ariel whispered. "At least some of them, poor bastards. Dumped here to rot beneath the city."

"What—"

Ariel's hand went over her mouth as he snapped off the flashlight's beam.

Sounds—faint, indistinct—wafted toward them from some unknown direction. Ariel stood very still; he seemed scarcely to be breathing.

The sounds came swiftly closer. Tori strained to hear what they were. As they neared, the sounds resolved themselves into male voices, then words, and Tori thought, My God, they're speaking Japanese.

"Perhaps Rega could have been of some further use," one voice said.

"His use was at an end," the other said. "Given half a reason, he would have betrayed us." A laugh. "Besides, it felt good to put the gun against the back of his neck, pull the trigger, and *boom!* Like snuffing out a candle in a church. In that instant, you know something significant has happened: the law has been transgressed."

"I am a Shintoist," the first voice said. "God and the devil mean nothing to me, like the blink of an eye seen in a mirror. All illusion."

"I am Catholic," the second voice said, "so I understand the meaning of punishment—and of sin."

"I don't understand. How can you be a Catholic and a sinner?"

That laugh again. "I cannot be redeemed if I haven't sinned, so these days I do my best to ignore the law. Also, as you must suspect, there is a measure of personal pleasure for me in violation."

"Let's get on with it," the first voice said.

It was impossible to say just how close the voices were. Perhaps they were around an unseen corner, perhaps much nearer than that—tunnel acoustics being treacherously unpredictable.

Tori suspected that Ariel was thinking the same thing. She

18

thought he wanted to get out of there but was afraid of being seen or heard.

Suddenly a light snapped on, and Tori and Ariel were caught in its piercing beam. Tori could make out the blossom of two black figures, faceless, on the move.

"Hey, look!"

"Who the fuck—"

The glint, dark and evil, of machine pistols.

"Madre de Dios!" Ariel breathed. He grabbed her hand, pulled her out of the circle of light. They began to stumble their way back down the tunnel.

The light flashed wildly, illuminating the tunnel in rhythmic bursts, casting their distorted shadows against the rough stone walls. They heard swift footfalls behind them.

"They're coming after us!" Tori said.

Ariel said nothing, pulling her after him down the twisting tunnel. They gained a flight of steps, raced down them. But they could hear the heavy footfalls, the panting breaths that told them their pursuers were gaining on them. Tori wondered what in God's name he had led her into.

"Faster!" Ariel's voice barked from out of the darkness. "If they catch us, they'll kill us!"

We'll never outrun them, Tori thought as they rushed past an open archway. Impulsively, she reached out, grabbed Ariel, brought him up short.

"What—"

"In here!" she whispered in his ear, and ducking down, they entered the pitch-blackness beyond the portal.

It smelled musty, and Tori could hear the scrabbling of tiny nails against loose rock. Ariel used his hands like a blind man, feeling the wall, following its contours.

Light flared behind them and they both froze, then it faded, and they continued on their way in the darkness, into another, smaller chamber, then a third, even smaller one.

For the first time Tori failed to scent a flow of air, and she was suddenly afraid that they had worked themselves into a dead end. On the other hand, coming in here had thrown the pursuers off their trail. She began to relax somewhat.

Light returned again to the outer corridor, and now she could hear voices talking in Japanese. The light increased so that the edges of it spilled into the chamber they were in.

Tori looked around; she had been right. There was only one

exit out of this tiny room, and in order to use it, they would have to get past the Japanese who were hunting them.

In the dim, inconstant light, she could make out a mounded shape against the far wall. Breaking free of Ariel, she went over to inspect it more closely—and was confronted by a veritable cairn of human skeletons.

The disappeared. More than she could count. In a brief glare of light tiny red eyes peered out at her from the labyrinth of bones.

The light increased, but the voices had ceased, a clear indication that the Japanese thought they were nearing their quarry.

Tori made up her mind; she turned back to Ariel, said, "Quick!" and taking him by the hand, drew him down to the cairn of bones and skulls. They burrowed their way through the skeletons. Tori heard a brief high-pitched squeal, and the red eyes were gone. The smell of putrefaction and earth was overpowering; it was as if they climbed into a grave that was now closing around them.

When she reached the far wall, she curled up in a ball. Ariel did the same. All around them the forest of the dead rose up in an angular chaos of arms, legs, spines. Buried beneath the bones, the two of them watched the arched portal through which their pursuers would emerge. Tori could feel the heat from Ariel's body curled against hers. They were like doomed lovers, breathing in the dark, breathing in the dead, waiting for death to claim them.

A beam of light entered the chamber, played across the cairn of skeletons. It penetrated the latticework structure, deeper and deeper, darkness and light, revealing layer upon layer of bones, as a spotlight pierces deep water.

Tori saw a bar of light touch her skin, the flesh white among the white bones, a glare in her eyes, dazzling her, and she closed them, praying that she and Ariel had buried themselves deep enough so the Japanese could not distinguish the living from the dead. At that moment she felt a kinship with these poor, murdered people. If their spirits were still here, she prayed they would reach out to protect her.

She breathed tidally, shut her mind down, diminished her *wa*, her inner energy which, if these Japanese had been trained as she had, they might be able to sense even though she was hidden from their sight.

Beside her, Ariel did not move. He might have been dead. He knew what to do, too.

20

"Bah! There's nothing here," one of the Japanese said.

"The dead are here," the other Japanese said.

"Mute witnesses. Let's go."

But they did not move. "Those two saw us," the first Japanese said. "I want them."

"Fine. I want them, too. But they're not here."

Still, they did not leave. The light continued to play over the cairn. Abruptly it increased in brightness, and when the first Japanese spoke again, he was heart-stoppingly close to where she and Ariel lay.

"Are you certain? What do I hear? Is it breathing? Is it you— or me? Are we the only ones in this room?"

Tori felt a trickle of sweat make its way down the indentation of her spine. She recognized this man as the philosophical one, the maniac who said he enjoyed living outside the law. He was more dangerous than the other one; his imagination was by far the keener.

She heard a metallic click, sharp, clear, echoing in the confined space, and she thought of the machine pistols they had been holding.

"All I have to do to find out," the first Japanese said, "is to spray this pile of bones."

Tori's heart threatened to burst through her rib cage.

A loud scrape as of a shoe sole. Then the second Japanese said, "Are you crazy? This is a death site."

"What do I care?" the first Japanese said harshly.

"These dead haven't been properly buried. Their spirits aren't at rest. To disturb them is a sin even you don't want to commit." There was a pause. "Why don't you admit we've lost them. It's a maze down here; they could be anywhere. We don't have the time to shoot up all the dark places in these tunnels. And we don't want to be heard. Come on. If we stay any longer we'll be in danger of missing our pickup. I don't know about you, but I want to get out of this hellhole."

"But those two—"

"What did they see? They can't know what we're up to. Forget them. They were probably tourists who wandered down here for a thrill and a shiver in the dark."

"Shit."

Then the light was gone, replaced by a glow in the tiny chamber, swiftly fading. Darkness descending, Ariel and Tori waited.

Ariel started to move, but Tori put one hand on his shoulder, a finger pressed gently to his lips.

Across the littered floor the rat was back, its bright, beady eyes shining, and Tori saw in their depths the possibility of betrayal. If the rat squealed now, and if, as she suspected, the Japanese were waiting with their light off just inside the adjoining chamber, then they would know that they had not been alone with the cairn of skeletons, and spirits or no spirits, the hail of machine-pistol fire would come, the end.

Tori continued to watch the rat as it made its circuitous way toward them through the maze of bones. It was clear now that the rodent scented them, and it was hungry.

Tori waited, patient, closing her eyes to slits. Her right hand lay relaxed along the line of Ariel's hip. The rat was very close now, and Tori, without seeming to move any other part of her body, whipped her right hand out to the rat and, in the same motion, neatly snapped its neck.

Time passed. Tori let her consciousness drift off. Semiawake, but with her senses more alert than before, she heard the tiny scraping sounds the Japanese made when they gave up their vigil, clambering back through the succession of chambers into the more familiar corridor.

Tori's lips touched Ariel's neck, and together they rose from the dead.

Ariel and Tori were standing on one of the two terra-cotta tile balconies of Ariel's magnificent house on Russian Hill in San Francisco. One hundred years ago Ambrose Bierce, Bret Harte, and Mark Twain frequently met in a cool salon atop this nearly vertical hill.

It was not quite forty-eight hours since the incident in the eighteenth century Jesuit tunnels. Ariel, who had been returning home, had invited Tori to accompany him, and she had accepted because she found that she had lost her taste both for Buenos Aires and solitude. Besides, though she was reluctant to admit it, Ariel intrigued her. Reluctant, because for so long she had gone out of her way to avoid even a hint of a relationship or complication with a man. But she had been presented with an enigma: what was a pair of Japanese Yakuza assassins doing in the tunnels beneath Buenos Aires, and how did Ariel Solares, the man who had told her so glibly that his life was prosaic, know they would be there?

Tori looked down. Below them, the city of hills swept away to the foot of Hyde Street and, beyond, the gray bay, dotted now with ships, where, no doubt, unseen dolphins played. The house's other terrace overlooked Lombard Street as it wound its serpentine way down to North Beach.

Behind them, filling up Ariel's vast living room, were mementos of the ancient civilizations of South America: painted pottery, carved stone statues of women and animals, diminutive wooden weapons set with blackened iron tips Tori knew had once been dipped in poison.

" 'Through the years,' " Ariel Solares said, " 'a man peoples a space with images of provinces, kingdoms, mountains, bays, ships, islands, fishes, rooms, tools, stars, horses and people.' " He was quoting a fragment of Jorge Luis Borges that Tori knew.

"This is the perfect spot," she said. "Away from everyone, above everything."

"My only regret," Ariel said, "is that I'm not here nearly enough." He turned to her, refilled her glass with more champagne. "Are you familiar with San Francisco?"

"Not really." Tori drank. "I'm afraid I have the native Los Angelino's reflexive distaste for it."

"It's not bad as American cities go," Ariel said. "I'd prefer Paris, but I've got to work."

"Don't the French need beef?"

"Not as much as we Americans. And they're a bitch to deal with. Very picky about imported meat. I'd rather deal with the Japanese." He laughed, then shivered as a cool breeze ruffled his hair. The sun had gone down minutes ago. "Let's go in, shall we?"

She had never particularly liked San Francisco, but she was wild about Ariel's house. She had never actually been up to Russian Hill; it was like living along the Royal Mile in Edinburgh. There was a peace, an apartness, in the height and the vistas, that appealed strongly to her.

Inside, he stood so that the purple sky was reflected in his coffee-colored eyes. He seemed about to say something, then turned away.

"What is it?" Tori asked.

For a time Ariel said nothing. He looked casual and relaxed in a white sport shirt, black slacks, a natural jacket of flax and silk. He seemed genuinely disconcerted. "I want to ask you to go to bed with me, but I know I shouldn't."

Tori laughed. "Well, that's a new one—a new line, I mean."

"It isn't. At least, I didn't intend it to be." He seemed so uncomfortable that Tori considered cutting right to the heart of

23

the matter. But then she thought that he would have to learn his lesson sometime, and that in the end he might be better off learning it from her.

"Look, you've made it obvious from the moment we met that you're attracted to me," she said seriously. "I appreciated your candor. I'm here, aren't I? Don't tell me you can't feel how attracted I am to you. What I don't understand now is the 'shouldn't' part. Why are you suddenly backing off?"

"You'd never believe me. I—" He stopped in mid-sentence. "Could we forget I ever said any of this?"

"I doubt it," Tori said, moving closer to him. "You'd better learn not to check your brains at the door before you open your mouth. You never know the trouble your own words can get you into."

"I think I'm going to be in enough trouble as it is," Ariel said.

"With whom?" Her breasts brushed against him.

"It's you, you know," Ariel said. "I'm usually a pretty fair liar. I think you bring out the best—or the worst—in me."

"Poor Ariel." Tori lifted her face to his. She could feel his heat. Her lips parted, only to be crushed beneath his.

After all the inner barriers she had erected to keep her own emotions at bay, she found it difficult to break away from him. But when at length she did, she walked away from him, stood staring at the book-lined shelves against an inner wall. Her eyes drifted over titles that had no meaning for her; her vision was filled with her own quickened pulse. Blood roared in her ears.

"Why did you do that?" Ariel asked.

Without turning around, Tori said, "Don't come any closer." She knew that she had to stop this now, before she got herself into something she could not control. This man had lied to her; he had known just what he was doing, taking her down into the tunnels under Buenos Aires. The only thing left to discover was where he meant to lead her.

But all the while she could feel the heat building, a heat she felt all the way to her fingertips. *Stop it!* she admonished herself. *Concentrate on what must be done here.*

She said, "Why do you live here, and not in Virginia? Doesn't Slade require face-to-face briefings anymore?"

For a long time there was no sound in the room, then she heard Ariel moving, and a moment later music drifted through the house. Melissa Etheridge singing "Chrome Plated Heart."

He came up close behind her, said in her ear, "How did you know I work for the Mall?"

Tori closed her eyes. "It wasn't just one thing. The Japanese who just happened to be in the tunnels. You said of them, 'If they catch us, they'll kill us!' Then, just now, you said you'd rather work with the Japanese. What would you know about the Japanese? But the biggest mistake you made was in not showing sufficient surprise at what I did down there: finding our hiding place, killing the rat, keeping you from making a sound when they were still out there waiting for us." At last she turned to face him. "I think it's about time you tell me what this is all about."

"Later," Ariel said. "When there's plenty of time." His lips covered hers, and this time she knew she lacked the will to break away.

She felt him around her, his arms coiling, a great masculine figure, hard and strong, a sanctuary within the heavenly aerie he had created for himself. And it was as if she had been dropped into the center of a whirlpool, in the grip of forces she could no longer hold in check. She was out of control; she knew it; and still the exhilaration rose in her, blotting out everything but Ariel.

She crushed herself against him, feeling her nipples erect, feeling the long dormant liquid heaviness in her thighs and pelvis. She trembled in his embrace, and he lifted her off her feet.

The taste of lust was in her mouth, the fire in her body given full reign, conscious thought driven away on the wings of her passion.

She was so hungry—not only her loins but her empty heart yearned to be filled again, to throb at the sight of a precious lover, to anticipate his love like the coming of night, and then to feel it gushing through her like a mountain stream at the first thaw of spring.

She wept as he kissed her breasts, her thighs, her wet sex. She murmured endearments when she, in turn, took him in her mouth, feeling him growing, growing, the taste of him intoxicating.

She cried out when he entered her, her nails scoring his back as he slid all the way up her and she was filled to bursting, her heart thundering, her thighs lifting, enclosing him. Their breaths mingled; he kissed her ears, her nose, the corners of her eyes where her flesh was as thin and soft as a baby's. He inhaled the musk at the hollow of her throat, licked the swelling tops of her breasts.

And, oh, it was good. Not only the pleasure they were creating together, but the letting go, like dancing in the rain or rushing naked into the sea. Tori's heart sighed, contented, as she was hurled breathlessly toward an ending, a thunder in her soul, the sun in her eyes, the rain of their sweat flying as they ground together, the sweet collision of flesh and emotion that only making love can produce.

Then he was gasping and heaving. She felt him shudder, arch into her, and something touched her core. Everything shattered, like walking into and through a mirror, arriving at a new reality, a plane of existence once only hinted at.

"Oh, my God . . . Ohhh!"

She moved—when she could gather herself to stir again—to the beat of his heart as well as her own. The feeling was so sweet, so intense, that she felt tears come again. It was something to feel like a woman once more, soft and vulnerable. It was so different from how she had been trained: she had been instructed to become as hard as a man, so she had become harder; she had been instructed to replace emotion with logic, so she had become harder; she had been instructed to replace logic with instinct, so she had become harder still, so immersed in her studies she had no time for personal considerations. An economy of movement, speech, thought had overtaken her, defining her new life.

And everything else had withered within her. She had seen this as good, a purging, an exorcism of the toxins that had embittered her previous life, that had driven her to Japan, to a land and a philosophy that was as far as she could get from what she had once been. Up until this moment.

Now she saw the other side: how the forging of her spirit in the crucible of her extraordinary training had distanced herself from everything—the good as well as the bad—that had dwelt inside her. And she was immensely grateful to Ariel Solares for giving her back that part of herself she knew she could not live without.

She wanted to make love again, now, before thought crept back through her drunk mind, but her bladder was bursting, and she staggered naked off the sofa, down the hallway, into the bathroom.

She was finished, splashing cold water on her face, when she heard the sound. Or, perhaps, felt it would be more accurate.

Her first thought was that an earthquake had hit. She lurched, grabbing onto the cool porcelain of the sink. Ariel's toothbrush rattled in its holder and a bottle of cologne crashed to the tile floor.

But dimly Tori was aware of the aftermath of a percussion. Alarm flooded through her. She pulled open the door, leaped over the shards of glass, ran down the hall.

All her senses were alert. The air was thick. Plaster dust, smoke, and the smell of burning filled the air, choking her. She smelled the acrid chemical by-products of plastique explosives.

"Ariel?" she called. Then more urgently, "Ariel!"

She found him crouched on the other side of the room. The sofa on which they had been making love but moments before was demolished, charred as if in a fire. Its pieces had been thrown halfway across the floor. The doors to the balcony had exploded outward; shards of glass glittered in the city light. There was a hole in the wall behind where the doors had been, and the cruel San Francisco evening wind whipped the tattered drapes, impaling them on the iron-tipped Amazonian spears.

Tori threw herself down beside Ariel. He was making hideous gasping sounds; he was covered in blood. She tried to hold him, but he shrugged her away, and she saw that he was desperately trying to get to something. His fingers scrabbled at a cabinet door. He fumbled it open, then seemed to lose all energy. His shoulders slumped heavily and his forehead rested against the carpet.

Tori turned him, stifled a scream. There wasn't much left of his chest. How he was still breathing, let alone able to open a cabinet, was beyond her.

Her mind refused to work. It was as if she were stuck in tar. What had happened? How could this have taken place in the few moments she had been at the other end of the house?

Ariel Solares was dying, but he did not seem focused on that; he had more urgent business. Still in her arms, he flopped like a landed fish until his right hand could reach into the cabinet. He drew out a hardwood box. It trembled in the grip of the spasm that racked him.

Then Ariel pressed the box into her hand. His lips moved, his eyes searching hers, and Tori bent down.

"What is it, Ariel?" she whispered. "Oh, my God, my God."

Because his mouth was suddenly filled with blood. Bubbles formed at the corners of his lips as he drowned in his own fluids.

27

And there was nothing Tori could do but hold him, rocking him gently, looking down at him to let him know she was there, thinking of the last line of the Borges fragment he had quoted before.

Shortly before his death, he discovers that the patient labyrinth of lines traces the image of his own face.

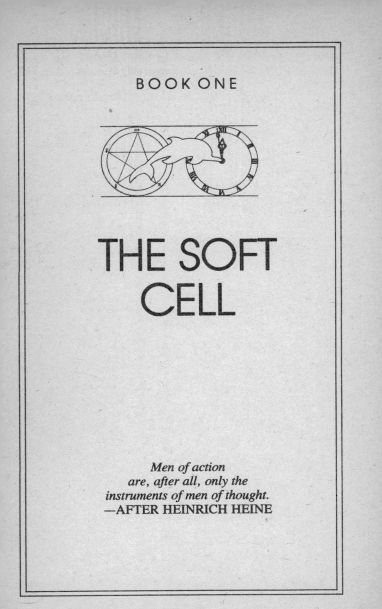

BOOK ONE

THE SOFT CELL

*Men of action
are, after all, only the
instruments of men of thought.
—AFTER HEINRICH HEINE*

ONE
VIRGINIA COUNTRYSIDE/LOS ANGELES

"She was meant to be canned—and she *was* canned."

"What you should say is that *you* canned her."

"*Should?*"

"Yes. This is, essentially, what is operative here."

The two men—one younger, black-haired, hawk-nosed, with penetrating blue eyes, the other, older, lanky, stoop-shouldered, with an aureole of cotton-candy hair—paused along the blue-stone path laid out in concentric circles around an immaculately manicured formal English garden.

The late afternoon sun slid in and out of the elms and alders, catching in its burnished glow a spray of hyacinth here, a twist of ancient vine there. Just behind the men a large Tudor-style stone and half-timber manor house was snuggled in among rustling beech, sheared cypresses, and well-established magnolia.

"I don't understand you," the younger man said. He was dressed in a white shirt open at the neck, the sleeves rolled up to expose his burly forearms, and blue jeans, the bottoms of which were tucked neatly into blue Tony Lama lizard cowboy boots. He wore a belt studded with silver Navajo conchos.

"You don't?" The older man could have added "That's odd," but didn't. He had the face of a born commander: powerful,

31

shrewd, disarmingly gentle in its deceit. Now, however, the fissures of time had scored his sunken cheeks, thinned his hair, unearthed the tic of a failing nerve. Only the eyes retained the full cunning of his youth. They were the eyes of the boy down the block who dared you to climb the tallest tree, to ride the back bumper of the local bus, and, maddeningly, disdained you whether or not you acceded to his dares.

"When I was somewhat younger than you are now," the older man said, "I spent a great deal of time with our cousins in London." He gestured at the cherry and hawthorn trees, the sea of crimson and lavender azalea bobbing beneath them. "That's where I discovered my love of gardens."

"But not gardening." Russell Slade, the younger man, could not keep the sardonic tone out of his voice. "The Brits love to tend their gardens."

"And so they should." Bernard Godwin, the older man, nodded approvingly. His summer-weight Henry Poole hunting jacket was as immaculate as his garden. His sturdy John Lobb country shoes positively glittered in the sunlight. "When one has little space one can call one's own, it is only prudent to mind it as best one can." Godwin swung abruptly around to face Slade; their eyes locked. It was essential, Slade knew, not to look away, for Godwin would take that as a sign of weakness. "But this is America, Russell, and here space is not a problem. This land goes on almost forever. The cowboys learned that the hard way a hundred years or more ago. But the same holds true today. That's our one absolute advantage over the English, the Europeans, the Japanese."

"What, our land?"

"Not the land, per se. But, rather, how *having* land as a natural resource makes us act and react. And it's our one true link with the Soviets." Bernard Godwin never said Russians. It was always Soviets—and there was a vast difference between the two terms. The Russians were only one people who inhabited the Union of Soviet Socialist Republics along with the Lithuanians, Estonians, Latvians, the people of the Baltic Republics, the Georgians and the Armenians, the trans-Caucasians, the Ukrainians, not to mention the Moslem minorities, who were part of a whole other microuniverse. Godwin had studied them all in depth. So, of course, had Russell Slade; it was just that his conclusions differed from those of Godwin. As long as the Soviet minorities were a collective thorn in Russia's side, so much the better, he believed. Let the Russian government be

32

distracted and drained by internal problems for as long as possible. Christ, he thought, why doesn't Bernard see how the minorities bedevil the Russian government? The thought of helping to resolve that immensely difficult issue for the Russians seemed absolutely insane to Slade. Glasnost or no glasnost, an off-balance Russia was, in his opinion, a manageable Russia.

"The Soviet people are not, thank God, the Russian people," Godwin said now, making his way around a carefully bordered semicircle of variegated pansies. "Each Soviet minority is like a fruit shaking itself free of the central tree. It is time for a forest to grow up in the wilderness surrounding that one tree."

Russell Slade shook his head. This is a dead issue as far as the Mall is concerned, he thought. Why won't Bernard give it up? He said, "Does this in any way bring us back to Tori Nunn?"

Godwin fluttered one rather feminine hand; its ridged back was covered with liver spots. "Tori Nunn was your affair from the beginning. She still is."

Slade recognized in that one snapped retort the edge of the boundary he had crossed. He took a mental pace backward onto safer ground. He was prepared to take his punishment like a man. He nodded. "All right. I admit that it might have been a mistake to bring her back like that."

"It certainly was for Solares."

"Yes. It was a shame to lose such a valuable agent."

Godwin said, "Let me remind you this isn't a baseball game. It isn't a run the opposition has scored against us. It's a death in the family."

So that's why the old man has summoned me to his summer house in the country, Russell Slade thought. Stone and thatch, birds and flowers, all very bucolic. But there isn't anything bucolic about the old man. He's as full of bile as ever.

Slade looked at Bernard Godwin. If he had ever been under the misapprehension that being made the director of the Mall meant it was his to run, here was the proof it just wasn't so.

Bernard Godwin, the man who created the Mall, despite rumors of ill-health and even imminent death, was still in the thick of it. His to command were the unknowable routes to power, and this power continued to hum inside him like a vast engine.

More than anything else, Russell Slade longed to possess this power. Through guile, cunning, and deceit—Godwin's trine of shadow virtues—Slade had risen faster and farther through the labyrinthine ranks of Bernard Godwin's hybrid brainchild—part espionage network, part global think tank—than anyone save the old man himself. There was no one better than Russell to interpret the disjointed data from farflung field operatives and discover the subtle strategies hidden there. Give him one piece of a puzzle, and he would eventually deliver to you the entire picture. Russell was also a gifted administrator, juggling budgets, maximizing men and matériel in a way no one before him had been able to do. Godwin admired those attributes, and had rewarded Slade for them.

But Slade could not help but suspect that the old man was jealous, too. Though his hands were bony with age, gnarled with arthritis, still they refused to relinquish the reins of power. For Slade had the one thing that the old man did not—indeed, could not—possess: youth. Though Slade was at the heart of the Mall, Godwin had yet to divulge to him the last level of his worldwide contacts, the ultimate power that made even presidents defer to him.

The Mall and its godfather, Bernard Godwin, were and always had been laws unto themselves, and this power was what Russell Slade coveted beyond anything else. The time has come, Slade thought as he watched the old man gazing at his sheared English yews. Damnit, render unto Slade that which is rightfully Slade's!

"Russell, let me give you a bit of advice," Godwin continued. "The moment you cannot control the lives and deaths of your field people, you know it is time for you to step down."

"You talk as if this is the first casualty we've had in the field."

The flapping of that feminine hand again. "Of course we've lost agents before. But in my day they were sacrificed for a greater cause. There was a meaning to their deaths. Everything was planned. Do you understand me?"

In my day, indeed! Godwin was as callous as they come, Slade thought. How quickly will he sever me if the situation gets too hot? Has he already got someone lined up to take my place? By God, I'll fight to the death to keep this position.

Slade understood that Godwin had abruptly distanced himself from the current situation, just as he understood that his own immediate priority was to regain the equilibrium Godwin had stripped from him. Godwin loved nothing better than to prod his people. Pressure, he firmly believed, sharpened the wits and brought out the best in his people—and if it did not, they were severed from the Mall.

Without betraying any of his thoughts, Slade said blandly, "You know, Bernard, it occurs to me that you've been spending

34

altogether too much time with the administration's spin doctors. Those presidential apologists who call themselves aides love to rewrite recent history, and so do you. I notice that you're deliberately ignoring the losses the Mall suffered at the hands of the KGB's Operation Boomerang.''

Godwin grunted. ''Ancient history.''

''Really? Your predilection—dare I say it, borders on obsession?—toward helping Soviet dissidents is all too well documented. It cost us ten good agents, lost to the KGB, who were running the bogus dissident cell inside Russia. The KGB sucked in a lot of people with that scam—including you, the expert's expert on the Soviet Union.''

''That was a bad dream, all right,'' Godwin said. ''I don't mind telling you it gave me some sleepless nights. But in the end, I put that slip down to a temporary loss of my acute sense of cynicism.''

Slade, thinking of how cynical Godwin's response was in itself, shook his head. ''No, your error was in placing too much trust in your friends over there.''

''In the end, friends are all that make a man a man,'' Godwin said firmly.

''Even in this shadow world of ours?'' Slade said skeptically.

''*Especially* here.'' Bernard, in the shadow of one of his hoary hawthorn trees, never seemed more mysterious. He had the kind of soft eyes that engendered trust, that completely masked his cynical heart. It was all too easy to believe what he said even when you suspected him of spin control: distorting the truth to suit his purposes. ''I don't know about you, Russell, but it's a friend I want at the other end of a three A.M. phone call when my ass is in the fire in Istanbul or Prague or some other godforsaken red zone when the opposition has blown my cover and is closing in, not some operative who may or may not have been turned while I was looking the other way.''

He gave Slade a tiny, ironic smile that made Slade's stomach contract. ''Sorry,'' he said in a gentle tone of voice. ''I sometimes forget that you have no field experience.'' A rebuke or simply a reminder of fact? With Godwin it was impossible to tell. ''That's the way I came up, because that's the way our shadow world worked in the old days.'' He grunted. ''You have your own areas of expertise, Russell, and believe me, I appreciate all of them. But it's times like these that make me long for the relative simplicity of the past.''

''Damnit, I know I made the proper decision,'' Slade said.

"I was sure that Ariel Solares would bring Tori in. A little honey on the end of the hook, because otherwise I knew, under the circumstances, she wouldn't consider it."

"Of course she wouldn't," Godwin said, pouncing on the opening Slade had given him. "But if you had made her a friend—an ally—instead of alienating her when she worked for you, all this would have been avoided. Tori would be here now, and Solares would still be alive."

The best course when Godwin delivered a verbal low blow, Slade had learned, was to ignore it. Godwin responded to points well made, not to cries of foul. "Solares was to pique her interest with a look at what he was working on," Slade said. "In addition, because there is still a question of her fitness, he was to maneuver her into a challenging physical and mental confrontation. He was meant to look for any deterioration of her skills. The plan was perfect: subtle and psychologically sound. But somewhere along the line Solares must have gotten careless, and someone took him out."

"Solares was your man. You ran him directly. In retrospect, you may agree with me that perhaps, given your lack of experience in the field, that was an error in judgment. It was your call to make, and I didn't interfere. But now's the time to examine your motives. That's why you chose to run him directly, wasn't it? To lure Tori Nunn out of her isolation, to be ultimately in control of her once more."

"As far as me canning Tori Nunn from the Mall," Slade said, "I recall you gave your blessing to the severance." Immediately, he regretted saying it. In trying to regain control of the conversation, he had walked into one of Godwin's verbal traps.

"I gave you my assent, Russell. Nothing more." The old man refused to give up an inch of territory; he was relentless. "It was your decision."

Slade looked at him. "Do you mean to tell me now that you disagreed with it?"

"Are you deliberately missing the point?" Godwin said, neatly sidestepping the kind of answer Slade was seeking. "It was *your* decision. You made it. Now you must deal with the ramifications."

"What ramifications?" Slade said. "This situation is without nuance."

"Bullshit," Godwin said, leaning toward Slade. "Your relationship with Tori Nunn is all unfinished business. Yes, you made the proper decision with Solares, Russell, but you must

36

see that you made it for all the wrong reasons. The 'situation,' as you choose to refer to it, is fraught with psychological nuance."

"I'll take care of Tori Nunn myself," Slade said angrily. "Okay? Will that satisfy you?"

"I want my director's full concentration on this crisis, that's all," Godwin said soothingly. He paused to allow the tension to dissipate; no one knew how to orchestrate a conversation better than Bernard Godwin. "What have the caretakers come up with?" The caretakers were the Mall's group of forensic specialists who were sent in to analyze "wet work" sites.

"Nothing as yet," Slade said. "For the moment, at least, the identity of Solares's murderer is unknown."

"Any guesses?" the old man asked.

"I don't deal in speculation," Slade said, annoyed that the old man still saw fit to test him. "You taught me that, Bernard. Speculation leads, more often than not, to false conclusions."

Godwin nodded. "You said that Solares got careless." He had paused to run his hand across the ruffled field of Hino crimson azalea. "Of course, there's another possibility." He watched, fascinated, as a furry bumblebee, its legs thick with pollen, took off from the center of a flower. "Someone is one step ahead of you." He glanced sidelong at Slade. "Now there's a disturbing thought."

"Jesus Christ," Slade said. " 'Disturbing' doesn't begin to cover that prospect. How does the word 'disaster' grab you?"

The old man frowned to show his distaste. "You know I dislike words of that nature, Slade," he said. "They smack of defeatism. Defeat is for the weak—it is not for us. What we need now is a sound offensive strategy."

"Of course," Slade said. "Every situation has its master, every speciality has its *sensei*. We need Tori Nunn back. We are lost in the middle of her field of expertise."

"Yes," the old man said. "And you've volunteered to get her back yourself. I appreciate that, Russell. Just make certain it isn't simply a gesture."

Slade suddenly saw how neatly he had been maneuvered into this personal involvement, despite his own conviction that personal involvement was dangerous and potentially lethal in the shadow world. In Russell Slade's opinion, emotion had no place in Mall business. That was a point he had tried to make over and over to Tori without the slightest success. It occurred to him—not for the first time, but now with increasing focus—that his sense of being in total control of the Mall was more illusory than real, and abruptly he felt the heavy yoke of servitude to this one man stamped upon his flesh like stigmata.

"One must consider the method of Solares's death," Godwin was saying. "Whoever killed him didn't just put a gun to his head. They made a lot of noise. They wanted us to know right away all the way back east. Goddamnit, they wanted to embarrass us." He tore off an azalea blossom and, making a show of it, used the pads of his thumb and forefinger to squeeze the petals. "There can only be one response to that." He shook the flower, and the bumblebee dropped at their feet. "Go for the throat, that's what's called for." Godwin placed the beautiful, unbruised azalea in his buttonhole. "When you've been set back on your heels, it's the only strategy that's worth a damn, take it from me."

Russell Slade, staring at the lifeless bee, wondered how he could free himself from Bernard Godwin's tyranny and still be privy to his secrets. He would discover who had murdered Ariel Solares in his own way but, being the brilliant administrator that he was, he would also devote himself to his own agenda. Why not? he thought. Bernard has his hidden agenda with his Soviet dissidents, why shouldn't I have mine?

Tori awoke to the sound of a bobwhite. It was sitting in among the bougainvilleas which, if she turned onto her right side, she could see through the open jalousied window.

For a moment she could not think where she was. Then she remembered: Los Angeles. Home.

The huge bed seemed like heaven; she did not want to leave it. She stirred, and as she did so, heard the door to the bedroom open. She saw her mother come quietly in. She was wearing a chic silk and chenille robe, calfskin slippers. She carried a tray filled with food, juice, coffee.

She smiled. "You're up, darling."

How did I get here? Tori blinked into the sunlight, closed her eyes, and remembered . . .

. . . the scents of cigar smoke and marzipan, exhaust fumes and expensive suntan oil. Decaying earth and mold. Light and shadow, a crazy quilt of images, a jumble of sound . . . The squeal of a rat . . . the stench of fear as they were buried alive . . .

I don't want to be back.

. . . the aromas of love, an intimate steam, a delicious dissolving of defenses, an intoxicating wine taken in through the pores of the skin. And then . . . a death's-head blossoming, and the stench of fear again, coming to claim her . . . plastique detonating, destroying her lover, shattering her aerie, her new-found peace; her sanctuary.

I don't want to be back.

"It's so wonderful to have you home again, darling," Laura Nunn said as she set the tray down across her daughter's lap. "We were so worried when we got your call. What *were* you doing in a San Francisco police precinct?"

But what Tori really meant was, Don't be dead, Ariel. Please come back. Greg is dead. It's more than I can bear for you to be dead, too.

Tori pushed the dark thoughts away from her as if they had an insupportable weight. She forced herself to sit up and say, with a mixture of apprehension and fatalism, "Where's Dad?"

"Ellis is at the office." Laura Nunn settled the tray around Tori. "He sends his apologies, but you know your father, he's like quicksand—" She put her hand over her mouth. "Did I say quicksand? Well, of course I meant quick*silver*." She gave a small, embarrassed laugh. "I never understood how a human being could get along on three hours sleep a night. But Ellis is a creature of habit. He still sleeps from three to six, and not an instant more."

Tori studied her mother: so beautiful as a young woman, so exquisite as a mature one; and now, in her early sixties, her hair was still a long chestnut cascade, her eyes brilliant green, her skin, devoid of makeup, without serious line or flaw. It was difficult to believe that any time had passed for her. Ah, well, Tori thought, that was L.A. for you. With a combination of good genes and even better plastic surgeons, the society here had banished age just as surely as God had banished Adam and Eve from Eden. Except that here sin was accepted—cherished, even, as a trait of success; hadn't Ellis Nunn's favorite twist on a phrase always been, *In Los Angeles, nothing succeeds like sin*? And, like undergoing a skin peel, it was acknowledged that you could always shed your immediate past, as long as you played the game. You could continually get away with stepping on the people you didn't need, as long as you kissed the asses of the people you did need.

Laura Nunn snapped out the linen napkin, placed it over the bedcovers. "Now, Maria has gone to great pains to cook everything you love."

Tori looked at the flower pattern Limoges china, the 1930s Tiffany silverware. They brought back dizzying images of her youth, growing up within the boundaries of Diana's Garden, this modern-day Xanadu that her parents had built.

Mistaking her hesitation, Laura Nunn said, "Darling, it would be a sin to leave all this delectable food. You know what a marvelous cook Maria is, and she's always had a tendency to spoil you."

Tori gave her mother a distant smile, slipping on a childhood mask so familiar she did it without being altogether aware of it. As soon as she took her first bite of food, she found that she was famished.

Laura Nunn watched Tori devour her breakfast with the kind of pleased attention one normally gives to one's key light, the light that illuminates the star. "Ellis promised he'd be home early today. Now, you promise me, darling, you won't get into a fight with him."

"*I* never get into a fight with *him*," Tori said as if in knee-jerk response.

Laura Nunn rose. "Perhaps you'd like a little time to yourself."

"No." Tori reached out, drew her mother back down to the side of the bed. "I'm just a little . . . disoriented." She smiled. "Of course I won't get into a fight with Dad. That's all over and done with. I promise."

"Good." Laura Nunn smiled at her daughter. "Now we can get to what really matters. Your happiness. I see that you're still alone. I was half expecting you to show up with a boyfriend or, well, a male friend of some kind."

Tori felt her heart contract. "Mother, I appreciate your concern. But I rather think I've given up men for a while." She saw her mother blanch, then laughed despite herself. "No, no. What I meant is, for the moment at least I feel like being on my own."

"Oh, darling, that's so sad," Laura Nunn said. There was a role in *Possessed*, one of her films, where she played the mother of an innocent outcast, that Tori thought her mother kept falling into. Or was that an unfair assessment? "But you must have companionship—*everyone* must. It's like heat or light, an essential one simply cannot live without."

As usual, Tori thought, Laura Nunn's opinion was the world's opinion. But perhaps she should not be so hard on her mother. It was true that she carried her mother's expectations for herself as if they could be a cure for her own heartache. "People do it all the time, Mom,'' she said with a minimum of conviction. Just another knee-jerk response.

"But of course they do," Laura Nunn said. "That hardly makes it right. I want you to be happy. That's all I've ever wanted for you and . . . for Greg."

"Whereas Dad—"

"Now, darling, you promised. Your father's like a dog with a bone. I'm afraid he'll never put anything like that away." Laura Nunn looked at her daughter, then hugged her. "Oh, Tori, you're so much like him in so many ways."

"Well, perhaps that's why he disapproves of me so strongly." She had meant it to come out in a light tone, but the bitterness was unmistakable.

Laura took Tori's hands in hers. "Oh, my dear, he doesn't disapprove of *you*. I can't think where you get your notions. It's just that he was so . . . disappointed"—was that a catch in her throat, or merely that she had almost used another, more appropriate, word?—"when Greg . . . failed to live up to his expectations."

"Jesus, Mom," Tori cried, "Greg didn't fail to live up to Dad's expectations. Greg was killed."

"Well, your father—"

"I know. He could never tell the difference." All at once she was aware of how soft her mother's hands were against her own callused ones.

"Now I've upset you. Darling, I never meant to."

What part was Laura Nunn playing now? Tori wondered numbly. "You haven't upset me," she said, slumping back into her pillows. "I'm just . . . tired." If her mother could use euphemisms, why couldn't she?

"Of course." Rising, Laura Nunn picked up the tray. "You get some sleep, darling. I've left instructions with everyone that you're not to be disturbed. There'll be no vacuuming on this floor today."

That was something, Tori thought. Her mother was notorious for demanding that her house be vacuumed daily, including Sundays. Tori had always harbored the suspicion that in years past she had had this done at least in part to keep her children from sleeping late on weekends. Sleeping late was, in Laura Nunn's opinion, a sign of laziness.

"Mom, will you be here this afternoon?"

Laura Nunn smiled. "I've got a meeting at the studio at three." She always said "the studio," whether it was Paramount or Warners or Disney. Just like the old days. "Traffic's sure to be impossible that time of day—the stockbrokers are all marching off like lemmings to their health clubs or tennis matches, so I can't imagine I'll be home before six. But I'll have Maria bring your dinner up herself well before then."

"No, don't," Tori said. "I'd like to wait until you get home, have it in the dining room."

Laura Nunn smiled the smile that one hundred million people the world over knew by heart. "We'll see, darling. Now get some rest, all right?"

When she was alone, Tori breathed a sigh, as if holding her breath the entire time she and her mother had been together. It was as if she had been in the presence of a high wattage spotlight. She felt flushed, her skin slightly singed from being so near the preternatural heat. She wondered, fleetingly, how her father had dealt all these years with his wife's power over people.

Actors were different from mere mortals. They tried on and discarded identities and emotions as easily as others did clothes. This chameleon quality so essential for success on the screen made for complex, unsettling, and, at times, eerie family relationships. It was often like being lost in a wilderness of mirrors.

The trouble with actors, Tori had learned at an early age, was that they never stopped acting. You never knew whether they were doing something—such as inducing an emotion in you—because they were genuine or because it was some form of unconscious exercising of their art. She did not envy her father's life with her mother.

The lace curtains blew against the window sash, bringing into the room the scents of the jacaranda, the lilac bushes, the bougainvillea outside. Drapes whipping, blown inward by a wind through a hole rent by plastique . . . scorched fabric and flesh . . . the scent of death clogging her nostrils like pollen . . . Ariel, we hardly had time. . . .

Convulsively, Tori threw the bedcovers off, let her feet touch the Isfahan carpet. She stood, felt a brief wave of dizziness, went immediately into *prana*, breathing deeply, slowly, completely.

She felt as if she had driven all night from San Francisco to Los Angeles, from the darkness into the light, from monochromatic fluorescence to multicolored neon. The sun struck her across the face, and she closed her eyes, breathing in the scents as if they were memories: cars and chrome, miniskirts and oversized jewelry, hot-rodding in the Valley, hot groping in the backseat, lipstick as bright as any neon sign, kohl as black and thick as pitch: desperate attempts to escape her sadness, her prison— Diana's Garden.

I don't want to be back.

She stripped, showered in very hot, then very cold water. Dressed in a sleeveless shirt and shorts, she put on minimal makeup, then ventured out into the hall. It was quite still. She could imagine the servants tiptoeing around the estate so as not to wake her. She put her hands on the polished antique mahogany banister, peered over the pillar railing down to the great entrance below. A sea of Carrara marble, bronze busts of Cesare Borgia, Niccolo Machiavelli, Cosimo de'Medici, Ellis Nunn's pantheon of the Florentine Renaissance. It amazed and saddened Tori that Michelangelo, da Vinci, Fra Angelico, Donatello, Cellini, had no place in her father's historical perspective, as if the Italian Renaissance was an age best remembered for its politics and internecine warfare.

Down the hall she opened the door to her mother's study; her father had his in the other wing of the house. Nothing much had changed here; it never would. The walls were coated with layer upon layer of black lacquer so that they shone with a kind of opalescence.

These walls, along with a baby grand piano, a Regency fruitwood escritoire and commode, satinwood side tables bracketing a sofa covered in French floral chintz, were all festooned with a galaxy of framed photographs, mostly in black and white, though some were in color. These photos were either formal publicity photos or stills from films. They were all of Laura Nunn.

In these shots, Tori's mother was bathed in a luscious combination of moonlight and dreams. It was an underappreciated art, Tori thought as she roved among the gallery, to manufacture such ethereal and subtle illumination. No wonder so many men fell in love with her, and so many women envied her.

The Hollywood Reporter had once dubbed Laura Nunn "the Last of the Great Movie Goddesses." Over the years, her films had not diminished in impact; in fact, many of them had taken on an added historical importance beyond being directed by Alfred Hitchcock, Howard Hawks, or John Huston. They were illustrative of a woman refusing to remain in the manufactured star mold that had characterized the studio-dominated motion picture industry. Laura Nunn might have been a goddess, which

43

made her something both more and less than most of her fellow performers, but she could also act. That had made her invaluable.

Tori tried hard not to see herself in her mother's visage, but, as always, she failed. Her childhood had left her with the vaguely superstitious notion that if she looked like her mother, she would end up being like her. Of course, her subsequent training had taught her the fraudulence of such notions, but the ties that bound child to parent were, like roots, often resistant to change.

Tori slipped out of her mother's study and into the adjoining suite. Greg's room. But here, oddly, things had changed. She saw the same masculine blue and white theme he had liked, the banners from Cal Tech, the medals, the sports trophies, firsts in the nationals in diving, track, and lacrosse. She saw the usual pictures of her older brother. But now there was more.

As if caught in time, Tori gazed at photos of herself, the quintessential cinnamon girl of California, long blond hair streaked by the sun, trim, athletic body with wide shoulders and powerful thighs. Green eyes, wide apart and so direct they are without a trace of guile, but filled with the spark of competitive fire. For the first time it occurred to her that all the shots were lit both by sunlight and by reflections from water. The swimming pool.

The pool at Diana's Garden was both a haven and a repository of memories. A kind of museum of the mind. Thinking of the pool, she remembered . . . the waiting, the tension at the edge of the diving board, the extension of her body, the launch through space, twisting and rolling as she plummeted down, taking one quick visual fix on the water as she spun, then her breath in her ears, foam in her nostrils, the cool water closing over her head, and her father bent over the side of the pool, saying, *Almost as good as Greg does it, Angel. Almost . . .*

I don't want to be back.

Then, stuck in a corner of a frame, she saw two yellowed bits of paper. Her heart thumped as she reached out, unfolded them. The first was a newspaper photo of Greg and the cosmonaut Viktor Shevchenko, their hands clasped triumphantly over their heads, smiling at the camera, in their space suits with the special combined NASA-CCCP logo, as they headed toward the launch pad at the Tyuratam/Baykonur cosmodrome in Russia. In the background it was possible to make out the gigantic launch vehicle, the SL-17 Energiya with its six strap-on booster rockets.

TYURATAM, USSR, May 17 (AP)—History was made today as American astronaut Gregory Nunn and Soviet cosmonaut Viktor Shevchenko successfully lifted off in their
Odin-Galaktika II module from this cosmodrome deep inside
the Soviet Union on the first leg of what is hoped will be
mankind's first manned exploration of the planet Mars.

So vast and expensive was this undertaking that the two
major superpowers decided to pool their technological resources in the effort. NASA officials had been on site here for
more than a year in preparation for this event. . . .

Tori stopped reading; she knew the events by heart. She returned to the photo of Greg and Viktor Shevchenko, and was
struck again by how similar their faces were, both handsome,
strong, confident, as if spacemen were a breed apart, unconcerned by the petty differences of race or nationalism. But then
again Greg, like Tori, was of Russian heritage. She thought that
somehow ironic now.

How proud she had been of Greg that day. She had been glued
to the television, watching the great white plume fill the bright
blue Soviet sky until the space vehicle was a mere point of light,
glittering like a star. Reluctantly, she folded the photo away.

Tori had known what the second newspaper clipping would
be even before she saw the reproduction, blurred by the news-
print paper, of Greg's official NASA photo. Perversely, she
forced herself to begin reading.

MOSCOW, Dec. 11 (AP)—Gregory Nunn, the American astronaut teamed with his Soviet counterpart, cosmonaut Viktor
Shevchenko, was declared officially dead, it was jointly reported by the Soviet news agency Tass and American diplomatic personnel Friday.

Mr. Nunn had been one half of the historic American-Soviet
effort piloting the Odin-Galaktika II module in the first
manned attempt for a landing on the planet Mars. That mission was aborted six weeks ago when "an event of unknown
origin" apparently killed Mr. Nunn and severely damaged
the Odin-Galaktika II module.

With the successful reentry of the damaged space vehicle,
and its subsequent recovery just after midnight yesterday
morning, officials were able to verify Mr. Nunn's death. There
is no word yet as to the condition of Mr. Shevchenko, although it is known that he survived the flight.

A severe winter storm in the Black Sea splashdown area hampered rescue operations following the Odin-Galaktika II's emergency landing, and, for a time, it was feared that the module would be lost at sea. However, the Soviet heavy cruiser, *Potemkin*, was called in when smaller ships began to founder in the heavy seas and near-zero visibility . . .

"Dear God," Tori whispered, jamming the news articles back in their niche. Abruptly, she could no longer bear to look at the bannered walls, the shining trophies, the photographs of who she had been and, in part, must still be.

Suffocating, she got out of there as quickly as she could. She leaned against the closed door, breathing hard in the hallway, in the presence only of the power-laden Florentines of old and of her own memories.

Late in the day, with the California sun slipping through the ornamental lime trees and the oleander, Tori was summoned to meet her father. As she walked through the familiar gardens she wondered at how quickly the spell of this place had overtaken her. It was already difficult to focus on the world outside, to think that anything existed outside this self-contained, all-encompassing environment. Just like old times.

Ellis Nunn was waiting for her at the near end of the sturdy teak pergola he had had built beside the Olympic-size swimming pool. It was overhung with knotty twists of white and lavender wisteria. Wisteria was a tough, drought-resistant plant whose beauty Ellis Nunn could admire.

He smiled when he saw her, embraced her hard in his typical bearlike way. "Hello, Angel." At least he hadn't spoken to her in Russian, as he often did despite Tori's protests—"so you will not forget where your family was born," as he used to say. He smelled of tobacco and cologne, a pleasant mixture that Tori remembered from years past.

Despite the fact that Ellis Nunn tried hard to be very American, he was invariably taken for a native in Europe. He had the kind of Nordic good looks combined with a typical Slavic thickness which marked him as a Russian on the Continent, where such things still mattered.

Tori's father had changed his name before he applied for admission to Stanford. It was not then the power university it eventually would be, but in any event, he received an outstanding education. He became Ellis Nunn not so much because he was ashamed of his real name, but because he loved America so much that he longed for what he thought of as an American name. Tori still did not know what an American name might be.

He was a big man, exceptionally fit despite nearing seventy; he worked out in his pool every day for an hour and a half. His hair was more gray than blond now, but it was just as thick as it had been when he was a young man. His vaguely almond-shaped gray eyes were set on a slight slant. His wide mouth could be as expressive as a comedian's.

The oddest feature of his face was his nose, which, to Tori's way of thinking, did not fit with the rest of his Russian features. No wonder—Ellis had had it redone in his youth to be the very paradigm of an Anglo-Saxon nose. Again, vanity had little to do with the change; his desire to fit into American society did.

Ellis Nunn was a man of light; *the* man of light, some said. He had taken his father's light bulb manufacturing business and, with the knowledge he absorbed at Stanford, brought it west, in the process turning it into the largest and most inno-vative creator of film illumination. If you needed low light to film by, dazzling light to illuminate a gigantic set, spectacular lights to augment explosions, lights to simulate night or any time of the day, delicate, fairy-tale twinklings to highlight a love scene, you called Ellis Nunn's This Magic Moment. His com-panies extended into almost every part of the globe that was a filmmaking center: Italy, France, Spain, even Hong Kong. To-day, his computer-generated networks of lights could do literally anything and everything Hollywood could ask of them, espe-cially now that he had the latest laser technology from his own R&D department to draw on.

His work had made him rich in his own right. He was not, and never had been, one of the sad Bel Air bassets, as they were cruelly known: husbands of movie stars who lived off their wives' breathtaking incomes.

As they strolled under the pergola, Tori thought of all the times she had seen her father walking here with Greg, wonder-ing what it was the two men were speaking of, wondering why she had only rarely been granted the privilege of walking and talking like this with her father, and never here beneath the twining wisteria, Ellis Nunn's favorite spot.

They reached a patch of sunlight and Ellis Nunn stopped. As if divining her thoughts, he said, "Do you know why I love it here in my pergola? Because here no one can see me, no one can hear me." He laughed. "There are too many people padding around my house." He shrugged, began to walk again. "Well, there's no sense in fighting it. That's how it's always been. Your mother's doing. Personally, I can't abide strangers in the house. Who knows where they are and what they're really up to when they're out of sight." He grinned at her. "They don't know what *I'm* up to when I'm here, out of their sight."

"Does that include Mom?"

"Of course it does," he said. "She's the nosiest of the lot. Trouble with her is she wants to run everything. Can't do it, no one can, but she's never learned. Not surprised. She's never been good with the basics. That's why she needs all these people, really. Her mind's on other, more esoteric matters. Who she'll be today. Flexing those prodigious emotional muscles of hers. Miss Emotional Universe. I used to call her that in the old days. Nothing much has changed since then, I suppose, but us. Well, not your mother. She never changes, not really—I mean, not deep under the surface."

The patch of sunlight illuminated the stone statue of Diana, a reproduction of the one in Mexico City.

Ellis Nunn pointed at it. "There is your mother: Diana, the Huntress. Did you know that she was born Diana Leeway? No? I'm not surprised. No one does. I can't imagine her telling you. No one left in any of the studios now to recall it, either. I can't remember whose idea the name Laura was. Anyway, the producers liked the sound of Laura Nunn, so that's what she became, in reality as well as on the screen. Well, as much as your mother knows what reality is."

"How did you put up with her all these years?" Tori asked. "You not only survived, but thrived."

"Well, I don't know about thriving," he said, "but as for surviving . . ." He put his forefinger against his lips, thought a moment. "Do you know the story of the Zen Policeman? No? Odd, with all that time spent in Japan."

"Dad—"

"My God, Tori, look at you." He only called her by her Christian name when he was angry with her. "You're a grown woman of thirty-six, and what do you have to show for it? No discernible job, let alone a career. And as for starting your own family—well, that's something of a joke, isn't it? Face it, Tori, you've made a mess of everything, and here you are standing in front of me, while Greg—" For a moment he could not go on. He looked apoplectic. Then he seemed to gain hold of himself. "You're the one who has studied Oriental philosophy. Tell

48

me, why is it that Greg, who had everything going for him, who had his whole life laid out as clearly as a road map, a career distinguished by—Jesus God, he was going to become one of the first two men to live in space, and then to land on Mars . . . Have you any conception of what that means?'' He passed a hand over his face. ''Why did it happen, Tori? Why is he gone?''

Tori said nothing. What was there to say?

''Greg was destined for great things, I knew it the moment he was born.'' Ellis Nunn seemed drained of the spasm of anger that had gripped him. He seemed genuinely confused. ''Why was he taken from us? Your mother says it's God's will. Well, if that's so, then God's an unforgivably cruel and capricious creature.''

Now Tori felt the words coming; she could not help herself. ''So that *is* what you think I've done with my life: nothing. Well, I'm not what you wanted me to be, an astronaut, stretching the envelope of space. I'm not like Greg. You trained him; he wanted to be just what you wanted him to be. It was the perfect union of generations. You were so proud of him. You understood what motivated him; Greg was like an open book to you. But you couldn't fathom why on earth I would want to go to Japan to study. Of course you couldn't. You've spent all your adult life here in L.A., in many ways as far from global politics and economics as Fiji. This is the original land of Nod, and you built yourself Diana's Garden, a dream within the dreamland of L.A. Is it any wonder that you have no conception of what makes me tick? 'Japan,' I remember you saying. 'What the hell could be so damn important in Japan?' You never understood. You never wanted to.'' She shook her head. ''I must be such a disappointment to you.''

Her father was studying the last of the sunlight as it slid down the folds of Diana's stone robe. He had that faraway look on his face he sometimes had during long meetings at the office, as if he were there only in body, not in spirit. It was a sad look, as well, so similar to the one she had caught in the corners of Greg's face now and again when he was sure no one was watching him.

Tori put her head down. Too late she remembered her promise to her mother not to start a fight with her father. What did it matter? she thought. This isn't about me or my father—it never was. It's about Greg. It's always been about Greg, and there's nothing I can say or do that will ever change it. As she let the silence of the encroaching evening steal up on them, she was aware of a great sadness welling up inside her. She recognized

49

that she was angry at her father, but also at herself for letting him get to her again and again.

She said, after a time, "Are you going to tell me the story of the Zen Policeman?"

Ellis Nunn nodded, but whether it was in simple assent or in acceptance of the fragility of their relationship, she could not tell.

"Many centuries ago," he began, "there was a young Buddhist priest who traveled to Tibet in order to further his understanding of religion and philosophy.

"He possessed the proper credentials as well as a letter of introduction from his superior at his temple in central China. When, at length, he came upon the monastery he was searching for, he had climbed so high he felt as if he had breached the very vault of heaven, and it took him some time before he was able to adapt his breathing to this dizzying height.

"In due course he was accepted into the monastery, but it was some days before he was summoned to the presence of the high lama. The old, wizened man looked three hundred years old.

" 'I understand that though you are a priest you do not believe that your spiritual education is complete.'

" 'That is correct, sir,' the young priest said in a somewhat overawed voice.

" 'What is it you seek to learn here?' the old lama asked.

" 'Why, all there is to learn,' the young priest said immediately.

"The old lama looked at him and smiled. 'We shall see,' he said. 'In the meantime, we require you to remain awake and on guard during the night.'

"The young priest looked confused. 'It took me two months to reach here. I know how remote this monastery is. How could you have enemies here?'

" 'The monk who brought you to this chamber will tell you where you must sit tonight,' the lama said.

" 'But I am a priest, not a guard,' the young man protested. 'Besides, I am a Buddhist. I have pledged never to harm a single creature. I cannot even till the earth for fear of killing a worm or an insect.'

" 'You do not yet know who or what you are,' the old lama said. 'That is why you are here.'

"That night, the young priest was shown to the spot in the exact center of the monastery where he must keep watch. A

50

pillow was placed for him to sit. It was a crossing of the four main corridors of the stone structure, and from his vantage point he could see most, if not all, the monks' tiny sleeping cells.

"The hours of the night crept by with agonizing slowness. Nothing happened. The silence became a weight on the young priest's eyelids, so that once or twice he found himself drifting off into a light slumber before starting awake. He yawned and stretched to keep himself alert. He began to wonder why he had come here, or if he had come to the right place at all.

"Then, all at once, he stood up. He looked from corridor to corridor, sure that he had heard a sound. But there was only the heavy awful silence, claustrophobic as the inside of a tomb. Then he became aware that the 'sound' was an ethereal stirring, as if in his own mind, and he whirled around.

"He was not alone. Something was in the west corridor. It came toward him but, in the flickering light of the reed torches, he could not make out what it was.

"Suddenly, it burst out of the corridor, coming upon him like a whirlwind, and he felt a chill race down his spine. It was as translucent as the wings of an insect; he could clearly see the corridor behind it, *through* it.

"The wraith brushed past him, careening down another corridor. Soon the intersection where the young priest now stood was thick with these wraiths. Sometimes it seemed to him that they had faces, bodies, hands and feet. At other times they were nothing more than pure energy.

"The young priest felt a fright welling up inside of him. What were these forms? Were they the enemies of the Tibetan monks? If so, how was he to combat them, when violence was anathema to him? These questions and ten thousand others crowded his mind in the same way the wraiths crowded the corridors of the monastery. The terrible fear built inside him, until he contemplated abandoning his post, turning tail, and putting this mad place behind him forever. But, as if in a dream, he felt rooted to the spot. He did not know whether to fear for the loss of his mind or his life.

"Then he noticed a curious thing. The fear was coming from inside him. When he concentrated his spiritual powers, he realized that the wraiths, whatever or whoever they might be, posed no threat to him or to the people of the monastery. The chaos of their rushing to and fro was, in a way, self-contained.

"And then he set about trying to turn the chaos into order. He found that, with continued concentration, he could move

51

closer to these darting wraiths, could feel where they wanted to go and, eventually, guide them on their way.

"It was at that moment that he recognized one of the wraiths as the monk who had led him to the lama's sanctuary, and to this crossroads. And then the young priest understood everything.

"These wraiths were the spirits of the monks. Unleashed as they slept, freed from the bonds of their daytime work, these spirits were prone to the chaos that lurked within the innermost recesses of even the most disciplined mind. They lacked but a single soul—a kind of Zen policeman—to see them on their proper paths, to keep them from the dangers inherent in chaos."

Tori and her father had come to the far end of the pergola. He turned around, took one last look at the statue of Diana, cloaked now in the robes of twilight. He said, after a long silence, "Does that answer your question as to how I have survived in Diana's Garden? I learned that I had to change in order to survive the demons peculiar to your mother's genius."

Tori thought for a long time. It was an amazing story, and even more amazing that it had come from her father. She simply had not thought he had such subtlety in him. The story also explained many things about her parents' relationship. But it also brought into focus some of her own childhood concerns. She said carefully, "I worry sometimes that I . . . Well, I still sort of lose myself when Mom's around. There's so much of her—her personality, her aura, her *wa*, as the Japanese would say—that there often seems no space left over for me."

Her father said, "You should try to understand your mother more. If you did, I'm sure you'd find it worth your while."

"I'm not sure you heard what I said." Tori was struggling to find a basis for communicating with him, but either he was misunderstanding her or being willful. Still, she pressed on. "I often end up not knowing how I feel about her." She looked at him, at that noble, almost primitive profile. "Do you love Mom?"

Ellis Nunn turned to his daughter. "I understand her, Tori. I think, in your mother's case, that's the same as loving her."

"Is it?"

"Well, you tell me, then," Ellis Nunn said testily. "How else do you love an icon? How do you bring something so monumental, so universally adored, into your reality? The answer is, you don't waste your time. Instead, you enter into *its* reality as best you can."

52

"I don't—"

"Look, my marriage survived where the marriages of people like DiMaggio and Arthur Miller did not. I've come to see that as accomplishment enough." He looked away toward the pool, as if he wished he were in there now. "Your mother needs to be what she has become in the same way you and I need air to breathe. Once you understand that, you understand everything."

Tori looked up into his face. There was just enough light left so that the reflections from the pool lit up his face and she was reminded of the photos of Greg, poolside, fresh from some diving triumph, his angel eyes aglow with the victory fever. Greg. It was always Greg. Even death could not stop them all from talking about him, thinking about him, trying to live up to the shining potential of his angel eyes.

"Spoken like a true Zen policeman," she said with all the irony she could muster.

Evening approaches. Tori, hidden away from her mother, behind the massive carved oak doors to the library, is again feeling trapped in Diana's Garden. She remembers a time of adolescence. She is trapped in the big house in L.A., in the sunshine, in her sleek tanned body. She is pinned by her beauty to the imagined future, the foregone conclusion that her father wants for her, that boys her own age imagine is already hers. They are the same, these images, and they dominate her life like a nun's vows.

She has all she wants within Diana's Garden, and increasingly she feels that there is no reason to venture outside its perfect, all-encompassing environs.

Until, one night during a party given by her parents, she discovers how completely she has fooled herself. Just about everyone who matters in Hollywood—except enemies—has descended upon the manor house, and the rooms are full of familiar faces, screen legends, movers and shakers. There are the money men and their exquisite women, as polished as gems, seemingly pulled out of the men's pockets like an expensive watch or a roll of thousand-dollar bills.

Gossip, which is the only approved mode of communication at affairs such as this, centers around who is sleeping with whom, and who is pregnant by whom. Gradually it dawns on Tori that these people who inhabit Hollywood like a race of gorgeous troglodytes run their private lives in sync with their professional careers. Love affairs, marriages, seduction—whatever the current voguish designation—last among these strange, alien life forms only as long as it takes to make a film. These people meet on the set, become immersed in each other in the same manner in which they become immersed in their roles. In order to differentiate reality from fantasy, however, they feel compelled to make tangible their love for one another, if not their commitment. A child follows, as surely as the night the day. But, invariably, with the advent of the baby, the love affair, marriage, seduction loses its luster. A mother is never as exciting as a lover; three takes the edge off the heat generated by two.

Tori understands at last that she hates these people, that she feels their coming as an invasion. That night, whether in the living room, the study, the library, the throngs of people overwhelm her. She feels suffocated. She flees the house, but the grounds, too, are choked with celebrities, and still she cannot breathe. Bent over by the side of the lighted pool, her sanctuary, where she had always felt closest to Greg, she wheezes like an asthmatic.

At last she stumbles to her car, a new Thunderbird, convulsively turns the ignition and, scattering gravel in her wake, speeds away into the night, the neon light of Los Angeles. Not Beverly Hills or Westwood, but beyond, where people who are not rich, pampered, privileged, work and play.

There is a rage inside her she can neither explain nor face. She feels inadequate in the face of it, and at the same time ashamed of it, as if part of her mother has broken off and, like a poisoned arrowhead, has embedded itself in her brain.

She hates the shame most of all, because it keeps her from embracing her rage, owning it and, thus, understanding it. Kept at a distance, it is nothing more than an arcane artifact living at the edge of her emotional horizon, a glyph-covered stele, marking what? She does not know, but tonight she is determined to find out.

Down twisty Mulholland to the freeway, rolling over the edge of the glen, coming upon the wide swath of smeary lights glowing in the Valley. The pollution, trapped by the air inversion between high ground, makes her eyes tear, her skin itch. She depresses the accelerator, bringing the horizon closer.

At a seedy bar she pulls in beside a line of scruffy Harley-Davidson motorcycles. She sits listening to the hot engine of the T-bird ticking over as if it is the beating of her heart. Sadness mixes with her rage, and she wishes that Greg were with her,

Greg who is always willing to listen to her, the one person in the world who accepts her as herself and nothing more. But Greg is away at Cal Tech, studying for finals which he takes more seriously than God.

I am alone, Tori thinks, the glyph-covered stele coming nearer.

She goes into the bar and orders drink after drink. She is underage, but she regularly passes for eighteen. In any event, her beauty is something no bartender can resist, and she is never turned down or asked for ID.

A jukebox is blasting "The Loco-Motion," and the dancing is ferocious. There are a number of black leather jackets. She sees tattoos, long, lank hair, thick, studded belts and armbands. One biker wears a miniature skull on a leather thong around his neck. A girl asks him something, and he laughs, fondling it, saying over the music, "It's real, man. Belonged to a rat that thought it could share my kitchen with me. What you think o' that?" The girl giggles giddily and shudders, but she cannot avert her gaze from the grisly talisman.

All the guys—and most of the girls—are staring at Tori. She sticks out here like a tea rose in a cabbage patch. Someone is pointing out the window, at her brand new T-bird, and the whispering begins. The artifact, once at the edge of her horizon, is almost close enough to touch.

The only guy who hasn't noticed her is the one with the rat skull around his neck. He is not handsome, not even attractive to Tori, but that is irrelevant. He is the one she wants. In him burns the fire she knows so well—yet does not understand at all: the rage of the beast caged, bound by the laws of a hypocritical society. He will be the one, her Rosetta stone, from whom she will obtain the secret of deciphering the glyphs of her rage.

He is dancing with the girl who asked about the skull. There is a fire in her eyes that Tori recognizes and envies, a fire she feels but must suppress in order to fit into the perfectly manicured life in Diana's Garden. The fire exhibits itself as simple, unadulterated, elemental, and it represents everything Tori is not.

With a sudden wrenching of the girl's wrist, Tori spins her away and begins dancing with the biker. He is huge, and she smells him, a rich, heady combination of leather and sweat. Primitive. The beast.

"Hey! Hey!" The girl has returned, her hair disheveled, her face twisted into an angry mask.

"Get lost!" Tori shouts as she dances. "I'm here now!"

"Bitch!" the girl shouts back, and reaches clumsily for her. The rage bursts its bonds, at last. Tori twists her upper torso, slams her balled fist into the girl's face. The girl's neck snaps back and her legs go out from under her.

Tori continues to dance with the biker. She has not once looked into his eyes. She does not want to. His eyes don't interest her.

"Hey!" he says. "Hey!"

Tori is dancing, and hardly notices that he has stopped.

The biker says to her, "Who the fuck do you think you are?" And, as casually as someone would swat a fly, he smashes the heel of his thick hand into Tori's nose, breaking it. . . .

Tori sat very still in the huge leather chair. It had been a long time since she had thought of that night in the Valley. Because her nose had healed slightly crooked, her mother had taken her to her own plastic surgeon. But after seeing the array of new noses he could provide her, Tori had run out of his office and never gone back. In the end, her imperfect nose had become for her a badge of sorts, a reminder of what she had never gotten and what she needed.

Freedom to be . . .

Be what? She did not know. But Adona was right: she needed a passion. Without it, she was suspended in limbo, surviving perhaps, but hardly living.

"Tori?" Laura Nunn poked her head into the library. She was wearing a pair of blue jeans with lines of rhinestones across the pockets and down the legs, and a plain white man-tailored shirt, both of which she had just bought at a posh store on Rodeo Drive in the mistaken impression this casual outfit would allow her to feel closer to her daughter. But this attempt at being a pal was a role as well, and the sight merely saddened Tori.

"Oh, there you are, darling! You seemed to have disappeared like a puff of smoke." Laura Nunn flashed her kilowatt smile. "There's someone here to see you."

"There is? I don't see how." Tori looked up from the book she was reading. She had one leg thrown over the arm of the oversized leather chair she was slouched in. She was barefoot, wearing only a pair of cutoffs and a Cal Tech T-shirt. "No one knows where I am."

"Nevertheless, he's here."

"Who?"

56

"Russell."

"Russell who?"

"Why, you know, dear. Russell Slade." Laura Nunn held the smile as if she were waiting for the director to yell, Cut!

"Jesus Christ!" Tori slammed the book shut, jumped off the chair. "I hope to God you told him to go to hell or, at the very least, that I wasn't home."

"I did nothing of the sort," Laura Nunn said. "I told him I was delighted to see him—which, by the way, I am. I told him I'd go fetch you. Now—"

"Mother, Russell Slade *fired* me!"

"Well, I'm sure that was just a misunderstanding," Laura Nunn said. "More a matter of internal politics than anything else. I'm certain it had nothing to do with the kind of job you were doing. New regimes, and all that. People who come into a new job want their own people under them. It's only natural, darling. I've seen it happen often enough at the studios. One just has to thicken one's skin. The last thing you need is to take this kind of unpleasantness personally."

"Oh, Jesus, I haven't even spoken to Russell since he canned me a year and a half ago."

"Not even when we were . . . in Washington last year?"

"No." Tori's mother could not bring herself to speak of it, but the President had presented them with the Presidential Medal of Freedom awarded posthumously to Greg, and she had carried it back here, put it away in a drawer in Greg's room. It was to her not a symbol of pride, but rather another reminder of the enormous tragedy of his death.

"I can't think why you haven't patched up your differences by now, darling. He's such an adorable man. Just perfect for—" Some sixth sense caused her to stop. She turned to look over her shoulder, said in a voice so bright it verged on being brittle, "Darling, look who's here!"

And Tori saw Russell Slade brush past her mother, neatly cutting off her own avenue of escape from the library.

"Hello, Tori," he said, just as if nothing had ever happened between them.

Tori, for the moment speechless, looked past him to where her mother still stood in the partly open doorway. Laura Nunn gave Tori a beseeching look, then quietly closed the door.

Russell looked around. "I haven't been here in a long time. It was good to see your mother again. My God, what a magnificent woman she is."

"You've got a set of brass ones," Tori said. "What the hell are you doing here?"

"Could I have a drink, do you think? It's a long drive from the airport."

Tori went to the wet bar along one wall, fixed him a Tom Collins without asking him what he wanted; she already knew. She handed him the drink, and he nodded. He was dressed elegantly but comfortably in a dark blue polo shirt, linen trousers, a beautifully cut lightweight silk jacket. Tori was acutely aware that she was barefoot and dressed like a waif. She seemed at a distinct disadvantage, like a naughty child being interviewed by her father.

"I've come to debrief you," Russell Slade said.

"*Debrief* me?"

He nodded. "Someone had to do it. I thought it might as well be me. Ariel Solares was one of my best field men. Since you were there when he died, you know it's standard operating procedure that you be debriefed."

"You're the director; you don't know the first thing about debriefing field personnel, they're too far down the food chain."

Russell ignored her sarcasm. "As I said, Solares was one of my best men. I thought it wise if I came myself."

"Don't bullshit me, Russell. You came here because it was me who was with him."

"I understand your anger, but—"

"You don't understand one thing about me!" Tori flared.

Russell, taking a sip of his drink, regarded her coolly over the rim of his glass. "In any event," he said at last, "I've got to talk to you."

"I don't work for you anymore."

He sighed as he took a seat on the leather sofa beside the chair she had been reading in. He picked up her book. *"The Nobility of Failure."* He looked at her. "I know this book. It's about Japanese heroes of myth and history, isn't it?" He did not take his eyes off her. "Sit down, Tori, please. I recognize you're angry that I've intruded on your solitude, but I came here because Solares's murder compelled me to come. I think even you can see that. Let's try at least to be civilized, get the interview over with, and call it a day."

"How simple you make it all seem."

Tori turned away from him, went back to the bar. She selected an oversized glass, dropped in some ice, poured single-malt scotch, then added some water. She recognized that she didn't

58

really want a drink, but she needed to buy herself some time to restore her equilibrium.

"The first thing I'd like to know," she heard him say from across the room, "is if you're all right. You must have been hurt in the explosion, yet the San Francisco police told us that you refused medical treatment."

"That's because I didn't require any," Tori said, taking a sip of scotch, then turning around to face him.

"Not even shock. I see." Russell regarded her for a moment, then nodded. "That would be like you," he said, as if to himself. "You were always adamant about doing everything yourself."

"I am more qualified—"

"Yes, yes, I know. Please let's not get into that all over again."

"What mask do you have on today, Russ?" Tori sat down beside him. "The mask of the invincible administrator, or the master chess player, sacrificing one pawn after another in the bloody field you've never walked through? Or maybe it's your favorite you have on today: the Bernard Godwin protégé mask."

Russell sipped at his Tom Collins. "That's the one you hated most, isn't it," he said, aware of Godwin saying to him, *Your relationship with Tori Nunn is all unfinished business*. "Because in a way we're victims of sibling rivalry. We both think of ourselves as Bernard's protégés. He never had children, Tori, he made us, instead."

Tori made a disgusted sound, sat back against the sofa, allowed the coolness of the leather to penetrate her T-shirt.

Russell got up, took a walk around the library. This was typical of him; he liked to get the lay of the land. He found the physical and the emotional space inextricably entwined, and he chose the ground for his interviews with meticulous care.

Tori saw him come at length to the French fruitwood table. He ran his hand across the chocolate-colored leather of its top, the brass and green glass banker's lamp, the chased-silver burl cigar humidor given to Tori's father by Samuel Goldwyn. In so doing, Russell passed near enough to touch the box Ariel Solares pressed into her hand just before he had died. Tori held her breath. She had no intention of telling Russell Slade about its existence, either now or in the future. Ariel had given it to her, and she was now its sole guardian.

He turned back to her. "What the hell happened in San Francisco?"

"Why don't you tell me."

59

"I don't follow you."

"Ariel Solares was pursuing me."

Russell's face was impassive. "Was he? Well, he had better taste in women than I gave him credit for."

Tori laughed despite herself. "You've gotten better, Russell, I'll give you that." She got up, stood face-to-face with him. "You know Ariel was pursuing me," she said, taking a stab in the twilight. "You sent him after me."

"Now that's an absurd notion."

"I don't think it is," Tori said. "Why else would you come to debrief me personally unless you were running Ariel yourself?"

"It happens that Solares was working on a first-priority mission for us. Actually, I was about to dispatch someone else to debrief you, but in the end decided that mine was the duty, sort of my way of taking responsibility for Ariel's death."

"That's a pathetic gesture, typical of a desk jockey who knows nothing of the dangers in the field."

"Don't be melodramatic," he said. "The truth is my people go because they want to go, not because I make them." He put down his glass on the table beside the box Ariel had given her. "But you already know that."

"What I know is that Ariel was working for you, that his picking me up in Buenos Aires wasn't happenstance. He was waiting for me."

"Well, that's an interesting surmise," Russell said smoothly. "But it's wrong. A bit too Machiavellian."

Tori laughed again. "That's an oxymoronic sentence I'd like to preserve in my diary." She finished off her scotch. "What was Ariel doing for you in Buenos Aires?"

Russell shrugged. "According to you, waiting to lure you into his web."

"I mean in the tunnels, Russell. The Yakuza assassins. Ariel knew who they were and why they were there. That means you know, too."

"Sure I do, but the information's classified. You don't work for me anymore."

"Thank God," Tori said. "But I have to wonder whether you were ever able to replace me. Skills like mine are invaluable."

"To a very select few."

Tori smiled. "No, I don't have to wonder. I know you've never been able to replace me."

Russell sat back, stared up at the ceiling. "That may or may not be true. But I would have thought you would recognize your role in helping us find Solares's murderers." He paused significantly. "If only for his sake."

Tori smiled. "That's right, Russell, give it the old college try. Give me one last shot of team spirit, see if it takes."

"I think you've misunderstood. Do you really think I'm as completely cynical as that?"

Tori rose, went back to the bar, poured herself some mineral water. "How is Bernard?" she asked. "He's still retired from the Mall?"

"Oh, not retired, never retired." Russell watched her carefully. "Bernard's maintained an unofficial consultancy of sorts. It's an arrangement that is beneficial to all concerned."

"Remember me to him, would you?" Tori said.

"Of course." Russell extracted a mini tape recorder from an inside jacket pocket. He snapped it on. "Now, can we get on with the interview?"

"All right," Tori said. "I'll tell you everything I know."

When she had finished, Russell said, "You're certain that's everything."

Tori said it was. She had not told him about the box or about going to bed with Ariel.

Russell snapped off the tape recorder. "Well, that's over with," he said in the tone one uses when one is finally finished making funeral arrangements. "Do you think we can call a truce of sorts?"

"What makes you think we'll need one?" Tori said, rising.

But as she passed by him, he put his hand gently on her left hip and said, "How does it feel?"

Tori went into *prana*, breathing deeply and easily. But to regain her equilibrium had cost her time, and the silence was unspooling rapidly, each second increasing Russell Slade's small victory over her. "I rarely think of it anymore," she lied.

"That's good," he said. "It means the healing is complete." He took his hand away, but still she did not move. "Tell me, can you do everything you could do before the, ah, incident?"

And, abruptly, it all clicked into place in her mind, scattered pieces that had made little sense on their own. Only when they were connected did the whole picture emerge. She turned to look at him. "It wasn't just that you sent Ariel after me, was it? You ordered him to test me. That's why he took me down into those tunnels. He knew the Japanese were going to be there.

And that's why he was so passive down there, to allow me the opportunity to figure a way out. I was a rat in a maze." She stared wide-eyed at him. "That's it, isn't it?"

Russell smiled at her. "Well, I see there's nothing wrong with your imagination." He pocketed the tape recorder. "But to put your mind at ease, I have no idea why Solares took you into the tunnels. In fact, he should have known better. Taking you into a Red Sector was a gross breach of security—and I'm afraid he paid for that breach."

"No you don't," Tori said. "Don't lay this off on Ariel." She came across the room, stood looking down at him. "You have no idea why he was murdered or even who did it, because if you did, you wouldn't be wasting your time debriefing me." No, she thought, you need me, Russell. *That's* why you're here. I passed your reentrance exams and now you want me back.

Russell was shaking his head. "What a waste. If only you'd consented to allow our specialists to look after you following the incident. Don't you see, by insisting on your own doctors— Japanese doctors who we could neither vet nor vouch for—you put the entire Mall network in jeopardy. I had no choice but to sever our ties at once. You brought on your own fate with us."

"I did what I had to do in order to save myself," Tori said. "I knew nothing about *your* specialists, but I *did* know mine. They are friends, *and* they are the best at reconstructive surgery."

"That all may well be true, but—"

"You still don't get it, do you?" Tori shook her head. "Without this body, without it being able to do everything it did before, I would have been nothing. I would not have been able to live with myself."

"I fully understand your concern for your body. But our people were just as good as your Japanese surgeons, *and* they had the highest security clearance. Who knows what you could have revealed about the Mall under anesthesia? I had all of my people to think about, not just you."

"Clever," Tori said, "but it's not enough. You used that incident, but that wasn't the real reason you severed me. That's the one thing you haven't lied about. We *were* like siblings. I was your major competition with Bernard, and you wanted me out of the way, and you got what you wanted because in the end the Mall's like every other place, a bastion of male superiority."

"Control was never a place for you, you're quite right about that." Russell stood. "But now you're not on any missions, either. That must be a source of considerable pain for you." His eyes were on her. "As far as the hip is concerned—"

"The Japanese surgeons put in a prosthesis of a material that's far superior to human bone. It's ten times more flexible and one hundred times as strong." She gave him a cold smile. "But since you asked, there's no pain on wet days, no unusual friction, nothing that reminds me that the hip had once been shattered. Except that I run, jump, and twist better than I did before the implant."

"In any event, you seem to have gotten out of the tunnels in an ingenious fashion." It was his way of saying he believed her, but at the same time he had confirmed her suspicion that Ariel had been ordered to test her. Under the circumstances, she felt it to be an inadequate victory.

She continued to study him. "You'll never admit that I did the right thing by going to my friends instead of using your people."

"The truth is you made a decision—one of many, I might say—with your emotions instead of your brain," Russell said. "Worse, you could not see the danger in putting yourself in the hands of those not under Mall discipline. I'm afraid you left me no choice."

"How convenient memory can be."

"We all believe what we need to believe, Tori."

"Except for Bernard."

"You give Bernard entirely too much credit," Russell said. "But that's no doubt because Bernard Godwin recruited you. He was your mentor. But, you see, Bernard handed the reins over to me. You never understood that, or never wanted to. You mistrusted me from the outset."

"I detested the callous way you used people."

Russell smiled at her. "You forget that Bernard Godwin was my mentor, as well."

There was a silence for a time. Tori digested both the tone and the thrust of the conversation. At length she said, "There's really nothing you can say that will change my mind."

"About what?"

"About returning to the Mall."

"That's not why I came here."

"Isn't it?" Tori said. She matched his smile, but all the time her heart was beating fast. "Perhaps you're right. In that case, you've got what you came for."

63

"Right," Russell said. "Don't want to overstay my welcome."

"You never had one."

He laughed. "Thanks for the drink. You've been the perfect hostess."

Tori said nothing.

"*À bientôt,*" Russell said. Until we meet again.

"That'll be the day."

The library, so cozy and snug in the daytime, was now wreathed in the shadows of evening, made gloomy and depressing by her dream as well as by the onset of night.

Tori sat curled in the huge leather chair, still feeling Russell Slade's presence as if it had somehow been imprinted upon her flesh. For a moment she was suddenly overcome by panic. Her hip! What if Russell had mentioned it to her mother? Tori had never told her parents that she had been injured, or that she had a prosthetic hip. She could imagine Russell saying, It's wonderful that your daughter has fully recovered, Mrs. Nunn. But no, she knew him better than that. Always security-conscious, Russell never said any more than he had to. He was the consummate spy; his lies were largely those of omission.

Feeling a bit calmer, Tori got off the chair, went to the desk. She put her hands on the box Ariel had given her. She opened it once again, took out the color snapshot, stared at it. It was a photo of Ariel, clearly taken recently, perhaps only weeks before he had come down to Buenos Aires. In the background Tori could see trees, walkways, benches, one of San Francisco's small parks. Tori could see Russian Hill in the distance, so the park was close to where Ariel had lived. His face was in partial shade, but it must have been quite sunny because his eyes were crinkled up against the light. He was smiling. Just behind him was what looked like a bronze sundial and, beyond, a child at play. At the edge of the park a couple was walking toward the camera, and a bit closer there was a man in the left-hand corner of the frame. They were all too distant for her to be able to make out their faces.

Tori had studied this photograph endlessly since she had come home, searching for a clue as to what might make it important enough for Ariel, at the point of death, to entrust her with it. But she could find nothing out of the ordinary. It was just a photo of a man in the park. Ariel. Was this the sum total of him, all that might pass for a legacy?

There was a soft knock on the library door, and Laura Nunn entered. "Darling, it's so late. We were waiting dinner for you."

Tori glanced at her watch. "But it's only six-thirty, Mother."

Laura Nunn smiled. "Seven-thirty. We turned the clocks ahead this morning. It's Daylight Saving Time. Summer's on its way." She cocked her head. "You're hungry aren't you?"

Tori, putting away the mysterious photo of Ariel, said, "As a matter of fact I am."

And speaking of Zen policemen, Tori thought, hours later when she was alone in her room, there was Bernard Godwin, the father figure in her life. She had met him and her life had changed, as if he had been a bolt of lightning, or a Zen policeman.

She was sitting at the art deco vanity—a Christmas gift from her mother—where, years before, Laura Nunn had put ribbons in her hair, tying them just so, the perfect mother making her daughter in her image. Perfect. Tori, running her brush through her thick hair now, shuddered. She stared at herself in the mirror, and remembered . . .

Almost ten years ago she had been, in the current street patois, a wild child—what the society of sixteenth century feudal Japan would have called a ronin—a masterless samurai.

Those were the days when Tori haunted the wicked back streets, the evil bars squatting in the putrid backwaters, bastard splinters of Tokyo's monolithic nature.

There were so many empty spaces in Tori's mind, she could afford little sleep, because in rest she would be forced to look into the emptiness and see, perhaps, what she was not ready to confront. Instead she walked the line closest to the abyss of death in order to prove to herself that she was still alive.

It was inconceivable to her, for instance, that she might be homesick. Oh, she missed Greg, but that was a given for her. It never occurred to her that she might long to see her father again, to gain from him what she never had been able to, a sense of her own worth, a knowledge seen in his eyes, heard in his tone of voice if not directly from his words, that he was proud of her, the way he was proud of Greg. There had never been room for her in a family fixated on continual praise for Gregory Nunn, pilot, astronaut, and it was far less painful to relinquish all hope than to be forever disappointed.

The fact was, had she been able to admit it to herself, Tori would have seen that she loved her father as she loved Greg.

Both were extraordinary people in much the same way. But Tori's burning need to be recognized in her own right by her father made it impossible for her to see him with the same objectivity she saw Greg.

In a way, it was odd that she put no blame on her brother for the praise lavished on him. Shouldn't she see it as his fault that when the family spotlight swung on him, it left her in shadow? Yet she did not. Perhaps her love for Greg was so complete that it never occurred to her to hate him. Certainly she envied his relationship with Ellis Nunn, and yet whatever her lack, she saw it as her father's fault, not Greg's.

But, in another way, it was perfectly understandable that she should hold her brother blameless for the excesses of her family. Greg was her lone ally in her skirmishes with her parents, and to exclude him from her life would be to threaten her very existence.

But with Greg gone from Diana's Garden, Tori discovered that her desire to get as far away from Los Angeles as possible overshadowed everything else.

Japan.

Where a fire awaited her, burning in the darkness of her night.

Perhaps *sensei* discerned the blackness inside her, but if so, he made no comment on it. *Sensei* was a believer in hard work—in discipline, he once told Tori, is the answer to every problem.

Either he was mistaken or Tori was unable to absorb his teachings deeply enough. In either case, Tori graduated from his arduous course of training—the only woman to make it all the way through—without having successfully confronted the specters within her own night.

This was the state in which Bernard Godwin found her: dangerous, her nerves hair-trigger fine, walking the edge between trouble and death, and getting a hell of a kick out of it.

In fact, when she remembered the moment of her first meeting with Bernard Godwin, what stuck out most was that she had almost gotten him killed.

He had found her in an *akachochin* called The Happily Ever After. The after-hours club was in the wrong end of Nihonbashi—God knows how Bernard even found it. Walking into the place was like being sucked into a whirlpool in the center of a cesspit.

A Yakuza underboss approximately as large as Godzilla was hitting on her. She didn't mind; she liked his tattoos: flames, everywhere flames, eating gods, demons, mythical animals, and fierce swordsmen with indiscriminate greed. The flames made her think of exorcism, turning filth to oily smoke, purging sacred ground that had been made profane, purifying the night.

Just before Bernard Godwin came down the stairs in The Happily Ever After, she remembered composing the first line of a reply to the letter she had just received from her brother: *It's all right, Greg. I'm doing the best I can.* Smiling up at Godzilla, the Japanese gangster full of fantastic flames. Yessir, she thought. He's evil, he's nasty, and he's all mine.

Then Bernard Godwin had introduced himself. It was not a happy moment, for either Tori or Godzilla. Neither of them wanted to be interrupted. Then Bernard Godwin said that he had a proposition for Tori, but first she must come away with him out of this place, and all hell broke loose.

Godzilla might have been huge, but he was astonishingly quick. This was his turf, and he was nothing if not intensely territorial. Bernard had muscled in on his property, and Godzilla was enraged. He displayed his displeasure by picking Bernard up in one meat-hook fist and shaking him until Bernard's teeth rattled.

"Stop it!" Tori said.

Godzilla ignored her. A small blade snicked into his left hand. It headed for Bernard's throat.

Tori drove her doubled-up knuckles into Godzilla's sternum while simultaneously smacking him in the groin with her knee. For a moment nothing happened, then Godzilla's eyes began to water, his mouth flopped open, and he dropped Bernard Godwin to the none too clean floor.

Tori knew her exit cue. She grabbed Bernard by the back of the neck and got out of there.

Across town in Roppongi, in an infinitely more savory neighborhood, they entered an all-night sushi restaurant. A sign over the door had imprinted on it the image of a round, spiky fish.

"You're buying," Tori said as they sat down. "You owe me."

"It will be a pleasure," Bernard Godwin said, inclining his head in a gesture that seemed both old-fashioned and appropriate. She was surprised that he appeared none the worse for his ordeal.

Tori ordered for them: bowls of baby eels to start, then an assortment of sushi that included abalone, flying fish roe, and sea urchin. Lastly, she ordered broiled *fugu*. All this was quite deliberate: the Japanese Unique Culture Test. Tori had been subjected to it on her arrival; she saw no reason why she shouldn't subject Bernard Godwin in the same way. She had taken him to one of the restaurants licensed to serve blowfish, which, in the wrong hands, could be lethally poisonous.

They were given hot towels. The hot sake came first, and Tori watched Bernard as he drank his. They were on their second bottle when the baby eels arrived: tiny white things in a clear broth. The eels were without doubt disgusting to look at, but really were quite tasty. Tori ate with gusto, and was mildly disappointed when Bernard dug in without so much as twitching an eyelid. Oh, well, she thought. There's plenty more to come.

All the sushi she had ordered was food for which, after a long time, one might possibly acquire a taste. It was true that many Japanese themselves did not care for sea urchin. But to impress Westerners as well as to prove their superiority and separateness, they ate it anyway, pretending to savor its strong rancid taste.

To her dismay, Bernard tackled the sushi with a good deal of aplomb. He even asked for more marinated ginger and *wasabi*, the fiery green horseradish.

"I once read a report," he told her, "that said this ginger was a natural protection from any nasty microorganisms that might be in the raw fish. Had you heard that also?"

Tori said she hadn't.

The *fugu* came, and Tori told him what it was. Bernard looked at the fish, shrugged, ate it. When they were both finished with their food, and Tori ordered their sixth bottle of sake, Bernard said, "Tell me, young lady, how did I do?"

"Pardon me?"

"How did I do on the test you just gave me?" he said patiently. "Did I pass?"

Tori looked at him for a moment, then laughed until the tears came to her eyes. "Jesus Christ," she said, wiping at her eyes, "you really are the limit."

"Funny," Bernard Godwin said with a serious face, "that was just what I was thinking about you."

Tori took him back to her apartment, a tiny place in an ugly, colorless building that looked like a cracker box stood on end. But inside it was comfortable, if cramped.

Bernard seemed content to settle in. He was an exceedingly magnetic man, for he carried with him a singular kind of power. He reminded her of images she had seen of Julius Caesar: the planular face, dominated by the long patrician nose, the prominent chin, the commander's eyes, so full of good humor as well

68

as power. It was a good face, strong and at the same time gentle. It was a glyph which, if you read it correctly, seemed to say, If you are my friend, I will take care of you forever, but if you are my enemy, I will take you down in such a way that you will not even know it's happening. Much later she would come to see the guile, lurking like a pike in deep water, behind his bright blue eyes.

Tori got a couple of Kirin beers from the half refrigerator, opened them, handed him one. She liked that Bernard was comfortable drinking it from the bottle. He was dressed in a pair of dark blue trousers, a polo shirt of the same color, and a handsome jacket of soft chocolate-colored lambskin. He wore highly polished John Lobb stalking shoes that made no sound when he walked.

Tori liked the way he moved—not quickly, but lithely, with a sense of purpose always. His were not the mannerisms of a young man, but they certainly weren't the mannerisms of an old man, either. Far from it. Bernard Godwin had obviously put his years to good use, learning as he went, from many sources. Tori found this interesting. In fact, she found Bernard Godwin altogether fascinating, but after the incident in the *fugu* restaurant when he had so effortlessly seen through her, she was careful not to let him know this. He wanted something from her. She thought that the chances were good that he would get it, but it was she who wanted to set the price.

"You said something about a proposition," Tori said, flopping down beside Bernard Godwin on the rolled-up futon she slept on that doubled as a sofa.

"Yes, indeed." Bernard had stretched out his long legs, crossing them at the ankles. His eyes were hooded, as if the sake was finally catching up to him or he had passed his bedtime. "This is something I've no doubt will pique your interest."

"First I'd like to know how you heard about me."

Bernard took a sip of the Kirin. "The Yakuza might call you the Wild Child, but there are others to whom you are known as the Female Ronin." He turned his head toward her. "In certain circles you really are quite famous."

"Like a celebrity." Tori got up, turned on the stereo. Jefferson Airplane. Stomping backbeat, swirling melody. Grace Slick singing "White Rabbit." Yeah, Tori thought. You tell 'em, Gracie. Who knows what evil lurks in the hearts of men? When Tori came back to sit beside Bernard, she said, "What circles?"

69

"My kind of circle," he said in his sleepy voice. "Yours, too, I imagine." He sucked at his Kirin.

"Yeah? What makes you so sure?"

"You want it straight? Okay. You're an angry young woman looking for direction. Right now, you'd as soon throw yourself in the furnace as someone else. Right now, it doesn't matter all that much to you as long as *someone* burns. But I'm here to tell you that it does matter. It matters very much."

"Why?"

For some time Bernard Godwin was quiet. Then he leaned forward, put the Kirin bottle on the free-form glass and iron coffee table. He put his elbows on his knees. "There was a guy I know," he said at last. "This was a long time ago. This guy was about your age, perhaps a couple of years younger. His mother had just died, and all through the funeral he was hoping his father would walk into the funeral parlor—just for a minute, even—to pay his respects.

"This guy's father had run out on his wife when his son was five years old. He found another woman, maybe, or maybe he liked to go from woman to woman, who knows? Anyway, the guy hadn't seen his father in all those years. He hadn't thought that he really wanted to—harboring in his heart this hatred for his old man—but now at the moment when the minister was speaking of the fulfilled life of the dearly departed, he saw the eulogy for a lie, and this guy knew that he had to see his father again.

"Soon after his mother was buried, the guy traveled west to Chicago, where his father had taken up residence. He ate lunch at a great rib soul shack on the South Side, where he was served by a black woman who had hickory ash in her hair, then he walked to the building where his father worked.

"His father was a reporter for a Chicago paper, and when his son asked to see him, the guy was told that his father was out running down a story. No one knew where he was or when he would be back.

"This guy said he was the reporter's son, that he hadn't seen his father in years, and that he'd wait. No one said a thing.

"He was shown to his father's desk, and he sat down in an old scarred swivel chair that squeaked when he moved it back and forth.

"He saw the clutter on his father's desk and thought of the clutter of his mother's life. He saw the old IBM typewriter on his father's desk and thought of how often his mother longed to

70

hear from his father, walking to the mailbox with an expression of hope, returning with the weight of a secret defeat. Only it hadn't been a secret from her son, who saw everything, and hurt when she hurt.

"This guy opened the drawers of his father's desk one by one as if he hoped to reveal the ghosts of the past he could not remember, the specters of a past that might have been. In the lower right-hand drawer, underneath a half-empty box of Kleenex, he pulled out a framed picture of his mother and himself as a small boy. He could not remember the picture having been taken. He put the photograph away, as if he were not really certain that little boy was him.

"Time passed, day into night. The son fell asleep, his head on his folded arms, his arms on his father's desk. When he awoke, he saw his father standing in front of the desk, peering down at him.

" 'Son,' his father said, 'what the hell are you doing here?' "

There was silence for some time. Even Grace Slick had the sense to keep quiet. Tori did not stir, though she felt the need to cut the silence with music.

At last Bernard Godwin got up, fetched two more Kirins for them from the refrigerator. Tori heard the tops popping, and it was a kind of music. She took the bottle Bernard offered her, but she didn't drink it right away.

Bernard said, "I guess in my case the truth was simple: my father was a dyed-in-the-wool sonuvabitch. People who knew him better than either I or my mother did said he had to be like that to be such a good reporter, but I didn't give a damn what they said. As far as I could see, he was an abject failure. But there you are, everyone has to have his own opinion."

"Maybe we're not so different," Tori said at last.

Bernard Godwin took a thoughtful swig of his beer. "Well, if life has taught me anything, it's this: truth is a complex animal. Every time you think you've caught it by the tail, it turns around and bites you on the ass."

Tori laughed, but she knew he was serious.

As the gray end of the night became the pearl-blue beginning of a new day, Tori and Bernard Godwin strolled through a Tokyo filled with the last rumblings of delivery trucks. The bridges were filled with them. From the Sumida River horns sounded as fishing boats neared the Tsukiji wholesale fish market.

Tori found herself recalling how Bernard had done nothing, not even twitch, when Godzilla had lifted him off the floor. Now

71

she wondered what would have happened if she had not intervened. She was not at all certain that she would have put money on Godzilla. She thought she would give anything to see Bernard Godwin at work.

"I guess now's as good a time as any to present your proposition," Tori said. The sky above Tokyo looked clean this early in the morning, and the city seemed immense, a world unto itself.

"I want you to work for me," Bernard Godwin said.

"Is the work legal?"

"I take it as a good sign that you asked." Bernard took a last swallow of beer, gave a little belch. "Pardon me."

Tori smiled.

"What I do—and what you will do should you decide to join me—is legal in the broadest sense of the word."

"Meaning?"

"Meaning that no matter what we become involved in, we would never be brought before a court of law."

"But . . . ?"

"What we do is, in another sense, amoral. We are beyond the laws man constructs. This does not mean that we are lawless. Far from it. Much like the Japanese, whom you obviously love and admire so much, we create and define our own set of laws." Bernard's eyes seemed to have closed, as if he were on the verge of sleep. "Interested?"

Tori almost said, God, yes, how soon can I start? Instead she drank half her Kirin, looked up at the forest of monstrous towers through which they were walking, and said, "I'll give it some thought."

Three days later Tori gave Bernard Godwin the answer she knew she would give him from the first. The trouble was, she did not want to go home. He understood this, just as he seemed to understand the rest of her character, carefully hidden from all others like an enigma in the center of a stone pyramid.

"I want you here in Japan," Bernard told her. "We have no one with your expertise in this quarter of the globe. We've found it impossible to infiltrate anyone of substance into the Japanese underworld. But you're already in it. You're already respected, and more importantly, feared."

Tori said, "I think you've got that the wrong way around."

"We'll see," Bernard said . . .

We'll see.

"Oh, God," Tori moaned softly. "Oh, God." And with Ber-

72

nard Godwin's voice still echoing in her mind, she stumbled to the phone, dialed a number she had long ago committed to memory.

There was a great deal of waiting while the switching was accomplished. But when at last she heard Russell Slade's voice, crackly with mobile phone interference, she said, "*À bientôt.* You were right. I'm coming."

TWO
TOKYO/MOSCOW

No one knew in advance that Kunio Michita's *nakodo*—his go-between—was going to commit ritual suicide, save Honno Kansei. Honno worked for Kunio Michita. As personal secretary to Tokyo's most prominent businessman, Honno was privy to many secrets: impending deals, mergers, acquisitions. She could easily have put this knowledge to work on the Tokyo stock market, but she didn't. Honno was adept at keeping secrets. She had made herself that way out of necessity. She carried a secret buried deep inside her: the horrific knowledge that she had been born during the year of *hinoeuma*. It had been a mistake, of course. Her father had never forgiven her mother, believing, of course, that the pregnancy was her fault. If he had come to love Honno, he had never showed it. He always made her feel *soto*, an outsider in her own family.

Why? According to the ancient Chinese zodiac, *hinoeuma* was a year of the horse that appeared every sixty years. Legend had it that women born in *hinoeuma* became husband killers. Consequently, there were far fewer births in Japan in the year of *hinoeuma* than during any other year.

Because of her keen intuition and empathetic powers, Honno was almost destroyed by superstition. Leaving her family had both strengthened and weakened her. The constant proximity to their fear and anguish had been like a knife cutting through her belly, and she had believed her sensitivity to be a curse. But years later it had also inadvertently exposed her to many more deeply buried secrets.

Such as the impending death of Kakuei Sakata, Kunio Michita's go-between.

Sakata, too, had been privy to many secrets. He had borne this burden, if not easily, then well, for the past four years. What had changed now to cause him to snap? If he had been a member of a different, more Western culture, Sakata would simply have resigned his position in the face of a scandal cracked open. He would have turned state's evidence against his boss, acquiring immunity, as well as vast wealth from the best-selling book he would then write about the affair. A film or television miniseries would merely be the icing on the cake.

But Sakata was Japanese, living in Japan, where the worth of a personal relationship created one's definition of what it meant to be a human being. His death, like Yukio Mishima's years before, was a means of communication, a statement, a symbol even of his own personal beliefs which would now be stamped for all time upon the collective consciousness of the nation.

All these ramifications, like ripples upon a pond, were on Honno's mind when she heard Sakata tell his assistant, "Your time has come. I wish you luck, though I doubt that in the coming maelstrom it will matter."

What maelstrom?

As she looked upon Sakata's calm face, Honno wondered what must be in his mind. What were the secrets that would unleash the maelstrom? Had he just unearthed them or had they at last become too difficult to bear?

He had come to Sengakuji to die; Honno was certain of it. This was the place one came to honor the memory of the forty-seven ronin who, in feudal times, had avenged themselves upon those who had wrongly put to death their lord. They had died in that pursuit, nobly, honorably, so that their deaths were as meaningful as their lives had been.

This, too, was Sakata's purpose. He could no longer live with what he knew or had done, yet he could not divulge these secrets. A betrayal of his lifelong friendship with Kunio Michita was unthinkable; the shame would be unbearable not only for him, but for the family he was leaving behind. Ritual suicide was the only honorable way out for him. Honno knew this and, therefore, did nothing to interfere. It would not have occurred to her to commit so dishonorable and disrespectful an act.

She had always revered this man who handled the fund-raising from Tokyo's complex bureaucratic and political arenas that backed Michita, but never more so than now.

On this very warm spring day the graves of the forty-seven ronin were covered in flowers. Incense rose in the still air. The combination of heady scents was almost overpowering, and for the rest of her life, Honno would equate this particular amalgam of odors—sweet and musky—with death.

What were the secrets Kakuei Sakata could no longer live with? As far as Honno knew, there was not even a breath of scandal. Connected as she was with Tokyo District's feared Tokuso—the Special Prosecutor's Office—surely she would have heard if an investigation file had been opened on Michita or Sakata.

It was a long road from Kasumigaseki, the district in central Tokyo where Sakata and Honno worked, to the ancient graves at Sengakuji. Sakata had chosen a time late in the day when the shrine was deserted.

He was dressed in white, the color of death. Honno saw him limned in the setting sun against the field of flowers covering the graves. A wind whipped his baggy cotton trousers about his legs. The contrast between the vivid color of the blossoms and the purity of the white material was striking, another memory that Honno would not forget.

She watched as Sakata knelt with his back to her. He withdrew from his waist a ceremonial knife. The blade, slightly curved, shot the sun's rays into Honno's eyes, so that for a moment she saw nothing. Then the glare was gone and Honno saw Sakata hunched over. She could see the acute angles his arms made, and knew that his hands, grasped around the knife's hilt, were already thrust against his lower abdomen.

All at once his head shot up. She could see his shoulders trembling as he sought to bring the blade, buried deep inside him, from left to right, in the ritual samurai's disemboweling cut.

Sakata's spirit was being purified, disentangled from the sins he had committed during the course of his duty. But even the strongest hand could falter. The mind's determination did not fail, but the body in trauma could betray the spirit, and this was what was happening now to Sakata.

76

Honno could see that, on the verge of death, his body lacked the strength to finish the cut. He tried again, but to no avail.

Honno could watch no longer. She stepped from behind the huge cryptomeria tree that had hidden her from Sakata and, hurriedly, she knelt by his side.

The lower half of his clothes were stained crimson. The veins at the sides of his neck were standing out like ropes, and his eyes seemed to be bugging out of his head with the massive effort.

Honno leaned over him and, placing her hands over his on the silk-wrapped hilt of his ceremonial knife, added her strength to his. She heard a terrible ripping sound like thunder as the blade crossed fully from left to right.

Sakata's red-rimmed eyes rolled toward her, locking on her. For one split instant his face registered gratitude. Then he toppled face first into the bed of fragrant flowers, placed there to honor the sacred memory of the dead.

Irina Viktorovna Ponomareva awoke not knowing where she was: Mars's large, dark apartment in Vosstaniya Square or Valeri's brighter but more spartan one in Kirov Street. She sat up in bed, looked out the window. There was narrow Telegraph Street behind the Ministry of Education, where she worked, and there was the Church of the Archangel Gabriel. Irina's coworkers referred to it as Menshikov Tower, but she could not, at least to herself.

But then again, Irina had nothing in common with anyone at the Ministry of Education. She had returned from an extended trip to the United States filled to overflowing with innovative ideas based on the American educational system.

She had spent the subsequent weeks painstakingly writing, revising, and annotating a lengthy treatise on how the Soviet educational process could be streamlined and improved. The paper had been duly passed around the ministry without so much as a ripple of comment.

At last Irina had sought an interview with the minister, who had spent twenty minutes circling around the fact that all the points she had made in her paper had been rejected. He had been so condescending that Irina had no difficulty in divining his message: stick to your computer models, to your statistical research. Use the American methodology to reform the ministry's medieval archival retrieval system—that was, after all, why she had been sent to the United States in the first place, the minister reminded her—but leave the important reform to the experts, the men.

Well, at least I don't have to worry about being stuck in that dead-end job anymore, Irina thought as she stared at the familiar landmark of the Church of the Archangel Gabriel. She knew where she was. She was in Kirov Street: Valeri's place.

Irina felt her pulse still racing. Thoughts of her job, the quotidian tasks of her life, had failed to calm her.

She had awakened from the same nightmare. In it, she is drowning at the dinner table. She jumps up, goes to the window, but there is blood on the streets, and when she looks up in horror, bars across the moon. She knows she must get out into the streets, something important is happening there, something that will otherwise leave her behind forever. But she cannot move and, looking down, she sees with a kind of sickening despair that she is shackled to the floor . . .

Irina closed her eyes for a moment, then stared again out the window, across the street to her church, beautiful, comforting, as if to assure herself that she was truly awake, that the nightmare was just a dream. Put it out of your mind, she reprimanded herself sharply.

Though it was in the Sadovaya, farther out on the periphery of Moscow—Mars insisted on living with the people—Irina actually preferred Mars's apartment. Or perhaps it was Mars himself that she preferred. That, indeed, would be ironic.

But this apartment had its charms. She loved to wake up in the morning to the sun shining on the remnants of the church spire, destroyed in a fierce electrical storm some years ago. It was a reminder of how even something so fragile as faith could survive in inhospitable soil. If the church could survive here, she had decided some time ago, so could she. It was a reminder that she did not have to end up like her parents.

Irina turned away from the window, and could hear Valeri bustling around the kitchen. What was he preparing? There was bread, but no butter or milk available in all of Moscow. It had been this way for months now, and Irina recalled her mother's harrowing stories of the war, when beets and turnips and perhaps a cabbage or two were all that were available to eat for months on end. *My God,* her mother had once said, *what we would have done for a bite of fresh food! Killed each other, like as not.* Although it was said—and Mars assured her—that great upheavals were occurring every day in the Soviet Union, Irina thought that some things never changed—and never would.

Despite perestroika, she found it just as difficult—and in some cases impossible—to obtain the essentials of day-to-day life: soap, bread, fresh vegetables, toilet paper—as she had in the years before the restructuring. The problem that no one seemed to want to face was that the old market centralism was so deeply entrenched that not even the president could dislodge it. Though it was clear to anyone that the produce grown by private enterprise was robust and healthy, whereas the vegetables from the old collectives looked soft and withered, even the president was reluctant to encourage the anathema of more private enterprise.

In Russia, after all, such structural transformations always were paid for by enormous political risks, so it was usually better not to act than to make a move at all. Instead, in typical Soviet doublethink, the decisions to enact new freedoms were quickly followed by decisions to severely limit those freedoms.

This would have been an utterly depressing scenario for an American—but not, it used to be said, for most Russians. Hardship, the long, bone-chilling winters, and the even colder heart of the state apparatus, inured the Soviet citizen to disappointment. When there is little hope, depression flourishes unwillingly. But flourish it does, in direct proportion to alcohol consumption, which warmed the body, numbed the mind, and destroyed the spirit.

Irina stretched, got out of bed, padded down the corridor to the bathroom. As usual, the hot water was not working, but she was used to showering in icy water. Nevertheless, her eyes opened wide under the spray, and she gave a little reflexive shout.

Toweled dry, she dressed in fresh clothes she kept in the bottom drawer of the magnificent mahogany chest Valeri had had imported from England.

Standing in front of the mirror, she carefully applied the American makeup she had bought in the local Beryozka store, where privileged citizens like herself could buy a limited selection of imported goods. She was a small-boned woman, with fine, high breasts, a tiny waist, and narrow hips. Her legs were shapely (the right genes), and had remained well-muscled (she still worked out at the ballet barre three times a week, though she could no longer harbor dreams of becoming a ballerina, her mother's wish for her). She had a peculiarly feline face, triangular, with large tawny eyes, a small nose, full, sensual lips, ears set close to her skull. She wore her shining black hair almost shockingly short. Altogether, she was happier with her looks than most women she knew.

In the kitchen, Valeri Denysovich Bondasenko was hunched over the illegal Toshiba 5200 lap-top computer he had smuggled into the country. The amazing Japanese technology had done away with the bulky CRT monitor. In its place was a flat gas-plasma screen. The battery pack—essential in a land where power outages were a fact of everyday life—bulged from the Toshiba's plastic side.

Irina peered over his shoulder, saw the food recipe up on the multicolored screen, kissed him on the tip of his ear.

"Almost ready," he said distractedly. He was a frighteningly large man, with a wrestler's meaty shoulders and the powerful forearms of a laborer. Irina had been terrified the first time she had gone to bed with him. His face and voice were as intimidating as his body. When he was angry, she could feel the tension in the same way she could just before a powerful storm.

She had not wanted to go to bed with him that first time, but she could not imagine what he would do to her if she did not acquiesce. They had met at a typical state function. She had gone because it was her duty to go, but all the time she had been thinking of renewing her flagging spirit on her knees at the font of the Church of the Archangel Gabriel.

Then Valeri Bondasenko had spotted her. He had herded her out of the throng as American cowboys did with cattle to the slaughter. She had read this in a paperback copy of *Lonesome Dove* that she had smuggled back into the country, and which she now kept with her wherever she went.

Valeri had been charming, gracious even. But beneath that veneer, Irina had been aware of another Bondasenko—the feared political tactician. It was he who had masterminded the brutal crackdown against the national separatists in his own native Ukraine. It was he who had counseled forging the still controversial compromise with the leaders of the Soviet Union's Baltic states that made the subsequent crackdown in the Ukraine possible. It was said that every move Bondasenko made was part of a sound strategy. Irina was intelligent enough to wonder what it was he wanted from her.

She had known full well that she was being seduced, but that knowledge did not stop the process from continuing. Whatever Valeri wanted, Valeri got, that was what everyone said. And it was clear that he wanted her. Irina did not have the political strength to resist him. No one did. Still, it had been a sad moment in her life, to be brought home to her in such concrete fashion that she was so helpless to determine her own fate. Sitting naked for the first time on the edge of his bed, she had prayed for guidance and for the moral strength to resist his corruption. Then, wiping a single tear from her cheek, she had climbed in beside him. He exuded the heat of a furnace.

She thought she might be crushed beneath his muscular bulk, but he turned out to be a surprisingly gentle and compassionate lover, as if the Valeri Bondasenko she met between the sheets was a different man altogether from the one who stalked through the halls of the Kremlin, consigning to purgatory—figurative and literal—those foolish enough to oppose his rise to power.

This gave Irina some semblance of hope. She had not hated him when he had taken her, had, almost despite herself, been swept up in the vortex of his lust. Soon she had found her own, and knew that she could come to find enjoyment on her own terms in this liaison, despite the fact that with him, as with all of her lovers, the moment of his physical parting from her brought a sense of emptiness and of sadness.

One night, in this apartment, with the sleet battering heavily against the outside walls, rattling the ancient windowpanes, Irina discovered another layer to their relationship. He had still been inside her, thick and hot. She was still pulsing to their accelerated heartbeats.

"Can I confess something?" she whispered. "I have never felt like this with any other man." She pushed the hair back from his forehead. "You frighten people, perhaps you don't know how much you frighten them. When you approached me that first night, I felt paralyzed. I couldn't say no to you. I was terrified if I said no to you I would come to work the next morning to find my job was no longer there."

"Didn't I attract you, even a little?"

"Yes, of course you did, but I— Don't you see that whatever I felt at the time didn't matter? I did what you asked me to do, that was the beginning and the end of it. And then, later, in bed the first time, I was so frightened I'd displease you. And then . . ."

"Then."

"I discovered a whole other Valeri Bondasenko," Irina said. "One nobody else knows about. It made me feel—I don't know—special somehow. In all the vast sea of women in Moscow, you had chosen me."

Valeri laughed. "Is that all there is to your confession?"

81

"No." Irina was quiet for some time. She listened in the stillness to the beating of their hearts, as if it were a language she needed to decipher. "For an instant, I felt a part of your power. Not a reflection, but one with it. Is that foolish?"

"Not at all," Valeri said, stirring. "In fact, your confession, as you call it, makes me more confident to confide in you. I had been thinking of bringing this up for some time, but I wasn't sure I could trust my instincts."

Irina snuggled closer to him. "What about?" She could feel the power radiating from him, bathing her, warming her. Was it so bad to want to get inside it?

"I want to get inside the head of Mars Petrovich Volkov," he said, startling her because in some way she could not yet fathom his thoughts had been paralleling her own. He was so close, his lips brushed hers as he spoke. "Volkov has gotten the inside track against me in the Congress of People's Deputies. He has lined up a formidable array of party officials behind him, and got himself elected. I still hold the edge because of my strong union and national district ties, but now that he is in the Congress, he is beginning to make life very difficult. With reform as the new history, and speaking one's mind being tolerated, certain people have become drunk on spewing criticism. Volkov is one of them. He's making a living directing it at me. He appears to enjoy branding me a Napoleon, claiming that I have designs on becoming the next emperor of Russia. He falsely claims he has no ego and I do. That is his problem, but he is rapidly making it mine." Irina could see his eyes glowing and her own image filling them up. "In order to defeat Mars Volkov, I must know what he is thinking. I have learned through bitter experience that there are things men cannot do or do well. This is one of them. I need you to become my protégé so that you may do to Mars Volkov what I have done to you."

"You want me to seduce him?" Irina had asked. "I cannot. I don't have the temperament."

"Temperament," Valeri said, "is forged through circumstance. I will teach you what you need to know."

"I will not prostitute myself in that way." Irina had grown angry.

To his credit, Valeri had felt this immediately. He crushed his lips to hers, then smiled. "The joke is that it is you, Irina, who has seduced me. Do you think that you are the latest in a long line of conquests for me? No. You know my reputation. I make these things open so that there cannot be any misunderstanding that my rivals might turn to their advantage."

"No one knows about us. You made certain of that," Irina had pointed out.

"True enough, but that, too, is for a purpose. I, too, have a confession to make. After my wife died, I found that I had little taste for sexual adventure. We had tried for the last several years of our marriage to have a child. Unsuccessfully. After my wife died, I came to see that being childless was just as well. In this terrible world, a child, too, might be used against me."

He rolled them both over so that she lay astride him. "I know the danger inherent in what I ask you to do, Irina. But when you say no so hastily, you ignore the rewards to yourself."

"What rewards? A reassignment? Money? Presents from the Beryozka? These things cannot tempt me."

"Oh, I know that." He looked at her in the semidarkness and laughed again. "You see, I felt something in you from the moment I first saw you. The reason I can ask you to seduce Mars Volkov is that I can understand the power it will bring you. Most women are content to bask in the reflection of the power of men, but you are different, Irina, you are special. You want the power for yourself. Now you understand that I can give you that power.

"So you will make pillow talk with Mars, you will get to know him, and you will report to me everything you learn. You will do it happily, Irina. Trust me."

Then the fear had crept through her like a worm burrowing into the core of her. He's right, she thought, I love this new world he can open up to me. No more Irina the boring academic, Irina the computer programmer, Irina the educator with ideas no one will listen to.

Now, entering Valeri's kitchen, Irina could smell onions and, startlingly, shallots sautéing in a skillet. She sat at the small black-and-white, marble-patterned Formica table that might have been at home in an American kitchen of the 1950s. Valeri brought her yogurt from the Ukraine, and tea into which she dropped two cubes of sugar, a perquisite in the sugar-starved Soviet Union even she was not privy to on her own.

She watched Valeri carefully stirring the eggs into the hot skillet. This was another benefit of spending the night with Valeri: she adored being served breakfast. She was an excellent cook in her own right—one of the few gifts her mother had passed down to her—and had the cook's special appreciation of being served food by another good cook. But it was not an unadulterated pleasure, because she always felt a pang of guilt, as if this small decadence indulged in while others starved would weaken her, would somehow make her unfit for the continual struggle of life here. She had spent much time in America, learning new educational methods, but also absorbing the Western way of life. Sometimes, when she was most depressed about Russia, she worried that she had been irrevocably contaminated by the West. Too often she found herself making comparisons between where she had been (Boston) and where she was now (Moscow), and becoming despondent over Moscow's shortcomings. Her sojourns in America had brought into question the validity of the entire Soviet way of life. This was her secret, her terrible burden, and she knew that she must never allow Valeri to know she harbored these treasonous thoughts.

She said, with all the patriotic zeal she could foster, "What progress have you made in penetrating White Star?"

Valeri delivered a rude expletive. "That bastard organization of minority dissidents. They're like ghosts. Can you believe it? White Star has remained hidden from us. This should be impossible in our country. My guess is that they are somehow being supplied by the West. How else to account for our failure to discover even one of their cells?"

"It seems to me that you don't even know if they exist."

"Oh, White Star exists, I've no doubt of that." He gave a short laugh. "We, the government, are the only ones adept enough at propaganda to create a phantom organization. God knows, we've done it often enough." He waved a hand. "No, no. The only real question is whether or not White Star is responsible for the wave of nationalist uprisings in Georgia, Uzbekistan, the Baltics, even the Bashkir Autonomous Republic. In every case, the rioters are well led and are even better-armed: handguns, machine pistols, even mortars are becoming common. They are being supplied by someone."

"Isn't Ufa, the site of that recent awful dual train disaster, in Bashkir?"

Valeri nodded. "Over two hundred people died in the crash. But it wasn't an accident. It was sabotage. A cadre of Red Army generals was on one of those trains. They were bound for a top secret military base in the Urals. All of them were killed."

"Sabotage?" Irina said. "I had no idea."

"Nor has anyone else, beyond a select few." Valeri cleared his throat. "The truth is, an alarming spate of terrorist acts has been proliferating since Chernobyl. An internal investigation, made immediately secret, proved that the nuclear event at Chernobyl was a deliberate act of sabotage. It was the first, but it was a disaster of such dimensions that it should have put us on notice that these people are quite serious, and quite mad. However, bureaucracies are the same the world over: overstaffed, underutilized, bloated with inertia. And never more so than here in Russia."

"My God, what you're telling me is incredible."

"Unfortunately, you're not the first to say that. It took me some time to convince the president of the need for an antinationalist task force. And that I should be put in charge of it."

"But White Star is supposed to be composed of Ukrainian nationalists," Irina said.

Valeri considered the rest of her unspoken question. "It is true that White Star's leadership is Ukrainian and so am I," he said at last. "But we want two separate things. My loyalty is to the state. Theirs is to themselves.

"Now, however, it appears possible that White Star's membership has became more eclectic. It might even turn out to be the first pan-minority nationalist group, embracing the Georgians, Estonians, Latvians, Lithuanians, even the Moslem minorities. That would naturally exponentially increase White Star's power, and its danger to us, the state.

"These people have no idea what it is they want. Anarchy. Chaos. Not a better, more cohesive dialectically consistent whole. If they gain autonomy, they will, like as not, begin warring with each other. They are primitives, misguided. Who better than me—a Ukrainian, a member of a Soviet minority—to show them the dangerous error of their ways?"

Irina did not know whether she felt admiration or disgust. Perhaps it was a combination of both. She suspected that there was a measure of truth to what Valeri said. Dissidents' motives were often muddled, because they stemmed from the irrational: anger and fear. And the sad truth was that revolutionaries rarely had any idea how to wield power once they got it, so they ended up making a mess of things. Yet she wanted to say, But can't you see that this White Star is a symbol, a yearning of the non-Russian people to be free? Don't you see it as a sign that a change must come, just as it has come on other Eastern European nations? Are you and your ilk so far from the czars, after all?

If only she could trust someone. It was awful having to bottle

85

up one's true feelings every hour of the day and night. A nightmare. *Her* nightmare: imprisoned in her own country. How she longed to confide in someone, but there was no one she could trust, not even the priest at the Church of the Archangel Gabriel. Certainly never, ever Valeri Denysovich Bondasenko. So she held her tongue, continued to play the good little Russian girl with him. "What a perfect pragmatist you are," she said evenly.

"Communism is the essence of pragmatism, so I must be an expert," Valeri said. "Now come, breakfast is ready."

He brought the omelettes and his own glass of strong tea. As was his habit, he had already consumed his portion of yogurt while he was doing the cooking.

"This is delicious," Irina said, tearing off a hunk of coarse black bread.

Valeri grunted. "The recipe is from the *New York Times*. It didn't help that I couldn't get butter. Pierre Franey says that butter makes all the difference. I had to use oil."

"It's just as well," Irina said. "Oil is far healthier. It's not full of cholesterol." Her fork stopped midway to her mouth. My God, she thought, we sound just like husband and wife. Have I actually begun to get used to this life of deceit and treachery? God forbid. But she thought again of what Valeri had said about her wanting to be free, and the fear gripped her again.

"What is it?" Valeri said. "You look pale."

Irina took a bite of her omelette to give herself some time. "I . . . was just thinking about tonight—and Mars."

Valeri delivered a colorful oath. "That sonuvabitch is out to bury me. And the sooner the better, as far as he's concerned. Now he's begun questioning my proposal for compromise with the Baltic states."

"Doesn't he understand that your compromise was the best thing that could have happened?" Irina said. "It proved to the world that our reform is for real, and it showed your colleagues in the Politburo the need to be elastic. Besides, everyone knows—although they're afraid to say it—that the Baltic states were never really a part of the Soviet Union. They were awarded illegally to Stalin by Hitler in the Molotov–von Ribbentrop accord of 1939. For years Estonia, Lithuania, and Latvia have had their own legations in the United States. Isn't it shameful that we have held on to them? Wasn't it time that they broke away?"

Valeri Bondasenko smiled sardonically. "Even though Lithuania and Latvia have succeeded in becoming independent, the Central Committee is not happy. It still calls these secessions, the virus of nationalism, and seeks some way—*any* way—to return these Baltic states to the Soviet fold.''

"Surely that's an exaggeration," Irina said. "I mean, we wouldn't go to war over it."

He wiped his mouth. "Lenin said, 'The interests of socialism are above the interests of the right of nations to self-determination.' He was just following in Marx's footsteps: 'the proletarian has no country.' ''

Irina hated him when he spouted ideology by rote. How could he, a Ukrainian, be so devoutly Marxist-Leninist when history—the history of *his* people—had so painfully proven them wrong?

"In any case," Valeri was saying, "we can't give away the world the way the American president Roosevelt did in Yalta. We have held on to Estonia. We'll hold on to the Ukraine and Georgia, Armenia and Moldavia, in the face of all nationalist agitation. This is the point that Mars Volkov continually avoids, as he hammers at me over and over. He's sounding as repetitive as a rock and roll record."

Irina laughed despite herself. "My God, Valeri, sometimes I forget just how backward you can be."

"Politics is my only concern," he said simply.

"One day, your obsession will be the death of you," Irina pointed out. "You cannot outthink enemies with blinders on."

"Does this expansion of my horizons include decadent Western rock and roll, then?"

"Perhaps." Irina looked at him. "But it's a good example. In the West, rock music is a great force. It not only generates a tremendous amount of money, it moves young people. It can galvanize them, mobilize them."

"Then the army comes in, and disperses them," Valeri pointed out.

"Only until the young people become their own army."

Bondasenko thought about this for some time. He knew that Irina's position in the Ministry of Education allowed her to observe firsthand many of the Western trends of which he was as yet ignorant. He would do well, he knew, to listen to her advice. "Your criticism I can take. It's constructive. It's Mars Volkov's criticism that must be silenced." He rose, but did not take his eyes off her. "Please keep that in mind tonight when your head is snuggled comfortably into his chest."

Two days after Kakuei Sakata's public suicide, a certain envelope arrived by mail. It was odd: square-shaped, of heavy handmade paper. Honno Kansei took it out of the mailbox on her way to work. The letter was from Kakuei Sakata.

It was dated the day he had killed himself. There was a folded piece of note paper inside. Honno opened it on the subway to Kasumigaseki, discovered a small key and nothing else. No note, no explanation.

Now she began to feel a wind rising, the first chill brush of the maelstrom that Sakata had spoken of. For thirty-six hours the television, radio, and newspapers had been filled with reports and spectacular photos of the death of Kakuei Sakata. And swirls of speculation rippled outward from that one violent and chilling act of social conscience. She had seen her boss, Kunio Michita, interviewed on the news, in much the same way that the former prime minister had been publicly grilled several years before, except that Michita was so telegenic, he emerged with increased face. One channel preempted its favorite nighttime soap opera to present a half-hour special live from Sengakuji, the site of Sakata's suicide.

That morning, Honno went to work and, with the key in the moist palm of her hand, brought Kunio Michita his mail and his cup of freshly brewed coffee. She watched Kunio Michita, a small, dapper man with silver hair and a neat mustache, pick through his mail. She dutifully took down the dictation he gave her, reminded him of his full day of appointments, meetings, conference calls, and interviews. In private he gave off conflicting signals. While he seemed genuinely upset at his go-between's unexpected death, he also appeared almost buoyant at the prospect of the media coverage. He was exceptionally skilled in front of the cameras, and he knew it. In fact, from his first interview on television, widespread support for him, both financial and otherwise, had begun to pour in. It was beginning to look to Honno as if Michita had found his métier at last.

"Our bid for the Osaka Ceramics has been approved," Kunio Michita said, "so, would you inform our contracts department." He rubbed his hands together. "That makes sixteen bids this year we've successfully negotiated." He handed her a thick file. "And I've decided to close our petrochemical division. We've got to gear up Michita Satcom to beat the satellite delivery deadlines. I have a hunch the government will give us a fat incentive for those moves." He handed her another file. "Also, the Kaga people will be here at noon, so I want you to make certain that everything is in readiness for the signing. Our joint venture with Kaga will give me great face.'' He still had not looked at her. "Oh, by the way,'' he touched his forehead, as if his memory had just been jogged, "I want you to squeeze in another appointment. I've got to see Aoki at Tandem Polycarbon at noon. Our new dye process is perfect for their entire new line of products.''

Honno was overwhelmed. "Thank you, sir.''

"Eh?" Michita at last glanced up at her. "What are you talking about?''

"Well, last week in the staff meeting I mentioned that I'd heard about Tandem's new product line and thought our dipole dye process would be a perfect match for it.''

"Really?" Michita's attention was already on other matters. "I can't say I remember that. Perhaps you are mistaken. I've got a memo here from Fujinami. Just got it. Shows research. He really did his homework. If the deal goes through, he's in for a promotion. Remind me, would you?''

"But sir—''

"Eight-thirty," Michita said, consulting the clock that dominated his desk. "It's time for my first conference call. You have set it up, I trust.''

Honno retreated from his office. Mr. Fujinami had been in that meeting last week. He had heard her idea, used it. She should have thought to put her ideas in memo form. Perhaps then Michita would have listened to her.

Honno sat at her desk and slowly unwrapped her fingers from around the key Sakata had sent her. Her sweat glistened on its surface.

Honno counted her blessings. She was in the heart of Tokyo, her favorite place on earth. She was secretary to the country's most successful businessman, and her face among friends, associates, and colleagues was great. Actually, she was lucky to be at Michita Industries during this past year of enormous expansion.

It seemed to her as if every time she looked up, Kunio Michita had negotiated another winning bid on a lucrative new government-sponsored project. The new focus on Michita Apparel was another example of how Michita always managed to have one division or another eligible for government incentives in high-speed growth industries. Six months ago Honno had been certain that Kunio Michita's massive string of good luck would rub off on her. It hadn't.

What had happened just now? She had gone into Kunio Michita's office fully intending to tell him of the key's existence, to give him a chance to explain to her the reason behind Kakuei Sakata's suicide. But now she knew that she would not do it.

Honno suspected that, at the very least, she should tell her husband, Eikichi, about the key, because some sixth sense was already warning her that the Tokuso should be notified. Her connection with the Tokuso—the Tokyo District Special Prosecutor's Office—was a personal one. Eikichi Kansei, her husband, worked there as deputy assistant to the chief of the Tokuso. "I am," he loved to tell her, "up to my armpits in investigations into political bribery, extortion, and influence-peddling." His job made his heart sing.

Everything in its place and a place for everything, could be Eikichi's prosaic but simple philosophy. He was a supremely organized man, a scion of one of Tokyo's best families, who, by virtue of hard work as well as his father's considerable influence, had gone to the right schools, had made the right contacts, and had ended up in the right job: prestigious, enviable, honorable.

Eikichi's mother had spoiled him while he was growing up. But because he wanted to live up to and even surpass his father's expectations for him, he was a fanatic, almost obsessive worker. From the time he had graduated university in the top five percent of his class, he had been on his own. On the other hand, with the generous annual stipend provided by his grandfather, he never had to worry about working for a living.

Eikichi's world had always been defined by two linchpins: money and influence, both of which his family had in abundant supply; and, with a good degree of accuracy, one could say that he took these things for granted, rather than seeing them as the blessings they were.

Honno knew all about Eikichi when she had been introduced to him by a mutual friend, and she had been attracted to him precisely because of his highly structured, rigidly compartmentalized life. She had never had much stability in her home life, and the idea of being married to a brilliant organizational wizard struck her as most appealing. Besides, the prestige accorded her by being Eikichi's intended bride changed her life overnight. Nine months ago, from the moment they had gotten married, her phone would not stop ringing, and she was obliged to install an answering machine to handle the flood of invitations from her friends and associates to lunch and dinner for her and Eikichi.

Eikichi was everything Honno could hope for in a husband. He was already cool, aloof, displaying all the signs of *ittai*, that special intimacy that came from the fusion of two spirits into one. He never praised her, and would never think to, since this would be akin to praising himself, which would have been unutterably embarrassing. His deep male silences, his coolness to her, proved the existence of their *ittai* feeling, their extreme intimacy. Like all her friends her age, she never referred to him by name at home. Rather, she called him "Oto-san." Papa. This was not particularly her choice, but what the culture dictated she do. Anyway, it was difficult for Honno to put into words, or even coherent thought, just what her relationship with Eikichi was. It was *ittai*.

Eikichi's private life was as rigid as his professional one. He liked his meals set out on the table at a certain time, and expected Honno to have remembered and have prepared his favorite foods each day. On those occasions when they went out to eat, Honno was expected to follow his lead in conversations, and to know when, in business discussions, it was time to remain silent. If she harbored opinions about business matters—she was, after all, the personal secretary to Kunio Michita—she was to keep them to herself. Every month, like clockwork, Eikichi had a dinner party at his home for his business associates and contacts. Honno was expected to arrange everything, and then, like a geisha, blend into the background.

No, the same stubborn streak that prevented her from confronting Michita kept her from alerting Eikichi. Besides, she had never told him about her friendship with Kakuei; she would never have known how.

The key. The key seemed everything to her. A message from beyond the grave, a terrible responsibility thrust upon her. She felt *giri*, the obligation too great to bear, weighing upon her. For some reason, Kakuei Sakata had chosen her to carry out his last wish. Why her? Honno did not know. Perhaps when she learned what it was this key opened, she would begin to understand.

Sakata had been a complex man. In their frequent talks together, he had impressed her as someone who understood the subtleties of the feminine mind. He was not like most samurai, disdainful of the contributions a woman could make. "Times have changed," he once told her. "Women were once thought

91

to be unclean. My father, who made sake, would not see my mother for many months during the crucial stages of brewing because he was convinced that she would in some way pollute the process and spoil the sake." He laughed. "Samurai tend by nature to live in the past. But the past was not always what it was cracked up to be."

Sakata was not prone to deep male silences when he was with her. He spoke to her often and at length. He seemed to derive pleasure from these talks, as if to him they might be a form of intimacy. Honno had listened, answered his queries, and eventually, at his prompting, spoke about herself. She was happy, too, to be with him, but without quite knowing why she should feel this way. It was odd for a man to talk to her so much and in such detail, as if her opinions were of some value to him. Kakuei liked modern-day Japan, or at least admired some of its new strengths. "We are more resilient now," he told her. "And so are better able to deal with adversity. For younger people, such as yourself, there are perhaps options that we oldsters never had. It's only when this newfound resilience is abused and turns into corruption that I, like Mishima, mourn the loss of the old Japan, as uncompromising as the blade of a *katana*."

The truth was, they liked each other, and she had counted Sakata as one of her few friends. Honno could not fail that trust now.

She felt a growing terror of the evidence that Sakata had left behind him: the dark heart of the maelstrom that had so abruptly, so cruelly overtaken him. What would it do to her if it had destroyed a samurai?

But she knew that she could not back down. Her feet were already set upon this particular path and there was no turning back. *Giri* dictated that she find the evidence that had destroyed Kakuei Sakata.

What, then, was she to do about the key? She could hardly handle this situation on her own.

Honno could think of only one answer, and it scared her to death.

Mars Petrovich Volkov was an altogether different breed of animal than Valeri Bondasenko. For one thing, he wasn't Ukrainian, or a member of any other Soviet ethnic minority. He had been born and raised in Moscow—in the White City, not so far from where Valeri now made his home. Accordingly, he possessed that sangfroid peculiar to Muscovites which only a

Parisian or a New Yorker would fully understand. Everyone else would have resented the kind of arrogance Mars Volkov exhibited were he not so smooth a talker and a genuinely sympathetic listener.

Mars Volkov liked to think of himself not as a lifelong politician or even a party member, though there was no doubt that he was both, but as a problem solver. "I am like a cryptographer in the KGB," he told Irina when they first met, "locked away in some subbasement of the Lubyanka, struggling to make sense of the incomprehensible. But unlike my somewhat clinical counterpart, I deal with real people in the full light of day."

This was not, strictly speaking, the whole truth, or in any event it was not as simple as that. For Mars Volkov sought to convert the subversive into the patriotic. Like Valeri, he dealt with the gray areas of daily life in the Soviet Union. It was he who decided the new coats of paint with which to cover the old.

And that, fundamentally, was where he and Valeri differed. For it was Mars's considered opinion that the old should not merely be repainted, but be done away with entirely. Valeri found this idea at best dangerous, at worst subversive.

Irina was up on all the latest rumors. It was all well and good for Valeri to be paying lip service to Mars's growing power in the Congress, but Irina knew who ultimately held the advantage: Valeri Denysovich Bondasenko. These days, though he was continually trying his best to pound home his views to the rest of the Politburo, Mars, like all of Valeri's previous enemies, was definitely coming out second best. Irina wondered how long it would be before Mars was removed from his seat in the Congress of People's Deputies, shipped off to God only knew where, far from Moscow, the center of power. No doubt that would be determined, in part, by how successful she was in the aftermath of her seduction.

Mars Volkov looked like a movie star. A Russian movie star, to be sure, but a movie star nonetheless. He was tall and slim, with the pale eyes and high cheekbones common to the people of the windswept northern Steppes. His hair was blue-black, very straight, and he wore it slicked back from his wide forehead. He had a generous, thin-lipped mouth, and a firm chin. His only oddity was his rather small ears. But this lack of perfection somehow enhanced his overall appearance, rather than detracted from it. In sum, he was more than attractive; he was desirable.

This made the task Valeri had given Irina far less odious. But

93

in the beginning it was almost irrelevant. What drove her—Valeri was so right, damn him!—was the sense of absolute freedom she gained by initiating the contact with Mars Volkov. She orchestrated his subsequent seduction with the aplomb of someone born to the role. By the time they went to bed for the first time, Irina was giddy with her newfound sense of freedom, but also a little afraid by how much pleasure she derived from this act of treachery.

She was no longer one among many coworkers at the Ministry of Education, some drudge, given work no man would do, accorded a minimum of recognition for either her initiative or her innovations. Up until this moment of separation, she had seen herself only in terms of being her parents' daughter or, briefly—until he had died in a training maneuver accident—her husband's wife. But something inside her had always whispered, *Is this the sum of what life is? Can this be all there is to Irina Viktorovna Ponomareva?* Now she knew the answer, just as Valeri had known. There was another Irina, independent, in control, yearning to be free. And at the moment of her triumph, when she knew that she had caused Mars Volkov to become enamored of her, to desire her beyond all other women, she had at last caught the first glimpse of her own true worth. And she knew with an immense thrill that the real Irina Viktorovna Ponomareva was just beginning to be defined.

Mars had been elected to represent Moscow in the Congress, a signal honor. His constituency included the Soviet Baseball Federation, as well as Zvezdny Gorodok, Star Town, the city built to house and train the Soviet cosmonauts. He had been one of the main architects of the space program for some years, which, Irina supposed, was why he had been chosen to help build the national baseball team.

Irina thought that Valeri had good reason to fear Mars. Their views differed in quite fundamental ways, and Mars was in every sense a charismatic figure. In America this talent would have caused Mars to go far in whatever field he chose, but this was Russia, and charisma was looked upon with a good amount of suspicion.

Where Valeri held sway through the sheer force of his personality, Mars charmed people. While Valeri easily forced other wills to bend to his, Mars had to struggle for every inch of political ground gained. He was, he said, always fighting against other people's innate fear of Valeri Bondasenko. "I feel like a salmon," he told Irina that night when she asked him why he had not eaten the meal she prepared for him. "Always swimming upstream. Valeri Denysovich will beat me, despite all my efforts, just as he has beaten everyone else." He looked up at her with a weary smile. "They say that beneath the Kremlin there is a pile of bones that is all that remains of his enemies."

"Defeatist talk," she said.

"Tonight," Mars said, "I feel like the defeated."

"Tomorrow—"

"Tomorrow will be different, yes? That was what you were going to say, Irina, wasn't it?" He shrugged. "Well, who knows, perhaps you're right."

She sat down beside him, took his hand. "Tell me what happened."

"No. It's too boring—and too depressing. And I've had enough of gloom for one evening. Let's go out, have dinner, get drunk on pepper vodka."

They did. Irina let him do all the talking. He seemed in the mood to do so, and she wanted to get to know him better. When he spoke, she was a student, soaking up information—the bits and pieces of his life—as if she were studying for a final exam.

He told her about his parents, who still lived in Moscow and whom he visited every Sunday, bringing them treats—tins of caviar, fresh Baltic herring—things they would never buy for themselves. He told her about his brother, who had died, and his sister, who was married with three children. "Sometimes," he said, refilling their glasses with vodka, "I think that my sister is the lucky one. She lives a simple, uncomplicated life, and her worries are small ones, common ones, not so much to bear. She had a little trouble with the last baby, it was born with a heart murmur, but the child is fine now. She lives under the signs of love, of contentment, of the family. These are everything to her; without them, she is lost."

Later, he said, "You know, it's funny about my sister. We weren't close when the three of us were growing up. My brother and I were inseparable, and she was, well, an outsider, I suppose. The enemy. We never confided in her for fear that she would pass on our secrets to our mother. Imagine my surprise when, years later at my brother's funeral, she recounted our boyhood secrets. She had known them all the time because she was far smarter than either of us boys had been. And she had kept them to herself. Our secrets had been sacred to her, even though we excluded her from everything we did, even though we teased her and made fun of her. Now we're very close. I have come to cherish our time together, because she is the one oasis of sanity in my insane world. Her love of the prosaic—this country, her children who will one day join the party, make their contribution to the Soviet way of life—constantly reminds me of the importance of what I am trying to accomplish.''

Irina wanted to ask Mars just what that was, but she downed more pepper vodka instead. She already had, like a professional, an instinct for when to ask questions and when to keep her mouth shut. The same instinct made for great military commanders: the need to attack had to be tempered with the necessities of parrying and of retreat, not only to cut losses, but to avoid casualties altogether.

Attack meant, by definition, exposure, and Irina did not think that the time had come for her to take that risk. Mars was not vulnerable enough; he was still watchful, too much in control, despite the vodka. His cheeks might be flushed, his eyes over-bright, but she could feel beneath it that his mind continued to function unimpaired.

Such was not the case by the time they returned to Mars's apartment. The vodka had had time to saturate his entire system, and his libido had usurped control from his mind.

As usual, he made love at the approximate speed of an express train, as if he could not wait to get to the conclusion, or in some secret way, could not abide the pleasure he derived from it. From the beginning of their relationship, Irina had felt this odd in a man who obviously felt deeply, a patriot who, as far as she could see, was far more straightforward than Valeri. In any case, whether it was his abrupt manner in bed or something inside herself, she could not bring herself to fulfillment with Mars. Instead she acted, somehow feeling more ashamed of this fakery than the more purely mental exercise of making him care for her. One was akin to being up on a stage, making an audience (of one) react; the other was much more intimate.

And, as usual, in the cool aftermath as he slipped out of her, she felt sadder, even more isolated, than she had before. She had an image of herself: a tropical fish swimming around and around a glass bowl. She squeezed her eyes shut, but the image remained. Around and around, until she longed even to feel dizzy, so that the emptiness would go away.

Afterward, Mars chain-smoked black Turkish cigarettes and drank black Turkish coffee, thick as honey, into which he poured a finger of vodka. He sat, naked, at a hideous Danish modern desk, all angles, blond wood and chrome, brought his gooseneck lamp down close and read through files he brought home in a battered leather attaché case. If he could work twenty-four hours a day, Irina thought, he would.

His face was half hidden by acrid smoke, but Irina continued to watch him as she lay belly down on the bed. "The only good news I've had all week," Mars said, "is that support for the United States' resolutions in the U.N. is at an historic low. Perhaps we will be able to isolate America, after all."

Irina, testing the atmosphere, scented an absence of defenses. The time seemed right to expose herself, and see if he suspected anything. "Where is all the bad news coming from?" she said casually.

"From right here," Mars said, flipping a page. "Right here."

Irina knew his files would probably be of interest to her—that is to say, to Valeri—but she was smarter than to try to gain access to them. That would be tantamount to suicide. Irina yawned. "How do you mean?"

Mars closed the cover of the file, raised his gaze. He regarded her for some time, smoking slowly, almost indolently. Irina was afraid that he already knew about her. But how could he? It was impossible, she told herself.

Then Mars opened another file, began to scan it, and Irina realized that he had not been looking at her, but through her. She relaxed.

"Hafnium."

Irina blinked. What language was he speaking? "What?"

Mars repeated the word without looking up. "It's a high-tech metal used to make control rods for certain types of nuclear reactors, especially those installed in submarines." He turned over a page, as if he were reading directly from the file. "We need hafnium. We never have enough. But the Western alliance, COCOM"—Irina knew he meant the Coordinating Committee for Multilateral Export Controls—"forbids its member nations to sell us any because it's classified a strategic metal, suitable for military purposes."

Mars lit another Turkish cigarette from the butt of the one he had finished. "It has taken us years, but we have found a reliable source in the West for hafnium. That is, until COCOM found out about it and cut off the supply at its source: Japan. At least, that's what we believed, since the hafnium supply line ceased to function shortly after the source was shut down."

He rose, poured himself more coffee and vodka. Back at his

desk, he sat sipping and smoking for so long that Irina became convinced that he had forgotten his train of thought.

At last she said, "What happened to the hafnium meant for delivery here?"

"Ah." Mars put his cup down. "At first we assumed that it had been confiscated by the Tokyo police and handed over to the Tokuso, the Tokyo District Special Prosecutor's Office. That's standard operating procedure there. A week later, however, we received a reliable report—which we were later able to verify from an independent source—that the last shipment of hafnium had gone out *before* the raid, and we were discreetly asked for payment. The trouble was, we had never received the hafnium."

Irina sat up. "You said the supply line had ceased to function."

Mars threw the file to one side, got up, came over to the bed. "In a sense, that's true." He looked down at her. "When we sent people back down the pipeline to trace the whereabouts of that last shipment, they found only death. Each link had had his tongue neatly cut off, jammed down his throat. To asphyxiate is far from pleasant, but to die in that way is monstrous."

Irina shuddered. But the fact was, she was fascinated. "Do you know what happened to the hafnium?"

"That is, as the Americans say, the six-hundred-million-dollar question." Mars sat beside her. He was staring at her nakedness, and she could clearly see the effect she was having on him. She could feel his tension like a song in the darkness. "It was logical to assume that terrorists from another nation had seized the hafnium, but inquiries were made, and this avenue of speculation eventually came to a dead end. That was three weeks ago."

"Then where is it?" Irina closed her fingers around the thickening snake between his thighs. She leaned over, kissed his nipple. "You know, don't you?"

"I do," Mars said thickly. "And I don't." He closed his eyes. "The hafnium is here, inside Russia." His breath quickened. "But oddly, frighteningly, we do not know who has it."

Honno Kansei had promised herself that she would never see Big Ezoe again, but converging events now dictated that she must. *Karma.*

Big Ezoe inhabited a large, almost warehouselike space on the eastern edge of Tokyo. Honno knew that he must be very rich to be able to have so much room around him. That was

98

unsurprising, since Big Ezoe was *ōyabun*, overlord, of Tokyo's most powerful Yakuza family. The Yakuza were gangsters, turning the shadowed alleyways of Tokyo into their own private underworld. But they were also close-knit families of gamblers, eternal losers when it came to tossing the dice of heaven, and thus, among the Japanese, they had attained something of the status of myth.

If the Yakuza inhabited an almost mythical underworld, then Big Ezoe was their Charon, for he had so many fingers in a multitude of legitimate pies that surely he had ferried more unsuspecting souls across the River Styx into the dangerous land the Yakuza controlled than anyone else. One of those unfortunates had been Honno Kansei's father.

Honno could never be certain, but she suspected that Big Ezoe had killed her father. Not directly, perhaps, but what did that matter? Honno's father had been an inveterate gambler. Nothing she or her mother could say had any effect on him. He gambled at the Yakuza parlors and lost. And when, at length, he had lost so much that he could not possibly repay them, he had slipped—or, Honno suspected, was pushed—off a crowded curb into the path of an oncoming bus. He had ended up beneath the wheels with his back broken and his blood running in a river along the gutter. He had died before the ambulance could get him to the hospital.

As Honno approached Big Ezoe's place, she could remember vividly their first—and only—meeting. She had walked meekly into the place, asked politely to see Big Ezoe. When she was refused, she said, "Tell him that Noboru Yamato's daughter is here to repay his debts."

Three minutes later she was shown into Big Ezoe's office. He had a huge smile on his face. Honno had stood in front of him, drinking in the sight of the man she believed to be her father's murderer. Then, her heart hammering painfully in her chest, she had pulled out a small pistol, aimed it at Big Ezoe's head.

Big Ezoe never ceased to smile, not even when she said, "You broke my father's back and his spirit. Why are you smiling at me?"

Big Ezoe said, "To show fear in the face of death would be shameful."

And it was at that moment that Honno had understood the full ramifications of what she was about to do. And, simultaneously, she knew that she could not do it. As much as she mourned the unnecessary death of her father, she could not avenge it in this way, by taking the life of another. She had lowered the gun, placed it on Big Ezoe's desk.

Now, just a year later, desperation had driven her to return here, the last place on earth she wanted to be. It sickened her to have to come here, but Big Ezoe had a power she needed. He was a monstrous creature and, like a mythical dragon, an unpredictable one.

As Honno entered the warehouse, she had a sense of displacement, as if she were returning to the past and, in so doing, everything else was about to be lost to her.

A garden had grown up in her absence. A skylight had been installed in the center of the high ceiling, and below it a perfect square was displayed: a pebble stream with a steep rock bank on one side, a grouping of ferns, hostas, a dwarf maple on the other side. A mini-stand of emerald-green moso bamboo filled one corner, creating asymmetry, the tension a counterpoint to the repose that was essential for contemplation.

Honno was taken past the garden, down the warren of corridors, into Big Ezoe's office. He regarded her silently as she was ushered in, left alone with him. The room was filled with rarities: antiques both delicate (a translucent Chinese celadon vase) and earthy (a magnificent suit of seventeenth century samurai armor); a wood-block print of the Great Wave by Hokusai, transcendant with power, hanging above a monumental black stone Noguchi fountain that gleamed magically with an endless rippling of water that appeared as black as the stone.

Honno took this all in, thinking, How could a man as base as he is have the good taste to surround himself with elements of such ethereal beauty?

It was a long time before Big Ezoe moved. When he did, it was to open a drawer, reach inside, and place on the desk the pistol Honno had aimed at him one year ago.

"I suppose," he said, "that you've returned for this."

Honno stared at the gleaming face of the pistol. Big Ezoe had carefully turned the barrel away from her. She saw in the bits of chrome and steel the mirror of her past, and the wound of her father's death seemed fresh and raw again.

"If the hate is still inside you," Big Ezoe said placidly, "you have another chance to act on it."

But Honno saw only another chance at damnation. "You keep it," she said thickly. She regained control of herself slowly and painfully. "Perhaps you'll find some use for it."

Big Ezoe nodded. "As you wish." His huge hand covered

the pistol, and he opened the chambers for her to see. "It wasn't loaded, but you thought it was. And that let me see what was in your heart." He laughed. "Is that all?"

Honno lifted her gaze, stared into his eyes. She took a deep breath, said, "May I have some tea?"

Big Ezoe arched an eyebrow, but all he said was, "Yes, of course." Depressing a toggle on his intercom, he spoke quietly into the speaker. Then, sitting back, he said to Honno, "If you continue to frown like that, you will be old before your time. I used to hear my mother instructing my ex-wife on how to smile." A laugh escaped him. "Perhaps I should take you home to meet my mother."

The tea arrived. Big Ezoe served it himself. When it was poured, the first cup consumed, the refills steaming, Honno said, "I need your help."

Big Ezoe seemed sad. "My hands are dirty. I am a gangster. You are convinced that I had your father murdered. What could I possibly assist you with?" He shook his head. "You have come to the wrong place. I think it is the police you want. Or perhaps the Tokuso."

So he knows about my marriage to Eikichi, Honno thought. She knew she shouldn't be surprised. Information was Big Ezoe's business, among other things.

She steeled herself. "Neither the police nor the Tokuso would be appropriate in this instance," she said. "You are my one and only avenue. I want to do the right thing, but I am afraid. I am bound by *giri*, but I am a woman in a man's world. Will you help me?"

Big Ezoe gazed at her for a long time. He was a large man in his early fifties who was so muscular that he seemed to be bursting out of his silk suit. He had a wide, open face that, oddly enough, inspired confidence. But there was also an aggressiveness about his mouth and chin. He had bristly, short-cropped hair, a neat mustache with just a hint of silver in it. He looked more like a law enforcement officer than a Yakuza *oyabun*.

He opened his huge hands. "Forgive me," he said, "but why should I help you?"

Honno was prepared for this. "What's in it for you," she said, opening her pocketbook. "I understand." She withdrew an envelope thick with yen. "I have money here. As much as I can afford."

Big Ezoe scowled.

"It isn't enough?" Honno said with a sinking heart.

"Put that away. I do not take money from nice young girls who should know better."

"Must you make a joke of everything?" Honno felt desperation grip her. If Big Ezoe would not help her, what would she do? "Your help—"

Big Ezoe came around from behind his desk. "My help, my dear Mrs. Kansei, is not bought. It is earned." He looked into her eyes. "You said it yourself. You are a woman in a man's world. It is like my mother used to say to my ex-wife: I think you must convince me that you belong here. If I agree to help you, I take on an obligation. This is a serious matter for both of us, and I suggest you consider this thoroughly before you continue."

"I have already considered it," Honno said. "If you agree to help me, I am in your debt. You have no concept of how violated that makes me feel."

"Now you insult me. You have a peculiar methodology for asking for help."

"I am obligated to carry out a samurai's dying wish," Honno said fiercely. "He was a friend. He was honorable, and I helped him die with honor. Now he has asked a service of me, and I am bound by honor—his honor as well as my own—to carry it out for him. I know I haven't the means to accomplish this on my own. That is why I am here."

"A samurai, you say." Big Ezoe pulled at his lower lip. He appeared intrigued. "Are you saying that you were Kakuei Sakata's second at Sengakuji? You pulled the blade across his belly when he could not?"

"Yes."

"I see." He was wreathed in thought. "A Yakuza taking up the fallen banner of a samurai. Now that is a fascinating situation."

"You will help me, then?"

Big Ezoe's eyes focused on her again. "You know, Mrs. Kansei, I had a feeling you'd be back. A year ago you walked in here and pointed a gun at my head. That was something I thought I'd never see a woman do. Maybe you were too dumb to know better. On the other hand, you were smart enough not to try to pull the trigger. Had you tried, my men would have killed you. And now . . ."

"I will do whatever I have to," she said.

"Will you? I wonder. I question whether you have any notion of what your boast might entail." Big Ezoe looked at her thoughtfully for a moment, then he laid her pistol in the flat of his hand. "Who knows where this path will lead you, or what may be required of you along the way?" He came around from behind his desk. "It is not for a small matter that a samurai takes his own life. You are about to take your first step into the darkness. Unknown forces undoubtedly lie in wait. Powerful, malignant forces, I suspect. You must be prepared to defend yourself against them." He hefted the pistol, curled his finger around the trigger. "What do you think now? It is not too late to change your mind."

Honno took out the key Kakuei Sakata had mailed her. She showed it to Big Ezoe and said, "This is where we begin."

THREE

VIRGINIA COUNTRYSIDE/MACHINE-GUN CITY

Russell Slade picked Tori up in his custom armor-plated limousine. It was still dark outside, even the birds barely awake.

In his arrogance, he had been at the Los Angeles airport, waiting for her to call. Russell had one of these cars—bulletproof, capable of running at 150 mph, filled with the most advanced communications center imaginable—in Washington, New York, and Los Angeles. They were a necessary—one could say vital—part of his work, a mobile office where, more often than not, he ate and slept while missions were running. Russell had an almost pathological dislike for being in one place for too long. He had, no doubt, picked up this peculiarity from Bernard Godwin, who had survived a KGB assassination attempt in his hotel room in Bonn. Russell detested hotels, principally because it was virtually impossible to arrange decent security inside them. There were far too many personnel to vet, too many passageways, deliveries, passkeys, people going in and out at all hours of the day and night to make even a token stab at keeping a room safe.

The only thing in Russell's favor was that he had not gloated, but had accepted her presence as a natural occurrence, which, once Tori took the time to think about it, said as much about him as she wished to know.

She had plenty of time to think on the flight back to Washington. Russell had his own private jet, of course. There were so many antihijacking devices, the Mall was obliged to order a 727 instead of a far smaller Lear jet. She wanted to sleep, but every time she drifted off, she was back in the same dream cycle, in Ariel's house on Russian Hill, on the couch when the explosion hit, the pain recalled from the other explosion, the one that had ripped apart her hip, when she had stared into the hideous eyes of death . . .

She snapped awake each time, her heart hammering in her ears. She sat up straight, watched Russell sitting across from her as he sent and received faxes from the Mall's situations room, buried far beneath the emerald Virginia hills. When she had known him, he had smoked, but now he confined himself to gnawing at the cap of a plastic pen.

Somewhere over Ohio or Missouri they were served sandwiches and coffee, for which Tori was grateful. She had no wish to return to her nightmare landscape, locked in an endless circle of fear and pain.

When they were finished eating, Russell said, "You still hooked into Japan's version of *la Famiglia*?"

Tori did not care for his sarcastic tone; she thought of him sitting in his limousine, so arrogant, so certain that she would call him and capitulate that he hadn't bothered to board his plane. She had the urge to hit him in the face; instead, she concentrated on her plan. Somewhere near dawn she had come to the conclusion that there was a way in which she could get everything she wanted for herself: reinstatement in the Mall on her own terms, and revenge on Russell Slade for severing her. What she would do to Slade would be a far better—and more fitting—fate for him than a mere broken face; although the picture of Slade with his jaws wired together did have a certain charm.

She smiled. "If you're talking about the Yakuza, yes, I still have my contacts."

Russell nodded, almost as if she had passed some kind of test. "Good," he said. "Because the Yakuza are involved up to their bushy little eyebrows."

"Are you talking about Ariel Solares's murder?"

Russell pushed the swivel light away from him, pressed the tips of his fingers against his eyelids. His face had retreated into the shadows. Outside, the clouds streamed by below them, rent asunder by their screaming passage.

"Remember the Yakuza assassins you and Solares overheard in the Argentine tunnels?" he said. "Well, they're just a tiny part of what is coming our way, and I'm afraid they've got something particularly nasty in store for us."

Tori said, "If the Japanese are involved in a big way, I can see why you came to see me yourself. You need my expertise." She peered into his face with mock concern. "That isn't flop sweat I see on your lip, is it?"

"Don't be ridiculous."

He seemed genuinely annoyed, and Tori was pleased she had found a nerve.

"Just how deeply *are* the Japanese involved?" Tori asked.

Russell stared at her. "You know, your Japanese friends are infuriating; they don't know how to play by the rules."

"Oh, they play by the rules all right," Tori said. "The only problem is you're like every other member of American government: you haven't the slightest idea what the rules are."

He stared at her in the way someone will contemplate an enigmatic work of modern art, with a combination of shock, confusion, and, certainly, a degree of anger.

Before he could say anything more, Tori got up, went into the lavatory to clean up and change. She emerged twenty minutes later dressed in a natural mohair cardigan over a pale lace camisole. She wore a short fawn-colored suede skirt, brown lizardskin shoes, heavy dull-gold earrings.

"Bit of a show, isn't it?" Russell said, taking her in.

"That's what L.A. reminds you," Tori said perversely, "that all of life's a show." She smiled. "Bernard will appreciate the effort, even if you don't."

A thick mist was rising off the Potomac when they landed in Washington. One of Russell's specialized limos was waiting for them on the tarmac beside the runway, its powerful engine purring, its blackened windows up as protection against the capital's humidity as well as an assassin's bullet.

Once into the Virginia countryside, Tori slid her window down over Russell's protests. "I want to hear the birds," she said, just before they turned onto a four-lane highway. Five miles farther the limo made a left into a vast mall. Tori saw the stores typical of a mall nearly anywhere in the country: Sears, JCPenney, Radio Shack, a huge chain drugstore outlet, Filene's. The limo cruised through the mall, entered an underground car park, kept descending. It stopped at the lowest level, pulled up against the far wall: painted concrete, blank. They waited while the limo was scanned. When a green light appeared on a small console by Russell's right arm, he punched in a ten-digit access code. A portion of the concrete wall rose, and the limo slid through.

They were in a tunnel built around a two-lane blacktop. Strip lights glowed orange-yellow on the far side of both lanes. Otherwise the road and tunnel were absolutely featureless. Ten minutes later the roadway sloped up and they once again appeared in the Virginia countryside. This time they were within the borders of a 150-acre horse farm. This was the true home of the Mall.

Bernard Godwin was waiting for them at the entrance to Central. His face lit up when Tori emerged from the dark confines of the limo. He looked to her to be not one moment older than when they had last met: a Roman general with all the cunning and deceit of a master statesman. She had never met anyone—including Russell, *especially* Russell—for whom the mantle of power was so well suited. She believed that Bernard Godwin actually thrived on what he had become; he needed the power just as her mother needed to slip in and out of her guises. Strip him of his power, and he would be dead within a day.

"By God, Tori, you look a damn sight better than when you left here a year and a half ago." Bernard embraced her warmly. "It's good of you to have come back," he said so softly that she was the only one to hear. Then he broke away. "Russell, you've done well to bring her home."

Briefings were traditionally held in a plush suite of rooms which were insulated from and surrounded by the Mall's own electrical generators. The entire complex was totally self-sufficient, a prerequisite—albeit an expensive one—that Bernard Godwin had insisted upon when the Mall was first founded. Besides anything else, the placement of the enormous generators ensured that no listening devices could penetrate to the suite.

The rooms were furnished in the typical style of a men's club, comfortable, broken-in, masculine. Which was, in part, why Tori had chosen to wear so provocative and feminine an outfit. She had not been back to this center of clandestine power in eighteen months, and now that she was, she wanted the men who ruled it to feel her presence in every way.

The three of them settled around a burl table. Sandwiches,

fresh fruit, coffee, juices were waiting for them, and they ate while they talked. Tori found that she had lost the sense of whether or not she was hungry, but she ate anyway out of force of habit. She automatically helped herself to the blueberries. They were one of a number of what was known in the Mall as "mission food." Blueberries had been fed to fighter pilots during World War II, they were filled with an enzyme that temporarily increased visual acuity.

Tori looked at Bernard, but he merely said, "Russell, you're on."

Russell Slade opened a buff-colored file. Tori saw that it was imprinted with the title ICE CREAM and had a scarlet band in the upper right-hand corner, signifying it contained "Eyes Only" documents, the most highly classified in the Mall: they could not be photocopied or taken from the premises, and one needed D.C.—"Director's Clearance"—to access them.

Russell cleared his throat, said, "Tori, I told you on the plane that our adversaries had come up with something particularly nasty. I wasn't kidding, and I wasn't exaggerating. This concerns the global transshipping of drugs."

"Cocaine?"

Russell and Bernard Godwin exchanged a brief glance. "Yes," Russell said, "and no. It was bad enough when the South American drug lords bribed their own governments into becoming witting accomplices to the growing, manufacturing, and shipping of cocaine, but now an entirely new element has entered the arena, and the implications are staggeringly dire for the United States."

He paused here to take a sip of orange juice. Russell was a good public speaker, Tori remembered. His sense of timing was impeccable.

"The first hint we had of something sinister," Russell continued, "was just under a year ago. A Washington kid died. Doesn't sound like much, I know. But the death got odder, its implications more frightening as the investigation went on. First off, the kid was a girl of about fifteen, a *white* girl from a socially prominent family. That, sadly, was a break for us. Had the victim been an inner city kid, her case most likely would never have come to our attention.

"But this girl's father has plenty of bread and—and this counts for much more—clout. He hires a forensic specialist— a former New York City chief medical examiner who's off writing his memoirs. This M.E.'s a smart cookie, and he

108

begins to dig. He delivers his prelim report to the father, who's so appalled he phones several of his government pals. At this point a red flag pops up on our computer screen, and I send someone—Ariel Solares—out to interview the principals."

Russell detached a sheet from the file, slid it across to Tori. "This is the M.E.'s report, but I can summarize it for you. This fifteen-year-old white girl died not of a drug overdose, which had been the original diagnosis, but of chronic cocaine use."

There was silence for some moments, and Tori thought that Russell had not lost his touch for the dramatic.

"Do you begin to see the conundrum we were presented with? A fifteen-year-old girl dies of chronic cocaine abuse. But the M.E. tells us it would take at least ten years of heavy usage to get her to that stage. Impossible. Yet we were all looking directly at the proof."

Russell's fingers fumbled in his jacket pocket, and Tori knew he was searching for a cigarette. But he didn't smoke anymore, so he poured himself some more juice, instead. "It took the M.E. the girl's father hired six weeks to come up with the answer, but the clever old dog got it. It was cocaine the girl had been using, but only for the last three months." Russell's eyes locked onto Tori's. "In three months her body had deteriorated ten years' worth. How? The answer lay with the cocaine itself. It was cocaine all right, but an exhaustive molecular analysis revealed differences. They seemed at first subtle, but when we re-created some in our own labs and fed it to mice, the results were astounding. This stuff is poison, plain and simple. Oh, it doesn't work like poison, rapidly causing death. In fact, the high it brings to the user makes regular cocaine seem like sugar. It is ultraaddictive, and it destroys the body within three months. Taking it is tantamount to swallowing a time bomb."

Tori considered all this. "Then this is the lead Ariel was working on in Buenos Aires?"

"Yes."

She said, "The two Japanese Yakuza in the tunnels?"

Russell glanced at Bernard, then back to Tori. "Ariel had assumed they were part of the pipeline. Then, according to his last report, he began to uncover another—and far more disturbing—link between the Yakuza and the supercocaine."

"Wait a minute," Tori said. "Are you saying that the Japanese are manufacturing this supercoke?"

"That appears to be the case," Russell said.

"Where did Ariel get this intelligence?" Tori asked. "Who were his contacts?"

"We don't know," Russell admitted. "He convinced me in order to get close to these people he had to be cut loose from all normal Mall procedure. That meant no day-by-day control, no timed dead-drop reports, no backup, no shield, nothing. He told me he was in a red zone, that if they suspected anything—" Russell stared down at the ICE CREAM file, but Tori could see he was looking at nothing. Perhaps he was remembering—and regretting—Ariel's death.

"This is why we need you," Russell said. "You know the Japanese culture, and the people. They can't invent anything, but give them a prototype and they'll refine it better than anyone else on earth."

"It isn't true that they can't invent anything."

"You know what he means, Tori," Bernard said. "This isn't a synthetic drug. The real thing is needed to metamorphose it into this most potent, untraceable, unstoppable weapon."

"This is insane," Tori told them. "Why would the Japanese create the ultimate cocaine? To make money, yes, that's understandable, but to create such a thing as a weapon—it's monstrous."

"I couldn't agree more," Bernard Godwin said. "There are elements within our own government who feel strongly that for years the Japanese have been waging systematic economic war on us, that they will stop at nothing to defeat us." He pursed his lips, as he often did when analyzing complex data. "Personally, I don't believe this, but you'd be surprised at who does in the White House and on Capitol Hill." He looked firm and resolute, a leader still. "All that seems clear at the moment is the intelligence Ariel unearthed that the Japanese created the supercocaine. We want you to find out the rest: who is manufacturing it, who they're selling it to, and why. Then we want you to shut the whole goddamned thing down."

"You should try to be more tolerant of Russell," Bernard Godwin said. "He's a good man."

"He fired me," Tori said.

"Yes, indeed. And he had my blessing."

"Your—"

"Tori, I trained you, and I love you. I brought you into the

110

Mall, and, I must say, I knew the risks involved when I did so. I was convinced that your extraordinary physical talents and your unique mind more than outweighed your rebelliousness, your unpredictability, your insubordination.

"But the fact remains that the Mall is an organization, not so very unlike the military in ways you already are quite familiar with. And like the military, strict rules and regulations have been instituted for the benefit of the Mall as a whole. No one individual must be allowed to rise above those rules and regulations. You tried to do just that, and you reaped the consequences. Russell did what he had to do as director, so stop blaming him."

They were walking out past the corrals where the striped wooden bars were set out to put the hunter-jumper horses through their paces. No one else was around, and by a bond of unspoken tradecraft, they kept near the trees and foliage, natural barriers against electronic listening devices.

"All right," she said, "perhaps I've been unfair to him. But I still want what I want."

"And what is that?"

"To come back on my own terms."

"That's too loaded a request for me to agree to outright," Bernard said. "Tell me exactly what it is you want."

Tori thought a moment. "I don't want to rise above the rules, I just want them bent a little. I want autonomy—"

"Impossible."

"You need me."

Bernard turned, and his eyes bored into hers. "Let's not dance. We know each other too well, Tori. The fact is, we need each other. If you deny this, I cannot under any circumstances allow you to come home, because in deceiving yourself, you're likely to deceive us. Not willingly, perhaps, but that possibility would be far more perilous for us. You love the hunt, the danger—even, yes, the blood being spilled so close to you. No, no, don't bother to deny it, we both know it's the truth. The dance so near death is your dance, Tori, and you do it better than anyone I ever met."

There was silence for a moment, broken only by the sound of a nearby woodcock. "If you'd have allowed me to finish," Tori said at length, "perhaps you'd agree to what I'm asking for."

"I doubt it," Bernard said, "but be my guest."

They began to walk again. They stopped within a copse of

huge maples. It was cool and dark within the eaves of the shade trees. In the sun-drenched distance they could see horses grazing, nuzzling one another. It was very peaceful.

"I want Director's Clearance, so if I need to, I can get Mall matériel without going through interminable red tape," Tori said. "And I want Russell with me in the field."

The silence between them was momentarily so deep that Tori could hear a horse snorting on the hillside a good six hundred yards away. This was her revenge on Russell Slade: to take the desk jockey into the warrens, get him muddy, let him see the face of the enemy, and, if she were lucky, have him stare death in the eye.

She had not for a moment been swayed by what Bernard said. He was an ex-actor. One of his talents lay in manipulating emotions with what he said. But Tori had grown up with such guile, and she was by now inured to it.

"A director's place is not in the field," Bernard said at last.

"Nevertheless—"

"I cannot allow it."

Tori gave him a little salute. "Then maybe I'll see you in another eighteen months or so."

"Tori, you need us as much as we need you."

She took a step away from him, into the sunshine. Bernard reached out, stopped her. "All right. You'll get your D.C." He closed his hand over hers. "I've never asked you for anything, Tori. But I am now. We *do* need you. Far more than Russell was willing to admit back there. He's only human; he's got his pride." He took her hand in his. "And perhaps you need us more than you're willing to admit to yourself. Damnit, you know there's truth in what I say."

Tori's eyes held his; she did not blink. "I want Russell with me, Bernard."

"Why?"

"He's ultimately vulnerable here, locked away on this impregnable farm, in his bulletproof limos, his terrorist-proof jets. He's out of touch with the world. You weren't like that. Think back. Your experience encompassed more than the think tank and the communications center. Once in a while you've got to put your ear to the ground instead of to a wireless grill. Russell will be a danger to me if he sits here and runs me, which is what he's got planned for me. He ran Ariel, so he'll run me. Let me bring him into the field. He needs the experience, and I'm going to need the help."

"I'm not sure this is the mission for him to get his feet wet."

Now it was Tori who impaled him with her eyes. "You mean you can afford to lose me in the field, but not Russell."

Bernard said, "I can't, at this moment, afford to lose either of you." But he seemed to be wavering.

"Neither can you afford to allow this new cocaine to begin flooding the country. Your own evidence shows that it's already started. Can you possibly imagine where it will end? If this mission doesn't get off the ground, there may not be another one for Russell to go out on."

"How did she talk you into it?" Russell Slade said. "I know this couldn't have been your idea."

"Don't be impertinent," Bernard Godwin said. "I sanctioned it."

Russell grunted. "You always did have a soft spot for her."

"With good reason," Bernard said. "It seems to me, Russell, that you never fully appreciated Tori's talents."

"To the extent that's so," Russell said, "it's because I've never fully trusted her. Oh, not in the usual sense. But she's chronically unpredictable. I know when you brought her in, you thought she'd grow out of her rebelliousness. But you saw, as I did, that she never matured."

"I'm not so sure 'mature' is the operative word," Bernard said. "She's got a healthy hatred of organizations of any kind. I'm beginning to see that's an asset in her line of work."

Russell snorted derisively.

Bernard said, "If you'd put aside your personal antipathy toward her, you'd understand what I'm talking about. Her hatred of organizations makes her one hundred percent secure. Do you think anyone could ever get to her to turn her? Not a chance. In that sense, she's pure, and that free spirit of hers guarantees it. Be grateful for that."

"All of this is bullshit," Russell said. "I'll be goddamned if I'll go into the field taking orders from her."

Bernard Godwin grabbed hold of the younger man. "Listen to me, Russell. You'll do it, and you'll be a good sport about it. Because if you aren't, where you and Tori are headed, I'll guarantee you'll be dead inside of thirty-six hours. There's nobody who's better in the field than Tori Nunn. Nobody. She's asked for you as part of her negotiations for returning home, and I've given you to her."

"What else has she negotiated for?"

"Leave that to me, will you? They're just details. Now I want you to take charge of this Japanese situation. I've got more than enough on my plate with White Star."

"I can't believe you're still on that, Bernard," Russell said.

"White Star is our first real link to a coordinated Soviet nationalist underground," Bernard said. "Of course I'm not going to let it go."

"But how can you do otherwise? Even you can't get a dime in appropriations, not when everyone believes you're walking into a similar situation to what happened years ago. What a fiasco for the Mall. That 'underground movement' turned out to be the KGB's Operation Boomerang."

"Must you continually remind me of that debacle?" Bernard said testily.

"I'm trying to protect you," Russell said. "The KGB's predecessors tried the same thing in the twenties, creating the Trust. They made believe the Trust's goal was the overthrow of Lenin. They did it so well, in fact, that they took in a load of Soviet emigrés, who were lured back to the motherland, only to fall into the hands of Felix Dzerzhinsky, head of the OGPU, who had created the bogus counterrevolutionary organization. This is a pattern, Bernard, and the KGB is known for repeating patterns. White Star—"

"This time I believe White Star is for real," Bernard said. "It wants nothing less than a union of independent but centrally linked republics—much like our own states."

"A true Union of Soviet Socialist Republics?" Russell almost laughed.

"No, no. Not socialist—and that's the point. Imagine, Russell! White Star envisions a *democratic* republic; the true death of socialism in Russia. I am convinced this is the only way Russia can become a viable, prosperous nation in the twenty-first century. Their very survival depends on change. Russia wants—and desperately needs—to compete with the likes of Japan, Korea, Taiwan for export dollars, but socialism is tying its hands and feet. It needs a free-market economy just as surely as it needs to free its nationalist republics from their slavery to Moscow. The leadership of White Star understands this. But now the temptation is to move too fast. When one does that, one gains unwanted attention." He waved a hand in dismissal. "But enough of White Star. We have more pressing matters to discuss."

Bernard had appeared to gain strength during their walk. He

114

said now, "You may think I'm overly sentimental about Tori Nunn, but you'll soon change your mind, believe me. Reviewing the files, I see now that you rarely utilized her to her full potential."

"Your opinion."

"It's the only one that matters." Godwin softened his tone. "In this instance, I happen to be more objective than you. No matter how often you may deny it, Russell, you hate Tori Nunn's guts. And I know why. You know that if she had 'matured,' as you so inaccurately put it, she would have been made director instead of you. And she's right, you know. You're atrophying sitting behind your desk. All too soon you'll be no good to me or the Mall. Neither of us wants that, do we?"

The two men resumed their walk. They were approximately in the same place where Tori and Bernard had spoken. But now it was later in the day, and the horses were gone. The hills seemed bare without them.

"Oh, don't look so downtrodden," Bernard said. "You've a chance to rectify your past mistakes. That's far more than most men are given."

"Still," Russell persisted, "I want some assurance. The possibility does exist that you are wrong about her. She may break the rules again and, in so doing, endanger us all."

"True enough," Bernard said. "And that's another sound reason for you to take the mission on with her. Who better to detect a false word or move than you, Russell?"

"And if you *are* wrong?"

"Oh, that's simple," Bernard Godwin said, heading back toward Central. "You're authorized to terminate her."

"Since our first stop will be Japan," Russell said on the way to the airport, "I'll need a crash briefing on customs, current style, idioms, so forth."

"We're not going to Japan," Tori said. "At least not right away."

"But it's the Japanese who—"

"We've got to start at the beginning if we're going to get anywhere," Tori said. "It's no good us sticking our heads in at the middle because we'll never know which way to go, upstream or downstream."

"But the Japanese *are* the source. They're the logical choice to begin."

"Logic is only successful in a laboratory maze," Tori said. "Out in the world, intuition bridges the gaps logic can't cross." From Central she had phoned Estilo, the Argentine businessman who had befriended her, asking him to meet them. She had spoken to him for quite a while. Estilo talked about Ariel Solares. He never broke down, never actually said how much he missed Solares, but then he didn't have to. Tori understood, just as Estilo knew she would. He had always said that she had the soul of a true *porteño*.

"All right," Russell said. "Where are we headed?"

"To Machine-Gun City," Tori told him.

"Medellín?" Russell said incredulously. "Colombia?"

"That's right," Tori said as they climbed aboard the private 727. The driver was stowing their luggage in the belly of the steel beast.

"D'you know that where you're taking us is off limits even for American diplomatic personnel? D'you know that down there it costs about eighty dollars to hire a mariachi band for the evening but only ten to buy a *sicario* for a hit?" Russell was talking about the local teenage assassins. "That hellhole has the highest murder rate of any city not at war."

"Medellín *is* at war," Tori said. She turned to him. "Look, Russ, Japanese or no Japanese, down to bare bones it's a cocaine pipeline we're after, so we've got to go right to the source."

"Yeah," Russell said, taking a last look at Washington. He was already feeling nostalgic for his comfortable surroundings, his daily routine. "Right down the barrel of a semiautomatic."

Medellín was in the west-central area of Colombia, not far from the Pacific Ocean. It was nestled into a deep valley within the lush pined ridges of the Andes. The 727 was obliged to circle for what seemed an eternity as it came closer and closer to the tops of those formidable peaks and then, breathtakingly, dropped below them.

Before landing, Tori and Russell had a good look at the scenery, as sun-drenched and gorgeous as anything out of a travel agent's brochure. They saw the spectacular terraced orchid farms, whose product was Machine-Gun City's other export.

They waited on the runway while the flight crew shut down the engines. Tori went forward to speak to the pilot. Everyone on board was a trained Mall operative.

Fifteen minutes went by; Russell began to chafe. He got up,

116

began to walk around the cabin. "Let's for God's sake get out of here," he finally said.

Tori said, "You don't want to go into the terminal. The *sicarios* who hang out there will spot your gringo face instantly, and attach themselves like leeches."

"So what are we going to do?"

"For the moment, we're going to do nothing," Tori said, pointing out the window.

Russell bent over, saw two uniformed *paisas*—natives—striding officiously across the tarmac. They clip-clopped smartly up the rolling stairway, entered the cabin.

"Let me have your passport," she said to Russell, and he handed it over.

Tori went to meet the *paisas*, and Russell could hear her softly spoken Spanish mingling with theirs. She did not sound like a gringo—he knew he did, even though he was fluent in Spanish, as well as several other languages. Tori had a peculiar facility for idiom and nuance that was beyond him. She spoke like a native wherever she went.

Russell saw packets of bills—U.S. currency—pass from Tori to the uniformed *paisas*. She handed them a stack of passports, hers, Russell's, those of the flight crew. All were stamped. A moment later they had left, without even having glanced Russell's way.

Tori nodded to him, and they went down the moving stairs. The uniformed *paisas* had already disappeared. Russell sucked in the air, clean and crisp, deliciously scented, and without any of the usual oppressive humidity found in the cities at a lower altitude.

Tori had a satchel of parachute cloth with her. While they stood there in the shadow of the jet, the flight crew was already in the process of refueling, going through the myriad maintenance checks necessary between flights.

A blue four-door Renault drew up. She had asked for it, because it had a larger engine and was heavier than either the Mazda or the Toyota that were available. "Are you armed?" Tori asked.

Russell shook his head.

Tori said, "Go back into the plane and requisition something from the pilot. He's also an armorer." She climbed into the backseat of the car.

Russell did as she suggested, but he was annoyed. He hadn't taken a good look at the pilot; he'd needed her to tell him who

117

his men were. He was beginning to regret his acquiescence to this madness. But what choice had he been given? None, he told himself glumly. Bernard had seen neatly to that.

Tori was already in the back of the Renault when he returned, huddling with the driver in front. As soon as he sat down beside her, the Renault took off. The driver, a fit-looking man with silver hair and mustache, wore wraparound dark glasses, an open-weave cotton shirt, and linen trousers.

"Welcome to Metra-lin, Señor Slade," Estilo said. He was using the only slightly tongue-in-cheek slang that had given Medellín its apocalyptic nickname, Machine-Gun City.

Russell turned to Tori. "Why not use a helicopter?" he asked her.

"The last people who tried that," Tori said, "were turned to cinders by *sicario* hijackers." She shrugged. "It's the gringo alternative. The natives—the *paisas*—go the way we will go."

The Renault was going very fast, bouncing along a scarifying switchback road that snaked through the forested mountains. Russell sneaked a look at the speedometer. Considering the terrain, he thought they were traveling at least twenty mph too fast. He was about to say so when Estilo said over his shoulder, "We're being followed."

Russell turned so fast his neck cracked. Out the rear window he could see a pair of chrome and black motorcycles gaining on them. "Jesus," he breathed, "so much for your security precautions." He began to recheck the pistol the pilot had given him. It was a large caliber weapon, deadly at medium range, absolutely devastating closer in.

"Try to lose them," Tori said to Estilo, and the Renault rocketed forward, hurtling this way and that down the winding road, tires screaming in protest. The world to either side had become a green blur, and the lushly forested mountainsides ahead were coming at them far too fast. In desperation, Russell turned to the rear window. The motorcycles, lagging for a moment, were already gaining back the ground they had lost.

"We'll never outrun them," Russell observed.

"We weren't meant to," Tori said to him. She turned her attention to the driver. "Slow down, Estilo," he heard her say. And then, "You know what to do." Estilo reached down between his legs.

"Are you insane?" Russell stared at Tori as she unzipped her satchel. "These *sicarios* will cut us to ribbons."

The motorcycles roared up beside the Renault, and now Rus-

118

sell could see that each held two *sicarios*, bristling with armament. None of them looked over seventeen. There were schools in the mountains surrounding Medellín that turned out scores of these fearless, punk killers, high on cocaine and the peculiar, frightening power of the killing lust. Russell caught a glimpse of a pair of sawed-off shotguns beginning to swing down, two MAC-10 machine pistols being leveled in the direction of the Renault.

Explosions from the shotguns. At that instant Estilo stepped hard on the brakes and, its rear wheels sluing back and forth, the Renault screeched to a halt. While it was still rocking on its shocks, Tori had opened her curbside door and, using it as a shield, whipped her arms up in the classic marksman's pose.

The motorcycles had meanwhile overshot their prey and were obliged to make sharp U-turns. This maneuver meant that the *sicarios* riding shotgun could neither aim nor shoot until the motorcycles had swung around and were heading back toward the stopped Renault. They fired.

Tori was holding some kind of long-barreled pistol that Russell was unfamiliar with. She squeezed off two shots, and the *sicarios* in the leading motorcycle were slammed backward off the bike. It roared erratically, running off the road and smashing into the underbrush. A gush of oily smoke rose into the flower-scented air.

The second motorcycle came on.

Russell could see that their driver, the man Tori had called Estilo, was either unarmed or was making no attempt to draw his weapon. Perhaps he had frozen. Russell was in no such position. He might be a desk jockey, as Tori had said, but he got only firsts on the target range, and he worked out in the unarmed combat *dojo* three times a week.

He raised his pistol, went to lean out his window. But Estilo whirled in the front seat and, putting his hand over the hammer of the pistol, pushed it down out of sight. "Orders," he said laconically.

"But the *sicarios*—"

"*Paciencia*," he said. "Wait and see."

Tori broke from the cover of the Renault and, slamming her door behind her, took off down the verge of the road, back the way they had come.

"What?" Russell twisted in his seat. "Tori, where the hell d'you—" He tried to get the pistol out of Estilo's grip, but failed.

He heard the blast of a shotgun firing. "Goddamnit, let go, you sonuvabitch! She'll be killed!"

Because now the remaining motorcycle had swerved off the center of the road and was traveling down the right verge in direct line with Tori's flight. The MAC-10 was chattering.

The motorcycle was almost upon them. In a moment it would zip right by their right side, and then it would be too late to do anything to help Tori. Russell redoubled his efforts to free his pistol, but it was like battling an octopus, and he was unused to unarmed combat in such restricted quarters. The intervening back of the seat prevented him from using the throws and holds he had learned.

He could see the faces of the *sicarios*, long hair streaming, huge grins splitting their faces as they rode the wind, the high their speed and their power brought them. They ignored the Renault and its occupants, focused as they were on the woman who had killed their compatriots. The MAC-10 resumed its thunder.

Just as the *sicarios* were about to draw abreast of the Renault, Estilo squeezed off one round through the open side window and, at the same instant, kicked his door open wide.

The motorcycle was far too close to avoid the obstruction, and there was a wailing scream as it plowed into the steel door, tearing it straight off its hinges. At the same time, the motorcycle rose into the air like a bronco spitting the bit. The vehicle squealed as if wounded, hurled itself over on its side.

Estilo was out of the Renault in a flash, and Russell saw Tori racing back. Estilo kicked the MAC-10 from the dead driver's hand.

As he got out of the car, Russell could see the bullet hole in the side of the *sicario*'s head, a clean hit, and he thought, Jesus, what a shot!

Estilo placed his left foot across the remaining *sicario*'s wrist, preventing him from getting to his shotgun. There was blood running from his nose and one ear. Nobody said a word until Tori came up. Russell noticed that she was not even out of breath.

Tori knelt down beside the last remaining *sicario* and said, "Who sent you?"

The *sicario* spat in her face, and she put the muzzle of her odd pistol against his right kneecap. She pulled the trigger. The *sicario* jumped as if speared. His face went white and his eyes rolled crazily in their sockets. Tears of pain streamed down his sweat- and dust-streaked cheeks.

Tori bent closer. "The next time I pull the trigger," she said, moving the pistol to his crotch, "it won't be your kneecap that won't work."

The *sicario* said one word, "Cruz." The bull. Then he began to shake as if he had contracted malaria.

The corrida was full by the time they got there. They had missed the drug lords and their shotgun-toting bodyguards lustily, patriotically singing the Colombian and Medellín anthems, but the first blood had not yet been spilled, and that was a good sign.

They could get seats only in the sun-drenched side of the bowl-shaped arena, and it was very hot. The place smelled of old stone, red dust, and fight frenzy. They were downwind of the red-eyed bull, currently facing a rail-thin matador.

"Can you tell me why the hell we're here?" Russell said to Tori as the three of them settled onto the backless bench.

"When Ariel and I were in the tunnels," she said, "we overheard a fragment of conversation between the two Japanese Yakuza. This was before they discovered we were there. They had just finished killing a man named Rega, who had seemed to be their local contact. It occurred to me, after the briefing you gave me, that this would be a good place to start. Who was Rega? That's why I called Estilo."

Russell glanced over at the silver-haired man. "Who is he?"

"Estilo is a friend of mine," Tori said. "That's all you need to know."

"It most assuredly is not," Russell said. "He hasn't been vetted, they aren't under discipline. I don't know him from a hole in the wall."

"But I do."

"Tori, I'm warning you," Russell said. "If this mission deteriorates into another one of your personal—"

"Go home, Russ," Tori said disgustedly. "I was wrong. You don't belong out here. Go back to your desk in Virginia and let me do my job."

The bull made a run at the matador, who turned a magnificent veronica three inches from the beast's left horn.

"I'm here for the duration," Russell said grimly. "You're not running me out of here. But this person—"

"Estilo saved your life and mine back there on the road to

the airport." Tori glared at him. "If you thought for a moment, you'd see that that was a far better test of his loyalty than any of your electronic vetting machines."

A roar went up from the crowd as the bull made another run at the matador, who this time stuck a lance into the powerful muscles of its neck.

"This is barbaric," Russell said. "Like something from the dark ages."

"It's the art of death, Señor Slade," Estilo said. "Beauty and death is what Medellín is known for. There is no violence here in the corrida, only grace and an honorable way to die. This is why the people come; this is what captures their fancy."

Russell shook his head. "I don't understand."

"Estilo told me who Rega was," Tori said, continuing their conversation. "A *paisa* runner who worked for one of the Machine-Gun City drug cartels. These are all family run, very powerful. Estilo can't understand—and neither do I—why the Japanese Yakuza terminated Rega. The Japanese need the real stuff in order to manufacture their supercoke, so why cut off their supply? It doesn't make sense, and until it does, we won't be on our way."

"But the corrida?"

"We have to find out who Rega worked for—Cruz, the most powerful of the Medellín family cartels, or the Cali-based Orolas, their rivals," Tori said. "We'll start with Cruz because he was the one who sent the four *sicarios* after us. We've got to talk to him, and this is where he is." She pointed to a fat man sitting in the section of the arena almost directly across from them, in the border between sun and shade. He was surrounded by *sicarios* wielding shotguns. Next to him was a beautiful woman with heavy-lidded eyes who kept checking her makeup in a compact mirror.

Estilo turned to Tori and, indicating the woman next to Cruz, said, "Medellín may turn out the most deadly men, but Cali, where Cruz's woman, Sonia, was born, creates the most beautiful women, don't you agree? It is said that when Cruz has that Cali-born body beneath him, he thinks only of his enemies, the Orolas."

"Considering what's happened," Russell said, "I don't think this Cruz wants anything to do with us."

"Sure he does," Tori said, watching Cruz and his party. "He just doesn't know it yet."

Below them, in the corrida, the bull's energy was finally flagging. It ran at the matador, but its head was lowered, and in triumph the thin man slid his blade as delicately and precisely as a surgeon just behind the back of the exhausted beast's skull, piercing its heart. The bull's eyes rolled, its forelegs collapsed, and it went down. The crowd was on its feet, screaming in delight and appreciation. Flowers rained down upon the matador, who pirouetted slowly, hands to the cloudless sky.

During this tumult, Tori kept her eyes on Cruz's woman. There was something odd about the way she kept looking in her mirror. Now she adjusted herself a little, and Tori saw a flash of reflected light, a spotlight brighter even than the sun, that illuminated the face of a dark-skinned man.

Tori leaned over, spoke briefly in Estilo's ear. Russell could see Estilo look in the direction Tori indicated. He nodded, said something to Tori that Russell couldn't make out.

The two of them got up. "Stay here," Tori said to Russell.

"But—"

"You'll be all right as long as you don't move." Her eyes fixed his. "Do you understand me?"

Russell nodded unhappily. It was perfectly clear. He was a gringo in the middle of a hostile environment. He needed the lowest possible profile.

Tori and Estilo made their way laterally across the tiers of cheering aficionados. The man who Cruz's woman had been looking at had left his seat. Tori knew there was a need to hurry, the noise was perfect cover. But they could not afford to divert attention to themselves.

"How do you want to do this?" Estilo asked.

"You go up behind him," Tori said. "I'll try to get between him and Cruz."

Estilo nodded, and the two of them split up. Estilo made his way up the tiers, higher and higher, working through the throng, which was still on its feet, applauding the beautiful death of the bull.

Tori was now near enough to the dark-skinned man to see the death stare in his eyes. It was a look she knew well, the mark of pure concentration, when the environment narrows down to one focus point: the kill. In this case, the victim was Cruz.

Estilo had identified the dark-skinned man as a member of the Orola drug clan, Cruz's bitter rival. The Orolas were from Cali, and Estilo knew them all.

The dark-skinned man was coming not with a shotgun or a MAC-10 machine pistol, but with a small-caliber handgun. It was a suicide mission, for sure, but it was the kind of surgical strike the Orolas preferred. It was the Medellín *sicarios* who loved to blow away half a city block to get their job done. Moreover, there was an elegant sense of irony at work here, executing Cruz at the corrida, in the tumultuous moment after the kill, that was typical of the Orola mind. Tori admired the strategy even as she worked herself into place to foil it.

She was very near the dark-skinned man now, and she stood still, contracting her *wa*, allowing his concentrated energies to pass over her. He was aware of nothing but his target: Cruz. He need not even concern himself with Cruz's bodyguards, who, in any case, were trained to look for weaponry, because he did not have to think about an escape. There was no escape.

The crowd was chanting, roaring, surging as the matador ceremoniously withdrew his blade from the heart of the beast. A single line of blood ran down his sword.

Tori waited until the dark-skinned man drew his gun. He raised it, aiming at Cruz's heart. With a great *kiai* shout, Tori lunged forward, the hardened underedge of her hand snapping the bone in the dark-skinned man's extended forearm.

She was aware of Cruz turning in a defensive crouch, the contraction of the circle of his bodyguards, their shotguns swinging down in concert. Screams from the crowd, the beginnings of a core of panic from those bystanders nearest the incident.

There was no reason for haste now. Tori twisted the gun from the dark-skinned man's trembling hand, held him up as his legs gave way beneath him. His head fell loosely in shock. As she saw the vulnerable spot at the back of his head, she thought of the bull, lying in its own blood in the red dust of the corrida below her. In this, she thought, Estilo is wrong, there can be no beauty, no artistry in this. Death is its own realm, it is finite, and when it comes, it comes, *finis*.

Cruz was shouting to his bodyguards, and they nimbly stepped around the fleeing people. All of them were focused on her. Cruz moved along the arc of the tier to where Tori stood, holding the dark-skinned man.

When she judged Cruz close enough, Tori grabbed a handful of the dark-skinned man's hair, jerked his head up so Cruz could see his face.

"Do you know this man?" Cruz asked her in a voice made hoarse by the proximity to death and by his innate suspicion.

"He is from Cali," Tori said. "He was to be a gift from the Orolas."

"A final gift, it would seem," Cruz said, taking the gun from her. He examined it, then looked full into Tori's face. "He had to get close to use this. He wasn't going to get out, was he?"

"Not today."

Cruz put the muzzle of the man's gun against the back of his head and pulled the trigger. "Not any day," he said.

Cruz lived in an enormous suite on the top floor of the Monaco Building, a glitzy apartment dwelling in El Poblado, Medellín's choicest district. His men patrolled the surrounding block, and there were two guards armed with shotguns in the hallway of his apartment. Inside, the living room was lined with bear and leopard skins, Flemish tapestries, and his lieutenants—more *sicarios*.

Because he had summarily executed the Orola assassin without first interrogating him, Tori had lowered her estimation of Cruz. But it would have meant a loss of face in front of all those *paisas* had he not killed the man immediately, and his business would no doubt have suffered as a consequence.

He was not a bad-looking sort, though he was flat-faced. His black hair came down in a widow's peak; he wore it slicked back, very long against his neck. But he scowled a great deal, he had an overactive trigger finger, and he was much feared in and around Machine-Gun City.

Certainly the Orolas found him something more than a nuisance. Just about three months ago he and ten of his *sicarios* had ambushed the youngest of the Orola brothers at the El Cerrito tollbooth. He had been making inquiries of Cruz's contacts with the Bolivian *cocaleros*—the coca farmers who grew the plant from which cocaine was ultimately refined. Cruz had not taken kindly to what he had seen as an act of war, and he had retaliated in the only true language he spoke. The five-minute hail of bullets fired from the massed MAC-10's of Cruz's *sicarios* had taken out not only their target, but his three bodyguards, a dozen human mules moving one hundred kilos of raw cocaine, and four bystanders, not to mention taking the concrete and tin tollbooth apart at the seams. Cruz had bragged about the kill for weeks afterward.

"This was not the first attempt on my life made by the Oro-

125

las,'' Cruz said as they seated themselves in his enormous living room. "But they are incompetent. They do not know how to refine the art of killing.'' He was bragging again, but what the hell, Tori thought, he was safe, in the center of his own turf, with the scalp of another of his enemies fresh on his fingers. He was entitled.

Tori made the introductions, and Cruz listened politely but, she thought, a bit disinterestedly. She was prepared to do something about that, but only at the right moment.

"Do you know what this country would be without me and the people like me?'' Cruz said. "Fucked.'' He laughed. "Ask the economists, if you doubt me. The Colombian economy is so fragile, like the glass of one of my Ming vases. Without cocaine trafficking to prop it up, our country would be plunged into a recession so severe I fear there would be no end. No, no, on second thought don't ask the economists, they're a bunch of *maricones*. Ask the people of Colombia, they will tell you the truth. They do not want this internal war the president has pushed on the country. They are sick of their government. And I am sick of planting bombs in post offices and government buildings. In my opinion the government of Colombia is dead.''

His self-promotion was like a cheap perfume, Tori thought, making everything around it reek. She already felt contaminated by his braggadocio.

Cruz's woman, Sonia, was servilely making the rounds, getting drinks for everyone. Tori thought she looked a little pale beneath her rich tan.

Tori sat next to Russell on a long sofa covered in pinto horsehide. A Chinese vase—one of several throughout the room—sat on the center of a Lalique crystal cocktail table just in front of her. She noticed that the brocade curtains half closed across the windows were lined with metal foil. She wondered whether this made them bulletproof as well as soundproof. "Do you know what you're doing?'' Russell asked her.

She said, "Are you good at improvisation, Russ? I hope so.''

Cruz grunted. "So. Now you are here.'' His tone and manner suggested that this was all she was likely to get from him by way of a thank-you for saving his life: an invitation to the great man's sanctuary. He gave the impression that he was already bored with their company. Perhaps he had come to believe that he was immortal, that her intervention had been irrelevant. Or, just as likely, his absolute power had corrupted him absolutely, and he was now nothing more than a pig.

Either way, Tori decided, she was going to shake him. This fat man, Cruz, was not so different from others of his ilk. She knew what made him tick: power and sex, in that order. But for him, as for the others like him, sex was not so far away from power, and often the two were inextricably entwined.

Sonia was important to him. When she ceased to be important, Cruz would see to it that she disappeared from his life. She would be thrown into the gutter and made to stay there. But for now he conferred his power upon her like a shadow, and she in turn gave to him the aura of her sexuality. And this aura of hers had about it a kind of magic. Like a dice shooter on a roll, Cruz was convinced he had luck on his side. Luck in the form of Sonia. This, too, made her his showpiece, in bed as well as out there in the streets of Machine-Gun City, where he cut his deals, cut down his enemies, where he was king. The *paisas* watched her coming and going, and they envied Cruz his ability to attract and keep this woman with the sultry eyes.

Cruz was looking pointedly at his watch when Estilo rose from the plush sofa and said, "Are you sure it's secure in here?"

Cruz looked up. "Secure? What do you mean by secure?"

"I was wondering about the Orolas," Estilo said. "Was that man the only assassin they have in Medellín?"

Cruz snorted derisively. "Are you crazy?" He pounded his chest like a gorilla, only with a good deal less charm. "This is my heart. My empire extends in all directions from this point. The Orolas are nothing. They have always been nothing. They do not have the *cojones* to worm their way into this building."

Sonia excused herself, and a moment later Tori did the same. Quickly, she followed Sonia through the apartment. As Sonia closed the door to one of the bathrooms, Tori stuck her shoe in the doorway, shoved the door open and stepped inside.

"Jesus." The place was as big as a football field. There were two of everything, including six-foot whirlpool spas and live palm trees. Tori could not tell whether there was more marble or mirror. She locked the door behind her, watched carefully the play of emotions on Sonia's face.

"Your days are numbered here," she said to Sonia. "Any fortune-teller would tell you that."

"In fact, one already has," Sonia said with surprising candor. "Her face was white when she told me." Sonia waited a minute, trying and failing to get the measure of Tori. "Did Cruz send you?" She seemed unafraid, almost defiant.

Tori laughed. "*Madre de Dios*, no."

"But you're a friend of his."

"I want something from him. That's not the same thing."

"Almost," Sonia said. "But no, not quite." Her shoulders slumped a little, as if she had been maintaining a pose. "You're just another business associate here to cut a deal."

"Maybe," Tori said. "But if I do, it won't be with Cruz." She put her back against the door. "Whose mistress are you?" She said it so abruptly and in such a different tone of voice that Sonia started. "Which one of the Orola brothers do you sleep with?"

"You must be crazy!"

Tori said, "There's someone in here who's crazy, but it isn't me. I saw you signaling the Orola assassin at the corrida. What do you think you're doing? This isn't a game."

"Of course it isn't," Sonia hissed. Her handsome face was twisted into a mask of hate. "The man who Cruz murdered at El Cerrito, Ruben Orola, was my lover. When his brothers told me what I had to do, I didn't think twice. Why should I? What is left of my life? Nothing. Nothing but revenge. I have a purpose now."

"What kind of purpose?" Tori took Sonia by the shoulders, faced her toward the mirror. "Look at yourself. You're a walking, talking automaton, nothing more."

Sonia licked her lips. "I appear just as Cruz wants me to appear. The man is crazy."

"So are a lot of people."

"You don't understand. This man is insane. All the cartel heads are. There is something in the air here, or maybe it's a by-product of the power they lust after with their very hearts. Cruz is dangerous—as much to me as he is to you. When maniacs move, you get out of the way. Period."

"Then you have to find some way to immobilize him."

Sonia stared at Tori in the mirror. "The moment Cruz is dead, I will put a gun to my head and pull the trigger."

Tori spun her around. "Is that so? Is your life worth as little as that punk assassin Cruz killed as casually as a fly? Then why haven't you killed Cruz yet? How many opportunities have you had lying beside him while he sleeps?"

"At night, after we have made love, when I hear his snores, when I see the rhythmic rise and fall of his belly, even then I am afraid to move. His power paralyzes me; his wealth surrounds me like a prison." She shrugged. "But I don't expect you to understand what I am telling you."

But Tori did understand, better than Sonia could ever imagine. "There must be a way for you to break his power."

"You know nothing," Sonia said. "Cruz is already dead, he just doesn't know it yet. But it is the *manner* of his death that is of importance to Ruben's brothers."

"A public execution," Tori said. "Like today."

"Why did you stop it? You're no friend of Cruz's."

"He has information I must have," Tori said. "After I get what I want, the war can resume. I am not involved."

Sonia gave her a cold smile. "But you are involved. It is not a matter of choice. Wars are enormous things, unwieldy, difficult to stop. You have gotten in the way. Now you and your friends are part of it."

When Tori said nothing, Sonia continued. "Tell me what you want from Cruz, and I will ensure you get it. But, in return, you and your friends must help me kill him."

"Why should I bother? This is your vendetta, not mine," Tori said. "I can get what I want from Cruz just by turning you in. Knowing you work for the Orolas will shake him to his core. He'll be so grateful, he'll give me anything I want."

"Then you don't know Cruz." Sonia took out a Marlboro cigarette but did not light it. She studied Tori's face much as a fencer will study her adversary before they put on their masks. "He takes, but he does not give. Unless proper payment is presented, you'll get nothing from him." She shrugged, placed the Marlboro on the vanity top, slit it neatly open. "Besides, I am not the only plant the Orolas have here. One of Cruz's lieutenants, Jorge, works for them as well. The Orolas are freer with their money than Cruz is. Jorge does not know about me, but I know about him."

Estilo was right, Tori thought. There is no loyalty here but to money. She said, "Why should I care about you or the Orolas?"

"You owe me," Sonia said. "You destroyed something that was mine: Cruz's death. Now you are obliged to re-create it."

For the first time her face held a measure of doubt, and Tori understood just how important her revenge was to her. It might destroy her, in the end, but it was the only thing she could call her own. She had already given up on herself.

Sonia produced a sheet of rolling paper, transferred the tobacco into it. To it she added what Tori recognized as cocaine base. She rolled the mixture in the paper, sealed it. Then she lit up, inhaling the smoke deep into her lungs. In a moment her brown eyes went opaque, the pupils expanding.

Tori wanted to help her, to reach out and show her that she, Sonia, still existed, independent of Cruz, the Orolas, even the ghost of her lover, Ruben. But she could see that it was useless. She had no illusions that Sonia was a good woman trapped in a bad situation. At the moment Sonia had agreed to the Orolas' plan, she had sold her soul to the devil. There was no turning back now, and Tori recognized that all she could do for this woman was to make her journey as painless as possible.

Tori wondered to what degree she could trust anyone here. For trust, one needed people, but there were none here, only soulless husks driven by greed, lust, vengeance. The sins of the damned. The cocaine-impregnated smoke filled the room, making her slightly sick to her stomach. The stink of corruption was everywhere in flower.

"All right," Tori nodded. But the tiny hairs at the back of her neck were stirring. This mission had become a two-edged sword, as perilous a situation as was possible. She might be helping out a woman in distress, but she knew that she had also just made a deal with a demon.

"You two girls have a good time in there?" Cruz laughed. "What is it you do together? Men don't want to see each other's pricks, so what is it you girls want to see?" He was being deliberately crude, baiting them, still feeling good after the kill. Blood did that to some men.

"Actually," Tori said, "Sonia discussed something important in there."

"Yeah?" The contempt was plain on his face. "What could that be? The name of a more effective douche?" Cruz guffawed, and his lieutenants grinned like trained animals.

Tori stood in front of him, said, "Sonia saw one of your trusted lieutenants signal the Orola assassin at the corrida."

"What? You're a liar." He yelled this with such vehemence that Sonia jumped. "Why didn't you say this to me right away?"

"She didn't really understand what she saw," Tori said, intervening. "But when I began to question her, it came out."

"This is impossible!" Cruz shouted.

"On the contrary," Tori said. "That's how the assassin was able to get so close to you. Close enough to use the handgun."

Cruz said nothing.

"Think. It's the only way the assassination attempt makes sense," Tori said. "The Orolas have someone inside your organization."

Cruz whirled on Tori. "Nevertheless," he said with a great deal of menace, "why should I trust you?"

"Besides the fact that I saved your life at the corrida, I can't think of a single reason."

Cruz leered at her. "Perhaps you saved me for a reason, eh, *chica*?" He rubbed his thumb and forefinger together.

"That makes no difference," Tori pointed out. "You've still got a lieutenant on the Orola payroll."

"So *you* say."

Tori made a show of considering his challenge. She said, "I think I have a way of proving to you that we can help you further." She nodded toward Russell. "Señor Slade here is our resident expert in moles."

"In what?" Cruz asked.

"Moles," Russell repeated. "Enemy agents placed within your cartel."

"Ah, yes, burrowing underground," Cruz said. "I see." He scowled at Russell. "What do you do?"

Russell remembered what Tori had said to him. *Are you good at improvisation? I hope so.* "I find moles," he said. He got off the couch, passed by each of Cruz's lieutenants in turn. He looked them straight in the eye. Some looked back curiously, others were overtly hostile. No one looked away.

Cruz came over beside Russell. "This is interesting," he said.

Tori said, "I will whisper to you the name of the lieutenant Sonia saw signal the Orola hit man at the bull ring. Without knowing what I have said, Señor Slade will find your mole."

"Is that so?" Cruz grunted. "Tell me, Señor Slade, what do you do when you find these moles?"

Russell felt an overwhelming desire to look at Tori, but instinctively knew that even making eye contact with her now would make the paranoid Cruz suspect they were working some kind of scam on him. His mind was racing. "There was a Soviet agent. I interrogated him until he dropped. That took nearly thirty straight hours, but in the end the mole broke and gave us everything we wanted to know."

"Like what?" Cruz said suspiciously.

"Like everything he knew about the operations of his own organization."

Cruz shrugged. "I already know much of what is happening inside the Orola cartel. But it would be beneficial to know everything." Now it was Cruz who was parading in front of his lieutenants, scowling, fingering an enormous hunting knife. "And just how did you discover this mole, Señor Slade?"

"Not any one thing," Russell said, "but many tiny mistakes. They build up, especially during an interrogation. There are signs I am trained to see."

Cruz nodded. "It is now almost four months since I executed Ruben Orola. Since then, his brothers have tried three times to kill me, the last one being today." He turned to Russell. "Therefore, I need you, the mole hunter, to track mine down for me. Here. Now."

Tori stood beside Cruz, whispered in his ear.

Russell went down the line of Cruz's lieutenants. He hadn't the slightest idea what to look for, but he found it peculiarly exciting to pretend this expertise. Moment by moment he could feel the power slipping into his hands, just as he could feel the tension and anxiety mounting as he spoke to each lieutenant in turn, watched the cast of his eye, the tic of a facial muscle, the thin sheen of sweat on upper lip or forehead.

He came at length to the last lieutenant and knew that he would soon have to give Cruz a name. Further, it had to be the same name that Tori had whispered in Cruz's ear. How was he to do that?

Russell stood at an angle to the last lieutenant, ostensibly to observe him better. But at the same time he could now see Tori out of the corner of his eye. Russell saw her left hand down by her side. Then he saw it move marginally. Her forefinger and middle fingers were extended, the others curled into her palm. Like a baseball catcher calling for a curveball, Russell thought. The second lieutenant.

Russell completed his interrogation, moved back up the line until he was behind the second lieutenant.

"This is the mole," he said without hesitation.

"Jorge," Tori said. "You see?"

"Lavaperro!" Dogwasher! Cruz screamed, and grabbing the man both Tori and Russell had indicted, slammed him back against the wall. Jorge was babbling his innocence, but Cruz was clearly not listening. Cocaine, whether as an addiction or a product in which to traffic, bred paranoia.

"Knife," Cruz said, holding out his hand. Another lieutenant stepped forward, slipped him a U.S. Marine KA-BAR.

Cruz took it, slashed the blade laterally across Jorge's throat. While the blood gushed onto him, Cruz pried open Jorge's jaws, cut out his tongue. The body slid to the floor.

132

Cruz held up the tongue like a trophy. Tori could see that he felt like the matador in the corrida as he withdrew the killing sword from the bull's heart. He said, "Send this to the Orolas. And make sure you pack it good in dry ice. I want them to get it fresh, like at the best restaurant." He erupted in a savage laugh. "I'm only sorry I won't be there to see their faces when they get it."

He turned to Estilo. "You feel more secure now?" He had begun to strut again, his old bravado returning. He turned to Russell and grinned. "I am grateful for your assistance. What would you consider proper payment? Money? Cocaine? A boat? Helicopter? A plane, perhaps? This is Medellín, gringo. Nothing is impossible here." His grin widened. "You are about to learn, Señor Slade, that here in Machine-Gun City our shopping malls are open twenty-four hours a day. And the price is always right."

"We want none of these things," Russell said, "though we are grateful for the offer. We need, instead, some information."

"Oh?" Cruz's expression showed that he was not pleased with the sudden turn in the conversation. "What kind of information? I am not an informer. I don't deal information."

Before his face darkened too much, Sonia stepped between the two men. She stood very close to Cruz, and reaching between her breasts, she drew out a stone on a gold chain. She took his hand gently in hers, squeezed it into a fist around the stone. "Listen to me, *corazón*," she said. "These people are lucky for us. I can feel it. Can you feel it, too, now? The stench of the Orolas is gone. And the sour taste of business since you sent Rega to Buenos Aires, since he was murdered, is about to end. These people are a sign of that change. Can you feel it, *corazón*? Feel it now. The rich taste of money is coming, coming back."

Tori, who was the only one close enough to Cruz and Sonia to hear this exchange, was both fascinated and repelled. The tone of Sonia's voice, the look in her eyes as they searched his, was so intimate, so blatantly sexual, that Tori could almost imagine they were making love right here in front of everyone.

But now she had one piece of the puzzle. Rega had been working for Cruz. Then why did the Yakuza kill him? What had one of them said? *His use was at an end.*

"When the Orolas killed Rega," Cruz said, "the war be-

133

gan in earnest. And war is profitable only for the armament suppliers.''

"Cruz," Tori said, "the Orolas did not kill Rega."

He scowled at her. "What could you know of it?''

"I ran into Rega's killers in Buenos Aires. In fact, they almost killed me, as well. They were Japanese gangsters.''

"Japanese?'' Cruz laughed in her face, then his scowl got deeper. "Are you trying to make a fool of me?''

"I'm sure she isn't,'' Sonia said, keeping his hand around her amulet. "Think. Rega had a rich source, a buyer flooding us with money. That's why you sent him—a lieutenant, not a mule—to Buenos Aires. She's telling the truth, *corazón*. Don't you see how it makes sense?''

"But the Japanese?'' Cruz said. "Why would they want so much coke?''

"That's what we've come here to find out,'' Tori said.

"You see, *corazón*,'' Sonia said excitedly to Cruz, "they *are* good luck for you.''

Russell said, "The question now is to find out why the Japanese killed Rega. He was their connection.''

Cruz considered this. "Only two answers are possible,'' he said. "One, they don't need supply anymore; two, they found a better connection.''

"They still need the cocaine,'' Russell said. "We're certain of that.''

"Could the Orolas be giving the Japanese a better deal?'' Tori asked.

"All that product?'' Cruz shook his head. "I'd know about it right away. If they have a new connection, it's not the Cali cartel.''

"Then who?'' Russell asked.

Cruz shrugged. "It may be nothing, you know how rumors are, especially here. But . . . over the last several months there has been talk of a major new cocaine factory establishing itself in the *llanos* of Meta Province, east of here, just past the Manacacias River. It's very wild there, difficult to track even rumors. Like I said, we had all dismissed the stories.''

"Whose territory is that?'' Russell asked.

Cruz shrugged. "Not Orola's, not mine. The Colombian army is in and out of there all the time. So is the DAS.'' He meant the Colombian Department of Administrative Security, charged with keeping the cartels and the shipments from the Bolivian *cocaleros* under control. "They do a shit job, but they can be dangerous nonetheless."

"No-man's-land," Estilo said.

"Llano negro." Black jungle. Cruz nodded. "A land of only shadows. One of the stories, more persistent than most, says that the army and the DAS patrol this area not to find this factory, but to protect it." He shrugged again. "But these rumors have a way of growing out of all proportion. There is no way to tell the truth from the fiction."

But, of course, there was one way. Tori, Russell, Estilo, and Sonia all looked at one another. Without saying a word, they had communicated everything they needed to know. It was to this *llano negro* they would have to go to find the beginning of the bizarre Yakuza cocaine trail.

Less than twenty-four hours later the three of them were lifting off from Machine-Gun City in one of Cruz's Bell JetRanger III helicopters.

Just before they left, Sonia took Tori aside without anyone seeing and said, "Remember your promise to me. You must help me destroy Cruz."

"I won't forget," Tori said. "When we get back."

"When you get back." Sonia nodded.

Sonia said something else, but the wind was already in Tori's ears. Was it her imagination or did Sonia have a doubtful look on her face?

They were all dressed in tropical paramilitary camouflage suits. Among the armament each carried was a machete, a Marine KA-BAR knife, a .45 handgun, and an Uzi machine pistol with three extra loads.

It was dark inside the helicopter, and the heavy vibrations penetrated to their bones. Russell was up front, quizzing Cruz's pilot, who was set to pick them up twenty-four hours after he set them down. If they didn't make the first rendezvous, he'd return the same time the day after. Estilo was stretched out, asleep, on the bench on the opposite side of the cabin. Tori put her head back against cold steel and closed her eyes.

"Don't look so worried, Señor Slade," Estilo said some hours later. "We Argentines have a saying, 'When Satan tries to walk on ice, he falls on his face. Ice is not his milieu.' "

Who is he kidding? Tori thought, as the JetRanger set them

down in a minuscule clearing in the *llanos* of Meta Province. She had a clear sense of foreboding.

Llano negro. The black jungle, where only shadows dwelled, where maybe the good guys rode shotgun for the bad guys. She thought, This territory isn't controlled by Cruz, or by the Orolas. So who does it belong to?

FOUR
MOSCOW/TOKYO

Mars called Irina at work and asked her to go to No. 1 Gastronome on Gorky Street during her lunch hour to pick up some provisions for his parents, which he planned to take to them on the following Saturday. He was in meetings all day, could not go himself, and he was afraid if he waited until tomorrow, the fresh sturgeon would all be gone.

Irina readily agreed. She loved Gorky Street, with its rush of sumptuously dressed tourists, its myriad shops and huge hotels, but she loved No. 1 Gastronome most of all. She felt like a child in a storybook, allowed to wander through a wonderland of magical displays. Foodstuffs from all over the Soviet Union, as well as from foreign lands, were stacked on shelves and behind glass cases. There were always lines here, but Irina never minded standing in them, because it gave her more time to soak up the atmosphere.

As Mars had asked, she purchased fresh smoked sturgeon, several tins of caviar, and on impulse, a half-pound of smoked salmon all the way from Nova Scotia. It was an extravagant purchase, but she thought the exotic salmon would make Mars happy.

Afterward she strolled down Gorky Street in the wan sunshine, happy merely to be out of her dim, cramped office and in the fresh air. Of course, one had to discount the traffic fumes, but like all city dwellers, Irina was barely aware of the clouds of exhaust.

She was perhaps fifty yards from the Druzhba bookstore when she saw Valeri emerge from the entrance. She raised her arm, about to call out to him, but he had already turned away. Irina hurried after him, excited to extend her lunch hour; anything to keep her from returning to her stultifying job.

She followed him up Gorky Street, past No. 1 Gastronome, through the Soviet Square, with its monument to Prince Dolgoruky, Moscow's founder. A few streets on he turned left, disappeared into a small building with a green facade, the old Moscow Arts Theater, where, years ago, Stanislavsky had taught the Method to Soviet actors, and thereby changed the face of modern theater forever.

Chekhov's *Three Sisters* was playing, and photos of the actors were posted just above the schedule of times. Irina went inside. The interior was cool, musty, filled with hushed voices, but she saw no one, the lobby deserted.

She pushed through the door into the theater proper. On stage, a series of spotlights shone down on actors rehearsing a scene. Irina looked around, saw Valeri sitting near the back of the semidark theater. She took two steps toward him, then froze.

There was a stunning woman with him. She had blond hair, blue eyes, and a nose Irina would have killed for. Irina recognized her as one of the stars of the current production, Natasha Mayakova.

Irina could not move, hearing in her mind Valeri saying to her, *The joke is that it is you, Irina, who has seduced me. Do you think that you are the latest in a long line of conquests for me? No.* But what was she thinking? Of course, this must be a business meeting, or a visit with a friend. But in the back of her mind a perverse voice kept saying no, no, no. He's lied to you. It is something else, not business, not friendship. It is an assignation.

They were sitting very close, their heads together. She could hear Valeri saying, "Time is difficult to come by, but not for you, *koshka*," and Natasha Mayakova's answering silvery laughter.

He called her *koshka*. Darling. Irina wanted to turn away, to run, but she could not. She felt like someone watching an accident, unable to avert her gaze, caught by a perverse fascination, observing their intimacy, an outsider. And all the while, Valeri's lie felt like a slap across her face.

It was not until she was back in her office, surrounded by the drudgery of her work, that she realized how angry she was with Valeri. But why should I expect anything different from him? she thought. He lives a life unlike mine. His coinage is intimidation, coercion, and deceit.

But this bit of psychological illumination failed to make her feel any better, in fact it unaccountably depressed her all the more. She tried to throw herself into her work for the rest of the afternoon, but it was useless. She was finished for the day.

"Nova Scotia salmon!" Mars exclaimed. "What a treat!" He impulsively gave her a kiss. "I should save this for my folks, but it looks so scrumptious, why don't you and I pull apart some black bread and dig in." They were in the kitchen of Mars's apartment. The lights were on, although it was only just twilight outside.

"You go ahead," Irina said without much enthusiasm. "I'm not feeling hungry."

"But of course you must be hungry," Mars said, taking down some plates from his cupboard. "It's after eight, and if I know Number One Gastronome, the lines must have prevented you from having time for a proper lunch."

"Actually, they weren't so bad," Irina said. "I had time to get these."

Mars took the small envelope from her, opened it. "Tickets to *Three Sisters*!" He grinned. "Well, you certainly are full of surprises tonight."

You don't know the half of it, Irina thought unhappily.

Mars put the tickets down. "But why so sad, Irina? Did you have a bad day at the office? No, no, don't tell me if you don't want to. I know you like your privacy. But come, I see dinner at home holds no interest for you. Let's go out!"

This was Mars's solution to all things: eat, be with people, get drunk, feel life in all its diversity flow like a powerful stream all around you, until it began to seep through you then into you, until the roof of your despair was made leaky and, whether you liked it or not, life began again to wash over you.

He took her to a tiny Georgian restaurant he had discovered, where they were happy to serve him even when it was near to nine at night and other, larger, restaurants had stopped serving hot meals. It was a boisterous place, filled with good smells, the combined heat of the nearby kitchen and its cheery denizens. They ate chicken *tabaka*, drank pepper vodka, and most important, Mars kept her talking.

"Tell me about your family," he said. "What was your home life like?"

"Lousy," Irina said. "My father was a secret drunkard, you know, weekends, days off. But he never missed a day's work. He's been dead now a long time. He worked in nuclear engineering, but he never brought his work home, never talked about it. I suspect he drank because he had watched his parents die in the Siberian winter, and I think he could never forgive himself."

"For what?"

"For living when they had died. He took the coat off his mother's body, the shoes off his father's feet. He remembered the feet so clearly, he said. They were blue, bloated, and cold as ice. It took him a half hour to get the shoes off. He told me once that those items of clothing saved him from freezing to death, but they couldn't stop him from remembering. He was eleven years old when that happened."

"Poor fellow," Mars said. "But he had his whole life ahead of him."

"I think a part of him died on the Siberian ice fields with his parents," Irina said.

"He was to be pitied, then."

Irina tried not to think. She could hear a voice calling, she knew what it was saying, but she didn't want to listen: *KGB. Keep calm.* The Siberian winter, bars across the moon, her country a prison. *He's dead.*

"Perhaps it all would have been different if my brother Yvgeny hadn't died," Irina said, not believing a word of it, and despising herself for dissembling. "He was killed not so far from here, on the bank of the Moskva, on a cold, clear night, a night of the full moon. He had fallen in with criminals, and he was selling—well, I don't know what, contraband of some kind, surely. He was knifed, but whether by a potential customer or by a rival, we never found out. Considering what my brother was up to, the police were understandably resistant to spending man-hours tracking down his killer. Frankly, they just didn't care. I got the impression they were glad he was dead."

"And the family?"

"Our family was so fragile anyway, the relationships so

140

close to cracking. My father had already been dead for many years. I think, now, that it wouldn't have taken much at all to send us spiraling down. But his, Yvgeny's, murder was like a detonation in our kitchen, our place of warmth and sustenance, the place I remember my mother always being, until the police brought us the news. She disintegrated. She ran out into the night without a coat or a care for herself. She beat her breast, tore her hair, and, on the spot where they had found Yvgeny sprawled with the knife still between his ribs, she wailed for her son. I remember dragging her away from there. She was hysterical, screaming invectives I never suspected she knew. I think she tried to bite me. At that moment, I don't believe she knew who I was."

Mars allowed a silence to close over them. The boisterous sounds of the restaurant seemed abruptly at odds with their own tiny world, and Irina found herself wanting to scream, Shut up! Shut up! Why are you all so happy?

At last Mars said, "Is she still alive?"

"Only after a fashion," Irina said.

"I'm sorry." He took her hand, stroked it with his thumb. "But words are so inadequate sometimes, aren't they?"

Irina looked into his eyes, aware of some subtle difference. It was like walking into a garden one had known all one's life, and finding that one rock had been shifted ever so slightly, but that this alteration had in some magical way transformed the aspect of the entire garden.

She said, "Sometimes nothing more is needed than being there." Something had changed in her relationship with Mars. But what was it?

The following Saturday, Mars asked her to go with him to visit his parents. Irina agreed, although she did not really know why. She suspected that she would be bored.

As it turned out, she was wrong. Mars's parents lived in a beautiful old cream-colored house on Bolshaya Ordynka Street. Its front was shaded with lime trees. It was quite near the 350-year-old Church of St. Nicholas of Pyzhi, whose architecture was so Eastern baroque, it reminded Irina of a wedding cake.

Mars's mother and father were wonderful people, warm and full of love for one another. Irina watched them covertly, almost shyly. And although they looked at each other or touched only rarely, they seemed always aware of one another's presence.

They loved the special foods she and Mars had brought, and

141

Mars went out of his way to say that the Nova Scotia salmon was a special gift from Irina herself. Irina helped Mars's mother in the kitchen, and found that they had an easy and almost instantaneous rapport that stemmed from cooking. They shared suggestions, then little secrets they had learned. They laughed together.

Near to dinnertime, Mars's sister and her family arrived. She looked like Mars, and was very beautiful. But she seemed shy, and when Irina at length arranged to talk with her, confessed to being unhappy with her thick-waisted, heavy-legged body. "I am just what the American magazines portray Russian women to be like," she said with a sigh.

Her children—two boys and a girl—were well-behaved, and they obviously adored their grandfather, who played games with them and loved tricking them, then telling them how he did so. Often, there were gales of laughter.

The children's father, Mars's brother-in-law, worked as an architect. Mostly, he said, he drew up plans for concrete housing developments, which Irina privately thought must be the height of boredom, like driving a bus back and forth along the same route all day long. He was an altogether ordinary-looking fellow, whose face was transformed when he watched his children.

Gradually, as the afternoon turned into evening, and as the evening became night, Irina found herself sinking into the warmth and homeyness of this family's life, with the kind of bliss one feels when lying back on an eiderdown pillow. For the first time in quite a while, she found herself relaxed. And then, with an electric tingle, she knew there was more to it than that: she was content.

At that moment Irina looked across the room at Mars Petrovich Volkov in an entirely different light. So what that the physical part of our relationship doesn't quite connect? she thought. He has so much more to give me. He can share with me what I've always wanted. With him I can be part of a family.

Kasumigaseki, the downtown Tokyo district where Honno worked, meant "Shrouded Gate." Big Ezoe was familiar with Kasumigaseki, though not in the ways Honno was. He showed her places within the district she otherwise would never have guessed existed.

Being in Kasumigaseki was the equivalent of living underwater. The light—what there was of it seeping through the steel and glass skyscrapers—had that aqueous quality that skin divers know well, and which can be approximated by peering through the bottom of a green glass bottle.

Big Ezoe had said, "Kakuei Sakata was a samurai, so you and I must begin to think like samurai. If we cannot put ourselves in Sakata's mind, we will never solve the riddle he has left you."

Big Ezoe had turned the key Sakata had sent to Honno over and over in his hand. "A businessman would have a safety deposit box in a bank. A Yakuza would have a lock box buried beneath the tatami in his bedroom. What would a samurai have to keep his most valuable possessions safe?"

Honno had looked at him. "I don't know."

Big Ezoe had grinned at her. "But I think I do."

And so he had led her back to the heart of the metropolis, to Kasumigaseki, the Shrouded Gate. They were consumed by modern Tokyo. There was industrial grit beneath the soles of their shoes, the exhaust of a half a million engines in their nostrils, a smog of pollutants in their eyes. And, of course, the dense night was dispelled by the nearby spin and sputter of gigantic neon signs running up the sides of buildings, adorning entryways large enough to accommodate a conquering army, squatting atop steel superstructures.

But hidden away on a side street, dwarfed by the steel and glass monuments to the nation's burgeoning economic success, was a remnant of another, older way of life, when simple traditions, not economic imperatives, ruled Japan.

"This is where Kakuei Sakata came when he needed to be alone, to contemplate or to invoke the *kami* of his world," Big Ezoe said, indicating the wood and lacquer Shinto shrine. He reached out, pulled a cord, and the clang of the bronze bell reverberated through the man-made canyons. "Wake up, spirits who inhabit the woods and the streams!" Big Ezoe laughed. "I wonder if there are modern *kami*, spirits who live atop steel girders and neon signs that say Sony, who ride high-speed elevators to the hundredth floor." His face crinkled. "I wonder if *kami* get acrophobia."

Honno was not amused. "How can you be so disrespectful?"

"I suppose it comes naturally to me," Big Ezoe said, but Honno did not know if he was serious or if this was just another of his endless jokes. Joking was alien to Honno, like being waited upon, or having Eikichi remember where she put his socks or where she kept the sugar.

"Nonsense," she said. "When you were born, you cried, ate, evacuated, and slept. These things were natural. Everything else you learned."

"Quite possibly," Big Ezoe said with some amusement. "But then it would have been my granny who taught me to laugh at the world. She raised me, you see. She liked to make fun of the world, she said, because it was such a somber place, she otherwise would have committed hara-kiri long ago."

"That's just what I mean," Honno said angrily. "I'm sure your granny harbored no such crazy notions."

"Well, I think she did," Big Ezoe replied. "And I'm in a better position than you to know it. Besides, what makes you think laughing at the world is a crazy notion?"

"It's either crazy or it's wrong," Honno said. "No wonder you became a gangster."

Big Ezoe grunted. "I don't think one *becomes* anything, least of all a gangster. My family is Yakuza; that is what I am."

"No," Honno said. "You say that as if you had no choice. But you did. It's perfectly clear why you became a gangster: you're in love with the life."

"Perhaps I am," he said thoughtfully. "But that's more than can be said for you. At least I'm in love with something."

"I love my husband," Honno said immediately.

"That birdbrain?" Big Ezoe laughed. "What is there to love in a drone like that?"

"I don't think it's any of your business. What do you know of Eikichi's world, anyway?"

"More than you could imagine." Big Ezoe looked up, past the Shinto shrine's roof, to the towering structures of Kasumi-gaseki. "I know you're reluctant to talk to me any more than you feel you have to, but I'm curious. What do you see in Eikichi Kansei that attracts you?"

Honno did not want to answer him, but she felt duty bound to defend her husband in the face of this mobster's insults. "There is great honor," Honno said. "Also, he needs me. And there is a solidness about him that makes me feel secure."

"Security. Ah, now we come to the heart of the matter. By security, don't you really mean submission? Isn't there, after all, a secret pleasure to be had in submitting to power, to giving up one's free will? Just as there is surely a similar pleasure in the sacrifices a mother makes for the sake of her child." Big Ezoe almost seemed to be talking to himself. "Eikichi makes you feel secure, no doubt, because of his strict adherence to rules and regulations. At home, he barely talks to you. When he wants you, he calls, *Oi!* Hey! He is your child, you see." Big Ezoe was still looking upward. "So he needs you. Yes. He needs you to make his food for him. To lay out his clothes in the morning. And you are, as we know, a working woman. How early do you have to get up, Honno, to make sure your husband's needs are met?"

"It isn't like that," Honno protested.

"Oh? How is it, then? Tell me."

"You are so good with words." Honno was so enraged she could hardly speak. "You twist them, turn them inside out so they suit your purpose. I am not that skilled."

He said, "Are you familiar with the *Hagakure*, the Book of Hidden Leaves? Yes? Then you may recall a key passage that tells of the clever samurai. When he gathers sufficient experience, he discovers, much to his dismay, that all the complex rules and regulations of society by which he has so scrupulously lived his life are nothing more than meaningless illusion. The *Hagakure* further counsels the samurai to hold his tongue once the truth is made manifest to him, so that he will not prematurely reveal it to those younger and more ignorant than himself."

Honno said nothing for a time. Her cheeks were unaccountably hot with shame. How she despised Big Ezoe at this moment. More than she ever could have imagined. At last she recovered sufficiently to say, "How is it you know where Sakata-san worshiped?"

Big Ezoe contemplated her for some time. "You know, Mrs. Kansei, you must learn to lighten your spirit. Burdens such as you evidently carry become insupportable over time." He moved inside the wooden roof of the tiny shrine. "The answer to your question is a simple one. I have many friends, even more contacts. More than one of them is a samurai. No doubt Sakata was seen here on a number of his midday pilgrimages."

"Is there anything you don't know?" Honno asked.

"Sure," Big Ezoe said, taking the key from her. "What Sakata was hiding." With some difficulty, he bent down, lifted up the cloth draped over the center of the shrine. He slid the key into the lock of a small door cut in the wooden side.

Inside he found two books that looked like ledgers. He handed them to Honno, who opened one, leafed through the pages which were covered by a tight hand-drawn scrawl. The second ledger revealed the same. The writing was not kanji or any other with which Honno was familiar.

"What is this?" Honno asked.

Big Ezoe, looking over her shoulder, said. "I'm not sure, but if I had to hazard a guess, I'd say it was some kind of code."

"Great," Honno said. "What am I supposed to do with these books? I don't even know what they contain." It was then she thought of Giin, and everything fell into place.

Honno had met Giin almost ten years ago, before she had known that Eikichi Kansei existed. At that time Giin was highly placed in a ministry, she was never quite sure which. She was meant to have married Ginn. She would have, except for the fact that he, like her father, was an inveterate gambler.

She had been so young then, still so full of mixed emotions about her father. His death last year had changed that, of course. Noboru's memory was purer than Noboru had been in life. All the contradictory emotions Honno felt for her father were swept away, to be replaced by the overriding virtue of filial piety. *Hino-euma* woman or not, she was her father's daughter.

But the one thing she would not do was to give her love to another man who gambled; a man who, more than anything else, reminded Honno of her father. While it was true that Giin was far more intelligent than Noboru Yamato ever had been—in fact, he was a genius, of sorts—there were other, more telling traits they shared. They both had obsessive personalities, they were tyrants in their professional lives, and they had an underlying weakness: they loved to gamble.

In fact, they couldn't stop. It was an axiom of their personalities: obsessive, domineering, certain they were always right. And, oddly, their mounting losses did not disabuse them of their vanity. Quite the opposite. They could not believe their losses, would not recognize the danger as those losses mounted precipitously. They were focused on only one thing: their passion to win. Because winning was essential to their personalities; they could not survive without it.

Indeed, Noboru Yamato had not survived his obsession. But Giin had, just barely. Honno had heard that he was no longer in the public sector, but whether that had been his choice or his masters', she did not know. He had been a *ronin*—an ex-minister looking for work in the private sector—for some time before he had found a job that suited him.

He had become a professor of philosophy at a Tokyo university, which was either laughable or pathetic, depending on your point of view. He would have been the least flexible person Honno had ever known—except for her father. And, considering that philosophy was a continual bending of thought, tenet, and ideology—a living dialectic with the universe, as it were—Honno considered it odd that Giin should end up teaching philosophy.

She insisted on seeing him alone, although Big Ezoe wanted to come with her. Privately, she would have been appalled to face Giin for the first time in ten years with a Yakuza *oyabun* at her side.

She met him in his office, late in the day, after his last class had ended. As his secretary announced her, Honno felt a hollowness in the pit of her stomach, the fluttering, almost humiliating sense of being brought before a judge, as if the first thing Giin might say to her was, "Well, my dear, what have you done with your life since you left me?"

In fact, he said nothing. He was grading test papers when she was shown into his office. It was no more than a cubicle, really, windowless, almost airless. It was jammed with books, papers, bound galleys, gigantic reference works.

Giin sat behind an anonymous desk. He wore an anonymous dark suit, his gray hair neatly parted, his round wire spectacles shining in the glare of the overhead lights. He did not look up when she came in, and she thought that rude. Somehow, this increased her sense of humiliation. But by now Honno had concluded that she felt as humiliated for him as she did for herself. Until this moment she did not appreciate how difficult this interview might be for him.

She had left him abruptly, unforgivably, after agreeing to marry him, after he had made her an integral part of his life, introduced her to his family and his friends. And, worst of all, she had done so without so much as a word of explanation. But how could she have told him that she refused to marry an inveterate gambler? It would have been too shameful for herself and for him.

Now, looking at him in this tiny office, grading papers of students who, no doubt, would never fathom the depths of his genius, Honno felt her cheeks burning. She sat silently, to meekly wait out his silence so that he could regain a measure of the face she had robbed him of ten years ago.

When, at last, he judged the silence to be of appropriate duration, Giin said, "So, I understand that you have married. Are you happy?"

"Of course I am!" Honno exclaimed, and immediately regretted her response. "That is, Eikichi Kansei is a good husband."

For the first time Giin lifted his head. Honno could see his eyes behind the lenses of his spectacles. He stared directly at her, and she seemed to wither, so intimidating was his gaze. For an instant she even wished, crazily, that she had allowed Big Ezoe to come with her. But it was only anger, and a hurt she knew she had no right to feel, so she closed off both these emotions, sealing them behind the facade all Japanese learn to construct almost from the moment they are born.

"It is good to see you, Giin," she ventured.

"It has been a very long time," he said, and she tried not to wince. "A lifetime for some."

"How have you been?" Honno was now dreading his every response.

Giin raised his hands, indicating his jammed cubicle. "This is how I am."

"Have you married?"

"There was no need to after you left."

"I—" Honno's nerve faltered. In the face of his pain and anger, what was there to say?

"I am pleased that you have found a life for yourself," Giin said in a lighter tone. "You seemed so lost, so confused when I knew you. I tried to help you with these things, but perhaps I did not know how to unlock the riddle of you." He smiled, and Honno was reminded of the man she had once known. "That's ironic, don't you think, considering my expertise in solving problems? But my work then involved cryptograms, codes, mathematical formulae. Complex matters, to be sure, but nevertheless, cut and dried. The truth is, I was never much good at handling people, or understanding them, for that matter. Perhaps that's where we went wrong."

"Yes," Honno said, lowering her head. "Perhaps."

"That's why I decided to come here to the university," Giin said sometime later. "Here I am not only surrounded by people, I am forced to interact with them. I suppose it was my way of admitting my faults, of trying to remake myself."

When Honno said nothing, he continued, "I'm glad you agreed to have dinner with me. I know I was rude to you earlier, but it was only my shock, and my shame at remembering."

Honno forced herself to look at him.

"I've stopped gambling, you see," Giin said. "Eventually, I came to understand how pernicious it was, how utterly it had ruined my life. It cost me my job, some of my friends. When I saw what I had been reduced to, my first thought was of you, and how grateful I was that you had left, so that I could not drag you down with me. I never would have forgiven myself if that had happened."

"I don't know what to say," Honno said, which was the truth. Giin's abrupt—and unexpected—confession had caught her quite by surprise. Her thoughts were in chaos. And her emotions . . . My God, she thought, the attraction is still there, deeply buried but unmistakable. She was utterly horrified by this thought, but no matter what inner contortions she went through, she was unsuccessful in suppressing it. I am happily married now, she reminded herself. It did not seem to matter. This was not what she had expected. She could see the love in his eyes, which he had never let die. Something unknown inside her was melting.

"You're not required to say anything," Giin said gently. "You are only required to sit here so that I can look at you once more for as long as the night will last."

"You did what!" Big Ezoe said.

"I gave him the ledgers," Honno said.

"I can't believe it!"

It was the next evening. Honno had come to Big Ezoe's warehouse.

"But that was the plan," Honno said. "It was what I was supposed to do."

"You were supposed to tell him about the *existence* of the ledgers! See if he'd agree to crack the code for us!"

"But he *did* agree," Honno said. "And stop shouting at me."

"I'll stop shouting," Big Ezoe shouted, "when we get those ledgers back from him!"

"You should have seen Giin. He was so eager to get back to what he had been doing years ago. That's why I gave him the ledgers right away."

"Your eyes are shining," Big Ezoe said. "It's disgusting."

Honno laughed. "You have no right to speak to me that way. And why should you care? Are you envious?"

"Of what? A beaten-down old gambler?"

"He doesn't gamble anymore," Honno said, somewhat stiffly.

Big Ezoe's eyes narrowed. "Where did you hear that?"

"Giin told me himself. He confessed—"

Big Ezoe groaned. "And you, you little lovestruck girl, believed him."

"Of course, I—"

"Fool!"

"Don't—"

"But you *are* a fool, Mrs. Kansei."

Angry and confused now, Honno said, "Would you kindly tell me what's going on?"

"It's simple," Big Ezoe said. "He's conned you."

"No, you're wrong," Honno said. "I know Giin."

"And I know gamblers. They don't change. Ever. They only say they do. I'm afraid, Mrs. Kansei, when it comes to human nature, you've got a lot to learn."

"If you'd stop making generalizations," Honno said, "you'd be far better off."

Big Ezoe shook his head. "I see you need to be convinced," he said. "Do you know where he lives?" And when Honno nodded, he ordered, "Take me there."

"Now?"

"Right now!" Big Ezoe said, taking her arm and guiding her out of his office.

"There's no answer," Honno said, ringing the bell to Giin's apartment for the third time. "He must be out to dinner."

Big Ezoe grunted. "Sure he is." He extracted a length of metal from his pocket, slid it deftly into the lock. As he began to manipulate it, Honno said, "What are you doing?"

"What does it look like?" Big Ezoe said, turning the knob and opening the door inward.

As they stepped across the threshold, Honno said, "Isn't there a law against this sort of thing?"

"If there is," Big Ezoe said, "I'm not aware of it."

He closed the door behind them, turned on the light. Honno gasped. Big Ezoe said, "Shit!"

Giin's apartment was in chaos. Furniture was upended, drawers were thrown here and there, their contents strewn around the floor. Cushions were ripped, as were sections of the carpet. The mess extended throughout the three rooms of the small apartment.

"In the name of heaven, what happened here?" Honno said.

"No Giin, no ledgers," Big Ezoe said. He looked at her. "They're both gone."

Honno was horrified. "Now do you see how wrong you were to suspect him? Someone's taken him, along with the ledgers. Dear God, what have I gotten him into? Giin could be hurt—or worse!" Her heart constricted. There were tears in her eyes as the past, for so long held in check, echoed through her like a crack of thunder.

"Did you enjoy meeting my family?" Mars Volkov asked Irina. "I hope you weren't bored."

"Not in the least," she said. "I adored every minute of it."

They were standing in the smoke-filled lobby of the old Moscow Arts Theater during intermission of Chekhov's *Three Sisters*. Irina had recognized Natasha Mayakova, the actress Valeri had had the assignation with, the moment she came on stage. There was something about her makeup that made her seem somehow sinister, like the Marquise de Merteuil, the older woman in *Dangerous Liaisons*, the film Irina had smuggled back from America on videocassette.

Irina wanted to burn this Natasha Mayakova with her eyes, although she could not quite understand why she should be so enraged. What could Valeri Bondasenko mean to her now? Nothing, she told herself firmly. Nevertheless, she had been tense all through the first act, and when intermission came, she embraced it with a profound sense of relief.

"Well, my parents can be trying at times," Mars said, "although I suppose I would be the only one aware of it."

"You look very much like your mother," Irina said. "There is a strength about her, a sense of her family and of herself that I admire tremendously. I'm afraid I'll never get around to the one, and I'm not very good at the other."

"Perhaps you're not one to settle down," Mars said. "I sense in you a restlessness of spirit."

They spoke for a time about mundane things: the play, the production, the acting. Irina mentioned that Natasha Marakova had played her namesake in the play, wanting perhaps to discover if Mars found her attractive, but all she got was a noncommittal answer. Mars made a joke and Irina laughed, but she was suddenly very uncomfortable. In a moment of sheer panic she realized that she had been contemplating blurting out her secret: her involvement with Valeri, seeing him on the street with the

151

actress, Natasha Marakova, her feelings of betrayal. What would Mars think if he knew she was betraying him in much the same way?

But, of course, that was different. She had not made any promises to Mars nor had she claimed purity. She had never lied to him, although she had no illusions that, sooner or later, she would be compelled to do so.

What she was doing was for herself, for Irina Viktorovna Ponomareva. Or was it? Had she been doing nothing but rationalizing to herself about her betrayal of Mars to Valeri? Because betrayal it was. It hadn't bothered her three days ago, but that had been before Mars had taken her home to his family, before she had seen how little Valeri thought of his relationship with her. Before it became clear how thoroughly Valeri was using her.

Now, she thought, everything's changed.

She looked at Mars Volkov as if for the first time, drawing aside the scrims of her own anger, selfishness, and power lust. What she saw was a very down-to-earth man, handsome, desirable, who, despite his immense charm, had to struggle in the Politburo and the People's Congress against the immense power of Valeri Bondasenko. A man who, unlike Valeri, was not obsessed with power, with imprinting his conception of the world on everyone around him, with power as the only consideration or form of currency.

One day, she thought, Mars would even be the head of his own family, and that would be enough to make him content. That idea made her feel warm and comfortable.

And, with that truth, came another one: it wasn't her own freedom that Valeri had offered her when he had enrolled her in his scheme to get inside Mars's mind, but a chance to take on a measure of his, Valeri's, own sins.

"Chekhov always sets me to thinking," Irina said, not only because it was the truth, but because she was determined to cover her unease. "I suppose that's because his plays are like modern paintings, they seem somehow unfinished or, at any rate, about such familiar themes they require your own participation to flesh them out."

"But it wasn't really Chekhov that seemed to interest you," Mars said. "It was the actress, Natasha something, isn't it?"

"I don't know her name," Irina lied. "I was just curious. She's a type; men often find actresses appealing, and I wanted a man's point of view."

152

"Too much makeup," Mars said as they were called in for the start of the second act. "I wouldn't know what she really looked like beneath all that paint."

The blue light from Vosstaniya Square filtered through the windows of Mars's bedroom. It was deep enough into the night so that the building's gastronome was closed and the cinema marquee below was dark. The sky was low with thick, metallic-looking clouds, and although it was late spring, there was a feeling in the air of snow that was somehow melancholy. Or perhaps, Irina thought as she undressed, it was the play that has depressed me. Of course, it can't possibly have been the sight of Natasha Mayakova.

She had been half hoping to run into Valeri at the performance, and now she wondered whether that had been her motivation for buying the tickets. Perhaps Stanislavsky would know, she thought wryly, but he was dead. She only knew that visions of her smiling at Valeri while she was on Mars's arm had filled her head all afternoon. Now that it hadn't happened, she felt deflated, empty. There was a bitter taste in her mouth, as if she had somehow taken a bite out of the clouds wreathing Moscow. And she could not figure out why. Here she was, with Mars, who could give her everything she ever wanted—well, almost everything—and yet her mind was filled with Valeri. Right now the man she wanted was Valeri—she wanted nothing more than to cleave herself to Valeri's musky body, twine her thighs around his, open herself to him.

She shuddered, frightened at the intensity of her emotions. It was as if she could no longer control her feelings. Did she love Mars? Then how could she still be lusting after Valeri? How could she still be jealous of his relationship with Natasha? What was happening inside her?

When she got into this situation she had been certain of who was right and who was wrong. She had allowed Valeri to co-opt her, partly because— Oh, he was so right about her!—he had made her see that she was more than a drone, one worker among many, undistinguished, unappreciated. It was so exciting to feel wanted by such a powerful man as Valeri Bondasenko. And then when he had so cleverly shown her that she could have more, that she could share in his power, she had been all too eager to do what he asked: spy on Mars.

But that was before she had come to know Mars, before he had begun to share his private life with her. Now he seemed to

153

be a wholly different person from the one she had set out to seduce. Now she felt ashamed of how she was betraying Mars to Valeri, and this shame caused her to be in constant turmoil, as if she could not relax even for a moment. She thought, My God, I'm headed for a nervous breakdown. And that frightened her even more, because then neither Mars nor Valeri would want her, and she would once again become nothing in her utter isolation. Now she felt as if only she—Irina Ponomareva—was in the wrong. Which way should she turn, to Valeri or to Mars? God help her, she did not know.

She felt Mars behind her. "What is it with you and windows?" he said. "You're like a cat who loves to stare at nothing. What is it you see out there that I cannot?"

Irina turned around. "I was just thinking."

Mars searched her face. "This sounds serious. It's too late in the night to be serious, *koshka*." Darling. What Valeri had called Natasha Mayakova.

"Don't you think that the darkness makes us more serious, more melancholy, sometimes?"

"I don't know." Mars cocked his head to one side. She could see that he was curious about her train of thought. "I often do my best thinking at night."

"There. You see?"

"But it's the quiet," he said. "The intimation of sleep all around me."

"And when at last you *do* sleep, Mars, what is it you dream of?"

"Electronic sheep," he said. "Powered by miniature nuclear reactors."

She could see, then, that he was making fun of her, but gently, trying to deflate her seriousness.

He gathered her into his arms. "What's gotten into you? Ever since we went to see Chekhov, you seem to have picked up his brooding soul. Is something the matter? Perhaps I can help. I'd like to help you, Irina." He put his lips close to her ear. "Do you know that my family has disapproved of every woman I have ever brought home. Everyone except you. My whole family loves you, Irina."

Irina felt a tingling, as if his words had galvanized her spirit. She found that she was holding her breath; she wondered if he could feel the thundering of her heart.

"I care so much for you."

She felt weak in the knees, as if he was saying in real life

154

what she had dreamed about ever since he had taken her home to meet his family. A family, she thought—what I wouldn't give to have a father, a mother who knew and loved me.

She allowed him to draw her away from the window, the kind of precaution against electronic eavesdropping he did without conscious thought. He took her down the hall and into the bathroom. He turned on the tub taps. There was even hot water.

Naked, they climbed in together, letting the hot water churn around them. The background of splashing water had a soothing effect. They sat face to face, their legs around each other.

He laughed softly, kissed the tip of her nose. "You see, Irina, I have an overpowering urge to trust you. That's a dangerous urge for one in my position in government, someone who has such a powerful enemy in Valeri Denysovich. But lately I find I want to tell you things I'd never dare tell another soul. Crazy, isn't it?" His lips came down over hers, crushing them, opening them. Irina gave a little moan.

"Not crazy," Irina whispered, her eyes half closed. "I think it's perfectly normal behavior for a man in love."

"But that's just it," Mars said. "For a man like me, being in love is the most dangerous state of all."

"Why?"

"You will become my weak spot."

Irina was aware of Valeri telling her that it was just as well he had emerged from his marriage childless because in this terrible world a child could be used against him. How similar these two men were, she thought, but how utterly different when one scratched the surface of their carefully prepared facades. Both were men who wore masks, and masks within masks when they faced the outside world. It gave Irina a fantastic thrill to have penetrated beyond those masks to see the true inner workings of two of Russia's most influential men. And now one, if not both, was in love with her. She was abruptly suffused with the scope of her own power, aware as if for the first time how in control she was, how more in control she would be once she unearthed the secrets that surely these men must harbor. She was not naive; even Mars was not a saint. Their power could not have been acquired without a degree of moral corruption.

The old Irina would have quailed from such a notion, but everything was different now. The power had changed her. She could see quite clearly that the rules for her—as well as for Valeri and Mars—were different than they were for everyone else.

Irina looked into Mars's eyes and, in that moment, she knew

155

that she would never tell him about how Valeri had sent her to spy on him. This was a measure of her power over both men, and she would never give it up.

"Irina, I will tell you a secret," Mars said, "something you must promise never to tell anyone."

"I promise."

"I can well imagine how Valeri Denysovich, for one, would chop me up for fish bait if he ever found out I harbor a secret affinity for the nationalist group, White Star."

Irina watched him through the steam and her slitted eyes. This was the last thing she had expected him to say, and, under the circumstances, it completely disarmed her.

Mars said, "You see, Irina, Valeri Denysovich pretends at compromise with the Baltics with his much publicized treaty. But he gives them only token freedoms. Then, with the other hand, he comes down like a mailed fist against the Ukrainians, his own people. Imagine." He stroked her hair. "You see, despite all the monumental changes taking place in the outside world, nationalism is still a dirty word inside the Kremlin—a treasonable offense. In fact, there are some who believe that the president encouraged the pro-democracy spin in Eastern Europe to divert the increasing pressure the West was putting on us for holding on to the Baltics."

Mars took her hand in his. "I want you to understand this clearly: White Star, if it's legitimate—if it's not being run by fanatics and terrorists—must be recognized. We must look to the Poland model. Solidarity could not be denied. Its rise to power was, in the end, the will of the people. Our strength—though our own government has yet to realize it—is in *our* people. The Soviet peoples. The longer we suppress their individual freedoms, the more we keep them at arm's length. We imprison them, rather than embracing them. White Star could change all that, given half a chance. I think it's worth the risk to give them that chance."

Irina looked into Mars's dark eyes. "It happens that I agree with you."

Mars smiled. "I knew you would." He wiped water droplets from her cheek. "Now I'm certain you'll agree to help me find White Star and talk to their leaders."

"Me? How on earth could I possibly help?"

"Well, it occurred to me that while you were on one of your trips to America, you might have stumbled across a White Star supporter or two. It seems apparent to me that elements inside

America would be only too eager to give what they could: money, arms, what-have-you, to White Star's cause.''

"That may be true," Irina said, "but I never met any.''

"Hmm. Well, it was just a thought," Mars said. He smiled, and wriggled closer to her. "I'll just have to muddle along on my own, then.''

"Why?" Irina reached under the water for him. "When we can muddle along together," she said.

Irina awoke with a start. It was very dark in the room. She could hear Mars's even breathing as he slept beside her. She lay for a time watching a pattern of pale light spiderweb the ceiling. Then she rose without a sound and padded over to the window.

She thought deeply for some time, her mind turning over the possibilities her power opened to her. She took her time, forcing back the desire to race ahead. At last she came to the conclusion that she would, indeed, help Mars in his quest to find White Star. The dissident nationalist organization seemed to loom with greater importance. Both Mars and Valeri were interested in finding White Star, each for his own reasons. But Mars wanted to help White Star, while Valeri was most concerned with the smuggled hafnium.

And now she could feel White Star exerting its own magnetic pull on her. It was fate that Mars had opened himself up to her tonight, a sign. I need to help him, Irina decided. The way each man has reacted to White Star has given me a regained sense of right and wrong. And perhaps in helping the peoples of White Star gain their freedom, I will find the purpose in life that has been missing ever since I returned from Cambridge.

She nodded to herself, beginning at last to see a way out of her terrible dilemma. She would continue to spy on Mars for Valeri, but now it would be a facade. Her facade. She would pass on to Valeri only what she wanted to, only enough to keep him from getting suspicious. In the meantime, she would work on Valeri like an archaeologist at a dig. She would find out all he knew about White Star. But first she needed some kind of insurance.

She did not delude herself. Turning on Valeri Denysovich Bondasenko would be dangerous; if she were not very careful, it could have dire consequences for her. She thought of her dream of the Siberian winter and shuddered, because she knew that Valeri could send her there with no more than a wave of his hand. No one would dare raise his voice in protest. There could be no help for her, no reprieve, even from Mars.

She was smart enough to know that there was a personal element in this decision. To deceive Valeri as he was deceiving her would, in some measure, make up for the hurt he had caused her by seeing another woman. Again, part of her wondered why she should feel so hurt by Valeri, and why she felt it necessary to exact a measure of revenge. After all, it wasn't as if she did care for him, was it?

Insurance. Irina knew she would need it. Some kind of leverage, should Valeri ever find out what she was doing. Power was the only currency Valeri traded in, and Irina knew she needed to make a deposit before she set out against him.

She would have to follow him. Valeri had claimed that he had no secrets; Irina was convinced this must be a lie. Everyone had a secret or two that he or she did not want made public. Why should Valeri be an exception?

He had to have a weakness, some crack, no matter how tiny, in the armor of his power. But what could it be? Irina stared out the window into the blackness of the Moscow night. The air was thick and heavy, almost as cloying as the atmosphere in the lobby of the old Moscow Arts Theater.

And Irina, in sudden inspiration, knew just where to start. Her name was Natasha Mayakova.

Honno said, "What if Giin is already dead?"

"Then we'll hold a funeral," Big Ezoe said.

Looking into her face, he laughed. "You know, being in love does something to you."

"I'm not in love with Giin, if that's your implication," Honno said. "Have you forgotten Eikichi?"

Big Ezoe said, "You're the one married to Eikichi Kansei, yet you aren't in love with him."

"Don't be an idiot," she snapped. "Anyway, why are we talking about me when Giin and Sakata-san's ledgers are missing?"

"Because my men are doing everything possible to find both. We have some time now. Just the two of us."

"Your tone is most offensive," Honno said. "Do all Yakuza deal in innuendo?"

"Our stock in trade, Mrs. Kansei." He grinned. "Sit down. If you keep pacing like that, you're apt to get a heart attack."

Honno stopped in her tracks. She was about to say something

acid, realized how useless her sarcasm would be on him, sat down instead.

They were in Big Ezoe's office. There was a great deal of activity outside in the warehouselike space. Honno hoped at least some of it was related to the search for Giin and the ledgers. She knew there were bodyguards around, but suspected that she would never quite manage to spot them all.

Honno had already spent two evenings out of the house, and, before Eikichi got suspicious, she knew she had to take some steps to ensure that she had uninterrupted time with Big Ezoe. Accordingly, she took a few days off her job at Michita Industries. She had to arrange for two women at Michita to cover her work while she was gone.

Eikichi often worked so late that rather regularly he went out afterward with some of his fellow prosecutors to eat, drink, and unwind. But on the nights he was home at a more or less normal time, he expected his dinner to be prepared and waiting for him when he walked in. If it was not there and, worse, neither was she, no explanation would be adequate.

Consequently, Honno told Eikichi that she was going to Osaka for several days to visit her aunt who was taken ill. Eikichi knew that this aunt was Honno's favorite relative, the only member of her family with whom she had a normal relationship, and he had not questioned her decision.

Big Ezoe shook his head. "You look even more nervous sitting down than you did pacing about." He came around from behind his desk. "This isn't the place for us." He touched his hip beneath his suit jacket. "I have a beeper. As soon as anything breaks, I'll be notified. In the meantime, let's go somewhere where you can get rid of some of that excess energy."

He took her in his gray steel-plated Mercedes to the Ginza, not to the great wide avenues clogged with tourists and traffic, enormous department stores, and neon signs, but to a quiet side street lined with ginkgo trees and wooden walls. Behind one wall Honno found a minuscule garden, immaculate, with a stand of mini-bamboo, moss-laden rocks and a wellspring of tinkling water.

This was the home of Tokyo's most exclusive club, on a street of exclusive clubs. There was a great deal of bowing and deferential treatment from the staff and from the managing director himself, who was immediately summoned from his inner sanctum on the second floor, which overlooked a stunning diamond-shaped atrium composed entirely of white marble slabs.

159

A man in a tuxedo was playing Erik Satie on a white concert grand piano. An enormous spray of red peonies was artfully arranged in a white porcelain vase on the piano's top. Behind him a very modern combination of glass and rice paper and ash shoji screens gave way to an inner courtyard of water, moss, ferns, and dwarf azalea, all amid rocks that suggested mountains, time, and great distance.

They were taken downstairs in a stainless-steel elevator. There Honno and Big Ezoe split up. "See you in the *dojo*," he said. Honno was escorted by a woman attendant into a rich, cedarlined changing room, given a white cotton *gi*—the traditional martial arts attire, loose-fitting and comfortable. She was shown where to bathe, and afterward she returned to the changing room, donned her *gi*.

Big Ezoe was waiting for her in a magnificent *dojo*. The walls and ceiling were paneled in kyoki wood, the space below the ceiling hung with banners of the ancient *daimyo*, the feudal warlords of old Japan. The floor was tatami mats, and the lighting was indirect, making the *dojo* evenly lit wherever one happened to be on the tatami.

"What do you think you're doing?" Honno asked. "How do you know I've had any martial arts training?"

"I'm good at this," Big Ezoe said. "Trust me." And when Honno burst out laughing, he said, "That's better. Let's get rid of some of your nervous tension, hm?" He began to circle her, watching her react to him as he did so. "Jiujitsu," he said. "Some tai chi. And, judging by the way you hold your hands, some aikido."

He moved in low and fast, going for her knees, but Honno used a basic *irimi*, a neutralization technique. Big Ezoe countered this, and Honno automatically went into a counterattack. As she did so, she felt the expansion of her *wa*, her central core of intrinsic energy. It was a wonderful feeling, a sudden release, an elation like a balloon rising into the air currents or a big fish breaking free of a line that had hooked it.

"That's better," Big Ezoe said, attacking again.

Despite his girth, he was light on his feet, agile and frighteningly quick. But Honno soon had a handle on his strategy. He liked to attack endlessly, giving no respite, figuring that eventually fatigue would cause his opponent to make a mistake. Soon after, she discovered the flaw in his strategy. The endless stream of his attacks left minute openings for a counter. One had to be so quick as to anticipate his next attack, or one would have no chance of getting through before its onset. But it could be done.

Honno bided her time, using one *irimi* after another to neutralize him, while dropping her earlier strategy of counterattacking. She needed the extra time to try to anticipate his next move.

She found him in a series of attacks familiar to her, and she thought, Now is the time. She deflected the first, the second, then, anticipating the third in the series, launched herself at the gap as it began to open.

But when, using the spirit of dawn, she came through the opening in his defense, she found him ready for her. Too late, she recognized the trap he had deliberately, patiently set for her. She could only marvel at his expertise as he took her down to the tatami, the callused edge of his hand against her throat.

He grunted, came up, pulled her off the mat after him. "Very good, Mrs. Kansei. But not good enough."

They met an hour and a half later, at the club's third-floor restaurant. In the interim Honno had been bathed, oiled, massaged, bathed again. She had found her clothes waiting for her, cleaned and pressed, in the fragrant changing room.

The restaurant was, in cool contrast to the club's white marble entrance below, a sea of gray unpolished granite, almost colorless, but vibrant with texture. A long line of narrow windows that ran its length overlooked the rigid grid of the city, the restricted view refining Tokyo's geometrics into a pattern that was so intense it became almost abstract, a kind of art.

"Has your office been in touch with you yet?" Honno asked as she sat down opposite Big Ezoe.

"You must learn patience, Mrs. Kansei," he said. A uniformed waiter poured chilled white wine into their glasses. "It was your lack of patience that betrayed you in the *dojo*."

Honno put aside the elegant menu, said, "I want to know what's happened to Giin. And I want to get the ledgers back."

Big Ezoe sipped at his wine, contemplated her. "Just so we get something clear—because this is quite important—is it your late friend Sakata's ledgers you care about or this professor Giin's life?"

"Well, both, of course!"

"But if it came down to it, and you could only retrieve one, the ledgers or Giin," Big Ezoe said as patiently as if he were explaining this to a child, "which would you choose?"

"Are you serious," Honno said, "or is this another one of your jokes?"

"I assure you, I am quite serious."

"But it's an impossible question to answer."

"It is not."

"What kind of creature are you?" Honno said angrily. Then, "All right. There's only one answer possible. Giin's life is far more important than a couple of books with chicken scratching all over them."

"Is that so?" Big Ezoe eyed her over the rim of his glass. "And what about your promise to Sakata-san, Mrs. Kansei? What about *giri*?"

Honno felt shame flood through her. In her anxiety over Giin's safety, she had completely forgotten about the burden of debt she owed Sakata. "But of course this is a moot question," she said hurriedly. "You're giving an imaginary example. It doesn't matter how I answer."

"Oh, but it most certainly does matter." Big Ezoe put down his glass. "I have given you a Zen riddle, and if you think answering it is a pointless exercise or it is merely complying with a whim of mine, you are gravely mistaken. Zen riddles, Mrs. Kansei, are meant as doorways through which one may resolve the contradictions of one's own spirit.

"I told you earlier that you must be prepared for anything. You assured me you were, you gave me your word. Now, when we come to the first difficult fording of a stream, you balk or give me an ill-considered reply. This is not the way of the warrior, Mrs. Kansei. What would your late friend, Sakata-san, think of your behavior?"

With that, Honno put her face in her hands, and began to weep. Big Ezoe watched impassively until her shoulders ceased to shake. Then he said, "Why did you do that?"

"I was a fool to attempt to act out of *giri*," Honno said. "The weight of burden is not meant for a woman. It takes a man's strength."

"Nonsense," Big Ezoe said. "What the performance of *giri* takes is a warrior's spirit. And a warrior is bound neither by age nor by sex. You have the warrior's spirit, Mrs. Kansei. I felt the expansion of your *wa* in the *dojo*. I felt how fiercely you fought. And I know just how much pleasure it gave you. Because I feel the same way."

"But poor Giin," she whispered. "I can't stop thinking about him. I can't stop worrying . . . What if—"

"A warrior's heart is pure," Big Ezoe said. "It is forged in

162

the crucible of combat, in the vise of *giri*, in the glory of honor. These are all that matter. Giin is only a man.''

"But I loved him once and, yes, perhaps as you have said, I still do. But I love Eikichi as well. And I am married to him.''

"Eikichi, too, is only a man. But the warrior's ideals are immutable, perfect, pure. Once you become one with them, they are yours for all time. There is no need to depend on anything or anyone else.''

"But I am married to Eikichi,'' Honno said miserably. "I owe him my honor.''

"Men—and women, too, Mrs. Kansei—are fallible. They lie, cheat, steal, betray. It is human nature, a way of life. To depend on a man—or a woman—is to invite disaster. A warrior avoids this, and therein lies his—or her—ultimate strength.''

"These are just words,'' Honno said. "Hollow words.''

Big Ezoe regarded her for a long time. At last he said, "You're perfectly right.'' He picked up his menu. "And tonight I think it's high time we turned them into reality.''

First there was the moss garden, verdant, lush, glowing like an emerald in the reflected light beneath the yellow and green cut-leaf maples. Then there was the pool, deep, dark, mysterious, in whose depths from time to time could be discerned the speckled back of a lazy koi. Like the arc of a curve, the koi's back appeared and disappeared, as full of meaning as the first brush stroke on rice paper, black ink spilled across the white page, a book yet to be written, yet to be read.

"Mama-san reads the portents here,'' Big Ezoe said, as if divining Honno's thoughts. "The koi dance and, in so doing, speak to her of the future. So she says.''

They had come to the northern outskirts of Tokyo, where there were still wooden houses from before the war, like this one. At this time of the evening the most extraordinary light existed in the bower beneath the carefully pruned maple trees, fusing leaf and pond, moss and butterfly, making even time seem to stand still.

"How do you know this place?'' Honno said. "Is this where you come when you need sexual release?'' It was that kind of place, an outpost of the water trade, the euphemism used to describe Japan's vast underworld of pleasure gardens, where even the forbidden was accepted.

Big Ezoe smiled. He led her away from the koi pool, across the courtyard, into the house. Mama-san was in the doorway, as if she expected them. She bowed to Big Ezoe and, when he introduced Honno, she was warm and welcoming. They took off their shoes, which were stored in a beautiful kyoki wood cabinet in the stone and wood entrance. Fresh flowers were everywhere. Some almost hid the *shunga*, erotic woodblock prints, hung on the walls. Mama-san showed them into a six-tatami room, dominated by a massive red-painted *tansu* chest with a great deal of intricate ironwork. A simple porcelain vase held a single yellow chrysanthemum amid a spray of dark green leaves. She had tea brought, but almost immediately Big Ezoe excused himself.

"Does he come here often?" Honno asked.

"Oh, no," Mama-san said. She seemed almost sad at the thought. She had gray hair, a round, pleasant face. She was dressed immaculately in the old fashion. The edge of a yellow under-kimono was visible beneath a kimono of spring green. Gorgeous wooden combs kept her hair in its complex pattern. Her face was white, black, and crimson with traditional make-up. "He almost never comes."

"How do you know him?"

Mama-san cocked her head, looking like a mockingbird on a branch. "My dear, Big Ezoe owns this establishment." She gave Honno the tiniest, most ingratiating smile. "Tell me, did he take you to his club in the Ginza for lunch today?"

"*His* club?"

"Oh, most assuredly." Mama-san's head bobbed, and her expression was that of a mother proud of the accomplishments of her son. "Big Ezoe owns many, many things. But he acquires nothing." She cocked her head again. "Do you understand?"

"I'm not sure."

"Well." Mama-san settled her hands in her lap. The light from the next room, filtered by the rice-paper shoji screens, fell obliquely across her face, softening it and, at the same time, making an abstraction of it, so that Honno was reminded of the restricted view of Tokyo from the Ginza club's restaurant. "Here is what I mean. A man acquires wealth, but of what use is wealth if he has no wisdom? Oh, he may ride in the grandest Mercedes, have his clothes made for him abroad, live in a house in Koji-machi, but if he owns no respect, then he is nothing, and his life is but coins sifting through his fingers."

"This is how you define Big Ezoe?"

"But I wasn't speaking of him, not in any direct way," Mama-san said. "I was trying to make you understand the nature of things. Events, often shocking, require an underlying logic so the mind can understand what the eyes cannot.''

At that moment Big Ezoe reappeared. "We must go upstairs now, Mama-san."

The old woman bowed. "I understand."

"Have you finished?"

She gave him an enigmatic look. "Well." The patterns shifted, black-white-black, across her face as she moved. "There won't be a finish to this."

Big Ezoe watched, as if suddenly wary, then he returned her bow and gestured for Honno to follow him. There was a man standing in the hallway, at the foot of the stairs. He had about him the air of one of Big Ezoe's men. He looked studiedly away from Honno as she followed Big Ezoe up the stairs.

"Where are we going?" she asked. "Why are we here?"

It was dark on the second floor. Their feet made no sound on the tatami mats. Sliding shoji screened off one room from another, so that the place had a sense of communality that spoke to the heart of the Japanese culture, where individuality was an uncomfortable concept.

"This is a sleepless place," Big Ezoe said softly. "And yet it is just the spot where dreams are born."

He stopped in front of a shoji near the end of the hall. He put his hand on the ash-wood frame, turned to her, said, "Trust, Mrs. Kansei, is too often misplaced. Won't you see my words turned into reality?"

He threw open the sliding shoji, and Honno stared into the room beyond. There were two people—a man and a woman—entwined on the futon. There was a crush of movement, rhythmic, primitive, unmistakable. Then the man, aware through the veil of his pleasure that he was being observed, flung the woman off his hips. The woman rolled out of the bedcovers, and Honno saw the woman was a man. He sat up, stared into Honno's face.

All at once Honno's blood froze. She was looking right at Eikichi. Her husband making love to another man. It was inconceivable. This must be a painting or a photograph, Honno thought. It cannot be real. She felt dizzy. And then Mama-san's words flooded back through her. Mama-san had spoken of Kojimachi. Kojimachi was one of Tokyo's poshest neighborhoods. It was where Eikicki had grown up, where he went to high school. It was where his parents lived, where he aspired to live. *If a man owns no respect, then he is nothing, and his life is but*

165

coins sifting through his fingers. Mama-san, in her oblique way, had been trying to prepare Honno for this scene.

"Honno-san!" Eikichi screeched. "How dare you come here! How dare you lie to me! How dare you spy on me!" The look of contempt on his face was acid. "Well, why should I be surprised? You're *hinoeuma*. Oh, yes, I know. Stupid you!" Seeing the look of dread and shame on her face, he was not about to stop now. There was a kind of gleeful malevolence that seemed to bubble out of him like lava from the mouth of a volcano. "Your father came to see my parents a month before our wedding. He was concerned, you see, for their reputation, their standing in the community. He wanted some remuneration for his information and, because I got to him before he had a chance to speak to my parents, I paid him off myself. Why not? His information was valuable to me, although not in any way he could suspect, the poor fool. I saw it as a lever to keep you in line, just in case you rebelled at some point, willful girl that you are, against my true lifestyle." He drew the thin young man back to him, lovingly embraced him. "Now, *hinoeuma* woman, get out of here, so I can finish what I've started!"

Honno wanted to cry out, but she could not. Just like that, with the thunderclap of Eikichi's voice, reality was brought home to her. She turned away, too horrified, too out of control, to answer him.

She tore past Big Ezoe, raced back down the stairs, through the entryway, out into the courtyard. Running barefoot into the darkness beneath the maples, where the tiny sounds of the koi pool could comfort her, where the lazy, somnolent fish could soothe away the fever burning inside her.

Then she turned away and, to her horror, vomited in a series of wracking convulsions. She gave a little moan, and crawling to the edge of the pool, lowered her face beneath the water. Coolness surrounded her, and she opened her eyes to the darkness, the life beneath the water.

When she rose, gasping, from below, she saw Big Ezoe sitting on the other side of the pool. He handed her her shoes. She was so humiliated she could not face him.

"You bastard," she said, "you knew about Eikichi all along." She was gasping for breath, as if she had been running for a very long time. "How long has he been coming here?"

"Three years," Big Ezoe said. "Nothing about meeting you, courting you, marrying you, changed his schedule."

"Because I am *hinoeuma*, born in the year of the husband killer," Honno said miserably.

Big Ezoe looked off into the night. There were fireflies out, and here beside the koi pool, beneath the maples, it was possible to forget all about Tokyo, the hypermodern superstructures, the official bribery and corruption, the race into the twenty-first century, which was the national task that the Japanese had set for themselves. Now only the essence remained, the hard, cruel lessons of a far simpler time, the time of the warrior for which Yukio Mishima longed, about which Big Ezoe knew so much.

"It has nothing to do with what you think you are," Big Ezoe said. "It is him. What Eikichi Kansei is: a product of the times. As Mama-san tried to tell you. She knows your husband far better than you do."

Eikichi's sadistic invective echoed in her mind. The humiliation of her pathetic lot in life overwhelmed her, and she thought she was going to be sick again. She had been systematically beaten down at home, first by her father, and then by Eikichi, whom she could see now was the only kind of man she could have chosen to be her husband: rigid, brutal, repressive. How could she have mistaken such inhumanity for honor? Obedience had blinded her.

And as for her job? Now she understood her role there, as well. She served the same purpose as the wallpaper in the halls: she was elegant, soothing, ever obedient. This was not only the definition of what she was, but what she would always be. She had as much knowledge and schooling as the male executives beside whom she served daily. But no one would listen to her opinions or ideas. What place did a woman have in business? Kunio Michita had given her the answer to that when he had ignored her idea for Tandom Polycarbon. Again she had been betrayed by her sense of obedience. And she realized in a thoroughly disheartening moment that she had always known what her place was in business, and at home.

Home? What home? Her childhood had been a cruel mockery, and her marriage an absolute sham.

She felt as if she had just awakened from a long dream, from a sojourn in a world where she must hold her tongue, underutilize her brain, instead look cool and beautiful, be the whipping girl for her bitter father, be an obedient automaton for Michita and a walking billboard for Eikichi.

Honno at last gathered the strength to look up at Big Ezoe. "Now I see there are worlds within worlds," she said. "Like this private bower within the city. And worlds within those worlds, like this koi pond within this bower. Which is the real world?''

Big Ezoe, sitting across the expanse of dark, lapping water, said, ''You have just learned that lesson, Mrs. Kansei. There is no real world. There is only *your* world.''

FIVE
LLANO NEGRO

On a tree at the near edge of the *llano negro*, Tori discovered a series of carvings. They were crude yet powerful. They depicted a baby; a bent, old man; a man with no legs; a man nailed to a cross; a man with no eyes: a dead man.

"What the hell does this mean?" Russell said.

"Myth," Estilo said.

"I don't believe in myths," Russell said, turning away. He was scanning the immediate environment, a quadrant at a time.

Estilo said, "Jorge Luis Borges, our most famous poet, wrote that myth is merely reality simplified to a point where it can be understood."

Russell turned around. "And you believe that?"

Tori, coming up to Russell, said softly, "It's important to believe it here in the field. *Especially* here in the jungle we don't know. It's dangerous to assume that reality and myth are two separate entities, because out here they serve the same purpose."

"Why do you always feel the need to show me how superior you are?" Russell said.

"Because," Tori told him, "you're a man and I'm not."

"So what?"

"So isn't that part of why you think I'm unreliable?"

"You're out of your mind."

"Am I?"

He looked at her for what seemed a long time. "It's getting late."

They pushed on past the carvings, through the trees and the encroaching underbrush, until they were swallowed up by *llano negro*, the black jungle.

Toward midday they paused for a break. It was hideously hot and humid, and all of them were drenched in sweat. They passed around food and water. Russell said, "Estilo, what did those carvings signify?"

Estilo grunted. "We are born, we age, are maimed, are punished for our sins, and die." He chewed on some dried beans. "It was a warning, I suppose. There is a great deal of superstition among the *campesinos* out here. This is the edge of the world as they understand it. The *llano negro* defines the boundary of what is known and what is unknown."

"Who d'you think put the carvings there?" Russell said.

Estilo nodded in the direction they were headed. "Whoever this land belongs to."

"Any idea who that might be?"

"Why speculate?" Estilo got up, dusted himself off. "We'll soon find out."

They set out again, and within the space of twenty minutes came to the bank of the Manacacias River. It was brown, sluggish, muddy. Downed trees, a forest of branches, clogged its flow, and it was not difficult, using these, to ford the water.

"According to Cruz's flight jockey, the cocaine factory shouldn't be far now," Russell said when they had gained the far shore.

"Estilo," Tori said quietly, "listen to me carefully. Don't move. And don't—*don't!*—turn your head." She walked around so that Estilo could see her. She could see Estilo's eyes opened wide with fear. "Look at me. Look at me! There's a stone beetle on you."

Estilo's lips barely moved. "Where?" He barely breathed it.

"The base of your neck."

"Tori." Estilo's eyes closed and a tiny tremor passed through him.

Tori could see he was praying. She could also see, out of the corner of her eye, Russell walking up behind Estilo. Without a word Tori reached out, caught him by the wrist just as he was

170

about to pluck the stone beetle off Estilo. It was very large, almost the length of her forefinger, blunt and ugly, its articulated carapace black and as shiny as chrome.

"I'm just going to get it off him," Russell said.

"If you try it, Estilo will die." Tori indicated the insect. "Do you see those forward pincers? They're already buried in his flesh. Even if you were fast enough, it would, at the point of death, reflexively release its poison." She looked at him. "Do you know why this is called a stone beetle? Its venom paralyzes the central nervous system of its prey. It's as if they've turned to stone."

"Just like Circe's gaze," Russell said. And when she did not answer, "I was thinking of the merging of myth and reality." He looked at her. "What are we to do? I have no experience with stone beetles."

"There's only one way," Tori said. "Don't move and, no matter what, don't make a sound." She turned toward Estilo, contemplated the giant insect at the base of his neck. It crouched there, dark and deadly. She could see its pincers with their lethal poison embedded in Estilo. She began to sweat.

She lifted her right hand and, separating her fingers, lowered the little finger toward the beetle's back. When the long, curved nail was millimeters from the creature, she paused. A tremor went through her; she knew she would have only one chance to paralyze the insect through the single chink in the armor of its carapace. If she missed, if she used too little or too much force, Estilo would die.

Tori, too, said a little prayer. She went into *prana*, extending her breathing, slowing down, allowing her *wa*, her intrinsic force, to expand, to explore the environment around her, and to wash away her apprehension and fear. Then, with a soft exhalation, she slid her nail through the slit between the plates of the beetle's carapace. There was some kind of obstruction, and she pushed on through it. For an instant she panicked, thinking she had gone too far and, in its death spasm, the beetle would shoot its venom into Estilo's bloodstream. Paralysis and death. She took another deep breath.

In a moment she said, "Estilo, are you all right?"

"Get that thing off me, damnit!"

Tori almost laughed in relief. The stone beetle was paralyzed. She grasped its sides with her left hand and, making sure to keep her fingernail in place, pulled on the beetle. She saw its pincers emerging from Estilo with agonizing slowness. At last

171

the pincers were out. In a blur Tori flung the insect away from them, into the underbrush.

"It's gone."

"Well done," Estilo said, clapping Tori on the back. Color was slowly returning to his face. "My God, that was too close by half." He kissed Tori on both cheeks.

"That was very impressive," Russell said to Tori as they prepared to move out.

"I didn't do it to impress you."

"Give it a break, okay?" he said. "What you did took a lot of guts, that's all I meant."

Russell walked away from her. He took point. He had gone over the terrain with Cruz's pilot, but he also must have completely memorized the topographical map in the helicopter, because he had not needed to refer to it once they were on the ground.

"This way," he said, pointing into the emerald and black jungle, and they pushed on through the dense foliage. Green light and darkness; shadows lying in layers, dense with mystery. It was slow going because they needed silence more than speed now. They could not afford to hack their way through with their machetes because the men guarding the factory would surely hear them coming.

They soon came to a huge tree. Again there was a carving on it. This time it was very large. It showed a man bound upside down to what appeared to be some sort of circle.

"The black wheel of death," Estilo said. "Endless pain, eternal torment."

"Another warning," Russell said. He took out his KA-BAR knife and, in three wide slices, gouged out the carving. "This time it's ours."

The first sign they had that they were close to their goal was a sight of an army patrol. They were bivouacked in a small clearing in which a *campesino*'s shack had been constructed. There were twenty soldiers.

As the three of them crept closer to the perimeter they could see that groups of soldiers were taking turns going inside the shack. It had been outfitted with a small generator, a TV and a VCR. The soldiers were watching a videocassette of *Apocalypse Now*, absorbing several scenes at a time before emerging like blinded owls into the intense sunshine, jabbering excitedly,

172

swaggering like Colonel Kilgore or blowing out their cheeks like Colonel Kurtz.

Russell guided the others with hand signals, and they gave the encampment a wide berth. It appeared that Cruz was correct about the army's use here—this detachment seemed to have no orders to patrol. They were within five thousand yards of a major cocaine factory, and they seemed happily on vacation. Who could command so much power? Tori asked herself as they headed toward the factory.

They encountered animals next: chickens, pigs, goats, enough to feed several hundred people. Then they saw the beginning of the compound. Russell, crouched beside Tori, whispered, "Jesus Christ, this isn't a factory, it's a goddamned city!" They counted a dozen long houses—no doubt dormitories—made of corrugated tin. Beyond, the jungle had been cleared to the south to make room for an airstrip. A Twin Otter airplane sat on the runway, being refueled.

As they continued to move around the clearing's perimeter, they came upon shedlike warehouses storing drums of acetone, aviation fuel, red gasoline, ether: the essentials of refining coca into cocaine, and of transporting it out of the *llano negro*. Farther along, three rows of massive generators hunkered in a huge shed cooled by the shade of a grove of trees. Other buildings housed washing machines, shower facilities, mess tables to accommodate a division. They found the lab itself, a long, low structure with a zinc roof. They moved on until they had identified every structure in the clearing.

The entire compound was dominated by the cloyingly sweet stench of "cooking" cocaine, a combination of ether and cocahydrochloride, which created its own kind of pernicious industrial pollution over this bizarre and scarifying jungle city.

"What the hell have we stumbled onto?" Estilo breathed. "This is more than we bargained for, Tori. The size of this place . . . You'd need a couple of army regiments to close it down."

"Maybe," Tori said. "Maybe not."

She led them back the way they had come. Twice they had to stop, melt into the jungle as guards in Jeeps thundered by, semiautomatic rifles at the ready. They were not soldiers, but they had the bearing of army-trained personnel.

Tori reentered one of the warehouses, checked the contents more carefully. When she returned to where the others were waiting, she said, "In any case, there's nothing more we can do now. Darkness is our greatest ally out here."

In the belly of the black jungle, Russell took the first watch. Tori and Estilo sat together, their backs against the bole of an enormous tree. Birds called to each other through the maze of tree branches, and the whir of flying insects was incessant.

Tori and Estilo passed a canteen back and forth, taking only sips at a time. They ate some concentrated food. Estilo put his head back, closed his eyes. "A long long time ago, when I was a little boy," he said, "I found a cat in the jungle. He was sick—you could see he had no flesh over his rib cage, and one eye didn't work right. But, my God, he was a magnificent fighter. I sat and watched him methodically attack, kill, and eat a seven-foot adder so poisonous I wouldn't have gotten within ten paces of it. When he was through eating, he licked his paws and, mewing, walked over to me. I sat still. His eyes watched mine, and I think that if I had made any move at all he would have attacked me.

"But I didn't, and he didn't, and so we became friends." Estilo shrugged. "For many years he was my only friend. My family lived with other German emigrés, and I hated them, with their stiff, formal ways, their arrogance of superiority. It was funny; they assumed that their superiority stemmed from genetics, but I knew the Argentines better than they did, and I knew what deference the Germans were given was bought with their stolen Nazi blood money."

Estilo turned and spat into the humid black earth. "One day the cat was gone, just like that. I found him that night in a back alley near my house. His neck had been broken. A swastika had been painted on his forehead, and then I knew who had killed him. There was a set of twins who lived in the house next to mine. They were bullies in school and in the neighborhood. They always stood by one another, so no one challenged them.

"I knew they had killed my cat, but I did nothing to let them know I knew. I decided to study them, and after a while it became clear to me that while they always provided a united front to the kids at school, when they were alone together—or thought they were—there was an intense rivalry between them. I was convinced that I had found their weak spot, but how to exploit it?

"It happened that the twins were both wild over one girl. She was a flirt, and liked both of them, or at least enjoyed the attention they gave her. Over the course of the next several months I secretly contrived to become her friend. She wasn't very good in mathematics and I undertook to tutor her.

"While I did so I drew her out so that she spoke about the twins. When she had given me enough intimate information about them, I used her to plant stories about how each of them was secretly trying to undercut the other in school, at home, with her. As I was certain she would, she passed on these stories. It did not matter that they were false; I knew the truth of the twins' rivalry, so the stories were believed.

"I set one twin against the other, until their enmity destroyed their connection, their love for one another. I drove them apart. In the end they became business rivals, and have spent their lives trying to bankrupt one another."

For a time there was silence in the jungle, the drip of moisture off the foliage, the whir and whine of insects, an animal call in the distance.

Tori wondered why Estilo had told her that chilling story. It occurred to her after a time that what he had been speaking about was not, strictly speaking, a cat—but rather loyalty, trust, friendship, and love. She recalled their talk on the telephone when she had still been in Mall Central, and she realized that this was as close as he could come to telling her how much he missed his friend, Ariel Solares.

Night in the *llano negro* was absolute. There was no moon, but illumination was provided by the factory's powerful arc lights. It was eerie to be deep in the jungle, and to see everything in terms of the powder-white sodium lights. There were no colors, no grays, only utter black and stark white.

Russell went with Tori into the warehouse. He said, "I'm not sure this is a good idea."

"It doesn't matter," Tori said, crouching down by the side of a barrel of acetone.

"I'm the commander in the field," Russell pointed out.

"You're nothing," Tori said. "You want to be a commander, go ahead. But you've got no one to command."

There was a small silence. Then he crouched down beside her. "I still think this is far too dangerous. We could all die."

"We could all have died in Cruz's copter, if the pilot had crashed," Tori said. "The idea is not to make a mistake." She nodded, held out a length of cord. "Cut this for me, will you?"

Russell did as she asked, and Tori dipped the cord into the

acetone. She looped it around the barrel and over to the one next to it that contained ether. She opened the barrel. Then she backed up, trailing the cord behind her.

"Ready?"

"Not by a long shot," Russell said, watching her light the end of the acetone-soaked cord. Then they got out of there.

The string of explosions began twenty seconds later. The three of them set out on the run, through the confusion of the compound, the screaming of the Jeeps' tires, the shouts of the personnel.

They had their Uzi assault rifles at the ready, but they made it to the lab without having to fire them. With the entire warehouse going up, no one was interested in them. Yet. This was a shut-ended situation, because the explosions would surely bring the army out of its *Apocalypse Now* torpor, and those in command surely would begin instituting a building-by-building search of the compound as soon as the post-percussion fire was under control.

Tori estimated they had five minutes, any more would be stretching it.

They hit the lab at once, smashing in the door, hearing bursts of semiautomatic fire and answering with their Uzis. Six guards went down in a hail of bullets, shards of glass, wood, and metal. A dozen lab workers stood cringing with their hands on their heads. The chemical stench was almost overpowering, even though the line of windows at the back of the lab was open.

Tori posted Estilo at the open doorway, where he could cover the workers while she and Russell roamed up and down the aisles. Zinc-topped trestle tables were filled with huge metal buckets of cured cocaine, but all the "cooking" was being done in vats outside. This was the end product.

On another table plastic bags were being filled with refined coke. "There's something odd here," Tori said.

At that moment Estilo came up. Keeping his eye on the workers, he said, "Did you take a look at the guards?"

Tori shook her head. "No time."

"They're all Japanese."

"Japanese?" Russell went over to where two of the guards were sprawled. He turned one over, looked at his face. "Japanese," he confirmed. Then he pulled back the man's sleeve. "Yakuza. What's this all about?"

176

"Protecting their investment?" Estilo offered.

Tori didn't think so. She took a look at the *irizumi*, the body tattoos on the man. She saw from the intricacy of the *irizumi* that this man was an underboss. He had been very powerful. That wasn't the way the Japanese Yakuza worked. The underbosses did not like to be so far from home. He'd be here only for the most vital of reasons. Coke was coke. He could just as easily have checked it at his end of the pipeline, or sent a trusted underling here to make certain of the quality. Then what was he doing in the middle of nowhere? What was so important—

Estilo gave a shout, then opened up with his Uzi. A worker who had drawn a pistol was thrown backward against the zinc-topped table where he had been stuffing cocaine into the plastic bags. As he collapsed, two of the ten-kilo bags fell to the floor. One burst open, and Tori made a sound deep in her throat.

She and Russell went over to the opened bag. Within the coke, something dark was just visible. Using the tip of her knife blade, Tori pushed aside the white powder.

"What the hell is that?" Estilo said.

"A soft cell," Russell said.

"What?"

Tori said, "It's a method of smuggling, unusual but invariably effective. It takes a convoluted brain to think of it. Contraband inside an altogether different type of contraband." She had uncovered a glassine tube. It was filled with pellets. They were of a metal that was almost black, almost totally without shine.

"What are they?" Russell said almost to himself. He took the glassine envelope, hefted it. "Heavy."

Tori was already slitting open the second ten-kilo bag. In its center, hidden by the powder, was an identical glassine envelope filled with the same metallic pellets.

"This must be why the Japanese are here," she said.

"This isn't about cocaine smuggling at all." Russell was staring at the pellets.

"No."

"But what *is* it about?"

At that moment Estilo said, "They're coming."

"Shit!" Estilo shouted at the workers, herded them out of the lab building. He took a look into the compound. "The goddamned army's arrived."

Russell looked at Tori. "Now we've had it," he said.

177

Tori said, "Take the pellets. Let's get going."

Gunfire began, and Estilo jumped away from the doorway, began to return the fire.

"Forget that way," Tori said. "Use the windows! When you get out, head for the airstrip."

They climbed onto the trestle tables, launched themselves through the windows. They emerged high up on the corrugated tin wall, but the underbrush cushioned their fall.

Immediately, more firing started, and the foliage around them began to fly apart. Estilo was nicked in the fleshy part of his arm, shouted a curse in German, pulled Russell backward to safety behind a tree.

There were shouts, and Tori moved in, Estilo and Russell behind her, fanning out, firing in short, accurate bursts.

Then they were through the hastily thrown-up cordon of guards, racing away from the compound, toward the airstrip where the Twin Otter waited, gleaming in the arc lights like an oasis in the blackness of the night.

They were halfway to the airstrip when the firing began again. A Jeep was careening out of the compound, heading toward them in a vector that would cut them off from the runway. The driver gunned the engine, and the two soldiers in back readied a machine gun on a swivel mount bolted to the side of the Jeep.

"Christ," Russell said.

"Keep going!" Tori called. She stopped, began to fire her Uzi with the blunt shock jammed hard against her left side. The Jeep did not veer toward her as she had wanted it to, but the machine gun swiveled in her direction. It began to fire. With her right hand Tori pulled the pin on a phosphorus grenade tied to the bandolier she wore across her chest. She ripped the grenade free, lofted it toward the Jeep.

The driver saw it, pulled hard on the wheel. The Jeep screamed, skittered on the rutted dirt track, lurched, bounced, came down just as the grenade made contact. The white-green explosion peeled back the nearside fender, impaled the wheel on hot metal, tore into the engine housing.

The Jeep bucked, shot upward, passing vertical, crashed down on its top. No one moved underneath its bulk. Flames began to lick upward, then the ammunition ignited.

Ducking the flying debris, Tori ran in a zigzag pattern, heading toward the airstrip where the others had gone. And ran right into a pair of soldiers who had burst at a full run from the underbrush surrounding the back of the lab.

One hit the point of her jaw with the stock of his machine pistol, the other kicked her legs out from under her. She fell to the ground, and one of the soldiers smashed the toe of his boot into her stomach. Tori doubled over, gasping for air, struggling for equilibrium.

Then she was hauled over on her back and one of the soldiers placed the muzzle of his pistol against the side of her head. His sweat dripped onto her forehead, into her eyes. He stunk from cordite and male sweat.

He grinned at her, and she could see the gaps between his teeth. *"Adios, puta,"* he said.

Tori heard the crack of the pistol and she jerked. But when she looked up, she saw the soldier with a stupefied expression on his face. Blood drooled from the center of his forehead. Then he toppled out of her line of vision, and she rolled into the second soldier, who had lifted his machine pistol.

Tori unsheathed her knife, drove it upward in a shallow arc, into the soldier's lower belly. He gave a cry, his machine pistol sprayed the air, then he fell to his knees.

There was plenty of life still in him. He smashed his fists into her side, and she grunted, twisting the knife, dragging it through his viscera. He hit her again in the kidneys and her strength momentarily left her. Then, gathering herself, she drew the knife upward and across, disemboweling him.

In a moment Russell was at her side. He put his .45 against the soldier's head, pulled the trigger. He hauled Tori to her feet.

"You okay?"

She nodded. "Nice bit of shooting. Right between the eyes."

He had to help her a little until the running could work out the soreness in her abdomen and side. Her jaw still ached from where she had taken the shot with the stock of the machine pistol.

They caught up with Estilo on the edge of the tarmac. The Twin Otter sat waiting, closer than ever. They trotted out onto the airstrip.

The airplane loomed up, and Tori thought, We've made it. Just then they saw another Jeep careen onto the tarmac. It headed for them at full speed, machine pistols blazing.

"Around the other side!" Estilo called. "Get the plane between us and those guns!"

They ducked beneath the wing of the Twin Otter. But as soon

179

as they did, they could make out an advancing column of troops appearing from out of the jungle on that side of the plane. They were caught in a tightening net.

"The plane's our only hope now," Estilo said. "We've got to get inside."

"But the moving stair is on the other side," Russell said. "Those machine pistols will cut us to ribbons if we show ourselves."

"Nevertheless," Tori said, "Estilo's right. If we don't take off in this plane, we're finished." She checked her Uzi. "Reload," she said. "Make sure you've got a full magazine. Okay." She looked at their faces, pale and grim in the reflection of the sodium arc lights. "Let's go!"

They began to fire even before they came around beneath the gleaming belly of the Twin Otter. The Jeep was closer than they expected, the fusillade from the soldiers withering. Already, they could hear the pop-pop-pop of semiautomatic rifles from the column of soldiers on the other side of the plane.

"We'll never get the moving stair in place!" Russell shouted over the din.

Tori saw that he was right. "Quick!" she shouted back. "In there!" she indicated the open cargo doors.

Russell grabbed Estilo, shoved him into the cargo bay. Tori got off a quick burst at the Jeep, saw one of the soldiers slump back. She covered Russell, still firing, as he climbed in himself. She shot off a final burst, scrambled in, closed the doors behind her.

The semiautomatic fire was like hail against the side of the plane.

"Shit, shit, shit." Tori, forward of them, was scrabbling at a plate in the ceiling. She pulled her .45, shot off the lock, shoved the panel aside, and light flooded downward. She clambered up, Russell right behind her.

They ran forward. There was no one on the plane, and she said a prayer for their luck. She slid into the pilot's chair, began throwing switches. "I'm not sure of the takeoff," she said. "Once we're in the air I'll be okay."

Russell sat in the copilot's seat, went through the pre-takeoff checklist. The engines started up. There was no problem, except for the semiautomatic fire directed their way.

"Time," Russell said, and they began to taxi down the airstrip. Faster and faster he fed the engines, adjusting the mix, then pulled back on the throttle, and with a great rush they were airborne, lifting slowly away from the *llano negro*, the insane cocaine city, the unknown enemy, powerful, plotting, hidden beneath layers of deceit, working the soft cell.

BOOK TWO

THE HARD MACHINE

*Perfection of means
and confusion of goals
seem, in my opinion,
to characterize our age.*
—ALBERT EINSTEIN

SIX
MOSCOW/STAR TOWN /ARKHANGELSKOE/TOKYO

The next time Irina saw Natasha Mayakova, it was face-to-face. As it happened, Natasha ran an acting school for women. There were four instructors, and she herself gave one class a week. Irina had enrolled in this class.

She had to audition, of course, but oddly, this had posed no great problem. Irina suspected that her recent work burrowing in between Valeri and Mars had made of her a fairly decent actor. She found that she had no fear or trepidation at all. She read from a scene in Chekhov's *Three Sisters*, which she privately thought was the height of irony. She must have done well, because the next day she was informed that she had been accepted into Miss Mayakova's class.

The class was attended by six women. They sat in a dusty back room of the new Moscow Arts Theater, which Irina did not like nearly as much as she did the old one, where Natasha performed five nights a week.

Irina had not, of course, given her real name. Her goal was to discover what Valeri was secretly doing with Natasha Mayakova, and to find some way to use it against him so that she could get out of him the information Mars needed on the nationalist group, White Star. Here, she was Katya Boroskaya.

Mars had been delighted to provide the false documentation Irina needed for enrolling in the acting school. It was too early to give him any information, and he had not asked why she required new identity documents. "I want you to think of yourself as a free agent," he had told her. "I trust you."

The first night, Natasha Mayakova had told her students that this class would not have been possible before perestroika. She said this with the kind of pride someone tells her girlfriends that her father has granted her the privilege of staying out past midnight. Irina thought the speech disgusting in its naïveté, frightening in its implied condescension.

"Here we will study such American playwrights as Edward Albee," Natasha continued. "I have chosen Albee because in plays such as *Tiny Alice* and *A Delicate Balance*, we can discern distinct Chekhovian antecedents. The characters' existential terror is not so far from the despair with which Chekhov imbued his characters in *Three Sisters* or *The Cherry Orchard*. Both Chekhov and Albee understood the dynamics of inertia, and its ultimate power to affect an audience."

Natasha asked them to do "cold readings," because, she said, "I want to see what you can do when I throw you without warning into an icy stream."

She chose two students, one of whom was Irina, to read passages from Albee's *Who's Afraid of Virginia Woolf?* Natasha asked Irina to play Martha, the role acted by Elizabeth Taylor in the American film version Irina had seen in a tiny Cambridge revival theater. Irina remembered sitting in the dark, surrounded by American students and the smell of popcorn, and feeling as if she were swimming naked in a sylvan mountain lake. She had felt so . . . free. And then the enlarged image of Elizabeth Taylor had sprung up in front of her, her acting transporting Irina away, away, away . . .

After class was over Natasha Mayakova asked her to stay behind. Irina was immediately terrified that, somehow, despite her precautions, Natasha knew who she was and was now prepared to confront her.

When they were alone, Natasha said, "Do you have time for a glass of tea?"

Because it was fairly late, they went to the night bar at the Metropole Hotel, one of the few places in Moscow to stay open past midnight. Muscovites often frequented the hotel because it had been a favorite speaking spot of Lenin's. Now it seemed faded, worn, almost shabby beneath the ornate gilt.

186

When they had ordered, Natasha said, "I wanted a chance to speak with you, Katya, because your reading of Albee intrigued me." She stirred sugar into her tea, watched the crystals melting. "It's from Finland, this sugar, did you know that? I don't know why there's never enough sugar and never any milk here. Where does it all go, do you suppose? I've heard that White Star hijacks the trucks and trains that bring these staples to Moscow, but it's difficult to credit such stories."

Irina said nothing, sensing that Natasha was merely musing, not asking a question. Instead she dissected the other woman with her eyes. Natasha was indeed a beauty: blond, blue-eyed, with a dynamic face that might have been judged overly aggressive save for her mouth, which was soft, gentle, inviting. Irina hated that face.

"*Who's Afraid of Virginia Woolf?* is not an easy play to decipher," Natasha said. She took a sip of her tea, wrinkled her nose. "Not strong enough. This must be for the tourists!" She gave Irina a small smile that was at once so shy and so genuine that Irina was taken aback.

"And also the characters are so complex," Natasha continued, "perhaps also stupefyingly American." She paused, as if momentarily unsure how to continue. "You handled the character well. Very well, indeed."

"Thank you." Irina thought Natasha so glamorous, with the actor's natural ease and grace in all situations, that she had begun to grind her teeth in envy and rage.

"As I've no doubt you are aware, Martha requires a certain inner rage, like a pot untended for too long, simmering on the stove, its contents about to burst out and scar the kitchen forever." She looked up at Irina and, with the actor's impeccable timing, said, "But I sensed in you a very real anger, a deep pool of rage from which you created your Martha. I wanted to speak to you of this anger because I wonder if you are aware how completely you are in its grip."

Irina did not know what to make of this; was she, perhaps, offended by it? But then she thought of her recurring nightmare, her living prison, where even the moon was barred. Sometimes she awoke from this nightmare so upset that she felt nauseous. Could that be the result of rage? She looked at Natasha Mayakova with renewed suspicion. She had had friends for years who would never think to ask her such a personal and disturbing question. "Is this more of your 'perestroika' talk?" she said.

Natasha gave her little laugh again, and there was the shyness

187

again, playing around her face like an imp, defusing Irina's deliberate sharpness. "Oh, that foolishness. Well, it's what my students want to hear, what they expect. It's harmless, really, but I've found it immediately puts them at their ease."

"It isn't foolish," Irina said. "It's dangerous talk."

"Really? In what way?"

"What your 'harmless' speech says is, shouldn't we be happy now, shouldn't we be content because today is the day we are allowed to run around Daddy's garden without a leash."

"What's wrong with that?"

"It's all wrong," Irina said. "Because the leash isn't the issue. Woof! Woof! We're still treated like dogs."

Natasha ordered vodka for them both and a platter of *zakuski*—a kind of Russian antipasto. When they were alone again, she said, "Olga, Masha, and Irina, Chekhov's three sisters, sit around for hours on end talking about how, one day, they will get to Moscow. They never do, of course, and by the end of the play we've discovered that they live only a few kilometers from the city. I think this is what you are speaking of."

Irina again felt overcome by the irrational wave of jealousy, as if she wanted to shriek at Natasha, What are you doing with Valeri Bondasenko? Are you making love to him every afternoon before rehearsals? Or do you share his bed on the nights when I am not there?

Ridiculous! Impossible! Yet why was she thinking it? Irina held herself together with an effort, wondering again whether she was on the brink of a breakdown. She said, trying to clear her mind of its disturbing emotional clutter, "How smug you are. You think you know just what you are and what you're doing. You run your little school secure in the thought that you're preserving a better place in the state for women. But the truth is, you're blind.

"You're part of the system, and, in a sense, you're worse than the KGB. Everyone knows what the KGB is and what it does. It's no secret. But you are one thing while pretending to be another. You perpetuate the system by telling your students how well off they are now, how grateful to the state they must be for their new, improved status. But what really is your message? Don't complain, be happy, do as you're told. Look how well-off you are. Look how free. It's bullshit!"

"You must want to leave my class, then," Natasha said, finishing off her tea.

"No, I don't. I can put up with the bullshit, just as long as I learn how to act."

"It seems to me," Natasha Mayakova said as the drinks and food were served, "that you won't need many lessons."

They ate in silence for some time. Irina was acutely aware of the tourists, especially their clothes, which she loved to look at and longed to wear. In Boston, in a lingerie store, she had tried on a silk Charmeuse teddy, and had almost passed out from the erotic sensation of the divine material gliding against her flesh. She shot a clandestine glance at Natasha. How she wished she could share her decadent memory with someone. Her whole mind ached to open itself up, to let the secrets piling up inside spill out, to share, to share.

"In acting," Natasha said softly, "we learn to dissect the different personality types found in lead and secondary roles. You have proved tonight that you already possess that talent."

She said it in such a way that Irina found herself saying, "I'm sorry," when she knew she could not possibly mean it.

"Don't be," Natasha said. She wiped her lips on a paper cocktail napkin. "I imagine I deserved it. I haven't been carved up as skillfully since my own first weeks in acting class. I had an instructor who was a marvelous actor, but he was an absolute ogre in the classroom. I worshiped him, and nearly died of delight when he accepted me into his class. From then on I burst into tears in front of him more often than not. I used to lie awake at night, replaying his murderous criticisms, miserable as could be. I could hear his rantings echoing in my dreams. His words stalked me like an apparition, until all I could think about was making him stop."

"Did you?" Irina asked.

"Yes. I became an accomplished actor." Natasha ordered more vodka. "That's all he ever wanted from me. He saw in me—as opposed to the majority of his other students—a potential for greatness. Those are his words, not mine. He made certain I lived up to that potential."

"By making you miserable?"

"By forcing me to look inside myself, to find that potential and mine it for the precious ore he knew was there." Natasha paused while the empty glasses were replaced. "You see, Katya, I was an orphan. I was brought up in a state institution and I had inside of me a ball of ice, a rage against an unknown source. Did my parents die or had they abandoned me? I had no idea. Either way I hated them, because they had rejected me. Their memory lived inside me like a living thing, a malignant growth, eating at me.

"Where did I come from? My mother, my father. My grandparents. Most people know. It seems, in fact, such an elementary bit of knowledge that nobody thinks of it, it's taken for granted. For me it was like walking around with a wound that never healed, a chunk of flesh that was forever gone, for which no one could ever provide an adequate prosthesis. I was different, an outsider. I was always aware of this, but never more painfully so than during holidays when families reunited, drank and ate together, rubbed elbows, laughed and told stories." Natasha was focused on something inside herself, and her irises had gone very dark. "I remember, I remember . . . An actor's curse, to remember everything." She touched her finger to the vodka. "When I was growing up, more than anything else I wanted someone to tuck me in at night, a mother to sing me a lullaby that she had learned at her mother's knee, a father to tell me stories of wolves and goblins, elves and princes."

Natasha pushed her vodka away with such violence that it spilled across the table. "Leave it," she said when Irina moved to mop it up. She sucked the liquor off her finger. "It's important to know it's still there—like memory."

There was a murderous look in her eyes, and Irina was abruptly concerned. Strange! How different people could be from how you imagined them. Natasha had seemed so content on Valeri's arm, so in command on stage. And yet here she was, on the verge of tears, admitting to being lonely and miserable. For a moment Irina forgot her own hate, a mask dropped away and she leaned forward. "Are you all right?"

"What makes you think I'm not?" Natasha snapped.

"You look as if you'd like to kill someone."

"That's interesting," Natasha said. "That's just how you looked this evening when you were playing Albee's Martha."

"Did I?" Irina was shocked. She shuddered. And she found herself thinking, My God, is it possible? I came here to bury this woman, and now I believe that she and I could be friends. I believe that if I told her how I felt when I was in Boston, she would understand. She would understand how miserable I've become here, and she would not immediately report me to the KGB for having treasonous thoughts. Isn't it funny how despair can unite people? How utterly odd and mysterious life is sometimes. "I believe I'll have another vodka," Irina said softly.

Natasha nodded. "I think we ought to make it *starka* this

190

time.'' She was speaking of the aged vodka that ran to 120-proof and beyond.

They were on their second glass of *starka*, still picking over their *zakuski*, when Natasha said. ''The truth is, Katya, I watched you playing Martha tonight, and I saw myself. It was like looking in a mirror, and being able to peer backward through time. My God, what a shock you gave me! And I thought: I must get to know this woman. I have no family; I have no one. Perhaps, in time, I will have her to welcome me at Easter.''

''You're not married?'' Irina asked. It was not merely that she was interested, as in, Are you married and sleeping with Valeri? She desperately needed some guidepost. She was feeling increasingly that being near Natasha Mayakova was like standing on the edge of a quick-following sea. With each roll of a wave onto the beach, the sand on which she stood was eroded further and further, and without seeming to have moved, she was being propelled away from shore, toward the blue-green deep.

Natasha smiled. ''The trouble is I was always far too beautiful for my own good. I attracted men to me like bees to honey. They came at me, and I was never able to determine whether they saw anything beyond my beauty. My face, my body, these are the things they responded to. I knew there was more to me, but did they? That was the question I never seemed able to answer.''

Irina said, ''But for someone like you, with no family, I would have thought marrying and creating a family of your own would have been most important.''

''I think it was *because* I had no family that I had so much trouble accepting the men who came my way. You see, I wanted—I needed—everything to be perfect. What if my husband left me? What if I felt compelled to leave him? I suppose the risk of perhaps repeating what my parents had done paralyzed me, made me incapable of being happy or content in a permanent relationship. I think, when it comes right down to it, I have no faith at all in personal relationships between men and women.''

''I have to admit that I don't, either,'' Irina said. ''Men are such bastards.''

''Yet we need them so much.'' Natasha sighed. ''I often wonder whether we need them because they *are* such bastards.'' She laughed, and this time a surprised Irina joined her.

But then, like a prick from a hidden needle, Irina thought of

Valeri. And her insistent memory dredged up the scene of happy, glowing Natasha strolling down Gorky Street with him. After that first time, Irina had watched, hidden, as they met once or twice a week. Why was Natasha with him unless they were having an affair?

And Irina thought, Either Natasha is lying to me, or Valeri—powerful, manipulative Valeri—has something on her. Which was the more likely possibility? Irina did not have to think twice about it.

Twice a week Mars Volkov emerged from his office, climbed into an official black Chaika, and was driven out of Moscow to Zvezdny Gorodok, Star Town. This was the ultramodern high-rise complex built to house and train Russia's cosmonauts.

There was surely nothing odd in this oft-repeated journey, since Mars's constituency in the Congress of People's Deputies was all of Moscow, including Zvezdny Gorodok, and Star Town was very important to Moscow in particular and the Soviet Union in general.

In Star Town, Mars did his obligatory movie-star turn, charming everyone: the bureaucrats who ran the mini-city, the technicians who thought they ran it, the theoreticians who thought they ran the technicians, and the cosmonauts who inhabited it.

All of Star Town's citizens were pleased to see Mars, save one, and he was the real reason that Mars made this trip twice a week. It was with him that Mars spent most of his time. After the glad-handing of the bureaucrats, the political smiles directed at the technicians, the cogent but not too probing questions asked of the theoreticians, and the backslapping of the cosmonauts in training, came Mars's real work. Interrogation.

The Hero of the disastrous Odin-Galaktika II mission, the first attempt at a manned landing on Mars, had his own building in Star Town. A city within a city within a city, it was manned by its own battalion of scientists, theoreticians, doctors, lab technicians, and security personnel. The place was like a fortress, and deliberately so. First, because of the wishes of the Hero, second, by order of Mars himself. Cleaning up in the aftermath of the Odin-Galaktika II mishap had been Mars's responsibility, and it had been no easy matter. In fact, twenty months after the event, it was still very much an open case, an ongoing—though highly secret—investigation.

The Hero's building was a four-story affair. The basement was filled with generators that powered every appliance in the structure. The first two floors were given over to laboratories and testing chambers, where the doctors read through reams of twice-daily medical readouts on the Hero: heart rate, respiration, EKG, EEG, stress, and the like. The top two floors were for the Hero's living, such as it was.

As Mars went through the elaborate security procedures that he himself had set up, he considered that he had been coming here for more than a year now, ever since this building had been erected, yet the Hero was still as much of an enigma to him as he had been the first day they met. How this was possible, Mars could not imagine. It was not that the Hero was recalcitrant in any way. He responded to interrogation with an openness, even sometimes an eagerness, that Mars found commendable. And yet Mars still had no idea what went on inside the Hero's mind, how he felt, what he thought of anyone or anything. It was as if they had shot a human being out into space and what had come back to them was some kind of an alien.

He had been changed.

Of course, there was the trauma to think of. Not only the sudden, heartstopping death of the man he had trained with, lived with, lifted off with—the man who had his life in his hands—but also the shock of the damage to the spacecraft, the certain knowledge that the mission had failed, and the nagging fear that he would never get to see Earth again. And then there were the effects—still unknown, still being debated by the theoreticians and the scientists—of the seepage of cosmic rays through the fault in the Hero's EVA suit.

All this had to be taken into account when one interviewed the Hero, and Mars, with great diligence, did make allowances when trying to decipher his responses. To no satisfactory conclusion.

"Where is he?" he said to Tatiana, one of the Hero's hand-picked female companion-guards, as he gained the top floor.

"In the pool, comrade," Tatiana said.

"Is he alone?"

"Lara is with him."

Mars nodded. The Hero insisted on women, and who was Mars to deprive him of whatever pleasures were left to him? Heroes had earned the right to take their pleasures wherever they could find them.

Increasingly, it seemed, the Hero preferred water to land. Not surprising, since, alarmingly, the scientists had discovered one of the effects of prolonged weightlessness was to weaken not only muscles but bones, damaging the bones irreparably. These days the Hero looked something like the Hunchback of Notre Dame. By all accounts, Lara and Tatiana, the women assigned to him, apparently did not find his physical appearance all that repugnant, another mystery for Mars to try to decipher.

He saw Lara first, her long, muscular form, clad only in a clinging American-style bathing suit, stretched intriguingly over the edge of the saltwater pool as she fed the blue dolphin. The dolphin had been installed in the pool about six months ago. At first Mars had balked at the outlandish request. But then, in her weekly debriefing, Lara had offered the startling opinion that the Hero required companionship on a plane other than the ones she and Tatiana could evidently provide.

Mars heard the odd, rhythmic clicking the dolphin used as its form of communication. Some weeks ago the monitoring had picked up two sets of this clicking in the dead of night, and upon checking, it had been discovered that the hidden microphones—the concealed cameras could not penetrate the water—had recorded the Hero in the pool, seemingly in verbal contact with the mammal.

Lara turned when she heard his approach. "Good morning, comrade," she said. But she did not stop her feeding of the mammal.

As Mars returned her greeting, he saw the Hero floating in the pool beside the dolphin. It was odd and, if Mars were honest with himself, a bit disquieting that there were so many similarities between the Hero and the dolphin. The radiation that the Hero had been inadvertently exposed to in space had caused his skin to become slick and utterly hairless. He dove and flashed through the water with the ease and apparent familiarity of one born to the sea. He had even, so Lara had reported, spoken to her about asking for an operation that would add membranes between his fingers and his toes.

Mars did not, in fact, know whether or not he was serious. The Hero was prone not only to making bizarre requests, but to playing eerie and disconcerting pranks on those who were observing and monitoring him. Once, for instance, he had placed his heart monitor over the dolphin's heart instead of his own.

The Hero, Mars had concluded, may have been physically maimed in the event, and as a result may or may not have been mentally scarred, but he was still an exceedingly clever fellow. Mars had no illusions concerning the underlying reason for the pool. The Hero knew he was being observed, listened in on, monitored. But in the water his time was his own, and the cunning electronic eyes that followed him were blind there.

"I am," he often told Mars, "like Odysseus stranded on the island of Polyphemous." The first time, to his delight and Mars's chagrin, he had been obliged to explain that Polyphemus was the name of the Cyclops who Odysseus, by cunning and guile, managed to defeat. "Don't be embarrassed," he had said with his poker face, "nowadays I have far more time to read than you do." Mars never knew whether he was being blandly pleasant or cynically ironic.

"Good morning, Viktor," Mars said. "How are you feeling today?"

"Lousy," the Hero said. "And I've told you, don't call me Viktor. I want no names connected with the event used here."

"I should use it," Mars said, sitting on the edge of the pool. "It's your name." He thought, Ah, nothing's changed.

"I'll tell you something which will, no doubt, come as a surprise to you," the Hero said. "I won't lie down. I lived through a horror no man was meant to see, let alone live through. But the fact remains, I did survive. I'm alive. And I will not go willingly into that unquiet night out there just because it may suit your purposes, just because it will salve your embarrassment for me to be swept under the rug. My comrades out there beyond these walls know I'm alive. You can't hurt me and you can't kill me, because they'll know. The cosmonauts. And they'll rebel."

"You are afforded many privileges," Mars said softly. "Lara. Tatiana. The pool. The dolphin. Especially the dolphin. I brought them to you and I can take them away."

"And I can stop talking," the Hero said. "To you and to everyone." He looked at Mars. "Now what have we proved?"

Mars took a small fish from the bucket beside him, dangled it over the water. The dolphin stared at him, then began a long series of clicks.

The Hero threw his head back and laughed. "You know, she's got a better sense of humor than the whole lot of you."

Mars wrinkled his brow in annoyance. "What did the dolphin say?"

"Her name's Arbat," the Hero admonished. "And she doesn't like you one bit."

Mars bit his lip, said as calmly as he could manage, "And did she say why?"

195

"First, you don't use her name. Second, she says you're not to be trusted."

Mars made a sound of disgust. It was intolerable that he should be forced into having a conversation—if that was what you could call this farce!—with a dolphin. But he knew that in order to engage the Hero, he had to make the effort. He said, "How would Arbat know whether or not I can be trusted? She won't even take the food I offer her."

A flood of clicking was followed by the Hero saying, "If you give the fish to Lara, Arbat will take it from her."

"I'm disappointed," Mars said, but he dutifully plopped the fish into Lara's palm. Immediately the dolphin dipped her head, scooped the fish up, swallowed it.

"Viktor," Mars said. "We must talk."

"All right." The Hero stared up at Mars. "But why must you insist on calling me Viktor? I told you not to use any of those names."

It was clear that he had once been exceedingly handsome. But something inexplicable had happened to him up there in the heavens. Mars had seen photos of the Hero before he had been fitted into the Odin-Galaktika II spacecraft and was launched into space. This was not the same man. Oh, surely, the configuration of skull and skeleton were the same, although he was far thinner now, and walked—when he could walk at all, rather than being confined to his special motorized wheelchair—with the lack of assurance and the brittleness of a man of ninety. In fact, that is what Mars would have suspected happened to him up there—the answer to the mystery: an unnaturally rapid aging—had it not been for the fact that the Hero's mind had not deteriorated one iota. It merely had been altered. And so the enigma continued to unfold like a complex origami in front of Mars.

"I call you Viktor," Mars said, "because I must. I have orders to do so." He shifted to keep the floating man in sight. "If it helps, I don't think of you as Viktor, but as the Hero, with a capital H."

"A generic," the Hero said. "Like a military rank."

"I don't see it that way. I don't think of you as the Cosmonaut."

"What can I do for you today, Volkov?" The Hero seemed to have had enough of light banter, and his change in tone put the dolphin on guard. She was, so Mars had been informed, extremely reactive to changes in the Hero's mental and emotional states. Arbat swam away from Lara and her fish, popped up beside the Hero. She started her incessant clicking.

Mars had to keep a rein on his temper. Basic interrogation techniques called for a rhythm to be established. Once you got the subject used to answering questions—no matter how innocuous—it was a much smaller step to get him to give you the answers you sought.

It was one thing to be interrupted by a colleague, but to deal with the interference of an animal was too much. He was about to shout when, looking into the Hero's bland upturned face, he began to suspect that this kind of disturbance was just what the Hero had in mind. The Hero was not unaware of the principles of interrogation, and it would be in character for him to use every method at his disposal to deflect his questions.

"Actually," Mars said, "I came here today to tell you that I'm tired of this little play we've been in. It's like being consigned to act in *No Exit* for eternity. Some kind of bizarre purgatory. I'm willing to call a beet a beet. You've been put here more or less against your will, but so have I. I didn't ask for this assignment, and I haven't been happy with it. As lousy as you feel day to day, I feel almost as bad watching you suffer."

"Do you actually expect me to believe that shit?"

"I'd be naive if I did." Mars rose and, walking about the room, methodically disabled every listening, watching, and monitoring device. Lara stared at him with a kind of terror, but the Hero's face was as bland as ever.

Within thirty seconds they heard shoes pounding on the stairs, and a clutch of the building personnel—two of them armed guards—burst into the room.

"It's nothing," Mars said. "I turned everything off. Go back to your posts."

"But with the machines down," one of the scientists complained, "we have nothing to do."

"Go have lunch," Mars said. "Take a walk. Do what you've never done before, enjoy the sunshine and the spring day with nothing on your minds."

"I hope you have clearance for this," another scientist said. "What you've done has serious implications."

"Get the hell out of my sight!" Mars bellowed in an uncharacteristic display of temper, and the clot of men disappeared.

In the silence that followed, the Hero said, "I want Lara to stay."

"As you wish."

"And I want to come out of the water."

Lara moved toward him, but Mars motioned her back. He bent down, gripped the Hero under his arms, brought him up over the coping of the pool. Lara went to get the wheelchair while Mars propped the Hero up, began to pat him dry with one of a pile of enormous towels.

The Hero wore no bathing suit when he was in the water, and Mars looked interestedly at his body. His hairlessness was somehow fascinating, and though he had to be pulled like a rag doll out of the damaged spacecraft upon landing, his subsequent muscular rehabilitation had been remarkable. (It was his bones that had been irreparably damaged.) And the color of his sleek skin, which could only be described as a kind of pale silver, like a star, glowed in the indirect lights. For the first time Mars could sense why, bent back or no bent back, Lara and Tatiana found the Hero sexually attractive.

Together Mars and Lara maneuvered the Hero into the wheelchair. Lara draped a fresh towel over his loins. The Hero disliked clothes; perhaps, Mars surmised, because they had become so damned inconvenient to get in and out of. And they, more than anything else in his daily life, reminded him of his disabilities.

"What name would you like me to use?" Mars asked, beginning the interrogation rhythm all over again.

"I don't know. But not Viktor. I'm not Viktor."

"Of course you're not."

"How about Odysseus?" That blank face. "I promise I won't call you Polyphemus."

Mars waited a moment, unsure whether this was a concession or another joke at his expense. "All right. How are you sleeping, Odysseus?"

"I don't sleep," the Hero said at once. This was a subject he liked. "I dream. It's not the same thing. When you dream continuously, you're not sleeping, you're living, but in an entirely different way. You're in another state of consciousness."

Mars had become used to this kind of talk. "And your dreams?"

"Are filled with the wonder of space," the Hero said, "and of the stars. I dream of the color I saw out there, the color between the stars."

"What color? Red, green, blue?"

"I can't tell you," the Hero said, "because it's impossible to

198

find words to describe it. It's not even as ephemeral a color as you know it.''

"What do you mean?''

"There's . . . I don't know, a substance to it.''

"A substance such as what? Like your spacecraft had substance?''

"No, not like that at all.''

There was a long pause during which Mars glanced at Lara. She was sitting with her wrists on her knees, gazing into the Hero's eyes. Mars wondered whether her loyalties were wavering. Then he immediately dismissed the thought. He had chosen Lara and Tatiana himself. He knew their backgrounds intimately, so he knew where their loyalties lay. It was just that he was paid to be paranoid. Nevertheless, he told himself, he mustn't allow the business of paranoia to become an obsession. That would clearly undermine his current work.

The Hero cleared his throat. "I've thought about this ever since I first awoke,'' he said after a long time, "and I believe that what I saw out there was the color of God.''

Mars was interested in this. "Why do you think that?''

"Because it's what the dreams tell me, over and over, in as many different ways as there are faces on the people of this planet.''

"Lara,'' Mars said, "do you believe him?''

"Yes.''

The Hero looked at her. "Tell Volkov what you would tell him if this was one of your weekly debriefings.''

Lara was clearly stunned, and Mars only a bit less so. How did the Hero know about the debriefings?

The Hero gave Mars a canny look. "Let's call a beet a beet, yes?''

Mars considered this challenge. Then he nodded at Lara. "Tell me.''

Lara looked from the Hero to him. "I believe him,'' she said, her voice echoing out over the gently lapping pool where Arbat was watching them.

Mars took some time to work this through. "Perhaps,'' he said to the Hero, "your dreams tell you that you *are* God.''

A smile spread slowly from the corners of the Hero's mouth. When it reached his eyes he said, "I'm not mad, Volkov. To intimate so is futile and, worse for you, foolish.''

"I withdraw the intimation,'' Mars said immediately, accepting this little defeat as gracefully as he was able. "You understand it was something I felt compelled to ask."

"And I ask myself why?" The Hero regarded him. "It's not such a great secret, although I'll bet anything *you* think it is. There's only one thing that makes this discussion meaningful, Volkov, and it's that, like me, you believe in God. No, don't bother to deny it—I know you're doing it for Lara's sake. You needn't bother. For one thing, Lara, too, believes in God. So does Arbat, so for once we're all agreed on one matter. And a monumental one it is, too. For another thing, Lara belongs to you, hook, line, and soul. Now isn't that ironic, in a country that professes to put no value on the capitalistic notion of possessions. I see your lips moving, Volkov. What's that? Speak up! Heresy, you say? All right. Then we both have heretical thoughts. You see? You're no better than I am, though I can hardly expect you to agree with me."

Mars glared at the Hero, as if with his gaze he could burn out the mysterious alterations the void of space had worked on that mind.

"The presence of God," said the Hero, "is something we all feel. It's what binds the four of us, even though four more divergent creatures could hardly exist in one place. Or perhaps it's our belief in Him that has brought us together."

"I don't want to speak about God," Mars said.

"Then by all means, we'll change the subject," the Hero said sardonically. "I wouldn't want you to feel discomfited in any way." He smiled, although it was hardly a benign expression. "But before we do, I'll say one thing more. I've got your weakness down pat."

Mars found to his shame that his mouth was dry. He longed for a glass of water, but to ask Lara to get him one would be unthinkable; he could just imagine the Hero laughing at him. "And what is that?" he managed to get out.

"It's essentially this: you don't know what happened to me up there, so no matter what stories I give you, *no matter what I say*, you cannot altogether disbelieve me. Because, even though I don't think of myself as God, in one sense I've become like God. You know absolutely nothing about me."

"You're a man, just like I'm a man. We're both human beings, nothing more." But Mars said this with far more conviction than he felt.

"You know, Volkov, the two of us remind me of a pair of rival Spanish Gypsies. We've challenged each other to a duel.

We're bound together by a six-foot cord. But we've somehow lost our stabbing knives, our conventional weapons, and now we're desperately trying to come up with an alternate way inside each other's defenses. Stalemate.'' That smile, hard as steel, widening. "Or is it? Have you figured it out yet? Haven't you seen its shape emerging from the darkness? Hasn't our duel, rather, evolved into a war of wits?''

"We're not on opposite sides,'' Mars said. "I'm not sure where you got the idea that I am your enemy.''

The Hero said nothing. He was watching Arbat in the pool.

"What do you and the dolphin talk about?'' Mars said suddenly.

"Arbat.''

"Arbat,'' Mars conceded.

"We discuss the universe,'' the Hero said, still looking at the dolphin. "The complexity of existence, the diversity of knowledge. We also contemplate the nature of death.''

Mars was staring at Lara, but apparently she did not think this exchange at all amusing or even odd. Mars abruptly felt an acute sense of dislocation. What is going on here? he asked himself. One of us in this room appears to be mad, but the curious thing is, I don't know who it is.

"What happened up there, in space, in Odin-Galaktika II?'' Mars said. "We lost contact with you; the event took place. I know it was a long time ago—''

"Not for me,'' the Hero said. "It happened yesterday.''

"Well, I know, in some circumstances it must *seem* like—''

"It happened yesterday,'' the Hero repeated. He raised his hands, cupped them into a hollow sphere. "Because I've learned how to bend time in the same way you've learned how to bend light rays.''

And that was another of his disconcerting, dislocating idiosyncrasies. The Hero kept saying "you'' instead of "us,'' as if he no longer belonged to the human race.

"How many times in the past fifteen months since I came out of the coma have you asked me what happened? And how many times have I told you?''

Too many to count, Mars thought. The trouble was, no one believed him. How could they?

He said, "Nevertheless, I'd appreciate it if you would tell me again.''

"Again?'' the Hero asked. "Or one more time?''

The two men grinned at each other, and Mars thought, He's

quite right, this is a war of wits. I must ensure that he doesn't win it.

"We had put the Mars module components together in Earth's orbit," the Hero began. "Everything was going just fine. We were working well together. I guess, in the end, you were right in paring the crew down from ten to two. We never would have made it in such a huge module. It was very difficult putting together the sections of the smaller module you sent up in different payloads.

"We blasted out of Earth's orbit into the Mars injection trajectory. We began the next phase of the mission. We were well past the gravitational pull of the Moon. How incredible it was to see that satellite up close. For those moments of the flyby, I was a child again, staring up through a clear winter's sky and wondering, What's it like up there? Now I knew, and it was giving me the chills. I was actually sick from the sight of it, as if it were too much to take in, as if I were Moses approaching the burning bush. But, of course, I was wrong. That would come later.

"We were in deep space. Mars was beckoning us like a red titan. We slept like dead men. We were told that would happen on a mission of almost three years. Day fatigue sets in. Because we were hooked up to Mission Control, you knew just when we were awake and when we were asleep. The funny thing was that I never dreamed. I know I've said this over and over to the psychiatrists and they don't believe me because the hard medical evidence refutes it. They told me your readouts showed I had REM every night cycle. They insisted I dreamed; that I just never remembered my dreams. Well, I may have had rapid eye movement, but I tell you that I *did not* dream. I have always remembered my dreams, ever since I was a little boy. And I think now that one reason I didn't dream was because I felt as if I was dreaming while I was awake.

"Another thing is that the psychiatrists said I talk altogether too much about dreams. They say I'm fixated on dreams. But in the scheme of what happened to me up there, I'm convinced that not dreaming is significant, even if no one else does. I know they think I'm lying or, at least, delusional about what happened during the event. Otherwise I wouldn't still be here, and you wouldn't continue to interrogate me. I know what you're like. You hate a mystery; you'll tear apart heaven and earth to solve it."

The Hero abruptly began to laugh, continuing in a crescendo.

Through his tears he gasped, "Heaven and earth, that's very, very funny. I don't know what's come over me. Before I lifted off, I never had much of a sense of humor. Who knows, perhaps being suspended between heaven and a living hell will do that for you."

Mars felt he had to pierce the encroaching silence before it got impenetrable. "What happened to Gregor?" he said.

"No names!" the Hero shouted. He was extremely agitated. "Goddamnit, I told you! I warned you! But you're a thick sonuvabitch, you never listen! Now fuck off!"

"I'm sorry," Mars said. "I apologize. I forgot."

"Like hell you did." The Hero turned away, began an incomprehensible conversation of clicks with Arbat.

Mars looked at Lara. Her face was calm, firm. Did he see the hint of a rebuke in her expression?

He tried again. "What should we call your partner who died? Odysseus, did you hear me?"

"Menelaus," the Hero said, without turning away from Arbat.

"All right. What happened to Menelaus?"

"He died," the Hero said suddenly. "He was outside. We were both suited up, although I was still inside the vehicle. It was a typical EVA, planned way in advance. Everything was fine. Until . . ." He was silent for a long time. "What I think happened was that we encountered some kind of storm in the form of a shower of tiny particles, like minuscule meteors. I heard a hollow sound, like someone throwing a handful of sand at the vehicle's hull. Then I heard his voice. It was already breaking up, and I knew it was an emergency. I put on my helmet, got out of the airlock as quickly as I could.

"What I saw . . . His helmet had been pierced by the burst of cosmic storm. We were hanging in darkness, but there was this light all around. I don't mean starlight, that's separate and distinct. I saw what had happened to him in the illumination of this . . . light between the stars. His visor had been riddled by the sand of space or of a far distant world. Who knows the truth? We never will, that's for certain.

"All the atmosphere, the pressure, had been sucked out of his EVA suit in the time it took me to get to him. He was hanging there, at the end of his umbilical. The expulsion from inside his suit had created a force, and he was spinning, spinning. His eyes were staring straight ahead, and he was . . . I don't know how to say this properly because it was so horrible . . . he was

203

smiling, as if in defiance of the bruises and contusions that puckered his face like the seas of the Moon. Then I had him, stopped his spinning and drew him back toward the vehicle. I knew he was dead. I knew there was nothing I could do for him.

"Then I got a good look at his face. It was as if, I don't know, something had blasted his eyes. At first I assumed some of the cosmic sand had penetrated him. But then I knew that couldn't be because only his eyes were affected."

Silence again, and Mars was obliged to say, "What happened to Menelaus's eyes? What did you see there?"

The Hero put his head down. "What's the use of going on? You won't believe me because your forensic evidence contradicts my story."

"No. The evidence doesn't corroborate what you've told us. That isn't the same thing. Forensics on Menelaus were utterly inconclusive. The truth is, we could tell nothing from his corpse. It was as if it had been wiped clean of evidence. How did he die, what happened to cause his suit to malfunction—or yours, for that matter—what happened to him during those crucial minutes when he was on the EVA, when you were struggling to get to him? Of one thing we're sure: there was an interplanetary disturbance of some sort. Our telemetry went down during the event. We had no monitoring capability. We don't know."

The Hero raised himself up in his wheelchair. "I've told you what happened."

"Yes," Mars said slowly. "You have."

"But no one believes me."

"Frankly, what you've told us makes belief somewhat difficult." Mars nodded. "Yes. There are some who think you're lying, or have misremembered, or are delusional."

The Hero's eyes locked on Mars's. "Are you one of those?"

He knew this was a crucial moment. There comes a time in every interrogation when the pendulum begins to swing the other way, when psychologically an enemy can be transformed into a friend. This moment comes for many reasons: the subject wants an end to isolation, or he can no longer distinguish the truth from fantasy, or his disorientation has become so acute he cannot properly recognize his own emotions. The Hero was far stronger and smarter than the average subject. In his case, he had asked the fatal question because Mars had allowed him to see partway inside of him. The Hero required a kindred spirit, someone beyond either Lara or Arbat, who were both incomplete entities, though in totally different ways.

Mars knew immediately that the Hero would sense a lie. He was vulnerable, but that only made him doubly dangerous. Mars would not fall into the trap that had destroyed many an interrogator: mistaking vulnerability for weakness.

Mars said, "The truth is, I don't know what to believe. The forensics are useless, and those of us who stubbornly cling to scientific principles are, I think, missing the point." He left his hands open and palms up as a subtle reinforcement. "I don't believe you're lying. What reason would you have to do so? And the chances of you misremembering are, in my opinion, too remote to consider."

"But I might be delusional."

"As you yourself said, no one knows what happened to you up there. All I'm certain of is, we can't dismiss outright what you've told us. Which is why I'd like to hear it again, not from a tape made a month or a year ago, but from you, now."

Mars could almost see the Hero's mind turning over what it had just heard. It was fascinating, like watching a snake digesting its prey.

At length the Hero nodded. "I remember this in the most minute detail. It was his eyes, Menelaus's eyes. There were no pupils at all. It was as if the irises had grown inward and outward. It was as if his eyes were now all color. And what color! His eyes had taken on that color, the color between the stars. The color of God."

Mars said, "He spoke to you, is that right? The corpse opened its mouth and—"

"No, no." The Hero shook his head. "This isn't something out of a science-fiction or a horror film. He didn't come back from the dead, nor was he animated like a zombie or a golem. This was something else, something that I think you'd have to see for yourself to fully believe. I still don't understand it, even after fifteen months of contemplating it from all angles: physical, metaphysical, philosophical, religious. It wasn't magic, Volkov. I'm not a fool. And it wasn't illusion."

The Hero took a deep breath. "The truth of the matter is, the corpse did not move its lips, it did not speak to me. But something communicated *through* it. Through its eyes. Do you begin to understand? We're not confronting any conventional method of communication as we know it. Not even telepathy.

"Nevertheless, there was a message in those eyes, in that world of unspeakable color."

Mars was aware of Lara leaning forward, slipping her hand

205

into the Hero's. Mars took his cue from her. "And what was the communication?" he asked gently.

The Hero's eyes were dark, swirling with emotion. He uttered a harsh Russian expletive. "Don't you people understand anything?" he cried. "That's what I meant by my being suspended between heaven and a living hell. I was given a message, *but I don't know what it is.*"

It was a perfect day for Arkhangelskoe: cool, crisp, cloudless. One arrived in the beautiful countryside surrounding the estate by taking the Kutuzov Prospekt out of the center of Moscow, picking up the Minsk road, making a right onto the Rublevo road, a left onto the Uspenskoe road all the way to the right fork that took you across the Moskva River, and thence southwest into Arkhangelskoe.

This was the route Valeri Bondasenko took. He went once a week, but never on the same day, and never at the same time. The estate consisted of a stucco-over-wood late eighteenth-century palace with its signature belvedere and a beautiful park on the verge of a vast pine and birch forest. Tourists flocked here in good weather to wander, take photos, and picnic.

Valeri came here to partake of none of those pastoral pleasures. Instead, he circumnavigated Arkhangelskoe, taking the narrow road that skirted the forest to the east and then curved north.

On the far side of the forest was a rather austere stone and mortar structure, through whose forbidding gates Valeri drove. He parked beside delivery vans, shabby Volgas and Zhigulis without windshield wipers.

Inside, the place smelled of disinfectant and, in places, vomit. White-coated nurses hurried to and fro, thick-shouldered, stern-visaged. Here and there a male attendant with a truncheon on his hip could be seen, peering through mesh-reinforced windows set in the doors at eye level. To call this place an insane asylum would, perhaps, be harsh, but it would nevertheless be correct.

Valeri hated this place. It reminded him of everything that was wrong with the world. The dimly lit halls might have smelled of chemicals and offal, but the place reeked of despair. The personnel were just as much to blame for this as were the inmates. This was a terminus point for them, worse than a backwater, a sentence to be served with the patience of the penitent. Except there was no escape from this place, either by the inmates or by their wardens. Everyone here was serving a life sentence, and their invisible secretions oozed through the corridors like putrefaction through a swamp.

When Valeri arrived back in Moscow from his sojourns here, he invariably found himself stripping off his clothes, plunging himself into an ice-cold shower, scrubbing himself with tallow-rich soap, washing and washing. What was he trying to get off?

Filth was easy to wash down the drain, but memories were another story altogether. Memory existed independently of conscious thought, or so it seemed to Valeri. He was an ardent student of Jung, and had seen in several of his interlocking concepts a compression of time, a commingling of past-present-future that was fundamental to all human beings, as if each culture were not, in fact, separate, but rather a different quadrant of one gigantic spider's web. And what was there, glistening at the web's center, but a central core, a past that was true for all men?

This included man's ability—yes, perhaps even a desire—to be inhuman to his fellow man. Homicide—mass murder—was such an inadequate way to describe, over the course of history, what man insisted on perpetrating against his neighbor—*especially* his neighbor.

Was it so very long ago, 1918, that Valeri's uncle had been shot in the streets of Kiev—the capital of the Ukraine—for daring to speak Ukrainian? A Bulgarian—can you imagine!—had been the president of the Ukraine then, cat's-paw to the rulers in Moscow, and he had stated publicly that to sanction the use of the Ukrainian language would be reactionary, of interest only to a minority: the kulaks—the Ukrainian peasants—who broke their backs to harvest wheat for all of Russia, and the intelligentsia. So a Russian soldier, one of so many in Kiev, had walked up to Valeri's uncle and put a bullet through his head. Guilty as charged, your honor! Boom!

And what of Valeri's father? It was, Valeri knew, better not to contemplate his ultimate fate. It was so very Russian, and so very terrible.

Valeri shook himself as he stepped outside onto the shaded lawn. His gaze followed the greensward as it ran down to the beginning of the pine and birch forest, on whose far side, invisible now, as unimaginable amid this noisome clamor as a fairy-tale castle, lay beautiful Arkhangelskoe. Why these dark thoughts?

"Comrade Kolchev?"

Valeri heard Dr. Kalinin's voice, and he knew. He turned, forced a smile onto his face, nodded. "Doctor."

"It's good of you to come," Dr. Kalinin said, in much the same tone of voice one hears in a funeral home. Valeri was convinced that Dr. Kalinin did not mean to sound like a mortician, he just couldn't help himself. It was this place or, more accurately, what inhabited this place, that was to blame. When one spent one's days and nights with the living dead, one could not help but be affected in some way.

Dr. Kalinin was a young man with thin, light hair and eyes sunken into his cheeks. Valeri could not imagine what he had done to be consigned to this purgatory at so early an age, and he had no desire to find out. Still, he pitied the doctor.

"You must get more sun," Valeri said, indicating the cloudless day. "Too much time indoors is bad for one's health."

"Ah, the long winter," Dr. Kalinin said. "Now that it's spring, things will be different." But his morose expression betrayed him as it told the truth: here it will never be different than it is right now.

Valeri stuffed his hands into his trouser pockets, led the way out over the lawn, which was dotted here and there with chairs inhabited by mentally and emotionally shrunken creatures, pathetic husks, overseen by attendants looming in their frail shadows. Valeri needed to get as much space as he could between himself and the godawful corridors of the place. He still had their stench in his nostrils, and he felt like gagging. That would be something to talk about, he thought, throwing up all over the good doctor's shoes, so sorry, comrade, but this place you work in turns my stomach, you do understand, don't you?

"She's awake," Dr. Kalinin said, broaching the subject they both knew was so fragile. "I'm sure she'd be delighted to see you."

Why does he keep doing this? Valeri asked himself. Why draw the veil of illusion over any of this? And then he had his answer. It was obvious, really. How else could Dr. Kalinin live with himself in this hideous den of horrors. Some sense of normalcy needed to be imposed on the abnormal, the heart of anarchy, the eye of chaos, otherwise the madness that crept through these corridors would one day curl around your spinal cord and infect you.

That explanation notwithstanding, Valeri would be goddamned if he'd allow this man to impose his lunatic set of rules

208

on him. He said, "Doctor, my daughter hasn't been delighted by anything in her entire life. She isn't capable of delight— although, God knows, the poor thing certainly feels despair. I'm aware of it as soon as I come near her." It's as palpable as the scent of a rose, he thought. It haunts my dreams.

"Perhaps these visits would become easier to handle if you could manage to come more often."

Valeri stood stock-still, his hands clenched into white fists. Do you understand me at all, Doctor? he thought. Do you know that there are times—like now—when I'd cheerfully shoot you between the eyes, and never feel a moment's remorse? Of course you can't know. Otherwise you wouldn't be standing here with that prissy superior expression on your face. It's true I pity you; but I also hate your guts. Your daughter is normal and healthy, and mine is . . .

"I come as often as I am able."

"Of course you do, comrade. I was only making a clinical suggestion. One that I think would be helpful for your daughter."

You idiot! Don't you understand that my daughter is beyond the help of your antiquated theories? Valeri wanted to shout. But, of course, he could do no such thing. He was here as a private citizen, Comrade Kolchev, a machinist with no ties to anyone in government, let alone to the Politburo. In his position—with so many enemies circling him at a respectful distance—Valeri knew that his daughter could only be a liability, a fatal weakness he could not afford, her existence a pry bar to lever him out of power. Otherwise, he thought, why in the name of all that's holy would I have allowed her to be put in a back-water pesthole like this?

Valeri said in a perfectly normal voice, "My daughter does not know who I am, Doctor. It makes no difference to her whether or not I come to see her, let alone how many times a week I come. She absorbs nothing from her surroundings. Am I getting through to you?"

"It's true that she has no manifest reaction, comrade, but can we really presume to know what goes on in her mind?"

Doctor, you're a bug, a worm, a slimy toad, Valeri thought. The way you look down on me makes me want to puke. But, you know what, I'll never let on that's how I feel. Through a complex set of circumstances even I can't undo, you're in charge of my daughter, and I don't want to antagonize you even a little, because even with a mind empty of thought, my daughter is precious to me.

"You're right, of course," Valeri said. "One mustn't give up hope, must one?"

Dr. Kalinin smiled. "Now that's the spirit. Why don't you wait here, comrade, as is your custom, and I'll fetch her for you."

"That's very kind of you," Valeri said, though he was quite certain that even one glance at his daughter's blank face today would set him to screaming. "I appreciate all your help."

"I'm glad to be of service," Dr. Kalinin said, striding off purposefully back to his house of horrors.

Valeri strolled farther down the lawn until he came to a large birch tree. There was a slat-backed wooden bench facing it, and he sat in it. Beside him, a slender young man sat with his face turned up to the sun. His hair was long and lank, and he had a strawberry birthmark on his cheek.

"Have you heard the latest, comrade?" the young man said. "The nationalist group, White Star, has forced the administration to abandon its underground nuclear testing in Semipalatinsk."

"Is that so?" Valeri said. "I thought it was stopped because of the protests of a Kazakhstanian environmental group."

"Hah!" the young man said. "Government propaganda. It was White Star, I tell you."

White Star. Everywhere he went, it seemed, Valeri heard the name White Star. He did not look at the young man, stared instead at the birch tree. He liked this spot; principally, he thought, because the old birch reminded him of the one outside his childhood home in Kiev. But then seeping into his thoughts: the gunshot, his uncle's blood staining the streets, the Russian soldier kicking the still-warm corpse, saying, *A lesson learned, eh, comrade?* And Valeri's father opening his mouth, about to say something, then turning away, tears in his eyes. How many times had his father told him that story, until it seemed that he had been there at his father's side, holding his hand.

Father.

How could they have done that to you?

Far better not to think of what had happened. So many years ago. But, as Jung would say, no time at all. Pain beat like a hammer on an anvil in Valeri's soul; a Russian as well as a Ukrainian soul, it never forgot.

Five minutes later Dr. Kalinin appeared. By that time Valeri was alone, the young man with the strawberry birthmark having wandered away. At Dr. Kalinin's side was a pale-skinned young girl.

It occurred to Valeri that it was impossible to tell his daughter's age from either her face or her unformed body. She was eighteen, but her years on this earth had been nothing more than a dream, a whisper of the wind, a cry for help, lost in the forest, echoing so far away that Valeri did not even know where to search.

Looking at her thick golden hair, her blue eyes, her pristine beauty, he resolved again to come to grips with the fact that she was beyond his help. But more than anything in the world, he wanted to communicate with her, and he, Valeri Denysovich Bondasenko, supreme pragmatist, could not reconcile himself to this reality.

Dr. Kalinin turned Valeri's daughter to face him, and Valeri said, *"Koshka."* Darling. And, despite himself, despite the presence of Dr. Kalinin, a tear leaked out of his eye, ran down his cheek to drop at his feet.

"My granny once told me a proverb, 'Strangers begin with your own family,'" Big Ezoe said. "You would do well to remember that."

Honno said, "There are only strangers in my world now." She used the word *hito*, which could be translated as "people," but always with a pejorative twist to it. *Hito* were never insiders; they were always strangers.

"I want to thank you for moving me out of Eikichi's house," Honno went on. "I have asked nothing of him except that I never see him again."

They were sitting on a sofa in an apartment of considerable size. Big Ezoe was in a dark business suit, Honno in a pair of natural silk city shorts and long shirt-jacket, an outfit she had just bought. Lamps of various sizes and shapes illuminated a room filled with chic contemporary Western furniture. They had just returned from a long, leisurely dinner in a rough, smoky restaurant, surrounded by sumo wrestlers busily consuming everything in sight.

Outside, the last vestiges of moonlight were about to be obscured by scudding storm clouds.

"I trust you're pleased with your new accommodations," Big Ezoe said, spreading his arms wide.

"It's magnificent," Honno said. She got up, went to the win-

211

dows. "I always dreamed of having an apartment that overlooked the Sumida. Look! Moonlight on the river! It's like a woodblock print." She felt as if she were seeing the city from an entirely new perspective.

She turned to face Big Ezoe. "I'm still in something of a state of shock, and part of that, I suppose, is intimidation. The size of this place is immense, so very American."

Big Ezoe laughed. "It's true that my American friends feel at home here. They always feel so crowded and cramped in Tokyo, they tell me. They're grateful to stay here."

"You needn't worry," Honno said, immediately concerned. "I won't be here long."

Big Ezoe waved a hand. "Stay as long as you need to," he said. "I have many such apartments all across Tokyo."

"Well, there's the expense to think of."

"Why should you think of it?" Big Ezoe said. "I don't." Honno looked at him, and he nodded. "Now you're thinking, Why is he doing this? What does he want from me, and when is he going to exact his price?"

"No, I—"

"It's perfectly natural to have such thoughts. First, I am Yakuza. Second, you hate my guts. You yourself said as much when we met again. This is not a combination to inspire a sense of trust, is it?"

Honno found it impossible to answer. She had never before encountered anyone who had the temerity to be so direct, to cut through the layers of ritualized fabrication that seemed an integral part of every conversation.

"But the fact is that my interest is a simple one: the evidence of wrongdoing your friend Kakuei Sakata left behind in those cryptic ledgers. I have many important ties to the business community. I don't know what Sakata knew, what he had gotten hold of, but it is important for me to find out, before anyone else does and leaks it to the authorities, such as your husband."

"But—"

"It is time to get on with things. Are you ready, Mrs. Kansei?" Big Ezoe produced a memo pad, tore off the top sheet of paper, handed it to her. "This is your itinerary for tonight. Please follow it. I promise you will be neither disappointed nor bored. There's a car waiting for you downstairs. The driver has a copy of the itinerary, and he's familiar with all the venues."

"But what about Giin and the ledgers?"

"I'll meet you at the Ginza club at six tomorrow morning,

212

and we'll discuss everything then." Big Ezoe rose. "Now I must leave you. Enjoy yourself tonight, Mrs. Kansei."

There was, indeed, a driver waiting for Honno outside. He bowed, opened the back door of a pearl-gray 560 SEL Mercedes with tinted windows. The night air was already heavy with hints of the coming bad weather. Honno ducked into the cool, dimly lit interior, found someone already in the backseat.

"Good evening, Mrs. Kansei," a thin young man said pleasantly. He wore his thick hair slicked back over his delicate ears; a pair of wide, masculine sunglasses was wrapped around his eyes. He was dressed in an immaculate dove-gray summerweight suit, with a starched white shirt and a rep tie. Honno noticed gold cuff links and a ring that appeared to be a nugget of gold. "I am Fukuda," he said. "Big Ezoe asked me to be your guide tonight. Will that be convenient." There was no interrogative at the end of the sentence, and therefore it lost its usual meaning.

The enormous Mercedes was already slipping effortlessly through the choked Tokyo streets. How it was able to do that, Honno could not imagine. It was as if she had entered another world, someplace that most people never knew existed, let alone ever got to see; a world where the natural laws of physics, economics, and social customs were void, a world of smoke and dreams. Honno put her head back, luxuriating in the feel of the German leather, and thought of nothing.

Their first stop was in Shinjuku. Honno and Fukuda rode the high-speed elevator to the fortieth floor. He led her down a corridor filled only with the hushed whisper of the air-conditioning.

Fukuda produced a key. They slipped through a small door just down the hall from a set of imposing double doors on which was painted one character in *kanji*, KAGA, along with the corporate logo in three-dimensional bronze, which was as universally known as that of Mitsubishi or Panasonic.

The rooms through which they passed like ghosts were silent, save for the battery of fax machines running, now and again, like arcane radios, picking up the random conversation of the cosmos, sending out their own messages in timed sequence to Australia, West Germany, the United States, on and on, a bizarre automated communication among masses of electronic circuits and silicone chips, whole cities of a new civilization.

At length Fukuda turned a doorknob, and as he did so, he put his forefinger briefly across Honno's lips. Shhh. Honno found herself in a secretary's anteroom. The window behind the empty desk had its blinds up, and a brilliant shaft of light shot outward. Fukuda led her around to an area of shadow where they could stand and peer into the inner office, assured of not being seen themselves.

Inside, a heavyset middle-aged man was busy on the sofa with a woman who had her skirt up over her hips. Fukuda put his lips to Honno's ear. "The man is Kaga's senior vice-president of finance. Does the woman look familiar?"

Honno looked, was stunned to recognize Mama-san from the house that Big Ezoe owned, where they had discovered her husband with his lover.

Honno watched, fascinated, as the Kaga vice-president worked assiduously on his own pleasure. It was odd, she thought, how incongruous, even grotesque, the act could appear without the elusive ingredient of sexual attraction. The one true magic potion—passion—was the great leveler that cut through race, religion, even class. Honno considered it the most powerful force on earth. How many great men had been laid low by their lust?

Fukuda gestured, and Honno followed him silently back through the maze of offices, the whirring fax machines.

Downstairs, the streets were slick with moisture. A kind of precipitation was falling on Tokyo that could not quite be called rain. It had picked up so much of the industrial pollutants in the air that it fell like sleet, though the temperature was warm. One day the Japanese would find a term for it, just as they would find a way to describe the automatic nocturnal conversations between faxes.

The purring Mercedes took Honno and Fukuda onward, through the nocturnal traffic, deep into the heart of Shinjuku, dark with forbidden pleasures despite the sprays of brilliant neon shooting up the sides of buildings, reflected endlessly in glass towers, spreading like dye along the wet tarmac of the streets.

The Mercedes slid to a stop in front of an *udon*—a noodle parlor. Fukuda took Honno through the dingy, steamy restaurant, down a long dark hallway that echoed with the tiny sounds of the city seeping through the walls like sweat.

They entered what was obviously a Yakuza gambling house. Long low tables were set out upon the floor, around which were arrayed an interesting melange of men. They were illuminated by wide-shaded lamps hung by cords from the ceiling.

Fukuda and Honno kept to the shadows ringing the walls.

Honno could see the *irizumi*-covered Yakuza, their fantastically conceived tattoos given a life of their own by the movements of their bodies as they moved packets of money around the tables.

This was no local gambling house; these were games played for the highest possible stakes. And now Honno began to concentrate on the faces that belonged to the gamblers: the conservatively dressed, immaculately groomed, sober-visaged men, men such as she had seen every day of her business week trooping in and out of Kunio Michita's office.

Fukuda leaned unobtrusively toward her, whispered, "The third man on your left. The one with the pencil mustache and the largest bets in the house. He is the senior vice-president for administration for Kaga."

Honno watched as if enwrapped by a kind of enchantment, as the senior Kaga officer proceeded to lose 6,500,000 yen—approximately $50,000—in just over an hour. By that time his hair was disheveled, his tie was askew, there was sweat beading his pencil-thin mustache, and he was frantically writing out a marker for an equal amount. The marker was passed from one Yakuza to another until, at length, it arrived at the head of the table.

A bald man with the image of a dragon tattooed on his shining skull took the slip, read it. Then he looked up, poker-faced. With a little thrill, Honno saw that he was looking directly at Fukuda. Fukuda gave an almost imperceptible nod, and the man with the dragon tattoo pocketed the marker, slapped three packets of yen onto the table, had them passed to the Kaga officer.

Honno was wondering just how deeply Big Ezoe's claws had penetrated the Kaga conglomerate when they arrived at their third destination. They were still within the precincts of Shinjuku, but this was the far side, where sleazy streets were inhabited by all manner of nocturnal creature, where it was often not safe to walk deep in the night when these creatures slithered out of their lairs. Honno had certainly heard enough stories of this section of Shinjuku—every resident of Tokyo had, she imagined—but she had never been near it.

"Have no fear, Mrs. Kansei," Fukuda said, as if reading her mind. "You are with me." They stepped out onto the rainswept streets. It was now well after midnight.

There was a scent Honno was not familiar with. It was the stench of the effluvia of a large city—any city—where a certain section of human wreckage congregated: the psychologically halted, the emotionally crippled, the perverse and the perverted, caged, sent down, inhabiting a nighttime netherworld in the bowels of the city.

The Mercedes had stopped opposite a dark bridge over which rumbled an endless line of trucks which only had access to Tokyo's streets during the night.

Fukuda did not lead Honno across the bridge, but rather took her down under it. She could hear the lapping of the river against ancient wooden pilings, and the stench of decomposition was very strong.

They went into a building. Honno recognized it as an *akachochin*, an assignation bar, where anything and everything could be bought—for a price.

In the unpleasant crimson illumination of its interior, Honno saw beautifully clothed and coiffed women whispering on the arms of salesmen, low-level businessmen who could not afford the more affluent after-hours clubs in Nihonbashi or the Ginza, where even the price of one drink could take your breath away.

"The man directly in front of you," Fukuda said unexpectedly, "the distinguished one with the thick gray hair, is the chairman of Kaga. He comes here because of his sexual proclivities. He is certain that no one who would recognize him would ever frequent such a dive."

"But he's wrong," Honno said. "You've recognized him."

"We are always wrong," Fukuda said cryptically. "Big Ezoe owns this *akachochin*. You would be astounded at the wide range of information that may be acquired in places such as this." Fukuda nodded. "Now watch as we walk past the creature who has the chairman's undivided attention."

Honno kept her eyes on the beautifully dressed woman on the Kaga chairman's arm. As they passed the couple, Honno stifled a gasp of recognition. The woman was a man. A transvestite.

Outside the *akachochin*, Honno breathed deeply. She welcomed the rain pattering down on her. How her perceptions had changed. The night air, filled with decomposition, seemed almost pure compared to the atmosphere inside, gravid with sinister lusts.

In the sanctuary and comfort of the Mercedes, they slipped across the river, headed toward the bright lights, the modern high rises of an entirely different Tokyo.

In the Akasaka district the Mercedes sped them toward the Capitol Tokyo Hotel. In the Origami Coffee House, Fukuda ordered them the justly famous German apple pancakes. Honno found that she had no appetite. She watched in a kind of numbed silence as Fukuda ate his food then, determining she had no intention of eating hers, cut into her pancakes.

Five minutes after he had finished, as if on cue, he turned toward the entrance to the restaurant. Honno followed his gaze, saw to her amazement her boss, Kunio Michita, walk through the door. He spoke briefly to the hostess, who seated him at a table with a man Honno had not noticed before. Now she did. He was the finance minister of Japan.

The two men bowed cordially to one another and began to talk in animated fashion. They ordered only coffee, but hardly touched their order. Minutes later they got up to leave.

Fukuda paid the check and took Honno out. They followed the two men out into the semidarkness of the night. All around them glittering high rises bespoke the enormous wealth of the new Japan.

Honno could find nothing strange in this assignation. She saw only two men meeting for a friendly discussion. It was then that she saw the buff-colored envelope pass from Kunio Michita's hand to that of the finance minister's. It was quickly put away in the finance minister's inside jacket pocket. The men continued their stroll, their talk, as if nothing had happened. Ten minutes later they parted.

Fukuda and Honno continued their walk through Akasaka. Honno thought of the fantastic run of luck Michita Industries had had over the past year: winning bids, coming in at just the right time on government-sponsored projects, always being eligible for government incentives in new and emerging industries, closing down divisions just before the ministries declared their product obsolete or nonpriority. Now she knew that luck had nothing to do with it. No wonder it had not rubbed off on her.

All around them, the superstructure of Tokyo rose into the clouds and the rain. The sky was so low, it was bright with the city's efflorescence. Tokyo stood as a modern miracle of terraforming. Honno had always loved this city, but now, as if with a twist of a kaleidoscope, she was seeing it from another vantage point.

She remembered, at the beginning of this evening, looking out the window of the apartment Big Ezoe had given her, seeing the moonlight play across the bosom of the Sumida River. A dream of hers had been fulfilled. But now she had been exposed to the opposite side of that dream, a nightmarish world that harbored every form of perversion, corruption, and deceit. And these two worlds were part of the same Tokyo. Her Tokyo. My God, she thought. What I've witnessed is monstrous. How will I ever fall in love with Tokyo again?

Fukuda led her into a small park. There was one stone bench. Honno could hear the soft tinkling of a stream but she could not see it. They sat on the bench, which had a view of the park's lone tree, a cryptomeria that leaned far to its right, as if caught in a high wind.

"I particularly enjoy this spot," Fukuda said, as if to himself. "Often, I find the grid of the city overly grim, like staring at a detailed blueprint for far too long. Its beauty is leached away by familiarity. Then I come here, and look at this cryptomeria."

"Poor tree," Honno said. "It looks as if the hand of God has mauled it."

"On the contrary," Fukuda said, "it seems to me that the cryptomeria's beauty is transfigured, made awesome by its pain. Look. The stark contrast of its bark and needles to the backdrop of steel and glass and neon; the twisting of its trunk arcs against the rectangles of the buildings. Whether nature or man is responsible for the tree's form, no one can say."

And then Honno understood what Fukuda meant. It did not matter which was responsible for the tree's form. Nature and man were here become one. This was the purpose of the cryptomeria, as if by its tortured appearance it could bring meaning out of the inchoate meaninglessness of the city.

"Yes," Honno said. "I believe I, too, would enjoy coming back here from time to time."

It was nearly three A.M. Their last stop was a bunkerlike building in Shimabashi. It was made of ferroconcrete and was absolutely featureless, an ultramodern edifice set off by the older buildings that surrounded it.

Inside was a world of semidarkness, similar to what one found in the heart of a forest. "You may change in there," Fukuda said, indicating a door.

Honno went through, stripped, bathed, clothed herself in a fresh white *gi*, the cotton divided skirt, the loose overblouse of the martial arts discipline. She was alone in the *dojo* for several minutes. It was very different from the one she worked in with Big Ezoe at his club in the Ginza. This space was darker, far more forbidding. She felt as if she were deep in the castle keep of the Shogun, Ieyasu Tokugawa.

Fukuda soon appeared. He was wearing a protective wire-mesh mask and carrying two *bokken*, the traditional wooden swords used in *kenjutsu* practice instead of the steel *katana*. He also carried another mask.

"How are your swordfighting skills, Mrs. Kansei?" Fukuda asked as he threw her a *bokken* and the mask and began his advance, all in one movement.

Honno did not even have time to answer him. He took her through the entire range of attack and parry strategies, from firecut to fallen leaves, from sea-land change to crossing at the ford. Honno did her best to respond, but she was unused to being up all night, and this, combined with the shocks she had received while walking Tokyo's seamy underbelly, caused her focus to wander, and consequently made this an inauspicious time to work on her *kenjutsu*.

However, as she well knew, one could rarely choose the time of battle, and so one needed to concentrate within and through every conceivable type of situation. So she gathered herself, bore down a little harder with her mind and with her body.

And from this determination, she discovered something interesting: Fukuda was toying with her. She could sense it now that she was concentrating, in the laziness of his parries, in the haphazard manner with which he chose to move from strategy to strategy.

There was, as a foundation of Honno's curriculum in *kenjutsu*, the necessity to unlock the secret of your opponent's strategy. With that knowledge, one divined weaknesses as well as strengths. Now one's own strategy was quickly formed: a series of attacks and parries, building in a kind of crescendo, to weaken the opponent bit by bit, to strip him of his defenses, and then to attack with the one, swift fatal strike.

What was Fukuda's strategy? His haphazardness made his intentions impossible to fathom. But the real question was, was he merely sloppy or was he being devious? Was he hiding his strategy or did he, in fact, have none?

Honno's *kenjutsu sensei* had told her that it was far better to overestimate an opponent than to underestimate him. With this in mind, Honno kept her concentration strong and slowly expanded her *wa*.

She did not seek in any overt way to take control of the match. This, she suspected, was just what Fukuda wanted her to do, and in becoming careless, to fall into a trap he had lying in wait for her. She had not forgotten the lesson learned in her *aikido* bout with Big Ezoe, and she was determined not to repeat her mistake.

To the untrained eye nothing appeared to have altered in the match. Fukuda was still dictating the random flow of strategies. But the slow expansion of Honno's *wa* was making its presence felt. She attacked with more strength, parried with greater swiftness, counterattacked with more fervor. Slowly, she was moving the field of battle across the tatami mats of the *dojo*, until Fukuda was nearly backed up against the edge of the battlefield. To step outside the perimeter onto the polished wooden floor would mean defeat.

Now Honno expanded her *wa* to its fullest and, as she did so, her body went limp. The *bokken* dropped from her hands, and as Fukuda's wooden sword slashed downward at her head, she reached up, caught it between the palms of her hands.

Fukuda immediately stopped, bowed to Honno. "Big Ezoe was indeed correct about your warrior's spirit."

"But I am a woman," Honno said. "And history records so few women warriors."

Fukuda took off the protective mask, and Honno gaped at the face beneath. "Is that you?" Honno whispered, coming closer. "The real you?"

The face that, without lipstick, behind a pair of man's sunglasses, had seemed so handsomely masculine, had now been transformed into a paradigm of feminine beauty. And in that transformation Honno saw the falseness in the concepts of "handsome" and "beautiful" with which she had been brought up. She saw only the truth of the reality that Fukuda had brought home to her: perception of the world, and how it was constructed, was nothing more than a spiderweb of lessons absorbed with your mother's milk.

"I, too, am a woman, Mrs. Kansei," Fukuda said. "I am *sensei* in sixteen separate martial arts." Her dark eyes shone, not with pride, but in reflection of the revelation she recognized illuminating Honno's face. "I have defeated more men than I can count in the kind of *kenjutsu* match we have just completed. I urge you to believe me when I tell you that the warrior spirit resides in us both."

Now they left the *dojo*, their field of battle, their place of coming together, and they showered together, dressed together, and went back out into the waning night. It was close to five A.M., and Honno wondered what they were going to do until six, when she was to meet Big Ezoe at his Ginza club.

She soon had her answer. The Mercedes glided back toward the futuristic colossi of Shinjuku. The streets were emptying even of the trucks. Their rumbling across the bridges spanning the Sumida came like distant thunder, endless, echoing through the deep canyons of the city.

In twenty minutes they were back in front of the *udon* parlor. In the rear, the gambling was still going full force. Honno thought they might have been gone five minutes rather than five hours. The place stank of stale cigarette smoke and staler bodies. The atmosphere of frenzy had not abated, and with a quick contraction of her stomach, she remembered her father. How many nights had he spent on his knees throwing away money in just such a gambling house? More than there were trees in the forests of Yoshino. His fate had been death by obsession, a finding no coroner could ever make, but it was the truth, nonetheless.

The same shirtless Yakuza knelt on the floor, their fantastic *irizumi* sheened with sweat, the same players pushed their packets of money onto the center of the low tables. Though the long night was near its end, the players were not weary. On the contrary, their eyes were fever-bright, their nerves at hair-trigger level.

Though their victory was still as far away as it had been when the night began, they saw it as being closer than ever. This was the dangerous delusion of their obsession, the one that always took them down, now, soon, or later. It didn't matter, because that one end would come, inevitably, tragically.

Honno focused on the senior vice-president of administration for Kaga without Fukuda having to tell her. He had just lost another round and was scrabbling in his pocket. He pulled out a pad, wrote out another marker, signed it. How many did that make tonight? How much money did the pile of markers, in concert, represent? My God, Honno thought, how often can he afford to do this?

The Kaga senior vice-president passed his marker, and he followed it with his avid eyes as it made its way from Yakuza to Yakuza, all the way down the table, until it came to rest before the bald man with the dragon tattooed on his gleaming skull. The dragon man did not even look at the marker. Instead, his gaze rose to meet Fukuda's.

Fukuda made no move. She whispered to Honno, "What would you have me do? Accept Kaga's marker or turn it down?"

"I haven't any of the facts," Honno said.

"They're irrelevant," Fukuda said. "Yes or no. Tell me."

"I don't know what to do."

"Yes," Fukuda said. "You know as well as I do what must be done. It is time you took the responsibility for it. Your warrior's spirit needs responsibility in order to survive and to flourish."

Honno stared from the dragon man to the Kaga official. She should have been thinking of her father, of his terrible agony, the suffering of his family, and perhaps she was, but hardly in the way she had expected. She found that she harbored no sympathy for the Kaga man. This was his obsession, and she knew from bitter experience that he was already too far gone to be helped. Besides, she discovered, much to her surprise, that she had no desire to help him. She saw her father's obsession, his fate now from a different window, and like the moonlight being chopped to bits on the face of the Sumida River, there were other realities besides the one that she had been living all her life. And in this last moment of indecision, she understood everything she had seen tonight, every cryptic sentence Fukuda had spoken. Now nothing was cryptic, all was revealed, and there was no longer indecision.

"Take his marker," the warrior with Honno's voice said.

Fukuda nodded, and the dragon man pocketed the marker, slapped three thick stacks of yen on the table. They made their way to the Kaga senior vice-president, who was already devouring them with his eyes.

The Mercedes pulled up in front of the unobtrusive entrance to Big Ezoe's club in the Ginza at three minutes to six. The rain had been blown away on a freshening breeze from the east. Dawn was already painting the sky high above Tokyo's towers a dove gray, the exact hue of Fukuda's suit.

"You're not going in with me," Honno said.

"No," Fukuda said. "I have other work to see to now."

"Will I see you again?"

The driver had come around, opened Honno's door.

"That will be entirely up to you, Mrs. Kansei," Fukuda said. "The power is yours. Your fate is in your own hands."

And Honno, stepping out into the brightening Tokyo dawn, thought, At last.

222

"We've found him," Big Ezoe said as Honno walked into the granite-clad restaurant.

"Do you mean Giin is still alive?" Honno slipped into the chair opposite him. "Has he been harmed?"

Big Ezoe laughed. "Your university professor is very much alive, Mrs. Kansei, and quite unharmed." He shrugged. "Why shouldn't he be? There was no one to hurt him."

"I don't understand."

Outside, sunlight was spreading downward, across the faces of Shinjuku's gigantic office towers. The nocturnal denizens among whom Honno had walked just hours ago would already be back in their lairs, sleeping, waiting again for the return of night. She was reminded of that lone cryptomeria, stark, bent in pain, an oblique counterpoint to the endless right angles of the city, and she wanted to return to it, to somehow pay homage to it, so that its suffering should continue to have meaning.

"Your friend Giin is a clever boy," Big Ezoe said. "He engineered his own kidnapping."

Big Ezoe must have already ordered, because breakfast arrived, American-style: orange juice, eggs, bacon, corn muffins, black coffee. Honno had never seen so much food at breakfast, but she found that she was famished.

She should have been surprised by what Big Ezoe was telling her, but somehow she seemed inured to surprise. The warrior's spirit, having surfaced, was now gaining ascendancy.

"Giin merely used the kidnapping as a way to disappear for a little while without you clinging to his coattails," Big Ezoe continued. "When he had made his plans and was ready to implement them, he surfaced. In the middle of my world. That was the easiest part, since he was already something of an habitué."

Big Ezoe looked at her. "You're taking this news with a great deal more equanimity than I expected, Mrs. Kansei. Didn't Giin swear to you that he had given up gambling, that he had put his past behind him?"

"He did. But then my father said the same thing to my mother. Many times."

"You seemed more than willing to believe your friend several nights ago."

Honno considered this. It occurred to her that several nights ago seemed more like a lifetime ago. She looked at Big Ezoe, said, "He wants to sell back the Sakata ledgers he stole from me."

"Yes," Big Ezoe said. "And no. I think he wants—needs—money very badly. His debts in my gambling houses have mounted of late. But I also think he's too smart to give up the ledgers for one score. He's had a chance to decipher Sakata's code. That's why it took him this long to surface with an offer. Now he knows what the ledgers contain, and he has no doubt discovered that they're far too valuable for him to give up."

"What does he plan to do?"

"Figure it out," Big Ezoe said. "It isn't so difficult."

Honno thought for a moment. "He's going to try to take our money and give us nothing—or, perhaps, just a little—in return."

Big Ezoe said, "Like all amateurs, Giin believes that he can outsmart the professional. That's a proven fact. Why else would he come back night after night to my gambling houses? He has set up a meeting for eight this morning, in the center of the Nihonbashi bridge. I will bring him the money, and he will give me one deciphered page from the ledgers. Then, when I'm satisfied as to their value, he'll give me an address where I'll supposedly find the entire ledgers, along with the rest of the decoded pages. Only they won't be there, and he'll begin the process of bleeding me dry."

"But that's so terribly dangerous for him."

"It certainly is," Big Ezoe said, "but in a way he doesn't yet begin to suspect. He's chosen to deal with me. That's because he knows me—or, at any rate, he thinks he does. In fact, he's very close to the edge, and in danger of falling a long, long way.

"You see, Mrs. Kansei, what Giin hasn't counted on is you."

"You loved Giin, once," Big Ezoe said in the tone one would use when beginning a fairy tale. "But now your warrior spirit has shown you that it wasn't Giin you loved at all, but an image of Giin. An image your own needs, desires, and misconceptions created. Just as they created the Eikichi Kansei you thought you had married. There, too, the truth was something altogether different."

Honno and Big Ezoe were in his limo, on their way to Nihonbashi. They passed through a city that looked as if it were waking up from a long, troubled slumber.

224

"What do you plan to do?" Honno said.

"I?" Big Ezoe looked at her. "I plan to do nothing at all."

The limo pulled into the curb, and the driver got out. In a moment Honno's door was opening. The driver handed her a slim attaché. It came as no surprise to this new Honno. She emerged into the busy street.

She said, "What is in the case?" But, really, it was a question to which she already had the answer. She could hear Fukuda saying, *Whatever you want to be in there,* and the warrior with Honno's voice repeated the answer out loud.

Behind her, she heard Big Ezoe's voice saying, "I will remain here until the matter is resolved."

Without a backward glance, Honno walked onto the bridge. Centuries ago the Nihonbashi had been the starting point of the Tokaido, the main road between the capital—Edo, now Tokyo—and Kyoto. She recalled as a child seeing the stylized rendition of the Nihonbashi in a woodblock print by Hiroshige. Perhaps it was at that moment, engulfed by the beauty of the artist's work, the point where myth and reality converged, that she had fallen in love with Tokyo.

Eight o'clock. Giin was at the center of the bridge's arc, waiting. Behind him all of Honno's beloved Tokyo was arrayed like a set of runes whose meaning she had at last begun to decipher.

He saw her coming and his face went white. He turned to run, then he hesitated, his greed gaining the upper hand, and he turned back. And Honno was already there.

"Why did you run?" she asked him. "Why did you steal the ledgers?"

"You don't understand," Giin said hurriedly. "I need money. Desperately."

"You could have asked me for money."

He laughed. "Don't be absurd. I need a great deal more than you could ever have."

"How do you know that?" She saw Giin pause. "You should have asked."

Giin gave her a tentative smile. He bobbed his head. "Yes. I suppose I should, now that I think about it. But it was such a shock to see you, and I—well, I found myself so smitten again. It didn't matter that you'd married. I wanted everything to be perfect this time. For you, only for you, Honno. That's why I need the money. I need to get this behind me—this emergency—and then everything *will* be perfect."

Honno seemed not to have been listening. "You're still gambling."

"But I'm not! I told you—"

"Why are you lying to me?"

"I swear—"

"You've always lied to me."

"Honno, what's happened to you?"

"Nothing," she said. She lifted the attaché case that contained nothing. "Money," she said. "To give you your perfect ending."

Giin nodded uncertainly. He handed a sheet of paper to Honno. "The information contained in the ledgers is fantastic. I can hardly believe it's true. But it must be. Every entry is cross-referenced several ways. Look. Times, places, numbers of meets, amounts transferred. The ledgers detail an entire network of bribes, extortion, a web of corruption so wide it's almost inconceivable."

"But to what end?"

Giin's smile widened. He sensed that for all this woman's new strangeness, he had regained the upper hand. "Ah, that will have to remain a mystery until I have the money, and you get the balance of the decoding."

"I want it all now."

"Huh?"

"I want everything you've decoded," Honno said. Without warning, she reached out, brought Giin toward her with such fierceness that his teeth rattled. "You'll tell me now, before the transfer of money, as an act of contrition for lying to me, and for stealing what is mine."

"You're mad," Giin said. "Absolutely mad. I've made my deal."

"You'll tell me what I want to know," Honno said. "Or I'll kill you right here, right now, as a public lesson, a reminder to those who lie and cheat and steal."

"I don't—"

"Your particular obsession has ended right here." Honno stuck her forefinger into that soft spot just below Giin's sternum. He winced, collapsed into her. Saliva drooled out of his gasping mouth.

"You've caused too many people far too much pain," Honno told him. The finger jammed inward again, and Giin's eyes opened so wide she thought the eyeballs would pop

226

out. "I'm the one, little Honno, who you thought so little of, who you condescended to. I am going to put an end to it."

Once more the finger moved, curling upward toward his heart. "To your own suffering as well, since you are obviously incapable of helping yourself. You're just spiraling deeper and deeper into deceit and self-delusion."

Honno brought Giin so close against her she could hear the frightened beating of his heart. Her *wa* was fully expanded, and there was a peculiar triumph burning like a fire inside her. She thought of Fukuda and transformations. Was she, Honno, fully transformed by the warrior spirit? Not yet. But soon.

"I'm going to break your back," she said. "Not kill you, not yet. You thought I was still trapped by your spell, that you could con me yet again with your soft voice and your honeyed words. But I know what you are now; you have no effect on me. And I want what I want."

"But I don't know." Giin's voice was filled with pain and tears. "I've, oh no, over the years I've lost my abilities to decode. Age was playing . . . playing tricks on my mind. So I found a protégé. He did the decoding. He . . . he has everything you . . . you want."

"Name," Honno said, tightening her hold. "Address."

Giin told her, his head lolling on her neck like an infant. And Honno, the warrior, was abruptly disgusted by his weakness—just as she had been disgusted by her father's weakness, she realized. All these years she had been too much the good girl, the Honno her parents had raised her to be, to question her own emotions, to recognize her disgust.

With a cry, Honno's arms contracted. She heard the *snap-snap snap!* like twigs breaking underfoot as Giin's vertebrae popped. Then she threw him over the side of Nihonbashi, the symbol of a beginning, into the sluggish waters of the Sumida, over whose pristine surface the moon had dreamily cast its light just last night.

Then the warrior had picked up the empty attaché case and walked calmly back toward the waiting limo. In her mind's eye she could see the lone cryptomeria, and now, truly, she understood all the layers of its existence. Just as the curve of its trunk softened the pitilessly hard edges of the city surrounding it, its strength lent meaning to her suffering. The cryptomeria was proof that purpose could be found in the thickest fog, the darkest night, the deepest pain. And with that, the past melted away, and only the future, shining and limitless, remained.

The city—her Tokyo—pulsed on all around her, its myriad streets radiating out in every direction, beckoning. But the warrior had already chosen her path. The one that had led her to what she wanted most: freedom.

SEVEN
MACHINE-GUN CITY/TOKYO

Estilo was all for killing Cruz the moment they landed back in Medellín, but Russell said absolutely not. Tori had told them, during the flight back to Machine-Gun City, of her promise to Sonia. Dawn was breaking, the heavy disk of the sun painting the clouds with golds and reds, as if it had set them on fire.

"We are not assassins," Russell said, being his usual meticulously logical self, reminding them point by point of how life must be led. "I do not want to involve ourselves with these people any more than we already are. And I can't see any reason to do the Orolas' dirty work for them."

"Forgive me for saying so, Señor Slade," Estilo broke in, "but you're missing the point. It is a matter of honor. This is no longer business, otherwise I would wholeheartedly agree with you. It's personal."

Tori glanced at Estilo. She had never known him to be so bloodthirsty before. He was a *chanta*, a slick operator. Pointing a gun at someone's head and pulling the trigger was not good business. Ask Cruz. He had done that to Ruben Orola, and just look what had happened: almost assassinated twice, stalked by his own mistress, about to be betrayed by everyone on this plane.

229

Not that he deserved anything less. It was merely a lesson to be learned.

"I'm concerned with neither honor nor emotion, merely with getting out of here in one piece," said Russell, the pragmatist. "The Medellín Cartel has bought the local police, the judiciary, maybe even members of the Colombian government and our own DEA, which was driven completely out of Cruz's territory two years ago."

"How about justice?" Tori asked him. "Without Sonia's help at Cruz's apartment, we never would have lived to get to the *llano negro* and the cocaine factory. We never would have found this." She lifted up the glassine tube filled with the dark metallic pellets: the center of the soft cell they had discovered in the bags of coke.

"Fuck justice," Russell said. "This is Colombia. No one here ever heard of justice."

Russell was reminded of how he had met Bernard Godwin. It had been near the end of his graduate studies at Wharton. Bernard had come to lecture on the nature of justice, which, he had contended, was a wholly man-made concept, and therefore subject to the distortions and rationalizations only humans could bring to something of their own creation. In nature, Bernard had argued, there is no such thing as justice, only life and death.

Russell recalled how taken he had been with the lecture, and with Bernard Godwin. Years later he realized that Godwin had come to the campus on a recruiting mission for the Mall, but even that knowledge could not diminish his admiration of Godwin's mind.

Godwin had known Russell's background: how his peculiar genius with logic and numbers had estranged him from his family. As prodigies often will, he had frightened his parents and had caused his brother to feel stupid.

"We're both people who are all alone," Bernard had said to Russell. "People who can understand the depth of commitment to an abstract: a concept, an ideal."

"Like justice?" Russell had said.

And Bernard Godwin had laughed, put his arm around the young Russell Slade. "Just so."

Now, sitting in a smuggler's airplane, on his way back from the *llano negro*, Russell could still hear Bernard's voice speaking softly, seductively, in his ear. So much power. Hooking up with Bernard had been like having a pipeline directly to God, Russell thought. But so much has changed since then.

The cockpit grew warm as the sun, lifting above the cloud-bank to their rear, streamed through the windows, following them back to Medellín. Tori broke off large chunks of a candy bar, handed them around. Estilo manned the radio, monitoring traffic, speaking softly into the mike now and then.

"Have you forgotten," Tori said to Russell, "that it was Cruz's *sicarios* who came after us on the way in from the airport?"

"Okay, while we're on the subject, it was Cruz who loaned us one of his helicopters so we could get to *llano negro*," Russell pointed out.

"Jesus," Estilo said.

Tori said, "Let's by all means kiss him on both cheeks the next time we see him. I don't think you're seeing this situation clearly. I made a promise to Sonia, and I'm going to keep it."

"You'll do nothing of the kind," Russell said. "You made one mistake, but I'll be damned if I'll let you make another. You had no right to promise that woman anything. She obviously got to you on an emotional level, but I'm ordering you to put aside your emotions—they're far too dangerous out here in the field. This is the end of your maverick ride, Tori."

"Like hell it is," Tori said. "If you won't help, Estilo and I will—"

"Forget it," Russell snapped. "You signed on with the Mall, and you've got to learn discipline. You'd better start right now. We're back to civilization, and my word is law."

"If you think Machine-Gun City is civilization, Señor Slade," Estilo said, "you're dead wrong."

Estilo's words turned out to be more prophetic than even he could have imagined. The plane was met at Medellín airport by Cruz and his cadre of *sicarios*. None of them were shy about brandishing their MAC-10's.

The engines of the Twin Otter were still idling when Cruz directed the moving stair against the airplane's side, began climbing it. Tori went aft, opened the door. The three of them were waiting for him when he entered the cabin. His *sicarios* piled in after him, immediately beginning a thorough search of the entire plane. Cruz watched them carefully while he waited. He said nothing.

"No cocaine?" he said at last when the *sicario* leading the cadre returned, shaking his head negatively. Then the *sicario* handed over the glassine packet of metallic pellets.

"We weren't there for the coke," Russell said, deliberately ignoring the glassine packet.

"Ah. Then did you discover who is running the cocaine factory?"

"No. We got something of a rude welcoming."

"Then you were inept." Cruz gave them a wide grin. He hefted the packet. "But I see for all that, you didn't come away empty-handed."

Russell said, "You mean this plane?"

Cruz's nasty laugh echoed in the confined space of the cabin. He stared at the packet. "This must be very valuable—to you." He lifted his gaze. "But then everything becomes valuable, sooner or later. Take information, for instance. While you were gone, I received some. It seems that Sonia had been the lover of Ruben Orola, the bastard I blew away last year. Now isn't that interesting? Of course, Sonia thought it interesting. She'd tell you so herself, but sadly, she could not be here with us today. She met with an unfortunate accident. She went for a walk in the wrong part of town, and someone shot her. Foolish girl. How many times was she warned?"

In the silence that followed, Cruz stepped up to Russell, stared him in the eye. "I don't know what your game is, but it's ended now. You have an hour to get out of Medellín. After that"—he shrugged— "I can make no assurances concerning your safety."

"We'd be only too happy to leave," Russell said amiably. "Just give us our package and—"

"But no," Cruz said. "I must exact payment for the use of my helicopter, not to mention the inconvenience your visit has caused me."

"That package is of no use to you," Russell said.

"Perhaps. But this plane is." Cruz studied Russell. "And it is enough to know that I have something you want. In a few days I may throw it away—who knows, who cares—but it is mine to do with as I wish."

He turned, was walking away, when Russell said, "I challenge you." Russell's heart was beating fast, and he felt a sick sensation in the pit of his stomach.

Cruz paused. Without turning around, he said, "You're a gringo. Why should I—"

"It was this gringo who found the Orola mole inside your organization. You'd be dead without me." Russell grinned. Somewhere, a voice inside his head was screaming for him to shut up, but he would not. He had to prove that he could pull his weight in the field. Along about the time when bullets were whistling past his head in the *llano negro* it had occurred to Russell that Bernard Godwin had deliberately sent him into the field as a taunt, a humiliation for not having come up in the Mall in the same way Bernard himself had. Russell was determined not to give Bernard—or Tori—the satisfaction of seeing him psychologically torn apart by field work. "Besides," Russell went on, "your *sicarios* might wonder at the reason you won't listen to my challenge. Is it that I'm just a gringo? Or have you become afraid? Are you becoming soft and weak?"

Cruz whirled around; his face was flushed with rage. "When I discovered what Sonia had been—an Orola spy—I shot her myself. I, Castro Cruz. I put the barrel of my gun into her mouth and pulled the trigger. I was looking into her eyes the entire time. I watched the coming of death; I saw it claim her. Does this sound soft and weak?" He walked up to Russell. "And now I have to ask myself if Jorge was indeed the Orola spy you claimed he was, or why you, the spy hunter, missed Sonia."

"I wasn't looking at Sonia," Russell said. In his mouth was the taste of metal, bitter and nauseating. "Take my challenge."

Cruz glanced around the cabin. His *sicarios* were watching him expectantly. He gave a perfunctory nod, then shrugged. "It's your death," he said.

The corrida was eerie. Silent and empty, it lay sleeping in the heavy sunlight. There was nothing going on in the bullring except on Sundays, when the Medellín natives crowded its stands to drink in the contrast of life and death when man faced bull.

"All right, Señor Slade," Cruz said. He and his men surrounded Tori and Estilo in the lower reaches of the stands. "You have challenged and I have answered." Cruz grinned down on Russell, who stood in the bloody dust of the corrida itself. Waiting. "I have instructed that my best bull be set loose. If you handle him, I will give you what you want. If, on the other hand, the bull has his way, whether or not I have this package will no longer matter to you. You'll be dead."

Tori tried to read what Russell was thinking by the expression on his face, but he was too good for that. She was thinking, If he dies, it will be on my head. I will never be able to forgive myself.

"Russell," she called out, "you don't have to do this!"

Cruz grunted. "But of course he does." He nodded to one of his *sicarios*, who pointed his semiautomatic at Russell. "A

233

man does not back out of a challenge. Oh, but Señor Slade, I forgot for a moment that you're not a man; you're a gringo. Anything is possible for one such as you."

Russell said nothing. His attention was fixed on the huge iron-bound wooden doors across the dusty floor of the corrida.

Cruz raised his arm, let it drop.

The wooden doors creaked open, and they could see in the semishadows a huge, hulking figure. It snorted heavily, then pawed the ground. Russell moved, and the bull came charging across the corrida toward him.

"Doesn't he even get a killing sword?" Tori said to Cruz.

"No. The killing sword is for a matador only, not a gringo. He will have to manage on his own."

"But he won't be able to," Tori said. "Not with just his bare hands."

"Well, I suppose that's the point." Cruz laughed, then shouted, "Olé, gringo! Olé!" as Russell whirled away from the bull's first charge.

Russell felt the burst of sweat breaking out all over his body. He had seen bullfights before, but he now understood just how enormous these creatures were close up. They were all muscle, all rage, chaos incarnate. The smell of the beast was in his nostrils. He had stared into the bull's red eyes, had seen there a sight that had jolted him: a kind of unthinking evil, elemental and absolute. In that first instant of recognition, Russell knew that there could be no middle ground here. Either he would kill the bull or the bull would kill him. No other possibility existed in those strangely magnetic eyes.

The bull charged again, his hooves thundering, kicking up dust dark with dried blood. Its head was lowered, and Russell saw its long horns aimed at his stomach. He could almost feel the agonizing rip of the gore, could sense himself being jerked off his feet by the beast's inhuman strength, the horn tearing through his abdomen as the bull flailed him along the ground or against the corrida's wall.

The thing was, it did no good to move right away, the bull would just follow. And since it was far faster than a man, it would run him down. Russell knew he needed to follow the dictates of the matador, and not move for as long as was possible, to whirl away only at the last possible instant, to constantly frustrate the beast. And yet, he told himself, what good would even this do? There was no one to cut the beast, to continually wound it, to wear down its prodigious strength, to bring it to the point where, exhausted and bleeding, it lowered its head in the middle of its charge to receive the killing thrust.

Russell waited as the bull came on. He felt his muscles rippling with tremors over which he had no control. His teeth were chattering. The beast's huge head loomed, rushing toward him at appalling speed.

He whirled, but he cut it a bit too fine, and the bull's outflung hoof caught him on the ankle. He staggered, fell into the dust. The bull snorted, so close that Russell could feel the damp heat on the back of his neck. The foam of madness overflowed its lips. The tip of its horn scored the wall just above him. The scent of the beast defined his world.

In the stands, Cruz and his *sicarios* were straining forward, fascinated, sensing that the dance of death was nearing its end. Even the guards posted high up in the arena were concentrating on the imminent death of the gringo. No one yelled "Olé!" now; they were rooting for the bull.

Tori leaned over, whispered in Estilo's ear. He nodded, as she knew he would. Estilo was as fearless as he was loyal. She counted silently to six, saw out of the corner of her eyes Estilo doing the same. Then she launched herself over the barrier in the stands, down into the corrida. At the same time, Estilo slipped the handgun from Cruz's holster, pressed the muzzle against the side of his head. "Don't move!" he shouted to the *sicarios*. "If you want to keep your leader alive, you'll just relax!"

In the corrida the bull had flung out one hoof. It was meant for Russell's head, but Russell had had the presence of mind to curl up, and the blow struck him on the shoulder instead.

He grunted, began to scramble away. That was a mistake. The bull charged after him, its head already down, its horns darting this way and that.

Tori landed on her feet and, reaching down, slid a knife from its sheath against her ankle. She leaped atop the bull's back and plunged the knife to the hilt in that spot she had seen the matador find for his killing thrust, between the massive muscles of the beast's shoulders and neck.

She was certain she heard the bull scream. It shuddered as a fountain of blood shot up, and its convulsions threw her off. She hit the wall, came down hard.

Then Russell had scooped her up, and the two of them were making for the doorway through which Russell had been shoved onto the floor of the corrida.

As they reached the door they heard the unmistakable sound of semiautomatic fire. Fearing for Estilo, Tori turned around and had a brief glimpse of the guards stationed high up in the stands, then Russell had pulled her through, from the intense sunlight of the corrida to the darkness beneath the stands.

"Someone's shot Cruz's guards," she shouted at Russell.

They raced around the semicircle, came up into brilliant sunlight, headed up the tiers of empty seats, but the gunfire had ceased. None of Cruz's people were left standing. Instead, Estilo and Cruz were surrounded by another set of men. The Orolas?

"It's all right," Estilo said as the men trained their weapons toward the oncoming figures, "they're friends."

"Are you all right?" Tori asked Estilo.

He smiled, jerking on Cruz's collar. "As you can see, *torero*." He was referring to her bravery in the bullring.

"What the hell is going on here?" Russell demanded.

Estilo said to one of his men, "Search them carefully, especially the woman. She is capable of many tricks." Then he turned his attention to Russell. "I took the liberty of ensuring the outcome of our little adventure. I radioed my people from the plane on our way back here."

"Your people?" Russell said. "Who the hell are you, anyway?"

"I am Tori's friend," Estilo said. "That's all you need to know."

Tori came up to him. "Once, that was all *I* needed to know, Estilo. But now everything's changed."

"Are you certain, *schatzie*? Nothing has changed, not really, not for the two of us."

Tori saw the love in his eyes, but beneath that she could discern something foreign, and her stomach tightened in a kind of precognitive warning. Because it was the hint of fear she saw in Estilo, an emotion she had thought him incapable of feeling. She could already feel him slipping away from her, and she knew that neither of them would ever be the same.

Estilo nodded. "So be it. Finding the cocaine factory in the *llano negro* came as no surprise to me. Why would it? I own it."

"You?" The word came out and almost choked her. She could hardly think straight.

Estilo smiled. "Didn't you think it a bit too convenient, this

236

Twin Otter refueling just as we had need of it?'' He laughed heartily. "Just like in a James Bond movie."

"I don't believe it."

"But I do," Russell said. "The whole escape from the factory was so easy. I should have seen it."

Estilo ignored him. "Friendship does that to people, *schatzie*. I think in your heart of hearts you are not so surprised. You knew that some of my business was not altogether legitimate."

"But cocaine—"

"Only a sideline for me, *schatzie*," Estilo said. "The soft cell, remember? I never would have told you, but this pig, Cruz, stuck his nose in where it didn't belong. He took the hafnium pellets. I could not allow you to be killed over them."

"The hafnium comes from you," Russell said.

Estilo nodded. "Very astute, Señor Slade. The metal pellets are what I'm really exporting. The Japanese buy the hafnium from one of my concerns in West Germany. I transship the hafnium down here, and they oversee the soft cell, making sure it's stuffed into the coke."

"But don't you know what the Japanese are doing with the coke?" Tori said. "They've made a supercocaine, one that kills in a matter of months."

"So? Tori, you know me better than that," Estilo said. "I'm a businessman, pure and simple. I'm motivated by profit, not ideology or politics. I thought you understood that."

The real horror was that Tori did understand. She had known all along what Estilo was, and what he was capable of. They had become friends despite that knowledge. What did that say about her?

"Isn't hafnium used as some kind of damper in nuclear reactors?" Russell said.

"I sell hafnium," Estilo said. "I don't research it."

"Who are you selling it to?" Tori asked. "Which Japanese? Bastard, tell me."

"There's something else I'd like to know," Russell said. "Was it you who ordered the hit on Ariel Solares?"

"Ariel was a friend of mine," Estilo said stiffly. "I still mourn his passing." He sounded as if Russell had insulted him.

"If you didn't kill him," Russell said, "who did?"

"You know, I should kill you both," Estilo said. "That would be the smart move. The businessman in me says I should get rid of you two before you do me more damage than you've already

237

done." He looked at Tori. "But you are my *schatzie*, and I could never harm you."

"I don't understand," Tori said. "What you're doing is despicable: you'll sell anything for a profit with no thought of the consequences."

"Forgive me."

"Never."

"But I forgive you, *schatzie*." Estilo looked at her sadly. "That is the difference between us. I accept you, Tori, all of you. The good and the bad. I am the true friend you never had before, but of course you can't see that. Perhaps in time . . ." He shrugged, said to one of his men, "They have a personal jet waiting for them at the airport. See they get there, and that nothing happens to them at Immigration or Customs. See them off. And, Tori, when you get to Japan, which I've no doubt you'll do, go see your old Yakuza friend, Hitasura."

"What do you know of Hitasura?"

"Wrong question," Estilo told her. "It's what does Hitasura know?"

Tori stared at him a long time. So many emotions were running through her she did not know where to begin to comprehend them. She knew that Estilo had protected her and Russell; and he had, in a major way, helped them with their mission. Then why couldn't she forgive him for having a part in the supercocaine smuggling? Or was it simply that he had lied to her about his business dealings? Could her hurt stem from something so personal as that?

Estilo said, "Adios, Señor Slade. *Auf wiedersehen, schatzie.* I have much to do now. I must see that justice comes to this pig Cruz, and I will see that Sonia is given a proper burial." He took one last look at Tori. "Perhaps you'll say a prayer for her."

"For her," Tori said as she and Russell were led away. "But not for you."

"Do you want to be alone?"

Tori looked up at Russell standing over her. The 727, at 35,000 feet, was whispering along. "Yes." But when he turned away, she reached out for him. "No. Sit with me."

She put her head back, sighed. It was good not to be alone, to put an end to the solitude—the isolation she had imposed on herself from the moment they had taken off from Machine-Gun City.

238

"Next stop, Tokyo." Russell looked at her. "I hope we haven't been sent by Scylla into the maw of Charybdis."

"What do you mean?"

Russell shrugged. "If Estilo is any yardstick by which to judge your friends, this Yakuza *oyabun* of yours, Hitasura, might be waiting to blow our heads off."

"If Estilo wanted that for us, he'd have done it himself."

"Speaking of Estilo, Tori, why'd he do it? From the moment you called him from my office, he must have known what you and I were looking for. He was it, or part of it, anyway. Why did he allow us to get so close, find out about his operation. And even more interesting, why did he get involved himself?"

"I don't pretend to have all the answers," Tori said wearily. "But Estilo knows me. He knew once I sunk my teeth in, I wasn't going to give up, and I think he wanted in some way to ensure my protection. He figured if he was along, he could do that. Also, Estilo was in a fundamental way lying to us when he said he's nothing more than a businessman. Underneath, he's the last of the adventurers. There are those who think the world's gotten too small for people like him. He gets a kick out of making fools of them by slipping through the international cracks they don't know still exist." She shrugged. "But maybe I'm wrong. He went with us, protected us, exposed his operation to us. But God knows, it's clear now that I never fully understood Estilo."

"On the contrary, I think you understand him all too well," Russell said. "Mainly, because you two are so much alike. You're wrong about only one thing, Tori. Estilo's not the last of the adventurers. You are."

Tori turned her head, stared out the window at the colorlessness at 35,000 feet. She looked upward, past the intense blue of the shell of Earth's atmosphere, and thought, What did Greg see in the darkness up there? What did he think when he looked behind him and saw the totality of home?

"There's something else," Russell said, and she turned back, away from the home of the angels. "Why in hell did Estilo tell us about the hafnium? What sort of devilish game is he playing?"

"I don't know," Tori said. "But knowing Estilo as I do, he told us because he wants us to know."

"Perhaps he was lying. It could be the pellets are something other than hafnium."

239

"No. That isn't Estilo's way. He merely would have kept his mouth shut. Those pellets are hafnium, you can bet on it."

Russell opened his hand, smiled. In it, wrapped in a small plastic envelope, was a small dark metallic pellet. "I don't have to bet," he said. "I have my own private sample." He pocketed the evidence, frowned. "What if Estilo *did* order the hit on Solares?"

"He said he didn't."

"No. Think back. What he said was that Ariel was his friend, that he still grieves for him. He gave us no direct answer."

"With Estilo, it's the same thing," Tori said. "It's a matter of honor. Ariel was his friend; Estilo could not have ordered him murdered."

Russell grunted, but he did not argue with her. "Well, then, it's on to Japan," he said. "You'd better brief me. Who's this other friend of yours, Hitasura?"

"Hitasura is the youngest of the Tokyo Yakuza bosses," Tori said. "He made his bones by leading a bloodless coup against the old *oyabun* of his family. There was a scandal the old man was involved in, and Hitasura used his influence among the young bureaucrats of his acquaintance to hush it up. The elders of the family were grateful, so grateful, they installed him as the new *oyabun*. Since then he's expanded his family's influence threefold. His chief rival is an *oyabun* named Big Ezoe. A real sonuvabitch."

"This is the Yakuza we're talking about," Russell said. "They're all sons of bitches."

Tori nodded. "That's more or less true," she said. "It's the 'less' you need to concentrate on. Once you do, you find some fascinating personalities. Hitasura's one. Anyway, he's in my debt, so you don't have to worry about his loyalty."

Russell waited for her to tell him how Hitasura happened to be in her debt, but when she wasn't forthcoming, he asked her himself.

"It's none of your business, Russ," she said. "You don't ask questions like that. They're too personal."

Russell could see that she was already reverting to her enigmatic Japanese personality, the one that drove him to distraction when he had first worked with her. He wasn't going to let that happen again. "This is different, it's business," he said. "It's my neck that's being put on the chopping block along with yours. Under the circumstances, don't you think I deserve an answer?"

"No," Tori said.

Russell leaned forward. "Look, Tori, do I have to point this out: if Hitasura is involved in the soft cell—"

"Russ . . ."

He stared at her. "I don't care if he is in your debt, the possibility remains that if Estilo didn't order Ariel's murder, then Hitasura did."

"Let's not get ahead of ourselves, shall we?"

Russell could see she was angry. He couldn't blame her. Both Estilo and Hitasura were her friends. One had already betrayed her. How much would it take for the other to betray her as well?

Tori stood up. "Excuse me. I've got to go to the bathroom."

Russell watched her go down the aisle. He wondered why he could never win an argument with her. Several minutes later it occurred to him that they hadn't had an argument, merely a conversation. Then he began to wonder why he saw their conversations as skirmishes, and, worse, why it was he found it necessary to win them all.

Something stirred inside him. He felt again the torn edges of the end of his life, blood covering his eyes, the stench of the great bull filling his nostrils, the corrida's red dust coating his mouth, the taste of death choking him. Russell had already given himself up for dead. He had been sucking the dust into his lungs, his vision clouded. There had been pain in his shoulder, his ankle. The bull was towering over him, ready to inflict its damage on his body. His mind could see it coming. His death. It was as if in that moment he had seen how out of focus his life had been up to that point.

He rose, went down the aisle to the door to the head. He knocked on it. "Tori?"

His hand twisted the turnplate, and the narrow door opened inward. He saw Tori hunched over the stainless steel john, her body racked with dry heaves.

When she turned to look at him, her eyes were filled with tears. "Get— Get the hell out and leave me alone!" she managed to say.

One of the Mall flight crew was coming up behind him, and Russell stepped inside, quickly shut the door.

"Oh, God!"

He knelt down beside her, held her head and shoulders while the spasms went on and on. At last she collapsed against him, and he winced as pain shot through the spot where the bull's kick had caught him.

He reached up, managed to get a paper towel soaking wet.

241

He gently wiped her face, her lips, her neck. She used the water he gave her to rinse out her mouth.

Russell could feel her heat, her softness, combined with the peculiar tautness she possessed. He felt a stirring inside him, the accelerated beating of his heart, and cursed himself for being a fool.

How could he let this happen? She was soft and vulnerable, lying meekly in his arms. Strong, capable Tori Nunn. He had her just where every man would want her. But that wasn't it, not at all. What he was feeling was something else, something new, and because he was already at war within himself as to the nature of it, he was at a loss as to what to do.

He was aware of the cloudlike swirl of her golden hair, still matted here and there with the blood of the terrifying beast she had brought down. He could not put aside the memory of her vaulting over the barrier into the red dust of the corrida.

He was aware of the delicate curve of her cheek, so like—yet so unlike—her mother's.

Her lashes fluttered against the bare flesh at the hollow of his throat. Her breathing, the beating of her heart, the heat of the insides of her wrists so close to his own, merging. He had seen the glint of the long knife as she had vaulted atop the beast, as she had plunged the blade with a matador's unerring skill into its skull. Jesus, but he had been frightened.

He had never known the meaning of terror until that moment. And something, he was certain, had happened to him then. In the instant when he was showered with the beast's blood, was assured of its death and, in consequence, the continuation of his own life, he had come to understand what ten thousand sleepless hours closeted in the Mall's operations room could not provide.

At last, he knew what it meant to have his head thrust down a hole, black, dank, menacing, and in that horrific darkness, come face to face with himself. So close to death, the veneer he had worked so assiduously to apply to his life had been stripped away. He had always considered that veneer to be a perfect confluence of sophistication, urbanity, and cunning. The exact mix required for the complex dance of quid pro quo the director of the Mall was required to perform.

But now he saw that he could no longer live with the true nature of the life he had built for himself: the *danse macabre*, a malevolent minuet designed and dictated by Bernard Godwin, the man to whom he paid constant homage. The man who owned Russell Slade completely.

And at last he came to the core of it all: he had been certain that he had challenged Cruz to prove Bernard Godwin wrong, to prove himself to Tori; but in the end he understood that he had faced death for himself. Because he could no longer stand himself, the old Russell Slade, boy genius, perhaps, but a man filled with insecurity at not being part of the veteran network presided over by Godwin, a man on the outside, forever cut out of the field operative's loop—isn't that why he had been so intensely jealous of Tori? Yes, Russell Slade had been just the man Bernard Godwin could subtly manipulate in almost any way he chose.

The horrific truth was that by appointing him director of the Mall, Godwin had made it possible for him to continue running his own agendas while giving the appearance of having moved back into an advisory capacity. Russell was filled with shame.

He felt Tori's arms around him, her fists clutching him, and something inside himself gave way. He put his head down, much as the beast in the corrida had done for the matador's killing sword, and his lips sought hers.

It was not a conscious gesture. Dazed by the ramifications of his revelation, Russell hardly knew what he was doing. His lips came down over Tori's, he felt hers soften, and searched for her tongue with his.

Then her mouth broke away. "No," she gasped. "No, please." Their eyes locked, and Russell was shocked not by how beautiful her eyes were, but by how he had never really noticed their beauty before. They were like misty jewels, translucent, luminous, a blue that was not truly blue, a green that was not quite green, and that special color appeared to him now like a doorway through which, more than anything, he longed to step.

"Tori—"

"Russell, I—"

The moment had seemed so right, but now he recognized how wrong it had been. He had the strong sense that if he insisted, she would give in, he had felt her melting against him. But if she did acquiesce, he knew that he would never know why. Was it vulnerability, despair, a need to be close to someone after two terrible losses? Or was it something else, a feeling, perhaps, that at some point she would not be able to control?

It was of paramount importance for Russell to know—and for him to be assured that Tori, too, knew what she wanted. Otherwise, what was the point?

Russell rose, pulled her to her feet. He did not say he was sorry, because he wasn't. He left her without a word, went forward to speak to the pilot and go over their route to Tokyo, feeling it was important for him to be aware of these things in case anything went wrong along the way. He always liked to know where he was. Which was ironic, considering the whirl of conflicting emotions flooding him.

When he returned to the main cabin, Tori was back in her seat. He ordered sandwiches and hot coffee, and when they were served, he and Tori consumed it in great quantities while she briefed him on her expertise: the tangle of modern-day Japan.

"The central issue in understanding the Japan of today," Tori said, "is to keep in mind that no one person is ultimately in charge of the country. Absolutely no one in America seems to get this, not the President, nor anyone on Capitol Hill, in business, or, God knows, the Pentagon. They're all so mystified by this new Japan that they had such a major hand in creating, and so self-righteously pissed off when nothing much happens in response to their requests.

"Putting aside for the moment the fact that they're not asking the right questions, what they're all looking for—and not finding—is a place where the buck stops. The truth is that no one in Japan will take responsibility for the buck stopping because, more often than not, buck-stopping is synonymous with loss of face.

"Japan's society is unique in all the world—in all history, for that matter. It is a country 'governed'—although that's too precise a term for so amorphous a concept—by a loosely knit organic conglomerate of entities including the prime minister and his ruling party, the Diet, the samurai bureaucracy, the corporations of the business world, and the Yakuza. The death of the great Tokugawa shogunate at the dawn of the Meiji era in the late 1860s, the nineteenth-century intervention of the Western world, and the post–World War Two MacArthur constitution, made certain this uneasy alliance would continue into the twenty-first century."

Russell watched her while she talked. He wondered what she must be feeling, how deep the facade she presented went. She appeared quite herself now, as if the incident between them had never happened. But could that be so? Could anyone be in such iron control of their emotions?

He had to admit to himself that he found Tori Nunn to be a complete enigma. She was like a code to which he was increasingly drawn yet could not break. Being close to her, working with her in the field, had given him no insight, no new understanding of her underlying psyche. Instead, he had merely bedazzled himself.

His attraction to her was suddenly so strong it had the potential to become an obsession. Up until now, Russell Slade's sole obsession had been the Mall. When he had been appointed director, Bernard Godwin had taken him to dinner, during the course of which he had said, *Now you'll know what it means to have a mistress, one who occupies you heart and soul. I trust you will be up to the task of managing her.*

Russell thought that because he had uncovered some of the lies his mentor had so easily told him, he had Bernard under control. But just the opposite was true. Bernard Godwin had attached invisible strings to him—just as he had to Tori—and he had been pulling those strings all along. Of course Tori and I fought like brother and sister, Russell thought. Bernard made certain that both of us saw him the same way: as a father figure. We were both "bred" to please him.

And now, watching her explain to him the inner workings of Japan, he knew he wanted to draw closer to her still. He saw how she still idolized Bernard, how she would do anything he asked. Russell, feeling his heart filling up with emotion, wondered when he would cut the strings Bernard had so painstakingly attached to her. He knew he must begin by telling her the truth about Bernard, that he was ready to sacrifice her if it came to it. But not now; Tori was not yet ready to hear anything negative about Bernard Godwin, her spiritual father. Besides, Russell thought, on a purely selfish level, there were more important matters to resolve.

In the electric moment when he and Tori had been closeted together, everything had changed. A door had been unlocked, and once opened, it could never again be closed. The world was different now, at least the world as Russell Slade knew it. And, in the coming days, he would have to determine just what he was going to do about it.

Tokyo. They had traveled almost nine thousand miles on the transatlantic route, touching down for refueling in Cartagena, Santo Domingo, and Frankfurt. They were only through Japanese Customs and Immigration, and Russell was already feeling like an alien. The Japanese had developed the uncanny ability of being extremely polite while firmly keeping you at arm's distance. And by so doing, they neatly managed to lock you out of anything of importance. Everything here was form; there was no substance. It was as if the entire country were in the process of enacting a gigantic Kabuki play.

Smiles without meaning; cardboard bows; saying yes when they meant no; an obsession with minute detail while talking around the edges of major issues. Could there be a more unfathomable people, a more opaque culture on the face of the earth? Russell asked himself on the long, traffic-choked drive in from Narita Airport. Well, the Chinese, yes, of course, but in a fit of self-mutilation, the Chinese had dealt themselves out of international play for years to come, so they didn't count.

"We going directly to Hitasura's?" Russell asked.

"No. I think it would be advisable to learn a bit more about hafnium first. If Hitasura is Estilo's buyer, I want to go into the first meeting with him with as much armament as I can."

For once Russell found himself in agreement with Tori. And, much to his surprise, it wasn't an altogether disagreeable feeling.

"This guy Deke is a little weird," Tori said.

Russell glanced at her. "How weird?"

"You tell me," Tori said as she led him down the steps into a grimy tattoo parlor somewhere in the incomprehensible tangle of Shinjuku. The sun was out, but you'd never know it this deep in the heart of Tokyo. There was only reflected light here, a colorless illumination bounced off ten thousand panes of glass.

Russell peered at phoenixes, dragons, lissome seminude ladies, spiders, serpents, warriors out of history and demons out of myth. All were on display in astounding detail on the walls of the shop, which was lit with sodium lamps, giving it the appearance of a highway or an industrial park.

A Japanese who improbably seemed to be in his late teens looked up when they walked in. He made no sign of recognition, returned to his work on the back of a very heavy individual. He had a punk's spiky haircut and a laborer's ink-stained hands. He wore sandals, long-legged Day-Glo surfer shorts, and a T-shirt cut off just above the navel that had PEPPERDINE U. VOLLEYBALL TEAM emblazoned across the back.

"Greetings from Tokyo General, dudette," he said without looking up.

"Howzit, Deke?"

"Bitchin'." Deke dipped a small circle of needle-sharp

246

wooden picks into colored ink, applied it beneath the skin. He was an artist with his canvas. "As ever."

Tori stood behind him. "Got a problem for you."

"Solution's my middle name, dudette."

Tori displayed the dark metal pellet in its plastic envelope. "A to Z." When he nodded, she slipped it into the pocket of his shorts.

"One hour," he said. "I just opened." Deke opened for business after noon, worked late into the early hours of the morning. He dipped the picks into the ink, applied it. "Go get a milkshake or something, you dudes are making my client nervous."

When they returned, just over an hour later, there was no one in the tattoo parlor.

"Where'd this weirdo split to with my evidence?" Russell said suspiciously.

"Deke's space goes all the way to the next street," Tori told him. "In the back of the shop is his lab."

"Isn't this kid a bit young to be running sophisticated diagnostic tests? I mean, he might set his diapers on fire."

Tori smiled. "Deke *is* young," she said. "But he's also brilliant. Don't let his age prejudice you. In Japan it's often best to keep an open mind."

At that moment Deke appeared. He had on thick rubber gloves, a heavy apron, and was grasping the pellet at the end of a pair of metal tongs. Around his neck was a filtering mask. He peered at Tori. "You still playing v-ball, dudette? We got a bitchin' game going this P.M."

"I'm a little short on play time this trip," Tori said. "Catch you next." She nodded at what he was holding. "First, you scope the traces of white shit on the pellet?"

"Colombian, mon. Happenin' premium stuff." Deke smacked his lips. "Mmm mmm good."

"Is that all?"

"What else were you expecting?"

Tori glanced at Russell, then said to Deke, "Let's hear the rest."

"Cool," Deke said. "This here's a pellet of hafnium," he said, nodding at the pellet. "Good quality shit." He looked at Tori. "You have any more of this stuff to sell?"

"Not in the business," Russell said tersely.

"Can you give us some background on hafnium?" Tori said,

before Russell's American aggressiveness could get them into trouble.

"No sweat," Deke said. He plopped the pellet into Tori's hand. "Hafnium is a by-product of zirconium mining. It's used to make control rods for nuclear reactors. These rods are like dynamic controllers, meaning they move in and out of the reactor core so that they can like absorb more or less of the neutrons given off by the atomic reaction. You like control the power output that way.

"Usually, boron is like used for the control rods, but boron wears out, and new rods have to be fitted. Hafnium's advantage over like boron and the other similar control rod substances is that it has an enormous capacity for absorbing neutrons. See, like the neutrons bombarding it change it into another substance which also has the capacity to absorb neutrons.

"Because of this property," Deke continued, "hafnium is used most often in like the nuclear reactors of submarines. The longer such a reactor can go without replacement, the longer the sub can stay underwater without refueling."

"What kind of time are we talking?" Tori asked.

"Boron would give you like maybe six months," Deke said. "But with rods of hafnium in your reactor, you could stay underwater like over two years."

"Okay," Russell said. "You said control rods, but these are pellets. Does this mean what we have here is raw hafnium?"

"Solid choice." Deke nodded. "But wrong." He looked at Russell. "What you gave me to analyze isn't raw, dude. It's the refined, finished stuff."

"Yet it's not a rod. This must be some special stuff," Russell said.

"Uh-huh. Now you're in the loop." Deke's eyes gleamed. "This here's something better than a rod. It's a fixed poison. Meaning it's like part and parcel of the reactor's core itself. Which means that this kind of core is something new. I'd sure like to get my hands on it."

"You'll have to get in line," Tori said.

"I hear you, dudette."

Russell said, "What would you use this kind of new reactor for?"

Deke shrugged. "Hard to say. A sub could stay independent for like five years, maybe more."

"Any other possibilities?" Tori asked.

Deke thought for a moment. "Well, with like a fixed poison

of this kind of hafnium, I suppose it would be theoretically possible to construct a miniature reactor of a much higher potency than what we already have."

"How potent?" Russell asked.

Deke scrunched up his face in concentration. "If you got the right brains together, I imagine you could come up with a backpack-size reactor that could—well, it could like power just about anything. Care to name your poison, dude?"

"Christ on the cross," Russell said sometime later. "One murder has taken us from a mission involving cocaine running to a multinational conspiracy to create the ultimate portable power source. Tori, imagine it! An atomic reactor you could carry on your back! Think of the possibilities!"

"I am." Tori shuddered. "And in this context they're all monstrous."

"Another bit of interesting news," Russell said. "According to the tests Deke ran, the cocaine being manufactured at Estilo's Colombian factory in the *llano negro* is normal, not the killer stuff the Japanese are manufacturing. So at least he's not involved in that side of it."

"Small comfort," Tori said.

They were sitting at a window table at a second-floor *kissaten*—one of thirty thousand such coffee shops in Tokyo—overlooking the trendiest street in the trendy Roppongi district. The decor was highly futuristic, both inside the *kissaten* and out in the street.

Red neon strips hidden by pink lacquer sconces that ran the length of the interior of the coffee shop lit stainless-steel sculptures of bonsai trees, waves, cranes in flight. Old symbols in a new medium. It was as if the Japanese, in stepping boldly forward into the future, were duty-bound to drag their past with them.

Outside, people passed like peacocks, their clothes so outlandish they could be considered costumes. Russell noticed that the futuristic clothes were almost colorless: black, white, putty, simple hues that allowed the fantastic cuts and shapes of the blouses, skirts, and jackets to take center stage and, like sculpture, to make their own impact in the purest state.

"Tori," Russell said, "why is it that everything in Japan is a symbol?"

"That's not so hard to figure," Tori said. "The Japanese fixation on symbols is merely a reflection of their culture: say one thing, act another way. Too many people in too little space. And because of chronic earthquakes, the traditional housing construction was of wood and paper—easier to rebuild after a quake has leveled your house. But both these factors made for an acute lack of privacy. Did you ever try to tell someone a secret in a room whose walls are made of rice paper? Don't bother.

"In Japan, everyone shares, everyone is part of a series of groups, so it was natural that an elaborate system of politeness and protocol should arise. The obsession with symbols is an outgrowth of these things. A symbol is easily identifiable for groups, something happily embraced by many."

"I'm with you so far, dudette," Russell drawled, and they both smiled. "But if you take the time to look behind these symbols, you find that they have no meaning."

"Right. And that makes sense, too, if you can learn to think like a Japanese. What is on the surface is to be admired, but not necessarily adhered to. As long as form and protocol are outwardly satisfied, what difference does it make what's really on your mind or in your heart? Under these circumstances, it's far better for the symbols to be meaningless. That way, there's no chance of an entanglement that could cause shame and loss of face."

Tori thought, I am so Japanese, yes. All the while I'm expounding like a professor on their culture, I am part of it, a living symbol. I am talking, hearing myself talk, but that is only the surface, the gleaming shell, all that I'm allowing Russ to see. To show him more would bring me shame, a loss of face.

Tori was trying desperately to come to terms with her own emotions. Ever since she had seen Russell in the Medellín corrida, about to die, something had changed inside her. She knew, deep down, that it was not merely a sense of decency or even guilt that had motivated her to leap into the corrida, climb upon the bull's humped back.

And later, in the 727 on the way to Tokyo, when he had burst in on her, had held her while she was racked with the pain of the trust she had lost in Estilo. She had been so certain that Russell would reprimand her, push her face into the uncertainty that now loomed before her: could she trust any of the network of friends she had so slowly, so painstakingly nurtured, cultivated, relied on? Her network was her eyes and ears on the clandestine movements of the world. And now that that network had so clearly sprung a leak, now that she was bleeding, was

250

the time for the Russell Slade she knew to hit her, hit her hard, so that he could at last wrest the reins of control from her. Because she had been convinced that this was Russell's weakness: he was a control freak, and the fact that she had her own way of running a mission drove him crazy.

And yet . . . Russell had not acted in character. Just the opposite, in fact. He had been gentle, kind, understanding, all traits she could not reconcile with the Russell Slade she had known in the past.

The fact was, she had gotten a great deal of pleasure from driving Russell crazy. And the fact that she was so obviously successful with her unorthodox methodology should have shown him his own weakness as clearly as if it were a mirror. It hadn't. She hadn't counted on his stubborn streak—and the depth of his weakness. Control was everything.

Tori had promised herself on the day he had severed her from the Mall, that one day she would create a laboratory experiment where Russell's sense of control was stripped from him.

This new mission had presented just the opportunity she had been looking for. Since it was clear Russell and Bernard were desperate to have her back, she had decided to exact her revenge on Russell. The field was the greatest laboratory she could hope to find. There was no control in the field, where one was continually bombarded with the randomness of life. The only problem was that she had herself forgotten how random a mission could be, and events had not gone as planned.

For one thing, Estilo had betrayed her. For another, Russell had turned out to be far more clever and resourceful in the field than she ever could have imagined. She had maneuvered Bernard Godwin into ordering Russell into the field with her just so she could show him up as the desk jockey he was, to send him back to Mall Central humbled and defeated by his incompetence. But, Tori thought, that's not how it's turned out.

She had been increasingly impressed by his expertise, his bravery under fire, both psychological—at Cruz's apartment—and physical, at the cocaine factory in the *llano negro*. And then in a stunning display of courage, he had challenged Cruz, throwing himself, weaponless, into the corrida in Machine-Gun City.

My God, she thought, sitting across from him in the second-floor coffee shop in Roppongi, this can't be happening. I don't know this man at all. Russ has been my rival, my enemy. Who does Bernard love most, me or Russ? That's the way it's been ever since Russell came on board—at least, I'm convinced that's how he's seen it. Bernard Godwin, the Mall's *eminence grise*, has been our surrogate father, and like disputatious children we've been yelling "Choose me! Choose me!" at the top of our lungs.

Staring at Russell across the table, watching him drink his ten-dollar cup of coffee, Tori could no longer see him as the man who had outsmarted her at every turn at Mall Central. I'm supposed to hate this man, she thought. Haven't I hated him from the moment he severed me? I hate him; I don't, I *can't* possibly—

But she could not even think it, and with an inner convulsion, she turned her thoughts in another direction, any direction to distract herself . . .

She remembered a time at Diana's Garden in L.A., late in the day, when the shadows grew long and as dark as plums, her favorite time, lazing by the pool after a ninety-minute workout on the board and in the water. She was in her second year of junior high, and Greg was a sophomore in college, home for Easter.

She was staring up at the glazed sky. Greg was at her side. She could feel him, his coolness close to the heat of her own body. She liked that he was always cool, always a contrast to her warm skin, because often, when she looked in his face, it was like staring into a mirror, two pairs of identical angel eyes reflecting.

Her workout had not been enough to calm her on that particular day, and Greg had caught her crying.

"What's up, Tor?"

"Nothing."

"You're crying over nothing?" He grunted. "That's stupid."

"I'm not stupid."

"I know."

She looked up, almost shyly. "I'm having a hard time in Russian. I can't seem to understand it at all."

"Don't give up on it. It's important to him that we know Russian."

"Uck!"

It had always seemed an enigma that her father, so desperate to be part of American society in so many ways, also wanted not to lose his Russian heritage. It was he who had insisted she take Russian instead of French, the elegant language most of her friends took. Russian classes were filled with nerds with Coke-bottle-bottom glasses, thick necks, and pimply faces. She hated them, and she hated the language in which nothing seemed to make sense. She thought she'd rather study Martian.

"You have a test today?" Greg asked.

"Mid-term. I got sick and threw up before I took it. I think I might have failed it."

"You've got to apply yourself," Greg said, stretching into the last patch of sunlight on the coping. "It's easy if you try. Everything's easy."

"For you, maybe."

"For you, too. We're not so different as you think."

"But I don't understand a thing!" she wailed. "I've gone to every class, I take notes, but I don't know what it is I'm writing."

"Maybe it's the teacher, then. Who've you got?" Having graduated the same junior high six years before, Greg knew everyone.

"Mr. Broker."

"Broker sucks," Greg said. "I'll go have a talk with Bob Hayes, the principal, tomorrow after classes. Hayes knows what a prick Broker is. Peter Borachov's the best Russian teacher. I'll get you transferred to his class."

"I'll still hate it."

"Don't be a dope. It's neat. You'll like it, I promise."

"Really?"

"Really."

"Gee. Great!" And just like that, Tori's insoluble problem had been solved. It had taken Greg to come up with the answer. Greg always had the answers.

All of a sudden that afternoon was so peaceful, so perfect. But not for long. Greg, laughing, rolling over, reaching out, taking her with him into the pool. Down, down, down, into the water, Greg's wide, powerful hand pressed against the top of her head, keeping her deep in the water while the air running out burned her lungs and a kind of animal panic gripped her so that she flailed out with her arms and legs and, at last, as she began to cry, feeling the weight come off her, Greg lifting her upward into the air and the light.

"Stop! Stop! Stop! Don't ever do that again!" She could remember him peering into her face while she wept and gasped, until she said, "Why are you looking at me?"

"To see your face change," Greg said.

"How did my face change?" Tori asked, wiping away her

tears. This was an altogether grown-up conversation, and she had already forgotten her fear and her anger.

"I can't tell you," Greg said, "but I can show you." He put her hand on his head. "Push me down into the water. Don't let me come up."

"Greg, don't be stupid. Why should I want—"

"Just do it, Tor!" he thundered, his eyes alight with energy, so that Tori was helpless to do anything other than comply.

She pushed his head under the water. It took both her hands, her arms rigid, her legs fluttering back and forth in the water for added power. Her head was just above the surface of the pool. She could remember how the sunlight cut a last dazzle on the water and then, sinking below the tops of the palms, left the pool in blue twilight. The pumps had cut off, and the water was utterly still, crystal clear.

Tori looked down at her brother submerged as, terrifyingly, she had been moments before. Was this some kind of test, she wondered, a way to improve his breath control? She liked being made part of his program; loved the sense of Tori and Greg versus Mom and Dad, his strength added to hers, another layer of callus to keep out the parental intrusions.

They were alone in Diana's Garden, alone in the cool water, just the two of them taking part in a mysterious process, like an ancient rite of which Tori had no knowledge. And the not knowing somehow added to her excitement, as if she were participating in a really adult thing, Greg trusting her as if she were already grown up; and she thought, it was worth being terrorized by him for moments such as these.

Time passed. Ripples on the skin of the pool, a string of tiny bubbles leaking from the corner of Greg's mouth. She could feel him trying to rise, and she fluttered her feet harder, gaining purchase and leverage at the same time, pushing down to meet the increased pressure.

And then a bluebird swooped down from its perch in a nearby tree, skimmed the water as if wanting to see what lay below, and Tori thought, What am I doing? I am holding my brother underwater, and I don't know how long he's been unable to breathe. She felt a shiver of fright.

With a convulsive gesture she took her hands off the top of Greg's head, dove down, pulled him back to the surface. His face was white, his eyes oddly dark. He looked like a different person, as if the proximity to death had somehow changed him. Something strange and cold crept through Tori's veins.

"There," Greg said, gripping her shoulders hard to be certain that she was staring directly at him. "Do you see? I couldn't tell you, but I've shown you, haven't I?"

Tori, sitting opposite Russell Slade in futuristic Roppongi, asked herself why she had recalled that specific incident. Perhaps it was because the emotions gripping her heart were so disturbing that she had to conjure even more disturbing thoughts to try to block them out. Wasn't it that moment, seeing Greg's changed face, when Tori's feet were set upon her path, that she knew she would not be satisfied until she stared death in the face?

Tori thought she wanted to explore this horrific idea further, but the essence of Russell kept insinuating itself into her consciousness—that new side of him she had glimpsed in the corrida when he had been near death; when, later, she had been so vulnerable, such an easy target for him, and instead of making the most of his advantage, he had gathered her into his arms.

Tori in Tokyo now, recalling Tokyo then, ten years ago, when she was ever so young, ever so smart, ever so vulnerable. She had walked a different road then. She had been cocky, so sure of herself, of her abilities. The thought of defeat was merely a dream, the contemplation of her own death inconceivable.

Greg had flown in, one of the few occasions he had had the time to visit her in Japan. It was odd, their worlds were so different, and yet so alike. They both trained vigorously, both had a kind of monodirectional bent that allowed them to concentrate on the flood of information they had to learn, then translate it into action. They were masters of both the cerebral and the physical, learning what a valuable commodity the combination could be.

Though they were in touch infrequently, and saw each other even less, they still remained close. Perhaps it was their parents that made them so, an unspoken mutual need to band together against the enormous pressures at home in Diana's Garden.

In Tokyo they had gone out drinking. It was a recreation neither had the time nor the inclination to pursue on a regular basis. Their lives were so disciplined, so regularized, so military, that the chance to kick back and break loose was irresistible. It was also Tori's firm belief—a very Japanese concept—that real truths, the full heart, not the empty symbol, could only be expressed while drunk. Everything could

255

be forgiven then; there was no loss of face, no shame at becoming sentimental or showing weakness.

They had gone from bar to bar and, as the night wore on, found themselves in darker and meaner sections of the city. They were not unaware of this; rather, they welcomed the proximity of danger. There was about the entire night a sense of machismo that Tori was unable to understand until she looked back from the perspective time gave her. At first she had believed that Greg, NASA pilot, astronaut in training, had been responsible for that febrile aggressiveness. But then she realized that much of the machismo had stemmed from her, and Greg was following her lead. That had been a switch.

She had followed Greg in everything: sports, mathematics, school, teams, the works. That had been their father's doing. Ellis Nunn had wanted to ensure that she was prepared for the hard, competitive world she would one day be thrown into. *If you can compete with your brother, you'll be ready for anyone,* he had told her. *Don't complain and don't try to weasel out. I'm doing you the favor my father never did for me.*

But, of course, she was doomed to failure at every turn. Greg was the golden boy, superb in sports, mathematics, excelling in each school he attended. Not that she didn't do her best to excel—and succeeded most of the time. She just could not match Greg's level. He seemed to revel in the milieu Ellis Nunn threw him into; she despised it.

So, in the end, she ran away, all the way across the Pacific to Japan, as if she needed to get as much distance as she could between herself and the life she had been forced to live. But her flight was more than away from pain; it was toward a lifestyle that in its enigma drew her steadily on. Like Odysseus on his arduous quest, Tori could hardly have done anything different. She was made for Japan and it was made for her.

For one thing, the stringent asceticism at the martial arts school she joined was such a welcome relief from the opulence and endless money, her parents' insatiable appetite for acquisitions, that she nearly wept for joy the first week at the school. Alone, lying on her simple futon bed after a full day's mental and physical work, staring up through the garden at the moon and the stars, Tori had at last known a peace she had once thought could never be hers.

For another thing, there was *sensei*, a small, quick-gestured man, who nevertheless moved with a deliberation so profound,

256

it actually seemed to be the opposite. His stratagems appeared to be inadvertent, haphazard, wholly unexpected.

"This is more difficult to achieve than you as a Westerner could possibly imagine," he had told her when she had reached the fourth of his six levels of training. "This is not a racist remark, merely the truth. You see, we Japanese abhor randomness. Nature in its pure, unadulterated state frightens us, which is why we have created deities such as the fox goddess to reinforce that fright."

"But *sensei*, look out there," Tori had said, pointing to the exquisite garden. "You are always surrounded by nature. I don't understand."

Sensei had smiled. "I urge you to look again at the garden on which I lavish so much attention. Is it nature? When we wander the lush hillsides of Yoshino, that is nature, when we climb the alps to the north, that is nature. But this garden? No. It is a product of my imagination. Everything is made, dwarfed, bonsaied, controlled by me or by one of my students. This garden is what I want it to be, nothing more, certainly not nature. Not yet.

"The perfect garden, Tori-san, is a simulacrum of nature; it merges with nature to become one with it. But there is no such thing as a perfect garden, and there never will be. The result, though we work all our lives toward it, is too frightening a prospect, because if it ever came about, we would, by definition, lose our control over it, and that can never be allowed."

Facades and a sense of control, these were the principles of Japanese gardens, microcosms of the Japanese culture itself. And these were what Tori thought of the night she went carousing the wild side of Tokyo with Greg. Because she was, at last, tired of both.

Sake was a good antidote to regimentation. Something quite strong was needed to blur the lines, the grids, the bars of the life of an acolyte. Because that was just what she and Greg were, acolytes: she had joined the samurai religion of the past, he the scientific religion of the future. The two of them met here at this moment in time, amid the neon burning of a Tokyo night, in the primitive jungle within the world's most civilized city, bound in the present they were creating.

Or so Tori had thought, until they hit a place called The Lemon Crush. It was at the wrong end of Shinjuku, a kind of *akacho-chin*, an after-hours joint, posh and potent, where the price tags were hot and the action even hotter.

They were, by this time, two liters into sake, and Tori felt as if an electric wire had been slipped into her veins. Greg's eyes crossed at intervals, and he couldn't keep the sweat from glistening in his short, blond hair.

"Wow!" he had exclaimed, when they had taken the Lucite elevator down to the main floor of The Lemon Crush. "I don't ever want to leave this place!" Greg had always been prone to theatrical overstatement, a trait he had unconsciously picked up from their mother.

They had been given a table on the upper level that circled the main floor. Blue and yellow neon rimmed everything: floor, tables, steps, railings, and on the gigantic screen of the ceiling, projected *origami* were continually unfolding like exotic flowers in yet another display of the Japanese trying to control nature.

Tori and Greg were on their second round of sake, soaking up the sights, the sounds of Heaven 17 singing "Fascist Groove Thang" at teeth-rattling volume, when Tori sensed Greg's attention wandering. She followed his gaze, saw him staring fixedly at a beautiful young woman, tall, lissome, exotic as the *origami* unfolding overhead.

"Hubba, hubba!" Greg said, and slipped out of his chair before Tori could do anything to stop him. This was Japan, but Greg had no conception of what that meant, especially in his current state.

"Damnit, Greg!"

But he couldn't hear her. As Tori watched him make his way down toward the beautiful young woman, she thought of the kind of place this was, and what that said about its habitués. Drug dealers and sex peddlers were only the tamer elements wending their way through the yellow-and-blue-lit throng. The Lemon Crush, it was whispered, was a favored hangout of the Yakuza.

Tori had never met a Yakuza, and even through her sake-induced buzz she thought that this was not the night to do so. Macho was one thing, suicide quite another. Greg would not understand this. Tori did not think they had enough time together for her to adequately explain the inner workings of the Yakuza mind to him.

Now she could see Greg talking to the woman, could see her smiling in return. Greg was so handsome; he had never had trouble getting girls; just the opposite, in fact. Tori could remember when he was in high school, there were too many girlfriends to make life simple. And at one point Greg's after-school and practice life became something of a slapstick farce, complete with slammed doors, lightning changes of clothes, and, at least on Greg's part, iron-man stamina. Tori had had an active part in this, playing—in Laura Nunn's parlance—the straight man who stooged for the star, making sure no two girls would catch him in the same room at the same time.

And, recalling this, seeing him laughing with the beautiful, exotic Japanese, Tori discovered that it wasn't only apprehension she was feeling, it was anger. She and Greg saw each other so infrequently, she thought it insensitive of him to go off and leave her like this. And from the secure distance of the future, Tori was able to see the truth: she had wanted to spend the night with her brother, matching his macho with hers, at last on her turf, showing Greg—and Ellis Nunn—that she could compete on his level.

Could she really be jealous of this creature? Tori had asked herself then. Yes, yes, as she slid through the crowd, moving toward them.

Tori was still some distance away when she saw the tall, square-shouldered young man heading on a collision course with her brother and the woman. He was a Japanese dressed in a stylish suit. His hair was shorter even than Greg's, almost a military cut. There was something in his direct gaze that disturbed her even before she was close enough to feel the power of his *wa*. That was when the fright took over. By that time she had had more than enough training to know a dangerous opponent when she saw one.

The young man was heading straight for Greg, his gaze fixed steadily on him. Tori watched him move through the crowd. It was like seeing a hot knife slice through butter. He did not have to fight his way through, did not have to elbow people aside. No one was disturbed, there was no ripple to mark his passage.

Then abruptly, shockingly, he reached out and the sleeve of his jacket rode up his arm, exposing a wrist covered with an *irizumi* demon spitting fire. And Tori's heart lurched. Oh, my God, she thought. Greg's making a move on the girlfriend of a Yakuza.

She and the Yakuza converged on Greg and the woman. Tori had just enough time to say, ''Greg, let's get out of here!'' before the Yakuza's hand clamped down on Greg's shoulder.

Greg spun, shoving the hand off him. Greg was in a semicrouch, the standard first position of the sort of unarmed combat taught by the United States government agencies. It would mean nothing to the Yakuza. Unless Greg pulled a gun and shot him dead, the Yakuza's skills would quickly overpower anything Greg could throw at him.

Greg grinned. "Hey, I don't want any trouble," he said suddenly, coming out of his crouch. He put up his hands. "No law I know of against talking to a beautiful woman."

"The woman belongs to me," the Yakuza said. He had gone very still. One arm was out from his body, rigid, the other one was close to the lapel of his suit jacket.

Greg said, "You've got it all wrong, pal. Slavery was abolished almost a hundred years ago."

"The world doesn't belong to America," the Yakuza said.

"Yeah? Well, it sure doesn't belong to Japan."

The Yakuza grinned. "Not yet."

"Greg, come on," Tori said. "We didn't come here to debate cultural differences."

"Stay away, woman! This does not concern you," the Yakuza growled, curtly dismissing her.

"Like hell!" Tori said, for the moment forgetting everything she had been taught. "When you threaten my brother, you threaten me."

The Yakuza slowly turned to her, said in the most condescending voice, "You're cute, you know that?" He produced a snub-nosed automatic. "But that's all you are, so—"

At that point Tori jammed the stiffened fingers of her right hand into the Yakuza's solar plexus. His eyes opened wide and he was jolted backward.

Greg lunged for the automatic, and the Yakuza's left hand chopped down on his forearm. As if in slow motion, Tori saw the Yakuza turn his gun on Greg; she went for the nerve cluster in his right arm, and using her own left arm as a brace, bent the Yakuza's gun arm backward until she heard the snap.

His savage kick caught her on the edge of her pelvis. She cried out in surprise and pain, slammed into him again and, almost simultaneously, heard the report of the single shot.

The Yakuza's face went white, he said something unintelligible in all the electronic noise and commotion, then slipped to the floor. Blood, a dark flower, spread its lethal petals.

Tori bent, touched him on the side of the neck. Then she

grabbed Greg and pushed her way through the throng, farther and farther, blue and yellow mutating the shadows all around, the *origami* unfolding, unfolding, the strained faces now so alien to her.

Outside in the spangled night she said, "Come on! Let's go!"

Greg hesitated. "But that guy's wounded. He might die. I think we ought to wait."

"Greg, he's dead. He had no pulse. The only thing that will happen if we wait is we'll be killed. That guy was Yakuza, a gangster of the most dangerous sort."

Greg seemed bewildered. "But we can explain . . . they'll understand—"

"The only thing his family understands is *giri*—obligation. And their obligation now is to destroy us. For the love of God, come *on*!" Pulling him away from The Lemon Crush. "Even if we run, there'll be trouble!"

Who had killed the Yakuza with the demon on his wrist? Tori? Greg? Or had he, himself, pulled the trigger by accident? No one would ever know. The simple fact was that he had died as a result of the bullet wound.

"That was really something!" Greg exclaimed later. They were sitting in a cheap dive somewhere in the sludgepit of Kitasenju. "I've never seen you defend me, Tori. It's always been the other way around."

"It was a stupid incident," Tori said sourly. "It never should have happened."

"But it did. The happenstance of life! It's like why I came here to a place I'd never been to before, a culture I know nothing about. Like fate. *Karma*, wouldn't you say?"

"It never should have happened. If you hadn't—"

"No, no. It showed me something. Something I was supposed to see."

"I don't know what the hell you're talking about." She was still angry with Greg, still partly in shock over what had happened. She had never liked guns; now she liked them even less. But staring at her brother across the dirty table, she saw another kind of light in his angel eyes. It was the same disturbing darkness she had seen that late afternoon years before when he had risen from beneath the water of the pool in Diana's Garden where she had held him as the air had leaked out of him.

It was as if the shooting had galvanized him—no, that word wasn't quite right. It was more like it had elated him. But that could not be possible, Tori told herself over and over. Her brother, the golden boy, the NASA astronaut, couldn't harbor such an antisocial, such an amoral emotion. No, not Greg. But she was facing the incontrovertible evidence.

"Don't you? But you must understand. You're the mystic in the family, Tori. That's why you came here to study, isn't it? Me, I'm the pragmatist. The mathematician, the pilot, soon to be the man in the moon. I hope. But first, I've come here to see you." He looked at her. "You *don't* understand."

"No."

Greg nodded. "Okay. After how you defended me, I guess you deserve to hear this, and anyway, we're far too drunk to have it make a difference." He took a deep breath. "I imagine you always thought I loved the pool, the diving."

"Well, sure," Tori said, confused. "You were always so good at it."

"Not always," Greg said. "You see, I never wanted to dive. Never. Never. Dad made me. He shamed me into it. I was afraid to get on the diving board, so one night he made me go with him to the UCLA Olympic diving complex. Dad had done all their new outdoor lighting, so he had access to everything on campus.

"He took me by the scruff of the neck and climbed with me all the way to the top of the high-dive board. By this time I had a good idea of what he was going to do, so I was crying. Even after all this time, I'm ashamed to admit that. I was so frightened, I almost wet my pants.

"Dad took me to the edge of the board. He pushed my head down, forced me to look. Arc lights on the water. It was such a long way down! My teeth were chattering, and he had to hold me up.

" 'Go on!' he shouted at me. 'The only way you'll learn to dive is to dive!'

" 'But I don't want to dive!' I protested.

" 'You're too young to know what you want!' he shouted. 'Do as I say!' And with that he shoved me off the end of the board.''

Greg shuddered. "Christ, but it was a long way down. I remember the wind whistling in my ears and the world turning, turning. I think, for just an instant, I saw him standing at the end of the diving board, smiling. Or maybe I just *thought* I saw him. I don't know. The lane lines painted on the bottom of the pool were rushing up, so goddamned clear I was sure there was

262

no water in the pool. Then I hit the water and all the breath exploded out of me.

"Dad came and got me. I was limp as a noodle, but he just slapped me on the back a couple of times to make sure all the water was out of me. And up we went again. This time I gritted my teeth and went down on my own. By the fourth clumsy dive, I ached all over and I was ready to listen to his instructions."

Greg's eyes were bleak as he looked at Tori. "That was how I learned to love diving."

"But it was horrible! How could you ever have loved it after such an introduction?"

"That," Greg said, "is what I've been asking myself ever since then."

"Tori?" Russell Slade said in the present of futuristic Roppongi. Across the *kissaten* the bank of Quotron machines—Free Use to Patrons!—flashed their minute-by-minute update of the progress of the stock market. "Where have you been these past several minutes?"

"I—" Tori made an effort to come fully back to the present. "I was thinking of what Deke said about the hafnium." Why am I lying to him? she asked herself. "All the terrible possibilities, given the kind of minds, the evil out in the world."

"Yeah, well, there's no use dwelling on nightmares," Russell said. "We'd just better make sure the nightmares never occur. Where is this hafnium ending up? That's what we've got to find out. The question now is, will Hitasura help us?"

"Let's go find out," Tori said.

Getting an audience with Hitasura was approximately as difficult as finding the treasure chamber inside the Pyramid of Cheops. He was a cautious man—some said paranoid, but these were his enemies, and their envy evidently distorted their judgment. There had never been an assassination attempt made on Hitasura, and this spoke volumes for his strategy and caution.

This was not to say that he was inactive. On the contrary, Hitasura was a hands-on *oyabun*. He was as yet perhaps too young to feel comfortable with delegating power to his lieutenants. Just as well. In the three years since he had come to power, he had already found it necessary to execute two lieutenants whose loyalty was to the yen rather than to himself.

Tori had met Hitasura ten years ago, when she and Greg had been hiding out from the members of the Yakuza family who had sought to avenge the shooting of the man with the fire-spitting demon on his wrist. That family was the chief rival of Hitasura's family, and Hitasura—a mere lieutenant then—had taken it upon himself to protect Tori and her brother.

Some years later Hitasura's sister had been kidnapped by members of that same family on an unrelated matter of *giri*, and it had been Tori who had penetrated the stronghold where she was being kept. The family had thought themselves clever, stashing Hitasura's sister in a Western brothel where they were certain Hitasura would never come because he would stand out like a peony in a patch of dandelions.

In the process of getting her out, Tori had killed four Yakuza of the rival family, and had been wounded in the left shoulder. At that moment Hitasura had sworn eternal friendship. The *giri* he felt toward Tori was immutable, absolute. It would be unthinkable to question his loyalty.

Tori made half a dozen calls, all from different phone booths on the streets and in hotel lobbies, before she got the response she had been seeking.

Twenty minutes later a red 750 BMW swooped them up in the Ginza. They were squeezed into the front seat while wax plugs were put in their ears from behind and they were blindfolded. The BMW stopped and they were transferred to the roomier backseat. It accelerated into the city.

Neither of them spoke. Tori had cautioned Russell against any untoward word or gesture. "Just sit back and relax," she had told him. "Let what's going to happen happen." Russell had not protested, yet another sign that the new side of his personality that had emerged in Medellín was gaining dominance. Now he sat with uncharacteristic calm while they hurtled through the innards of Tokyo.

A sense of acceleration, the centrifugal force generated by turns, and the passage of time, were the only clues left to give them an inkling of where they were being taken. Tori had an intimate knowledge of the city, but this was like trying to back down a mountainside in a snow storm: calculating vectors and distances was next to useless; memory and feel were the only things that mattered.

Where would I be if I were Hitasura?

Somewhere on the streets. Tori started at this point and let her intuition unravel the puzzle. While one part of her brain was busy with time, turns, and speed, the other part was occupied with solving the mystery of where they were being taken. She knew of three of Hitasura's bases, but she had to take into account that she might be a year out of date. It could be very useful to know where Hitasura was taking them, especially if he had no idea that they knew.

This was basic tradecraft: knowing where you were at all times, whether you were with friend or foe. Still, Tori had another motivation, one that disturbed her profoundly. After Estilo's betrayal, she was unsure of everything and everyone. Caution was one thing, but full-blown paranoia could paralyze you. You had to know which way to jump at any minute, or, not knowing, sometimes trust. If trust was gone, only a great black chasm remained, yawning below her, waiting for the moment when she would fall.

The BMW came to an abrupt stop and Tori and Russell were bundled out of the car. Tori could not shake the odd feeling that they had gone around in circles. But she knew that the Ginza was not Hitasura's territory, so that was out. Or was it?

They were helped up a short set of stairs and, kept bent almost double, ushered through what seemed like a tunnel. Then they were allowed to stand up. They were pushed backward until they felt something soft behind their legs. They sat.

At last their earplugs and blindfolds came off. At the same instant a muffled roar of a diesel engine sounded. A moment later the unmistakable sensation of motion.

Of course, Tori thought. A vehicle! We *had* been driven in a circle to confuse us, to make us think we had gotten to another part of the city, when all along this van had been waiting around the corner. As soon as Hitasura's men had determined that she and Russell had not been followed, they had called for the van.

Tori looked around, blinking in the dim light. They were in what appeared to be a miniature living room. They were sitting on a sofa upholstered in an Oriental cotton print of blues, greens, and deep yellows. There was a brass coffee table, Chinese ginger jar lamps on matching mahogany side tables, a pair of dark blue upholstered wing chairs, even a couple of pleasant well-framed landscape prints on the walls. No windows, however. It was surprisingly comfortable, nonetheless.

"Where in the hell are we?" Russell said.

"A moving van," a deep rich voice said. They looked up, saw Hitasura, a tall, slender, dark-skinned Japanese, enter the mobile living room. "One of many in my fleet." He smiled warmly. "Should the need arise for you to move, one of these vans will handle everything in one load, you here in comfort, while below and behind you, your containerized possessions are safely stored, fumigated, and sanitized."

Hitasura sat across from them in one of the wing chairs. It was large enough to accommodate his height. "Tori, it is good to see you again." He might have been a handsome man, but there was no moderation to his features. He had hard eyes, a sharp nose, and an unforgiving mouth. There was a tea-colored melanin birthmark on the left side of his neck that ran up his jaw and encroached on the lower portion of his cheek.

"Hitasura-san," Tori said formally, "this is Russell Slade. A friend."

"Mr. Slade." Hitasura inclined his head. "Perhaps you will forgive the melodrama when I tell you that these rather elaborate precautions were necessary."

"What's happened?" Tori said, picking up on his tone.

Hitasura sat back, made a bridge with his fingertips. "I hardly know where to begin. It may be a war is brewing, Tori-san, though I hope I am overreacting." He looked at her. "My only brother is dead."

"How?"

"He was murdered," Hitasura said. "Much more than that I do not know. It happened sometime shortly after midnight. His apartment was broken into. Some things, perhaps, were stolen, although we can rule out robbery as a motive. His money and valuables were not touched."

Tori said, "Have you any idea who's responsible?"

"Nothing conclusive," Hitasura said. The pain was apparent in his dark eyes, in the new lines in his face. The pressure of being an *oyabun* was massive. "But yesterday morning, early, a woman hurled my brother's mentor, a university professor named Giin, from the parapet of the Nihonbashi. Giin had been teaching my brother his method of deciphering codes."

"Who killed this man, Giin? Fukuda?"

"That would have been my guess, since Fukuda works for Big Ezoe, and he is my chief rival. But the odd thing is that Fukuda was busy elsewhere at the time of Giin's demise.''

"Another female assassin?" Tori said doubtfully. "Who?"

"You've come back to me at a most propitious time, Tori-san." Hitasura's eyes were burning. "I have begun to mobilize all of Tokyo to find out."

"We have a fix," Hitasura said with the receiver of the mobile phone to his ear.

"On who?" Tori said. "You have no description of the woman who killed Giin, and you can't even say whether it was she who murdered your brother."

"We know where Fukuda is," Hitasura said. "Fukuda knows. We must persuade Fukuda to tell us what she knows."

"Who is this Fukuda?" Russell asked. "Did I hear you right? She's some kind of female Yakuza assassin?"

"That's right," Tori said.

The anonymous moving van rumbled through the streets of Tokyo. Hitasura was on the mobile phone, getting the latest information on the citywide search for his brother's murderer.

"But I thought the Yakuza had no use for women," Russell said.

"Generally speaking, that's true," Tori said. "But Fukuda is an exception."

"In many ways," Hitasura added. He had cradled the phone receiver. "Fukuda has a—oh, shall we say, a history in Yakuza lore."

Tori grunted. "What Hitasura-san means is that she broke her way into Yakuza society. Forcibly. She made the Yakuza *oyabun* notice her, and accept her."

"Some," Hitasura corrected. "Others will never accept a woman doing a man's job."

"Better than most men can do it," Tori said.

Hitasura glowered at her, then abruptly laughed. "Tori-san, too, is an exception. I do not hold her sex against her." He said this in a tone of voice that indicated he should be congratulated for his insight.

"If I read Hitasura-san's thinking right," Tori explained, "he feels sure that if there is another female assassin working, she had to have been trained by Fukuda. Fukuda is the key."

"Wait a minute." Russell looked from one to the other. "Even if you manage to capture her, what makes you think that

267

this highly trained assassin is going to tell you anything?''

Hitasura glanced at Tori.

Russell said immediately, "What am I missing?" He looked at Hitasura, but the *oyabun* turned away. "Tori?"

Tori said nothing. Instead, she took his hand in hers, placed the flat of it over her left hip. It was an extraordinary gesture, full of echoes of the past: their meeting in the library in L.A. when he had come to re-recruit her, and had touched her there. *How does it feel?* But there were also intimations of the future, an intimacy about which neither of them was at the moment able to speak. It was in some sense a tribal gesture, a tremor of intent, primitive, powerful, a symbol full of meaning, in a land composed of meaningless symbols.

"Fukuda broke your hip?"

It was a whisper, but Tori winced, as if she were experiencing again the bright blue-white-green flash searing her eyes, singeing her brows and fuzz of hair on her arms, feeling anew the weird sense not of falling, but of floating in the subway tunnel far below the streets of Tokyo. Feeling nothing for an instant, and then as if the percussion is hitting her all over again, the agonizing, teeth-grinding pain as the shock dissipates. Then the extreme heaviness of her own body, as if it now weighs tons. Crashing to the tracks, the shining steel coated with a hot, sticky substance, dark, running out of her in a stream. And Fukuda pausing a moment in the semidarkness of the subway tunnel, her face alight with triumph. *I told you not to get in my way, but you didn't listen. You took from me something that was very precious. Now that you'll pay with your life, perhaps you will understand just how precious.* The gloating is cut with her rage and her hate. *You backed the wrong horse. Sooner or later, we'll take Hitasura down, just as we've taken you down. No big thing. Easy does it.* Then she had disappeared, and in her place was the rumbling of the oncoming train, sweeping around a curve, its startlingly brilliant headlight firing the steel tracks, the light racing toward Tori, who lay on the tracks, immobile . . .

"Tori! *Tori!*" Russell was shaking her. "Are you all right?"

White-faced, Tori turned her head toward him. "No," she said, her voice a hoarse whisper. Her eyes locked with his. They were dark, swirling with emotion. "I've come full circle, Russ. I beat death once. Now I see I've got to do it all over again."

EIGHT
ARKHANGELSKOE/STAR TOWN/MOSCOW/TOKYO

"Comrade, have you heard the latest news? They've done it again."

"Who's done it again?" Valeri said.

"White Star," the young man with the strawberry birthmark said. "Their elite cadres are better armed, more well-trained. White Star is no longer merely a ragtag guerrilla organization made up of disparate dissident minorities. They are a full-fledged army now. And elements of this new army have attacked the Kyshtym Industrial Complex. It is entirely destroyed!"

Valeri Bondasenko was sitting on the bench overlooking the large birch tree, outpost of the forest on the other side of which were the grounds of Arkhangelskoe. On one side of him was the young man with the strawberry birthmark, on the other, his daughter, silent, imperturbable. At their backs, up the sloping incline, hulked the almost Victorian exterior of the insane asylum.

"Is that so?" Valeri said. "I had heard the story differently. I had heard that there was a low-level nuclear event at the complex, but that it was under control." Kyshtym, for almost fifty years, had been the site of the Soviet Union's main military atomic reactors. Three years ago, a massive overhaul of the

270

aging units had begun. But only after a series of scrupulously unreported events—leaks, explosions, and the like—had killed one-third of the people who worked at Kyshtym, and who lived in a nearby city so secret it was without a name.

The young man laughed. "Where do you get your information, comrade? Tass?" He chuckled, shook his head in disbelief. When he spoke he looked ahead, never at Valeri. "Really! The gullibility of some people."

He seemed to have drifted off, and was talking to himself, and Valeri began once again to consider the enormous miscalculation the president made when he began to replace the central Communist party with his own handpicked people. Cults were dangerous. If anything in Russia's recent history had been made manifest it was that.

The president had needed some form of stability to hold the center together while he gathered his cult around him, and he had most unwisely chosen the military to aid him. In return for their help, he had promised—and delivered—more and more money to the generals' annual budget. This had created a serious shortfall in the other national sectors in dire need of money.

Now the president was paying the fearful price of consolidating his power in the form of strikes, local uprisings, the disintegration of the economy, the appalling Western characteristic of the polarization of the classes, and the concomitant rise to power of White Star.

Valeri shivered, trying to free his mind from its turmoil. He slipped his hand into his daughter's, as if this could reassure her that he was here with her. He wanted so much to see even the slightest hint of a reaction, a sense that there was the spark of consciousness in her mind, that she might be thinking, *I know you're with me, Daddy, and it makes me feel better.*

But then the young man spoke directly to Valeri. "No, no, comrade. It was White Star. They blew apart the concrete lake prison labor helped pour. They exposed cracked reactor cores, defective rods that caused partial meltdowns, and enough carelessly dumped plutonium sludge to irradiate all of Siberia. I'm told the entire area has been evacuated. The officials won't get any more idiots from the city without a name to come in and clean up like they did after the disaster of 'fifty-seven. Within two years, over a thousand people had died of radiation poisoning. Within ten years, twenty-seven hundred more died of cancer, almost everyone who had been brought in for the cleanup in exchange for promises of extended vacations." The young

271

man laughed again, but this time there was a disturbing edge to it. "The workers got vacations, all right. Only they were a bit *more* extended than they had bargained for."

Valeri gripped the white hand of his daughter all the tighter. The tracery of blue veins beneath the translucent surface of her skin reminded him of the skein of birch branches, bare, traced with snow, pale against the dark Ukrainian sky in winter.

"The stars," Valeri's father had said during the last nights of his life. "Perhaps our salvation lies in the stars. The stars look cruel, I know, but Valeri Denysovich, I know they are not. Here is where the cruelty reigns, in Kiev, in the captive Ukraine."

Valeri had stayed with his father, until his nights became hours, then minutes, and at last his eyes closed for the final time. A moment later the red sun rose over the snow-covered roofs to the east, bloodying their tops.

Valeri, sitting next to his only child in this pastoral, almost peaceful setting near Arkhangelskoe, could not remember his father without also conjuring up the dreaded specter of Solovki.

In the late 1920s and early thirties the Solovki Islands in the White Sea had been turned into one of the most infamous of the Russian death camps. Into the forbidding universe of Solovki had been thrown the so-called "anti-Soviet" elements, chief among them the rebel Ukrainian kulaks—the peasants.

Valeri's uncle had been a kulak, but after he had been shot by a Russian soldier in the streets of Kiev for daring to speak his native language, Valeri's father decided on another course of action. He joined the army. Not just any division, mind you, but the fiercely independent First Siberian Cavalry Corps.

He had seen that as his revenge against the Russians, but instead it proved his undoing. Six months after he joined, in the autumn of 1931, the corps was overrun by Russian "loyalists," who were sent by Moscow to punish the unit for spreading anti-Soviet propaganda. The truth was the First Siberian had gotten too powerful. It had made Moscow nervous in a nervous time, and Moscow had acted accordingly.

Valeri's father was imprisoned for a short time, then sent summarily to Solovki. There was no trial, no chance to refute the charges. In fact, charges were never read to him; he never knew what he had been accused of. That scarcely mattered to Valeri's father. He was Ukrainian; that alone was enough to mark him as a potentially dangerous criminal.

"That's just what the Russians had made me," he would tell Valeri many years later. "A dangerous criminal."

In Solovki, Valeri's father and his fellow inmates were fed—when they were fed at all—on nine ounces of moldy black bread and a bowl of something akin to hot water with a lump of frost-blackened turnip floating in it. Clothes were out of the question, as was any form of heat, save the occasional fire.

A week after his father arrived in Solovki, there were already so many inmates that the overcrowding became intolerable. As a consequence, inmates were herded out in order to be sent to another camp. Valeri's father watched with bleak eyes as his fellow criminals pushed, shoved, clawed, and fought each other to be chosen. Anyplace, the reasoning went, would be an improvement over Solovki.

His father was chosen in the last batch herded out, but in the turmoil he managed to slip away, secrete himself beside a mother and child, blue-skinned and stiff, dead for a day and a half. He had no desire to be trekked to another place he knew nothing about. Better the devil you know, he told himself, than stepping out blindfolded in the dark.

It was two months before he received word through the camp grapevine as to the fate of those who had left Solovki. They had been sent to Siberia. Marched up the narrow ice-clogged Vasyugan stream, they had been left on the ice fields and the barren bogs without food or clothes. All of them had died.

His father spent just over three years in Solovki. Though he lost two fingers and four toes to frostbite, though he lost sixty pounds, he was a survivor. He stole food from the dead, ate the flesh of the odd guard dog that died of exposure, and eventually learned how to snare fish from the icy waters.

He escaped, finally, one moonless winter's night, with the snow falling eerily on the water, the guard dogs barking frantically, the darkness aflame with automatic gunfire.

He was wounded but managed to escape. It took him six weeks to make his way back to Kiev, and by that time he had lost the feeling in both his legs.

In order to save his life, the legs had to be amputated. "Do it! Do it!" he had shouted at the surgeons, shaking with rage at the indignity of what was about to happen. "What's the difference? I only have six toes, anyway. That's not so much to miss!"

But Solovki had done more than take his legs, it had dehumanized him. Living with the dead, eating frozen dog meat, watching day by day as his fellow Ukrainians wasted away or were shot by guards bored, drunk, or both, had scarred his soul. He could never again think about his country in the same way.

Just as the murder of his brother had caused a violent reaction in him, so had his time in Solovki. But instead of turning his burning rage outward, now his isolation had turned it inward.

It had been his son, Valeri, who had saved him from taking a pistol and putting it to his head. Valeri had said the only thing that would make his father want to keep living: "I want to learn, Father. I want to know what it means to be a Ukrainian, and I can only do that from you."

Now I am the father, Valeri Bondasenko thought, sitting beside his mute, unthinking daughter on the wide lawn of the asylum near Arkhangelskoe. I want to teach her what you taught me, Father, but even if she hears me, she isn't listening.

Does this mean they've won, Father? The Russians who systematically beat us, stripped us of our culture, our past, who have entangled us in hopelessness, who have tried their best to exterminate us? No, no, no! I haven't forgotten what you taught me, how to bury my hate so deeply no one would ever find out what was in my heart.

No. They haven't won, the Russians, but they haven't lost. Not yet. Not yet.

Another day, another visit to the man who would be God, Mars Volkov thought as he drove up to the Hero's fortresslike complex within Star Town.

He did not immediately get out of the Chaika limousine, however, but instead listened again to the tape recording he had made of his last conversation with the Hero.

"I don't know what's come over me. Before I lifted off, I never had much of a sense of humor. Who knows, perhaps being suspended between heaven and a living hell will do that for you."

It had been a rather nice touch, Mars thought, to make such a theatrical display of disabling the monitoring equipment in the Hero's living quarters. Of course, it was quite real. Mars had actually shut down the system. And he had been correct not to inform the dolts downstairs. Their display of genuine pique had put the icing on the cake. No amount of acting, no matter how expert, would fool the Hero or his idiot manqué, Arbat. (Mars had to admit that the bloody dolphin had been his one major mistake, but now that it was done, he could hardly take it away.)

"There are some who think you're lying, or have misremembered, or are delusional."

"Are you one of those?"

All in all, Mars thought, the last interrogation had gone well.

Mars was far too clever to try to fool the Hero at this late stage. It would, he knew, be another mistake to underestimate the Hero now, even though he, Mars, had finally gained the high ground in their battle of wits. Mars's own sentiments about being fed up with playing their no-win game had been real, as well. But he was not as much the maverick as he had led the Hero to believe—it was far more convincing to tell a semblance of the truth than to try to put over a lie. Consequently, Mars had come prepared to his last meeting. He had been wearing a body mike attached to a portable microcassette recorder. The same was true today.

"The corpse opened its mouth and—"

"No, no. This isn't something out of a science-fiction or a horror film. He didn't come back from the dead, nor was he animated like a zombie or a golem. This was something else . . ."

Mars reached over, shut off the tape. What had happened up there between the stars? He was becoming consumed with this puzzle.

He sat for a moment longer, lost in thought. Then he got out of the Chaika, went through the laborious but necessary security procedures to allow him entrance to the Hero's complex.

Inside, the Hero was with Tatiana. She was a short blond woman, with a ruddy complexion and wide-set, direct gray eyes. She had the wide shoulders, narrow waist and hips of the athlete. She was as attractive as Lara, though in an entirely different way.

"Good morning, comrade," Tatiana said when she saw Mars enter the pool area. Her swimsuit was quite shockingly brief, cut very high around the tops of the legs in the Western manner, and Mars made a mental note to order different, more modest suits for his guard girls.

He nodded to her, said, "Where is Odysseus?"

Arbat surfaced, sped across the diameter of the pool, spewed water all over Mars. Tatiana put her hand over her mouth, turned her face away, but not before Mars caught a glimpse of her laughing.

"He's in the shower," she said when she had recovered. She brought him a towel. Mars glowered, making quite sure her face was solemn.

"What the hell does he need to shower for?" Mars said tightly. "He's in the goddamned pool all the time, anyway."

275

"He never goes in the pool without showering first," Tatiana said.

A buzzer sounded, and she went across the room. She opened a translucent glass door, and Mars could hear the shower cut off. Then she reappeared, carrying the Hero in her arms.

Odysseus said nothing until Tatiana had deposited him into the pool. He slid from her arms as if he were a slippery eel. His sleek, hairless body, so pale and unearthly in color, was sheened as if with oil as well as water. Arbat immediately began a series of clicks, to which the Hero responded briefly.

He turned to Mars. "You're early."

"Good morning to you, too," Mars said sourly.

The Hero bobbed in the water, eyed him. "Did you fall into a puddle? I don't believe it's raining."

"The dolphin—" Out of the corner of his eye, Mars saw Tatiana stifle a laugh. "It was your bloody dolphin's idea of a joke."

"Oh, not a joke," Odysseus said when Arbat's clicks had ceased. "It was her way of saying 'Hello, comrade!' "

"Don't be idiotic. You're trying my patience."

"And you," Odysseus said, "have been trying mine." He smiled. "That makes us even, though not in any way you'd understand. But maybe you still feel at a disadvantage. You're wondering, I'm willing to bet, what it is that Odysseus sees in being in the pool all day. Am I right?" Before Mars had a chance to answer, the Hero had pressed on. "So here's your big opportunity, Comrade Volkov. Take off your clothes and join us. See firsthand what it's all about."

When Mars hesitated, the Hero said, "Still undecided? Let's give you a hand in making up your mind. Arbat?" The dolphin leaped up and, at the top of her arc, spat a long stream of water into Mars's face. When she landed, she did so broadside, sending a wave over the side of the pool, inundating Mars.

"Guess you don't have much of a choice now, comrade," Odysseus said, clearly delighted.

Mars, in an inner rage, resolved to do nothing outwardly to show the Hero he had won this round. But simple human dignity dictated that he say, "I have no bathing attire."

"That's a quaint thought," the Hero said. "I don't need 'bathing attire,' why should you?"

Mars could think of no appropriate answer, so instead he stalked across the room to the shower area and disrobed. He wrapped a towel around his middle, reemerged.

"Welcome, Volkov," Odysseus said, "to the isle of Polyphemus, the Cyclops."

Grim-faced, Mars approached the pool and, deliberately ignoring Tatiana, who was already bobbing alongside the Hero, dropped the towel and slid into the water.

Arbat made quite a fuss, clicking and diving. For a moment Mars was uneasy. It suddenly dawned on him that he was in the creature's domain. What would the dolphin choose to do to him? Nothing, it seemed, but click and dive. Arbat never approached him.

"It's easier here in the water," the Hero said in the silence after the dolphin's last outburst.

"What is?" Mars found himself asking.

"Life," Odysseus said, staring up at the arched ceiling, alight with reflections from the water. "I thought that would be self-evident once you were in here." His gaze lowered. His eyes, Mars saw, were the color of gun metal today, and seemingly just as hard. "But perhaps I have overestimated you."

"I hope not," Mars said.

"We'll see."

Mars said, "I'd like to return to something you spoke about last time. The unspeakable color you saw in . . . Menelaus's eyes after he died." Mars had almost forgotten the name the Hero wanted him to use. Menelaus, another of the Greek chieftains who took part in the sack of Troy, and, so Homer would have us believe, Odysseus's alter ego. "The color of God, so you said. I'm interested to learn why you used just that term. Surely there are others that would do as well."

"Are there?" Odysseus said. "If so, it's clear you wouldn't know them. You're in the dark here, all of you. I'm the only lamp to guide you."

"That's true," Mars conceded. "But God?"

"We're back to Him, I'm afraid," Odysseus said. "And you said you no longer wanted to talk about God."

"I've changed my mind."

"Really? Well, that's mighty adaptable of you. I'm impressed." The Hero closed his eyes for a moment. "All right: God. Do you know that dolphins believe in God? Arbat has quite a cogent concept of Him, much more sensible than the clumsy versions humans have been able to come up with." There it was again, not "we" but "humans," as if he was no longer human.

"I chose that phrase 'the color of God' because it was the only one that is appropriate," the Hero said. "We return to

277

Arbat, to dolphins in general. Their minds don't work like humans', Volkov. Arbat's mind works in a kind of wave pattern and, beyond that, spirals. Linear thinking is unknown to her. Interesting, no?" His eyes popped open. "So. God to her is Time. Not day and night, dolphins don't conceive of such categorized sections. Time as in movement—the movement that has extended before life, that extends through life, and will extend after life has been terminated."

Mars tried to absorb this circumlocution. "And what has this to do with the color in Menelaus's dead eyes?"

"They weren't dead," Odysseus said. "Oh, yes, Menelaus himself was an empty husk, embalmed by the winds of space. But his eyes had become a conduit."

"What precisely did you see in them?"

"That," the Hero said, "is the fundamental mistake you've all made. I didn't see something *in* them. I saw *through* them. It was as if they had become a telescope of fantastic power. I saw Elsewhere. I saw Elsewhere."

Mars closed his eyes, pressed his fingers against the lids. He was getting a headache. The essential problem was that he couldn't tell whether this discussion was too profound or too laughable for him. Was he confronting a madman or . . . what? What had happened to the two men of Odin-Galaktika II during the event, when all telemetry and monitoring went down? That was what Mars had been ordered to find out.

Had the Hero in some way been transformed, or was he merely pulling everyone's leg, amusing himself at the state's expense as some kind of sick reparation for his disabilities?

The truly frightening thing, Mars thought now, was that there was at least the possibility that the Hero *had* been transformed by the event. In that case, what had he become?

"Can you give me even a hint," Mars said at last, "of what 'Elsewhere' and 'Elsewhen' mean?"

Odysseus held out his arm. "Tatiana," he said, "would you come here?"

Tatiana obediently swam in his direction so that she was in front of him. Then the two of them swam forward until Tatiana's body was pressed so firmly against Mars's that he could feel her hard breasts, the slight swell of her stomach, the press of her pubic mound.

"What—"

"Bear with me, comrade," Odysseus said firmly. "And don't back up; this is all in the name of so-called science." He peered into Mars's face. "I want you to imagine that still being you, you feel Tatiana's breasts as if they were your own, you feel her sexual organs as well as yours, swim in the pulse of her blood as well as your own, wander through her thought patterns. Can you do that, Volkov? No, I suppose not." He let Tatiana go. "But that is what I meant when I said 'Elsewhere.' "

"This means," Mars said slowly, taking it a step at a time, "that in Menelaus's dead eyes you sense the presence of another entity."

"Yes."

"And during the event you merged with the entity."

"Not merged," the Hero said. "It was more as if I was allowed in for just a moment to take a look around."

"I want you to be absolutely clear about this," Mars said. "By 'entity' do I take it you mean an extraterrestrial?"

"I can't think what else it might be."

This is rapidly becoming infuriating, Mars thought. He's so clear about this that I'm beginning to believe his madness. Perhaps I'm coming here too often. Can madness be communicative? No. Impossible. But then he reminded himself that if Odysseus were, indeed, mad, it was an entirely new form of madness, which the scientific team had yet to identify, let alone begin to define.

"All right," Mars said. "Let's leave the issue of 'Elsewhere' for the time being. What about 'Elsewhen'?"

"In an odd way, that's simpler to explain," the Hero said, "because it more directly relates to the color between the stars; the color of God. God is Time, and Time is what I saw. Not the present or the past or even the future."

"Now you're talking in riddles," Mars said testily. "Einstein proved that—"

"Einstein was wrong," Odysseus said matter-of-factly. "His mind, brilliant though it was, was human, and therefore bound by certain limitations."

"But when it comes to time, there *is* only past, present, and future."

"Not so, Volkov," the Hero said. "What I saw was all three at once: past, present, and future merged, not three streams, but a continuum. It was like coming to the edge of a dense forest and, beyond, walking down a shoreline to a vast ocean that I never before imagined was there."

Now Mars felt a peculiar crawling in his belly, an icy fear

gripping his bowels, for as he spoke, the Hero's face had become transfigured.

Odysseus said, "There I was wading in it. In Time. And I came upon Existence. I saw myself existing in past-present-future all at once. They were the same, not different. There was no younger or older. There was no death. Age and death are myths, Volkov, but they're not the only ones." He reached down, plucked at his sleek, silvery flesh. "The body, too, is a myth. It's what inhibits us, what gives rise to the myths of age and death. Without the body, we can step freely into the ocean of Time."

Mars experienced once again that vertiginous sensation that comes with the proximity to madness, but he still did not know which of them in the pool was mad.

"You don't believe me," Odysseus said. "I can see it in your face." He shrugged. "Well, you asked for the truth. Don't blame me if you're unable to accept it." He gave Mars a pitying look. "However, I can't, in all good conscience, blame you. You weren't there. How *could* you believe?"

Mars took a long time thinking over what the Hero had said. At last he said, "One thing disturbs me."

"Only one?" Odysseus said sardonically.

"From what you claim you experienced during the event, it would seem as if you would have returned to Earth in a kind of state of grace, in possession of a great peacefulness. Yet if I remember correctly, you have said that you are suspended between heaven and a living hell, and it's obvious you have a great deal of rage that you barely suppress. How do you explain these discrepancies?"

Odysseus turned to Tatiana. "I want to get out."

Immediately she launched herself onto the coping. Still dripping, she went off.

"Are you going to—"

"Be patient, Volkov."

Arbat's head bobbed upon the water, looking inquisitively between the two men.

Tatiana returned with the Hero's special wheelchair. Then she bent down, lifted him out of the water. Arbat began a long series of clicks, her nose bobbing incessantly, as if she were distressed.

When Tatiana had settled the Hero in, draped the oversized towel across his loins, he said, "Wait here for a moment, comrade. Talk to Tatiana. I'm sure you can benefit from her insights.'' He threw the wheelchair's engine into gear, motored off across the huge room.

Mars, at the edge of the pool, crossed his arms over one another on the coping. He gazed into Tatiana's face for a long time before saying, ''What do you think is going on here?''

''What you want to know,'' Tatiana said, ''is whether or not he's mad.''

''In a sense,'' Mars conceded. ''I have to know whether or not he's telling the truth. Did he come face-to-face with an extraterrestrial or has the cosmic radiation he was exposed to affected his brain?''

''Oh, yes,'' Tatiana said unhelpfully, ''he could be telling the truth as he knows it, and also be quite insane.''

Her tone was so like the one the Hero used that Mars was momentarily nonplussed. By the time he recovered, the Hero had returned. He stopped at the outer edge of the coping and, looking down at Mars in the water, said, ''Rage and a sense of a living hell.'' He threw down a packet of photocopied papers. ''This should answer your question.''

Mars's hands were dry, and he leafed through the pages. As he did so, the icy ball in his stomach expanded. What he was looking at was a Limited Distribution Kremlin report that not only should not have been copied, it should never have been known to exist. The document was so top secret, fully two-thirds of the Politburo were ignorant of it.

Mars saw that his hands were trembling, and he immediately fought to gain control of himself. How in God's name had anyone—let alone the Hero, locked away in this fortress—gotten a copy of this document? He thought again of the Hero knowing about Tatiana and Lara and their weekly reports to him; how the Hero had known about the extent of the monitoring, and had used the pool to give himself a measure of freedom. He stared up at the Hero as if seeing him for the first time. Holy Mother, he thought, what have we let in among us?

Mars's mouth was dry, and he had to swallow several times before he was able to say, ''You never should have seen this.'' It was futile asking the Hero where he had obtained the copy. Mars knew he wouldn't divulge his secret, just as he knew he could not force the Hero to tell him. The thing was to somehow get the Hero to tell him of his own free will.

''But I did see it,'' Odysseus was saying. ''It's a report detailing one of the experiments done during the Odin-Galaktika II mission. Funny. Neither Menelaus nor I were ever told of it.''

281

"No one else was, either."

"Is that supposed to make me feel better? That we weren't the only ones in the dark?" Odysseus cocked his head, as if he were listening to a voice only he could hear. *"But we were the guinea pigs!"* he roared so abruptly that Tatiana flinched.

Below him, Mars fought for control. He was acutely aware of how vulnerable he was floating naked in the pool while the Hero sat above him.

"You set up cosmic ray experiments," Odysseus continued. "Built into our EVA suits was a kind of filter to expose us to a minimum dosage of cosmic rays."

"No, you're wrong." Mars cleared his throat. "This plan was discussed. But it was never implemented."

"You're dissembling, comrade." Odysseus clucked his tongue against the roof of his mouth.

"Think about it," Mars said. "Would the Americans have ever let us perform this kind of experiment? They have an almost holy reverence for their space program. Your exposure to cosmic rays was purely accidental. Something went wrong."

"I'll tell you what went wrong!" Odysseus thundered. "We were never meant to make it to Mars. The Odin-Galaktika II was meant for this cosmic ray experiment alone!"

"No, no, no!" Mars was shouting himself now, but he could not seem to stop. "We're not monsters! Why must you persist in seeing us that way? What's happened to you?"

"You know very well what's happened. I'm irradiated with cosmic rays—at your instigation." The Hero's expression was withering. At last all his pent-up rage was being played out. "You've made me into a fucking laboratory experiment. All because some of your people got the idea that minute dosages of cosmic rays could counteract the damaging long-range effects of weightlessness."

The Hero's fists were clenched tight. "Do you have any idea what you've done to me?" He shook his head. "What's the difference? Even if you had a clue, you wouldn't care, would you? You're all heartless bastards. 'No heart, no soul,' that's what the dolphins say, did you know that?"

His right fist opened. "Here's a little present for you." Something glowing dropped from his hand into the water beside Mars. "A little plutonium."

"Christ! Jesus Christ!" Mars heaved himself out of the water. "You *are* mad! You're homicidal!" He began to shiver. No one made a move to hand him a towel, and he was too paralyzed with fear to move. He felt the racing of his heart. His guts had turned to water, and he was certain he had begun to involuntarily urinate before he made it out of the pool. He was only too familiar with the fearful effects of radiation poisoning.

"Relax," Odysseus said, looking at Mars's white face. "It's just a marble I coated with a harmless radium paint." He seemed calmer now. Arbat gave out with a short burst of clicks. The Hero smiled thinly. "Arbat says you peed into her water. Gave you quite a fright, didn't I? Now perhaps you have some sense of what you did to me."

"But we didn't—"

"Save it," Odysseus said, swiveling abruptly away, "for another day."

End of interrogation.

In the aftermath of what she had done—unleashing her rage, murdering Giin—Honno dreamed. Suspended between sleep and consciousness, she dwelled in the shining field she had been taught to search for and to make her own. And she once again walked the path of her awakening . . .

When Honno was eight years old she overheard a conversation between her parents. It was night, and she was awake, being in the midst of a fever that had left her so pain-ridden she could not sleep.

For a while she stared out her window. The moon was full. The mountains of her home, which she loved to climb, were visible, stark sentinels in the blue light. Once she saw lights in the mountains, moving as if of their own accord, and because it was said that gods lived there, she was certain that they were the source of the light. Often she would pray to these gods to release her from her curse.

It was summer, and the fusuma from her parents' room out to the garden was open. Cool moonlight slipped into their room, and through the translucence of the rice-paper shoji walls, Honno could make out her parents as silhouettes, their movements throwing shadows against the rice paper, oversized, slightly distorted, as if they were characters in a theater play illuminated by stage lights.

"I had a dream," Honno's mother was saying. "It was about our daughter."

"I do not want to hear anything more about Honno," her father, Noboru, said.

"But you must!" The hand of one silhouette reached out,

grabbed the sleeve of the other. "This was a significant dream. I dreamed that it was the dead of winter. Snow covered the ground in every direction but, curiously, the trees were as black and bare as if they had been set on fire, there was no snow on them at all.

"As I said, it was winter. We lived in a desolate place, I can't say where. Honno awoke. She was ill, as she is now, and needed to defecate. I took her outside, in the snow, don't ask me why. She squatted down and I watched her, as protective as could be.

"Then, out of the corner of my eye, I saw movement. There was a stoat staring at me with red-rimmed eyes. She was as black as the blasted trees, and as gaunt. She had never grown her white winter fur, and I could see her swollen teats hanging down from the loose skin of her underbelly.

"But it was her face that terrified me," Honno's mother went on. "Her muzzle was dripping blood, and I knew that she had slain her mate so that her cubs might eat. Now she was looking hungrily at Honno.

"I looked from the stoat to Honno and, to my horror, I saw that what was spilling out of Honno was not feces, but blood. It soaked into the pure white snow, the stain spreading farther and farther."

"*Hinoeuma*, the husband killer," Noboru said. "Foolish, foolish woman for not taking the proper precautions."

"We must do something," Honno's mother said. "My dream was an omen, a warning of evil."

"What would you have me do?"

"Take her," Honno's mother said, "to the Man of One Tree."

The Man of One Tree was so called because he lived on an island off the southern coast of Japan. It was a singular place, rocky, bleak, lashed by wind and rain in the summer, wind and sleet in the winter. The island seemed to be built not upon bedrock, but rather the gigantic root system of the ancient pine tree that overspread nine-tenths of the island.

Having made the journey south with Honno, Noboru had hired a small boat, which had deposited them on the rock-strewn beach of the Man of One Tree's island.

The Man of One Tree was a hunchback with a head far too large for the rest of his monkeylike body, and his appearance frightened Honno. She hid behind her father's legs while he addressed the Man of One Tree.

"My daughter," Noboru said, "is *hinoeuma*, having had the misfortune to be born in the sixtieth cycle of the year of the horse. My wife and I fear that she is destined to murder her husband."

The Man of One Tree peered at Honno with his frightful, opaque pitch-black eyes. It was said that he was Indonesian or, in any event, had emigrated many years ago from that mysterious archipelago. Now he produced five shards of half-blackened tortoiseshell. He threw them onto the ground three times, after which he squatted down, his thick brows knit tight as he read the runes inscribed on the insides of the shells.

He looked up at Noboru, his wrists on his knees, accentuating even further his simian aspect. "You could kill her," he said in a high, quavery voice.

Honno whimpered; and Noboru put a protective arm around her, holding her tight to him. "Are you mad?" he said. "This is my flesh and blood. Whatever she may be, she is my child. I would not have her harmed."

The Man of One Tree nodded sagely, as if he had been presented with the correct response. "Or," he said, "you can leave her with me."

"For how long?" Noboru asked.

The Man of One Tree stood. "When she is ready, she will come to you."

"But my wife—I must be able to tell her when she can see Honno—"

"Tell your wife," the Man of One Tree said, "to forget she has a daughter. Tell her to turn her mind to other matters. She will not survive the separation, otherwise."

Honno had cried bitterly when her father had left. She had run onto the beach, the sharp rocks slashing through her thin-soled shoes, cutting the bottoms of her feet.

"Daddy!" she had wailed. "Daddy!"

But Noboru had already turned resolutely away as the boat took him out over the gray sea toward home.

Honno collapsed at the edge of the water, weeping uncontrollably. Then she was aware of being lifted into the air, and opening her eyes, saw to her utter astonishment that the Man of One Tree had hefted her in his arms as easily as if she were a sack of rice.

"Why do you cry, little one?" he said. "This is a new beginning for you, a chance for life instead of death."

"I want to go home!" Honno had cried.

"I understand," the Man of One Tree had said. "Home is where I am taking you."

It took Honno less than a year to think of the island as home, but then children are so much more adaptable than adults. Noboru, for instance, would never have been able to make the adjustment.

The thing about the Man of One Tree was that he was so interesting. Even when Honno could not quite grasp everything he said, she filed it away, to ponder over late at night when she was alone, staring up at the stars glittering through the overarching branches of the One Tree.

And that was another thing that surprised her. She enjoyed being alone, having time to listen to the rhythm of the surf on the rocks, the crying of the terns and gulls, the rising and falling whisper of the sea wind through the tangle of the One Tree, the ticking of her own mind.

"Thought takes time," the Man of One Tree had told her early on in her stay. "And it takes effort, because you must decide which thoughts will improve you, which will impair you. You must think of your mind as a garden that needs constant attention. You must study and discuss your studies to feed it, you must regularly seek the silence and isolation essential for periodic weeding."

Honno used the stars as her focus. They were so far away that even her *wa*, which each day she and the Man of One Tree worked to expand, could never reach them. But stretching over such a distance allowed for the deepest weeding.

In the night, Honno recalled her lessons for the day, turning them over and over, as if they were jewels of great value which she must observe from every facet.

In this manner she absorbed everything she was taught. She proved to be an extraordinary pupil. Her memory was prodigious, and as long as her interest was piqued, she never grew tired or unresponsive.

The Man of One Tree instructed her in the basics of Zen and Shinto, for he felt strongly that religion was the backbone of any successful education. From there he moved outward in what he saw as concentric circles to the Tao and the philosophy of Lao-tse. Now came the warlike, more secular philosophies of the master strategist, Sun Tzu, and the master swordsman, Miyamoto Musashi. Concurrent with these mental studies were the physical exercises: tai chi, jiujutsu, aikido, karate, *kenjutsu*.

One might think of this as a rather traditional curriculum, and it was: for a young boy studying the martial arts. It was totally unconventional for a female. In addition, the Man of One Tree

286

added to Honno's studies the somewhat more esoteric philosophies and physical disciplines he had acquired during his years crisscrossing the Indonesian archipelago.

"You will never be a woman in the traditional sense," the Man of One Tree said to Honno one night. It was six years since she had come to live with him. She had breasts now, and the place between her thighs was covered with fine black hair. She had bled for the first time that evening, just as the sun was sinking with the colors of a peacock into the turbulent ocean.

She had known what the blood flow was, and what it meant. But some other part of her, the *hinoeuma* child hanging on, had remembered the horror of her mother's dream, how she had squatted in the snow and, under the baleful gaze of the starving stoat, had squirted blood.

"I am still *hinoeuma*," she had said in despair to the Man of One Tree. She was trembling, and her callused hands were rough and red from scrubbing herself. "I am still unclean."

To which he had replied, "You will never be a woman in the traditional sense." He took her to the center of the One Tree, where its trunk was as large as a house, where even the stars could not be seen, and sat her down with her back to the rough bark. "But that is all to the good. I have done my best to cleanse your spirit. Never mind your body; it will only betray you."

"It will never betray me," Honno had said naively.

He spread his arms wide. "When you return to the mainland, all this will fade in time."

"No, no!"

"It will come to seem as a dream," the Man of One Tree persisted. "That is only natural; it is the way of life. You will continue to mature until you become a woman. Then will your body betray you, and you will want what every woman wants: a husband, a family, a home.

"But your path leads in other directions. For you, normality will bring to the fore your *hinoeuma*, and only evil can ensue. Therefore, I counsel you to be strong within yourself. When you feel the urge to fall in love, to marry, return to that place in your spirit I have taught you to find, for only this will nurture you, and protect you from the fate of the *hinoeuma*, the husband killer."

Honno, opening her eyes in the present, stared out into pale sunlight, except she was still seeing the body of the young man whose larynx she had crushed. Had it been only hours ago? It felt like years.

But, yes, it must be only hours. In her mind's eye she could still see his blood fresh on her hands, and behind her Big Ezoe saying, almost gently, "Mrs. Kansei, I have the Sakata ledgers and their decoded pages. It's time to go."

Now Irina and Natasha Mayakova went to dinner almost every night. Even on those days when she wasn't attending Natasha's acting classes in the back of the new Moscow Arts Theater, Irina met Natasha after her performance of *Three Sisters*.

Often, in fact, they did not have a proper dinner, they preferred to stroll through the streets and parks, talking, endlessly talking. They would stop, eventually, for a bowl of cabbage soup in some tiny neighborhood shop filled with steam and gossip, then move on, drifting through their city, a part of it yet somehow apart, creating their own world.

Now more than ever Irina was burning with curiosity about Natasha's relationship with Valeri. She could not be seeing him at night, unless they met very late, and as Irina was coming to understand, an actor could allow neither drunken days nor sleepless nights while she was working.

At the same time, Irina found herself feeling guilty at having lied to Natasha about her name. It was no longer exciting to hear Natasha call her by the name of Katya Boroskaya; instead she longed to be called by her real name. Yet she could think of no way to tell Natasha that her name was Irina Ponomareva. What excuse could she give for her falsehood? Besides, despite her growing friendship with Natasha, she was loath to give up her reason for contacting her in the first place: to find the link with Valeri.

It was so incredibly wearying to be a spy and to be feeling close to the person on whom you were spying. Often, on their walks, Irina forgot why she was there and, for a brief time, would luxuriate in her newfound friendship. Then reality would intrude and in some subtle way that disturbed and depressed her, she would withdraw from the shared intimacy with Natasha.

At night in bed, alone, Irina would think of her relationship with Natasha. It seemed terribly unfair that her one chance at true friendship should be tainted, so distorted by lies and deceit.

Her nights with Valeri became more fevered, fueled by a kind of desperation pulled from Irina's very core. Their lovemaking was increasingly wild, animalistic, exhausting, so that afterward

Irina would plunge into the most absolute slumber, from which Valeri was obliged to shake her awake in the morning.

Then, over his protestations, she would climb upon his naked body, spread her legs across his loins, moving until she felt his response, then engulf him with her mouth until he arched off the bed, exploding.

In an orgy of self-destruction, she could no longer tell the difference between lust and love. And Valeri's groans of sexual arousal and release would haunt her all day, echoing in her ears while she watched him talking intimately with Natasha Mayakova, until tears of hatred and self-pity clouded her eyes.

Irina, Irina, Irina. She would recite her name silently as if it were a prayer or an enchantment that would ensure she remembered who she really was. The trouble was, she no longer knew who Irina Ponomareva was. Somewhere along the line her identity, her *self*, had been misplaced or covered over so thoroughly that she had forgotten where to look for it.

At Mars's apartment, after he fell asleep after their tepid lovemaking, she would stare at the ceiling and, before she herself fell into a shallow, troubled sleep, she would promise herself that tomorrow would be the day when she would confess everything to Natasha, so that they would have an opportunity to start all over.

But she awoke each morning knowing that she could never go through with it. What was done was done. She could never go back, sanitize the emotions that were sure to be raised by the truth. Would Natasha forgive her for using her, or would she never want to see her again? With a profound sense of foreboding, Irina knew that she could not take the chance to find out. Her relationship with Natasha was already too precious for her to jeopardize it in any way.

And yet she knew that she was jeopardizing it every time she and Natasha were together, when there was a possibility that she might slip or that someone she knew would recognize her and use her real name. Worse, she suspected that she hated Natasha as much as she cared for her; despised her for her relationship with Valeri, the unknown nature of which Irina found increasingly maddening.

Irina had begun to experience an odd sense of fragmentation, as if her life had been an eggshell that had abruptly been struck against a stone, turned into jagged bits, all with their own structure, but each with far less than the whole. Some essential truth was missing, and had been, she realized, for some time, even before she had met Valeri.

Irina knew that she had been given a glimpse of that truth—that heart of things that, when she understood it, would come to mean more to her than anything else—in America.

In Boston she had watched the kids pouring out of the universities. She had walked the tree-lined Cambridge streets with them, had eaten pizza and Coke alongside them, had bought clothes where they did, had listened to their music, first in snatches from passing cars, then in jukeboxes in the pizzerias, then in the dance clubs late at night.

One evening she had been invited to a party along with everyone else—including the chef—of the local pizzeria. She had, of course, declined, but moments later thought, Why not?

It was as close to all-out chaos as Irina had ever been. The noise level was tremendous. Her glass shook in her hand and her teeth ached from the vibrations. It was wonderful, as liberating, in its way, as sitting in the darkened movie theater, watching Elizabeth Taylor being Martha in *Who's Afraid of Virginia Woolf?* But different. So different.

Everything was spontaneous, from the laughter to the comings and goings of people, from the informality to the wide range of conversation topics: Kierkegaard on the meaning of death; Woody Allen on the meaning of life; Tom Cruise on the meaning of sex. It was dizzying, wild, captivating. Irina had not wanted to leave.

There was a young man there, with hair the color of a bear's pelt. He wore it short on the sides, long and flowing on top, so that he was continually brushing it back from his forehead. He had watched her drifting slowly from group to group in the party with a shyness that made Irina's heart ache.

At one point, when she was standing on the edge of the crowd and he was dancing with a thin, sandy-haired woman, he had accidentally brushed against her, spilling the contents of the glass over her.

"Oh, I'm sorry," he said. "I'm so sorry."

"It's all right," Irina said. "It's only club soda." And then, because he obviously could not take his eyes off her, "Shouldn't you get back to your dance partner?"

She ran into him again in the kitchen. It was late, and the crowd had begun to thin out. Irina was putting a slice of cold pizza in the microwave, and he had stopped her.

"Don't you know anything?" he said. "You can't use foil in

290

there, it'll pop all over the place." He put the pizza on a paper plate, shoved it in, turned on the microwave.

They shared the slice.

"You're the Russian, aren't you?" the young man said.

"Yes."

"Your English is excellent. I wish my Russian was as good."

"How good is it?" Irina asked him in Russian.

"Only so-so, I'm afraid," he said in the same language.

"You need to speak more, that's all," Irina said, switching back to English. She found that she wasn't in the least nostalgic for anything Russian.

All of a sudden the young man leaned forward, kissed her on the lips. "I've been wanting to do that all night," he said in a rush.

"Did you think I'd be offended?"

"I had no way of knowing."

And in that one sentence he had summed up for her the disquiet she had been feeling there. Why was she so comfortable, so free in Boston? Why did she not feel homesick for Moscow? *I had no way of knowing*. Tucked away in Russia, she had had no way of knowing what America would be like, let alone Boston, or this wondrous Cambridge area, delightfully old-fashioned, yet at the same time, so excitingly avant-garde. A world within a world within a world. All scrupulously hidden from her by her government.

Oh, how she had wept that night when at last she had crawled into her bed, because she would never feel the same about her home anymore. Doubts so fundamental that they questioned her entire way of life had crept into her consciousness. And, once there, they could never be dispelled.

The very worst of it was that as soon as she got back to Moscow, it all seemed like a dream: the silk Charmeuse teddy she had swooned over, the magnificent Martha brought to life by Elizabeth Taylor, the endless pizza and Cokes, the equally endless curious minds, the shocking music and even more shocking clothes, the young man at the Cambridge party who had loved her from afar, who had dared to kiss her, who had said to her, *I had no way of knowing*, all were swept away on the gray tide of minutiae that was her daily life.

A dream, that's what it had become. She would dream—when she was released from the recurring prison nightmare—of Cambridge, and would awake weeping, as if it were as lost as Camelot or as mythic as Avalon.

So painful had this sense of loss become that even Irina's feelings for Mars could not quench them, sex with Valeri was an inadequate opiate, and, more and more often, she would seek the only solace she had ever known, kneeling before the altar at the Church of the Archangel Gabriel. There she prayed for guidance, and for some measure of peace which she now suspected was beyond her.

And then, one evening in the midst of a sleety rain that had driven them off the slick Moscow streets, the miraculous occurred. Natasha said, "Do you know that my greatest moment on the stage came not in Moscow, not in Russia at all, in fact, but in the United States. I was asked to perform at Lincoln Center in New York City. Do you know it?"

"I've never been to New York City," Irina said with her heart in her mouth. She knew this was the time to mention Boston, but she could not.

They were in Praga, a restaurant on Arbat Square. It was a touristy place, so the food was good, and because the owners knew Natasha, the service was, too. Irina stared out the windows at the people hunched over, hurrying along the rainswept street. She found, to her utter amazement, that she felt no connection with those people. It was as if she were now separated from them all the time by this plate-glass window, as if she were here, safe and dry, while they were there, cold and wet.

But if they were here in Moscow, she asked herself, then where was she? In some kind of terrible limbo or purgatory, serving out her sentence in the prison that barred even the moon.

"Katya?" Natasha put a hand over hers. "What's the matter? You look as white as winter."

Irina's depression was so intense that she completely forgot who Katya was and, for an interminable moment, stared blankly into Natasha's concerned face.

"Katya?"

"Yes, yes," Irina said, breathing again, in out, in out, everything quite normal now, and yet not normal at all. "I'm fine. I . . . don't know what came over me. For a moment I was so dizzy. It's passed now."

"Nevertheless," Natasha said firmly, "it's a glass of *starka* for you, my girl. And, for God's sake, eat. You haven't touched a thing."

Later, after the plates were cleared and the strong, dark tea had been served, Natasha said, "America is such an unusual place. How I wish you could see it! So filled with delicious sights, sounds, tastes. Quite naughty, really." She chuckled. "There was, for instance, the divinely decadent French bustier I wore the night that Texas financier and I—" She stopped abruptly, waved a delicate hand. "But, no, I think I've already shocked you quite enough for one evening."

"I don't think I'm easily shocked."

Natasha laughed. "Oh, but of course you are! You're such a naif, Katya. After all, education in this country is so appallingly primitive. In some ways, I'm afraid we're still not much better than all those third-world countries we're always professing to help. It often seems to me that we're the ones who need assistance."

Natasha sipped her tea. "Let me tell you something, darling. When I was in New York I met Edward Albee. He had come to watch me perform. Can you imagine? My God, what an opportunity! And do you know what? I made the most of it. I'd be damned if I was going to talk with one of the most brilliant theater minds of this century while my flock of KGB babysitters was hovering all around, eavesdropping.

"I took Albee, and we ducked away, lost them all. What I learned from him I could never have gotten from thirty years with my Russian acting teacher. He spoke in truths. His language was a kind of music that I seemed to absorb through the pores of my skin. I felt as if I had never before been alive, had never known what it was to don a persona and walk out on the stage. He showed me how to speak not only his words, but all words."

Natasha poured herself more tea and, as she stirred in the sugar, her eyes shone with an inner light. "We talked all night. What a risk, darling, but what else could I do? It was hell to pay, I'll tell you, when I got back to the hotel. But who cares? I have a guardian angel who watches over me." Irina wondered whether that guardian angel was Valeri.

"My whole point," Natasha continued, "is your rage. It was my acting teacher's point of view that rage is frustration stifled. The older I get, the more I am inclined to agree with him." She took Irina's hand. "Your rage is such that, sooner or later, you will be unable to control it. Then it will boil over and, well, who knows what the consequences might be?

"That night in New York City, Edward Albee showed me what I was meant to be. And that knowledge has made me a different person. He opened up the world to me—not only his world, but mine.

293

"Oh, darling, don't you see what I'm saying?" She searched Irina's eyes. "One day you will meet your Albee, and he will change your life utterly. The answer for you is to seize your moment as I did mine. You must say to yourself, 'Damn the risks!' and plow straight ahead. Believe me, there is a time to consider the consequences, and a time to ignore them. Do you understand me, Katya?"

"You have no idea how frustrating it is," Mars said to Irina two nights later, "knowing that somewhere out there the leaders of White Star are going about their daily lives—and I can't get to them." He turned to her. "Have you gotten any leads?"

"Not yet," Irina said.

They were in Mars's apartment on Vosstaniya Square. It was very late at night. The streets were deserted. Every so often a military truck or troop carrier would rumble by.

Irina thought, I even miss the traffic in Cambridge, the blasting rock 'n' roll, the kids swinging their hips, laughing, drinking their Cokes, eating their pizzas. These days, hardly an hour passed without some memory of Cambridge surfacing like a fish through the ice, appearing like a specter, pulling her further and further from her own world. There was a tautness inside her, like a steel cable singing with vibration. It was always with her, disconnecting her further from everyone and everything around her. Once she had even found herself unable to breathe, as if she were stuck in a black, airless place.

Irina felt guilty, having indulged her appetite for friendship rather than exploiting the closeness that had developed between her and Natasha Mayakova. But what was she to make of her relationships with Mars and Valeri? She had no idea now what she felt for either of them. She felt as if she could not now exist without them, as if they—and Natasha—were her only lifelines. She loved and hated them at the same time, not yet understanding that her sense of them was distorted by the turmoil writhing inside her like a live thing. She felt trapped on the other side of the mirror, in a place where there were no signposts to tell her which way to go or how to feel.

The situation seemed far too complex for her to untangle. She was in over her head, and now she appeared to be drowning in an alien sea beyond her understanding.

Mars grunted. "Perhaps my trust in you is misplaced."

"Don't say that."

"Isn't it true? I have given you everything you wanted, false papers, a private car, leave from your work when you need it to careen around God only knows what sections of Moscow. And for what? Have you anything to show for it?''

Irina thought, I have all these things from Valeri, too, but I can never let Mars know that, I won't ever give up an ounce of my power over these men. But I want to give Mars something, I know he's counting on me, and I don't want to disappoint him. I have to stop procrastinating; I can give him Valeri because, after all, it's Valeri Mars is interested in, Valeri and his hunt for the nationalist dissidents of White Star. Yet still she hesitated, as she had during the weeks she had followed Valeri and Natasha. She did not want to be sent back to her unutterably boring job, her previous drab existence; she knew she could never bear that now. Yet she lacked the courage to plunge all the way into her new exciting life.

Mars was studying her carefully. ''As I thought,'' he said, as if he were passing sentence on her. ''I think you should return to your job at the Ministry of Education.'' He shrugged, clearly disappointed. ''Too bad. Under the circumstances, it would have been extremely helpful if you had made some progress. I have made an excellent beginning at finding the leaders of White Star, but now I need to move faster because there seems to be some sort of deadline now where White Star is concerned.''

''What do you mean?''

Mars's face, in the warm lamplight, was a patchwork of shadow. ''I have learned there is a major counterstrike being mounted against the nationalist group by the KGB.''

''What kind of counterstrike?''

''I don't know,'' Mars said. ''That sort of information is classified, even for me. And if I began to ask questions or pull in favors, I'm afraid I would attract the wrong kind of attention. If Valeri Bondasenko should hear—''

''What does Bondasenko have to do with this KGB initiative?'' Irina asked.

Mars said, ''Valeri Denysovich is KGB.''

''You must be mad,'' Irina said. She thought she was going to throw up. KGB! No! It couldn't be! ''Everyone knows who Valeri Denysovich is. His career is an open book, deliberately so.''

''Yes, *most* deliberately so,'' Mars agreed. ''But have you ever wondered why? Let me explain something to you. Two years ago the head of the KGB came out in the Congress of Peoples' Deputies as saying that his organization should follow

295

the American CIA model and be regulated by the Congress. Consequently, the KGB's modus operandi has had to change. Now the KGB does, indeed, operate like its American counterpart. On the surface it pays lip service to the constraints put upon it by political committees, while clandestinely going about its business as usual.

"It's the same KGB that it always was, Irina. It will take more than perestroika to change the KGB. The only difference is that now its chief operatives work behind efficient smokescreens. Like Valeri Denysovich Bondasenko."

Irina shuddered. My God, it was her worst nightmare come true. The icy winds of Siberia, the bars over the moon, her country as one huge prison, everything.

Mars reached over, leafed through the report he had been reading. He came to the page he wanted, showed it to her. "You needn't take my word for it."

And there it was, typed across the page. Irina was holding an original document, stamped with the red Cyrillics of the Politburo master files she had occasionally seen on some of the other documents Mars had left lying around.

—Valeri Denysovich Bondasenko, Colonel, Second Chief Directorate, Komitet Gosudarstvennoi Bezopasnosti, is hereby granted the authority to create and/or redesign a Department to be under his control.

This Department, [hereinafter] referred to as Department N (funds for which see Appendix B: Special Appropriations) will consist of approximately 1600 people, including administrative personnel.

The Chief of Department N shall report directly to the Chief of the KGB. The Chief of Department N shall have powers including, but not limited to, the selection of personnel from other Departments within the Second Chief Directorate; access to all sections of the KGB master files, including those "Limited Distribution" dossiers under the control of other Directorates; the ability to call upon the advice and services of personnel within all other Directorates; at his discretion, he may commandeer any and all hardware he deems necessary from the Border Guards Directorate . . .

Irina could read no more. The letters were blurring before her eyes. Shaking as if with the ague, she heard again down the long corridors of her memory those horrific words: *KGB. Keep calm.*

"This is the charter," Mars said, taking the paper from her hand, "for Valeri's counterintelligence initiative against White Star." He put it carefully back in the report. "Fortunately, Valeri's new department needs appropriations just like any other. It's covered in the Congress of Peoples' Deputies' budget hearing under 'Baltic Reapproachment,' but through a stroke of luck I was able to get my hands on the real charter."

KGB. Keep calm.

Irina rose suddenly, walked unsteadily to the window. She could not breathe. She threw open the sash, and the damp night air blew in. She shivered in the cold. Then she felt Mars behind her, strong, solid, warm. "You see, *koshka*, the KGB has set a time bomb for White Star. I can't find a way to warn their leaders because I can't find them. But the existence of this strike against them proves that Valeri already knows where they are."

Then he was turning her around, cradling her. He pushed her hair off her face. "You're trembling so," he said. "What's the matter?"

"You couldn't possibly know," Irina said. She took a deep breath. She could hear again the tromp of the military jackboots, the pounding on the front door, awakening her in the middle of the night.

"I remember," she began. "The moon was obscured by clouds—what an absurd thing to remember! I can hear my mother's voice, raised, shrill with fright. And, peeking out of the doorway to my room, I see a man in a black leather trench coat, his face obscured by the wide brim of his hat.

" '*KGB. Keep calm.*'

"My mother is screaming as the uniformed men under Trench Coat's command drag my father from his bedroom.

" 'What do you want with him?' my mother cries. 'He's done nothing!'

" '*KGB. Keep calm.*'

"The uniformed men are beating my father as he begins to resist them.

" 'This must be some kind of mistake!' My mother is shaking as she moans. 'You're making a mistake!'

" '*KGB. Keep calm.*'

"The rubber truncheons are lifting and falling, lifting and falling, and I can't ever forget the awful thick sound they make as they strike my father on his shoulders, his back, his upper arms, his head. He does not say a word, but I can hear his involuntary grunts with each blow of the truncheons.

"The uniformed men start to drag my father toward the door, and my mother steps in front of them. I see her eyes opened wide with panic. They are filled with a kind of primitive terror I once saw in a rabbit's glazed eyes as it was caught in the beam of my flashlight.

" 'You can't take him!' my mother sobs. 'I won't let you!'

"The man from the KGB reaches out and, in an almost lazy arc, slams the back of his hand into the side of my mother's face. She staggers back, one leg collapses under her, and she crashes into a side table. A lamp shatters, and she screams. I can still hear the rage and terror in her voice. Tears stream down her face.

" 'KGB. Keep calm.'

"The man in the black leather trench coat drags her out of the path of his men, and they take my father away. My mother offers no further resistance. She does not even take a last look at my father as he is manhandled down the stairs of the apartment building. Her eyes are blank.

"The man from the KGB is about to leave, but at that moment his head turns. He had heard something. Me. He moves slowly through the small apartment until he finds my room. I hear him coming in, coming closer.

"I am curled up in bed, hugging my pillow. He is across the room in one long stride. He pulls the covers back, exposing me.

" 'Irina,' he says. 'Little Irina.'

"I can't understand how he knows my name. I am so terrified I don't know what to do or think. His black leather trench coat is billowing around him like the wings of a gigantic bat. I can feel my heart beating painfully, like a trip-hammer.

"His white hand closes over my ankle so that I am stretched out across the bed. 'How old are you, little Irina?' he whispers. The wide brim of his hat hides his face completely, so that he seems to be a part of the shadows of the room. A shadow that holds me fast.

" 'Eight.' I hardly know how I squeezed that one word out.

"His hand moves up to my thigh. He touches me there, between my legs. 'Take care of your mother, little Irina. She needs you.'

" 'What—What did you do with my Daddy?' I asked him.

" 'Forget your father,' the man from the KGB says, straightening up. 'He's dead.' "

298

Irina had recited this horrific tale in a dispassionate, detached voice. But as soon as she uttered the words "He's dead," she broke down, sobbing hysterically into Mars's chest.

He held her, gently swinging her back and forth, as a mother will comfort a child with night terrors, until at last her sobbing subsided.

"Irina," he said gently, "tell me, did the man from the KGB force himself on you?"

"You mean sexually?" Despite her best efforts, her voice cracked.

"Yes."

She shook her head no. After a moment's pause she said, "But, in a way, what he did was just as bad. It made my flesh crawl, and when, years later, my first lover touched me there for the first time, I screamed just as if he had thrust a knife into me."

"My God," Mars said, "what a nightmare."

Mars was right, she thought, though the nightmare was continuing in the present in a way he could not imagine. Her first instinct was to break off with Valeri. Then, almost immediately, she saw why she absolutely must *not* break with him. In the first place, she saw quite clearly that she must not give Valeri any reason to suspect that she had been spying on him, or that she knew what he really was. If she broke off with him now, with no good reason, he would undoubtedly become suspicious. She knew well that paranoia was the KGB's middle name.

In the second place, she thought, Valeri is evil. Just as the man in the black leather trench coat was evil. They're one and the same, and if I run from Valeri, I'll just be giving them another victory over me. I don't want that. I'd like nothing better than to give them back a measure of the pain they gave my father and mother. I'd like to finally free myself from this nightmare.

She came to her decision: I'll give Valeri to Mars. Of course, that means implicating Natasha, but perhaps that won't be so bad; what could Natasha mean to Mars? If I give him Valeri, that's all he'll focus on.

"I may have found a way to track White Star," she said abruptly. "It concerns Valeri Bondasenko."

"What?" Mars frowned. "Is this how you have been spending your time, *koshka*?" His frown deepened. "I know I told you that Valeri Denysovich is also looking for White Star, but you see he is dangerous, too dangerous for—"

299

She said, "There's a woman Valeri Bondasenko secretly sees during the day."

"Aha!" This clearly interested Mars. "A chink in the iron man's armor."

Irina said, "He obviously cares for this woman, so there is an obvious weakness there I believe I can exploit. If I can find what Valeri Denysovich and this woman are up to, I think I can use it against him, get the information you want in return for my silence."

Mars looked dubious.

"I know what I'm doing," Irina said, "and I'm doing it well."

"No, Irina. I can't let you continue your surveillance of him, especially now that I know your background."

"You think I haven't the nerve, but you're wrong," Irina said. "I see now this is something I have to do; I have to face my fear of the KGB in order to overcome it. If you think me weak, Mars—"

"No, I don't think that." He smiled. "Otherwise I never would have allowed you to follow your instincts in trying to find White Star." He nodded. "So be it, *koshka*. Well done." The sudden look of admiration on his face flushed her with warmth. "My little dove," he said, using the common Russian slang for a female spy. He embraced her, kissing her on both cheeks as she had seen Red Army generals do when they greeted one another within the precincts of the Kremlin.

Valeri said, "I hope you're not falling in love with Mars."

"What an extraordinary thing to say."

"Is it?" He eyed her. "He took you home to meet his parents."

Irina was startled. "Are you having me watched?"

"Only when you're with Mars," Valeri said. "And only to make sure nothing happens to you."

"What could happen to me?"

Valeri turned down the stove burner. How much more bear-like he seemed to her now, almost like a Titan, the implied strength in his massive shoulders, chest, and upper arms so much more intimidating because he had the infinite power of the KGB behind him. "When it comes to women," Valeri said, "Mars can be dangerous."

Mars can be dangerous? Irina thought. Holy Mother, how he can twist the truth. She was sitting in the kitchen of Valeri's apartment, watching him prepare breakfast.

300

He said, "Do you know, even I couldn't get peppers or zucchini at the street stand yesterday. I had to settle for cucumbers, and they looked none too fresh to me." He poured the contents of a frying pan onto a platter. The Toshiba computer was on, and he regularly consulted its screen while he was cooking.

"How do you find time to get all those recipes in memory?" she asked, because she was uncomfortable now talking with him about Mars.

"I get some help." Valeri laughed. "There's a ghost in the machine."

Of course, Irina had a great deal of expertise with computers; that was one of the reasons she had been sent to Boston. Now she was in charge of the new computer system at the Ministry of Education. It was rudimentary by American standards, but still it made life so much easier.

Valeri said, "I hope you're going to eat better than you slept."

Indeed, for the first time since she stayed with him, she had not slept well. In the middle of the night Valeri had reached over, put his arm around her. Irina had gone rigid. How could she possibly make love with him now? And yet when he turned toward her and she felt his heat against her, his central core of hardness like a bar of iron pressed against her lower belly, she melted. It was as if she were two women: one who was now terrified by Valeri, the other who had found something deep inside him, something not only tremendously exciting, but also, in a way she could not fathom, redeeming.

Valeri was so gentle, so tender as his lips covered her body, moving from the hollow of her neck to her breasts, her stomach. By the time he reached her thighs, she was trembling in anticipation. Her mind was on fire. No, she realized later, not her mind. For she had put her rational mind on hold, locking away for the moment her terror and her shame, while her heart seemed to merge with her sex at that precise moment Valeri's tongue found her open and wet.

She moaned, reached back, holding onto the brass bars of the bedstead while her head whipped from side to side. When she felt on the verge of exploding, she reached down, ran her fingers through his thick hair to pull him up.

Mindlessly she guided him into her, arching up hard against his groin so that not one millimeter of him was left outside. She was wild, wanton, so abandoned that she could not remember later what she had said or how long it had lasted. It had seemed like forever, an endless moment, ripped from the cloth of time, when the both of them hung on the brink of ecstasy, their muscles tight and jumping.

At the end Valeri's lips sought hers, kissing her as the delicious, aching, febrile end came, as she groaned into his open mouth, tasting him as she cried out, their twined bodies spasming on and on and on . . .

And in the long silence afterward, with Valeri still inside her, with her licking the aromatic salt from his shoulder, she could not help but think of Mars, beautiful, handsome Mars, and wonder why sex with him was so uninvolving, so disappointing.

She had fallen asleep on top of Valeri, his hulking body her bed. And when she awoke at dawn, when her rational mind was again in control, she wept silent, bitter tears at the weakness of her flesh.

Now, as Valeri set their breakfast on the table, Irina found that she had no appetite. Valeri watched her toy with her food, said, "I want you to break off your relationship with Mars."

Irina felt her heart skip a beat. "I can't do that," she said.

"You not only can, you will." Valeri tore off a chunk of black bread, took a bite of it. "That's an order."

Irina looked up at him. "Why are you doing this?"

"I made a mistake," Valeri said. "It's as simple as that."

"Don't lie to me."

He raked some of the sautéed cucumber onto his bread, dipped it into a pool of pale yellow yogurt.

Irina said, "Whatever your motives are for wanting me to stop seeing Mars Volkov, they're far from simple. I don't know what's going on in your mind—I never do—but it's sure to be convoluted."

"I don't want you getting involved. Isn't that simple enough for you? Nothing convoluted there."

"You sent me off to Mars to get involved—"

"I did no such thing!" His outburst was so vehement that Irina jumped. "Don't you understand anything?" he said in a more normal tone of voice. "I wanted him involved with you, not the other way around. Now I think I've made a fundamental error in sending you into the lion's lair. I think, Irina, that the lion's had you for supper."

"You're judging me unfairly. You think I'm weak, a pushover for whomever—"

"Mars Petrovich isn't just anybody!" Valeri thundered.

Irina could not bring herself to look into his face. She felt disoriented by this conversation. Valeri her protector? No, no! He was KGB; he was lying, always lying. She steeled herself.

"I can take care of myself," she said.

"Perhaps from your point of view," he said. "Not from mine."

"But my point of view must have some validity!" she cried. "You can't think of me as just a method to unlock Mars's secrets!"

"Of course I don't." He finished off his bread and cucumbers, wiped his fingers. "That's why I want you away from his influence. It's clear to me that you haven't the willpower to resist his movie-star charisma."

"That's a typically male thing to say. Women don't fall in love with men just because they're handsome."

"Charisma," Valeri said, "is more than skin deep." He grunted. "Take it from me. It's my business to know such things."

"Well, whatever you may think, I'm not in love with Mars Volkov."

"Then what have you been doing with him? Fucking his brains out and that's all?"

Irina stood up. "Why you—" She was trembling with rage, but could not find the words to hurl back in his face.

"Sit down, Irina," Valeri said in a softer tone of voice. "I haven't called you a whore."

"No. But I imagine that's next."

Valeri watched her. "It seems to me that you enjoy it when we make love."

Irina sat back down. "I do," she said. It sickened her to think that it was the truth.

"Irina, I don't want to fight with you."

"What *is* it you want, then?"

"Can't you see that I'm trying to protect you?"

"Protect me?" If she were not so afraid of him, she would have laughed in his face. "From what?"

"Mars Volkov is the enemy. He wants to destroy me. I think perhaps you've forgotten that."

"I have forgotten nothing," she said, angry despite herself.

"Irina, what's happened to you?"

"Nothing, I'm just—" With a chill that froze her soul, she realized how dangerous Valeri could be, and knew she was taking the wrong tack with him. "I'm tired, that's all. The strain of keeping up pretenses, of lying to Mars, of having to remem-

303

ber through layers of identities, has frayed my nerves. Sometimes I'm not sure who I am anymore.''

Valeri nodded. ''You see? Your own mind is telling you that you weren't cut out to be a spy. And that's all the more reason for you to break it off with him. Now. Do you understand me, Irina? I see that I gave you more than you can handle, and I'm sincerely sorry for that. Now I want you to forget all about Mars Volkov. I'll think of another way to get to him. I'm not about to sacrifice you; nothing's that important, not even Volkov.''

Now Irina had no choice but to look at him. She could barely think straight. ''What are you saying?''

Valeri pushed his plate away. ''You must know how I feel about you. Haven't I made it perfectly clear every time we make love?''

''Valeri, I—''

''I care for you, Irina.'' His hand enfolded hers. ''I made a terrible mistake in trying to use you against Mars Petrovich. My overwhelming desire to destroy him put you in grave danger, and I'm ashamed of myself for doing that. That's why I must take you out of harm's way now—immediately—before you're in too deep for me to get you out.''

His voice was so soft, go gentle, that Irina felt her disorientation return. She felt her original desire for him rising and, with it, her own power waning. Again she had to remind herself of what Valeri really was behind this compelling, seductive mask. The specter of the papers Mars had shown her, revealing Valeri's true identity, rose up, towering over everything, and Irina shuddered inside, clamping down on all feeling, concentrating on what she must do to help Mars destroy Valeri.

I have not told Mars Natasha's name, Irina said to herself, so I have not betrayed her.

She was standing on a corner later that day, concealed within the shadows of an ornate doorway. She was watching Valeri and Natasha Mayakova talking in the lobby of the old Moscow Arts Theater.

She no longer felt the intense jealousy she once had at their clandestine meetings. But, then, she no longer felt the same way about Valeri Bondasenko. Now he revolted her.

Or did he? Then how is it, she asked herself, that you adore him when he makes love to you?

Irina had tried all morning to answer that question. There seemed an essential paradox in all her relations that she was not

304

understanding or seeing. It nagged at her; she felt as if her thoughts were spinning around in circles. She understood dimly that she no longer seemed capable of distinguishing right from wrong, good from evil. It was wrong to continue sleeping with Valeri, knowing what she knew about him. She had told herself that she did not want to go back to him, and she had meant it. Yet the moment she did go back to him, the moment he put his arms around her, her insides turned to water and the sexual hunger inside took over. Did that make her evil, as well? Even her devotions at the Church of the Archangel Gabriel were no longer of any solace.

In an intense spasm of guilt, Irina imagined Valeri in a black leather trench coat, and thought, You are doing a first-rate job of scaring yourself.

But she was also frightened for Natasha. Did she know what kind of man Valeri was? Did she know that she was kissing a colonel in the KGB when she met with him once a week in the afternoon?

The last time they had met, Irina had followed Valeri when he had left her. But he had merely returned to his office, staying there the rest of the day, except for when he appeared at the Congress of Peoples' Deputies.

Irina watched Valeri now, saying good-bye to Natasha. *I care for you, Irina. I made a terrible mistake in trying to use you against Mars Petrovich,* he had said. More lies.

If she were going to be truthful with herself, Irina had to admit that she could not read Valeri at all. How did he really feel about her? Why had he seduced her? What was it he wanted from her? Did he care about her? But, no, that was impossible.

She concentrated more deeply. She wanted to think like a spy, to prove him wrong when he had told her she wasn't cut out to be a spy, so she worked at getting inside his head. He seemed to be a bundle of contradictions. If he had picked her up in order to use her against Mars, then why had he suddenly ordered her away from Mars? Had something changed? Was she missing a step in the equation? She could not say. She only knew one thing: she *did* want a measure of revenge on the KGB for what they had done to her father, to her entire family.

Irina had never before dreamed she would be in a position to exact revenge, but her relationship with Mars had changed all that. She saw clearly how she could use his power to destroy Valeri. Some kind of evil animal was whimpering inside her, re-creating the scents, the emotions of sex. How can you think of destroying all this? the evil animal said. Are you mad?

Irina blinked. How long had she been standing here? She took a step out of the shadows, then immediately retreated. Across the street Natasha was emerging from the old Moscow Arts Theater.

She glanced at her watch. Now that's interesting, she thought. Rehearsals aren't half over with yet. Where can she be going?

Irina set off after Natasha, watching as she headed up Gorky Street, through the crowds. At the last instant Natasha ducked into Druzhba, the Freedom bookstore. Irina waited a moment, then followed her inside.

The bookstore was crowded with tourists, but Irina did not see Natasha. She went quickly through the store and out the back, caught a glimpse of Natasha turning a corner. Irina hurried after her and found herself, more or less, back at the old Moscow Arts Theater. There she saw Natasha getting into a black Zil which pulled immediately out into the street.

Irina turned away as the car passed, then ran to the anonymous-looking blue Volga that Mars had procured for her from God only knew what government stockpile. While it had been parked, someone had stolen the windshield wipers, which were in short supply and consequently in great demand by Moscow motorists. She cursed herself for forgetting to take them with her.

Irina followed the Zil through the city, then out of it. Forty minutes later they were entering the environs of Zvezdny Gorodok. Star Town.

When Mars saw the blue Volga he had loaned to Irina parked across from the Hero's compound, he ordered the driver of his Chaika to pull over fifty yards away. He sat in the darkened interior and watched the Volga with the kind of suspicion one reserves for the broken lock on one's apartment door.

Across from where the Volga sat, a shiny black Zil was parked in front of the entrance to the Hero's building. As Mars watched, Natasha Mayakova came down the steps, ducked into the backseat of the Zil, and it began to turn around.

Mars got out of the Chaika and, as the Zil drove away, he came up to the Volga. He pulled open the door, stared down into Irina's face, white with fear, and said, "What the hell are you doing here?"

"Mars!" Irina put a hand to her throat. "You scared me half to death!"

He smiled. "I'm sorry, *koshka*, but you gave me quite a turn when I saw you here in the Volga. Are you interested in cosmonauts now?"

Irina stepped out of the car. "Why is it," she said, "that there are no peppers or zucchini to be had in all of Moscow, but there is always plenty of money for cosmonauts and rockets to the moon?"

He frowned. "To Mars," he corrected. "We've already been to the moon." He shrugged. "The system has been around for over seventy years, and it isn't yet perfected. But we're getting there."

"Rockets or food, is that it?" Irina said. There was a silence for some time. When she saw that he wasn't going to answer her sardonic question, she decided she'd better switch topics. "Actually, I'm working," she said.

Mars's frown deepened. "Working? How so?"

"I've been following that Zil all the way from Moscow."

"Natasha Mayakova's car? What on earth for?"

"You know her?"

"Certainly," Mars said. "I know everyone who goes into that building."

"Isn't that where the Hero lives?" And when he nodded, she added, "How does Natasha know him?"

"The more pertinent question," Mars said, "is why you are following Natasha Mayakova all around Russia." Then he snapped his fingers. "She isn't the woman Valeri has been seeing."

Irina nodded.

"Good night," Mars said. "Now there's an intriguing thought."

"Are you going to see the Hero?" Irina asked. "I'd love to meet him."

"I'm afraid that's out of the—" Mars hesitated. He looked at Irina. But why not? he thought. What more perfect way to assuage the Hero's burning animosity than to let him talk with Irina. She was ingenuous enough to appeal to him, more than intelligent enough to keep him engaged. And since she was his friend, she might in some way offset the damaging effects the Limited Distribution report on the Odin-Galaktika II cosmic ray experiments had had on the interrogation. The bond of trust that

307

had been forming between himself and the Hero, no matter how tenuous, had been ruptured.

Mars decided that Irina being here at this moment was just the stroke of good fortune he needed. Though he did not altogether believe in omens, this seemed to be as close to one as he was likely to encounter.

"All right," he said, taking her by the elbow. "If that's what you'd like, I'm sure it can be arranged."

Irina heard the lapping of the pool first, then the siren call of the dolphin. "My God," she exclaimed, "what a magnificent creature!"

She went to the edge of the pool, knelt down, held her hand out to touch the dolphin's bottle nose. "What's your name, handsome?" Irina said, then gave a tiny startled scream as the Hero's head burst up through the water.

"Her name's Arbat," Odysseus said, laughing at the expression on Irina's face. "What's yours?"

Irina forgot all about the dolphin. She stared wide-eyed at the Hero, at his chiseled features, the pale, almost phosphorescent skin, the wide-apart eyes.

And what eyes! Filled with all-color/no-color, she saw and didn't see (perhaps imagined) in their depths colors she never suspected existed. His eyes were absolutely translucent, like scrims across the front of a stage, at once revealing and concealing what lay behind them.

Irina was utterly captivated; she could not take her eyes off him, as if she could devour him, absorb into herself the timeless wavelength that she felt emanating from him.

The long lashes of his eyes were the only hair on his face. There was not even the shadow of a beard on his cheeks or lips, but rather than making him seem effeminate, the smoothness somehow increased his aura of sensuality. It was almost, Irina told herself, as if she were face to face with a merman, some mythical being, half human, half dolphin.

There was a playfulness about him that seemed similar to Arbat's, but Irina could sense a darkness that the chattering mammal did not possess. And it was this darkness at noon, this anomaly, this black hole in his human horizon, that drew her inexorably, until he was the only thing of which she was aware.

She heard Natasha saying, *One day you will meet your Albee, and he will change your life utterly. The answer for you is to*

*seize your moment. You must say to yourself, "Damn the risks!"
and plow straight ahead.*

"Irina. My name is Irina," someone with her voice whispered over the water.

"Welcome, Irina," the Hero said, pulling her into the
pool with him so that Irina felt surrounded by the sun, the
moon, the stars. A universe of strange music was washing
over her, making her vibrate with an unknown excitement
from the inside out. "Call me Odysseus."

Honno, staring out over the vast grid of Tokyo, thought how
much the city resembled a pachinko board. Sunlight coruscated
across the tops of the massive forest of high rises, steel and
mirrored glass behemoths, leaving their middle floors in the
pale, filtered light of an undersea world, their lower floors in
deepest shadow.

She thought, I have only to open my hand, flick the ball of
my *wa*—my intrinsic energy—outward, set it careening through
the gutters and trenches I see down there. Just like pachinko.

How far she had come! How distant her other life seemed to
her now, a set of fading photographs, ill-lit, slightly out of focus,
best packed away in some dust-strewn attic, forgotten. Another
person's life, surely.

"Mrs. Kansei."

Who is Mrs. Kansei? Honno thought as she watched a
747-SP, silver in the brilliant sunshine, begin its descent
into Narita Airport miles away.

"I want another name," Honno said abruptly, turning away
from the glittering, enthralling grid of Tokyo. "Isn't there something of a custom for Yakuza to take a new name?"

Big Ezoe nodded. "Sometimes, yes." He was watching
Honno carefully, trying to absorb the changes firing through her.
Each moment she seemed to alter, flickering like a series of
dynamos being switched on one after another, illuminating the
darkness of the night.

"Koi," Honno said at length. "I like Koi." The name she
had chosen had many meanings besides the magnificent species
of Japanese carp; it meant, variously, dark, strong, the power
of the Imperial throne, even, as a verb, to change one's clothes.
All these meanings seemed, in some fashion, to fit this new
Honno.

"Koi," Big Ezoe said from his seat behind the massive black

rosewood desk, a kind of free-form sculpture which Americans would recognize and cherish as retro.

"Your samurai friend, Kakuei Sakata, had good reason to commit ritual suicide." He shuffled the papers he had taken from the apartment of Asaku Hitasura, Giin's protégé. "These are the complete translations of the ledgers Sakata kept. He was a meticulous man. Everything is here, details of corruption: bribes, extortion, ministerial appointments for private profit and professional gain. This is a veritable catalogue of sins: greed, lust, envy, gluttony, pride, you name it, it's certain to be here. And the trail goes from the industrialist, Kunio Michita—your former boss and Sakata's—all the way to the Ministry of International Trade and Industry. And what do you know? The one link between them all, the go-between, was not your friend Sakata—though he served that purpose as a facade—but my old enemy, Hitasura."

"Hitasura," Koi said, running her fingers over Kakuei Sakata's ledgers which she had liberated. "Isn't that the last name of the man I killed last night?"

For a moment Big Ezoe said nothing. He was astounded by the matter-of-fact tone in her voice. Had she felt nothing at all when she had crushed Asaku Hitasura's windpipe? Well, good. Fukuda had done her job well, then. But Big Ezoe's finely tuned sense of *wa* sent off a distant alarm.

This woman is an addict, he thought. She devours power in the same way others consume food. She cannot help herself; she needs it now simply in order to exist. For one such as she, there can be no such thing as honor or *giri*. She is bound on the wheel of her addiction as surely as a heretic was bound to the rack. I pity anyone who is foolish enough to get in her way.

"Asaku was the *oyabun* Hitasura's younger brother," Big Ezoe said. "Hitasura's people are already becoming meddlesome, combing the city for a clue to the identity of Asaku's murderer."

"Let them look," Honno said. "No one knows what happened except you, me, and Fukuda."

"I'll say one thing about Asaku," Big Ezoe said, "he was a genius at cryptography."

"He was arrogant," Koi said. "He dismissed me because I was a woman. He laughed in my face."

310

"That was because he was so angry at how easily you got into his apartment. You scared the shit out of him."

"That's not all I did to him," Koi said.

Big Ezoe thought of the moment when Honno, or Koi, as she now wanted to be called, crushed Asaku Hitasura's windpipe. He had seen in her face the image of a mask in a Bunraku puppet play. It was the mask of a god—though which god, Big Ezoe could not now recall—and it had been cleverly painted with features that managed to exhibit both ecstasy and despair. He had marveled at that mask. How he had wanted to meet the artisan who had so masterfully created it. And yet Big Ezoe had never inquired, afraid that the man would turn out to be mundane, altogether dull, not at all what he had pictured in his imagination.

Then, last night, he had magically found that expression reproduced on the face of a human being. How absolutely extraordinary! Big Ezoe, who loved and admired rarities, had decided that Koi was the rarest of the rare. He had sought to transform her, to make her—as he had Fukuda—into an extension of his psyche.

Fukuda had come to him essentially as Koi had, emotionally maimed. People—especially women, Big Ezoe had discovered—were peculiarly vulnerable when they were bloodied. Blood meant wounds that had not been able to heal, a flaw in the psyche.

Until last night, when he had seen the godlike expression on Koi's killing face, he had considered Fukuda to be his crowning achievement. It was then that Big Ezoe began to suspect that Koi would far outstrip his first model.

And later, when he had taken Koi back to the apartment he had given her, he had watched her while she took her cleansing bath. He had rolled up his sleeves, had covered her with soap, then sponged her down. Spraying her with cool water, watching the suds spiral down the drain, uncovering in sections her hard, unblemished body, Big Ezoe had caught himself eyeing her enviously.

After hosing down the tub to get rid of the residues of dirt and soap, Koi had filled it with steaming hot water, lay back to soak, and spoke the first words since her second act of murder. She said, "I was taught that women enter this world already bearing a guilt we can never fully rid ourselves of. We are unclean. Our bodies regularly run with blood, proof of the evil passions we cannot control." She stared at Big Ezoe. "How much more fully this applies to me, a *hinoeuma* woman, born in the year of the husband killers."

Big Ezoe had said nothing. He was content now to watch and to listen as he had done the night of the Bunraku play, as if he were again one of many, sitting in the darkness of the huge theater.

Koi had raised her arms, bringing her hands out of the water. Her clear skin was steaming, gleaming in the bathroom lights, center stage. Water dripped from her fingertips, and for the first time Big Ezoe noticed that her nails were lacquered the color of blood.

"But now," Koi had said, "now I know I have the power to exercise my evil passions as I see fit. I can exploit them, as I did tonight, or I can make them lie quiescently by my side like a slumbering lover." She put her head back, her eyes closed as she slipped lower into the water, so that to Big Ezoe her body already seemed insubstantial, its outline wavering. "The choice is mine."

And today she had chosen her new name: Koi. Like stepping out of old clothes, into new. Darkness. Depth. Power.

"No one knows," Koi said again now.

Big Ezoe came around from behind the desk, stood with her as she surveyed the city. The sky had already clouded up. Pollutants turned the pristine morning blue sky to a sickly yellow-gray. Fujiyama, the great mountain that symbolized Japan, was swallowed whole in man-made mist.

"But Hitasura will suspect my involvement." Big Ezoe was acutely aware of Koi as he stood beside her, aware of the enormous power of her *wa*, and he felt as gratified as an artist with his masterpiece. "It is only inevitable. Sooner or later, he will come. And when he does, he will not be alone."

"So? Let him come." That extraordinary expression was re-forming on her face, the confluence of ecstasy and despair that had about it now an air of expectancy. The air around Koi seemed to alter, as it does just before the onset of a storm. "I will welcome Hitasura with open arms."

With an enormous sense of satisfaction, Big Ezoe could see what happened: he had made of Koi a warrior whose scars he had annealed by his own form of cauterization, until, unlike Fukuda, Koi had absolutely no room for the soft emotions of pity, sympathy, or compassion.

312

And Big Ezoe, giving a tiny shudder, thought with enormous satisfaction, Yes, you bastard Hitasura, come. I have a surprise for you. I want you to meet my darling creation. My hard machine.

NINE
TOKYO

Tori was once again studying the photograph of Ariel Solares as he stood, smiling into the camera lens, in the tiny park near his house in San Francisco.

She kept studying the people in the background—the man and, farther away, the couple—as if in their faces she could discover what it was about the photo that Ariel had found so significant. But she could not make them out. She turned the photo over, saw the date it was taken digitally printed on the back, March 21 of this year. Was the date important? Not according to the Eyes Only dossier on the manufacture and distribution of the Japanese supercocaine she had been shown at Mall Central.

Russell and Bernard Godwin had been desperate to bring Tori back into the Mall because Ariel had determined that the Japanese had created this lethal new form of cocaine, and were beginning to disseminate it. Bernard wanted her to find out why. But Tori saw now that this was not the only question she needed to find an answer to. The new coke was in some way bound up with the hafnium pipeline. When the coke left the factory in the *llano negro* of Colombia, so did the hafnium. But what happened to the soft cell when it reached Japan?

And who was manufacturing it? From Deke's tests of the residue on the hafnium pellet Russell had taken from the *llano negro* factory, it was clear the coke being refined there was "clean." If Estilo was telling the truth about Hitasura being the buyer of his soft cell, then Ariel's intelligence was correct: the killer coke was being manufactured here in Japan. And Hitasura would know where and why.

Tori closed her eyes, went into *prana*, deepening and strengthening her breathing, slowing her pulse. She had to admit to herself that because her trust in Estilo had been shaken, her big fear was discovering that Hitasura was involved in what the Mall had termed "Ice Cream," the supercoke. If that turned out to be so, another important link from her past, her network, would have proved unreliable.

She knew that Russell must be impatient for her to begin interrogating Hitasura on the subject. But the crisis of Hitasura's imminent war with Big Ezoe—and the reemergence of Fukuda—was providing Tori an excuse for procrastination.

Part of her wanted more than anything to steal a moment, to take Hitasura aside, to get it over with and find out the truth. But it was not only her fear that made it impossible; this was Japan, and the iron dictates of custom made such a direct Western approach unthinkable. Tori knew that she would have to find just the right moment, just the right way to approach Hitasura.

Russell came up to her while Hitasura was receiving last-minute information on the mobile phone. "Isn't it about time you told me the origins of your blood feud with this female assassin, Fukuda?"

"She tried to kill me once," Tori said, but Russell only stared at her. It's only fair I tell him everything, she thought. "Do you remember what I was doing for you when I got hurt?"

Russell nodded. "Sure. You had picked up the improbable rumor of a joint Japanese-Russian venture hidden from even the ubiquitous Japanese bureaucracy. To be frank, I thought it was a waste of your time and the Mall's money to keep you on it, but Bernard insisted. You know how fanatical he is about the subject of the Soviets. Even more so now, if that's possible." He looked at her out of his penetrating blue eyes. "I wish I had held my ground on that one. You'd still have both your hips."

Tori studied him for a moment, as if she could not make up her mind about him. "That's kind of you to say, but the fact is I wouldn't be able to do physically what I can do now without the aid of the Japanese-designed prosthesis, so you see, in a way

315

you did me a favor." She gave him a tentative smile, as if she were afraid to allow him—and herself—to see what she was really feeling.

"Anyway, it seemed there *was* something to the rumor of the Japanese-Russian venture," she said, "though I ran into Fukuda before I got in deep enough to find out what exactly was happening."

"How did you happen to meet her?"

"There was a man," Tori said. "He was no more than a boy, really. Just twenty. But there was something about him, both personally and professionally. I had heard of him through Deke, who said he was *tsukuru-hito*, a 'maker.' In street slang, that means a go-getter, someone who is admired, who has great *hara*, great inner strength, which the Japanese prize above everything else."

"Was this young man Yakuza?"

"Now that was the most interesting part," Tori said. "He wasn't. And yet it seemed, because he was *tsukuru-hito*, many Yakuza sought his advice in complicated affairs of business. I suppose, in ways to circumvent international law, because the *tsukuru-hito* was an international lawyer. He called himself Yen Yasuwara, though it seemed to me he had taken that first name as a kind of joke. Yen was like that, sardonic, always laughing at the world through which he moved with such ease, though always in a dark way.

"He despised convention, an odd bias for a Japanese. And he hated burying his true nature beneath the countless layers that convention required him to form in order to survive in Japanese society.

"But Yen's goal wasn't to survive, it was to succeed, to blaze like a shooting star across the firmament of the Japanese business community. I use those words because of their poetic nature. Yen used them, and it's essential you get a complete picture of him.

"Yen once confided in me that his dream was to put together an international deal of such proportions that it would stand all Japan on its ear."

"Like maybe a Japanese-Russian deal?"

Tori nodded. "That's why I went to see him. 'What this country needs is a swift kick in the ass,' he told me after I got to know him well, and I'm certain he meant it."

"Just how well did you get to know him?" Russell asked.

"Don't get ahead of the story," Tori told him. "Yen worked

at Budoko Associates, an exclusive Tokyo law firm. It isn't large, but its prestige is first-rate. Yen came from the right family—his father and Budoko's senior partners were born in the same Honshu village; he went to the right schools, and got the right grades. In short, until the moment he was hired by Budoko, Yen was the very paradigm of Japanese convention.

" 'Then,' he told me, 'when I got where I wanted to go, I started the process of fomentation.' "

"Fomentation?" Russell said. "What the hell did he mean by that?"

"I'm not certain," Tori said. "But making an educated guess, I'd say that Yen wanted to in some way undermine the modern system of Japanese society. Like the author, Yukio Mishima, who committed ritual suicide to protest what he saw as the softening of the powerful Japanese martial culture, Yen saw the problems hidden within the astounding economic successes of modern-day Japan. I think he saw the Japan of today as complacent. I think he was sickened by the sight of his countrymen running all over the world, buying out Tiffany's, Fred's, Cartier's, Ungaro's, you name it, gathering up real estate, building resorts—mini-Tokyos—all over Hawaii, unwrapping their endless rolls of money to snap up anything that caught their fancy. 'The Japanese,' Yen said to me, 'are the technology-rich Ugly Americans of the fifties, the oil-rich Arabs of the seventies. Now we are no better than the rednecks of any culture. Progress has made a shambles of us.' "

"Christ, just what was this philosopher turned international lawyer up to?" Russell said.

"Now you're beginning to see the attraction," Tori said. "But there was another side of Yen that you wouldn't be able to see. He was enormously charismatic in a physical sense. I didn't count on that when I first approached him.

"I did it in the prescribed method. I manufactured a seemingly accidental meeting while he was away for the weekend in Kyoto. I did my homework, and contrived to bump into him on the bullet train.

"He was exceptionally charming. He had this way of engaging you in conversation that was actually a two-way street. He thrived on dialogue, not, as is true with so many people, in telling you what he thought.

"He was on his way, he told me, to the Kokedera, the famous Moss Temple, whose magnificent garden is composed of forty varieties of moss. Unless you've been there, you cannot imagine

317

the peacefulness of that place: the mist dusting the pellucid lake, the sunlight filtered through the tall cryptomeria and black pines, spreading a light like fairy dust over the low-mounded emerald moss. It's a heavenly spot, and a holy one as well. When you're at Kokedera, it's impossible to imagine time moving. It's as if the temple's reality is so powerful it defeats even time's march.

"I don't expect I'm describing this adequately," Tori said, "but I suspect that the effect of that singular place had something to do with how quickly I was drawn into Yen's universe. Understand, there was nothing boyish about him, save his looks. And even then the lack of lines in his face only served to keep at bay the hardness that sooner or later life inflicts on most countenances.

"At that moment, in that spot, Yen seemed perfect, just as the moss garden was perfect, almost as if he were an extension of the spirit that pervaded the place. He was irresistible."

"Tori—"

"Oh, Russ, don't tell me it's never happened to you. Haven't you ever found a woman irresistible?"

"Not while I was on the job."

Tori automatically thought of Ariel and the legacy he had left to her safekeeping. "You mean pushing the papers around your desk? I'm hardly surprised."

"Thank you very much."

"Sorry," she said. "You don't deserve that. But the old Russell Slade, the one I used to know, was so judgmental—and thought himself so perfect."

"God, no, never perfect."

"But that's just the mask you'd put on."

"Did I?" Russell was surprised. "It seems you're describing another Russell Slade."

Tori looked at him. "In a way, that's true."

"It seems to me he died somewhere in Machine-Gun City. In the red dust."

"Yes." Tori looked at him. "I never told you how you surprised me that afternoon at Cruz's apartment, when you took the lead and won him over by being the famous mole hunter." Russell laughed and Tori joined him, for the first time realizing that she was enjoying his company. "And then in the jungle, and in the corrida. I thought you'd fall apart—that's why I coerced Bernard into ordering you to come into the field with me. I was sure I could humiliate you."

His blue eyes had turned dark. "Just as I humiliated you when I severed you from the Mall for my own selfish reasons."

"It almost seems as if Bernard deliberately set us against one another." And she was suddenly aware again of Estilo's story of how he had set the German twins against one another, destroying their intimate bond. But this was so different. Of course, Bernard hadn't meant her or Russell any harm. Yet it was odd how the story seemed to remain in her mind.

Russell seemed to think about what she had said for some time. He was about to say something, abruptly changed his mind. "It's funny the curves life throws you," he remarked. "No matter how organized, how ready you are, you're never prepared for what happens."

"Yes," Tori said. "That's what happened to me with Yen." She waited for him to make a comment, but he was silent. "We had a glorious afternoon," she went on, "and then we parted company. But not forgetting why I had made contact, I doubled back and followed him.

"It was twilight, near the dinner hour at that time of the year, and I followed Yen into a restaurant in Kyoto. Someone was waiting for him."

"Don't tell me. It was Fukuda."

"Yes. She and Yen were having an affair."

"Dear God."

"You're not wide of the mark," Tori said. "Once I determined the nature of their relationship and that Yen's real purpose in coming to Kyoto was to meet his girlfriend, I backed off.

"But I got some background on Fukuda, and I began to worry. The more I found out about her, the worse the situation seemed to be. I already knew enough about Yen that I realized I couldn't let him go. If there was a Japanese-Russian connection, surely it was flowing through him. But how was I going to avoid Fukuda?

"Back in Tokyo, I contrived another ploy. I approached Yen again, this time as a client. Remember those dummy corporation papers I asked you for?"

"Yeah," Russell said. "They put our myths department in a snit. They worked straight through the July Fourth holiday for you."

"I tried to keep our relationship strictly business," Tori said, "but Yen wouldn't let me. He even admitted to seeing Fukuda. He said it didn't matter. He wanted me, and no one was going to stop him."

"Sensitive guy."

"The odd thing was, he was sensitive," Tori said. "Just selectively so. He was like a searchlight. Whatever was illuminated by his attention was so well taken care of. But as soon as the beam moved on, the subject was left alone in the dark."

"Like Fukuda."

Tori nodded. "Yen said the affair was winding down, at least as far as he was concerned. It was fun, he admitted, getting off on the danger. Until it got too intense. Perhaps that was his way of giving me a warning for what I might conceive of as our future together."

"In other words, there wasn't to be any," Russell said.

"Not necessarily. I think he was saying there was going to be a future only if he wanted it."

"Nice."

"But isn't that typical of men?"

"Tori, don't start. Most women have minds of their own, too."

"Yes, but it's what's been drummed into those minds that troubles me." She shrugged. "Anyway, as far as Yen was concerned, he wanted us to start where we left off that afternoon in the Kokedera. I did my best to dissuade him."

"I'll bet."

"All right. Part of me wanted to be with him. I've never aspired to sainthood. What possible good would it do me? I'm only human."

"From this confession can I assume that you allowed the affair to continue?"

Tori was silent for some time. "In a matter of speaking," she said after a while.

"You're going to have to do better than that," Russell said. But there was no edge to his voice, for which Tori was grateful.

"The affair continued," she said, "only under my conditions. Which were that we not be seen in public together, and that I never under any circumstances come to his house. And it worked, for a while. I continued to mind the business aspect, hoping at some point to hint to him my interest as an investor in unconventional multinational deals.

"I never got the chance to make my pitch. A territorial war erupted between Hitasura and Big Ezoe. Fukuda was recalled from Kyoto, where she had been managing a large, complicated arms deal for Big Ezoe, and that was that.

"Within twenty-four hours of Fukuda setting foot in Tokyo,

she knew Yen was seeing someone else. Within forty-eight hours, she had discovered that that someone was me."

"Efficient bitch," Russell said.

"You don't know the half of it," Tori said. "She methodically tracked me down. She had more contacts than I had, and a great deal more obsessiveness. In the end, it was Deke who warned me, but by then it was too late. Fukuda was locked on to me, and I couldn't shake her."

"What happened?" Russell's expression showed that he was plainly fascinated by this dance of death.

Tori described the confrontation in the tunnels below Tokyo. "When the explosive she threw tore open my hip, Fukuda knew I was helpless. Then she heard the train coming, and she left me on the tracks to die."

"Stupid of her."

"Yes. Hitasura got to me before the train did."

"That's too bad for Fukuda," Russell said.

Tori couldn't help laughing at his bravado, even though she knew that where Fukuda was concerned, nothing was amusing.

Then he said, "Damnit, you should have told me all this at your original debriefing."

"You wouldn't have listened," Tori said. "At that point in time you weren't interested in my views about anything."

"That judgment wasn't for you to make."

"It's the truth."

"You were under discipline," Russell said. "The truth has absolutely nothing to do with it."

He was right, of course, but Tori was damned if she was going to give him the satisfaction of eliciting an apology from her.

"Hitasura is coming," Big Ezoe said in Fukuda's ear.

"I can see the vehicle now," she said into the pinpoint mike wrapped around her head.

"Where are you?"

"At the Kinji-to," Fukuda said. It was amazing, she thought, what the new fiber optics could do. Big Ezoe sounded as if he were inside her head instead of some miles away.

"Good," the voice in her head said. "Everything is ready. You are the guide."

"Yes," Fukuda said. She could see the moving van coming her way, and she stepped inside the glass-doored entrance to the Kinji-to. "That is what you trained me to be."

"Hitasura has an ally."

"From your tone of voice," Fukuda said, "I'm sure it's someone I know."

"Tori Nunn."

There was an exhalation from Fukuda, soft, but with an instant sense of forewarning. "In that event," she said, "don't bring Koi in too quickly. I want my chance."

"Last chance," Big Ezoe said.

"Not mine. Tori's."

Hitasura said, "We're here."

"Where's here?" Russell asked.

The moving van had pulled over to the curb, and Hitasura was ushering them out of the mobile living room. He pointed upward as they climbed off the rear of the van. They were parked in front of a massive postmodern structure that soared upward in pyramid fashion, an artistic chunk of twisted chromium, steel, orange-rusted iron, all dominated by enormous green-tinted windows.

At this time of the night the building acted like a mirror, reflecting the spectroscopic patterns of the city's skyscrapers, neon lights, the movement of its traffic in odd, skewed angles.

"This is the Kambata Museum," Hitasura said. "But for obvious reasons, everyone calls it the Kinji-to, the pyramid." He began walking toward it. "It's new since you were last here, Tori. It houses quite an amazing array of martial arts antiquities." He glanced at the entrance. "It's Monday. The museum's closed to the public."

"This is where Fukuda was last seen?" Russell asked.

"It's where she is," Hitasura said.

"Then she's here for a reason," Tori said.

Hitasura nodded. "You're the expert on Fukuda."

"Do you think there's any chance she's been tipped off that we're after her?" Russell asked.

Tori looked at Hitasura, who shrugged. "In the end, it doesn't matter," she said, moving up the granite and steel front steps. "We've got to go in and get her."

But Russell, right behind her, caught her shoulder, spun her around. "You're wrong, Tori," he said. "It matters a great deal. If she knows we're coming, there's a good chance she's prepared for us. Knowing that should change our strategy."

"Okay," Tori said, "how should it change?"

"I'd like to get more people here, for one thing."

Tori shook her head. "We've got to make as little noise as

322

possible. The more of Hitasura's people we call in, the better chance we have of bringing the Tokyo Metropolitan Police down on us."

Russell thought about this for a moment as his eyes searched hers. At last he said, so that only Tori could hear him, "I don't like being involved in vendettas. They're invariably unhealthy from any point of view."

Tori gave him a brief nod. "I understand." Then, for just a moment, her expression softened, and she said, "Russ, did you ever have an itch you couldn't get to? Tell me, what would you do if you suddenly got a chance to scratch an itch like that?"

Russell's hand fell away from her shoulder. "Well," he said, "at least you'll have me to look after you."

Tori grinned at him, and the three of them went up the steps. The front doors were closed but unlocked. Russell looked briefly at the lock to see if it had been jimmied open; there was no damage that he could see. Had Fukuda picked the lock or did she somehow have a key?

Clandestinely, Russell checked his armaments: .32 caliber Colt, lightweight titanium-handled boot knife, garroting wire with wooden handles. Everything checked, but somehow he did not feel all that much better. This Fukuda sounded more like a ghost than any woman he had ever met. He could feel the fear emanating from both Hitasura and Tori, and it worried him.

Tori, leading them slowly into the interior of the Kinji-to, was thinking of Sun Tzu. If you cannot choose the ground for war, he had written, make certain you choose the time. Tori wondered whether she would have that option. Not, she knew, if Fukuda had anything to say about it.

They were moving through the vast hall that made up the centerpiece of the museum's main space. Enormous slabs of green-tinted glass hung suspended three stories over their heads. Their intervals and angles brought to mind a futuristic version of the assembly of war banners arrayed in the great rooms of medieval castles.

On either side of the central aisle down which they made their way, the hall was filled with exquisite examples of armor from as far back as the tenth century all the way to the early nineteenth century.

Tori, Hitasura, and Russell moved through this thrilling yet somber reminder of Japan's past, a unique entity in which the lines of history and myth were often blurred and, more, exchanged places.

Tori paused. She could hear what at first sounded like the rough soughing of a storm wind through pine boughs. Then, as she listened more closely, as the sound built, guttural, throaty, it became the noise of the stalking lion, a great predatory beast about to open wide its jaws as it came upon the exposed flank of its prey.

"What in God's name is that?" Russell said. The short hairs at the back of his neck had begun to stir.

"She's here somewhere," Hitasura whispered.

"*Yo-ibuki*," Tori said to Russell. "In karate there are two forms of breathing. *Yo-ibuki* is the hard, aggressive style used in attacks."

"I never learned that in the Virginia courses," Russell said.

"Naturally." Tori did not take her eyes off the interior of the hall stretching away from them. "Isn't that why you're out here in the field?"

Green light saturated the hall in degrees, thick swathes, deeper or lighter depending on whether at any given place the glass slabs overlapped one another. The effect was spectral, in some ways sinister, as the thick, unnatural illumination highlighted cuirasses of iron here, or there an ancient ornate *kawara* corselet of layered leather "scales," cured to the hardness of metal.

These magnificent suits of armor were pieced together with intricate laces of differing patterns and colors whose styles, over time, had been the way samurai differentiated between clans and rank within an army.

Now Tori could see in the dimness ahead of them the *hi-odoshi* suit of armor of the Empress Jingo, known as Red Lacing, because of the dark crimson laces used to tie the pieces together.

As she watched, she saw the headpiece move. The mask below the high, horned helmet—dark, the old leather stained with the blood of enemies—turned in their direction. At the same time, the Empress Jingo's suit of armor came down off its pedestal. The sound of the *yo-ibuki* filled the hall, echoing through the centuries of battle attire.

Beside Tori, Russell was already in his semicrouch. Tori saw the Colt in his hand, yelled "No!" but he either didn't understand or didn't care. Russell had his own ideas of protecting her from being embroiled further in her blood feud with Fukuda. He pulled the trigger.

Tori had an instant's glimmer of the suit of armor being thrown backward by the impact of the bullet before the hall was lit up in a blinding glare.

The percussion hurled them off their feet. Tori felt as if a gigantic hand had been slammed into her chest. The noise of the percussion rattled her eardrums, making them ache, then, in its aftermath, filled them with white noise.

Fukuda was an expert in miniaturized explosives; Tori had thought that her story had made that evident to Russell, but apparently not.

As she struggled to regain equilibrium, Tori knew that Fukuda would not have been foolish enough to attempt a frontal assault on them. But the rigging of the armor told Tori a great deal. For one thing, Fukuda had some forewarning of their arrival, so her network of contacts must be stronger than ever: Tori and Russell's entrance into Tokyo had been highly clandestine. For another thing, Fukuda had chosen the Kinji-to, this pyramid, as her field of battle. Tori knew they had to be doubly careful.

How many more surprises did Fukuda have lying in wait for them? Tori knew Fukuda's strategy. She loved the convoluted, the oblique forms of assault. What she could not abide was a direct frontal attack. Tori would keep this in mind.

Tori rolled over, heard a groan.

"Russ?"

The groan came again, and Tori, drawing herself onto her knees, pulled Russell into a sitting position. "Are you okay?"

He nodded, but his eyes still looked slightly dazed.

Tori looked around, but there was no sign of Hitasura amid the rubble. Christ, she thought. What's happened to him?

She got to her feet, Russell beside her.

"Stupid," Russell said.

"What?"

"Remind me not to go off half-cocked like that."

"Very funny."

They made a careful search for Hitasura, but they could find no sign that he had ever been there. Russell looked at Tori.

"Don't say it," she said. "I won't believe that he's betrayed me, too."

"I hope you're right," Russell said. "But the evidence suggests that he led us straight into a trap."

They moved off, heading farther into the dimly lit interior of the hall. Soon the hall narrowed into a corridor; the deeper they got, the darker it became. Russell took out a pocket flash, handed

325

it to Tori. She flicked it on, played it in a shallow arc ahead of them—and immediately stopped in her tracks.

The concentrated beam of the flash picked up a shining strand, a thread like a spider's webbing, strung across their path. Tori touched Russell, pointed wordlessly: the monofilament was strung approximately at waist height. Even at walking speed, the monofilament would cut deeply into flesh.

Tori went down on her knees, then lay on her back. Russell followed her lead. Using the flash pointed upward, she began to slither beneath the deadly monofilament.

She was halfway past it when she felt a pressure across her shoulders. Her scalp began to prickle and she felt a line of sweat snake itself between her shoulder blades. She tried to turn her head, but she could not see what was directly in front of her.

"Russ!" she hissed. "I'm stuck! Get up here!"

He began to slither up on her right, but she stopped him with a guttural noise. "Get on top of me!" she whispered. "Whatever's stopped me goes from shoulder to shoulder."

Russell moved, scrambling over her.

Tori felt the comfortable fit of his body on hers, looked upward into his face. "What do you see?"

"Another monofilament," he said softly. "I guess it was meant to get you at the ankles."

"Or stop anyone alert enough to have seen the first monofilament."

"What do you want to do?" Russell asked. "I can easily drag you backward."

"No!" Tori said. "I can feel an odd tension that came into the monofilament as I stretched it. I think there's some kind of trigger that will go off when the tension's broken."

"Okay." Russell slithered forward and, using Tori's body as a base, passed over the second monofilament. Then he reached back.

"Don't use your fingers," Tori warned. "The monofilament will cut right through your skin."

"Right." Russell lay on his stomach, took out his knife, slid the blade between the monofilament and the hollow at the center of Tori's back. Carefully, he brought the blade back toward him until it took the monofilament to the same tension it was at against Tori's shoulder blades.

"Move," Russell said. "Now."

Tori moved gingerly away from the monofilament, and Russell immediately felt that odd tension transferred to his arms. It was like being near an electric current. Then Tori had scrambled across the monofilament and had joined him on the other side. She crouched down beside him, whispered in his ear, "I'm going to get behind you. On my signal, take the blade away from the wire."

"What?"

"Don't worry. Trust me."

Russell closed his eyes for a moment. The sweat was burning on his face, and he could feel his hands beginning to tremble with the task of maintaining just the right amount of tension on the monofilament.

A moment later he felt Tori gripping his ankles.

"I'm going to count to three. Ready?"

"Ready."

"One. Two. Three. Now!"

Russell, breathing a prayer, jerked the blade from its position against the monofilament. At the same time, he felt himself being slid backward, hard and fast.

There was an ugly breeze against his face, a blur in front of his eyes as the monofilament flew to his left, and he heard a soft *thock!*

Tori played the beam of the flash along the right wall, and they saw embedded there a *shuriken*, a miniature steel dart, a thorn dark with an unknown substance on its tip.

"This is one mean woman," Russell said, wiping the sweat off his face.

"Yes," Tori said. "Clever, too."

"I'd say diabolical." Russell stood. "No wonder Hitasura split. You picked one hell of a nemesis."

"*Karma.* I must have sinned like a sonuvabitch in a previous life."

Russell grinned at her. "Time for atonement."

Tori came close to Russell, her eyes glittering. "I think you should stay here. You've come far enough. This is between Fukuda and me."

"Like hell!"

"Russ, try to put your male ego aside for the moment. There's no sense—"

"Forget it," he said curtly. "How would you have come through back there without me?"

"I'd have found a way."

He gripped her shoulders. "Tori, I told you my feeling about vendettas—they have a way of eating people alive. *Everyone* who gets involved in them.''

"Nevertheless, I know Fukuda, and you don't. I'm afraid that from now on you'll be more of a liability.''

Russell sighed, then nodded. ''Go on,'' he said. He put his hand on her hip, as he had in the library at Diana's Garden, which now seemed a lifetime ago. ''I understand the need to pay her back for what she did to you.''

"Thanks.'' Tori kissed him quickly on the lips, then she was gone, swallowed up by the darkness.

Russell stood quite still for a moment, then he said, ''Bullshit,'' under his breath. ''I'm going to protect you whether you like it or not.''

When Tori left Russell, she removed her shoes, tying them to her belt; then she went very fast down the corridor. Her steps were utterly silent across the marble squares. It seemed as if she were barely touching the floor. In fact she was using only the extreme outside of her soles, never putting her full weight on either foot. The principle was akin to the way in which four-legged animals ran. At times all their hooves were off the ground at once because they were able continually to redistribute their weight as they ran, their center of gravity rotating away from each leg as it struck the ground.

At length the corridor ended and Tori found herself at a bank of elevators. She could see that they were all shut down. To her right was a wide flight of sculpted marble stairs curving upward in the classical style that in this venue seemed wildly out of place.

Tori mounted the stairs. The way to ascend under these circumstances was with her back to the wall. The idea was to put herself in Fukuda's mind and try to outthink her.

One quarter of the way up, Tori paused; she could feel a kind of grit on the stairs. Otherwise the marble was immaculately smooth. Just in this spot . . .

Tori squatted down. Another *shuriken*! In the feeble light she saw the glint of the miniblade not two paces in front of her, stuck between two squares of the marble wall. She examined the blade. It, too, was dark with some kind of herb toxin.

Tori reached down beneath her feet, picked up some of the grit on her fingertip, rubbed it. Fukuda had cleverly carved out a slitlike niche for the blade in the grout between the marble slabs.

Keeping her fingers away from the darkened tip, Tori carefully pulled the blade from the wall, took it with her.

Now she went directly up the center of the stairs, peering intently ahead as she wound her way up to the second-floor gallery.

She was almost at the top of the stairs when a ball of darkness came hurtling down at her. It struck her fully on her chest, and she crashed backward down the staircase until she landed painfully against the curved marble wall.

Hot breath in her face, claws digging into the flesh of her shoulders, she had no space in which to work and, worse, her position left her no chance to use either momentum or her greater weight against the creature.

She saw the red eyes of the Akita, knew immediately it had been trained as a guard dog. It was utterly silent, all its efforts directed at subduing her. It was very powerful, and she was still slightly dazed from its initial attack. She knew she had to disable it quickly or its teeth would eventually find her throat.

She jammed her elbow far back into its mouth, reached down for the poisoned blade she had taken from the wall, slammed it all the way into the Akita's belly. The paws scrabbled at her, but their full power was already waning.

Tori threw the creature off her, scrambled over it, gaining the second-floor gallery.

Silence.

Then a slight singing, as of a draft through a grate or a cord being vibrated. Tori looked around; there was something odd about the bank of elevators.

As soon as she moved cautiously toward them, she saw that one of the doors was open, revealing a gaping shaft, the source of the singing. Tori could see the main cable moving against the auxiliary one. Gripping either side of the doorway, she looked down, and could just make out Fukuda, already below the first-floor level, descending the cable.

Tori leaned out and, gripping the cable, wrapped her legs around it. Down she went. It was not easy. The cable was thick, coated with grease. She put a great deal of tension in her thighs, knees, and ankles.

It took her several moments to get the hang of it, but then she was making good progress. She had just passed the main floor when she felt the cable grow taut. Beside her the auxiliary cable began to move and, soon, she saw the counterweight soaring

329

upward past her and knew what was happening. Fukuda was sending the elevator car down.

Tori, trapped between the main floor and the basement, looked up, saw the car plummeting down on her. Its shadow was already covering her, and she could feel the kineticism in the cable she was gripping so tightly.

She realized there was only one thing to do, released her grip with ankles, knees, and thighs and, using only her hands to guide her, shot down the cable.

Without the grease coating, she knew the friction would have flayed the flesh off her palms. As it was, she felt the abrasion building, but the elevator was still gaining and, in the instant she raised her head to glance at its progress, she missed the basement level, shot on past, heading for the subbasement.

Here there were no doors, and the shaft ended abruptly. With mounting horror, Tori looked down at the concrete bed of the elevator shaft: a dead end.

Shadows descending, a hot wind on her neck. She felt the encroachment of the oncoming car, thought, What have I to lose? and let go completely.

She dropped the last fifteen feet, willed herself to relax. She landed in a ball on the oil-stained concrete, rolled, came out of her tuck, took a great leap sideways. Behind her, with a whir and a whine, the elevator settled into its bed.

Tori heard swift footfalls echoing in the chamber of the subbasement. She turned, headed in their direction. Bare bulbs burned in sockets along the walls. By their light she could see that the subbasement of this new building was far from finished. Rough concrete walls were interspersed with spackled wallboard on which hurried instructions for electrician or plumber had been scribbled.

She put on her shoes; the floor was poured concrete, filthy with oil and debris. But, often, gaping holes opened into noisome trenches strung with enormous bundles of cables, the lifelines of the Kinji-to.

Tori leaped over these holes, moving farther into the building's interior. Abruptly she came to the far side of the Kinji-to, the end of the subbasement. There was no wall, but rather a vast space opening onto the Japanese solution to the utter lack of parking space in Tokyo. An automated parking tower had been incorporated in the design of the Kinji-to. It was made up of a kind of vertical Ferris wheel of steel slots onto which cars were driven, then parked, which were then rotated like a dry cleaner's rack to get to the car needed.

Tori turned briefly back the way she had come, but she could neither see nor hear any sign of Fukuda. She stepped onto the steel slot of the parking tower, and it immediately began to move upward.

Behind her, through immense green glass windows, Tokyo glittered like a toy city within a glass ball.

Tori looked above and below her, but she could not find Fukuda. It seemed unsafe to stay in one spot, so she began to climb from slot to slot. This was not difficult, as the slots were immense gridworks of iron and steel, affording ample hand and footholds.

To be the master of your enemy's fate, Sun Tzu wrote, one must be as unknowable as one is silent.

Fukuda is doing a good job of it, Tori thought. So far. She is leading me in circles: up, down, up. Why is she doing that? Tori looked down, past the gridwork of the parking tower, past the skeleton of the Kinji-to's subbasement, into the deep strata below Tokyo itself, and she knew: up, down, up, *down.*

Thoomp! Her head jerked up at the sound. She had just enough time to glimpse Fukuda in the center of the parking tower where the machinery was housed, before her grinning face was blotted out. A black sphere, expanding as it approached. Tori saw immediately that the sphere—some kind of gas-propelled and inflated projectile that Fukuda had invented—would fill the entire area of the slot on which she stood by the time it hit.

There was no time to climb upward. Tori leaped downward onto the next slot. But by then, with the movement of the parking tower, she was again level with Fukuda.

Thoomp! The sphere exploding, expanding toward her.

Leap down onto the next slot.

Thoomp! The sphere exploding, expanding toward her.

Leap down onto the next slot. She had a vision of Sisyphus rolling his burden up the hill, only to see it roll down again.

Thoomp! The sphere exploding, expanding toward her.

And Tori, coiled into a ball, leapt backward, kicking out at the last instant, the soles of her shoes crashing through a window panel. She extended herself, reaching out and backward simultaneously. Gripped a horizontal steel rim. Glass cut her hands, and she gritted her teeth. Blood ran down her wrists.

She was alone in the night, hanging from the sloping side of the pyramid of Kinji-to. Wind brushed her cheek. She could hear the sounds of the city, a vast engine humming on like a star spinning endlessly in its orbit. It seemed so far away.

But at least she was off Sisyphus' hill, the dreadful treadmill that Fukuda had devised for her.

Tori refused to look down; she did not want to know how high up she was, how far away the pavement was from where she hung. The weight on her shoulder sockets was increasing with every moment she stayed in one position.

Carefully, she felt for purchase with her feet; she encountered nothing but smooth glass. Her only chance was to curl upward so that her thighs were pressed tight against her chest; until her feet were over the sill of the steel window rim. In her contorted position she could barely breathe, she was sweating profusely, and her heartbeat was dangerously high.

She hung on a moment more, going into *prana*, her deep, controlled breathing. Then, having marshalled herself, she gave one final heave, felt herself launched upward and forward toward the building. Her backside cleared the steel rim, and she let go with her hands, flew back through the rent window.

The parking tower had ceased its movement, and Tori climbed through one slot into the center of the conveyance where she had seen Fukuda. She threw the switch to start the engine, then climbed aboard a slot for the ride down.

She pulled out the small *shuriken* blade she had used to kill the Akita, sliced strips from her blouse, bound her bleeding palms. As she did so, she saw a small cut on the middle finger of her right hand. What differentiated it from the other cuts and abrasions on her hands was the flesh surrounding it. It was dark and swollen. Tori flexed the finger. Motion was restricted, and when she touched the cut, she felt no pain, nothing.

She looked down. She was almost back at the subbasement. She saw, to her surprise, that Russell was standing at the edge of the parking tower, looking up at her.

"Tori!" he called.

"Jump!" she shouted, coming abreast of him.

"What the hell—"

"Jump, damnit!"

Russell jumped down, landing on her slot. They passed below the level of the subbasement; Tori knew where they were headed, she had known it the moment, ascending Sisyphus' hill, she had looked down, past the subbasement, into the tunnels of Tokyo's subway.

Tori and Russell jumped off the parking tower at its bottom, before their slot began its ascent. This is the place she's chosen, Tori thought—the place where she left me to die. Now she's intent on finishing the job.

"What the hell happened to you?" Russell said, taking her roughly bandaged hands in his.

"I tried to fly," she said, trying to laugh it off, "but I didn't quite make it." She was thinking of her numbed middle finger, the knife thrust into the Akita's belly, her hand slipping in the blood, riding up the tiny hilt of the *shuriken* onto its blade.

"Fukuda's down here," he said. "I saw her riding that thing you were on."

"I know where she's headed," Tori said, leading him into the tunnels. "This is approximately where she left me the last time."

"The subway tracks?" Russell looked around. "But these tunnels are obviously long-abandoned." At that moment they heard a rumble, felt the vibrations coming up through their feet. Russell looked down. "Underneath us?"

Tori nodded.

"This is madness," he said.

"I warned you. I told you to stay behind."

"But this is personal. It has nothing to do with what we're supposed to be invest—"

"It has everything to do with it!" Tori snapped. "As long as Fukuda knows I'm in Tokyo, she'll give me no rest. Do you seriously believe she'd allow us to continue with our investigation?" Her eyes were almost black, as if they had absorbed the darkness of the tunnels through which she and Russell now crept. "One thing you can be sure of, one of us is going to die here. *Karma.*"

"Fuck *karma*," Russell said hotly. "That nonsense is only in your mind."

"You think so? I told you you wouldn't survive here without an open mind. I meant it."

"I could knock you out, put you over my shoulder, and carry you out of here," he said.

"Then do it, hotshot."

"Think, Tori. You're reacting emotionally, and Fukuda is counting on that."

"Don't get in my way, Russ. I won't back off."

Russell stood very still. He was livid with rage, but he also recognized that most of his anger was displaced fear. He was so

333

frightened for her that he did not know what to say or do. *One thing you can be sure of, one of us is going to die here.*

Finally, he nodded. *"Karma."* And he thought, If your final meeting with Fukuda is meant to be, Tori, then my presence here now is part of it. My *karma* and yours, bound together. When this is over, who will tell them apart?

They pressed on and, almost immediately, came upon a poorly shored-up section of the ground. Here wooden boards had been hastily placed over a length of track bed that had fallen through to the next level.

Russell got down on his knees, peered through a gap in the boards. "Christ, it's a long way down."

"That's where she is," Tori said.

He looked up at her, the determined expression on her face, nodded. "I'll go first."

He pushed the boards apart, produced the garrote wire and jammed one of the wooden ends into the gap between the boards where it narrowed to a crevice. He unspooled the wire into the abyss, lowered himself until his shoes hit the other wooden end. Using it as a foothold, he slithered down until he was hanging at the end of the wire.

Tori lowered herself after him and, locking her legs around him, moved slowly down his length. She climbed down his body, dropped, finally, off his ankles onto the track bed of the subway system. From somewhere beyond a connecting wall she heard and felt the passage of a train.

She reached up, said, "Now!" and softened his fall as his bulk hurtled down at her.

"Which way?" Russell said.

"Fukuda will tell us; the more she shows me her strategy, the more I learn about her."

Russell said, "I'm beginning to like this concept of *karma* less and less."

Tori gave him a thin smile. "Wrong approach. You can't like or dislike *karma*. You accept it."

"That seems to be something of a paradox," Russell said thoughtfully. "Is this acceptance supremely pragmatic or supremely delusory?"

"Russ, remember our talk about the merging of myth and reality?"

"Yes, but how does that apply here?"

"When you can tell me," Tori said, "then you will understand."

"Is that a Zen riddle?"

"You mean a *koan*?" Tori laughed despite herself. "In a sense, I guess it is."

A rumbling filled the tunnel.

"This track?" Russell asked.

"Next one over."

He relaxed somewhat. "It's only a matter of time before a train comes through this tunnel."

"We'll let Fukuda worry about timetables and schedules," Tori said as they moved off down the tunnel. "She's so good at it."

Privately, Russell thought this was a mistake. He could not understand why Tori was refusing to take the initiative. He had been taught to attack whenever possible. Why was Tori allowing Fukuda to dictate the pace of the encounter? All this esoteric talk of strategy made little sense to him. I've got to find a way to end this, quickly and finally, he thought.

Ahead of them, they saw a light.

"Train?"

Tori shook her head. She had one foot on the rail, and there was no vibration. "Fukuda," she said. They had, at last, come to the killing ground.

"Sit tight," Russell said, so unexpectedly that when he pressed Tori back against the damp tunnel wall, she made no resistance.

Russell, keeping to the shadows, gun drawn, ran quickly and silently down the extreme edge of the tunnel toward the light.

Russ, you idiot! Tori thought, heading after him. I thought I'd persuaded you to give up being my protector. Didn't you promise that you weren't going to go off half-cocked again?

Tori heard the crack and, almost simultaneously, Russell's sharply indrawn breath. As she came up to where he had been, she saw the cleverly disguised hole beside the track bed; he had fallen into it, had stumbled to his right onto the tracks, catching his right ankle between two rails where they branched into an adjacent tunnel.

"Don't touch him!" a voice cried, and Tori stopped on her way to try to free Russell. She stared at Fukuda, who was standing not fifty yards down the track, her hand on a chrome lever.

"This is the manual override to the automatic switching," Fukuda said. "If you don't do as I say, I'll put this lever and crush his ankle."

"Tell her to shove it," Russell said, frantically searching for

335

his pistol, which he had dropped when the ground had given way beneath him. He cursed his stupidity, thought of what his impetuosity had caused. He sat up, tried to free his ankle. Christ, but it hurt!

Tori said, "What do you want?"

"You know the answer to that." Fukuda's hand was curled menacingly around the lever. "I want you to die." She beckoned with her free hand. "This way."

Tori moved toward her.

"That's enough!" Fukuda commanded.

Yes, Tori thought, she's still afraid of me. She doesn't want me too close. A useful bit of information. She had a few weapons at her disposal, but she suspected now that they would not be enough.

Her right hand was at her side; surreptitiously, she flexed the fingers. The middle three were completely numb. She still had some feeling in her thumb, but her little finger was a mass of tingles.

Tori thought, Dear God, she's already won.

"One doesn't often get a second chance in this life." Fukuda cocked her head as she stared, black-eyed, at Tori. "I can't tell you what a wonderful feeling it is to see you down here again. I knew you'd get past the *shuriken* and the dog, but how you outmaneuvered me in the elevator shaft and on the moving carpark, I'll never know." She laughed. "But, you see, it doesn't matter, because here you are, and here you'll die. In just the way I want you to."

She's gloating, Tori thought. She's human, after all. Tori began to breathe again. There was no point in formulating a strategy; the place, the time, the circumstances had dictated what she must do, in any case. *Karma*. And, as she launched herself toward Fukuda, she found herself wondering if Russell would at last understand the nature of acceptance.

She saw Fukuda's eyes open wide in shock, saw the tension come into her left hand where it grasped the manual override, saw the lever begin its descent, the squeal of the rail behind her a harbinger of the pain Russell would suffer.

Then Tori was on Fukuda, her left hand, the fingers stiffened like a bar of steel, chopping down in a percussive *atemi*, breaking Fukuda's hold on the override. Tori and Fukuda crashed as one onto the tracks.

Tori had several advantages beside surprise: Fukuda would be reluctant to let go of the lever, since it was her primary hold on her. That meant she was stationary and essentially one-handed. Fukuda was also afraid of her, which would slow her response time to any sudden attack. And her aversion to frontal assaults made her hesitate a fraction more before reacting. Just time enough for Tori, with the help of her artificial hip, to reach her.

Fukuda's wrists were crisscrossed against Tori's throat in the cloudmaker. Her own pulse beat wildly in Tori's ears, and Tori fought for breath. She used her knee against Fukuda's thigh, bending it outward, then drawing up her foot, stamping down.

Fukuda grimaced as the tendons connecting her thigh to her pelvis strained, then, as Tori delivered another foot *atemi*, they snapped. But she did not release her grip. Rather, ignoring the attack, she pressed Tori back against the rails, pressing down on her windpipe.

Tori struggled for air. Her entire right hand was numb, the wrist feeling like it had bloated to three times its size. Pain was lancing up her arm.

She kicked again, felt and heard the bone pop, dislocating out of its socket in Fukuda's hip. Fukuda began *yo-ibuki*, the aggressive hard breathing from deep in her throat in order to block the excruciating pain.

It was then that Tori understood that nothing short of death was going to get Fukuda to release her hold.

Blackness, an acute sense of dislocation, threatened to engulf Tori. She was insensate on a black wind, beginning to float away, and it was with a supreme effort that she drew her drifting mind back to her predicament. *Hang on!* she commanded herself. *Hang on!*

And then, against her back, she felt the vibration come into the tracks, and she knew with an acute sense of déjà vu that a train was on its way.

Russell had screamed when he felt the increased pressure on his ankle bones. Oh, Christ, he thought. He was panting, and the sweat was rolling down his body. He heaved with renewed effort to free himself. In fact, he had made some progress when the squealing rail had caught him in its grip.

Out of the corner of his eye he could see his gun, glinting dully in the work lights of the tunnel. It was ten feet away, but in his position it might as well have been ten miles.

All right, he told himself as calmly as he could. Forget the fucking gun; how can I help Tori? He didn't know. He took out his knife, wedged the blade between the rail and his sock, tried to pry himself free. The blade bent, and when he felt the tension building in it, he gave up. There was no point in having it break off.

He could see Tori and Fukuda locked in what looked like a mortal embrace. He could discern no movement. It was as if their bodies had turned to stone and they were grappling with the force of their wills and their *hara*.

Then something made him look past the two antagonists. Light streaming, at first pale, but brightening rapidly until it was thick as lacquer, pushing back the darkness along the curving outer wall of the tunnel. The train was coming!

Mother of God, Russell thought. We are all going to be killed!

Myth and reality were blending. In Tori's oxygen-starved brain thoughts flashed like lightning in a darkling sky, random energy, losing direction. For greater and greater periods of time she had no memory of what had taken place. Surely her body, following the commands of her autonomous nervous system, was keeping on with staying alive, but that task was becoming more and more laborious. There seemed to be a better way, a sinking into a quieter time, a pool of silence where the seconds stopped their ceaseless ticking.

Wake up!

Tears of silence enveloping her, and the dark, comforting and warm, cradled her.

Darkness is death. . . .

So what?

"TORI!"

She awoke to see Fukuda's face, horrific with the effects of her efforts to kill her before the pain of Fukuda's dislocated bone rendered her unconscious.

Drifting away . . .

"TORI!"

Awake again, and thinking. Russell's shouting keeping her from going under. Something about Fukuda's face. What? So hard to think, like walking in quicksand, not worth the effort.

Slipping . . .

"TORI!"

Fukuda. What about her? That face so close to hers. Look! It was full of desperation. Fukuda was almost as near her end as she was.

Almost or more?

338

Up to me, Tori thought. She brought her knee up into the place where the bone was protruding from the inside of Fukuda's thigh, kicked as hard as she could.

Fukuda screamed and, for just an instant, relaxed her hold on Tori's windpipe. Tori already had her hands in position, inside and beneath Fukuda's cloudmaker, and now she used an aikido immobilization, blocking Fukuda's right arm with her left, then crossing her own right arm over, grabbing Fukuda's wrist.

The problem was immediate: she had no sensation in her right hand, so as quickly as she could, she jammed the heel of her left hand against Fukuda's elbow, rammed it upward until she heard the bone break.

Fukuda's jaws snapped shut and tears of pain squeezed out of her eyes. She tried to counterattack, slipping through Tori's guard with her good left hand, but Tori blocked her with a series of rapid-fire *kites* to her rib cage.

Tori sucked in air in deep bursts, put all her weight into a foot *atemi* against the right side of Fukuda's pelvis. Fukuda passed out.

Tori, almost spent, lowered her forehead against Fukuda's chest. Then she was up. The tunnel was brilliantly lit by the headlight of the train as it roared around the curve.

Tori ran to the manual override, but the automated switching was in progress, and the lever refused to budge. But she saw that it was no longer partway down. The switching had reset itself to the position it had been in before Fukuda had threatened Russell with moving it.

She ran to where Russell sat, grimacing in pain. She was so dizzy now, she could barely stand. He had managed at last to extricate his foot from the track, and they held on to each other as they limped to the nearest of the worker niches that lined the subway walls at regular intervals so that the maintenance men could get out of the way of trains.

The train shot by them, rattling through the tunnel, its whistle screaming. When it had passed, they emerged, and Tori headed for the spot where she had left Fukuda. The track was clear. She looked around, then shouted as a hand grabbed her leg from the side of the track bed.

She saw Fukuda's twisted pain-filled face, black and white, ribbons of soot streaking her pale skin, devoid of blood. The face, more like a mask, striped like a giant cat's, opened its

339

mouth, and Tori saw her own death mirrored there, the tiny metallic dart about to be shot out of its mouth tube.

Tori tried to pry Fukuda's fingers from her flesh, but they were like iron bands, pulling her down to the track bed. Fukuda's mouth raised, her cheeks hollowed to expel her final, deadly breath.

The noise of the explosion, magnified by the confines of the tunnel, made Tori jump. Fukuda's mouth closed with an audible snap, her body convulsed, and Tori saw the bullet hole flower blood just over her heart.

Tori began to shake, sat right down where she had been standing.

Russell hurried up to her, limping on his good leg. He pointed the gun at Fukuda's head, as if for a moment he could not quite believe that she was dead. "Come on!" he shouted. "Can't you feel it? Another train's on its way!"

Tori did not move. She was staring at the blank face of Fukuda. It seemed in that horrific instant that she saw her future, black and bitter, there. The end of the path she had set out on when she had discovered that in some way she needed to confront death again and again.

"Tori, goddamnit, get up! Your vendetta's finally over!" Russell knelt down beside her. He picked her up, carried her back to another worker box, shoved her in, crawled painfully in beside her. The darkness was electric with sound and vibration.

"She's dead." Russell's voice was hoarse. He was shivering with shock and pain. "I hope you're satisfied."

He was trying to examine her, but the lack of light made it impossible. "How badly are you hurt?"

"If you hadn't kept calling to me," Tori whispered, "I would have been the one left lying on the tracks." She put her head wearily on his shoulder, felt his arm come around her. She closed her eyes, but that only made her more dizzy. She felt unutterably sick.

"Russell, your leg—"

The tunnel was lit up as if by a display of fireworks, and they were shaken by the train's rumbling passage. When it was gone and semidarkness had descended again, Russell said, "Everything's all right. We'll make our way out of here now."

But when he pulled Tori to her feet, she immediately collapsed, and seeing her stricken face, he said, "Tori, what's the matter?"

"You're wrong, Russ. It's not over." Tori thought again of

340

her hand slipping in the Akita's blood, sliding up the narrow hilt of the *shuriken* knife that she had removed from the stairway wall, being cut by the blade.

"I can't move," she said, showing him the swollen wound, black as death, on her middle finger. "Fukuda's damned home-made toxin has poisoned me."

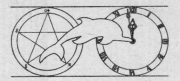

BOOK THREE

THE ZEN POLICEMAN

*It is always with the
best intentions that the
worst work is done.*
—OSCAR WILDE

"That bastard Hitasura."

Big Ezoe, standing in the wet subway tunnel beneath the Kinji-to, looked down at the broken body of Fukuda. He saw the blow tube still gripped between her teeth, noted with sorrow that the tiny steel *shuriken* had not been launched. On the other hand, her ferocious expression, not unlike a tigress about to strike its prey, filled him with satisfaction. She had died a warrior's death.

"That bastard Hitasura."

Still, he did not like losing a member of his family, especially one as valuable as Fukuda had been.

The rumble of the subway trains in adjacent tunnels filled the flickering semidarkness, building to crescendos, then dying away in echoes.

"That bastard Hitasura came in here with his troops and did this."

Koi, the hard machine who had once been Honno Kansei, knelt by his side. Her fingers touched the crepuscular flesh of Fukuda's cheek. "Hitasura's men didn't do this." Her voice was cool, detached. "Before she was shot, she went one on one with someone. Someone better than she was."

"Tori Nunn." Big Ezoe spit out the name. "That's why, at

the first sign of the trap, Hitasura escaped the Kinji-to to get his men. He brought them back into the museum, down here into the subway system where Fukuda had lured Tori Nunn. He risked the Metropolitan Police for that woman. She's teamed up with Hitasura again. That's bad news for me."

"No," Koi said, rising. "It's bad news for her."

The first streaks of sunlight, pressed like orange pulp through the gun-metal gauze of the clouds, filled the eastern sky. When they struck the curve of the Sumida River which Big Ezoe's apartment overlooked, the sluggish water was transformed into a ribbon of molten lead.

Koi stared out and down at the increasing dazzle, broken now by the pewter bow wave of a fishing boat heading toward the Tsukiji Fish Market. There were so many shades of gray on the river, in the long shadows along its banks, that Koi kept counting them, as if there was a lesson to be learned in attempting to measure infinity.

"We have several tasks before us," Big Ezoe was saying. "First, I want us to find a way to usurp Hitasura's deal with Kunio Michita. Michita must be paying Hitasura a fortune for his go-between work. The breadth and depth of the political corruption Sakata's ledgers revealed is breathtaking; the tapestry of bribes they recorded is priceless. Why should he have his fingers in that pie and not me?

"But it will not be easy. As you know, there is a gap in Kakuei Sakata's ledgers. The physical connection between the two— Hitasura and Michita—is never mentioned. Is it because of ignorance or by design?

"Second, we must punish Hitasura for his transgressions against members of my family. Third, we must destroy Tori Nunn for her part in all this. She murdered Fukuda."

There was a gull on the river, Koi saw, whose body incorporated every shade of gray in its environment as it passed from shadow to light to shadow again. I am like that gull, Koi thought. I am every shade of gray. I am my environment.

"I would have liked," she said, "to have had more time with Fukuda. I was looking forward to that."

Big Ezoe stared at her. She was lit from behind by the early morning light coming in through the windows. Her features, cloaked in darkness, seemed unreal to him, so much like the god mask at the Bunraku play that, for a moment, he was transfixed, for he could not tell one from the other.

346

Then she moved, and orange light brushed her cheek, warming her flesh, illuminating one dark eye. And, with a shock, he saw in there the hint of some mad thing, a black force like a maelstrom still far off on the horizon of night, and it made him shudder, for he suspected that it would be a struggle for him to control it.

Big Ezoe pushed these disturbing thoughts aside, said in a businesslike voice, "I want you to think back to when you were working for Kunio Michita. Can you give me a list of names, important clients and associates he saw with some regularity—say, more than three times a month?"

Koi began, just as if she were a computer sorting through vast files. "Of course," she said, reeling off more than a half-dozen names. "But that's not counting the Kaga people involved in the joint venture with Michita," she said.

"What kind of joint venture?"

"A combined research and development laboratory," Koi said. "But I don't see how that could be of interest to us."

Big Ezoe looked at his watch, made a quick call. When he hung up, he said, "I think it's time we went to breakfast."

"Bathe me first," Koi said. Her eyes were glittery with hunger. "Then we will go and do what must be done."

Big Ezoe was unused to being ordered around. He found that he did not much care for it. He opened his mouth to protest, then closed it again, deciding that at this point it was far better to humor Koi than to oppose her. With Fukuda gone, he needed Koi—not that he could ever afford to let her know this. But, with the manner in which Fukuda was disposed of, if he did not retaliate quickly and successfully, his loss of face would be devastating to his authority over his people. So he acquiesced as obediently as if he were a woman.

The bath was modern primitive: an S-shaped curve of translucent glass blocks created a wall of aqueous green light that shimmered its diamondlike reflections on the gushing water. Outside, the geometric grid of Tokyo was reduced to smears of gray, an incomplete template for a city of the future which Koi would, through the force of her will, perfect.

Rare Ainu fetishes hung on the wall opposite the glass bricks, the stark faces of dark gods now consigned to myths already forgotten. But for Koi, in these hard visages of the gods of Japan's indigenous ethnics lived the souls of the clouds, the rain and wind which for centuries had scoured Nippon, carving it into its present image. Here were the keys

347

to the kingdom, the real Japan, lying in wait with its breathless heart beneath the modern iconographic facade where image and symbol were melded to create a new language devoid of significance.

Naked, Koi climbed into the steaming water, sinking down until she sat in the lotus position, the hot water streaming onto the top of her head, surrounding her in spray.

"Now, at last, I see beyond all the lies, to the buried truth," she said. She was not looking at Big Ezoe nor at anything in the room. "Being born *hinoeuma* was a blessing, not a curse. Because I was *hinoeuma*, I was taken to the Man of One Tree, and there learned the ways of the warrior. But when I returned to the outside world, I was thrust once more into the caldron of my family, and I was obliged to suppress much of what I was taught by the Man of One Tree. I learned to fit in, to be the model daughter as preparation for being the model wife. I was no longer afraid of being *hinoeuma*, because the Man of One Tree had given me the strength I needed to combat it. He told me that I was now strong enough to decide *not* to be *hinoeuma*.

"But he was wrong—or, in the end, because he was a man, he lied to me. Here is the Truth: I am *hinoeuma*, and being so gives me an altogether different power. My evil passions, my bloody nature, is a divine gift."

And with this she rose up out of the bath, the water purling down her taut muscular body, a dark-haired leviathan, opal-eyed and omnipotent, emerging from the deep.

On the Tokyo waterfront mist was rising off the Sumida. It was already too late in the morning for the daily fish auction at the Tsukiji Fish Market, but the stalls were busy as the city's best restaurateurs continued to buy provisions for the afternoon and evening meals.

Big Ezoe and Koi emerged from the gray steel-paneled Mercedes, walked across concrete slick with water sluicing away fish entrails. They went to a little row of stalls, numbered 5 through 9, entered the tiny restaurant in the middle of the row.

It was more a coffee shop than a restaurant, a tiny kitchen behind a plain counter fronted by no more than a dozen stools in a sixteen-by-seven-foot area.

There was only one customer at the counter. A middle-aged executive with a pencil mustache wearing a regulation dark gray three-piece suit appropriate for corporation work. With a start, Koi recognized him as the senior vice-president for administration for the Kaga conglomerate, the man she had seen lose so much money at Big Ezoe's gambling house, the one she had had a hand in sending into debt.

The two men nodded to one another, but otherwise there was no traditional greeting. No names were exchanged, and Big Ezoe did not in any way seek to explain Koi's presence. Koi got the eerie sensation of being back in Kunio Michita's office because, for this moment, she had ceased to exist.

Big Ezoe ordered *asari*, a soupy dish made with a ladleful of fresh baby clams, white and briny. Koi asked for *oyako-ni*, a hot dish of eggs and browned onions, and three slices of toro sashimi.

Big Ezoe said, "There is a great deal of money outstanding."

"I cannot pay principle," the Kaga vice-president said.

Big Ezoe nodded. "I understand. I will be satisfied with a payment of interest."

This exchange sounded to Koi as if it were a rote call and response. Nevertheless, the Kaga vice-president's head seemed to sink between his shoulder blades. But he nodded. Koi could not see his face.

Big Ezoe said, "Your company has a joint venture with Kunio Michita. What does it involve?"

The mustachioed man seemed to consider this for some time. At length he said, "Our people stumbled upon a technology about two years ago. They thought it was a dead end, until Kunio Michita showed up and began talks with them."

"How did Michita know about Kaga's technology?" Koi asked.

The mustache twitched. "Good question. We are still trying to find the answer. I have no idea how Michita did it. Perhaps like your friend here, he's got a spy inside Kaga."

"And yet," Koi said thoughtfully, "Michita must have obtained the information from someone."

"In any event," the Kaga vice-president went on, as if this point were of no concern to him, "it seems Michita had a use for this technology even though it involved nuclear devices. We did not want to give him the technology, but we could see no conceivable use for it. It seemed logical, then, for the two companies to form a joint venture."

"I see." Big Ezoe worked a tiny clamshell around his mouth until he had gotten all the delicious juice out of it. Then he spit

349

it out. "So this joint venture isn't research and development at all."

"No," the Kaga vice-president said. "It's a manufacturing setup."

"What is it manufacturing?"

"I don't know. All I'm aware of is that we are getting illegal shipments of hafnium into the joint company."

Big Ezoe said, "What the hell is hafnium?"

The Kaga vice-president told him about hafnium being used to manufacture control rods for reactor cores, and how hafnium kept absorbing neutrons long after other materials became saturated and had to be replaced. "It seems evident that the setup must be manufacturing parts for some kind of nuclear reactors," the Kaga vice-president concluded.

"Nuclear reactors?" Big Ezoe shook his head. This wasn't turning out as he had expected. "Kunio Michita's business doesn't include atomics."

"I guess it does now," the Kaga vice-president said.

"Who is selling him the hafnium?"

"A West German firm owned by an Argentine named Estilo."

Koi said, "Does Estilo's company manufacture the hafnium?"

"How should I know?"

Big Ezoe looked at her, and she said, "I know of this West German company. It's had a number of dealings with Kunio Michita. Estilo is a middleman, a broker for all sorts of hardware and esoteric raw materials like hafnium."

Koi thought for a moment. Then she looked at the Kaga vice-president. "Who does Estilo buy his hafnium from?"

"I have no idea," the man said. "I doubt that even Ten-san knows." He meant Fumida Ten, the chairman of Kaga. The vice-president shrugged. "I don't even know anything about this West German company, except that it's represented in this country by Budoko Associates."

"That law firm is huge," Big Ezoe said. "Who at Budoko is handling the transactions?"

"I don't know. I shouldn't even be aware of Budoko. Normally I have to approve all corporate bills before they're sent on to accounting, but these were routed around me. I only came across one by accident."

Big Ezoe finished his *asari*, making smacking sounds of satisfaction. "Is there anything else that might be of use to me?"

"I can't think of anything," the Kaga vice-president said. He had not touched his breakfast. He looked at the food wistfully, as if he could recall a time when he had had an appetite. "Well, the only thing was, I don't think Michita was the original instigator of the joint venture talks. He brought an American with him."

"A businessman?"

"I don't think so. No. The American was introduced to us as Mr. Smith. What does that tell you?"

Big Ezoe nodded, threw some yen on the table, and he and Koi left the coffee shop. They strolled for some time amid the thinning throngs at the fish market. It was a good place to talk.

Big Ezoe said, "Now there are some intriguing new players to the game. It isn't just Michita and Hitasura we're chasing, it's Kaga and someone in the largest law firm in Tokyo. And where does Hitasura fit into all this? It seems we're no closer to finding the link between him and Michita. Not to mention this mysterious American. Do you remember a 'Mr. Smith' or any likely American who did not fit the typical businessman mold being in touch with Michita?"

"No."

"Let's leave that for the moment," Big Ezoe said. "Why were you so interested in where the hafnium is coming from?"

"I'm not sure," Koi said. "But it seems to me that none of this quite hangs together."

"Do you think our man's lying?"

"No. He's too frightened of you to lie. But I don't think he knows what's really going on. Neither do we, yet. What we're beginning to get a look at is flesh without any bones. It's not yet making sense."

They walked in silence for some time while Big Ezoe digested this. At last he said, "Does anything else occur to you?"

"Yes. I think we should put the deciphered pages of Kakuei Sakata's ledgers to good use. Let's use them as leverage to find out what Hitasura is up to."

Big Ezoe was already shaking his head. "I can't be certain that Hitasura doesn't already know what the ledgers contain. After all, it was his brother who did the deciphering. I can't take the chance of losing face."

"Then use the ledgers against Kunio Michita."

"Perhaps at some point. But not now. The ledgers are all we have. I resist the idea of shooting a gun with one bullet if I can achieve the same result merely by aiming the weapon."

351

Koi considered this a moment, then nodded. "There's something else," she said. "When the Kaga vice-president mentioned Budoko Associates, it rang a bell. I didn't think of this before when you asked me about people Michita saw with some regularity, but now I'm beginning to see its significance.

"There was a young lawyer, Yen Yasuwara. He's now a partner in Budoko Associates. Have you heard of him?"

"Yes, but it's interesting that you have as well." Big Ezoe's mind was racing. Yen Yasuwara had been at the heart of the blood feud between Fukuda and Tori Nunn. Fukuda had been seeing Yen Yasuwara, primarily because Big Ezoe had been given information that Yasuwara was somehow involved with the sort of deals Big Ezoe would find attractive. Big Ezoe had sent Fukuda to find out what she could in any way she saw fit. That she had decided to open her legs for him had not presented Big Ezoe with a problem; that she had not been able to discover what Yasuwara was up to had. Then Tori Nunn had arrived on the scene and that particular line of inquiry had been blown because, as it turned out, Fukuda had some personal feelings left, after all.

Now it seemed that Yen Yasuwara was tied in with Kunio Michita. Could he be the link missing from Kakuei Sakata's ledgers?

"What was Yen Yasuwara's business with Michita?"

"I don't know," Koi said, thinking back. "Michita never met Yasuwara in the office. In fact, I never made the appointments. I wouldn't have known who Yasuwara or Budoko Associates were except for the fact that during the particularly difficult negotiations for the joint venture with the Kaga conglomerate, Michita left me the same number each time he left the office when there was a hole in his daily schedule.

"I remember he had asked me to keep the hours of two to three open. Of course, I didn't ask why. But when the Kaga negotiations were at a crucial stage, I had occasion to call him several times."

"And the phone number he left you was for Budoko Associates?"

"Well, that was the most intriguing part," Koi said. "Each time I called, a woman answered. But it was obvious from the way she spoke that she was no secretary, and the call was not routed through a switchboard. I assumed it was a private residence, but I was wrong. One afternoon when Michita was out, papers arrived by messenger from Kaga. They were so important that they did not come over the fax. The envelope was sealed with red wax in which was imprinted the Kaga logo.

"I phoned Michita at the number he gave me, and told him what had come in. He told me to come right down. He also told me to take the subway, not a company car."

Koi paused a moment. "I assumed he was concerned with traffic—the subway was far faster than sitting in a car trapped on a crowded street. But now I'm convinced his main concern was security. He and Yen Yasuwara were at a private club in Shinjuku. The woman who answered the phone presided over their private room like a hawk with her young. She was a mama-san who had owned her own *akachochin*. This job, she told me, was far more lucrative. She looked after 'special' clients for whom the need for 'absolute privacy' was paramount."

"This puzzle is becoming more fascinating by the moment," Big Ezoe said. "Whatever Michita and Yasuwara were working on was so secret they had to keep it from their respective offices." He thought a moment. "How was it that Michita trusted you with knowing where he was?"

"To be honest," Koi said, "it never crossed his mind. I was so good at what I did that I was next to invisible. He thought of me as a computer with hands, nothing more. Certainly not as someone who might possess independent thought."

Big Ezoe grunted. "More fool him."

Yen Yasuwara lived in a sleek, modern house in Hiroo in Minato-ku. Apparently he was undisturbed by the influx of trend-minded foreigners, opting for the flash the nouveau riche the world over seemed to prefer. It was important, Big Ezoe reflected as he guided the Mercedes up the tree-lined street, for those who were new to money to show how much they had to as many people foolish enough to take notice. Insecurity. That made Big Ezoe happy. He thrived on other people's insecurities.

Big Ezoe nosed the Mercedes into the curb, pulled to a stop, but he didn't cut the ignition. He said over the purr of the idling engine, "Will you recognize him?"

"Yes."

He didn't doubt her. He didn't doubt anything she said. Koi, it appeared, was totally unconcerned about the need now and then to lie. She seemed, in fact, totally oblivious to other people's reactions to what she said or did. This was, to a large

353

extent, an enormous advantage, but her disconnectedness continued to concern Big Ezoe. Koi was like a tap gushing water: that was all well and good for as long as one needed the force; but what happened when it was time to end the flow and the tap would not close?

It was just after eight in the evening. The sky was the color of bronze, burnished by the ten billion lights of the city. There seemed to be no night at all. They had spent the day trying to get close to Hitasura and Tori Nunn, but even with Big Ezoe's vast network of informants, they could not even find out where they were. A day that had begun in a most promising manner had turned aimless and frustrating. On the other hand, Big Ezoe's lieutenants had assured him that, one way or another, an answer would be forthcoming before midnight as to the whereabouts of Hitasura and Tori Nunn. Until then, Big Ezoe knew he must content himself with what was about to happen.

Koi slipped out of the car, walking toward a young man in an impeccable three-piece suit who was approaching the front gate of Yasuwara's house. She had not said, "That's him," but had moved on her own, as if once having been given the objectives by Big Ezoe, she was now making her own way toward them without seeking his counsel. Big Ezoe again thought of the water tap that would not turn off.

Koi stopped Yen Yasuwara. He did not seem pleased to be intercepted. Koi said something to him, and Big Ezoe saw the young lawyer's face go white. Big Ezoe smiled. A moment later Koi had put Yasuwara into the backseat of the Mercedes, slid in beside him.

"You're a very handsome man, Mr. Yasuwara," Big Ezoe said as he threw the Mercedes in gear, pulled out into the street. "You must attract many women."

"Who are you people?" Yen Yasuwara said in a tense voice. "What do you want?"

Big Ezoe noticed that Yasuwara could not take his eyes off Koi. All the better, he thought. I want to remain as invisible as possible. It's Koi's job to take the heat of any fallout that might result from this interview.

Big Ezoe said, "It is my opinion, Mr. Yasuwara, that being handsome is something of a gift. It shouldn't be taken for granted."

"What nonsense are you talking?" Yen Yasuwara was trying

354

to seem angry, but he only succeeded in sounding more frightened.

Next to him, Koi hooked a bloodred fingernail, jabbed it into the center of his cheek. Yasuwara yelped, jumping in shock and pain. But Koi's left hand was already clamped firmly on his shoulder. She twisted her fingernail in Yasuwara's flesh.

"You . . ." he wailed. "You, what is this?"

"It's a picnic, Mr. Yasuwara," Big Ezoe said in a jaunty tone. "At least it is for us. We're out for a little fun."

Koi slit open the lawyer's cheek so that blood ran down his neck, soaking into his neat white shirt collar. Eventually it began to dribble onto his blue and cream tie, beading on the expensive silk like tears.

"Oh, God," Yen Yasuwara said.

"This might be an appropriate moment to begin our talk," Big Ezoe said.

"Talk? Is that what you want to do? Why didn't you say so at the beginning?"

Big Ezoe said, "We wanted you to understand the seriousness of our intent, Mr. Yasuwara. I make money from information, and today you are going to make me rich."

"I think you're mistaken. You must have the wrong man. These things happen."

Big Ezoe ignored him. "You are doing business with two men, Kunio Michita and Fumida Ten, chairman of Kaga. Is that not so?"

"You're Yakuza, aren't you?" He stared in morbid fascination as Koi lifted her bloody fingernail in front of his face. It was as curved as a hawk's talon.

"It makes no difference who we are," Big Ezoe said, "especially to you. Now, I have asked you a question. I expect a prompt answer."

Yen Yasuwara said, "Let me go. I don't know either of those men."

Koi's fingernail again buried itself in his cheek. This time she did not wait to drag it all the way down. Now there were two bloody parallel furrows along his right cheek. They could hear his gasping breath in the car.

Big Ezoe said, "Michita and Ten. They are clients of yours."

"Yes," Yen Yasuwara said immediately. His eyes were almost crossed in their attempt to keep sight of the bloody talon.

"What do you know of a West German firm owned by an Argentine named Estilo?"

"Look," Yasuwara said, "I could get into trouble if I answered that."

Big Ezoe laughed. "Mr. Yasuwara, you could not be in more trouble than you already are."

"But you don't underst—" His words were cut off in a scream as Koi's fingernail pierced his flesh just beneath his right eye. Yen Yasuwara gave a reflexive jerk, but Koi held him fast.

"Yes, yes," he cried. His right eye was bloodshot, and tears were streaming from it. "All right. Estilo's firm employs me to facilitate moving unusual cargo from place to place."

"By unusual," Big Ezoe said, "I take it you mean illegal. By place to place I take it you mean across international frontiers without being monitored by customs."

Yen Yasuwara said nothing until Koi dipped her fingertip into his blood, smeared it across his dry lips. Then he whimpered, said "Yes," in a voice made hoarse by fear.

When Koi said, "Where does Estilo's hafnium come from?" Yen Yasuwara jumped. Perhaps he had not expected that she could speak.

"Please, please, please," he said.

Koi leaned toward him, and Yen Yasuwara began to tremble.

"Estilo buys all his hafnium from a French firm, named La Lumière d'Or," he said. "It is a privately held French company, but its parentage is American."

Koi said immediately, "Is the American who accompanied Kunio Michita in his dealings with Kaga the owner of this French firm?"

"I don't know."

"But he might have been."

"I don't think so," Yen Yasuwara said. "I could tell the American was in control, although the two of them took pains to disguise the fact. I'm far too knowledgeable about such things for me to have been fooled. No, La Lumière d'Or is simply the conduit through which the hafnium flows. This man, you could see, was not a businessman."

Koi was thinking that Yasuwara was the second man who had said the mysterious American didn't give the appearance of being a businessman. The Kaga vice-president had made the same observation. In a moment she said, "Does Kaga buy the hafnium outright from Estilo?"

"No. That's part of why I was retained. Michita buys the hafnium from the West German firm by withdrawing funds from a blind offshore trust held at a bank on the Caribbean island of

Monserrat. I found a way for Michita to be involved without him having any connection with the account.''

''What do you mean?'' Big Ezoe said. ''He has to make the deposits.''

''He doesn't,'' Yen Yasuwara said. The sweat was streaming down his face, mixing unhealthily with the coagulating blood. ''That is taken care of by a third party.''

''Yeah?'' Big Ezoe said. ''Who?''

Yen Yasuwara hesitated only long enough to see Koi's talon come up to the level of his eye. He blinked furiously, swallowed hard. ''Hitasura.'' He said it as if it were a sigh and all the air was escaping from inside him.

There it is, Big Ezoe thought. The link no one wanted to admit to, the one even Kakuei Sakata had not dared commit to print in his ledgers.

Big Ezoe looked at Yen Yasuwara in the rearview mirror. The lawyer's terror filled the interior of the Mercedes like a perfume. He said to Koi, ''Can you believe this? Hitasura, Michita, and Kaga are all in on this sweet deal.''

He turned his gaze back to Yen Yasuwara. ''Why,'' he said carefully, ''are Michita and Hitasura using illegal offshore profits to fund the manufacture of nuclear reactors no one knows about?''

''Because of the strict laws here against atomics,'' Yen Yasuwara said. ''Also, they're building them for export.''

''Selling them to the highest bidder, right?''

''No. It's on consignment for a single vendor.'' There was a weariness now in Yen Yasuwara's voice, as if he had seen the future and understood that it held nothing for him. ''I put the deal together, so I should know. The items are being shipped to Russia. To an anti-Russian underground organization there known as White Star.''

The lights had gone down in a simulacrum of night, but in the starless darkness Irina could see Odysseus all the better. It was as if his skin, luminous during the ''day,'' picked up a phosphorescence in the absence of light. Irina, comfortable in the saltwater pool with the Hero and his blue dolphin, scissor-kicked slowly, languidly.

''I have to warn you,'' Odysseus said, ''I've been irradiated. I was exposed to cosmic radiation while I rode between the stars.''

''Do you mean to tell me even heaven has its pitfalls?''

The Hero gave her an ironic smile. "You're not concerned?"

"Why should I be?" Irina said. "Lara and Tatiana certainly aren't."

"It's their job to be with me," Odysseus said seriously. "They're prepared for the consequences."

Irina touched him. "I'm sorry I was so flip."

"Don't be." She could see his smile widening, and it was like the sun striking water. "I miss humor so much here."

"I'm afraid that is a failing of Mars's." She gave a little squeal as Arbat, the blue dolphin, raced between her treading legs.

"She likes you," Odysseus said. "Odd. I'd have thought she'd be jealous."

Arbat surfaced, clicking furiously, and Irina put her hand on the bottle snout. "She knows I don't want to take you away from her."

"Yes," Odysseus said. "She knows."

Waves lapping all around them. The scent of salt and phosphorous. Irina's mind, in proximity with this astounding human engine, had begun to unfold in skeins, stretching itself like a hermit at last emerging from her cave.

"What else does Arbat know?"

Odysseus's eyes were pale against his pale skin. "Did Volkov tell you to ask me that?"

"No. Why would he?"

There was a silence for a time; even Arbat was quiescent.

"No reason," Odysseus said at last.

"You don't like him much."

"Let's not talk about Comrade Volkov," Odysseus said. "The subject's so tiresome."

Irina tried to accept this. "Tell me how you know Natasha Mayakova."

"In the early days after my return from space, there was no pool, no Arbat. I was bored, so I was taken into Moscow, often to the theater. I saw Natasha in *The Seagull*. I was quite moved, and asked if I could go backstage to meet her. I was taken with her right away."

"Yes, indeed," Irina said. "I thought at first that I was going to dislike her, but then people have a way of fooling you once you get to know them."

"And others," the Hero said, "only fool themselves."

Irina swam closer to him. "Is there anybody here with us?"

"Volkov's gone. Lara and Tatiana are sleeping. There's only

358

us, and of course the monitors. But they can't pick up anything that goes on in the pool except for Arbat's clicking, and the technicians can't make heads or tails of that."

"I think it's awful that you have to be monitored," Irina said.

"Join the line."

"I'll ask Mars if he can do something about it."

Odysseus threw his head back and laughed. "You do that," he said. "I only wish I could be there to hear his reply."

"Why do you laugh? Mars has a great deal of power, you know."

"Mm. Well, if you can persuade him to call off the dogs, I'd be very grateful."

"Don't you get tired of this pool?" Irina asked.

"Don't you get tired of Russia?" he said, mimicking her tone.

"Is that a joke?"

"Not in the least. I don't consider freedom a subject suitable for humor."

"Yes," Irina said. "I do get tired of the life here."

"Well, that's a step in the right direction."

She longed to say more, to tell him all about Cambridge: the students, the Cokes and pizzas, the rock 'n' roll, but the words got stuck in her throat.

Odysseus floated for a time in silence. He was staring up into the darkness as if he could see the stars through the roof, through the dull cloud cover over Zvezdny Gorodok, as if his eyes were beacons or radar dishes.

Irina was getting used to his silences. It did not mean that he wasn't listening to her; on the contrary, his silence was a sign of his intense concentration. It came to her after a time that his silences were not like normal gaps in conversation, but, if only one knew how to listen, contained their own form of communication.

"What was it," Irina said now, "that you left behind up there in the space between the stars?"

Odysseus went very still. His eyes, much like the dolphin's, glittered in the bits of electronic light that, here and there, were scattered throughout the pool room. "How did you know that?" There was astonishment in his voice.

"I don't know. I knew." Irina seemed as bewildered as he was. "I . . . heard something in the silence. Or perhaps it was an image I saw."

Odysseus said, "I was thinking of the part of myself that did not come back to Earth with me."

"Which part was it?"

"I don't think it's definable, like a leg or a hand." Odysseus thought for some time, grappling with finding the right words. "A piece of what I had been was burned away during the event, I know that for a fact. But something new was added, and then a piece of it was taken away again, and that is far more terrible to live with. Is this making any sense to you?"

"As much as anything in the world makes sense," Irina said.

Odysseus said carefully, "But what I'm talking about is not from this world—or any other you can conceive of."

Irina said nothing. She was acutely aware of floating, hanging in a phosphorescent space, detached, more apart than ever from the people around her. It was as if a moat had been added to the pane of glass that separated her from the people in the Moscow streets, as if now she were moving through an altogether different medium—and, without knowing it, had been for some time.

"Let me try to explain," Odysseus continued, "because I want so much to share this with someone other than Arbat, and Comrade Volkov is incapable of any real form of understanding." He licked his lips. "If I tell you 'Here is a flame, put your hand in it,' you would fully expect to be burned. But what if you weren't burned? If I take you to the top of a building and say, 'Walk over the edge,' you would fully expect to fall to the ground. But what if you didn't? It is six in the morning, time for sunrise, but when you go outside, there is no sun.

"All these are answers to what I was given up there in the space between the stars. But they are only partial answers." He stirred beside her. "If the universe is vast, then the inculcation of ideas is even more vast. And the only thing that is infinite is the inception of 'reality.' Because reality encompasses even time. Reality is so unimaginably huge, so pervasive, that it defies even the dictates of time."

Irina pondered this for several minutes. Then she said, "In an odd way, you're a refugee, aren't you? Something happened to you up there. As if you stepped through a doorway into a new reality, and now you no longer belong here."

Odysseus said, "That's it precisely!" Something that had been hidden or absent before had come into his face, softening it,

360

giving it more of a human scale, instead of the massive intensity of a fifty-foot-high image.

I shouldn't be understanding this, Irina thought. But I do. Isn't my own sense of a changed reality what's at the heart of my discontent? I am, like Odysseus, a displaced person, living in one reality, while inside being part of another. It all makes so much sense, although I doubt if I could say why to an outside observer. She shivered, thinking, I hope we are alone here. What would anyone else make of this discussion? Probably that we were both mad as czars.

There were tears in Odysseus's eyes. "You can't know how I despaired of ever finding someone who would understand." He kissed her cheeks, her eyes, her lips. He laughed. "And to think it's Volkov himself who's provided me with my salvation."

Irina, who had begun to shiver when he had touched her, now quaked beneath his kisses. She felt consumed with fire, not only in her body, but in her mind as well. It was as if the line of communication they had together threaded had now sewed their souls into one combined whole.

"Space is a harsh mistress," Odysseus said. Irina could feel his words as well as hear them. "It draws you like a magnet, a siren, until you have no choice but to open up your soul to it. And then . . ." He put his head into her neck. "And then you step into the black water—the silence between the stars—and find that there is no bottom. You disappear into that silence, only to find that it isn't silence at all, but a riot of communication you have been too dull-witted to comprehend."

She felt his teeth on her flesh, his words in her ears in exactly the same way. "Immersed in a thunder of communication, your sense of humanness slips away, its importance diminishing to a point on the new horizon. Now comprehension is all that matters, understanding and being understood. An end to isolation, a chance to become one with the angels."

Irina was dizzy with sensation. The sensuality of his body was combining with that peculiar silent communication of his to create a whirlpool toward which she was being all too willingly drawn. Concentric circles of reality/time/energy seemed to surround her, pulsing in the darkness of the pool, heating the water she swam in, the air she breathed. Oxygen was being forced into her lungs as if through a bellows; there was a singing in her blood instead of a pulse.

The world disappeared.

In its place Irina hung suspended like a star in the blackest of heavens. And there was Odysseus, beside her, part of her, in her.

Sliding in as easily as if he had always been there. Irina, filling up with him, felt the moat disappear, the wall of glass dissolving. *An end to isolation, a chance to become one with the angels.* Her own isolation was at an end, as if her making love to the Hero was more than a physical act, as if it were emotional, as well as symbolic. She had at last found the strength to embrace something with every cell of herself, unequivocally, unreservedly, accepting it all, wanting it all, the good and the bad, the light and the darkness, because she was no longer terrified of the darkness inside herself, because in embracing Odysseus, she was also accepting all of herself, even the part that she had hated, feared, had tried for so long to disown.

Her breasts crushed against him, her erect nipples brushing his smooth, smooth flesh, her arms surrounding him, feeling the odd shape of his curved back, but not being afraid, accepting that as part of him.

Her eyes opened to watch his face lovingly, startled when his amazing eyes opened and she stared into their pewter depths, seeing behind them the images in which he had been immersed ever since the event in the nonsilence between the stars. Irina saw what he saw, felt what he felt. She was aware of their two hearts, beating in unison—surely an illusion—the ticking of a cosmic clock in the dark sea of reality/time/energy.

Her muscles were tensed as her hips moved, as her breath came in hot, excited spurts, but beneath that her bones had turned to liquid, as if she has been somehow transformed from human being into a creature of another design, as if the places where her bones were had been turned into conduits, filled with an alien fluid pulsing with the beat of their two hearts.

And in that shocked instant, when her hips speeded up but felt heavy with lust and longing, Irina saw/knew/sensed what it was that Odysseus had encountered in the space between the stars, the entity that had given him the tantalizing glimpse of its world/time/reality: a double-pumped engine like a heart, liquid "bones" beneath muscle as hard as a carapace, sense organs in a star-shaped cluster in what might be called a head, but with a body shape that was incomprehensible because it slipped back and forth between two and three dimensions.

Odysseus was not mad—or perhaps he was mad, and she was mad as well. But if so, then this madness was a state of grace, and Irina was grateful that it had come to her.

This thought exploded in her mind like lightning as her body spasmed, as the Hero exploded inside her, so deep that she felt him hard against her inner core, and this set her off again, moaning and thrashing against him, hearing his own deep-felt groan in her mind as well as in her ears.

Ripples, black in the starless darkness that immersed them, held them fast, protected them from everyone and everything, purled outward from the engine of their bodies, filling the water's surface with purpose.

At the other end of the pool, Arbat floated, still, silent, feeling the ripples wash endlessly against her, happy because the Hero was happy, content because the Hero was content.

After a very long time Odysseus slipped from Irina's warmth, but, strangely, she did not feel the emptiness, the sting of sadness she usually did at that moment. She was left with the image of what she had been exposed to, what she had become. She reached out, touched him, wondering if, instead of calcium, there was fluid running in the conduits of his bones.

Odysseus laughed. "Not yet," he said, reading her mind. "Though maybe one day."

Irina was still trembling. Waves of emotion rippled through her, but it could not dissolve the dark undercurrent that left a bitter taste in her mouth. And she thought, I've lied to Valeri, to Mars, even to Natasha. I cannot lie to him. She clamped down on her dread of the repercussions, said, "Actually, Mars *did* want me to find out something."

The Hero was silent. Arbat moved closer, watched Irina with a peculiar, disconcerting intensity.

Irina swallowed hard. In sudden panic, she wanted to turn back time, but instead she pressed on. "He wanted to know where you got some papers you showed him, a top-secret file." Watching Odysseus, she held her breath. She could feel the blood pounding in her temples. "Are you angry with me?"

"On the contrary," Odysseus said, "I'm grateful you told me."

Irina put her hands on him. "It was wicked of me not to tell you right away."

"Was it?"

"I don't want to ever lie to you."

He smiled. "That's a wonderful ambition." He said it as if he meant "impossible," instead of "wonderful."

"I want—" She stopped abruptly, marshalling her thoughts. "I need someone I can trust, someone I can confide in."

"You mean Comrade Volkov isn't the one?"

This is it, Irina thought. I want to—I *must* tell him. I know he will understand. And, taking a deep breath, she stepped off the edge of her world.

"I have spent some time in America, Boston," she said. "The Cambridge area is filled with students from many wonderful universities. I got drunk on the atmosphere and the variety of opinions. At least I thought I was drunk. But when I came home, and sobered up, I realized that I had left a piece of myself in Cambridge. I had fallen hopelessly in love. Can one fall in love with a place? Why not? But ever since, that love has been like a stone in my heart." Drifting. Arbat close, listening it seemed, too. "Now I know just how Shakespeare's Juliet must have felt. Love and pain are sometimes inseparable."

"Yes," Odysseus said. "It is true that sometimes memories hurt. Memories of paths not taken, memories of what might have been."

Irina watched the play of light across his face, tiny crescent reflections off the surface of the water. She could not decide whether she saw the sadness in his face or felt it emanating from him. After a time she said, "Are you here of your own free will?"

"That sounds like a metaphysical question," he said. "I don't know if I'm qualified to answer it."

She cocked her head inquisitively; she was getting the knack of manipulating silences.

"The question of free will is an important one," Odysseus said carefully. "We all may believe that there is free will, but I doubt now that it's the case. We are—have become—what we have been made into, what has been implanted in us in an unconscious, a subliminal sense at a very early age. And, as adults, the way in which we respond to people and to situations is determined by the nature of that subliminal information we may not even know is there."

As he spoke, Irina felt a tiny shiver race down her, and she sought to be closer to him, as if so near his presence she could beat back the unpleasant truth that seemed so uncom-

364

fortably near now. She had seemed so close to freedom when he was inside her, but now the old sad Irina was trying to reassert herself. Don't think about it, she told herself.

"I wonder," Odysseus said, "whether you hold me as you hold all your men?"

"Are you jealous of Mars already?" Irina said. She had meant it humorously, a light touch to a conversation pulling her ever deeper into the heart of her own darkness.

"Jealousy has nothing to do with it," Odysseus said.

"Of course. One of my men is KGB."

"Yes."

"You know?" Irina was startled.

"The KGB knows many things," Odysseus said. "But I know more." His eyes were light; she could see pinpoints dancing in their depths. "I know how we are joined. There can be no deceit in such openness, just as there can be no duplication of it with another. No, Irina, I am not threatened. But I am concerned by your dependence on men."

"What are you talking about?" But her heartbeat, out of sync with his, accelerated painfully, as if she already knew what he would say.

"Nothing." There was so much sadness in his voice that Irina's heart broke.

"Won't you talk to me about it?"

"No," Odysseus said. "I'll talk to you about space. The final frontier, isn't it?" He laughed, but there was an unease to him that Irina found unnerving. Arbat splashed nervously near them.

"But what have I said to offend you?"

"Not a thing."

"Then why do I suddenly feel cut off from you?"

"You are cut off from yourself," Odysseus said.

"You can help me, then."

"If I try, I'll only succeed in plunging you deeper into the woods in which you are lost."

Irina, on the verge of tears, said, "I don't understand."

Arbat, swimming fast beneath the water, surfaced at Irina's side, pushed her head against Irina's hand, as if she could feel Irina's distress.

"Arbat," Irina whispered. "What am I to do?" But she was staring into Odysseus's dark eyes.

Arbat chattered in her high dolphin voice, and Irina said sadly, "If only I could understand what you're saying."

"I'll translate," Odysseus said. "She says life is short but lessons are not quickly learned."

"Is that true of dolphins as well, I wonder?"

Odysseus looked at her. "Dolphins have no lessons to learn," he said, "except when it comes to dealing with man."

"I believe, Mr. Yasuwara, that we are finished with you," Big Ezoe said.

"Just like that?"

"Just like that," Big Ezoe said.

"You're going to let me go?"

"Oh, no," Big Ezoe said. "How can I? You've lied to me from the beginning."

"But—"

"You would have me believe that Hitasura, Kunio Michita, and Fumida Ten—all of whose profit motives are highly honed—are putting together an organization to make some kind of nuclear reactors, and then they are shipping them into Russia, a country so poor it has to buy wheat from the Americans to feed its own people? What do you take me for? It simply isn't logical."

"But it's the truth. I swear it!" Yen Yasuwara's eyes were bulging, his hands vibrating with his terror.

"For a start, why would Hitasura sink capital into such an insane venture?"

"Ask Hitasura or Michita. I don't know."

"Of course you don't," Big Ezoe said, then to Koi, "Kill him."

"Wait!" Yen Yasuwara closed his eyes. His face was completely devoid of color, and he was whispering "Dear God" over and over. His eyes opened, his tongue brushed his dry, cracked lips. "There's a way to prove I've been telling you the truth."

"Oh, Mr. Yasuwara," Big Ezoe said, "how can you expect me to trust anything you tell me?" He watched Koi edge closer to the lawyer.

"Please!" It was a croak. There was a wild look in Yen Yasuwara's eyes, more telling than if he had been hooked up to a lie detector.

Big Ezoe waited, turning the emotional screws, before nodding. "You have one chance, Mr. Yasuwara. I do hope you'll make the most of it."

* * *

The old wooden slats were drawn across the windows, and the acrid smell of iodine and sickness filled the room like dead flowers. Irina stood on the threshold of the one-room apartment in an unlovely, massive post–World War II building in Sadovo-Chernogryazskaya, and for a moment her mind was blank. She could not even remember what time it was or how she had come here.

Then she stepped into the room. She could see the form, sitting upright in the ladder-backed rocker that for years had belonged to *Babushka*. Wan light fell across the silhouette in thin, damaged strips, illuminating a scrawny shoulder here, a gnarled finger there.

Irina took a deep breath, said, "Hello, Mother."

"Is that you, Yvgeny?"

"It's me, Irina," Irina said, coming to kneel beside her mother.

"Yvgeny, you've been away so long," the old woman said. "You bad boy, why have you stayed away?"

"Mother, it's Irina. Your daughter."

"My daughter?" The narrow head moved, and light lit up its features, ravaged, wasted by time and memories that would not fade. "Have I a daughter?" The head moved slowly back and forth. "I cannot remember."

Irina reached across to the windowsill, took down the tin of dusting powder her mother loved so much. Softly, gently, she applied the duster to the translucent skin of her mother's shoulders.

"That smells nice, Yvgeny. I am reminded of my mother. She used to smell of boiled potatoes and cabbage. Even after she bathed, she smelled of boiled potatoes and cabbage. I wanted never to smell that way. No, never." Her eyes fluttered closed. "So nice."

Then her eyes flew open and her false teeth clacked together. "Mother of God, Yvgeny, what have they done to you! There is blood on the snow!" Her voice was rising in pitch. "Oh, Yvgeny, don't leave me! Don't leave me!"

"I'm here, Mother," Irina said. Her palm stroked her mother's brow. "Nothing can take me away from you."

"Yes." The old woman was calmer now. "Yes, that's the way it should be, of course. A boy needs his mother beside him, to take care of him, to protect him from the harm others might do to him. My Yvgeny." Her eyes closed again, and in a moment she was asleep, her head nodding, soft and warm, against the palm of Irina's hand.

Irina stared at her sleeping mother for a long time. In slumber she was so peaceful, her face suffused with the carefree peace of a child. How much like a child she was now, in her old age, the circle closing.

For an instant Irina allowed herself to come back from behind the mirror, from the blackness of her other reality, into the all too familiar horror of this reality, and she saw in the curve of her mother's lips, the line of her nose and brow, the qualities she liked in her own face. But she did not see her own destiny there, the ending of her life. Instead she became acutely aware of the branching of her fate. She saw how she had stumbled off the path that had been set for her, and then, less clumsily, had begun her journey to the other side of the mirror. The flesh may be the same, she thought, but the desires that animate us are so disparate.

She thought, then, of what Natasha had said: *Where did I come from? My mother, my father. My grandparents. Most people know.* I know, Irina thought, but it makes no difference. I am, like Natasha, an orphan now. My mother no longer knows who I am. I am dead to her—even worse, I have never existed.

Irina could remember her grandmother, splashed with thick lemon light, bustling about a kitchen warm with heat and good smells. There was always a bit of food on the tip of *Babushka*'s finger for Irina to taste, and when Irina begged for more—as she invariably did—*Babushka* would laugh, scoop up some more, blow on it to cool it sufficiently, before offering it to her granddaughter.

Irina remembered her grandmother as a strong woman in the way Soviet peasant women are strong: stolid, beefy-cheeked, hands as hard as concrete, with all the life sparkling in her eyes.

Irina did not remember her as smelling of boiled potatoes and cabbage, even when she was rocked against her grandmother's ample bosom, when, her belly full of *Babushka*'s delicious cooking, she fell asleep to songs from *Babushka*'s youth.

In the summer there was an emerald-green grasshopper who lived by the hearth. Irina's father was forever trying to kill it, but *Babushka* kept it safe, or so she told Irina.

"Grasshoppers are good luck, especially in the kitchen," *Babushka* had said. "They talk to you; yes, it's true, little one. Grasshoppers tell you when it's time to sow, and when it's time to reap your crops. Grasshoppers are very valuable."

When *Babushka* died, everything changed. Irina's father was transferred to a more modern nuclear plant, so the family moved to Moscow. Irina, who had made something of a pet of the grasshopper who lived by the hearth, had tried to take it with her, but it had not survived the trip. But then again, in Moscow there were no crops to sow or reap.

The afternoon sunlight was red as it squeezed through the slats in her mother's one-room apartment. The young student whom Irina had hired to take care of her mother came in from shopping.

"The lines are so long, one might as well camp out in the streets," she said, piling her meager packages beside the sink. "And then the shops are out of anything one wants to buy." She shook her head. "There's really little point in shopping anymore."

"She's worse," Irina said.

"Don't blame me," the student said, stowing what food she had bought in the tiny refrigerator and cupboards. "Her medicine is in short supply." She began to boil water for tea. "But, to be truthful, I can't see that the pills are doing her any good. It's clear she has no idea where she is or what's happening around her. If you ask me, she'd be better off dead."

"No one's asking you," Irina snapped.

"I only meant that this is no way for a human being to live," the student said hastily. She poured boiling water over loose black Russian Caravan tea, waited for the cut leaves to settle to the bottom.

"Have you ever eaten a pizza?" Irina asked impulsively.

"What?"

She looked into the student's dull face, trying to see any hint of the spark she had seen in so many of the young faces lining the streets of Cambridge. "Nothing," she said. "Drink your tea. It's all right, I don't blame you. She's just worse, that's all."

"Everything's worse," the student said, turning away.

And Irina, glancing from the student to her mother nodding in the rocker, thought of the grasshopper that had lived by her hearth. I am in a vise, she thought, that is slowly squeezing the life out of me. I must take some action before there are no seasons left for me to sow or reap.

The revelation hit her like a rifle shot. All at once she understood why it was so important for her to find White Star. It wasn't to help Mars, and it wasn't to get back at Valeri, although those motivations were still in play. She needed to get to White Star for herself.

Irina knew the answer to her feelings of imprisonment: freedom. Freedom not from people, but from the oppressive life in Russia which, despite all her attempts to lie to herself, she could no longer abide.

And, for her, freedom could mean only one thing: White Star. The underground nationalist movement was her one chance to find her way to America. To Cambridge, where every form of idea, theory, and philosophy was freely expressed, embraced, or rejected as the individual saw fit.

It was White Star, and White Star alone, Irina saw now, that could get her back to paradise.

"There she is," Mars Volkov said from the interior of his black Chaika. "Pick her up."

He was speaking into a mobile phone, and when he gave the order, three plainclothes men stepped out of the shadows. Two moved to either side of Natasha Mayakova, pinioning her wrists. The third moved behind her.

"What is this?" Natasha said, astonished. "What do you want?"

"KGB," said the plainclothes man behind her. "Keep calm."

Mars watched Natasha's eyes go wide with fear when the man whispered in her ear. There was a measure of satisfaction to be gained by that, as if fear were a form of energy that could be ingested like food.

Mars's men brought Natasha to the Chaika. The door opened, and with a stiff hand behind her neck, they pushed her inside.

One of the plainclothes men sat in the back so that she was sandwiched between him and Mars. The man who had whispered in her ear climbed into the passenger's seat in front, and the Chaika took off.

"Mars!" Natasha said, struggling to gain her equilibrium. "You needn't have been so melodramatic. Where are you taking me?"

"The Lubyanka."

It was interesting, Mars thought, to see how her brave face began to crumble. They all did it in different ways, his subjects, but like a catalogue of petty sins, there was an underlying correlation that bound them all together.

"You've been a bad girl, Natasha. I'm quite cross with you."

"What gives you the right to speak to me as if you were my father?"

"This gives me the right," Mars said, sending the back of his hand across her face in a stinging blow that sent Natasha's head whipping back against the seat back.

"My God!" she gasped. "You animal!"

"We're both animals, Natasha," Mars said. "You and I." He watched the blood seep from the cut in her skin just below her cheekbone. He thought the flash of color did her good. "You are gnawing at the underbelly of the state. But there are rules to be observed. The state demands obedience from one and all, I as well as you. If, one day, I am found wanting, as you have been, I, too, will wind up in the Lubyanka."

"What a load of shit," Natasha said. "You and I are like night and day. You are KGB. Are you surprised I know? The Hero told me, but how he knew I can't imagine, locked away like a prisoner or a laboratory experiment. Surely you didn't tell him, Mars. You're far too devious for that. You've been hoping to be his kindly uncle, haven't you? 'Put your head on my shoulder, old son, and tell me everything,' that's more your style. But you haven't fooled the Hero, and you haven't fooled me. The foul stink of the KGB is all over you, no matter how you try to hide it beneath cordiality and greasepaint. Like all the other members of the secret police, you enjoy all the perquisites your thoroughly corrupt nature can gobble up. Oink! Oink! Comrade Volkov!"

"I see," Mars said, nodding as if to himself. "I imagine that you are still under the misapprehension that the same guardian angel who protected you when you made such a dangerous fool of yourself and us in New York City will extricate you from this situation. Put such fantastic thoughts from your mind, Natasha. I am in the process of stripping your guardian angel of his power. He doesn't know it yet, but he is ready to take his fall from grace. And, as he is about to learn, it is a long, painful way down."

The black Chaika turned a corner, came gliding into Dzerzhinsky Square. Natasha's last look at the outside world was of the place on the corner of Kirov Street, where once had stood the Church of Our Lady of Grebvev, demolished, like so many houses of worship, as the Communists rebuilt areas of Moscow.

In the Lubyanka, the KGB's fortresslike prison across Dzerzhinsky Square from Detsky Mir, the world's largest children's store, Natasha Mayakova was divested of her possessions,

371

stripped, searched, given threadbare prison togs, delivered to a cell that measured eight feet in each dimension. There was no window, but a large light, protected by a metal grill, protruded like an exophthalmic eye from the center of the ceiling. It was off when Natasha was placed in the cell, but some time afterward, when she had lain down on the board that served as a bed, it went on. She turned toward the wall, put her hands over her eyes, but she could not block out the light.

It was very cold in the cell, and Natasha began to shiver. She thought she should be hungry, but she was not. The cold made her tired, but the light cut inside her closed eyelids as if prying them apart. Her mind refused to let her sleep, but when she sat up, she was abruptly dizzy, and had to hold on to the board to keep from pitching headlong onto the stone floor.

She put her back against the wall, closed her eyes. She could hear the accelerated beating of her heart, was aware of the blood pulsing through her veins. She tucked her feet under her in an attempt to keep them warm. The light went off. She drifted into a light sleep. An instant later—or so it seemed—the light came on again, but she could not shake herself fully awake. Instead she lapsed into a kind of limbo that sapped her of more strength.

Some time later—she had no idea how long—she was pulled from her cell. It was done during a period when the light was out, so that she was pulled out of sleep. She was taken three floors up, led into an interrogation room. Mars Volkov sat behind a scarred wooden table, an open dossier in front of him. There were two wooden chairs in the room; Mars was sitting in one. Natasha sat in the other one.

"Stand up," Mars said.

"What?"

"I said stand up!" he shouted, so that Natasha jumped to her feet. "You do not sit until told to do so."

"Bullshit." Natasha was regaining a semblance of her self-possession. She sat. Almost immediately, she screamed, leaped out of the chair as a jolt of electricity shot through her. She looked down, saw the wires coming up out of the floor, enwrapping the chair legs.

"I think you've got the seating arrangements wrong," Natasha said.

"Sit," Mars told her, "if you feel you have to."

Natasha remained standing.

"Do you see," he said, smiling hungrily, "how easy it is to

get you to do what I want? I don't have to use electricity or rubber truncheons or even threats."

Natasha sat. "It's a miracle you can live with yourself." She studied him. "No, I was wrong. It's not a miracle, it's an abomination."

"Are you hungry?" Mars asked. He seemed absorbed in the open dossier in front of him, and his refusal to engage her directly had the effect of making her will seem nonexistent.

"Where is your uniform, Colonel?" Natasha said, pressing on because she suspected that to be silent now was tantamount to giving up.

Mars ignored her. "If you do not answer my question, I will assume that you have no use for food."

"Are you certain you wouldn't be more comfortable with the KGB rank boards on your shoulders?"

"No food, then." Mars ticked off a box on the top sheet of the dossier, turned to the next page. "What is your relationship with Valeri Denysovich Bondasenko?"

"Valeri is my brother."

Mars looked up. He seemed genuinely startled. "Your brother?"

"Did I say brother? I meant lover."

Mars frowned. "Which is it? Brother or lover?"

"Both."

Mars put aside his pen, folded his hands, one over the other. Natasha, with the kind of heightened sense that often comes in such life-threatening situations, noticed with revulsion how his small ears made him look more like a beast than a movie idol.

"Natasha," Mars said carefully, "I assure you that talking with me will be far more preferable to the alternatives."

"My alternatives," Natasha said, "are life or death."

Now Mars smiled. "Out there, in the streets of Moscow, I would be inclined to agree with you. But you are here now, with me, and please believe me when I say that there *are* other alternatives to answering my questions. All of them are extremely unpleasant."

" 'Unpleasant,' I take it, is the current KGB euphemism for painful?"

"Why are you bent on making this difficult for yourself?"

Natasha said, "I am only doing what I have to do."

"I can see in your eyes, Natasha, how frightened you are."

"Oh, yes, I'm exceedingly frightened. But that will hardly change my mind."

Mars stared at her for some time. "What is your relationship with Valeri Denysovich Bondasenko?"

"Valeri is my brother or my lover, or both."

Mars flipped over another page. "And what is your relationship with the Hero?"

"Oh, there's no doubt there. I'm fucking his brains out."

"The vulgarity hardly suits you, Natasha."

"Now, now, Mars. Your prudishness is showing."

"Are you providing the Hero with access to official government limited distribution documents?"

"I'm an actor, Mars. Not a spy."

"Natasha, do you know what the penalty for spying is?"

"If it's being incarcerated in this shithole for the rest of my life, I'd rather die, thank you very much."

Mars nodded. "All right," he said. "I've done what I can."

"You certainly have."

Mars pressed a buzzer on the underside of the table. "It's time for the hard man," he said to no one in particular.

Natasha was so frightened, she had been on the verge of vomiting throughout the interrogation. She had always known what consequences her actions might bring. She thought she had been prepared for them. But, like the death of a parent, she reflected now, one can never truly prepare for the reality of this kind of nightmare.

It was odd, she thought, how disorienting being without a semblance of time could be. Without watch or clock, without a window to know whether it was dark or light, let alone the hour, with the random switching on and off of the cell light, she had already lost an important guidepost to reality. She had entered a new realm, where time did not seem to exist. Had she been picked up an hour ago or half a day? She tried to work it out but could not, and this loss frightened her even more. But she knew that she must never show her fear to Mars. If she did, she knew with a profound conviction that he would eat her alive.

"Here comes the hard man."

Natasha's head snapped up, and she saw, to her horror, an ugly dark-haired man approaching her with a hypodermic needle.

"No!" she cried.

But the needle had already pierced the flesh of her arm, the plunger was depressed, and a moment afterward an uncomfortable icy chill slipped through her like a wraith. Natasha's spirit convulsed as if already in torment.

"Kunio Michita's not at home." Yen Yasuwara was in a panic. He put down the receiver of the car phone.

"Perhaps that's the way you planned it," Big Ezoe said.

"No, no." Yen Yasuwara threw a fearful look Koi's way. "I know I can find him." His brow furrowed. "Why don't we try Kaijin?"

Both Big Ezoe and Koi were familiar with Kaijin. They knew Yen Yasuwara meant Kaijin ni Kisuru, which was the full name of one of Tokyo's most exclusive tea houses. It was an after-hours place, but unlike most *akochochin*, it clung tenaciously to the older, more sedate term so that a facade of respectability could be maintained. Nevertheless, its name, loosely translated, meant "to be reduced to ashes, to burn to the ground," which had nothing at all to do with drinking tea.

Kaijin was in Shimbashi, and without a word Big Ezoe turned the Mercedes around, headed there.

Like most of Japan's exclusive and expensive clubs, Kaijin had a wholly unprepossessing exterior. All that was visible, in fact, was an oversized door made of thick vertical kyoki wood slabs bound in hand-beaten iron. Though the door was obviously very old, it glowed, bespeaking the care lavished on it. Local legend had it that this was the original door from the first Shogun, Ieyasu Tokugawa's castle keep. In fact, the truth was unknown. As was typical of a country where much of its history was oral, Japanese scholars found it impossible to discern fact from myth.

Stone steps were guarded by a pair of gnarled dark green Hinoki cypresses, trimmed to resemble fantastic creatures. A buzzer one pressed sounded deep within Kaijin's heart, and it might be many minutes until the door was opened. And then, unless one was known by sight or was accompanied by a member, one would not gain entrance. Thus were the elite of Japan guarded against any unwanted intrusion.

Keeping a handkerchief to the side of his face, Yen Yasuwara rang the buzzer, waiting impatiently on Kaijin's doorstep. When the front door at last opened inward, a voice from the darkness inside said, "Welcome, Mr. Yasuwara. Two guests this evening?"

Yen Yasuwara nodded, mumbled something unintelligible as he stumbled over the threshold.

The kind of silence that enfolded the interior of Kaijin was sepulchral, almost holy, as if one had entered the innards of a church. Lights were few. What there was of them created indirect pools across whitewashed stone walls on which hung scrolls so ancient they depicted landscapes from China rather than Japan.

This stark, rather cold shell was in direct contrast to the furniture in the rooms, which was sybaritic. Long leather couches with sensuously curved backs, plush chairs wide enough to accommodate two, luxurious chaise longues across which were thrown animal pelts—all contributed to the bizarre, almost schizophrenic interior design.

"Mr. Michita is expecting us," Yen Yasuwara said to a heavyset man with a scar on the lobe of one misshapen ear.

The man looked from the young lawyer to his two companions and back again. Then he nodded. "This way," he said, beckoning to them. "Mr. Michita is taking tea in the Green Room."

Each environment within Kaijin was named for a different color which corresponded to either its design or location. The Green Room happened to be set as a traditional tea house overlooking a minuscule but dense interior garden. Though the garden was surrounded by walls on all sides, its design and tiered lushness fooled the eye into believing that one was at some countryside *ryokan*, where, in the distance, wooded slopes stretched away into the distance.

They were led down a hallway with polished wood floors. The walls were painted a mottled pewter and beige to resemble the plaster-cracked walls of an ancient villa. More facade to fool the eye.

Koi noted that they were taken past seven rice-paper and ashwood *fusuma* doors. All were closed. She paused outside each one, pressed her fingertips against the rice paper to see if she could pick up any minute vibrations that either movement or conversation would impart. She felt nothing.

And yet she fell farther and farther behind. Once she glanced over her shoulder. What was bothering her? Perhaps it was that the man with the misshapen ear had made no comment concerning the condition of the side of Yen Yasuwara's face. Perhaps it was because he did not seek the identity of Yasuwara's guests. (Of course, it might be that he was already familiar with Big Ezoe, but Koi refused to make such an assumption.) But most of all, she did not trust Yen Yasuwara.

The three men had stopped outside the sliding *fusuma* to the

Green Room, and Koi hurried to catch up. When the man with the misshapen ear put his hand on the door, Koi stopped him.

"I'll do that," she said and, before he had a chance to refute her, she whipped the *fusuma* back and slammed the heel of her hand into the small of Yen Yasuwara's back, catapulting him into the Green Room.

Nothing happened.

The man with the misshapen ear stared at Koi, and, turning around inside the room, Yen Yasuwara did the same. Big Ezoe ignored them both. He was looking at Kunio Michita, who, sitting cross-legged on the tatami mats, had twisted around.

"What is the meaning of this?" Michita said in a voice of flint.

"I'll tell you," Big Ezoe said as he stepped across the threshold.

Koi heard the soft *phut!*, saw Big Ezoe's body stagger backward into the hallway. He fell to his knees. His eyes were turning upward in their sockets, and there was blood on his chest where his frantically pumping heart was sending it through the hole made by the bullet from the silenced gun.

Koi did not step into the trap so carefully laid out for them. She saw that she could no longer help Big Ezoe, grabbed the man with the misshapen ear, pushed him hard into the Green Room, and took off back down the pewter and beige hallway.

Behind her, Hitasura stepped carefully over Big Ezoe's body, smiling on the corpse's opaque eyes. In his hand was a Beretta.

"One shot," he said. "That's all it takes to silence anyone."

Then Russell Slade was beside him, saying, "I've got to get back to Tori." Hitasura nodded.

Three of Hitasura's men rushed from the Green Room down the hall. "That's right," Hitasura told them, still staring at Big Ezoe with satisfaction. "Track her down. Then make quite sure you kill her." But it was clear that he had already found the most important measure of his revenge.

Comrade Volkov is incapable of any real form of understanding. What did Odysseus mean by that? All of a sudden it seemed important for Irina to find out. She felt like Methuselah, stirring from a centuries-old sleep, her brain still not at full speed, still partly cobwebbed, moving through a world she had not made, of which she would never be fully a part.

Using the key Valeri had given her, Irina let herself into his apartment on Kirov Street. It was silent. There was the smell of boiling cabbage down the hall, and Irina quickly shut the door behind her.

She went methodically through the apartment, looking in all the rooms, in the closets as well, feeling somewhat foolish, but less anxious, for all that, when she had determined the place was empty.

She paused at the bedroom window that overlooked the Church of the Archangel Gabriel. She knelt, then bowed her head, made the sign of the cross. She said a little prayer, then rose, turned away.

I am concerned by your dependence on men.

. . . Seeing the future as the past, Irina thought of the devastation visited on her family when her father had been taken away by the KGB. *How are we to live!* her mother had wailed. *Holy Mother, protect us!*

Irina's mother did not sit around the house for long, however. A week after her husband was taken from her, she dressed in her best clothing, went out day after day. Irina assumed she was petitioning the state for the release of Irina's father. Later, when her father did not return, she assumed her mother had found a job.

As it turned out, Irina's mother was far more pragmatic than Irina could have imagined, because one day she came home with a man, and introduced him to Irina and Yvgeny. Pavel was a short, glowering man of partial Lithuanian descent. He was a hod carrier, and his bulging muscles and hulking posture frightened Irina.

Pavel was only recently widowed, Irina's mother told her, and he was very sad. Irina's mother had determined to provide Pavel with a new family.

Though Irina's mother said nothing of this, Irina understood immediately from her mother's demeanor that it was vital that they all do their best to make Pavel happy and content so that he would not leave them.

Yvgeny, older than Irina by four years, reacted badly to another man's presence in his father's house. He was twelve, an age of rebellion. Yvgeny was, by nature, a rebel anyway, and Pavel's presence merely served to drive him further along that path, so that he began to disappear evenings, staying out most of the night.

Irina's mother was so visibly distraught that, once or twice, Pavel went out after Yvgeny, bringing him forcibly back. But after Yvgeny set fire to Pavel's shoes, in the process almost burning down the apartment, Pavel gave up.

"He's not my son," he said with a shrug. "Why should he listen to anything I tell him?"

"But he will get into trouble," Irina's mother said, wringing her hands.

"He's already in trouble," Pavel said. "But you can't chain him to the bedpost."

"Dear God, he needs his father."

Pavel got up and left the room.

Irina's mother and Pavel were married some weeks later. That event hardly helped matters with Yvgeny, who did not show up for the ceremony. During the next months, Irina's mother spent more and more time at church, praying for her son.

Irina found Pavel to be kind but dull-witted. He had no ambition, seemed unaware, in fact, that a world existed beyond the confines of Moscow. Irina remembered him coming through the door each night, white with concrete dust. She used to watch him at the kitchen sink while she was preparing his dinner, meticulously washing the flesh beneath his fingernails free of ground red brick.

His hands were so large they seemed swollen, and when she ran her fingers over his palms, they felt like slabs of wood. He was invariably gentle with her, though he spoke very little, mumbling something unintelligible when she set his dinner before him.

Irina would watch him eat, longing for him to say something, or even look at her, but he seemed totally absorbed with eating, as if he would die if he did not cram every bit of food on his plate into his mouth as quickly as possible.

One night when Irina was alone with him, she chanced to pass the bedroom, and saw Pavel undressing through the partly open door. He had his back to her, and as he raised his shirt over his head, she stifled a gasp. The ridged muscles of his curved back were disfigured by the crisscrossing of many scars. They were not new, but the cuts had been so deep that they never healed properly.

Hearing her, Pavel whirled around, stared hard. Irina was terrified that he would be angry at her, but instead Pavel sat down on the end of the bed, held out his hand to her.

Irina walked hesitantly into the bedroom. She saw her mother's wood and gilt icon on the wall over the headboard, the cheap prints of the Russian countryside her father had loved so dearly, the rocker that was always *Babushka*'s when the family had lived outside Moscow.

Pavel took Irina's hand in his scarred calloused ones. "Have I frightened you, *koshka*? I am sorry. I am not a handsome man. I know I am lucky to have found your mother. Most women would not look at me. My first wife used to mock me, but I like to think she loved me nonetheless." He frowned. "Do you understand this? No, perhaps not." He shrugged. "Well, it has nothing to do with the scars on my back, except that when my father used to beat me, he'd say, 'You beast, you monster! You cannot be mine! What nightmare did you come from!' "

"Oh, how awful!" Irina had cried.

"In a way it was," Pavel said softly. "But only in a way. You see, I was happy to take my father's anger, because I knew that then he would leave my mother alone. On the nights when he would come home drunk and couldn't find me, he'd start on my mother. I can still hear her screams. Oh, but they were terrible! They would make me weep. My brothers would huddle together in the far corner of our room, but I would go out into the hall because I had to help her." Pavel's eyes were turned inward, and at last there was a spark in them. "One night I couldn't stand it anymore. I ran into the kitchen, grabbed a carving knife and—"

"You killed him?" Irina's eyes were opened wide.

Pavel's eyes returned to the present, focusing on her. "No, no, *koshka*. My father took the knife out of my hand and whipped me. Oh, how it hurt, but I had stopped him from beating my mother, and that was a good feeling, I can't describe how good."

"What happened to them?"

"My parents? My father died of a liver disease brought on by his drinking. But that was three years after my mother had died."

"That time must have been bad."

"Bad, yes. Very bad." Pavel looked at her, then impulsively hugged her to him. "But do not think of these evil things, *koshka*. I am here to protect you and your mother."

Pavel had kept his promise for as long as he had lived. But he, it seemed, like Irina's father, was in a hazardous profession. He developed acute emphysema from the quantities of harsh dust he inhaled each day on the job. By then Yvgeny was dead, and the family, spinning helplessly out of control, fell apart. Irina's mother was not good at taking care of him—she was not even capable of taking care of her own children.

Irina stared now at the Church of the Archangel Gabriel,

where her mother had taken her so often. Abruptly, it, too, seemed alien, part of another time, another place, a sanctuary for another Irina, not this woman who stood here, at last breaking free of her memories, her rage at the helplessness of being a child, and far worse, a female child, set adrift in a world made for men. All this emotional baggage seemed removed, a distant report like thunder booming far off, diminishing with each moment.

White Star.

Irina turned back into the apartment. Somewhere in here, she thought, there must be some hint of the information Valeri held on the nationalist group. She crept carefully through every inch of his closets, looking in the pockets of his trousers and suit jackets, opening unmarked boxes, sifting through piles of linen, old photographs. At his desk she leafed through official papers, personal correspondence, blank paper.

Her exposure to the films of James Bond—a favorite of the students she knew—while she was in America had taught her to look behind pictures hung on the walls, inside the medicine cabinet in the bathroom. In the living room she unzipped slipcovers, got down on all fours, running her hand around the bottom part of the furniture frames.

She ended up in the kitchen, peering inside metal canisters of flour, sugar, and tea to make sure there wasn't some bit of paper secreted there. All her sleuthing came to nothing.

She sat wearily down in a dinette chair, stared blankly at the dark screen of the Toshiba lap-top. An hour and a half of combing through Valeri's apartment, and nothing to show for it.

Sitting here, alone, reminded her of all the mornings she had sat in this very spot watching Valeri prepare wonderful breakfasts. In the winter it was always warm in here, as it had been in *Babushka*'s kitchen, the mouthwatering smells irresistible. It was difficult if not impossible for Irina to reconcile this image of Valeri—and the one of the man so tender and loving in bed—with the knowledge that Valeri was a colonel in the KGB. She recalled his saying that the KGB's new accountability to the Congress of Peoples' Deputies had changed nothing; it had merely swept KGB operatives further underground. She shuddered.

The computer screen, witness to everything, repository of all truths, sat silent and dead, mocking her.

All of a sudden she recalled an American film called *Charade* she had seen in the small Cambridge art theater, and she began to look for anything in plain sight that would be so familiar the eye would automatically pass over it.

Then her eyes focused, and jumping up, Irina whispered, "My God, it *has* been visible all the time!"

She turned on the Toshiba. She was familiar with the software Valeri had had installed. Quickly she got a list of the directories on the hard disk, but nothing looked sinister. In fact, all that came up were recipe files. She looked for Macros—"hidden" strings of commands activated by a double keystroke—but could find none. Her excitement faded. Well, naturally, she thought sourly, this isn't a movie. Of course, Valeri could have the White Star material secreted on a hidden floppy disk; but she had been all through the apartment without turning up anything.

Then a fragment of a recent conversation surfaced. *How do you find time to get all those recipes in memory?* she had asked Valeri. And he had replied, *I get some help. There's a ghost in the machine.*

Irina approached the computer again, and this time pressed the Reveal Codes key. Nothing. She frowned. She had been so sure that Valeri's "ghost" would have been in Reveal Codes, an "invisible" mark held in the text.

Text!

What an idiot I am, she thought. She cleared the screen, retrieved the first text file in the directory. A menu for "Southern Fried Chicken" came up. Irina hit the Reveal Codes, and there it was, hanging at the very top of the screen: three consecutive signs for Underline that had no business being there.

She went back to the text. Then, holding her breath, she hit the Underline key three times in succession. Nothing. Damn! Now what? Those three Underlines must mean something.

She returned to the Reveal Codes screen, hit the Underline key three times. The "Please Wait" message appeared in the lower left-hand corner of the screen. That meant the computer was pulling an unusually large file out of the hard-drive memory. Irina's heart skipped a beat.

A moment later the computer began to spew out an enormous list of food menus. The file kept scrolling until Irina hit the Scroll Lock key. Then the screen held steady.

Irina studied the menu but could find nothing amiss with it. It was what it appeared to be: a menu for some kind of frozen dessert. In disgust, she depressed the Scroll Lock key. But instead of continuing to scroll, the screen went black and again the message "Please Wait" appeared.

Times, dates, places, names. When the new text came up on the screen, Irina's heart leaped in her chest because she was looking at what appeared to be the inner workings of White Star.

"With Hitasura's men all over the city looking for us, I can't afford a face-to-face rendezvous," Big Ezoe had said early that morning. "There is a way to get information from my informants. It's safe and utterly undetectable."

Koi was in Shibuya. It was just after eleven at night. Still, she was surrounded by such masses of people that she could not see the street. The sky was a yellow-gray, the air as opaque as miso soup, and it came as no surprise when the electronic pollution billboard near the NHK Building—one of fifteen in Tokyo—monitoring the levels of carbon monoxide, nitrogen, and sulphur oxides, began to issue an alert, advising children, the elderly, and the infirm to stay indoors.

"I refuse to sit in my office or in my car, waiting for a Hitasura hit team to blow me apart," Big Ezoe had said. "Hitasura is not so old-fashioned that he will kill me only with his own sword. That's for the old days, and the old days are alive only on movie screens."

Not his sword, Koi thought. His gun. What a world, she thought. If honor was dead, what use was living?

Outside the Seed Building, Koi stopped at the public message center. This was her third pass since she had come here by a circuitous route. She had doubled back many times, using the subways and the crowds in the streets to keep herself free of the hit team Hitasura had sent after her.

The public message center consisted of six CTR monitors connected to a sophisticated interactive computer program. Using an electronic pen, she touched the box marked READ. The screen changed, showing a list of four functions. She touched number 2, which read: MESSAGE TO YOUR FRIENDS WITH SECRET WORD. The screen asked her to enter the code word. On each pass before this, nothing had happened. She wrote KAMI with the electronic pen, the code word Big Ezoe had told her about, and the screen changed once again. This time a handwritten message appeared. It said: "Deke, the tattooer. Shinjuku."

Koi immediately touched the Eraser bar, and the message disappeared into the electronic heart of the machine. A moment later Koi, too, disappeared—into the electronic heart of the city.

* * *

"The first thing I want to ask you," the Hero said when Irina slipped into the pool with him, "is whether Volkov is with you." He had taken her out to the middle of the pool where the listening devices could not pick up their speech.

"I came alone this time," Irina said, staring at him.

"Do you know where Volkov is?"

"No. He doesn't tell me everything."

The Hero looked at her curiously for some time.

"What is it?" Irina said, uncomfortable beneath the intensity of that otherworldly gaze.

"I am wondering what you see in him."

"In Mars?"

"Yes."

Irina noticed that Arbat was restless, but she swam back and forth at the other end of the pool, as if she had no intention of coming near them.

"I said that I wouldn't lie to you," Irina said, "and I meant it. I have no family. Mars does. He's made me part of it, and I like that. It makes me feel secure."

"I don't understand."

"Wasn't I making myself clear?"

The Hero shook his head. "It's just that I can't see any way that the KGB can make you feel secure."

"Oh, you're talking about Valeri."

"Valeri who?"

Irina laughed. "Valeri Denysovich Bondasenko, colonel in the KGB's Second Chief Directorate, Chief of Department N, in charge of counterintelligence against the nationalist underground organization, White Star."

For a breathless moment nothing seemed to move, not Arbat, not the Hero, not the water in which they floated. In the silence that built itself like a spiderweb in the room, Irina imagined that a black abyss of immense proportions had opened up beneath her, and that she was in the process of falling into it.

"What have I said?"

Her heart beat on, seemingly the only motion in a place where even time had given up the ghost.

At last, when the silence had become so agonizing that Irina was about to scream, the Hero said, "Who told you about Department N?"

"Why, Mars did."

"And he said that Comrade Bondasenko was in charge of it?"

"No. Mars showed me a document. It was a charter, I think.

Department N's internal KGB charter. It named Valeri as the department's chief."

"You don't know." The Hero closed his eyes. "Mother of God." Arbat, perhaps in response to his inner turmoil, popped up next to him, but she wisely kept silent. She looked at Irina with what could only be described as astonishment.

"What is it?" Irina said in a strangled voice.

The Hero looked at her, and Irina did not know whether she saw pity or anger in his eyes. Perhaps it was both, or neither, perhaps it was some other emotion, one that he had learned in the space between the stars. "How best to put this," he said slowly. "I suppose," he said, continuing his inner dialogue, "there is no best way. There is only to do it." Arbat clicked briefly, and he nodded. "Irina, the monitoring that is done on me here is scientific, but it is also overseen by the KGB. Lara and Tatiana are KGB. They are my handlers as well as my companions. Twice a week I am interrogated by a high-ranking colonel in the KGB."

"Do you want me to see if I can stop it? Perhaps Mars—"

"Irina, Mars *is* the KGB."

For a moment Irina was certain that she had misheard him. Then it occurred to her that he was making a joke. But there was no smile on his grave face, and Arbat was silently watching her from the other side of the pool.

"You're joking," she said, feeling more and more foolish. "It's impossible. Mars showed me documents that—"

"They were false," the Hero said forcefully. "Or I should say, more accurately, they were falsified. I've no doubt the document itself is the real Department N charter. It's the name of its chief that's been changed. The original bears the name: Mars Petrovich Volkov, Colonel, Second Chief Directorate."

"No! It's impossible!"

"I'll call for Lara and Tatiana. Let them verif—"

"No!" She could see the truth in his eyes, his fear for her. "Don't move! Don't do a thing!"

Irina remembered the night she and Mars had gone to see the performance of Chekhov's *Three Sisters*, Mars saying to her, *The actress, Natasha something, isn't it?* And then, later, when he had come upon her here in Star Town after she'd followed Natasha to the Hero's building from Moscow, and wondered why she'd been following Natasha, Irina had asked him, *You know her?* And Mars had said, *Certainly. I know everyone who goes into that building.*

385

Irina hung suspended. Beneath her the abyss waited only for her to finish her fall, to close over her, suffocating her in its immense black belly.

God in Heaven! She was trembling all over. Abruptly, she began to gag, and the Hero turned her, hoisting her up so that she vomited onto the coping of the pool.

He gave a piercing whistle and, almost immediately, Lara appeared. "Your Comrade Volkov has claimed another victim," the Hero said to her.

Lara came to the side of the pool, pulled Irina out. She lay her by the side, then went to get materials to clean up the mess.

"Are you all right?" the Hero asked Irina.

Arbat poked her head out of the water, pressing her bottle snout against Irina's shoulder.

"No," Irina said. "I'm not in the least all right." She sat up as Lara knelt beside her. She opened her mouth, but the Hero put his forefinger across his lips, pointed to his ear as if to say, Remember the listening devices.

Lara turned on a portable wet-vac. The noise ate up the silence of the room.

"How long have you been working for the KGB?" Irina asked the young woman.

"All my life," Lara said. "Tatiana, as well. We were orphans, wards of the state. We were raised by the KGB, trained in their schools."

"How long have you been working for Mars?"

"Tatiana and I are part of the team Comrade Volkov put together when he was given the assignment of finding out what went on during the EVA event." She kept on scrubbing. "Not long ago Odysseus was able to procure for us our KGB dossiers. Tatiana and I discovered who we were, who our parents had been. Tatiana is Estonian. Her parents were killed in a nuclear accident of suspicious origin. The KGB file mentions negligence, a complete cover-up of the incident." She sponged more soapy water onto the coping, worked the wet-vac back and forth. "As for me, I'm Ukrainian. My parents were sent to the Perm political prison in the Urals."

"What was their crime?" Irina asked.

"I don't know," Lara said. "Their dossiers say that the KGB arrested them for espionage for talking to American diplomatic personnel, but that is a euphemistic catchall charge. It means nothing in itself. Perhaps my parents didn't know why they were arrested, either. Perhaps it was because my father was a professor of political science and held strong views at odds with the state. Or perhaps the state just needed more wards to bring up as they saw fit. The truth in these matters is impossible to determine, so I try not to dwell on it.''

''Do you at least know whether they are alive or dead?''

''No. No one knows.''

''But someone must,'' Irina said.

''I think Comrade Volkov knows,'' the Hero interjected. ''But he's not telling.''

Irina said to Lara, ''You're awfully open about all this.''

''Not to everyone.'' Lara finished her clean-up, but kept the wet-vac running.

The Hero said, ''I think to some extent Lara and Tatiana have been changed by their proximity to me.''

Lara nodded. ''We find it prudent not to report everything that we hear at our weekly debriefings.''

Irina said to the Hero, ''I see that you have been quietly assembling your own team.''

''In a way,'' the Hero said. ''Volkov thought he could win my confidence by disconnecting all the listening devices in the room. But he was wearing a body mike. The next time he came, I forced him into the pool, and while he was with me, Lara made a copy of the cassette he had on him. Would you care to hear it? There are all sorts of—''

It was then that Irina felt an icy stab through her heart, a wave of panic so strong that all the blood drained from her face.

''Irina, what is it?''

She looked into the Hero's eyes, pale now with anxiety. ''Oh, Odysseus, you don't know what I've been doing. I've been spying on Natasha Mayakova. I've told Mars everything. How Natasha has been secretly meeting with Valeri; how I followed Natasha here after she and Valeri met. My God, what have I done?''

In the ringing silence that ensued, only the wet-vac's drone could be heard. Then the Hero turned to Lara, said, ''Make the call.''

Her eyes were wide; she was clearly startled. ''Are you certain?''

''Now.''

Lara obeyed.

When Natasha failed to make their next scheduled rendezvous, Valeri drove out to Arkhangelskoe as fast as he could

387

without attracting attention. He did not take his usual route, and he made sure he wasn't being followed.

All the way out to the insane asylum he thought of the sinking feeling he had gotten as he waited for Natasha in the lobby of the old Moscow Arts Theater. It was still with him, and it was accelerating.

Natasha was absolutely reliable. On the one occasion when she could not make their rendezvous, she had used the dead-letter drop at the International Post Office in Komsomolskaya Square he had described to her. Before every rendezvous, Valeri went to the post office box there to make sure there was no message from her. There had been none today, and she hadn't made the scheduled rendezvous. He could not ask about her at the old Moscow Arts Theater without calling attention to himself, so he had left, fearing the worst. Then, at the public phone bank at the post office, he had called her apartment. A man had answered in an officious voice. His blood turned to ice, Valeri put down the receiver as if it had turned into a serpent.

All the way out to Arkhangelskoe, Valeri was thinking like a chess player, three, four, five steps ahead. He was moderately successful in keeping his mind free of Natasha, because surely she was lost to him now, and there were larger issues at stake, something Natasha knew and accepted when he had recruited her. Because her beliefs coincided with his, she had made herself into a professional. But, as he well knew, even professionals had their breaking points.

It was a question of time now.

If the KGB had picked her up—which it appeared they had—they would break her, no question. It was merely a matter of how long before she broke. There was no blame here. Valeri knew that were he in Natasha's position, he too would eventually break, tell them everything he knew, everything they wanted to hear. There would be no shame in it, only the secret knowledge of how many more lives would be saved by holding out that much longer before the will gave out and the damaging information began to flow.

He arrived in Arkhangelskoe free of ticks, and skirted the magnificent estate, the birch forest, but he did not park in the lot outside the insane asylum. Instead he pulled into a badly rutted dirt track that cut diagonally through the forest and switched off the ignition.

He sat listening to the ticking of the hot engine. The bluebirds and cardinals sang in the trees, the insects droned and whirred, life went on here no different than it had the day before, than it would the day after. If only that were true for Valeri Bondasenko.

Valeri pulled open the locked glove compartment, extracted the handgun. It was of West German manufacture, and extremely reliable. He slid it into the waistband of his trousers. It was uncomfortable there, but that was good, he thought as he began his nerve-racking trek toward the grim Victorian facade of the insane asylum; it would remind him of what had to be done now.

He took out a slender switchblade with a long, wicked blade. He tested the action of the blade, then strapped the knife in its sheath to the inside of his wrist.

If he was expecting a contingent of KGB Border Guards to have surrounded the place, he was mistaken. By the time he arrived near the front steps, he had almost convinced himself that Natasha was still holding on, that she hadn't spilled everything in her mind into their laps. He said a little prayer as he turned away from the main lobby, entering the building through the rear service doors.

He was immediately hit by the familiar noxious odors, but he was too concerned to be repelled. He went quickly up the south staircase to the third floor. He stood just outside the door to the floor corridor, peering through the meshed square of glass. In a moment he saw a plainclothes man coming in his direction. Valeri ducked back into the stairwell. The man passed by the door, and Valeri watched him as he went into his daughter's room.

His heart sank. Natasha was as good as dead. She had told them everything she knew. Poor Natasha.

The only good news for him was that it appeared that she had just been broken, otherwise all entrances would have been guarded, the place would have been surrounded. Time was running away. He knew that the Border Guards contingent must be on its way.

Valeri opened the door, looked first to his left, the direction from which the KGB man had come. The corridor was clear in that direction, but to his right another KGB man stood guard outside his daughter's room.

His heart thundering in his chest, Valeri ventured out into the corridor. He walked directly up to the KGB man, said, "I'm looking for Dr. Kalinin. Have you seen him?"

The KGB man opened his mouth to reply, and Valeri depressed the stud that opened the switchblade, shoved the blade between the man's third and fourth ribs, in a slight upward tilt so that the blade pierced his heart.

The KGB man's jaws snapped together as he collapsed into Valeri's arms. Valeri dragged him quickly across the corridor, parking him just inside the door to a room occupied by a co-matose woman in her eighties. He went through the KGB man's pockets, taking his ID folder, his weapons.

He strode swiftly, confidently, back across the hall and through the door to his daughter's room. The second KGB man looked up, said, "Stop where you are," then looked down in astonishment at the hilt of the knife buried in his chest.

He went down on one knee, but still had the presence of mind to draw his pistol. Valeri kicked it out of his hand. The KGB man grabbed Valeri's foot, twisted it from the heel.

Valeri felt himself going over, and the man was upon him. Blood was seeping from the wound in his chest, but Valeri could see how his aim had been off. The man's sternum had been pierced, but the bone had taken the brunt of the wound.

His hands were around Valeri's throat, and Valeri used his knee, kicking the man in his crotch. Pink froth flew from the KGB man's mouth, and his eyes almost bugged out of his head. He growled like an animal, but did not relinquish his strangle-hold on Valeri's throat. His spatulate thumbs were pressing into Valeri's windpipe.

Valeri used three *kites* to the man's rib cage, felt it stave in on the third blow. The man toppled to the floor. Valeri scrambled to his feet, went to the bed, gazed down at the placid face of his daughter. He was never so happy to see her. Bending down, he scooped her up, stepped over the body of the fallen KGB man.

He peeked out into the corridor. It was clear. He ran to the stairwell, headed downstairs. It took him seven minutes to ferry his daughter out of the asylum, back to where the car was hidden among the birches.

Then he hurried back. There was more to be done.

He skirted the building, heading around back to the long, sloping lawn. He looked back toward the open doors to the main lobby. There was the usual activity, with nurses passing this way and that, some with their charges in wheelchairs, others shep-herding slow-shuffling figures in tatty robes from one corridor to another. There was a clot of doctors to the left who seemed to be huddled over a chart.

Valeri saw Dr. Kalinin among the clot of doctors and, at almost the same moment, Dr. Kalinin saw him.

Valeri saw the doctor's face go white, then he began to surreptitiously edge away from his colleagues, away from the spot where Valeri stood.

Valeri ran down the lawn toward the bench that overlooked the large birch tree where he always sat with his daughter. It was empty. He turned, looked beyond the tree, toward the birch forest, and he saw to his horror the young man with the strawberry birthmark on his cheek running from two plainclothes men. The young man was heading toward the forest, but Valeri could see that he was not going to make it.

Valeri drew his pistol, went down on one knee, held the gun in both hands. He sighted, squeezed off one shot, two. Both the KGB men fell.

"Comrade!"

He heard the shout behind him and whirled. Dr. Kalinin had come down the back steps onto the lawn. He kept shouting, pointing at Valeri. Valeri shot him. Dr. Kalinin threw his hands into the air as he spun around. By the time he hit the ground face first, Valeri was already off and running toward the forest of birch trees.

He crashed into the underbrush, then was within the woods, the light dimmer, speckled with deep shadow. The rich scents of moss and humus perfumed the air.

"Halt!"

Valeri came up short.

"Hands!"

Valeri raised his hands.

"Stay right where you are or you will be shot!"

In a moment the young man with the strawberry birthmark emerged. "Valeri!"

Valeri put down his hands. "You gave me a start, Sergei!" Valeri's voice was filled with relief. "What are you doing waiting around here?"

"I wanted to make certain you got away clean," Sergei said. "That was some shooting, comrade!"

They laughed together, clapping each other on the back, but Sergei quickly sobered. "What has happened?"

"Come," Valeri said, leading him through the forest. "The KGB picked up Natasha."

"But how? How could they know about her? If there is a leak of such proportions, we're finished."

Valeri found the rutted dirt track, followed it back toward where he had hidden his car.

"Let's not get ahead of ourselves," he said, but Sergei could see the concern on his face.

"This is Volkov's doing," Sergei said. "I can smell his duplicity from a mile away." He shuddered. "That charm of his. How many people he has gulled."

And, of course, that was when Valeri thought of Irina.

Deke was no problem. He was a scientist, not a hero. Koi left him hanging by his ankles in the lab at the back of his tattoo parlor. His face was purple, bloated beyond any easy recognition, but it looked a good sight better than did his body.

Twenty-two minutes, Koi thought as she emerged into the teeming nighttime streets of Shinjuku, from the time I walked in there. She had been fascinated by the smells in the lab: formaldehyde, sulfuric acid, acetone. They spoke to her of death and destruction by increments, breaking down the building blocks of life one at a time. She had used some of these substances on Deke, rubbing them into his skin as if she were in the process of pickling him.

Koi rode the subways, advertisements everywhere: on long cards overhead, on banners hanging at eye level, even on the straps standing passengers held on to while the train was in motion. Koi read them all, but they were meaningless to her. She was outside of time, traveling down her own dark tunnel even as the train she was riding snaked through the tunnels beneath the city.

Her mind was empty, her expression approaching the one of the mask of the god that had so entranced Big Ezoe: the combination of ecstasy and despair. But not yet.

She emerged onto the street near Hammacho Station. The killing ground.

In her mind a roll of thunder, Big Ezoe saying, *We must punish Hitasura for his transgressions against members of my family. We must destroy Tori Nunn for her part in all this. She murdered Fukuda.*

Deke had told her how Tori Nunn and a man named Russell Slade had come to him with a pellet he had identified as hafnium. They had returned later, along with Hitasura. The two men were carrying Tori Nunn. According to Deke, she had been poisoned by a complex organic *doku*, a toxin, usually lethal,

392

whose main elements had been distilled from monkshood and the poison in *fugu*, Japanese blowfish.

Fortunately for Tori Nunn, she had been exposed to a very small amount of the *doku*. That, combined with her own inner resources, had prevented her from dying immediately. Deke had prevented her from dying at all. According to him, she was recuperating in one of Hitasura's safehouses near Hammacho Station. Deke had not wanted to give Koi the address, but she had finally persuaded him. By that time he had looked like meat ready for the slaughter.

Koi found the house with little difficulty. It was one of those expensive postmodern ferroconcrete structures, angular, minimalist, higher than it was wide, with windows inset like those of a medieval castle, and a heavy iron gate fronting a tiny courtyard dominated by a slender cryptomeria tree, a bonsaied dwarf juniper. A powerful grouping of rocks provided the negative space, and thus made the courtyard appear far larger than it actually was.

She spent forty-five minutes watching the house from all angles, noting who walked by and what cars passed on the street in front of it. Parking on this street was nonexistent. No one was loitering about, but she knew that Hitasura's men must be hidden somewhere. She understood that she must solve that puzzle before she could confront the one waiting for her inside the house: how to kill Tori Nunn.

Less than an hour after she had arrived in the vicinity, Koi spotted the first of Hitasura's street men. It had taken him quite a while to make a second circuit of the block, which meant—as she suspected—he was not the only one guarding the house.

Koi watched his movements, thought with a little luck she could avoid him. Her instinct from the moment she saw the house was to get to the roof, and now, an hour later, the roof was still her first choice. The front door was out of the question, and when she had made her way around to the rear of the house, there was a vehicle with two of Hitasura's men stationed at the back entrance. Besides, for security reasons Hitasura was sure to have put Tori Nunn on a top floor.

Two more of Hitasura's men were waiting for her on the roof. They heard her only when she was very close to them. She broke one man's neck instantly, but the other one, she saw, was going to be a bit of a problem. He was a bull of a man with a bald head and an evil look in his eyes. He grinned at her, ignoring his fallen comrade. He beckoned for Koi to come to him.

Instead she melted into the shadows on the rooftop. The bald man looked around, then unfurled a *kyotetsu-shoge*, a particularly nasty weapon composed of a chain with a spiked ball on one end, a curved double-edged blade on the other. He began to whirl the spiked ball around as he made for the spot where she had disappeared.

When he reached the shadows, Koi had had sufficient time to work her way around behind him. She leaped at him, slamming her elbow into his side, then locking her forearm across his throat.

It was a mistake.

The huge man bit into the flesh of her forearm with such force that his front teeth scraped the bone.

Koi stifled a cry, whirled off him. The bald man swung his weapon at her, and she rolled as the spiked ball slammed into the tarred roof where she had just been.

Immediately it struck and missed; he reacted, arcing the double-edged blade down at the spot between her eyes. Koi swung left with her head, kicked right with her feet. The soles of her shoes cracked the bald man's shins just below the knees.

His legs buckled; he reached out instinctively to break his fall, and Koi took up the double-edged blade of his *kyotetsu-shoge* and slashed his throat.

Now she had the roof all to herself. The thick layer of industrial smog that had caused the pollution alert blurred the lights of the city, running the colors together so that Tokyo seemed embedded inside a giant clamshell. The sky was the largest sheet of mother-of-pearl she had ever seen.

From up here she had a good view of the Hammacho Station itself, where so many customers embarked and debarked each day. The overhead rail lines shone like quicksilver as a train pulled into the station. Crowds surged forward. Koi turned away.

She tore a piece off the bald man's shirt, wrapped it tightly around her forearm to stop the bleeding. When she was satisfied, she took a careful look around her immediate environment. There was a small raised ferroconcrete structure in which was set the metal door down into the house, but she did not want to use it. Too vulnerable. If she were caught in the narrow stairwell, there would only be one way to go: back to the roof, and that could all too easily prove to be a deathtrap.

On the other hand, all the windows were illuminated by the streetlights, making it far too risky to seek entrance through any of them. But during her initial reconnaissance she had spent some time studying the facade of the house, and thought she had noticed a vulnerable point: a small pebbled-glass window in back—probably leading into a bathroom—that was in the shadow cast by a large building opposite. It was too small for a man to get through, but she thought that she might be able to make it.

She took the *kyotetsu-shoge*, walked to the rear of the roof. Knotting a length of nylon rope she carried around the center of the weapon's chain, she wrapped the *kyotetsu-shoge* around a metal flue. Paying the rope out slowly until she tied the other end around her waist, she went over the side of the house.

When she got level with the pebbled-glass bathroom window, she braced herself by placing her feet on either side of it. It was partly open, but this was of no help to her, since the metal frame impinged on the space she needed to crawl through.

She spent the next two minutes detaching the window from its hinged brackets. Then she slid it carefully into the bathroom, followed it in.

It was a tight fit, but she made it. She untied herself from the nylon cord, stood absolutely still for ten minutes. While her eyes adjusted to the gloom inside, she accustomed her ears to listen to the natural sounds of the house: creaks, doors opening, closing, footfalls in the hallway, muffled voices. No TV, no radio, no stereo, no VCR. No loud sound, no doubt in deference to their sick house guest.

When Koi was certain that she had catalogued every sound, no matter how minute, and that she would pick up the slightest deviation, she opened the bathroom door a crack.

Again she was still for ten minutes, allowing the scents of the house to come to her while the repetition of the tiny sounds reassured her that all was as it should be.

She had come in on the fourth and top floor. It seemed logical to her for Hitasura to put Tori Nunn as high up as he could. Also, that he would put her in a room as near to a bathroom as possible.

Koi stepped out into a hallway. To her right was the landing of the open iron spiral staircase down to the third floor. Beyond were two rooms, both with their doors open, both dark. Koi forgot them. To her left was only one room, the door to which was closed. A crack of dim light filtered out into the hallway from the far edge, which was not quite fitted into the frame.

Still Koi did not move. Her peripheral vision had picked up

395

a shadow moving. It crept up the open stairwell, illuminated by the lamps below. Someone was coming up the stairs.

She contracted her *wa*, stilled her breathing to the minimum. She watched as the top of a man's head came into view. It stopped, and she could hear voices talking softly. She craned her neck without otherwise moving, saw the top of a shorter man's head. He had been guarding the staircase, but because of his lack of height, she had not been able to see him from where she stood.

Koi waited. Eventually the conversation ceased, the shadow moved down the spiral staircase. The shorter man remained at his post, but he was concentrated on someone trying to come up the stairs. Koi slipped down the hallway to her left, out of his field of vision.

She stood by the lone door for a long time. She could hear nothing from inside the room. Her fingers on the door, a spider's deft touch. She pushed it inward.

Koi stepped into the room. It was a bedroom, furnished in Western style: mahogany bed, masculine dressers, a dark red and black patterned rug covering most of the floor. A mirror hung on the wall, along with several modern abstract prints. A lamp glowed on a night table beside the bed.

On Koi's face now spread that singular expression: ecstasy and despair.

In the bed was the sleeping form of a woman. Koi drank her in, the face beautiful even if her skin was still unhealthily pale. Her breasts rose and fell evenly from beneath the covers. Her long cinnamon-colored hair fanned out across the pillowcase. Very exotic, very American.

Tori Nunn.

Tori Nunn, lying unconscious in the big bed in the fourth-floor bedroom of Hitasura's safehouse near Hammacho Station, was dreaming of one moment in time, when she was the Wild Child.

It was nine years ago, the year after she had stumbled across Hitasura, who had pulled her out of hiding after she and her brother Greg had been involved in the death of the young Yakuza; three months after she had been recruited into the Mall by Bernard Godwin.

The then-managing director of the Mall—and Godwin's right hand man—was Tom Royce. Royce was a lanky, rawboned man, a sunravaged Texan who rolled when he walked, and chewed rather than smoked small black cheroots. It was easy to imagine him in a ten-gallon hat, lassoing a dogie. Bernard had sent him to Japan to brief Tori on Mall procedure and discipline.

In Tori's opinion, Royce was entirely the wrong man to send to Japan. After the first interminable week with him, she cabled Bernard this conviction, but all the reply she received was a terse "Carry on. You're under discipline. Follow orders."

In the end, however, Tori was proved correct. Japan got to Tom Royce.

397

Royce fancied himself a real cowboy. Wyatt Earp. When Tori found him in the alley behind her apartment shot to death with his own Colt pistol, she was hardly surprised. But she was angry. This was Tokyo, her city, and she had been charged with Royce's safety. Besides, the murder had come on what was the equivalent of her back porch.

She knelt beside Tom Royce's body, pulled the barrel of the Remington out of his throat. What a way to die. Yakuza, Tori was willing to bet. She went to see Hitasura.

The Yakuza *oyabun* was not forthcoming. "I do not know who killed this American," Hitasura said after they had had green tea and, as civilized protocol demanded, had spoken of many other unimportant matters, "but I will shed no tears for him. And neither will you," he added shrewdly.

"My personal feelings for Royce are unimportant," Tori said. "I was responsible for him. Whoever killed him knew that, and threw him up into my face."

"The American was without manners," Hitasura said, as if he had not heard her. "He was loud, aggressive, he made passes at our women and insulted our men. I would think that the suspects in his murder would be many."

"Only one person killed him," Tori said, rising, "and that person must answer for the insult."

Hitasura had poured more tea. "This time, Tori-san, I would think it better if you let the matter drop."

"It is a question of honor," Tori said. "If I back away, then I am worth nothing. To my employers, to myself."

Hitasura said nothing, and she left him pouring more tea for himself and for a guest who was no longer there.

Over the next several weeks Tori dived deep into the bowels of Tokyo. She wheedled, cajoled, threatened, plied her contacts with drink. Nobody knew a thing about Tom Royce's murder. Either that or they were involved in a conspiracy of silence. It could happen. For all of Tori's fame, and the respect she was given by the Japanese, she was still *gaijin*, an outsider. And now, trying to run down Tom Royce's murder, she came to the realization that as much as she wanted—needed—Japan to be her home, it was not. She was born Caucasian, and here that alone counted too heavily and irrevocably against her.

With a kind of relief she never thought she would feel, she flew back to the States, spent ten days being debriefed by Ber-

398

nard himself in Mall Central in Virginia, then headed west to Los Angeles and Diana's Garden.

Ellis Nunn didn't say, What the hell are you doing here? He didn't say anything; he was on a business trip in Europe. Greg was off on some top-secret assignment for NASA. That left Tori to fend for herself with her mother.

Within a week that familiar stifling feeling had returned, and Tori packed her bags, flew directly back to Tokyo.

It was good to be back. The city seemed scoured clean, bright with nervous energy, a beating heart that never faltered. It didn't matter that in her absence so many buildings had been torn down, others built in their stead, that she hardly recognized certain districts—that was part of Tokyo's uniqueness, and she felt immediately at ease.

She threw herself back into her work, but the specter of Tom Royce's murder continued to haunt her. Now she could not get her interview with Hitasura out of her mind. What if it was one of his lieutenants who had murdered Royce, or even worse, Hitasura himself?

Tori asked herself what she would do if the worse came to the worst. Would she try to bring Hitasura down, or would she back away, as he had first suggested?

This was the essential question that gnawed at her the night she was at The Neon Starfish. It was a club just this side of respectability, on the outskirts of the Ginza, starlit with colored lights, with a transparent floor beneath which lusciously colored tropical fish swam in lazy circles.

There were two Japanese businessmen, drunk on sake, who she had been aware of for some time. They looked as similar as bookends, though one was shorter than the other. They had already taken off their suit jackets, hung them up on seat backs. They wanted women, but were apparently too drunk to make it down the block to the local *akachochin*, where they could have their pick of the litter in return for a sum of money equal to a month's paycheck.

Instead they had begun a series of obnoxiously maudlin reports on the pathetic state of their home lives. Tori had just about had it with stories of their suckling at their wives teats as they had done with their mothers, when, as drunks are often wont to do, without warning they veered off on another topic entirely.

Now they were intent on impressing one another with tales from the office where, latter-day samurai as they apparently considered themselves, they were rife with legends of their board-room prowess.

This also proved to be boring, and Tori was considering changing tables to escape the white noise, when the shorter man said to his pal, "That's nothing. My boss killed a man. Yes, yes, of course, it's true. I swear it! We got drunk together last week, and he told me so himself. 'I killed an American,' he said. A drastic resolution to a problem, I said, but you know my boss, very old-fashioned, comes from *the* Murashitos—his ancestors it is said were samurai at the court of the first Shogun, Ieyasu Tokugawa. But now he tells me that this American raped his daughter, and I say, did you go to the police? 'What?' he said crossly, 'and involve my poor daughter further? Do you think I would consider holding her up for public inspection, or dragging her through the courts? No, no, not a chance.' This had to be settled quickly, privately, absolutely. I agreed. Yes, yes, I believe he did right."

Tori moved closer to the shorter businessman, and at one point, in leaning over to find something in her handbag, she palmed his wallet out of his inside jacket pocket. She dug out one of his business cards, and five minutes later slipped the wallet back without having been detected.

The next morning she presented herself at the executive offices of Tandom Polycarbon. They had a dozen floors in a huge building in Shinjuku, and the chairman's suite was on the top floor. She asked to see Tok Murashito, but was told that the chairman was in the middle of a board meeting and, furthermore, would be tied up all day. There was an appointment book on the secretary's burlwood desk, but she did not ask Tori if she wished to make an appointment. Tori was apparently beneath her notice.

Tori said sweetly, "Just tell Mr. Murashito that Tom Royce's sister is here to see him."

"I'm afraid that Murashito-san has left instructions not to be disturbed," the secretary said.

Tori leaned over the desk, put her face close to the secretary's, expanded her *wa* to its limits. "Call him. I'll wait." The secretary jumped as if poked with a hot fork. Her hand trembled as it picked up the receiver. She dialed an internal number, spoke briefly, waited a moment, then spoke again at length. In a moment she hung up. She seemed frightened. "Murashito-san will see you in his office," she said, getting up. "I'll show you the way."

The secretary led Tori through thick wooden doors, down a hushed carpeted corridor whose walls were covered with color blowups of microscopic views of different man-made fabrics that Tandom Polycarbon had designed, created, and patented. These photographs were matted and framed like works of art.

Tok Murashito had an office that faced west and south, a magnificent view that was in itself a major work of art. But the inner walls of his office were adorned with a Braque, a Schiele, and a Manet. Tori was impressed, as she was meant to be, both by Tok Murashito's wealth and his good taste.

Fuck good taste, Tori thought as the secretary withdrew.

Tok Murashito made certain that she had the office to herself before he made his entrance through a discreet side door hidden within the walnut paneling that housed a wet bar, a magnificent Olmec head that belonged in a Mexican museum, and six shelves of books more suitable to a lawyer's office.

He was shorter than the short drunk man who had spilled the beans the night before at The Neon Starfish, but he was thicker, too, with the wide shoulders and upper arms of a bodybuilder. The way his muscles stretched his suit, he seemed to belong in a *dojo* or a gym rather than a boardroom. The way he was built, Tori saw, he'd have to have all his clothes made to order.

"Well," Tok Murashito said without preliminaries, "what is it you want?"

Okay, Tori thought. "You murdered an American named Tom Royce."

Murashito didn't blink. "I had just cause."

"I wonder whether the police will think so."

"The police won't be called."

"Oh? What makes you think that?"

Tok Murashito walked past his desk, looked out his windows. It was a magnificent view, but it was also a long way down.

Murashito put his hands behind his back. "Why would the police be called?"

"They usually are when a murder has been committed."

He nodded. "That's true. In fact, they're already on the case." He smiled. "Surprised, Miss Royce? The police have been in contact with me. You see, we knew one another. Royce and I did business from time to time."

Tori recalled Tom Royce's cover as a textile salesman, thought, Fronts have to be maintained in order for them to seem legitimate. "So you knew him," she said. "Do the police also know you had a motive?"

Tok Murashito went very still. "Who are you?" he said.

Tori ignored him. "You didn't report the rape of your daughter, did you?"

Now an odd thing happened. Murashito's face changed, and if Tori hadn't known better, she would have sworn it relaxed. He turned quickly away, as if embarrassed. "She's already endured more pain and suffering than any young woman should."

Tori went silently up behind him. She said, "I'm not Tom Royce's sister. My name is Tori Nunn. Do you know me?"

Tok Murashito shook his head no.

"I'm the Wild Child. I could kill you right here and no one would know about it. Do you understand me?"

Tok Murashito said nothing for some time, then he said, "You're a foolish young woman. There is too much fire burning inside you. Go home." When she did not move, he turned to face her. "One of these days you'll discover that there are alternatives far preferable to violence."

"That's curious advice, coming from you."

"*Giri*. I did what I had to do."

Tori looked him in the eye. "Just as I do," she said.

Tok Murashito stared at her for a long time. Then he shook his head. "Time makes fools of us all, Miss Nunn. I strive to remember that, but all too often it slips my mind." When she said nothing, he said, "Will you kill me now?"

"If I did," Tori said, "your daughter's pain would forever be on my conscience."

"Well," Tok Murashito said, "after all, perhaps there is such a thing in the world as justice." He never took his eyes from her. "Tell me, why did you come here, Miss Nunn?"

"To let you know that I was here," Tori said. "To see how you would react."

"You were testing me."

"In a manner of speaking."

He passed a hand across his face. "I must say that this is the first time I have been tested by a woman."

"How does it feel?"

"To be truthful, it makes me uncomfortable."

Tori nodded. "The traditional roles have been reversed."

"That's not what I meant," Tok Murashito said carefully. "What makes me uncomfortable is your easy acceptance of violence."

"You think that because I am female I should hate violence."

"That is my experience, yes." He shrugged. "Someone has

402

to fight against violence, don't you think? If women abandon their traditional role as peacemakers, where will we be?''

"Mr. Murashito," Tori said, "you are something of an enigma.''

"I think I shall take that as a compliment, young lady.''

Tori frowned. "No one's ever called me young lady before.''

"Well," Tok Murashito said, "I think it's about time they did.''

The dream of the past began to dissolve in much the same way as a reflection of the moon on water breaks up with the coming of rain. Tori became aware of something dark and metallic impinging on her consciousness, and she rose through the layers of sleep, from delta to beta to alpha.

Her eyes fluttered open and she saw the figure standing at the foot of the bed, half illuminated by the lamp at her bedside. She was far more aware of the figure than she was of her surroundings. She hardly knew where she was or how she had gotten here. What had happened to her? Slowly, in patchwork fashion, she remembered the nightmarish chase inside the Kinji-to, leading to the final confrontation with Fukuda.

But, again, the dark metallic rings brought her out of the well of her memories, and at last she understood that what she was feeling was the expansion of the figure's *wa*, a dangerous weapon that was about to be used against her.

"Who are you?''

Koi moved closer. "I am Fukuda's spiritual sister. I have come to repay you for killing her.''

And immediately Tori thought of her encounter with Tok Murashito. Now, it seemed, in an eerie replaying of the scene, she was Tok, and this woman was what Tori had been so many years ago.

Tori saw a rather small handsome woman with wide shoulders, narrow hips, black, glossy hair. Her black eyes seemed opaque, or perhaps they were utterly transparent, and the darkness was the ghost hidden inside herself.

Tori allowed herself to touch the other woman's *wa*, felt an engine that would not stop, something so relentless that it would not give even its owner surcease. She felt what Big Ezoe had defined as the water tap that would not shut off.

"What is your name?" Tori said.

"I have given myself the name of Koi.''

"You are a foolish woman. There is far too much fire burning in you. Go home.''

403

Koi said, "I will leave when you are dead."

"So much violence inside you, eating you alive. Don't you see it?"

"Not before."

"No, of course you don't. I didn't, either, years ago. I'm not sure that even now I do."

"I don't understand you."

Tori looked at Koi. "In respect to Fukuda's death, I did what I had to do. *Giri*. She stalked me, laid a trap for me. She was determined that only one of us was going to leave that tunnel."

"This is irrelevant to me. I, too, must do what I have to do."

Grasping, at last, what Tok Murashito had meant, Tori said, "Listen to me, Koi. There's a difference between doing what you have to do and doing what you have been told to do."

"There is no difference."

"If that's so," Tori said, "then there is no self. In that case, you don't exist at all, but are purely the creation of someone else—who would that be, Big Ezoe? Of course. Big Ezoe. There is no Koi, only Big Ezoe's automaton." She watched the other woman. "Tell me, Koi, who are you?"

"I am the hard machine."

"That may be *what* you are, but it isn't *who* you are." Silence. "You can't tell me because you don't know. I'll bet there was never a time in your life when you were you, plain and simple, with no one else telling you what to do and what to be."

Koi said nothing for a long time. Her eyes seemed to have fixed on that peculiar middle distance that exists only in the back of the mind. At last she said, "I was trained by a *sensei* known as the Man of One Tree. He adopted me, or so it seemed, when my parents no longer knew what to do with me. I am cursed. I was born *hinoeuma*, in the year of the husband killers."

Her head moved slightly, but her eyes did not change their focus. "The Man of One Tree taught me how to combat my curse. He told me that *karma* was mutable, that if my will was sufficiently developed I could change my *karma*. I believed because I had nothing else to believe.

"I stayed with him on his island for many years. I came to think of myself as his daughter, and it seemed that he thought of himself as my father. I liked that. My real father was always so afraid of me, whatever paternal instincts he might have had were channeled away from me, toward my brothers and sisters.

"Then, one day, the Man of One Tree announced that we were leaving the island for several days. He took me to the

404

mainland, where his daughter was getting married. Watching the look of love transform his face as he gazed upon his daughter, I knew what a pathetic fantasy I had been living all the years I had been with him. I was nothing to him, not a daughter, not family. Nothing. But I hid my disappointment and anger by covering myself with shame. Of course he did not think of me as his daughter. How could he? I was *hinoeuma*. I was unworthy of his love.

"I said nothing of this to the Man of One Tree. I needed him as much as I had before—perhaps even more. Now that I knew he had not adopted me as his own, I had even less than I had thought. And I needed every scrap of attention I could find, otherwise I was sure I would shrivel up and die."

Koi stood very still, paralyzed by memories.

Tori could feel the awesome strength of her *wa* purling outward in waves, but she did not try to fend it off. Instead she said, "Koi, tell me something, why is it that you accept violence as your only alternative?"

"My nature is steeped in violence, in blood. I am unclean."

"And yet," Tori said, "I bleed every month the same as you."

"And you embrace violence as if it were your lover."

"No," Tori said. "That's not true."

"But it is," Koi said. "I feel the fire of rage in you. It's easy to identify something that is so familiar to me."

"We're women," Tori said. "We should do whatever we can to find alternatives to violence."

"Why?"

"Because fire without the requisite water to put it out occasionally is madness," Tori said, beginning to work the enigma out for herself. It had not been Tok Murashito who had been the enigma; it was herself. "Nature cannot long tolerate something that is so out of balance. Yin without yang will not long survive."

Koi said, "Then I will be a star, burning bright in the blackness before winking out."

"Is that what you want for yourself?" Tori asked. "Death?"

"In a world without honor, death is the only honorable solution."

"No. You're wrong. Bringing water to the fire is the preferable alternative."

"Banking the fire is impossible for me."

"For people like us, nothing is impossible," Tori said.

Koi put her hand on Tori. "You cannot even bring the water to your own fire, how can you counsel me to do it?"

Tori said, "In life, only failure breeds success. If, in the past, I have tried and failed, it does not mean that I will stop trying."

"And making the same mistakes over and over."

"No." Tori struggled now to sit up, but Koi's powerful hand prevented her. "The circle of defeat must be broken. I cannot tell you how to make yourself better. Too many people in your life have already done that, and look at the result."

"I cannot be better," Koi said. "I am *hinoeuma*. I am doomed."

"Superstitious nonsense. You're no different than I am, except that you've been totally cut off from people. You've had too many mentors, and no one to trust. It's so terrible to be disconnected. Life seems so desolate, you begin to survive only on desperation. But all you're doing is feeding on yourself." Tori's eyes caught Koi's. "If you trust me, I can help you. Perhaps we can even help each other."

"Impossible," Koi said, tightening her hold on Tori. "I must avenge Big Ezoe's death. *Giri.* I must kill you."

"Then," Tori said, "you truly are doomed." Her eyes had not left Koi's. Koi did nothing.

The two women, locked in a silent duel, heard the noise at the same moment.

"It's Big Ezoe's assassin. Kill her!"

Tori recognized Hitasura's voice, saw, at the same moment, Russell step into the room, aim a gun at the back of Koi's head.

"Shoot me," Koi said calmly. "Before I die I will take Tori Nunn with me."

Into the ringing silence Tori said sharply, "Back off!" She risked a glance at the men in the open doorway. "I mean it, Russ! Back off and take Hitasura with you!"

"She's a killer, Tori," Russell said. "She came here to kill you, for Christ's sake. She's got to go."

"I'm sick of you men and your solutions to problems!" Tori cursed in Japanese. "Get the hell out now!"

Russell dropped his arm. "Tori . . ." Tori said nothing. The men withdrew.

"Why did you do that?" Koi said.

"Because this has nothing to do with them. This is between us."

"I think they found the right spot, they could have killed me before I had a chance to get to you."

"Perhaps."

"Yet you insisted they back off." She shook her head. "Why?"

"I told you before. It's a matter of trust."

"I could kill you now."

"I know."

"It's what Big Ezoe wanted me to do."

Tori said, "What the hell is Big Ezoe to you?"

For a moment Koi did nothing. Then she began to laugh. She laughed and laughed, collapsing on the bed beside Tori, holding her sides, gasping, tears streaming down her face.

Then, abruptly, she was weeping bitter tears, tears pent up for years, tears of rage and self-loathing, and she put her head in the crook of Tori's shoulder while Tori stroked her hair as she would a frightened child.

"It's going to be all right," Tori whispered.

But Koi shook her head. "No," she gasped through her sobbing. "It won't. I don't think I'm capable of trusting anyone."

"But you're already trying, aren't you?"

Koi nodded her head yes.

"Then," Tori told her, "if it won't be all right, at least it will be better."

"I feel all right."

"You look like death warmed over."

"My, what a charmer you are."

Tori and Russell sat facing each other in the room where Tori had awakened to find Koi standing over her. However, now, thirty-six hours later, the bed was empty. Tori was dressed, had eaten two normal meals.

"Just trying to make a point," Russell said.

"Which is?"

"You're not a being from the planet Krypton."

Tori groaned. "Don't worry. I don't think I could leap over a fireplug, let alone a tall building. But we've still got work to do. Now where's Koi? Have you kept her and Hitasura apart as I asked you to do?"

"Yes, though this is his turf, so it wasn't all that easy. But, I must say, your poisoning has unnerved him."

"Is that so?" Tori said. "We'll see about that."

"What did you and Koi talk about? You and she were up here for hours."

"I need to do a couple of things before I tell you," Tori said.

"First off, I need a hookup to the computers at Mall Central. Can you fix that up?"

"No problem. I'll go make the call now. We've rented out space in the Sumitomo Building for about a year now."

"Good. Then, I'm going to want to interview Hitasura. That's long overdue."

"You bet it is," Russell said. "I have some questions to put to him."

"No. Trust me on this, Russ. I've got to do this alone."

But Russell was already shaking his head. "No way. For one thing, you've just got off a sickbed—"

"Want to arm wrestle?"

"For another, this is a situation of totally unknown consequences. I can't take such a risk with your life."

"Don't worry," Tori said. "Whatever happens, Hitasura won't kill me."

"I don't know that," Russell said firmly, "and despite what you tell me, I can't believe you do, either. No. If you speak to Hitasura at all, it'll be with me in the same room."

"Be realistic, Russ. Hitasura won't talk to you."

"Well, one way or another, you're going to have help when you meet with him."

But Tori wasn't listening. "Christ," she continued, "if he's involved in cocaine smuggling, he might not even talk to me."

"But he's got to," Russell said. "He owes you, doesn't he?"

Tori gave him a small smile. "If only it were that simple." She shook her head. "No matter what *giri* Hitasura feels toward me, I am still *gaijin*, an outsider. That fact outweighs everything else, even *giri*, because to a Japanese a *gaijin* might speak of *giri*, but it is impossible to believe that he will live by it. That gives *him* the leeway to speak of *giri* to me, without actually meaning it."

"Christ. If he feels he owes you nothing, how will you get him to admit to his involvement, let alone tell you what's going on?"

"Right now, I haven't the faintest idea," Tori said.

Russell sat on the bed, took her in his arms. "You scared the hell out of me, you know."

"Russ, you're losing your director's perspective."

"Fuck being a director. I'm a field executive now."

She smiled. "You've been demoted."

"Is that how you see it? I don't. I've gotten a sense of the Mall that I never had before. It seems that the higher you get in

408

any hierarchy, the less you know about the nuts and bolts of running it." He leaned forward. "That's because you have to turn off and disconnect yourself from one set of alliances in order to plug yourself into the political sockets needed to keep the jackals on Capitol Hill at bay."

"Dangerous stuff."

Russell nodded. "But a month ago I would have wasted my time and yours by shouting you down. Being out here in the field has allowed me to finally see the danger in what I and Bernard do. We get more and more insulated, devising policies—theoretical canvasses which we then order you to color with your blood. I'm beginning to understand that Bernard and I have lost all perspective. Politics and life are often wildly out of sync, that's what being out here in the wild has taught me."

Tori kissed him lightly. "We all have expectations of things: people, events, situations, you name it, but the reality is so often different. You know, there was a story Bernard told me about when he was younger."

"You mean when he supposedly went to Chicago to look up his long-lost dad, and Dad turned out to be a sonuvabitch after all?"

Tori stared at Russell. "He told you, too."

Here we go, Russell thought. I'm never going to get a better shot at this. "Tori, Bernard loves to tell that story, but it's bullshit, pure and simple. He tried it on me, only I had done my homework. I knew he came from bluebloods in Virginia. His father was a wealthy and successful attorney, founding a dynastic law office. Until his death some years ago, he had been happily married to his wife—Bernard's mother—for more than fifty years."

"But that story . . ."

He could feel her drawing away from him, a familiar coldness coming into her, but still he persisted; it was time for her to know the truth. "Bernard thinks it makes him seem more human. He tells it to people like you to help bind them to him."

"Oh, come on," Tori said. "Bernard's not that cynical."

"He doesn't think of himself that way," Russell said. "According to Bernard, business is conducted in any manner that gets the job done."

"I don't believe you," Tori said.

"Then you certainly won't believe that before I left with you on this assignment Bernard told me what to do to you if your undisciplined methodology got in the way." Russell rose. "He told me to terminate you."

It was dusk by the time Tori returned from the Mall offices at the Sumitomo Building in Shinjuku. By that time it had begun to rain, fine silver needles spraying the sidewalks, streets, and car tops, smearing the city grit across windshields. Gray water dripped from building facades. The sidewalks were a sea of umbrellas. Neon had taken over from daylight.

Russell had remained at the office to transmit a progress report and clear up the mountain of paperwork that accumulated during a transcontinental trip.

Tori was shaken by her foray into the Mall Central computers. Her suspicions had been made all too real. The travel information contained there confirmed everything that Koi had told her about the coalition between the industrialist Kunio Michita, Fumida Ten, chairman of Kaga, and Tori's friend, Hitasura, with Estilo acting as willing middleman supplier.

Koi's repeated mention of the mysterious American "who didn't have the appearance of a businessman" had set off warning bells in Tori's mind. Now she recalled her and Russell's puzzlement over why Estilo would give them information that seemed detrimental to him. In revealing his involvement, he had not only implicated himself—thus risking a termination of what must be a lucrative business deal to supply the decidedly odd Michita-Ten-Hitasura coalition with illegal hafnium—but he also had pointed them toward the one person in Japan who could help them further: Hitasura. Why?

Now it seemed clear: he had been warning Tori. If Estilo had betrayed their friendship, he had more than made up for it by what he had done. Tori thought now that she owed Estilo an enormous apology. He could have told her outright what was happening, but he knew that she would not be able to bring herself to believe him. He knew that she had to be led step by step toward the inevitable conclusion.

The information in the Mall Central computer confirmed that on the dates that the Kaga-Michita negotiations were commencing, Bernard Godwin had been out of the country. But there was some other reason why these dates seemed familiar. Tori racked her brain, but could not think of where she had come across them before.

Giving it up for the moment, she returned to the most immediate problem: where had Bernard Godwin gone? A search through the travel facilities of the Mall revealed that he had not used the company's services to book his flights.

Linking up to the American airlines computers had been more enlightening. A week before the Kaga-Michita negotiations had begun in earnest, Bernard Godwin had bought a first-class ticket to San Francisco. He was there just overnight. The next day he was on a flight to Tokyo. His return to the States was three weeks later.

Tori did not believe in coincidences. Bernard Godwin was the American who had instigated Michita's inquiry into the new Kaga process that had led to the forming of the coalition.

Bernard Godwin!

But that was patently impossible. For one thing, Tori could not believe that a man like Bernard would ever involve himself with cocaine trafficking. For another, even if the impossible had occurred, Godwin—along with Russell—had had a hand in bringing her back in order to track down the source of the lethal supercocaine. Recalling Bernard's outraged face as Russell described the effects of the new drug, Tori was more certain than ever that he had nothing to do with that part of it.

And yet Hitasura was an integral part of the coalition that Bernard must have put together so that he could supply these new nuclear weapons—whatever they were—to his precious nationalist movement in the Soviet Union. And Estilo had said that the untreated coke was being bought by Hitasura.

It's still not making sense. What am I missing? Tori asked herself.

There was only one path to take, and it led right through Hitasura.

Hitasura's tea-colored melanin birthmark, which ran up the left side of his jaw onto his cheek, seemed darker on this dark twilit day. The pachinko parlor in the Ginza was vast, as large as a castle. It was one of many owned by Hitasura's Yakuza family. The weekly amount of money Hitasura took in from just these betting game parlors, Tori knew, was astronomical.

Lights flashed on the rows of vertical game boards as steel balls whizzed through the maze of the pachinko. Men and women—especially women—stood enwrapped, playing game after game. The hardened veterans were sure to stake out one of the game machines that had a tiny color TV screen set in the middle of the game field so that they would not miss their favorite soap operas while they lost their money.

Hitasura sat in a glassed-in booth two floors above the action. The entire back wall of the booth was a bank of TV monitors which scanned the aisles and rows of players, making sure the house odds were not being tampered with.

"We got a kid in here last month," Hitasura said as Tori put down her dripping umbrella, came to sit beside him on a plain metal and green vinyl office chair. "You should have seen him, the sonuvabitch was some whiz. He had made a tiny electronic gadget that zapped the pachinko machine's circuits. He won every other time he played. Then he got carried away with himself and began to win every game. That was too much, don't you think?"

Tori said nothing. She ignored the TV monitors reproducing the frantic play going on below her. She had changed clothes at the Mall offices in Shinjuku. She wore a pair of tapered chocolate-colored leather pants, a man-tailored cream cotton blouse under a waist-length fawn-colored quilted rain jacket.

"How are you?" Hitasura inquired. He was wearing an expensive but ill-fitting sharkskin suit that was still rain-stained. "When we got to you in the tunnels and Mr. Slade told me you had been poisoned, I moved heaven and earth to make sure you wouldn't die."

"Deke's dead," Tori said. "Yen Yasuwara is maimed."

Hitasura rocked a little in his chair, as if he had developed a Western manner of mourning. "I am sorry you learned about Deke's death in this way," he said. "I had wanted to be the one who told you."

"Under the circumstances," Tori said carefully, "I agree that would have been proper." She noticed that he had not acknowledged in any way her reference to Yen.

Hitasura looked at her. "Perhaps you should speak to your newfound friend, the assassin who calls herself Koi. She killed Deke."

Tori said, "I have talked to her."

Hitasura turned his head away. His gaze was flicking from screen to screen on the wall of monitors. Suddenly Tori saw him start. "She's here," he said.

Tori looked at the screen that held his attention. It showed Koi making her way down one of the aisles on the floor below.

"What is she doing here?"

"I asked her to come," Tori said.

"You?" Hitasura's head swung around.

412

Tori watched him. "It's time to settle our accounts, to honor old debts."

Hitasura's face was now devoid of all emotion. It was as if his eyes had slid behind a veil. He reached behind him, produced a pistol from a holster strapped to the small of his back. He balanced the pistol on his right kneecap.

"Is that necessary?"

"When old friends reveal themselves as enemies," Hitasura said, "all precautions must be taken."

"What makes you think I've become your enemy?"

Hitasura gestured with his chin. "You bring Big Ezoe's assassin here to my ground, you have become friends with a monster who would murder you where you lay helpless in my bed. *My* bed! What else am I to think?"

"I don't know," Tori said. "I'm not the one whose conscience lies heavy."

Hitasura made a dismissing sound between his teeth.

Tori watched Koi as she passed from monitor to monitor, as she moved toward the metal staircase to the booth. Tori said, "As long as you brought up the notion, tell me, what kind of monster is it who concocts a new kind of cocaine so powerful its effects destroy the human mind and body in months?"

Hitasura sat very still, and with an icy crawling in the pit of her stomach, Tori had her answer. Estilo had not lied. Hitasura was the man.

Hitasura said, "If she begins to climb the stairs to this office, I'll order her shot, I promise you."

"And then you'll shoot me, and all your problems will be solved." Tori shook her head. "But, no. There's Russ to think of. What will you do about him, Hitasura? Kill him as well? What good will that do you? There will only be more people from the Mall come to avenge his death—and mine. You can't win this time."

Hitasura allowed himself a tiny smile. "Is that how you see the situation? Well, good. Then I have nothing at all to fear." Now a laugh leaked out of his mouth, quickly stifled, as if it had popped out unexpectedly. Hitasura wiped the smirk from his face. "Pardon me for laughing at you, but I could not help myself. You are so far off the mark, you have added a moment of unexpected amusement to an otherwise serious discussion."

"What's struck you so funny?" She had not wanted to give him the satisfaction of asking, but she, too, could not help herself.

"Mmm. I suppose you could not have forgotten Tom Royce. No, I see by the expression on your face, you have not. Then there is Tok Murashito. I know you remember him. What an interview you had with him, you the avenging angel out to nail him for killing that idiot Royce."

Tori was astonished. "How do you know about my meeting with Murashito?"

"Well, it wasn't from you, was it?" Hitasura cocked his head. "Figure it out for yourself. Having trouble? Okay, I'll go on. Murashito killed Royce, all right, but he didn't do it because Royce had raped his daughter. The funny thing is that I think Tom Royce was fully capable of rape, but Murashito was far too clever to allow his daughter anywhere near Royce.

"No, Murashito killed Royce because he was ordered to. By whom? you are about to ask. Why, by Bernard Godwin. Royce had begun his own investigation into Godwin's involvement here in Japan, and the deeper he got, it seems the less he liked what he saw. That's why he angled to take the assignment to come to Japan to brief you. Godwin let him come; until that moment, he had not been sure that Royce was the one doing the burrowing behind his back. Once he was sure, Royce's fate was sealed. He was a dead man. So you can see how empty a threat you've just made. No one from the Mall will come to avenge your death— or that of Mr. Slade. There will no doubt be an investigation, but Bernard will handle it himself. The circumstances dictate it, after all." Another laugh was squeezed out of him, and Tori shivered.

Hitasura cocked his head again, responding to the dumbfounded look on Tori's face. "Are you shocked? Perhaps I've gone too fast and you're not following me. Shall I slow down?"

All she could think of was Bernard Godwin: how he had manipulated everyone around him, including her. She had thought of him as a surrogate father, when all along he had been using her. She heard Russell's voice, *Bernard told me what to do to you if your undisciplined methodology got in the way. He told me to terminate you.* How right Russell had been about him.

"Go on," she said, concentrating now on the present. "I assume, then, that you've been working for the Mall for years."

"Oh, no. Not the Mall. For Bernard Godwin himself." Hitasura permitted himself another small smile, as if he were a dieter doling himself sweets. "Working with individuals, I've found, is far more rewarding than being part of a machine. I

414

think you understand that well, Tori-san." He shook his head. "I must admit I never understood your consenting to come back to them. Why did you do that?"

"Because," Tori said, "I had nothing else."

Hitasura pursed his lips. "Poor girl. If I had known—"

"Forget it. I wouldn't have been interested." She put her head in her hands. "How could I have been so wrong about Bernard. He's trafficking in that supercoke, after all."

"Are you kidding?" Hitasura said. "He'd try to skin me alive if he knew what I was up to."

Tori raised her head, staring at him. She had the sensation of her heartbeat being slow and painfully heavy, as if her heart was being set in cement. "What are you saying?"

"In some important matters, Bernard is slightly behind the times. I attribute it to his essentially altruistic nature. I find that odd in a man who must, in his chosen profession, be so profoundly pragmatic. But there you are. People are often far more complex than you ever give them credit for being."

"You were supplementing what he was paying you, is that it?"

Hitasura nodded. "Essentially, yes. Bernard's an excellent business partner in some respects, but in others he's sorely lacking. His obsession to free the Soviets from their Russian masters has blinded him to many things, including my method of getting the hafnium into Japan. He didn't ask, and I didn't tell. He was too busy making sure those teeny-tiny hafnium-controlled reactor cores were being fitted inside some kind of prototype nuclear devices."

"My God." Our worst nightmare has come true, Tori thought.

But either Hitasura didn't get it, or he didn't care. He laughed. "It was rather neat, I thought, using Bernard's altruism to make me rich. Until you came back, nosing around. What a pest you've become, Tori-san. Such a disappointment, especially in a friend."

Tori was appalled. Her head was throbbing, and she felt as if she had been struck in the stomach, but she knew she had to press on, get all the poison out at once in order for some sense of healing to begin. "And Ariel Solares?"

"Oh, him." This discussion appeared on the verge of boring Hitasura. "He was like Royce, nosing around, getting suspicious of what might be happening under his nose, behind closed

415

doors. He had become a liability to Bernard—and to me. I had him killed.''

With her heart in her throat, Tori said, "Did Bernard order Ariel's murder?''

Hitasura laughed. "God, no. Bernard hadn't the stomach for it. We discussed it, of course. But he was too afraid of Solares's friendship with Estilo. But I knew better. I knew that Solares had got further in his investigation of us than Bernard suspected. I did what had to be done for the good of all of us.''

Tori slumped in her chair. There was a feeling of desolation inside her, the same terrible sensation one got when one squeezed the life out of another human being. Every time it happened, she felt somehow diminished, as if a piece of her soul were being chipped away, falling into a fathomless blackness from which it could never be retrieved.

Now she saw another reason had prompted Estilo to warn her. It was not only a question of friendship, of his caring about her. It was also revenge. Tori remembered the eerie story Estilo had told her about the German twins in Buenos Aires who had been so cruel to him, and how he had waited to gain his revenge on them by turning their love and trust in each other into fear and hate. Estilo lived by his own unique brand of justice. Not for him the bullet in the back of the head, that was too quick. His definition of revenge was dominated by the verb "to suffer.''

It seemed clear now that Ariel had told Estilo of his suspicions about Bernard, and when Ariel was murdered, it was natural for Estilo to think that Bernard had ordered the hit in order to protect himself.

This was to be Estilo's revenge: he wanted her to find out everything so she could bring Bernard down for him.

With an effort of will, Tori brought herself back to the present. "You were Bernard's eyes and ears inside Kaga, weren't you?''

Hitasura nodded. "My people are very highly placed in many useful industries. We may not control them yet, but we certainly can manipulate them when there is a need.''

"And me? Why did Bernard seek me out all those years ago? If he had you and Murashito, what did he need me for?''

"That I can't say for certain," Hitasura admitted, "though knowing Bernard as I do, I suspect he wanted someone to keep an eye on me.''

"I guess I didn't do such a hot job.''

"I don't know about that. You know what I'm doing, and Bernard doesn't."

Tori said, "Tell me something. What would have happened to me if I hadn't bought Murashito's bullshit about Royce raping his daughter? What if I had gone ahead and killed him?"

Hitasura shrugged. "Nothing, I'm quite certain. By exposing Murashito, you effectively killed him, anyway. He became useless to Bernard."

"So you two had to find someone to take his place," Tori said. "Enter Kunio Michita."

"That's right. In fact, you did us a favor. Kunio Michita's far more venal than Murashito ever was. He's more powerful, too."

"God, what a fool I've been."

"In America," Hitasura said, "history shows that your countrymen make heroes of fools." His hand slid around the grip of his pistol. He lifted it, aiming it at Tori's chest. "It's a pity you'll never see America again."

Tori stood up, and she felt his tension soar.

"Don't," he said, tracking her with the muzzle of the pistol.

"Why not do what I want," Tori said, "if you're going to shoot me all the same?"

"I don't want to kill you," Hitasura said. "Not really."

Tori shook her head. "Too late for remorse."

"Not remorse. Regret. You were a good friend, while it lasted."

"While it suited you, you mean."

Hitasura shrugged. "I have no interest in semantics."

"I've no doubt," Tori said. "You can't make a profit on it."

"It's exceedingly odd," Hitasura said with some admiration, "but in many ways you are not at all *gaijin*—not at all the foreigner." He shrugged. "I suppose there are still some things in the world I do not understand."

"I would like to know one thing," Tori said. "Who are you sending the nuclear units to? Who is Bernard's contact inside Russia?"

"A last request," Hitasura said, then shrugged. "Why not? Who are you going to tell?" He laughed. "Bernard's befriended a man named Valeri Denysovich Bondasenko. The man's a Ukrainian; he's spent his entire career, it seems, suppressing minorities for the Kremlin while secretly working for their unification. Sounds like my kind of guy, but I don't know. From what Bernard says, Bondasenko genuinely hates the Russians, but then again he could be KGB. It's happened before, I understand. I don't personally trust any of these Russians. Far too inscrutable. What is it they want, anyway? To bury the West or to make money from it? It's tough to put your trust in a schizophrenic, but apparently that's just what Bernard's done.

"And now God help him, because we just got an emergency coded cable: something's happened in Moscow, and the situation is rapidly getting out of hand. Bondasenko's White Star organization has sprung a serious leak. Knowing that, I've washed my hands of Bernard as quick as you can slide a clam down your throat. There's a dead drop we use at the Hotel Rossiya in Moscow, addressed to a Mrs. Kubysheva. I wouldn't use it now if you paid me fifty million yen. I don't need any of the complications that inevitably come from trying to be a saint. In this day and age, a saint is synonymous with a sucker."

Hitasura looked at her. "Is that it for your last request? Can we get on with it?"

"Yes," Tori said.

Hitasura pulled the trigger. The explosion was loud in the booth, but amid the sound and vision of pachinko, no one noticed. Besides, the booth's glass panels were both bullet- and soundproof.

Tori was slammed back against the glass, a hole torn in her jacket just over her heart. She collapsed, and Hitasura was across the booth in one stride. He stood over her, much as he had stood over Big Ezoe in the corridor of the Kaijin tea house in Shimbashi.

He kicked Tori's thigh with the toe of his shoe, but there was no sign of movement. He squatted, put the muzzle of his pistol against her forehead in preparation for the shot that would make certain she was dead.

At that moment Koi tore open the door to the glassed-in booth. Hitasura, hearing her, swung the pistol in an arc toward her.

And in that instant of hesitation, Tori's right hand blurred upward, her hardened heel smashing into the base of his nose with such force it drove the cartilage in one piece back through his sinuses, into his brain cavity.

Hitasura's expression was one of dismay. It was frozen on his face as his upper torso tumbled backward. His head hit against the leg of one of the chairs, but he was past caring.

Koi came over to where Tori sat with her back against the glass panel. Koi stared down into Hitasura's face, then she knelt beside Tori.

"Are you all right?"

418

"He's dead, isn't he?" Tori's voice seemed far away.

"Yes."

"Another part of me gone." Tori closed her eyes. Her heart was pounding furiously, and no amount of *prana* would slow it. "I didn't want to hurt him. I never came to hate him." Then she looked up into Koi's face. "This killing must stop."

Koi nodded, reached over, picked Tori up. She put her hand beneath Tori's jacket, her blouse. "Wearing this Kevlar vest was a risk," she said. "What if he'd aimed his first shot for your head?"

Tori said, as they stepped over Hitasura's body, "Then that would have been me lying there. It would be all over."

Tori's knees buckled, and Koi caught her.

"Now you must repay me for helping you," Koi said. "There is something I must do, and I fear I cannot do it alone."

Sengakuji. The resting place of history's revered heroes, the splendid forty-seven ronin. The place where Kakuei Sakata had purified his spirit, where he had regained his honor by committing *seppuku*, ritual suicide.

In-ibuki, Koi's soft abdominal breathing, changed to *yo-ibuki*, the hard, aggressive breathing of battle and stress. Wordlessly, she pressed the translations of Sakata's ledgers into Tori's hands, then knelt on the carpet of grass.

Among the gaily waving flowers her white garb stood out starkly. She hoped that this one spot of purity among the vibrant colors would remain in Tori's memory as it had in hers from the day of Sakata-san's death. She could still remember the wind whipping his loose white leggings, the glare of sunlight on his blade at the instant before he reversed it, plunging it into his lower belly.

Tori bent down, closed her hand over Koi's where it clasped the short killing sword. "Don't do this," she said urgently. "I beg you to reconsider. There are alternatives."

"For you, perhaps," Koi said, "but not for me. I see now that I have trod too long and too heavily down one path."

"But you have a friend now," Tori said. "Your life is already changing."

But Koi was already shaking her head. "An illusion. A pleasant one, I've no doubt you think, but also a treacherous one, for no matter how much I may fight against the violence inside me, it will overtake me. If not today, then tomorrow or the day after. My spirit is unclean. It longs to be purified."

419

She turned her head toward Tori, and Tori could see the tears in her eyes.

"Oh, my dear," Tori whispered.

The tears ran. "It's not me I think of now, but others I no longer wish to harm. You."

With that, Koi plunged the blade to the hilt into herself.

"Koi!"

Koi's lips rounded and a tiny "Oh!" escaped her bloodless lips. She drew her elbows in. Her whole body was shaking. With an effort that Tori found unimaginable, she dragged the buried blade from left to right, cutting herself open.

The stench was appalling. Steam came from her, like a mist over spectral fields. She slumped over the buried blade, her bloodied, white-knuckled fists. Blood crawled down her thighs, soaking into the grass.

"It grows dark," Koi whispered. "Don't go."

"I'm here," Tori said. Despair and helplessness mingled inside her. In her mouth was the nauseating taste of fresh blood.

"It grows darker still. But the mountains . . . the mountains are alive . . . with light."

Death came to Koi like a cloud obscuring the moon, a film covering her staring eyes, seeing their mysterious mountains, alive with a light only she could see.

It took a long time to fill Russell in, but after what had happened in the pachinko parlor, it was no longer in Tori's interest to remain in Tokyo, so Tori locked herself in with him in the main cabin of their 727 and, as the jet took off, went over everything she had been told and had discovered a step at a time.

She told him about the coalition of Michita, Yen, and Hitasura that Bernard had created. She told him about Hitasura having Ariel Solares murdered because Ariel, like Tom Royce before him, had begun his own investigation of the clandestine affairs within the clandestine affairs of Mall Central. She even detailed her own unwitting role in playing watchdog to Hitasura and in helping Bernard come up with Kunio Michita, a far better and more powerful business partner than Tok Murashito had been.

It was good for her to have to explain everything to someone else. She had had so many shocks in so short a time, she needed to talk about these things out loud in order to make sense of them. Still, it surprised her how calmly Russell took the revelations.

420

"You were right on target with Bernard," Tori said. "It tears me apart to think how he used both of us. How I hate him now."

Russell was quiet for some time. Then he said, "I wish you could learn to respond with your brain and not with your heart. This is a time to consider objectively what has happened." He sat forward. "Think, Tori. Bernard put together this bizarre coalition of Michita, Yen, and Hitasura for a reason. He saw what no one else did: an unprecedented opportunity to seize what appears to be the ultimate chance to free the minority peoples of the Soviet Union."

Tori's face was pale. "I never suspected a thing. My God, all along Bernard never retired from the Mall. He had his own agenda hidden away from even you, the director he appointed in his place."

"You're quite right," Russell said. "Hidden agendas are Bernard's stock-in-trade."

Tori stared at him. "How long have you known?"

Russell gave her a thin smile. "Not long enough."

"I can't wait to bury the bastard!"

"Tori, it's no good hating Bernard. He is what he is, a man totally obsessed with freeing enslaved peoples."

"I wish there was some way I could help the nationalist movement inside Russia," Tori said. "It's Bernard's methods I disagree with, not his goals."

"So often said." Russell kept her close. "But it just goes to prove that Bernard's as human as the next person. He's made mistakes—grave ones, like allowing Hitasura to run his own supercoke smuggling operation under Mall auspices."

Tori turned away, looked out at the clouds streaming by below them.

"Russ, how can you defend him after what he's done to us? He took our trust and our love, and in return manipulated us."

"I'll tell you something," Russell said. "Bernard is a master of using all the resources available to him. At first, that's what I thought he was doing here. But now I'm not so sure. You see, he made a point of telling me how angry he was not only that Ariel Solares was murdered, but that it was done with such a bang we heard it all the way back in Virginia. He said they wanted to embarrass us, that there could only be one response to that." Russell made sure she was listening. "But Bernard knew all along who had ordered Ariel's death: Hitasura. 'Go for the jugular,' Bernard said. Jesus, he wasn't kidding. He made sure that every step of the way it was my idea to bring you back, but I could see how he planted that idea, how he manipulated conversations so that I would take that extra step to ensure that, one way or another, you'd come back to the Mall. I didn't know why then, but I do now: he knew that you were the only one who could take care of your old friend Hitasura for him.''

"Go on."

"But Bernard also must have known that for you to get close enough to Hitasura to terminate him, you'd have to have learned enough to implicate him—Bernard. So you were a two-edged sword, Tori. On the one hand, you were the only agent skilled enough to bring Hitasura down. On the other, you would come away knowing enough to send Bernard away for a very long time.''

"That's why Bernard ordered you to terminate me!"

Russell shook his head. "You're still not thinking clearly. I said Bernard *told* me to terminate you under certain circumstances. He didn't order me to do it, and further, he knew that I couldn't possibly hurt you. You see, Bernard—who knows everyone's weak spots—knew before I did that I was in love with you.''

Tori said nothing for a time. At last she put her head into her hands. "I can't think. There's too much—''

"This is your time in the corrida, Tori." And when she lifted her head to look at him, Russell said, "The bull is so close upon you you can feel his hot breath.''

"Yes," she said. "Yes."

Russell took her hands in his. "This is the time when you must think for yourself. Think not as Bernard wants you to do, but for yourself.''

She knew he was right in everything he said. And yet a stubborn, obtuse part of her was still committed to hating Bernard Godwin for his betrayal of her trust.

She said, "Whether he asked you, told you, or ordered you to terminate me, makes no difference. Bernard still wanted me dead in order to protect himself.''

"No, Tori." Russell caught her gaze with his own. "If Bernard wanted you terminated, he certainly wouldn't have asked me to do it. I'm a desk jockey, remember? And he knew I was personally involved with you. I'd be just about the last person he'd contract with to make the hit.''

"That makes sense," Tori said. "Then why did he tell you to terminate me?''

"Well, I've been thinking about that," Russell said. "What

he said was so wildly out of character that it was as if he was trying to tell me something. It took me a while to figure out the puzzle Bernard had set out for me, but I think I have it now. It was as if Bernard was saying to me, I've given you this picture, what's wrong with it?

"He knew that Hitasura had turned bad on him—Hitasura's murder of Ariel Solares was a major break in discipline. Bernard may not have known that Hitasura was behind the supercoke, but he sure as hell knew that he suddenly had a rogue agent on his hands—a rogue agent, I might add, who reported only to Bernard. Bernard knew he had to terminate Hitasura as quickly and as efficiently as possible.

"He knew he couldn't tell you openly about Hitasura because you wouldn't believe him, and he wouldn't have told me for fear I would tell you. That would have made you walk straight away from us. Bernard knew you needed to discover the truth about Hitasura for yourself, but he was warning me that things were not as they seemed in the hope that I would stay one step ahead of you. You see, Bernard was still concerned by your volatility. He set me up to be your watchdog just as, years ago, he set you up to be Hitasura's watchdog."

Tori gave an ironic laugh. "And now Bernard has given me the means to exact my revenge on him for manipulating me for so many years."

Russell nodded. "Now you understand that Bernard knew he was doing just that when he manipulated me into bringing you back to the Mall. It says something about the man that he trusts you—and me—with that power over him."

Tori thought about that for a long time, then she nodded. "I guess I still can't believe that I could have been so wrong about Hitasura. He used Bernard as Bernard was using us and everyone else around him. We have confirmation from Hitasura himself that Bernard never wanted Ariel murdered. And it's true that Bernard had no conscious knowledge of the supercocaine Hitasura was selling. It will just about kill him when he learns to what extent he's been involved in that."

Russell said nothing.

Tori exhaled slowly. "There is an Argentine saying: 'The devil can see at midnight, but revenge is blind even in the noonday sun.'"

Russell knew what she meant. She was moving away from the emotionally volatile adolescent filled with weaknesses that Bernard Godwin recognized and exploited. She was becoming

423

more whole and, therefore, more powerful with each breath she took. She had met her bull head on, and was riding it, facing herself at last, instead of turning away from herself to face death over and over.

"Look, we're not trying to excuse Bernard, are we?" Tori said at last.

"I think you'll have to make up your own mind about that," Russell said. "I'll only remind you of what you said just a few minutes ago. You told me that you wished there was some way for you to help the nationalist movement inside Russia. Bernard's shown you the way."

"You think we should help him?" Tori said. "Bernard's been selling nuclear devices of unknown and unproven design to White Star, a nationalist underground movement that might or might not be controlled by the KGB itself."

"You've just given the best reason I can think of for helping Bernard. Those miniature hafnium-damped nuclear devices could easily be the means to a revolution inside the USSR or the spark that ignites a world war.

"White Star has become the nexus point of this assignment. Either way, we have to penetrate White Star and find out whether Bernard has become a saint or a fool."

"Now there's a hell of an idea."

Russell pointed out the plane's Perspex window. "Welcome to hell, Tori," he said. "We've just crossed over into Soviet airspace."

TWELVE

MOSCOW/STAR TOWN

"We've lost him."

"Lost him?" Mars Volkov clenched his fists. "This man—this *traitor*—has killed four of my men. He has kidnapped a helpless psychotic from her bed in a state institution. And all you can tell me is that you lost him? How is that, Captain?"

Anatoly Nikolev, captain of the Eleventh Division of the KGB Border Guards, temporarily under the command of the chief of Department N, shifted uncomfortably on the hard wooden bench.

He and Mars were sitting in the otherwise empty stands of the baseball field at Moscow State University. They were watching the burgeoning national team work out. Beyond the stadium were the green-tiered Lenin Hills, where the vast Mosfilms sound stages and some of the city's finest old villas—Mars had one—were gradually being surrounded by squat modern-style multiple residences.

In the opposite direction was the stolid, ugly facade of the university dormitory and student facilities building, one of the many constant reminders in Moscow of Stalin's indelible influence on this stolid society.

Captain Nikolev looked resplendent in his gray uniform with

the red accents. There were medals on his chest, but he knew from experience that Mars Volkov was not impressed by past accomplishments. The man lived entirely in the present.

Captain Nikolev loved this place, especially a beautiful spot not a hundred yards from here where, on a promontory overlooking the river, it was said that Napoleon gazed down upon Moscow on September 14, 1812, before marching into the city.

"I can never come here," Mars said, interrupting Captain Nikolev's thoughts, "without thinking of Nikolai Ivanovich Lobachevsky. Now there was a great man. I see his bust in front of the university and I feel a great pride in being Russian."

Of course, Captain Nikolev thought with some cynicism. I come to the Lenin Hills and am filled with history. What fills Comrade Volkov? Rhapsodic thoughts of a non-Euclidian geometrist.

Mars said, "I understand that the last tank units have been drawn up. Which means we're ready to cross the mythical borders into Lithuania and Latvia."

"True enough," Captain Nikolev said. "It's a daring plan, but one which is also timeworn. It worked in Poland decades ago, so it should work now."

"Have you reservations, Captain?"

"I am not a military tactician," Nikolev said neutrally, "so I have no worthwhile opinion on such matters."

Mars regarded him with some surprise. "Yet you are a military man. Such action should set your blood on fire."

Nikolev grunted. "I think the time is long past for the heyday of the military man."

"I know," Mars said with some amusement. "A commission as an officer in the Roman legion would have suited you more."

Captain Nikolev watched the baseball players at their strenuous calisthenics, and thought glumly that the military should adopt such daily exercises.

"We lost Bondasenko's White Star contact at the institution in Arkhangelskoe, as well," he said when he felt he could no longer prolong the inevitable. "It was our ill fortune to have Bondasenko show up just as we were about to get the man. Apparently, Bondasenko was using the institution where he had so successfully hidden his daughter as

426

a meet to exchange intelligence with other members of White Star.''

"Very clever," Mars said. "I must remember to commend him before I put a bullet through the back of his head.''

Captain Nikolev said, "I think we can assume that Bondasenko is White Star's commander. We have gained that information, at least. It's not an inconsiderable bit of intelligence.''

Mars grunted his assent. "All right," he said now. "Bondasenko's gone to ground. But he can't stay hidden indefinitely. He's going to have to surface sometime, and, Captain, when he does, I want his head snapped in a rat trap. Is that clear?''

"Yes, comrade.''

Mars and Captain Nikolev lapsed into silence. They watched a pair of thin, chain-smoking professors from the university circulate among the young members of the national baseball team. They were not the coaches; the best coaches were still, to Mars's shame, mainly Cubans, who had many years of invaluable baseball experience. These chain-smoking professors were sports specialists in eye-hand coordination and musculature conditioning. They had determined that quickness of reflexes, not endurance, was the most desirable trait to breed into the new generation of ballplayers that the Soviet Union hoped would dominate world play in the 1990s.

But perhaps it would take longer to field a world-class team than had first been anticipated, since endurance was a trait already bred into the young Russians graduating from the extant state-funded sports academies. But Professor Kutateladze, who spoke eloquently and at length of the "technology of building a baseball player," had promised that the young men coming out of his baseball school would be different. Mars hoped he would be right. He always had been in the past.

Mars said, "Have you as yet located Miss Ponomareva?''
"No.''

Where has Irina got to? Mars asked himself. She was not at work or at home. She had not been at Valeri's and she wasn't with the Hero. Captain Nikolev had checked these places himself. Irina might continue to be very useful to me now, he thought. My surveillance has shown that she's been the closest to Valeri Denysovich over the past several months. If anyone might know where he was holed up, she might.

Well, Mars thought, stirring, perhaps it is time I took a more active role in finding out where she is.

It was very quiet when Mars entered the Hero's fortress in Star Town. He came across Tatiana first. She was folding the Hero's newly laundered shirts into a neat pile. The homey smells of soap and bleach were in the air.

"Comrade," she said when she saw him. Her wide-apart gray eyes were neutral. She did not stop her folding.

"Is he alone?" Mars asked brusquely.

"Lara is with him," Tatiana said. "You left orders that one of us should be with him at all times now."

"Yes," Mars said. "Of course."

He sat on a steel folding chair, watched her dispiritedly while she worked.

Tatiana cocked her head. "You look like you could use a drink, comrade," she said. "Can I bring you something?"

"Have you any pepper vodka?"

"I'll see." She went out of the room, returned in a moment with a pair of thick water tumblers and a bottle. She grinned, hoisting the bottle. "I didn't think a shot would be sufficient."

Mars drank the first slug of pepper vodka gratefully, felt his throat begin to burn, then his stomach. He held out his glass for a refill. "You know, Tatiana, I believe that the Hero has won."

"Won what, comrade?"

"Oh, our little battle of wits." Mars sipped. "I confess that he's still a complete enigma to me. Is he mad or sane? Did he make contact with an alien entity during the event or is he so enraged at what we've done to him that he's been pulling our leg all this time?"

"If you want my opinion—"

"Yes. Of course, I do."

"Well, then." She took a long gulp of her vodka, as if she needed fortification to go on. "I think the Hero *is* mad. Whatever happened to him up there in space has made him mad. But he's not insane in any way that we can understand. He's not, for instance, psychotic or schizophrenic, something our scientists can put their finger on. No. The Hero's different from you or me."

"Of course he is. He's—"

"No, you're not understanding me," Tatiana said. She looked down into the bottom of her glass.

"What are you saying? That he's no longer human? Don't be idiotic, Tatiana. I'm beginning to think that you and Lara have been too long with him."

"But that's just it," she said. "We know him better than anyone. And I'm telling you that even if his physiology is the same as yours or mine, his mind is not. It's been altered."

Mars watched her in silence for a long time. Why is it, he asked himself, that every time I come here I feel as if I've entered a whole new dimension? Has the Hero turned everyone around him mad, or is what Tatiana is telling me the truth?

Abruptly he stood up, put the glass aside. He'd had more than enough liquor. "I'd better go see him."

He left Tatiana as he had found her, carefully folding the Hero's shirts.

Upstairs in the pool room it was very still. Even the water seemed to have ceased its constant lapping. It was dark, and Mars groped in the gloom for the light switch.

"Comrade, don't turn it on." It was Lara's voice. "The Hero's eyes have become sensitive to light."

Mars fumbled his way toward the pool. "Have you informed the doctors?" Now that he was closer, he could see the slight phosphorescence of the saltwater.

"Yes, they've examined him extensively," Lara said. "They're baffled."

"Bah," Mars said with a dismissive gesture. "They're baffled by almost everything. What use are they? What use is anybody?" He squatted on the coping of the pool.

Lara swam up to him. He could see her dark eyes, her dark hair gleaming, plastered back against her skull. Her face was an almost perfect oval. Mars wondered why he had never noticed that before.

"Something's happening."

The way she said it, low, deep in her throat, made the short hairs at the back of Mars's neck stir. "What do you mean?"

"I mean that this sensitivity to light does not seem isolated, but rather part of an ongoing process."

"What nonsense," Mars scoffed. Then, looking at the expression on her face, he said, "Is it the cosmic radiation affecting him so quickly?"

"The doctors say no."

"What do they know? Nothing." But Mars felt a peculiar writhing in the pit of his stomach. He remembered Tatiana telling him that it was her belief that the Hero's mind was no longer human. *It's been altered.* He recognized the tiny flame of his fright flickering in the phosphorescent darkness. "Lara, what is happening?"

"I'm not sure, but I think he's in the early stages of some kind of change."

"You mean—"

"He's metamorphosing."

Mars worked his jaws for a moment until he was able to whisper, "Into what?"

But he was greeted only with silence.

"Where is he?" Mars said after a time.

"In the pool," Tatiana said. "Around the other side with Arbat."

"Stay here," Mars ordered her. He got up, made his way around to the other side of the pool.

"Odysseus?"

Mars heard his voice in echo. It resounded in the darkness that now seemed alive with a hidden pulsing—of life, but what form of life? Mars gave a tiny shudder, squared his shoulders, called to the Hero again.

"Here I am, comrade."

The lapping of the water, a small splash over the coping at Mars's feet.

Mars looked down, saw the pale, pale flesh of the Hero's face and shoulders. Was it his imagination or was the Hero's skin even more colorless than usual, more metallic looking—more alien.

At that moment Mars felt a hand clamp around his left ankle.

"You're too far away, comrade."

The grip on him tightened. "What are you doing?" Mars said.

"Why stand aloof at a distance?"

The Hero gave a mighty pull, and Mars lost his balance. His backside hit the coping with a painful smack. At the same time, he felt himself being dragged into the pool. He fought to resist, but it was as if his muscles were paralyzed, his body of no use at all.

The saltwater rose over him, and he felt the drag of the water on his clothes. He waved his arms, scissored his legs, but his shoes were weighing him down. The water closed over his face.

Then a fist grabbed his shirt and he was pulled upward. His head broke the surface of the pool and he spluttered. Saltwater ran down his face. His eyes cleared slowly. He was face to face with the Hero.

"It's a strange world," Odysseus said, "don't you agree, comrade?"

"Exceedingly strange." Mars was struggling with his fear. It had been bad enough when the Hero had scared him with the fake radium pellet he had thrown into the pool, now Mars was in here with the Hero himself—and what was the Hero becoming?

Odysseus guided him to the side of the pool. "Thank you for not turning on the lights."

Mars said, "You're welcome," then realized that this was the most civil exchange—brief though it was—that he and the Hero had ever had. He heard the small splashings beside him.

"I don't seem to need as much light as I used to in order to see." It was the Hero's voice, all right, Mars assured himself. But what was he saying? "Also, I see things I never saw before."

Mars opened his mouth to say, Like what? but no words would come out. He recognized, with a shudder, that part of him did not want to know. The same part of him that wanted to get out of here as fast as it could, and stay far away. With an act of will, Mars clamped down on that part, shoved it back into the shadows of his subconscious where it belonged.

"I can see underwater without opening my eyes." It didn't matter, he saw with a mounting horror he could not control, the Hero was going to tell him anyway. "Arbat says that I'm developing the kind of sonar that she has."

Mars forced himself to say, "All this sounds like so much fantasy, Odysseus." But there was no conviction in his voice. "Don't you think perhaps you're imagining these changes?"

"Just as I imagined the color between the stars?" His face was very close to Mars's. There was a sharp, distinct scent like cloves, but not cloves. "The color of God?" His eyes were like steel pellets, hard, highly reflective. "Perhaps this

431

is all a dream, eh, comrade? My training, the flight of the Odin-Galaktika II, the EVA, Menelaus's death, the event." He spread his hands. "All this. The building, the pool, Arbat. You.

"If I were a solipsist, Volkov, I tell you that's what I would believe. But my experiences have made me into something as far from a solipsist as possible. I am not alone. Man is not alone."

His voice, though soft, had the quality of a tolling bell, as if there were reverberations like sparks filling the space above the pool even after he had ceased to speak.

Mars had had enough of this. He needed to establish control of the interview, give it a certain rhythm, to turn it from a conversation into an interrogation. That would calm him, he was sure.

"I am afraid to say, Odysseus, that your days of uninterrupted information gathering have come to an end." Mars was watching the Hero's face for a sign of reaction. He thought of Natasha Mayakova's face when he had announced that he was taking her to the Lubyanka. Too bad he couldn't do the same with the Hero, but he could not afford a revolt from all the cosmonauts in Star Town. With the burgeoning breakdowns in farflung parts of the Soviet Union—the strikes, the pro-nationalist demonstrations, the acts of sabotage against government installations—he could not risk such a protest so close to home and from the symbols of Russian pride and superiority.

So it was to be no hard man for the Hero. Just Mars Volkov.

"You've been very clever, I'll admit," Mars said. "But I've been more clever. I have found the source of your illegal information."

"Is it your intention to isolate me, then?"

Damn him, Mars thought. I can discern nothing in his eyes. No emotion at all. "For a time," Mars said. "Punishment enough, I would think, for becoming involved in an illegal activity. And I assure you that I am being lenient, because I am ignoring entirely the charge of espionage that no doubt someone more rigid and zealous than I could level at you." He shook his head. "KGB files are off-limits to everyone other than ranking KGB personnel."

"Even members of the Kremlin, so I understand."

"We are not here to debate the fine points of Soviet policy!" Mars thundered. Seeing the look on the Hero's face, he immediately regretted his tone. He was ashamed that he had been led to lose his temper.

"It seems self-evident," Odysseus said blandly, "that far too often Soviet policy and KGB policy travel two separate paths."

"For the good of the state," Mars said stiffly. Another error.

"And the labor camps, as well. They exist for the good of the state."

Mars glared at the gleaming ashen face which he found so impenetrable. All right, he thought. Both barrels. "We have Natasha Mayakova, your courier."

"By 'have her,' I take it you mean you have put her under articulated interrogation."

"And we know her source," Mars pressed grimly on. "Valeri Denysovich Bondasenko. I'm afraid you're going to be information dry for some time to come."

"So that's how it's going to be."

"Yes."

"No more trying to be my kindly uncle, cajoling me out of the intelligence stored in my brain, pulling it from me like taffy, centimeter by centimeter."

"The traitor Comrade Bondasenko has caused the situation to change," Mars said. "It's clear that—"

He stopped, horrified. The Hero's expression had gone slack, his eyes had rolled up into his head, and his head lolled on his left shoulder.

At the same time, Mars felt a stirring against his legs, something cold and rough like a shark's skin scraped against his flesh where the purling water had lifted his trouser leg. He kicked reflexively as he turned this way and that to see where Arbat was. He saw her across the pool looking curiously—somewhat hostilely he thought—at him.

When he turned back, the Hero's eyes had cleared. He was looking directly at him. Mars said, "What the hell happened to you?"

The Hero opened his mouth, spewed out sounds that had no meaning.

Mars felt the small hairs at the back of his neck stir again. He thought of Lara saying, *He's metamorphosing*. And his own response, *Into what?*

"Odysseus," Mars said, "can you understand me?"

The Hero said nothing, and Mars called for Lara. In a moment she swam up. "Look at him," Mars commanded her. "A moment ago I asked him a question and he answered me in a nonsense language. Has he ever done that to you or Tatiana?''

"No," Lara said. She was staring curiously at the Hero. "He looks different somehow."

"Different?" The icy crawling had returned to the pit of Mars's stomach. "How do you mean?"

"His eyes," she said, swimming a bit closer.

Mars reached out, pulled her back beside him. "What about his eyes?" His fright had made him angry with himself, and he was impatient with her.

"I can see right through them."

"Impossible," Mars snapped. "A moment ago they were as opaque as ball bearings." But he peered into the Hero's face anyway. Had those eyes changed? In this low light he couldn't be certain unless he went closer. He wasn't going to do that.

He swam to the edge of the pool, hoisted himself out. Water sluiced from his sodden clothes, filled the spaces in his shoes. His tie was ruined. He rubbed at his leg where he had felt something mysterious scrape him.

"Lara," he said, "where is Irina Ponomareva?"

"I don't know, comrade." Lara was still staring into the Hero's face. "She left here some time ago."

"She had transportation?"

"I think she said she had a car."

Mars nodded. He had loaned her the car, so he knew where to find it. It had a homing device hidden in the innards of the engine. Perhaps when he found the car, he would also find Irina. He stood up. He thought it imperative that he do so as quickly as possible.

"I need some dry clothes," he said imperiously.

"Right away, comrade." Lara tore herself away from her contemplation of the Hero. She got out of the pool, went quickly across the room, disappeared into a cubicle.

Mars stared down at the still, floating figure of the Hero. He thought with a shiver of the thing that had brushed against him in the pool. What is happening to you? he asked silently. What are you becoming? He suspected that even the Hero did not know the answer to that.

At the end of Red Square one crosses the Moskva River via the Moskvoretsky Bridge. From there one is confronted by the illusion of choice, for it is no choice at all: two streets which,

434

though their paths immediately diverge, end up in precisely the same place: Dobryninskaya Square.

This is part of the great Sadovaya ring that girdles central Moscow, and here is known as the Zamoskvorechye, or the District Beyond the Moskva.

Centuries ago the Zamoskvorechye was the residential quarter not only for the czar's servants, but for the court artisans. Nowadays it is very different, like most of Moscow, having gone through a period of intense industrialization during the early part of the nineteenth century.

However, many delights still abound here, not the least of which is the Church of St. Gregory of Neocasarea. One arrives at this seventeenth-century triumph of Gothic architecture by passing over either one of the Kamenny bridges, following halfway down Bolshaya Polyanka Street.

The church is surrounded by modern one-story houses with their wide porches and cool inner courtyards, its five-domed sanctuary and tented belfry soaring over the shaded houses and narrow streets to the right, where, startlingly, one comes upon the Institute of Geography and the Atomic Energy Administration.

Valeri Bondasenko could not have found a better hiding place in all of Moscow than the Church of St. Gregory of Neocasarea. Though its gorgeous interior had been defiled—the sublime sanctuary's decorative frescoes and ceramics had been confiscated by the state—the church was a popular spot for foreign tour groups. Intourist buses were always parked not far away, and the ringing voices of sour-faced state tour guides could be heard during the day, as regular as the belfry's chiming, echoing through the interior, repeating by rote the authorized version of this particular piece of history.

Below the shuffling crowds, in the long-forgotten church crypts, Valeri and Sergei hunched in the dust and the cobwebs. Beside them, on a crude pallet, Valeri's daughter lay as if asleep. Her face was peaceful, utterly blank.

"God must be testing us, eh, comrade?" Sergei said with a derisive laugh. "Otherwise, I can't think why I feel like Job."

"It appears that the testing will be over soon," Valeri said in a serious tone, "one way or another."

Sergei sobered quickly. "Is White Star doomed, then?"

"I don't know," Valeri admitted. "Comrade Volkov—"

"May he rot in hell for eternity!"

"Comrade Volkov may have squeezed Natasha Mayakova dry,

435

but there is only so much she knows. We have sprung a leak, to be sure, but we're not yet sinking. As long as my log of White Star activity is safe, so are we."

Sergei said, "I don't think I care for the look on your face, comrade. What are you thinking?"

"I'm thinking that as long as my computer is in my apartment, it is a liability to us now."

"The log is in there?"

Valeri nodded. "Hidden safely away from inquisitive eyes. But still . . ."

"Yes. I understand completely," Sergei said. "Still, it is there." He shrugged. "Well, one thing is for certain, with Comrade Volkov's people scouring the city for us, neither of us can risk going to the apartment to get it. All of Moscow has become a danger zone. I doubt if we can risk anyone."

"Anyone who is involved with White Star."

"Well, of course, that's what I meant," Sergei said. "But who else could we use?"

"There is someone . . ."

"Who?"

"A woman."

Sergei groaned. "Not another woman, comrade. Look at what has happened to Natasha Mayakova. Doesn't her torture mean anything to you?"

"Yes," Valeri said. "It means a great deal. I cared about Natasha—"

"That, if I may say so, is the problem with you, comrade. Emotional involvement—"

"—is a clear and present danger," Valeri finished his thought. "Yes, I know, Sergei. But I find it imperative to continue to see people as people, not as pawns to be pushed around a chess board."

"But for the sake of all of us, you'll push this woman around the board, won't you, comrade?"

"I'll tell her what needs to be done, but not why," Valeri said. "I'll give her a choice."

"The illusion of choice, you mean," Sergei grunted. "By the time you're done with her, holding her tight, kissing her, I'm quite certain she'd jump off the Moskvoretsky Bridge if you asked her to!"

"She is not someone to manipulate," Valeri insisted.

"Neither was Natasha Mayakova, comrade, but you manipulated her just the same. For the good of us all."

436

"It was wrong of me to so shamelessly use Natasha in that way."

"Wrong? But no, you have mistaken my intent." Sergei put his hand briefly on Valeri's arm, a sign of solidarity. "You did what needed to be done. It might have been dirty, but there is no shame involved, my friend. It was necessary."

"I am not often certain of that, Sergei."

"Think of Volkov, man! Without your constant cunning, that monster would have defeated us already."

"Perhaps you're right."

"The times of revolution are desperate times," Sergei said. "They call for desperate measures."

"I think, comrade, that we are done with revolutions. You see the results of our original 'glorious revolution.' Would you have us repeat the mistakes of our forebears?" He shook his head. "No, comrade. These may, indeed, be desperate times, but I will not condone desperate measures. The cycle of mindless violence and hidden greed must be broken, once and for all time. I will not bring down one form of tyranny only to replace it with another. Do you understand this? Are you with me?"

Sergei nodded. "For forever and a day, Valeri."

Valeri clapped Sergei on the back, but his gaze was far away. "Ah, Natasha," he said softly into the musty darkness of the crypt, "if only you knew how important your pain was for White Star. Volkov has broken you, but now he believes that all you were doing was bringing the Hero KGB dossiers. Our truth is still safe." He turned to Sergei. "Still safe, eh, comrade?"

"Is he gone?"

"Yes."

Irina crept out of the Hero's shower where Lara had hidden her when Tatiana had warned them of Mars Volkov's arrival in the building.

"Don't be frightened by what you may have overheard."

Irina slipped into the pool beside him. "Nothing about you could frighten me."

The Hero touched her as they moved out into the center of the pool. "Mars was looking for you," he said.

"Did he say why?"

"I don't think it would be a good idea to let him find you," Lara said.

"But why is he looking for me?"

"He thinks you know where Valeri is hiding," the Hero said.

"He'll kill Valeri if he gets the chance," Lara said.

Irina shivered. "Now I *am* frightened."

"So you should be," the Hero said. Then he put his hand on her again, and she felt a warmth flow through her. "Don't worry. You have a guardian angel looking after you."

"That's what Natasha said." Irina squeezed her eyes shut. "Why must there always be violence, pain, suffering, death?"

The lapping of the pool; four entities in the faintly phosphorescent darkness, linked by an invisible umbilical.

The Hero said, "All these things are part of human nature."

"You're wrong," Irina said. "You must be."

"People want things," the Hero said. "Usually they are things they shouldn't have, such as too much money, too much power, dominion over other people, dominion over other nations. It never ends. There is a cycle of human existence that must be played out."

"Nothing is so inevitable," Irina said. "Now you sound like a god talking about his mortal charges."

"Mars has accused me of wanting to be a god, but that is not my intent."

Irina looked into his extraordinary opalescent eyes. "What is your intent, then?"

"Freedom," the Hero said. "That's simple, enough, isn't it? Or it should be. But human nature being what it is, the concept of freedom becomes entangled like a crab in a net, and now that crab crawls and crawls and never comes to the end of the net."

Irina was about to answer him when she became aware of Tatiana slipping into the pool. She was their sentry. Both the Hero and Lara looked toward her.

"She must go," Tatiana said, indicating Irina.

"Now?" the Hero asked.

"At once. It is vital."

"Where am I going?" Irina said. "I don't want to leave."

The Hero ignored her for a moment. He said to Lara, "Make certain she exits as she entered so she is not seen."

Lara nodded, climbed out of the pool. Tatiana followed her. Irina could hear the padding of their bare feet against the tile. Water dripping in the darkness.

"Must I go?" she repeated.

438

"It is most important," the Hero said, "or the request would not have been made."

"I won't go. I refuse to be ordered around. I'm done with being a marionette, dancing on the end of strings that men pull."

"It's freedom you want, isn't it?"

"Yes."

"Well, so do I," the Hero said. "So do we all. Even Arbat." He looked at her. "If you consent to go, you'll be helping us get there."

"Then how can I refuse?" But Irina felt the fright, like an engine that would not stop, churning inside her.

The Hero smiled. "Bravely spoken."

"But where am I going?"

"I don't know," he said. "It's better that way, I assure you."

Irina stared at him with wide eyes. She was fighting back the tears.

The Hero swam up to her. He took her in his arms, kissed her hard on the lips. "Come back to me, Irina," he whispered. "I don't know what I'd do without you." Irina's heart was beating so loud she could hardly hear him. She searched the universe in his eyes, spoke to him wordlessly in that peculiar silence of communication she had learned from him.

Then Lara and Tatiana were standing on the coping.

"It's time," the Hero said.

Bending down, they pulled Irina from the pool.

"What is it," Mars said to Captain Nikolev, "that is of paramount importance to you?"

"The sovereignty and security of the Soviet Union."

"You did not hesitate."

"No, comrade."

Mars nodded. They were sitting in the command center of Department N. Mars was at a small desk, reviewing the monitored communications of suspected White Star personnel over the past twelve hours. Captain Nikolev was manning a sophisticated electronics console. "It's good to be sure of yourself, Captain," Mars said. "That is something that fades with stamina as youth gives way to middle age." He looked at Captain Nikolev. "You are, what? Thirty-five?"

"Thirty-two, comrade."

"There you have it," Mars said almost wistfully. "Youth must have its day." He smiled enigmatically. "Like perestroika." Almost immediately his mouth twisted as if he had tasted spoiled food. "Tell me, Captain, how do you feel about the Americanization of Russia?"

"I beg your pardon?"

"Don't do that!" Mars barked. "Don't play the loyal but dull-witted soldier with me, Captain. You may gull your superiors, but they are only army men, after all. You can't fool me. I know the extent of your intelligence. I know about your studies, your passion for history that has led you to unearth the levels of 'authorized' histories down through the decades."

"Comrade—"

"Not to worry, Captain. Your secret is safe with me. But don't tell me that you are unaware of the Americanization of our country. The military must now go begging to a committee formed from the Congress of Peoples' Deputies if it wants to change anything, including the location of post latrines. Budget increases? Oh, no, it must go before an oversight committee which knows nothing about capabilities, liabilities, national security.

"Then there are the independent farmers who are now being paid in *foreign* currency in direct competition with the collectives."

Mars shrugged. "And what about the KGB? We are forced to endure the excruciating, nit-picking examinations of our present structure while submitting meekly to the grossest of theatrical public lamentations by known dissidents and subversives allowed into the Congress, berating us for what they see as our past sins."

He grunted. "This is not perestroika, it's America."

"As I understand it," Captain Nikolev said, "perestroika is merely an experiment."

"An experiment that has gone terribly awry," Mars said. When Nikolev made no further comment, he continued. "We have gone from trying to emulate a perfect model, to wanting to emulate a thoroughly corrupt one. In terms you can easily understand, Captain, it is akin to the ancient Britons wanting to base their culture on that of Rome in the time of Caligula. Utterly incomprehensible, utterly reprehensible. What is happening to us, Captain? Are we to lose all sense of ourselves, of what makes Russia unique in all the world? Our culture is being subverted by the very people who govern us. The CIA no longer needs Radio Free America, it's got the president to do its subversive work for it."

"I suppose it's all in how you look at things," Nikolev said.

"It's a telling lesson in how interpretation subverts intent, don't you think?"

"Spoken like a true diplomat." Mars laughed. "You're wasting your talents in the Border Guards, I can tell you."

"As you no doubt have suspected," Nikolev said, "my job affords me the luxury of time to pursue my own interests."

"It is altogether beyond my comprehension how you can hold any love for history, Captain, when our so-called scholars keep rewriting it."

"I would have thought that you, of all people, would see the necessity for revisionism."

"You interest me, Captain," Mars said. "Perhaps you, too, understand what an elusive and treacherous beast the truth is."

"Comrade, I am not even certain that I understand the definition of truth."

Mars laughed. "Yes, indeed, Captain. There *is* more to you than meets the eye." He nodded toward the bank of electronics. "What news?"

"The same," Captain Nikolev said. "Irina Ponomareva's car is still in the same spot. It has not moved since we began monitoring it. It is parked six blocks from your apartment. I have four of my men watching it."

"You do?" Mars's head came up. "Who told you to do that?"

"No one, comrade. I thought it would be pru—"

"You thought wrong," Mars snapped. "Get your men out of there at once. All we need is for one of them to be spotted. Irina does not know I am KGB. If she sees one of your men—and believe me, if your men are there, this woman will spot him—she will never go near the car."

"Yes, comrade."

While Nikolev made the arrangements, Mars thought of Irina. He had to laugh at himself, paranoid Mars. How often in the past had he wondered whether she had made any clandestine contacts, perhaps with American White Star sympathizers, while she had been abroad in the United States? After all, she had had mid-level security clearances, and therefore had not been monitored by the KGB as closely as, say, Natasha Mayokova had been during her tours of New York.

But he had had cause to be suspicious, he reminded himself righteously. Did she not have definite opinions about the national minorities inside the USSR, opinions that, frankly, had concerned Mars? Oh, yes. And Mars cleverly had made those questionable opinions work for him when he had sent her off to try to pry open Valeri Denysovich.

And, ultimately, Irina had proved her worth to him when her amazing amateur sleuthing had uncovered Natasha Mayakova, the link between the traitor Valeri Denysovich and the Hero.

Damn Valeri Denysovich!

Mars's fist crashed onto the tabletop, making Captain Nikolev start.

"Comrade?"

Mars was already looking over the monitoring of White Star transmissions. "They seem to have sent some kind of distress message into the West." Mars rubbed at his face. "We haven't fully broken their code yet, but we have enough to make some sense out of the garble." He looked up at Captain Nikolev. "Do you think that White Star is desperate enough to ask for direct help from the West?"

"Even if they have," Nikolev said, "who would be foolish enough to respond?"

"Hmm." Mars contemplated the transcripts as if they were tea leaves from which he could divine the future. After a time, he picked up a small interoffice memo, said, "An American diplomatic mission has logged a flight plan into Moscow."

"So? American diplomatic missions happen all the time."

Mars flipped the memo over to Captain Nikolev. "But take a look at where this particular mission is coming from."

"Tokyo."

"Yes," Mars said. "Interesting, because Tokyo is where the White Star S.O.S. we intercepted was sent to."

Captain Nikolev shrugged. "Could be a coincidence."

Mars took the memo back without saying a word. Captain Nikolev watched him as he clipped the memo to the transmission transcripts. In a moment Mars raised his head. "The mobile units are standing by?"

"Yes, comrade."

"The moment Miss Ponomareva's car begins to move, I want to know about it. If I'm sleeping, wake me. If I'm eating, pull the fork from my hand. Clear?"

"Absolutely, comrade."

The Hotel Rossiya, an enormous twenty-story structure built in an undistinguished style that in Russia passed for modern, took up the south side of an entire block of Razin

442

Street. The street was named after a well-known Cossack leader, a scourge of czars, and somehow it seemed appropriate to the state to house so many tourists here.

Irina went into the front entrance to the Rossiya and, as Tatiana had instructed her to do, went up to the front desk and asked if there were any messages for Mrs. Kubysheva.

There were.

Irina took the plain white envelope, went across the lobby, up the stairs into one of the many restaurants in the hotel. Locating the rest room, she went in, locked herself in a stall.

She slit open the envelope, read it twice through. Her heart was hammering so hard in her chest that, when the door to the rest room swung open, she wondered how the ladies who came in didn't hear it.

Memorizing the instructions, Irina tore the paper and envelope into tiny bits, threw them into the toilet. She flushed twice, making certain that not one scrap of paper was left in the bowl. In the rest room she rinsed her hands, but she did not look at herself in the gilt-edged mirrors.

She went out of the Rossiya by a side entrance. The onion domes of the Cathedral of St. Basil dominated the near distance. She was not far from the Kremlin, and she shuddered as if it were winter, and she without her fur-lined coat.

The instructions had urged her to go by foot and by bus, and Irina scrupulously heeded this advice. Sensibly, she did not want to look around to see if she was being followed, but she found herself staring like a cat into windowpanes, the glass of passing cars and trams, in order to catch the reflections of as many of those around her as she could see.

She made a circuit of trolleybuses, using routes that paralleled one another, ending up essentially where she had begun. Then she set off by foot and, at length, came to the far end of Red Square. The Moskva was dark and muddy, and the sky was so full of clouds that she could not see her reflection in the water as she crossed over the Moskvoretsky Bridge. That was all right with her. It seemed, anyway, as if another Irina Ponomareva was engaged in this terrifying espionage enterprise.

Past Dobryninskaya Square she came at last to the Zamoskvorechye, the District Beyond the Moskva. She saw the Intourist buses, exhausts bluing the heavy gray sky, and on Bolshaya Polyanka Street, the lovely facade of the Church of St. Gregory of Neocasarea.

In the sanctuary, Irina prayed for Valeri, for herself, but especially for Odysseus. The lies of the Intourist guides fell on her ears like acid. The tourists shuffled behind the guide like sheep to the slaughter.

Death and destruction were never far from her consciousness now, and she was frightened for herself, as if she could no longer recognize her own moral center, let alone the moral centers of those around her. Every step I take down this path, she thought, I am more lost, as I push back the boundaries of what I will and will not do. Will there be no end?

She was finished with her prayers. She walked from the sanctuary into the sacristy. It was quiet here, the droning of the Intourist guide indistinct, far away. The shadows hung like shrouds, thick, embroidered with threads of black among the shades of gray.

Irina started when a robed priest touched her arm. She was about to say something when he put his finger against his lips. His hood hid his face. He beckoned, and she nodded, followed him out of the sacristy, down a dark, musty hall, through a wooden door, down worn stone steps. It became cold and dank. She smelled tallow, fermenting wine, and mold. She sneezed.

At the foot of the stairs the priest pushed back his hood, revealing the strawberry birthmark.

"This way," Sergei said. He did not offer his name, and Irina did not ask.

Sergei took her by a circuitous route through the crypt until they came to the place where he and Valeri had made their temporary camp.

Irina saw the young girl on the makeshift straw pallet.

"My daughter," Valeri Bondasenko said, stepping out of the shadows. "I know you believed that I had no children. A necessary lie. No one knows about her. My daughter's . . . illness could have been used against me."

"Why is she here?"

"The KGB discovered her existence and her whereabouts in one terrible blow."

Irina looked at him. "They made Natasha tell them."

Valeri nodded.

"My God, is she alive or dead?"

"I have no way of knowing."

"Oh, Valeri, I may have killed her. I've been such a fool."

"No, not a fool, *koshka*. You'd been lied to so much, you

444

just lost your ability to tell fact from fiction.'' He gave her a rueful smile. "Don't blame yourself, please. You were up against the best. You had no chance to come through this intact.''

"You and Mars.''

Valerie came closer to her. "Yes.''

"But you, '' she said. "Why did you have to lie to me?''

"I thought I was protecting you,'' Valeri said. "At least, that's what I told myself. I had read your dossier; I knew about your family background, what you had suffered at the hands of the KGB. I convinced myself that, though I sought to use you against Mars, I would spare you knowledge about him that would cripple you. I felt that if you were ignorant of who Mars really was, you would be more natural with him.''

Valeri shook his head ruefully. "You see, *koshka*, I've become such a skillful liar that I had no trouble fooling myself. I didn't understand that I was falling in love with you, that each day I was sending you out into incalculable danger. What happened to Natasha—her arrest and interrogation—could have happened to you, had Mars begun to suspect you were spying on him for me. In the beginning I ignored that danger because I was obsessed with destroying Mars.'' He moved toward her. "Then, at last, I understood what I was doing to you—and to myself.''

"Don't,'' Irina said. "I no longer know whether I want to be close to you. You hurt me deeply, Valeri.''

"I didn't mean to. You must believe that.''

Irina said nothing.

Valeri said, "You must have forgiven me. You came, didn't you?''

"I came because Odysseus asked me to. He said it was important, that I would have a chance to actively work for freedom.''

"He was right.''

Irina stared at him. "But right now Odysseus is beside the point.''

"Is he?'' Valeri said. "Why? We are working toward the same end.''

"Perhaps it is your methods that I find so offensive. Frankly, from where I stand I don't see all that much difference between you and Mars.''

"Mars Volkov has been systematically interrogating Odysseus ever since he came out of his coma. Mars Volkov picked up Natasha Mayakova and subjected her to articulated interrogation. What does that mean? Even I don't know, but it could include beating, starving, sleep deprivation, electric shock, drug inj—''

"Stop it!" Irina put her hands to her ears.

"I'm just trying to set the record straight."

Irina's shoulders slumped. "Your efforts are noted."

"Thank you," he said formally.

There was a deep, almost hostile silence between them. Before it went on long enough to become irrevocable, Valeri said, "How did we come to this point, *koshka*?"

"You tell me," Irina said wearily.

"Do you want me to say it's my fault? All right. It's my fault. I never should have lied to you. But how could I have known what you'd be like? How could I possibly have trusted you?"

"You don't see it, do you?" Irina shook her head sadly. "You condemn yourself with your own words. Look at what your work has made of you, Valeri. You are suspicious of everyone. You can't allow anyone to get close to you for fear they may turn out to be your enemy."

"But you're wrong, *koshka*. I was close to Natasha Mayakova. My heart breaks for what happened to her. And you, Irina. I love you."

"No, Valeri. I don't believe you know the meaning of the word love. But I don't blame you. Your work comes first, it always has, and I see the necessity of it. Truly, I do. I don't know how I feel about you, and that's all right. I don't think it a good idea to examine that part of me right now—maybe ever."

"Forever is a long time, *koshka*."

"Especially in your line of work," Irina said. "And now that it's mine—however temporarily—I suppose we'd better get on with it."

"Then you'll help us?"

"Oh, Valeri, how your face lights up. Like a child at Easter." Irina smiled. "I had forgotten how nice your face is when you're happy."

Valeri gripped her arms. "Irina, I cannot overemphasize the element of danger involved. Mars is out for my blood. He's mobilized the KGB Border Guards to find me."

"If you're trying to frighten me, you're doing a first-class job of it."

"You'll be more careful if you're frightened," Valeri said. "Now listen, you need to get to my apartment. You know the Toshiba lap-top? You must somehow get it out of the apartment."

It was at that moment that Irina almost told him that she had found his ghost in the machine, that she knew much of the inner workings of White Star, including the identity of its leader. But she bit her lip instead, sure that he would not allow her anywhere near his apartment if he knew she had so much critical information inside her head.

"Once I get it out of your apartment, then what?" Irina said. "I can't very well walk around the streets of Moscow carrying an illegal computer."

"Of course not," Valeri said. "Do you have access to a car?"

"Yes."

"Ah, good," Valeri said, breathing a sigh of relief. "At last, the tide seems to be turning in our favor."

"Don't you just hate Americans?" Mars said.

"I met an American once," Captain Nikolev said. "I was off duty, of course. The Border Guards is not something the state wishes tourists to be aware of. I met him outside the gates to the Kremlin. He seemed a decent chap, really. Full of questions, but he had no real idea of how this country works."

"That's just it!" Mars said hotly. "Americans have no idea how anything works, not politics, not economics, not even social dynamics—*especially* not social dynamics. They're far too busy rooting around Bloomingdale's and Tiffany's to be of any value to their fellow man."

"Like Khrushchev, you want to bury them, comrade."

"No, Captain, not bury them," Mars said. "I want to eradicate them."

"Then you've set yourself an impossible task."

Mars looked at him. "Do you really think so? That's interesting, coming from a scholar of history. Rome fell, so did Byzantium. Why not America?"

"To be brutal, comrade, because it is not Democracy that has been found deficient as a form of government, but Communism. The theories of Marx and Engels are simply inadequate. It's a fact, sad though it may be to contemplate. Poland, Hungary, Rumania, Czechoslovakia, East Germany. We've had

447

to relinquish control of our colonies as the Western nations were once obliged to do with theirs.

"And why not? Desperate men must resort to desperate measures. Our own economy is in a shambles; we cannot even feed our own people, corruption and alcoholism are rampant throughout a bureaucracy that is second to none in its bloatedness, self-importance, and obstructionism. We simply have to face facts. The path we have set out on is a dead end."

"And where are we to go then?" Mars said fiercely. "Where will it end? With a Bloomingdale's and Tiffany's opening on Gorky Street? With our women wearing designer blue jeans and sequined jackets?" His face was livid. "That is not the solution, to lose ourselves in the mania of Americanization. I reject that despicable notion!"

"In the days of the ancient Britons," Captain Nikolev said, "the lure of Rome was irresistible. It was an endlessly fascinating place."

"A pit full of quicksand," Mars said. "There's the truth."

"If only," Nikolev said with an ironic tone, "we could recognize it." His eyes darted to the electronic console he was manning.

"What is it, Captain?"

"Irina Ponomareva's car," Nikolev said. "It's begun to move."

When Irina got to Valeri's apartment, she circled the block three times, cruising slowly, doing what Valeri had advised her, looking for KGB men who might be staked out, watching the place.

"If they have spared anybody at all, it won't be more than one man," he had told her. "They know I'm not stupid enough to try to get back there."

In any event, Irina used a great deal of caution. She parked around the back, went into the rear entrance of the building next door and down into the cellar. Valeri had told her that his building and the one next to it had once been one, and the cellars still connected.

Ten minutes later Irina emerged into the hallway of Valeri's building.

She stood quietly in the open doorway to the fire stairs, slowing her breathing, trying to listen for small sounds beyond the

448

thumping of her heart. Her eyes were open all the way around and their pupils were fully dilated.

Someone came out of his apartment, and Irina ducked back into the stairwell. She could smell boiled cabbage and stale tobacco. The door closed, a key turned, and heavy footfalls sounded in the corridor. The elevator whined, opened, closed, whined again, descending to the lobby.

Stillness creeping like shadows with the movement of the sun across the afternoon sky.

There were no *dezhurnayas* in either of these buildings, snoops who, in years gone by, would keep track of everyone and everything going in and out. Unofficial adjuncts to the KGB. Some things, at least, had finally changed in Moscow.

From where she stood, Irina could see Valeri's front door. It looked all right. Closed. Just as she had left it. But was that an illusion? Mars's people must have been through the place, if only to be thorough, searching for clues to Valeri's whereabouts.

KGB. Keep calm.

Irina shuddered, and for a moment her resolve wavered. She could just turn around, go down the stairs to the basement, cross over, and leave via the building next door. Simple. No one would know that she had even come near the place.

But the fact was it wasn't so simple. Freedom was a complex issue, one that, she saw now, she had been obsessed with ever since she had returned from Cambridge. How could she turn her back on freedom now?

If she turned away, where would she go? Back to her apartment to wait for Mars Volkov to find her and debrief her about her conversations with Odysseus? What would she do when Mars was finished with her? Return to her drone-like job at the Ministry of Education? No, no. She could not go back. She would choke to death on her own despair. Her feet were set on this new path, and she knew that she must follow it to its end or she would never be able to live with herself. The other side of the mirror was too tantalizing, too filled with wonders for her ever to contemplate stepping back.

Irina stood trembling with fear as she inhaled the smells of the building. The elevator hummed, on its way toward another assignation on another floor. A baby cried. A radio played a snatch of martial music, then was still.

Gathering her courage like a cloak around her, Irina ventured

449

into the hallway. She went quickly to Valeri's door, slid her key into the lock, turned it. She closed her hand over the knob and, turning it, let herself into the apartment.

She knew immediately that people had been here. The stillness was the same as when she had been here before, but there were smells lingering in the air, half-remembered reminders: a whiff of body odor in the dusty air of the hallway, a hint of cheap tobacco in the stale air of the bedroom. She saw no butts anywhere, and she did not notice anything out of place. Whoever had been in here, searching, had been circumspect.

Irina held her breath until she reached the kitchen. But there it was, the illegal Toshiba lap-top, sitting comfortably where it had always been, on the corner of the chopping block.

Crossing the kitchen Irina slammed down the top of the computer, unplugged the cord from the current converter, stuffed both into the computer's carrying case, then fit the computer itself in, zipped the case closed.

She had just grabbed the case by its soft handles when she heard the scrabbling sounds at the front door. Her blood froze in her veins. The contents of her stomach threatened to return to her mouth.

KGB. Keep calm.

Mary, Mother of God!

Irina looked around her. I'm trapped, she thought. Then, No! The window!

She threw open the kitchen window, ducked, stepped quickly out onto the fire escape. She turned, shut the window behind her, stood with her back against the filthy concrete and brick facade of the building. Below her was Telegraph Street. Irina closed her eyes, imagining herself kneeling in the sanctuary of the nearby Church of the Archangel Gabriel. She was there, as a child with her mother, inhaling the heady incense, hearing voices raised in prayer, listening to the incomprehensible sacraments. If only she could turn back time . . .

Her eyes flew open as she heard a voice say, "Is there any evidence that she was here?"

"The front door was unlocked, Captain."

"Search the apartment."

Irina turned her head, strained to get an oblique look through the windowpane. In a moment she saw a young good-looking man in a gray uniform with red accents. Valeri in the dankness of the crypt saying, *Mars is out for my blood. He's mobilized the KGB Border Guards to find me.*

How did they find me? Irina asked herself. Was I followed or were they watching the apartment? I thought I had been so careful. Oh, God, how stupid I am.

"She's already left, Captain."

"Why did she come here?"

Silence

"Is anything missing?"

"Just the computer, Captain."

"Ah," the young uniformed man said. "The computer." He turned away from the window. "Find her," Irina could hear him say. "If she slips by us, comrade Volkov will have the lot of you reassigned to Sinkiang."

KGB. Keep calm.

How many of them are there? Irina wondered, shaking with terror. They're like ants crawling over a picnic blanket. I've got to get off the blanket before they eat me alive.

When she could no longer see anyone through the kitchen window, Irina began to climb down along the rusting catwalks. At any moment she expected shouts to be raised as one of the Border Guards contingent spotted her. But nothing happened.

She gained the ground without incident. The Toshiba computer pulled at her left arm. If only I can make it to the car, she thought, I'll be all right.

She went along Telegraph Street, fearful that someone would wonder what it was she was lugging around with her.

It had begun to rain. Instead of heading directly for the car, Irina sought shelter. She stood, hidden within the deep shadows of a building doorway, the Toshiba tucked behind her legs, invisible to anyone passing by. She watched the street with frightened, haunted eyes. She could feel the bars across her moon, heading downward to close around her. She could feel the arctic cold of the winter that never ended, bones strewn across a bleak field of ice, frozen Siberian tundra catching the snow as it silently fell from a featureless sky. Her nightmare taking shape around her.

Irina scrutinized the faces of everyone who passed by. She peered into rain-streaked car windows. Everyone was a potential enemy, and she thought, It's happening to me, so soon, so soon. I have become afraid of everything and everyone. Must this be the price of freedom? Haven't I any other choice?

Thunder rolled through the canyons of the city, and it became as dark as midnight. Once or twice a flash of lightning lit the street in a sickly, colorless burst of energy, making Irina start nervously.

It was pouring. The KGB must be nearby, she knew, and she suspected that the longer she remained in the area, the greater her chance was of getting picked up. Such was her anxiety and single-mindedness, it never occurred to her to ditch the Toshiba in the nearest trashcan. Besides, even she knew that making a run for it on foot now would be foolish. The KGB would spot her within minutes.

The car was her only salvation. Once she was in it she could blend into traffic, take back streets, shortcuts, be able to double back on herself to make certain that no one was following her.

Picking up the computer and ducking her head, Irina ventured out into the rain, heading for the car.

It was slow going. The drainage in this section of the city was due for repairs, but they had not come through as scheduled and as a result, every time it stormed, rainwater would sluice through the gutters, occasionally slopping onto the sidewalks.

Irina passed several babushkas dragging their net shopping bags behind them. A street merchant huddled with sodden newspaper over her head, dancing from one foot to another to avoid the water as best she could, as her pathetic display of dried-out beets and blasted turnips was battered by the foul weather.

Once, when Irina suspected that she was being followed, she ducked into a small building, clattered through the worn tiles of the dismal lobby. At the rear entrance she glanced back, saw the obvious trail of water and nearly burst into tears.

I'll never get the hang of being devious, she thought miserably. Then she remembered that she had still eluded the KGB, and she took some solace from that fact. Perhaps I'm not as inept as I think, she told herself bravely as she pushed out the rear door.

She found herself in a filthy back alley. Someone had forgotten to take in their laundry, and linen flapped wetly over her head in the sodden wind. For a moment she was at a loss as to which way to go. Then, glancing down the end of the alley, she saw part of the rear of the Church of the Archangel Gabriel, and regained her bearings.

Irina hurried down the alley. The Toshiba was growing heavier by the minute, but she tried not to think of the weight. She concentrated on getting to her car, slipping through the net the KGB had thrown around Valeri's apartment.

She emerged from the alley, turned left down the block. A black Zil turned onto the street, came cruising toward her, its speed far slower than was normal, as if its occupants were checking each side of the block.

Irina ducked back into the alley, held her breath as the Zil came abreast of where she was hiding. She wished she were twelve again, thin as a rail, able to disappear in a sliver of shadow. She imagined herself gone from here as the Zil stopped abreast of the alley. Her pulse thundered in her ears and she was certain it would give her away. The Zil sat for what seemed an interminable time. Its windows were tinted black and she could not see inside. Truth to tell, she did not want to look inside. What was happening in there? Had they spotted her? Were they playing with her as they would a mouse?

At last the Zil rolled on. Irina took a deep, shuddering breath as her eyes followed the Zil down the street. It turned at the far corner, disappeared.

She headed down the street in the opposite direction. She would have liked to stop at the church, sink to her knees, pray for safety for Valeri, the Hero, as well as herself. But there was no time. Still, she spoke to God as she rounded the corner to the street where she had left the car.

She stopped, cautious again. The street was deserted. The car sat where she had left it. But suddenly it didn't seem like a sanctuary: this was, after all, the car Mars had given her; what if it had been followed, or worse, was bugged?

Irina looked furtively around, her heart pounding in her chest. What was she to do? She had to get back to Valeri with the computer, yet with the KGB out, she could not walk there or take a tram. But if the car was bugged, she would lead them straight to Valeri.

There was so little time. Sweat rolled down the back of her neck as she worked through the problem. She stared at the car. It seemed to beckon her on, a safe haven. It occurred to her that she was already thinking like a fugitive, and that frightened her further.

Behind her she heard the soft swish of car tires on the wet asphalt of the street, and she jumped, thinking of the black Zil.

All right, she thought, I'll use the car but abandon it well before I get to the church. Once I get to the other side of the Kremlin I'll be all right. I can walk the last few blocks, making sure I'm not followed.

Having made up her mind, she hurried to the car, dropped the keys in her anxiety, retrieved them, unlocked the driver's door. She threw the Toshiba on the passenger's seat, slid in herself, shut and locked the door behind her.

The ignition turned, and when she heard the engine cough to life, she breathed an enormous sigh of relief. She stared out the windshield. It was already fogged, and she used the cuff of her coat to wipe away the condensation. She wondered vaguely why there should be so much condensation when she had just now got in the car. That kind of mist came from human breath.

That was when she became aware of the slight stirring behind her. A hand clamped her shoulder and she gave a little scream.

"Did I startle you, Irina? That was thoughtless of me."

She saw his movie-idol face in the rearview mirror, and she thought for a moment that her heart had ceased to beat. Then it thudded home, and she felt as if she had been punched in the chest.

She said his name involuntarily, like a sigh. "Mars."

THIRTEEN
MOSCOW/STAR TOWN

Tori was dreaming of Koi, of the purity of whiteness stained red, of shiny innards slithering into sunlight, steaming like an Aztec sacrifice; she was meditating on the uncompromising will of the warrior spirit; she was wondering how it was the Japanese, among many other ancient peoples of the world, had determined that blood could purify the most corrupted spirit, when Russell woke her. Had she dreamed about the blood of Koi or the blood of Christ?

"We've just landed outside Novosibirsk for refueling," Russell said. "We're halfway to Moscow."

Although they were at a civilian airfield and had logged an official flight plan, the military commander of the nearby air base had sent his adjutant, who was in the company of a lean-faced plainclothes man. An obvious KGB agent, the lean-faced man's cheeks were scarred by a severe case of adult acne, and his cheap suit seemed to grab him under the arms and in the crotch. Tori wondered, stifling a guffaw, whether after eight hours in that flexible torture chamber he would talk in a falsetto.

The two men scrutinized the false diplomatic documents the Titles and Legends section of the Mall office in Tokyo had prepared, just as the Soviets in Ulan Bator, their first refueling stop, had done. Everything had been preprinted; all that had to be done by Titles and Legends was to insert the proper names, titles, border frankings, and so forth, add several sets of official orders, and the documents were ready to go.

The two men made a great show of taking notes, conferring among themselves, quizzing Russell. Mostly, they stared at Tori's legs. Then, apparently frustrated, they went forward to grill the flight crew. Forty minutes later they exited the plane, but not before scowling menacingly at Russell and taking a last, lingering look at Tori's legs.

"Horny devils," Tori said.

Russell, smiling at the scowling angry faces, said, "You'd be horny, too, if you were stuck in the back of beyond with only your Kalishnikov to keep you warm."

When the Russians were finally gone, Russell relaxed. "There's one thing that still bothers me about this whole affair Bernard's lost himself in. If he isn't part of Hitasura's supercoke scheme—and I'm as convinced as you are that he isn't—then how the devil is he getting the funds to buy these nuclear weapons? You can bet the coalition isn't giving them to him. And I can tell you unequivocally that he isn't using the Mall's money. Even Bernard—if he'd a mind to—couldn't embezzle the amount he'd need without my finding out pretty damn quick."

"That's a good question." Tori considered this. "I hadn't thought of that, but even if I had, I doubt whether Koi or Hitasura would have provided any help on that score. Bernard knew nothing of Hitasura's finances; and, knowing Bernard, you can be damn sure the reverse was true, as well."

Russell looked thoughtful. "You know, I don't believe I'll ever really understand what happened between you and Koi. What kind of bond could there possibly have been between the two of you? Frankly, it scares me to think that you could have related to anything about her."

"Oh, Russ, there was a whole other side of Koi you never saw."

"Koi was a stone killer."

"So am I."

"She enjoyed torturing Deke."

"There you're wrong," Tori said. "When she tortured Deke, she was torturing herself. She loathed what she did, but she felt she was cursed, that she deserved to be loathed—by everyone. Someone like that is to be pitied, not despised."

"She had to be stopped from repeating what she did to Deke."

"I stopped her, Russ." Tori's eyes held his as if in an invisible vise. "And that felt good—I can't tell you how good—because I didn't have to resort to killing her."

He nodded. "I can see that, sure. But—"

"Look, Russ, Koi was driven by demons. Maybe they weren't the exact same demons that drive Bernard, but they're close enough. Do you think Bernard is any less haunted than Koi was? The only difference between them is that Bernard has found a way to live with his demons."

"But don't you see that in time Koi would have become another Fukuda?"

"And what has Bernard Godwin become over time, Russ? Can you answer that with any degree of certainty? No? Then I'll tell you. Bernard is as much a stone killer as Koi was."

"But his motives are so altruistic—"

"That's Mall Central thinking," Tori said. "Motives don't count here—morality does. At least Koi had the courage to face what she had become—"

"And killed herself." He shook his head. "I don't understand a person who prefers death to life."

"Preference has nothing to do with it." Tori's eyes blazed. "Death was an atonement for her sins. For Koi, to die in so honorable a fashion as *seppuku* was to cleanse her spirit. If I compare her to Bernard, I think she had the right idea."

Russell rose. "All this talk of death is making me claustrophobic." He went off to the head.

Tori looked out the Perspex window, stared at nothing. "Christ!" she breathed. "How can he be so obtuse when he's also so insightful?"

Then she shook her head, followed him. She wanted him to understand, to at last grasp a concept that was not grounded in logic, mathematics, binary languages.

"Russell."

For an unbearably long moment they stared at each other. Then Russell grabbed her shirtfront, pulled her inside the head, hard against him. "Nothing's going to save you now," he said hoarsely just before his lips came down over hers.

"I don't want to be saved," she moaned into him.

Tori's mouth opened and her tongue twined with his. Her back was arched and her breasts were crushed against him. She felt dizzy and weak, as if she had lost all strength in her upper body. At the same time, her legs felt heavy, as if they were

457

buried in sand. Her thighs were on fire, and she could not seem to catch her breath.

Russell was pulling apart her blouse, his hands running roughly over her breasts. She moaned into his mouth as he found her nipples.

She could not wait, her own hands searching for his belt and fly, frantically pulling down his trousers, feeling him rise deliciously into her hand, cramming him beneath her short skirt, her other hand pulling aside her underclothes, ramming him full length inside her.

They both cried out at the same time, and Russell slammed her repeatedly against the bulkhead. If they were making noise, neither of them cared; if they were to be discovered, it did not matter. They were beyond caring about anything but their joined hot flesh, their liquid union, the mutual fire that threatened to consume them.

Tori felt filled to overflowing. She wrapped her arms around his head, filled the spaces between her fingers with his thick hair.

"Russ, Russ, oh!"

His mouth was at her throat, the sides of her neck, her ears, her jaw. He gathered her hard breasts in his hands, squeezing them as he hammered at her until Tori almost fainted with pleasure.

Her eyes were closed; she rubbed her face against the coarseness of his cheeks, and jolts of electricity penetrated all the way into her lower belly.

She could feel the tension come into him in increments, not the tension of conflict and strife with which she had become all too familiar, but the tiny ribbonings of a luscious tautness in the last few indescribable moments before release, a desire to drown in bliss.

Then he groaned, deep in his throat, a growl, really, drawn out and heartfelt, and she felt him draw in against her so tightly that she could not breathe as he convulsed. This, in turn, set her off, her eyes flying open, her mouth gasping, all thought obliterated.

Then, all too quickly, he was sliding out of her.

"No," she moaned. "Oh, no. Not yet."

But he had dropped to his knees, his mouth found her, burrowing in and up, his tongue like an adder flicking at the core of her, and she almost screamed.

She worked her hips around and around, her hands on either

side of his head, lovingly stroking him as she shuddered again and again, her upper torso folded over him, her legs shaking and jerking, her head heavy, spinning in the full flux of desire.

"Oh, God . . ."

Tori collapsed against him, and they tumbled in a heap to the floor. She took him in her hands, whispered, "I want you hard again. Right now."

Russell laughed. "Only one of us is from Krypton, remember? Give me a couple of minutes to recover."

Tori kept her hands on him, moving, and as it turned out, he didn't need a couple of minutes.

When at last they were fully sated, Tori rested her head against his chest. She liked hearing the beating of his heart, running at such a different pace from hers. It was as if, from this one percussion line, she could determine the scope of the music that moved him—what he liked, what he didn't; what made him happy, what made him sad; what comforted him, what frightened him. It was an illusion, she knew—people were far too complex for all their secrets to be revealed in such a way—but it was a lovely illusion, for all that.

"Almost to Moscow," Tori said wryly when they had returned to their seats, "and all we can think about is sex."

"It's a survival instinct," Russell said. "We both know where we're headed, that there's nothing but trouble waiting for us when we land, and yet we're still going. There's a part of us that does what it has to to remind us we're still alive."

"Is that what our making love was to you? A primitive instinct?"

"I see that once again I've said the wrong thing."

"You bet you have!" Tori said, pulling away.

"Calm down," Russell said.

Tori shook away his hold. "Don't tell me what to do!"

"I'm not for Christ's sake telling you what to do."

"Well, how do you expect me to act when we've just made such wonderful love and you tell me that! Didn't it mean anything more to you than some kind of anthropological mating dance?"

"Of course it did!" Russell shouted. "Haven't I already told you I love you? But I haven't heard a word in reply."

In the ringing silence they stared at each other.

"Sometimes I wish I didn't love you," Russell said in a low voice. "We're so different. You're such a mystery to me. You can be quite frightening at times. The things you're capable of . . . I don't really know what I'm letting myself in for, loving you."

"We never do know," Tori said softly. "Isn't that part of the excitement of love, the not knowing, the future of finding out together?"

"Tori," Russell said. "Do you love me?"

"Oh, Russ." She kissed him hard on the lips. When she pulled her head away, she said, "I'm afraid, too."

"Of what?"

"Of losing myself in you."

"I'm not your father."

She stared at him. "What do you mean?"

"Isn't that what happened to you? You wanted to lose yourself in him, and because you couldn't, you lost yourself in Bernard Godwin?"

"What a horrible thing to say."

"Perhaps, but it's the truth." Russell held her. "Tori, this is what Bernard saw in you—the Wild Child of Tokyo. Do you think he came upon you by accident, that he hadn't studied you for months? Understanding your particular psychology was how he was able to snare you, keep you loyal to him. This is Bernard's specialty."

Tori sought to digest all this. She watched water droplets streaking the window. It seemed to her as if that horizontal rain represented the strange new world opening to her. "I'm still the Wild Child, Russ," she said. "I don't want to lose her."

Russell stroked her hair. "It seems hard to realize, I know, but you won't lose her, no matter what happens."

Tori closed her eyes, shuddered. "Is that why it's so hard to pull away?"

"Partly," Russell said. "There's also the fear of there being only you now to rely on."

Tori opened her eyes. "But that's not true, now, is it?" She was crying. "I love you, Russ."

They held each other in silence for some time. At last he stirred and said, "You know, discipline dictates that we turn this plane around right now. Love and fieldwork are deadly companions."

"It's too late for second thoughts," Tori said.

"Is it?"

"Always serious. Always duty first, that's you, Russ."

"Not always," he said, reaching for her. "Not anymore."

The 727 flew on toward Moscow.

* * *

Captain Nikolev was at Department N headquarters, immersed in the drudgery of paperwork connected with the Bondasenko-Ponomareva stakeout, when the routine report came over the wire. It concerned the American diplomatic mission from Tokyo being held up at Sheremetyevo Airport because of bureaucratic red tape.

He immediately got up from the typewriter. He was thinking of the memo Mars had shown him, and Mars's firm if unstated belief that this "diplomatic mission" had more to do with White Star than it did with international diplomacy.

He rang downstairs to the garage for a driver and car, grabbed his hat off the rack, and took the concrete stairs two at a time down to where the black Zil waited.

It was pouring, and traffic was snarled. He instructed his driver to take the Chaika lane out of the city so they could make good time to Sheremetyevo. It was important now that he arrive before someone from the American embassy did to bail the "diplomatic mission" out.

But even with all the cynicism KGB foreknowledge provided, he was unprepared for the two Americans he found enmeshed in the exquisitely inefficient Soviet bureaucratic machine. It was not the big handsome American male with the hard eyes and sharp tongue of a professional—although hardly a professional diplomat—who threw Captain Nikolev, but the stunning, well-built blond with eyes so fantastic that Nikolev had to force himself to look away or forever be mesmerized.

If possible, her tongue was sharper than that of her companion's. She was wearing a short skirt and a sleeveless blouse. Captain Nikolev stared at the definition of the muscles in her arms. He had never before in his life seen a pair of legs like those. His mind was busy, flicking past possibility after possibility. Who was this singular woman?

The two Americans were surrounded by a clot of suspicious, dull-eyed officials. Shaking off his amazement, Captain Nikolev waded into the mess with the assurance and aplomb of a member of an invisible club which operated by an entirely different set of rules from the rest of the local citizens.

He glanced at the diplomatic mission's papers, and though he was convinced that they were forgeries before he even saw them, he could find no hard evidence to back up that suspicion. The papers seemed genuine to him, and he was certain that should he hand them over to the KGB lab, its results would likely not

461

differ from his first visual impression. The lab could do the same with any American—or British, French, Japanese—document one could name, so what was the point in trying to spot a forgery? One had to go by instinct in these matters, Captain Nikolev had learned, not by evidence. Though, of course, one needed to be thorough, experience had taught him that professionals rarely gave you any evidence to work with, so it was useless to waste too much time searching for it.

"Mr. Slade, Miss Nunn," Captain Nikolev said in Russian, as he introduced himself, "do either of you speak Russian?"

"I speak it passably well," Tori said, "though I admit it's been some time since I had cause to use it."

Captain Nikolev smiled, inclined his head. "Your accent is not terrible, Miss Nunn. How is your vocabulary?"

"We'll have to see."

Yes, Nikolev thought. That we will. He closed their documents, handed them back. "Everything seems in order," he said.

"Really?" Tori was surprised. "Then why have we been sitting here wrangling with Immigration for over an hour?"

Nikolev shrugged. "It seems to me that bureaucracies are the same the world over." He smiled. "Someone perhaps was concerned that your flight plan overflew the military air base outside Novosibirsk."

Tori said, "The fact is, we were detoured around it."

"Of course. I understand local security outside of Moscow is quite good, quite stable, but nevertheless . . ." He smiled again. "I hope it would not be too much of an inconvenience if I had some of my men check your aircraft."

"I'm afraid that's impossible," Tori said. "We are on a diplomatic mission. Our carrier is United States government equipment. We—and it—have immunity."

"I promise you nothing of a personal nature will be disturbed. I suppose some of my superiors are understandably disturbed that we might find long-range lenses or cameras—"

Tori said, "I can assure you there's nothing of that nature on board."

"Not to dispute your honesty, Miss Nunn, but policy dictates—"

"You'll leave our airplane alone, Captain, unless you're prepared to initiate an international incident. Our government takes a dim view of the violation of diplomatic rights."

Captain Nikolev hesitated for just a moment, then a smile

broke out on his face. "Of course," he said. "You're quite right. I can't imagine what I was thinking of." He gestured them through Immigration. "Won't you follow me? I have a car waiting to take you to Tchaikovsky Street. To make up for the inconvenience."

Tori saw his expectant look. She knew she was being tested. She already had the disquieting sense that this Captain Nikolev of the KGB Border Guards did not for a moment believe that she and Russell were diplomats. But how was that possible?

For a moment she had the odd, even more disquieting sensation that this man had been waiting for them to land. But all that had been logged with the Soviet authorities was their flight plan. That could hardly be enough to alert the KGB. And that nonsense about the air base at Novosibirsk had not fooled her. Had the ever-paranoid Soviets really been worried, they would never have approved the flight plan in the first place. She wondered what was going on behind the carefully erected facades.

As they headed through the terminal, Russell said in English, "What the hell's going on?"

Tori grinned like an idiot at him. "This nice KGB captain has been kind enough to offer us a ride into town."

"He's too kind," Russell said, catching her expression, which said, Who knows who understands English around here?

"My thought exactly."

Captain Nikolev's driver had the black Zil's curbside doors open, and they all piled into the car. Nikolev had previously told his driver not to take the Chaika lane inside Moscow, and the man did not take the route that would have brought them directly to the American embassy on Tchaikovsky Street.

"I thought," Nikolev said, "that you might enjoy a spot of sightseeing before I drop you at your destination."

"That's most kind of you, Captain," Tori said after she had translated for Russell's benefit. "Neither of us have been in Moscow before."

"A first diplomatic mission!" Nikolev enthused. "Now I must make this sightseeing something to remember."

Why is it, Tori asked herself, that I'm hearing sinister undertones in everything he says, as if he's saying one thing, and meaning something altogether different?

He took them past the Lenin Hills and the State University, where yesterday he and Mars Volkov had had their discussion. Along the Moskva, past Gorky Park, so green and lush in the full onset of summer.

Captain Nikolev stuck his head out the window. He could almost taste the ice cream as he watched children with their mothers queuing up to the mobile stand, clamoring for their treat.

"Such a beautiful time of year," Nikolev said to Tori. "You are so lucky to be here now."

"Luck has nothing to do with it," Tori said. "Our orders from the State Department brought us here."

"Of course." Nikolev brought his head back inside the Zil. It was odd, he thought, fencing with a woman. He would have much preferred to deal with the man, Russell Slade, but since Slade obviously did not speak Russian, Nikolev knew for the time being he'd just have to make the best of it.

"You know," he said now, "all this sightseeing has made me hungry—and you, well, you've just come off a twelve-hour plane ride. Please allow me to take you to lunch."

"Much as we appreciate the offer," Tori said, "I think we'd better be getting to our first appointment."

"I believe the time change has made you confused, Miss Nunn." Nikolev shot her his best smile. "You missed your first appointment while you were unfortunately held up at Sheremetyevo. In fact, were it not for me, I'm afraid that you and Mr. Slade would have been stuck there the whole day. Besides, it's lunchtime now. And I know the best restaurant in Moscow."

In fact, Tori and Russell were famished. But the moment they turned onto Krasnokursantsky Street, Tori was all too aware of the joke being played on them. She had heard of Lefortovo, the state security police interrogation center and prison, had even seen photos of its forbidding exterior. So had Russell.

"What the hell is this?" he said, sitting bolt upright.

Captain Nikolev laughed. "You do not think I am taking you *there*, do you?" He shook his head. "*That* Lefortovo is only for spies and criminals." The black Zil pulled up across the street. "You are to be my guests at the Lefortovo *restaurant*."

"Charming," Tori said as they stepped out onto the rain-washed sidewalk.

"Not really," Nikolev said, apparently ignorant of her sarcasm. He led them up the steps. "The place has little charm, I admit. But the food is good, the service even better—most important in Moscow, I'm afraid. And it's cheap. We who are dependent on military salaries must constantly count our rubles." They went through the doors. "I suppose it's the same with you and Mr. Slade."

464

"Why would you say that?" Tori asked.

Captain Nikolev took off his shiny-billed hat and, sticking it under his left arm, spoke for a moment with the maître d'. They were immediately led to a superior corner table.

When they were settled, Nikolev studied Tori for a long time. Then he said, "It is my understanding that government personnel of all types are underpaid. Is this not so?"

Tori chose not to answer him. Instead she said, "Captain, I would very much like to know why you chose this restaurant to take us to. Surely you knew its location—not to mention its name—would be repellent to us."

"Well, yes, that did occur to me," Nikolev said. He paused to order them all vodka. When the waiter had gone, he continued, "But we have business to discuss, and in Moscow one must choose one's negotiation site with the utmost care."

"Negotiation?"

"What's he saying?" Russell asked, concerned by the expression on her face. When she had translated, he said, "Just what the hell does this bozo want?"

"This bozo," Captain Nikolev said in almost accentless English, "wants a chance to make a proposal."

The silence at the table was deafening. Tori shot Russell a glare that would have taken off his head if her eyes had been lasers.

Nikolev cleared his throat. It seemed as if he was as uncomfortable as they were. The vodka came to save them all—at least temporarily. He raised his glass. "What shall we drink to?"

"The dismantling of Lefortovo prison," Tori said.

"An inquiry into its questionable practices," Captain Nikolev said.

They drank to that, but it was a compromise that made Tori uneasy. This man was, after all, a captain in the Border Guards division of the KGB. He was on to them, no doubt about it, but what was his game? Tori expanded her *wa* in an effort to catch a glimpse of his strategy. She did not like being wholly in the dark.

She and Russell had no sooner stepped into the Red Sector—the enemy's territory—when they had been picked up by that very same enemy. Or *was* Captain Nikolev the enemy?

That was the danger, she recognized: to be able to differentiate the enemy from a friend was a cardinal principle of espionage. The idea of successfully couching the one inside the other was what made this clandestine world continue to tick in

465

this electronicized, computerized age. When you got into trouble—whether it was an individual, a department, a country—it was because you had trusted the person who was selling you out to your enemy.

She felt nothing from this man, neither hostility nor camaraderie, merely a kind of coiled tension. It was different from Russell's tension when she and he were fighting. The Russian's was more intense, darker, more opaque. And it had many layers. It seemed interesting to her that this man should be under so much stress. What was he frightened of? she wondered.

"I want to at least attempt to explain," Captain Nikolev was saying now, breaking in on her thoughts. "Look around you. By and large, you will see only military men. Most of them work across the street. I know many of them, though not well. We have never shared an evening meal, our children are not friends. But they know me, and therefore this is a safe haven for me. I can take anyone here and no one will talk about it because it will be assumed that these people are my friends, my guests, or are business associates." He cocked his head. "Do you understand?"

"I think I'm beginning to," Tori said. "But you'd better spell it out for Mr. Slade. He isn't as quick as I am."

"Is this true?" Nikolev asked Russell anxiously. "Perhaps my English will be inadequate."

"Your accent isn't terrible," Tori said. "But Mr. Slade will, I think, tax your vocabulary."

Nikolev laughed softly. "I like humor," he said. "Especially in a woman. It's very comfortable, don't you think?"

"I think you mean comforting," Tori said. "And that depends on the type of humor."

"Perhaps if I get to know you better, I will receive an entire catalogue of humor," Nikolev said, clearly delighted. "I would welcome that. It's said the Romans of Augustus Caesar's day had much humor."

Nikolev patiently watched the silent interplay between Tori and Russell before saying, "I know. You're thinking again, 'What does this bozo want?' By the way, what is a bozo?"

"Know what a clown is?" Russell said. "Same thing."

"I see." Nikolev seemed to frown a little. Then the first course came, and he brightened. "It's a set menu here. I hope you don't mind not being able to choose."

"We're getting used to it," Tori said.

They ate more or less in silence. When the plates were cleared of the last course, Nikolev said, "Was it so bad?"

"Lutèce it isn't," Russell said, plopping sugar into his strong Russian tea.

"Ah, a restaurant in Paris."

"Close," Russell said.

Captain Nikolev nodded, apparently satisfied. "In any case, I think we all feel better now, yes?"

"Maybe some of us do," Russell said pointedly.

"What Mr. Slade means," Tori said hurriedly, "is that we're still a bit bewildered. Obviously you want something from us, but we still have no idea what it is."

"That's all right for now," Nikolev said. "Can we say that this time together has proven that we can . . . talk to one another?"

Russell said, "Depends about what."

Captain Nikolev looked at him for some time, as if he could not make up his mind about something important. "It's a matter of trust, isn't it?" he said. He took out a handkerchief, wiped his brow. "I have no idea whether I can trust you."

Russell, who had just taken some tea, was so surprised he almost choked on it. He began to cough, and his eyes teared. Tori just sat and stared at Nikolev as if he were out of his mind.

"Have I said something odd?"

"You bet you have," Tori said.

Russell said, "You, Captain, are the goddamnedest Russian I have ever met."

"Yes? Well, perhaps that is something to be proud of."

"You said something before about a proposal," Tori said.

"Have I your assurance that you'll listen to what I have to say?"

"I'm more paranoid than she is," Russell said. "What kind of proposal?"

"An . . . exchange of information."

"You first, Ivan."

"Russell!" Tori said.

"What?" Russell retorted. "Remember where we are, Tori. In a country where we're guilty until proven guilty. Anything we say or do from now on will be used against us in a place not unlike the building across the street. Talking to this guy's like trying to stand in quicksand. I think he's as loony as Daffy Duck."

467

"Excuse me," Captain Nikolev said. "This Daffy Duck, is he a bozo as well?"

Tori put her hands over her face.

Russell said, "Yeah." Then he turned to her. "This isn't happening."

"It isn't?" Nikolev said, clearly confused.

Russell said, "Where are the guys in baggy pants to squirt us with seltzer?"

"They have seltzer here," Nikolev said, calling a waiter. He was trying to be helpful.

"That's all right," Tori said. She told the waiter in Russian to forget it, and he retreated. Tori hunched over the table. "Captain, we have nothing to hide. I want that understood from the outset."

Nikolev nodded.

"On the other hand, Mr. Slade and I have no way to know whether we can trust *you*."

"Tori, for God's sake—"

"I understand," Captain Nikolev said. His expression showed something of his relief. "It is like a . . . Mexican shootout, yes?"

"Standoff," Russell said. "A Mexican standoff."

Captain Nikolev nodded soberly. "Thank you. I will remember that. American idioms are so . . . incomprehensible."

"Tell me about it."

"Pardon? I just did."

"Let's not start this all over again," Tori said. She spread her hands on the table palms up. "How do you wish to proceed, Captain?"

"I would like to make my proposal . . . but not here."

"Where?" Russell said.

"A villa. In the Lenin Hills."

Tori smiled. "Captain, please try to see this situation from our point of view. We have had no assurances from you—"

"I am speaking English," Nikolev said immediately. "KGB agents are not supposed to reveal such things. We are to pretend ignorance of English so as to learn more."

Russell said, "To my way of thinking, that's damn little in the way of assurances."

"Be fair," Tori said. "We haven't given him much, either." She said to Nikolev. "We'll listen to your proposal, Captain, but that's all we'll agree to."

Captain Nikolev nodded.

Russell groaned. "Great. Either way, I think we're about to get fucked."

At approximately the time that Tori and Russell were stuck at Immigration at Sheremetyevo, Mars Volkov was embracing Irina. Then he pushed her from him, held her at arm's length so he could look into her eyes. "I was getting worried about you," he said. "Your amateur sleuthing is all well and good—and believe me when I tell you I owe you an enormous debt of gratitude—but with Valeri and his KGB stooges on the loose, when I didn't hear from you, I feared the worst. In fact, I was just about to call the police when you showed up. How fortuitous!"

"Fortuitous, indeed." *KGB. Keep calm.* Irina was careful to let none of the terror she felt leak into her voice. *He's not yet ready to reveal himself,* she thought. *That means he wants something from me. What?* "It seems that the KGB were watching Valeri's apartment. They almost caught me."

"It's a good thing I'm here, then," Mars said.

The rain beat against the windshield of the car. The world was contracting into a tiny gray ball the size of a prison cell. Irina felt the irrational urge to look at the Toshiba portable to make sure it was still there. Of course it was. She stared steadfastly into the teeming mist.

"You're without wipers," Mars said.

"They were stolen. It's my fault. I forgot to take them with me one day."

He shrugged. "There are more in the trunk. I'll get a pair."

Irina watched him as he slid across the backseat, got out, went around to the rear of the car. She put her hands on the steering wheel, then let one slip to the gear lever. She saw Mars open the trunk, bend down.

All she had to do was release the hand brake, throw the car in gear, and crash out of the prison Mars was contemplating for her. Simple. Irina felt her muscles tighten in preparation for the move. Or was it so simple? Where was the Border Guards contingent that had had Valeri's apartment cordoned off? Surely they hadn't gone and left Mars here on his own.

Her hands were shaking so badly that she did not believe that she could drive properly. Not in this downpour. Not without windshield wipers.

She heard the trunk slam, and she gave a little cry as her heart skipped a beat. Then Mars was coming around, attaching the

469

blades. He did this with one hand. When, a moment later, he returned to the car, he slipped into the front passenger's seat. He put Valeri's Toshiba between his legs.

Irina looked down, saw a pistol in Mars's right hand. It was pointed toward the floorwell.

"I thought I saw one of Valeri's KGB men," Mars said when he saw where she was looking. "A kind of war has broken out between the two of us." He put the gun away. "I'm afraid you almost got killed coming between us."

"I've done what you asked." Irina wondered whether her voice sounded as brittle to Mars as it did to her. She hoped not. "Didn't I discover the connection between Natasha and Valeri?"

"Yes," he said. "You did. And, as I said, I'm grateful. Valeri and I had come to an odd kind of stalemate. Surveillance on either side had become virtually impossible. We knew each other's people far too well." He smiled. "Then you came to me like an angel from heaven. For that I am also grateful."

The interior of the car had begun to steam up, and he rolled down his window a bit. Rain pattered against the edge, sending a fine spray onto his shoulder. He took no notice. "But I'm also puzzled, Irina. What were you doing in Valeri's apartment?"

"Trying to find the answer to the mystery of White Star." She turned to face him, thinking, Was it you who tortured poor Natasha until she gave up the dark secret of Valeri's daughter? And did you kill her when she was no longer of use to you? Bastard! She said, "Isn't that what you asked me for?"

"And what have you found?"

She was acutely aware of the gun in his pocket. "I searched his apartment and came up with nothing."

"Except this," Mars said. "What is it?"

"Valeri's computer," she said.

"An illegal computer," Mars said. "That would be just like Valeri Denysovich." He stared at Irina. "Why did you take it?"

KGB. Keep calm. Irina fought the numbing terror, fought to make her mind work, to figure out what she must say to him, to appease him yet not to give away—

"I'll answer for you," Mars said. "You thought the computer might contain White Star's secrets."

Her mind was like a sheet of ice. "Yes." What else could she say?

Mars said nothing for a time. Then he put his head back

470

against the seat rest, closed his eyes. A slow smile spread across his lips. "Why don't we give it a try?"

Too late, Irina realized her mistake in not throwing the computer away when she had had the chance. Better it be lost to Valeri than land in the hands of the KGB. She wept inside for Valeri, for Natasha, for White Star, for herself, because this monster had won. Now she knew what he wanted from her.

She set the wipers going, and the windshield cleared as much as it was going to with the car's primitive and inefficient defroster. She held her breath, said, "Where shall we go? Your apartment?"

"No," Mars said. "Star Town."

Arbat was swimming in a circle.

"What's the matter with her?" Lara said.

"I don't know," the Hero admitted. He spoke to her in the peculiar clickings that Lara did not understand but had grown used to. Immediately, Arbat ceased her nervous circling, lifted her nose, let out with a long string of speech.

"Something's wrong," the Hero said.

"What?"

"I don't know. Neither does Arbat. But something very bad has happened."

"Volkov?"

"Yes, probably," the Hero said. He swam over to where Arbat was, put his arms around her. She nuzzled his face. "Don't worry," he whispered, then repeated it in her language.

It was then that Lara understood the depth of his concern. He had been trying to comfort himself.

Lara came close to him. "Perhaps we need not fear Comrade Volkov as much as we have in the past. I think we have succeeded in making him believe you are turning into something beyond his ken."

The Hero smiled. "That was a neat trick, you swimming underwater to scrape his leg while I went into my 'seizure.' "

"You played your role to perfection," Lara said.

"Comrade Volkov has seen to it that I've had enough time to work out the rough edges."

Lara was abruptly serious. She touched his arm. "All this playacting is one thing, but what worries me are the real effects of the cosmic radiation you were exposed to. What happens when its effects are made manifest?"

"What happens when we die?" the Hero asked her rhetori-

471

cally. "It might be interesting to contemplate, but there's no solid answer, is there?" He smiled reassuringly. "We'll just have to wait and see."

"Do you think Irina will have the courage to wait with you?"

"I don't know," the Hero said truthfully. "I've tried to explain as best I can what I'm up against. But you know as well as anyone that there is no way to explain the unknowable."

"You love her, don't you?"

The Hero was silent for a long time, hanging in his void of saltwater. "I love the color between the stars," he said. "That is where much of my mind now dwells, in the time/no time, the dimension where time is twisted like taffy around a spindle. I've been shown the limitations of being part of only the taffy. Now I long to join those inside the spindle."

"You do not need to worry about making me jealous," Lara said. "Tatiana and I would never betray you now, not after what you've done for us. You have shown us the power of our past, the weaknesses of our present. You are our family."

The Hero reached out, twined his fingers in Lara's. "If I do love Irina, it is in a way that neither of you can understand. Certainly I cannot explain what I feel."

"You talk to her without ever speaking."

"That's true."

"As you did with the entity who discovered you between the stars."

"Yes."

"What was it like, that communication?"

The Hero smiled. "I've told you so many times."

"It's like a bedtime story," Lara said. "I never grow tired of hearing it."

"All right," the Hero said, and his face screwed up in concentration. "It was like lying on a bed of nails, like running barefoot across a room filled with shards of glass; it was like eating so much chocolate at once that your brain boils, like hanging in a sensory-deprivation tank, your body sloughed off like a memory, connected to nothing but the processes of your own mind." He closed his eyes, and it was as if the world had winked out. Blackness reigned. "It was *like* all of those things happening at once. Yet it wasn't any of that at all."

"What, then?"

"All right. Another image. I was farther out in space than any human being has ever been. But when the communication began, I knew that I had journeyed so far only to have come to

472

the center of things, so deep inside that I had found an entirely new existence.''

"But inside *what*?''

"I don't know," the Hero said. "Perhaps time itself."

Lara was very close to him. "I wish I could understand."

"Yes," he said softly. "I wish you could, too."

"Arbat understands."

"Arbat is special."

"And Irina. She understands, too, doesn't she?"

The Hero's eyes were like stars in the blankness of space. They radiated warmth as well as light. "Irina knows how the entity and I communicated."

"How I envy her."

Arbat was pushing her nose insistently against the Hero's hand, and a moment later Tatiana slipped into the pool with them.

"Volkov's back," she said quietly, ominously. "Irina is with him. And so is Valeri's Toshiba portable."

"Ah, God." The Hero's voice chilled them all.

On the doorstep to the villa, Captain Nikolev turned to Tori and Russell, said, "This place belongs to the man from whom I take my orders."

Russell said, "You mean your superior in the Border Guards unit."

"No. My division has been seconded to Department N of the KGB. Mars Volkov, the Chief of Department N, is the man who commands my unit."

"He's got wide-ranging powers," Tori said.

"I want you to understand that," Captain Nikolev said, "as part of your assurances. This is an enormous risk I am taking." He looked at them both, then turned, unlocked the front door.

He went immediately across the tile floor, showed them where the microphones were hidden. He opened up a blond wood console. Behind a mirrored bar with a false back was a professional reel-to-reel tape recorder. Nikolev took the tape reels from the recorder so that Tori and Russell would know nothing that was said here was being recorded.

"There's always the possibility of body mikes," Russell said. "I suppose we should all strip."

Nikolev laughed. He eyed Tori. "That's jake by me."

They looked at him, and he said, "Have I mixed up my idioms again?"

"If I were you, I wouldn't try to pass for an American just yet," Russell said.

Tori said, "You're just a little behind the times, that's all."

When they had assured themselves that none of them was taped with a body mike, Tori and Russell sat on an ugly Scandinavian couch hideously upholstered in a dark brown tweed. Captain Nikolev fixed them drinks. He was obviously nervous and in need of something to do with his hands, but neither Tori nor Russell touched their vodka. On the other hand, Nikolev knocked his back, poured himself another.

He paced back and forth, and Tori could feel his tension reaching a new pitch. She shifted uncomfortably as his nerves affected her.

Abruptly Nikolev faced them, said, "In a world full of lies, how are we able to recognize the truth?"

"Truth comes with trust," Tori said.

"Which is in short supply here," Russell added.

There was silence for some time.

Nikolev nodded. "Department N of the KGB, of which Mars Volkov is the chief, has been given a mandate to root out the elements of White Star and eradicate them."

"Succinctly put," Russell said.

"I am trying," Nikolev said with some desperation, "to establish an atmosphere of trust." He took a deep breath. "Before we go further, I must know something. Did you come here in response to White Star's request for aid?"

"Is this your proposal?" Russell asked.

"It is the beginning of our exchange of information." Nikolev looked pained. "I am under the gun, Mr. Slade. I wish you could appreciate that."

"We're all under the gun," Tori said.

"Keep still," Russell said as he got up. He prowled around the villa.

When he disappeared into the other rooms, Nikolev and Tori watched each other like gladiators unsure whether to fight or join forces to assassinate the emperor.

"He's a hard man," Nikolev said. "Full of suspicion."

"That's what they pay him for."

"And what do they pay *you* for, Miss Nunn?"

Tori got up, made her own slow circuit of the room. When she returned, she stood in front of Captain Nikolev, stared him in the eye. "They pay me," she said, "to know who our friends are."

474

Nikolev's gaze flicked to her arms. He licked his lips. "What happens to those who you decide aren't your friends?"

"I kill them," Tori said with what she hoped was an expression of great relish.

"I am a friend, Miss Nunn. Do you believe me?"

Tori said nothing.

When Russell came back into the living room, Nikolev said, "What were you looking for?"

"KGB goons," Russell said. "But I guess I'm looking at one, huh?"

Nikolev said, "You have yet to answer my question. Before I proceed further, I must know whether you have a connection with White Star."

"We do," Tori said.

"Christ almighty!" Russell was clearly not happy. "Here comes the death squad."

"Why?" Tori said, keeping her eye on Nikolev. "For all the captain here knows, we could be working for Mars Volkov. I could be lying to draw him out so that he can incriminate himself as a traitor to the state." She smiled into Nikolev's anxious face. "Isn't that so, Captain?"

Nikolev licked his lips again. "Yes. It could be either way."

"But now, one way or another, the die is cast. We must see whether the trust on both sides is justified."

Nikolev's gaze faltered. He stared for a time into his glass. "I come to bury Caesar, not to praise him."

Russell said, "What?"

Nikolev looked at them. "I feel a bit like Brutus, Mr. Slade, so forgive me if I take my time about this."

Tori, so close to him, could feel the constriction in his chest, the conflict of emotions battering him. If he was being duplicitous, he was a master.

Nikolev could bear standing still no longer. He walked to the windows that looked out on a balcony and a steep drop as the Lenin Hills fell away into brush beneath slender pines and larch. Tori could see his shoulders hunch involuntarily as if he were expecting a blow.

He said at length, "There is a plan—hatched within the KGB, but fully agreed to by the military—to march into Lithuania and Latvia. We are now on the cusp of this mad campaign to return the Baltic states, which the president, in the euphoria of perestroika, allowed to slip away from the Soviet Union."

Russell rocked back and forth on his heels, whistling softly. Tori said nothing.

Nikolev turned to face them. He was haloed by the pristine light that fills the sky after a violent storm, and his face seemed so young that one could almost imagine peach fuzz on his cheeks instead of whiskers. "This is, of course, treason," Nikolev went on. "No matter. The campaign will begin in thirteen hours. Dawn tomorrow. There will be wholesale slaughter. The official story is that the new and as yet unstable Baltic governments have been infiltrated by dangerous Western elements that threatened the national security of the Soviet Union."

In the charged silence that ensued, Tori said, "What about the president?"

"The president, it is felt by these factions within the KGB and the military, has become obsessed by the same cult of personality that enveloped Yuri Andropov. At precisely the same moment that the order will be given to invade the Baltic states, the president of the USSR will be assassinated by his own guards. It is the Rome of Claudius all over again."

"This is madness," Russell said. "Do you expect us to believe some cock-and-bull—"

He stopped as Tori clutched his arm. "What has all this to do with us, Captain? Surely we are even more powerless than you are at this moment."

"But you're not," Nikolev said with some urgency. "Not if I can believe you. Not if there is trust between us. You see, for a while we've known that White Star has been receiving aid in the form of matériel from the West. If you're here on behalf of White Star, then you are a godsend. Mars Volkov has forced Valeri Bondasenko, White Star's leader, into hiding. We cannot find him, but as representatives of White Star's Western support, I have no doubt that you have the means to get a message to Bondasenko.

"If you can do this, tell him what is happening, then we have a chance. White Star is the wild card in this whole equation. That's why Mars Volkov has been given carte blanche to find White Star and eradicate it.

"Only White Star has the power to stop this madness. It has the popular support throughout the Soviet Union, it has the people. All it has been lacking is the proper armaments. But now we believe that . . ."

"What were you going to say, Captain?" Tori said. "That it now has the weapons?"

476

"Yes," Nikolev said. "We have no idea what they are, but we suspect that they have been amassing some kind of arsenal to use when they felt the time was right." His fist clenched. "But the time is now. You must convince Valeri Bondasenko of the extreme jeopardy the entire country is in. He must use his new weapons to bring White Star's power into the Kremlin."

"And what will you be doing," Russell said, "while we're unearthing White Star's leader for you?"

"Not for me, not for the KGB," Nikolev said, for the first time showing his impatience. "For all of the Soviet Union."

Russell turned to Tori. "Can't you see this guy is trying to use us? Bondasenko's gone so successfully to ground no one can find him. Nikolev will use us as his bloodhounds. As soon as we find Bondasenko for him, he'll come in with his goons and—"

"No, no! That is not my intention! I am telling you the truth!"

"I think he is," Tori said, but Russell waved away her words.

"Prove it," he said to Nikolev.

"But how can I . . . ?" Nikolev thought a moment, then nodded. "I will make a proposal. Mars Volkov has captured Valeri Bondasenko's personal computer. It is believed that White Star's entire infrastructure is contained in the computer's software. Under no circumstances must Volkov be allowed access to that material. With it, he could break White Star inside thirty-six hours.

"I was going to get that computer out of Volkov's hands while you were running down Bondasenko, but now I have a better idea. You'll come with me, you'll see firsthand that I am telling the truth. I will be putting my life—and the lives of my hand-picked men—on the line by defying Mars Volkov. As outsiders, you cannot know what an enormous risk that is. If we fail, we will be summarily executed. No trial, no incarceration, no recompense for our families. In the blink of an eye, we simply will cease to exist."

"If we go with you," Tori said, "we'll be wasting valuable time. We've got to get to Bondasenko well before the dawn deadline."

"Yes," Nikolev said. "So we will all be taking enormous risks. There is an increasing chance we will not get to Bondasenko in time. That is why I resist taking you with me; we will be gambling with an entire nation. But I see no other method of fulfilling Mr. Slade's demand."

"Russell?"

"I don't want to back down," Russell said.

Nikolev said, "You must help me. You must. If the invasion and the assassination are allowed to take place, I fear there will be no recourse for us. We will return to the repressive government of the nightmare days of Stalin. We will be lost forever."

"We are lost," the Hero said the moment before Mars walked into the pool room with Irina.

Tatiana was already out of the pool. She had an oversized towel wrapped around her middle, but her chest above the line of her swimsuit was beaded with saltwater.

"Comrade," she said. "Irina."

"Good afternoon, Tatiana," Mars said. "Look what I have." He lifted the Toshiba portable. "Would you help Irina set this up on the table over there? Make sure the power source is secure."

Tatiana did as she was told. She glanced at Irina out of the corner of her eye. Irina was afraid to say or do anything that Mars might misconstrue. There was still a chance, she felt, that he believed she was loyal to him. While that possibility existed, she was determined to make the most of it. She certainly was not going to give him any cause to doubt her allegiance.

Irina unzipped the case, took the Toshiba out, handed the power cord with its adaptor to Tatiana. While she was setting up the computer, Mars walked over to the coping of the pool, peered down into the phosphorescent depths.

"Odysseus," he said, "are you feeling any better?"

"I wasn't aware that I was at all unwell."

Mars knelt down. "You had a seizure. You don't recall that?"

"No."

"During the seizure you spoke a whole bunch of nonsense."

"The color between the stars," the Hero said. "I remember speaking their language."

Mars swallowed hard. "Whose language?"

"Not yours, comrade."

Mars stood up as if abruptly repulsed. He turned, went over to where the computer sat. Irina had pulled up a chair.

Lara came up, told Mars he had a call. Out of the corner of her eye Irina watched him as he went to the wall phone, spoke into it briefly. He seemed to listen for a long time and, though Irina could not be certain, she thought his face shut down tight. Mars made one final curt reply, hung up the receiver.

478

Irina went back to work. Her fingers danced over the keyboard and a string of recipes began scrolling across the screen.

Mars came up behind her. "What is this?" he demanded.

"Pineapple upside-down cake." Irina wondered what the call had been about. Whatever it was, it had put him in a sour mood. Good news for her or bad?

"Idiotic," Mars commented. "Where in the world would one get a pineapple?"

"Perhaps Valeri has them flown in from Cuba," Irina said.

Tatiana said, "I don't believe Cuba has pineapple trees."

"Idiotic," Mars repeated. "What else is in the machine?"

"More recipes, it seems."

"Bah. Valeri Denysovich wouldn't use an illegal computer merely to store his recipes." Mars shook his head. "What a woman he is."

"Apparently he is a woman you cannot find."

In the wake of the Hero's words, everyone froze.

Mars stood up, walked on stiff legs back to the pool. He glared down at the Hero. "Who told you that?"

The Hero said nothing. He floated placidly in the saltwater.

"I said, who told you that?"

Arbat began to chatter in alarm.

Mars had drawn his pistol and was now aiming it at the Hero's head.

"You'll answer me, Odysseus, or I'll blow your head off."

Irina got up, went across the room. "Mars," she said softly. She put her hand on his arm. "Mars, don't."

"No one told me, comrade," the Hero said. "You've quite effectively cut off my information gathering, remember. Besides, no one had to tell me. I can read your mind."

"What are you talking about?"

"You've manipulated the final showdown with your archenemy, haven't you, Volkov? No, don't bother denying it. I know. I can see it as clearly as I can see that ugly expression of hatred disfiguring your face. You pushed and pushed, and what do you have to show for it? Bondasenko's beyond even your reach."

"Shut up!" Mars said, and Irina, with a flash of intuition, understood that he was abruptly terrified that Odysseus would blurt out that he was KGB. Mars had no idea that Odysseus had already told her that.

Irina knelt beside the pool, looked into the Hero's eyes. They spoke silently for the instant before she said, "Let it be for now, Odysseus. You've provoked him enough."

479

The Hero sank beneath the water, and Arbat followed him.

For a long time Mars stared into the pool. "How does he do that?" he said. "Stay underwater for so long?"

"Perhaps he's half dolphin," Irina joked, but the stricken look on Mars's face told her that for him on this subject there was no room for humor. She thought that quite interesting, and remembering the Hero's last conversation with Mars, she began to see the strategy Odysseus had formulated for combating Mars.

"Come away now," she said gently. Her fingers closed over his where he still gripped the pistol with white knuckles. "There's no need for that. Come, Mars. Come."

And Irina led him back to the computer where every secret Mars lusted after lay hidden, waiting to be unlocked.

"It's the waiting," Russell said, "that I hate the most."

"You're thinking of Nikolev, aren't you?" Tori said. "You still think he's using us as bloodhounds."

"I only wish I was as sure of him as you are."

"Yeah, well, I thought I was sure of Estilo and Hitasura."

They stared out at the glorious view of the Kremlin and the golden domes of St. Basil's. They were sitting at a window table at the twenty-first-floor restaurant of the Rossiya Hotel. They had been there for forty-five minutes and had still to receive their drinks. That was all right; they were in no hurry.

Tori had left a handwritten message, sealed in an envelope, and as Hitasura had told her was to be done, had addressed it to a Mrs. Kubysheva, handed it in at the front desk. The young man who had taken it from her had looked at the name she had printed on the envelope, said carefully in English, "Perhaps you'd care to have dinner at the restaurant upstairs, miss. The twenty-first floor offers unparalleled views of the city."

Tori and Russell did as he suggested. Upstairs, Tori went to the ladies' room while Russell went to get them seated. How he had procured this choice table at the crowded restaurant she could not guess, but as she was learning, Russell was adept at such things.

"Hitasura outfoxed everyone," Russell said, still staring out the window. "And, as for Estilo, perhaps you weren't so wrong about him. After all, without his help we might never have come this far."

"But, oh, poor Ariel."

"Yes." Russell nodded. "Poor Ariel. He was a seeker after truth, and he died for that."

480

Tori pulled something out of her pocket, put it on the table between them. She smoothed out the creases. "I didn't tell you about this before, but Ariel made sure I had this before he died. He obviously thought it was significant."

Russell looked at the photograph. "It's of Ariel. That's San Francisco, isn't it?"

"Yes. It's a park very close to his house."

He looked on the back, read off the date: March 21.

"Jesus!" Tori snatched the photo out of his hand, studied it carefully. Now she knew why the dates of Bernard Godwin's trip had rung a bell. They coincided with when this picture was taken. She moved the photo closer, peered intently at the people in the background. And there, just to the left of the couple, in the extreme left-hand corner of the frame, was a man. Bernard Godwin.

Russell could see it, too. You had to be looking for Bernard, but once you did, you could recognize him.

"Ariel had him pinpointed, all right," Tori said.

Russell nodded. "It would seem so."

"And was murdered for it?"

"Do you think so?" Russell was not convinced. "But there must be something more to this photo. What's so incriminating about it? I mean, Bernard could have gone to San Francisco for a vacation, to see a woman, any of a million reasons." He studied the photo again, handed it back. "Can you make out this couple?"

Tori shook her head. "They're further away than Bernard is, though they seem to be headed his way."

"We could use a darkroom," Russell said. "If we could blow this picture up, we might be able to identify this couple in the background before the film got too grainy."

"We could always go to the KGB. I'm sure they have darkrooms to spare."

"Very funny." Russell looked morose. "I'm sorry, Tori, but I can't help thinking that Nikolev is something less than totally sincere."

"I think you're wrong, Russ, and like it or not, we're both gambling our lives on it. Nikolev has already revealed enough of himself to make us reasonably sure of him."

"Then I'm an unreasonable person."

"No," Tori said, giving his hand a squeeze. "Just a careful one."

At last a waitress showed up and they ordered.

"Don't get your hopes up," Russell said. "The food won't be coming any time soon."

"It'll be getting dark soon," Tori said, watching the lights come on in Red Square, the onion domes of St. Basil's glow a burnished gold at the waning of a long afternoon. "This is a cold city, even in the beginning of summer."

Russell grunted. "That's because the temperature has nothing to do with it." He sat back abruptly. "It's the waiting I can't stand."

"Unfortunately, that's all we can do until we get a reply from Mrs. Kubysheva."

"*If* we get a reply. With Bondasenko gone to ground, the organization won't be taking many chances."

"I think the dire situation is exactly why we'll hear from them," Tori said. "They wired Hitasura for help, we know that. Now that we've come, they'll see us."

"Yeah, but according to Nikolev, it seems we're not the only ones who know about that communication. The KGB must have broken the organization's code. I wonder what else the KGB knows?"

"I think Nikolev told us as much as he dares—perhaps, from his point of view, too much."

"He's the goddamn KGB, Tori."

"He's also a human being. He's obviously unhappy with what he has been doing. It seems to me he wants the best for his country. I think he's not so very different than we are, Russ. He's caught in a spiderweb of deceit, and now he's doing the best he can to crawl out of it."

"Christ, I hope you're right about this guy."

Tori stared out at the domes of St. Basil's. She was struck by how alien this city seemed to her. She remembered stories her father used to tell her that his father had told him, legends of valiant Ural mountain wolves in winter, tales of courageous Georgian peasants in high summer, sagas of brave soldiers caught on the ice fields of Siberia. How different this strange and unpleasant place seemed from the settings of those magical stories.

How she had hated when her father had spoken to her in his native Russian. She had known he was only trying to help her in her studies, but she despised the Russian classes she was taking—hated everything Russian. She had wanted her father to speak English like the fathers of all her friends. Now, to her surprise, she found that she wished he were here with her to talk

482

with her in Russian, and to guide her around this remote and forbidding metropolis.

She wondered whether he would like it here if he ever came. She suspected that he would be depressed by modern-day Russia, as she was. Perestroika or not, it was still as backward as a third-world country.

It was not until ten that they were finished eating. Night was coming down at last.

"It's not going to happen," Russell said. "And now we've lost Nikolev as well. He's off in some place called Zvezdny Gorodok."

"Star Town," Tori said. "Where they train and house the cosmonauts for the Soviet space program."

"We never should have allowed him to go without us."

"Too late for that."

The bill came on a small tray. Tori picked it up, saw a piece of paper, smaller than the bill, lying on the tray. She scooped it up, read it quickly, excitedly. Then she looked up, said softly to Russell, "We're in business."

"Irina," Mars said, "come here for a moment."

Irina gratefully abandoned her faked search through the hard disk of Valeri's Toshiba, went across the room to where Mars was standing. He was in deep shadow, and she could not make out his face.

"In here," he said, pushing open a door for her to step through.

Inside the small cubicle he said, "Now that Odysseus is asleep in his bed, I want to have a talk with you."

Irina nodded, keeping herself as calm as she was able. She wished she could control her heartbeat as she had read the priests of Tibet could.

"What did he tell you about his sources of information?"

Irina blinked. "Sources? I thought Natasha Mayakova was his source."

"She was a courier, yes, that's clear." Mars said. "But I don't believe she could have brought him all his information. He's always too up-to-date when I see him. Natasha saw him only perhaps once a week. I see him more often."

"He didn't say anything, and in any case, I felt I couldn't press him."

"He didn't say anything about Lara or Tatiana."

Irina could feel her heart skip a beat. "No."

483

"Was he suspicious when you asked him about his sources?"

"No," Irina said. "I didn't word it as a question. Anyway, he seemed to have other things on his mind."

"What, for instance?"

Irina looked away. "He's very . . . sexually active."

"Ah."

"Are you angry?"

"Ask me that in half an hour," Mars said.

Irina's head swung around. She kept her eyes on him. "What will happen then?"

"I'll know unequivocally whether you have betrayed me to Valeri Denysovich."

There was a buzzing in Irina's ears, and she thought she would faint. "What are you saying? Valeri is KGB. You know how I loathe them."

Mars said, "I am now prepared to say that I don't know as much about you as I would like."

"You're very different here," Irina said, trying to break off this inquisition. She hoped she was able to keep all wariness out of her voice.

"Not here," Mars said. "Now. Valeri has declared open war on me." He shrugged. "This will be a difficult and trying time for us all." He moved with the casual grace Irina was used to, but she noticed that he always kept himself between her and the door. "You should take that as a warning."

"But how can you suspect me?" Irina said. "Didn't I give you Natasha Mayakova?"

Mars nodded. "Indeed you did, but that could have been a mistake."

"Mistake? I knew exactly what I was doing."

"I wonder," Mars said. His gaze seemed to penetrate her defenses layer by layer. "The work you have been doing is tremendously strenuous even for a trained professional—which most certainly you are not. You have to be mentally and emotionally tough to be able to befriend people and then on command betray them.

"You spend so much time pretending to be someone else that often you actually *become* that someone else. Isn't it so, Irina? Admit it, it happens to even the most hardened professionals. Illusion becomes real and vice versa. In a way, it's a form of camouflage. If *you* believe your false identity is real, so will everyone else around you. Surely you can see the logic of such a trap. In any case, I'm told by experts that it's a sound psychological principle."

"No matter," Irina said somewhat defensively. "It hasn't happened to me."

"No?" He was very close to her now. Close enough to hear the rapid pounding of her heart? "Who are you, really? The sweet Irina Ponomareva my family knows? Or the devious Katya Boroskaya who is using Natasha Mayakova? Or the tough Irina Ponomareva who is spying on Valeri Denysovich?" He cocked his head sagely. "You know, even I get confused trying to sort through all these different personalities. It certainly would be understandable if you did, as well."

"I don't understand what you're doing," Irina said. "Why are you trying to put words in my mouth?"

Mars spread his hands. "I'm just trying to sort out illusion from reality, fact from fiction, myth from certainty. I'm like an archaeologist at an important historic dig. Many people are counting on the acuity of my skills."

"I don't know what you're getting at."

"You know, I blame myself most of all, Irina. I'm afraid I pushed you into this triple life. I see now the foolishness of my action. But it was compulsive. Surely that absolves me, if only a little. Valeri Denysovich pushed me to it. Because of him, you've been walking a perilous tightrope, and now you've fallen off. You've lost your center, you've forgotten who you really are, what your true allegiance should be.

"As I said before, it's perfectly understandable. Certainly, there's no hint of a criminal act involved, nothing you could be charged with, no matter what your confession might bring to light. I'd see to that personally." He reached out to touch her comfortingly. "You can count on me, Irina, to be your guardian angel."

The odd and terribly frightening thing was that Irina almost believed him. There was so much essential truth in what he was saying that it was easy to accept the entire package—believe everything: that she would be off the hook, that she would not be charged, that he would protect her no matter what. No endless Siberian winter, no bars over her moon, after all. It was so very tempting.

He made it so difficult to see the lie hidden away beneath his version of the truth, but Irina did see it at last and, imagining him torturing Natasha, she wondered how on earth she was going to fight this enormously powerful and charismatic creature.

She could see that she was out of time. It was obvious to her that Mars was pushing for a resolution—soft or hard—one way or another. She had to fight him, but how? Then she thought of Odysseus, Mars's prisoner for almost eighteen months. He had successfully fought Mars. How? By applying Mars's own psychology and boomeranging it back at him. Mars might on the surface seem invulnerable, but Odysseus had certainly proved that to be an illusion.

Mars was now frightened of Odysseus because Odysseus had convinced him that he was metamorphosing into another kind of being. Was that a complete lie? Irina did not know, and she suspected that, for all his bravery and bravado, Odysseus did not know, either. After all, he had been made into an experiment to see the effects of cosmic rays on the human body and mind.

And he had had the communication, he had seen the color between the stars, the color of God. Who could know how that had altered him, or even whether the changes were not still going on? Certainly not Mars.

So there was a way to fight him, then.

As Mars's fingers wrapped around her wrist, she collapsed in his arms.

"I don't know what more you want from me, Mars," she whispered. "I've given you everything you've wanted."

"I want the truth, Irina. Only the truth."

She put her head on his shoulder, molded her body against him, not as a siren, but as he would wish for, a helpless, confused female dependent on him for guidance.

"Irina," he said in her ear. "Just tell me everything. It will be all right. I promise you."

"Oh, Mars." Bringing to mind images of her betrayal of Natasha Mayakova, she began to weep. "When Odysseus took me by surprise in the pool, I was helpless, you must believe me."

"I do, *koshka*. I see his physical effect on Tatiana and Lara."

"I was at that time of the month. I was fertile."

She felt him stiffen, and she clung to him all the more.

"There is no way to know for certain, of course," she went on relentlessly, "but a woman can often tell these things far sooner than even a doctor can. But now I am afraid. I don't know what Odysseus is any longer. I don't believe even he does, though he puts on a brave face. Now I don't know what is forming inside me. What if it's—but that is too unspeakable to even contemplate. I would kill myself. I would—''

She stopped as Mars thrust her convulsively away from him. He stared at her for a long tension-filled moment.

"How could you?" he said at last. "How could you be with him at just the wrong moment?"

"I told you. He took me by surprise." Irina made herself shiver. *Who am I?* a tiny voice reverberated in her mind. "He gave me no time to think. He made me helpless."

"I—"

At that moment a sharp rap on the door interrupted them.

"What is it?" Mars showed his nerves by nearly shouting.

"Captain Nikolev is here," Tatiana said.

"Tell him I'm busy. I'll see him—"

"He says he must see you now, comrade. It is most urgent."

"Shit!" Mars said. He looked at Irina. "Get back to the computer. Find that White Star information. Now."

He went out into the pool room, ignored Irina as she slipped past him.

"What is it, Captain?" he said tersely.

Nikolev took Mars aside. Both Tatiana and Lara were staring at them.

"We have located Valeri Bondasenko."

"Excellent," Mars said, for the moment forgetting the sliver of terror Irina had handed him. "Bring him here."

"I am afraid that is impossible, comrade."

"Nothing is impossible, Captain. Do it! That's an order. I must have the secrets of White Star contained in Valeri Denysovich's computer."

"You and I will have to go to him," Nikolev said.

"I won't leave here," Mars said flatly. "I do not trust the Hero alone with Lara and Tatiana."

"Bring some of your men in."

"No," Mars said. "Such an overtly aggressive act would destroy everything I've worked for here. The Hero is far too important to us. He is a doorway to a whole new technology."

"Then take the computer and come with me."

"Do as I order!"

"But you don't understand, comrade," Nikolev said. "There was only one way to get to Bondasenko, and I used it. Remember the American diplomatic mission from Tokyo? I intercepted them at Sheremetyevo. They are the Americans that White Star asked for in the coded cable we intercepted."

487

Nikolev leaned closer. "I convinced them of my sincerity. They believe I am on their side. They told me they know a way to contact Bondasenko, and they are at the Rossiya Hotel doing so right now."

"Is that where Valeri Denysovich has gone to ground?"

"No. The hotel is apparently one of White Star's dead drops." Nikolev watched the play of emotions flicker across Mars's face. "We must go in as friends. Or, at least, I must. The Americans can convince Bondasenko to access the computer. I know that you do not want to let it out of your sight, so I suggest the two of us go."

"Valeri Denysovich and his people will not allow me to get anywhere near him."

"True enough," Nikolev said. "You will be thoroughly hidden from them along with my people. I will go in with the Americans and the computer. When they have convinced Bondasenko to access the information, I will signal you electronically. You'll bring my men in and we will have them all."

Mars spent some time digesting this. "It seems flawless," he said. "Except for one thing. How will the Americans convince Valeri Denysovich to access the White Star information?"

"I've told them about the coup."

"You *what*?"

Nikolev thought Mars was going to have a stroke. "It was the only way to hook them," he said. "Didn't you teach me that the truth works better than lies to catch human prey? Believe me, these are no ordinary Americans. They would not have believed a lie. Entanglement in the truth brings defeat, that's what you often say, eh, comrade?"

Mars thought a moment longer. Then he nodded. "Come," he said. "Take the Toshiba and let's go."

Downstairs the two men strode to Nikolev's black Zil. Nikolev got in behind the wheel, and Mars, with the Toshiba on his lap, slid into the passenger's seat.

"Where is your driver?" Mars asked.

"I drove myself," Nikolev said. He engaged the ignition. He was about to throw the car in gear when Mars put a hand on his arm.

"Just a moment, Captain. Regulations make it clear—"

"All my men are with the Americans," Nikolev broke in, heading out of Star Town. "Not so the Americans would notice, mind you, but that's why I've had to use so many. I've thrown an invisible cordon around the six square blocks surrounding

488

the Rossiya. What do the American soldiers say? An ant's ass couldn't get through there without my knowing."

Mars laughed. "Good work, Captain. You'll gain a promotion yet."

Out on the highway there was almost no traffic at all, and the Zil made good time. Several miles from Star Town, Nikolev pulled over to the shoulder and turned off the ignition.

"Is something the matter, Captain?" Mars asked.

Nikolev turned, and there was a pistol in his hand. It was aimed at Mars's chest. "I'll take the Toshiba now, comrade."

Mars's eyes did not flicker. "Why, Captain, you disappoint me."

"Never mind that," Nikolev snapped. "I want the computer, and I want it now."

"I hope there are a great number of treasures in here," Mars said, "otherwise you're throwing your life away for nothing."

"That's yet to be seen," Nikolev said.

"What did you do, Captain, foolishly make a deal with the Americans? I should have known. A rampant devotee of history could not be a true Marxist."

"You're a bit behind the times, comrade. There is no such thing as a true Marxist anymore. Can't you see that you're the last of a dying breed? A dinosaur in a new, enlightened age."

"If that's so," Mars said, "then my teeth are huge. The better to bite you with."

The muzzle of the pistol flicked slightly. "Give the computer over."

"And once I do, what is to happen to me?" Mars nodded, reading the look on Nikolev's face. "I see. So that's how it's to be. You'll leave a lump of dead meat for the animals to tear apart."

"You're a dangerous man, comrade," Nikolev said.

"You're telling me," Mars said, firing the small-caliber pistol he had hidden in his lap under the Toshiba.

The report was deafening inside the Zil, and the two men were rocked on its shocks. Captain Nikolev's face registered surprise, and he gaped at the blood pouring out of him. But the bullet had been slightly deflected by the computer, and it had entered Nikolev's belly, quite a bit below where Mars had been aiming.

Mars slapped at Nikolev's pistol and it went off, tearing a hole in the Zil's roof. Nikolev grabbed Mars, slammed the heel of his hand into Mars's throat. Mars's grip on his pistol loosened, and Nikolev slapped it away.

The Toshiba crashed to the floorwell of the car. Mars balled his fist, smashed it into Nikolev's belly where the bullet had entered. Nikolev shouted, and tears of pain came to his eyes.

Mars immediately bent to retrieve his pistol, but Nikolev caught him in a lock meant to break his arm. Gritting his teeth, Mars jammed his elbow into Nikolev's face, heard the sharp crack of the jawbone splintering, and thought, I have him now.

It was a mistake. Nikolev, almost blind with pain, used two quick, percussive blows to Mars's solar plexus. Bright spots of noncolor danced in Mars's head and he felt himself begin to black out. He fought to gain control over his spasming diaphragm, winced as the third blow robbed him of desperately needed air.

He used the heel of his hand in an attempt to break Nikolev's nose, but the lack of oxygen in his system had robbed him of strength and he had nothing behind the strike.

Meanwhile, Nikolev was hard at work trying to separate Mars from his ribs. Mars felt a searing pain lance up into his chest and neck. He was losing feeling in his right side, and he began to panic. He had nothing to work with, so in desperation he slammed his forehead into Nikolev's nose. Blood and cartilage splattered, but the pain in his chest would not abate.

Mars, losing control, hit Nikolev again with his forehead, and this time Nikolev's neck snapped back, the top of his head smashing into the Zil's windshield and breaking it. Nikolev, stretched unnaturally backward across the dashboard, blinked heavily, momentarily stunned.

Mars, taking great gulps of air, made the most of this respite. He drove his fist into Nikolev's side over and over until the rib cage gave way.

Nikolev fell sideways into the floorwell. His face was streaked with blood, and shards of glass were embedded in his cheeks. His eyes stared upward.

Mars, almost weeping with the enormous expenditure of energy, cursed him mightily, kicked the side of his head. He bent over, put his head between his legs so that he wouldn't pass out.

It took him some time to recover. The smell of fresh blood, as sickly as decaying flowers, reminded him of how close he had been brought to the brink of death.

"You sonuvabitch, Nikolev, you thought you were more clever than I was, but in the end you didn't have a clue. I had a man on the inside of your division since before the time I had you seconded to Department N. That's one of the reasons I picked the Eleventh Division of the Border Guards.''

He spat onto Nikolev's face. The captain was beyond caring, but just the same, it made Mars feel better.

Mars opened the passenger's door, bent down, rolled Nikolev's corpse out onto the verge of the highway. ''Dead meat, Captain,'' Mars said. ''You were right about that at least.''

He took the Toshiba off the floorwell. The case was covered in blood and bits of bone, but Mars didn't care about that. Hurriedly he unzipped the case, cursed harshly as he saw the damage his bullet had done to the computer. There was a large chip taken out of the hard disk.

Christ, he thought, this is useless now, the White Star information is locked away in there for all time. Now I need Valeri Denysovich more than ever.

Throwing the Toshiba aside, he activated the Zil's two-way radio. He identified himself, asked to be patched through to Lieutenant Pokov. His fingers drummed impatiently against the bloody dashboard. Come on! he thought. Come on!

The radio crackled to life. ''Pokov.''

''This is Volkov,'' Mars said without preamble. ''You are now commanding the Eleventh Division, is that clear, Lieutenant?''

''Perfectly, comrade.''

''You have the Americans in sight?''

''I do. Everything is under control.''

''Excellent. They will lead you to Bondasenko. Bring as many men as you feel you need. I give you the authority. And, Pokov, I need Bondasenko. I'd like to have the Americans as well, but if they give you the least problem, kill them. The less witnesses the better, do you follow me, Lieutenant?''

''Yes, comrade.''

''Volkov out.''

Mars replaced the receiver, slid over into the driver's seat. He started the engine, swung the Zil around, headed back for Star Town. It was difficult negotiating the highway with the shattered windshield, and he was soon obliged to pull over, use the butt of his pistol to knock out the remainder of the glass so he could see.

The guards gaped at him as he pulled into the Hero's fortress, but he had no time to give them an explanation. He was thinking of how Anatoly Nikolev had believed himself more clever than himself. He expected Irina did, too. She thought she had convinced him of her loyalty, but he knew better. He was willing to bet that someone, somewhere, had given her proof that he, not Valeri, was KGB. He could see the fear in her eyes, feel it in her body when she touched him.

Had she been fertile when she had allowed Odysseus to take her? He did not know if she was capable of such a terrible lie. But why not? he asked himself as he raced up the stairs of the Hero's fortress, wincing at the pain from his broken ribs. She had proved herself capable of so many dangerous things. He admired her for that, even as he hated her in the same unthinking way he hated the traitor, Valeri Denysovich Bondasenko. It was the antipathy of the cobra for the mongoose. There was no reason to it, just an elemental fire that could be temporarily banked, but would never go out.

Now, Mars thought, opening the door to the pool room, it's time to see just how far Irina is capable of taking her triple life. He decided it would be most interesting to see whether she clung to her smooth lies even at the edge of death.

Having crossed both the Moskva River and the narrow canal at the end of Red Square, having come cautiously down to Dobryninskaya Square on the Sadovaya ring, Tori and Russell now found themselves on the edge of the Zamoskvorechye, the District Beyond the Moskva.

Behind them, they could see the four handpicked men Captain Nikolev had left behind to make sure they got safely to their destination. He had been most persuasive. "With Mars Volkov using the bulk of the Eleventh Division to comb Moscow for Valeri Bondasenko, you'll never make it on the streets on your own," Nikolev had said.

Lieutenant Pokov got out of his Zhiguli, came over to them. It was one of those typical Russian cars, tinny, uncomfortable, a piece of junk, really. Yet another manifestation of the third-world atmosphere. "We are close to a number of Volkov's patrols," he said. "Are we near our destination?"

"Fuck off," Russell said.

Pokov looked hurt. He was a stolid-looking dark-haired Russian with the kind of musculature one often saw on amateur wrestlers. He appeared very quick on his feet. "I'll lock the car and leave it here. It will attract too much attention closer in."

Russell glanced over his shoulder at Pokov, drew Tori away from him. "I'm liking this less and less," he whispered to her.

"We're out in the deep water, and we can't even tell the good guys from the bad guys. This seems to be an excellent way to get ourselves killed."

Tori said, "You still think Nikolev's full of shit, don't you?"

"Believe me, I would like to think he's telling us the truth, but I can't. Face it, the odds are against it, Tori. Look at this setup. In all honesty, we've got to figure he had more reason to lie than to tell us the truth. Or he could have been telling us the truth but for the wrong reasons."

"Is that the same thing?"

Russell looked at her. "Do you see what's happening? We're getting so enmeshed in sorting out the truth, we've lost our way in the forest of lies. And let me tell you, Moscow is not a city to get lost in. You do, and chances are you never come out."

"Either way," Tori said levelly, "we've got to reach Valeri Bondasenko as quickly as possible. It's after one in the morning; less than four hours to the start of the Russian invasion of the Baltic states."

"If Nikolev wasn't pulling our leg."

They fell silent as Lieutenant Pokov approached them. "Excuse me," he said, "but we must go quickly. It is very late. Not many people are still on the streets, and so you will become too conspicuous to remain out yourselves. One of Volkov's patrols could pick you up at any moment, and I would be helpless to stop them. My men and I can only try to steer you clear of the other Border Guards patrols."

"He's right," Tori said. "We'd better go."

Russell said, "Goddamn this to hell," but he did not stop her as she headed down Bolshaya Polyanka Street.

And so at length they came to the Church of St. Gregory of Neocasarea.

"Stay here, understand?" Russell said to Pokov.

"Is this where Bondasenko is hiding?" Pokov said. "A church?"

Something in his voice warned Russell, and he grabbed Tori by her arm, dragged her quickly around to the front of the church. He got out a small instrument, twisted it into the lock. Russell pushed, and the huge door swung inward.

They stood inside, in the utter darkness, listening for shouts, the shouts of running bootsteps on the gritty pavement outside.

They heard nothing.

"What happened?" Tori whispered.

"Maybe we're okay, after all," Russell said.

Then he saw the silhouette of one of Nikolev's Border Guards insinuate itself through the front door. For a moment it was outlined against the faint blue light filtering in through the stained-glass windows, and Russell pointed to it. Then the silhouette was gone, and so was Tori.

Tori spent the first few moments doing nothing but listening. It was impossible to see the Border Guard, but she could hear him well enough. He was taking all the proper precautions, and in fact he was quite good, but Tori heard him nonetheless.

She had already taken off her shoes, had tied the laces together so she could hang them around her neck. She listened a moment more, then, when she was certain of where the Border Guard was and how he was moving, she went after him.

He thought he was being clever, crawling between the pews. Tori climbed onto a pew's back and, like a tightrope walker, put one foot carefully in front of another. She felt without having to see the straight line of the wooden pew back against the soles of her feet, which she relaxed around the inch or so of wood, molding them to the shape of the carved wood.

When she was above and just behind the crawling Border Guard, she dropped onto him, as silent as a bat. The Border Guard already had his knife out, ready to stab whoever he came upon first, her or Russell. He twisted as he felt her weight come down on him and, as he did, he swung the knife up in a vicious arc toward her belly.

Tori, using an aikido immobilization, guided aside his thrust, grabbed his jaw on either side, and, as he reared back in surprise, twisted once very hard to the left. His neck snapped like a dry twig, he convulsed a moment, and was still.

When Tori had left him, Russell stole behind the front door. He was waiting for the next Border Guard to come through when he felt the pistol in the small of his back.

"*Stoi!*" a voice commanded.

Russell, not understanding, moved. He turned around and found himself face to face with a cowled figure. "Have all priests in Moscow a need for a gun, Father?" he said.

"Only if they are in hiding," the figure said in heavily accented English.

"Valeri Bondasenko?"

"Yes."

Russell tried to penetrate the penumbra of the cowl, but the darkness of the interior of the church defeated him. "I am a representative of Bernard Godwin. My colleague is—"

"If what you tell me is the truth, why have you brought the KGB Border Guards with you?"

"It's a long story," Russell said, "and I haven't the time or the understanding to explain it all now. You must help us with the Border Guards."

"How many are there?"

"Three enlisted men, one officer, Lieutenant Pokov."

"So few? That's odd. They are usually deployed in much larger groups."

But Russell was no longer listening. He was staring into the muzzle of a Kalishnikov semiautomatic machine gun.

Tori took the knife out of the dead Border Guard's hand. She considered taking the gun as well, but thought better of it. She did not care for guns, and in any case, the firing of just one shot would alert the authorities and bring disaster on them all. She opted for pocketing the gun's ammunition so no one else who found it could use it.

Then she moved off into the depths of the darkened church.

The impenetrable blackness was like the shroud of a forest. She could recall the winter in Hokkaido, where she was tested: to find *sensei*, who was living in the dense forest of pitch pines there. It took her ten days, a long time in her estimation, but *sensei* told her she had beaten the next best record by eighteen hours. Most of his students never found him at all.

Lightning burst, reflection off a length of metal. Tori watched the progress of the telescoping steel truncheon as the Border Guard made his way through the darkness.

A moment later she could make out his face and, seeing the fixed look in his eyes, saw that he had spotted Russell. She creeped along the edge of the pew she was on, and was just about to break toward him when she became aware of the presence behind her.

She leapt off the back of the pew as the steel truncheon—the mate of the one she had been staring at—whipped through the space where an instant before her ankles had been.

Tori whirled and, as she hit the floor, struck out hard with her left leg. She felt it strike flesh and bone, heard a sharp intake of breath, and then she attacked with the stone, a two-handed percussive *atemi*.

495

His stiff arms, the gun held in both his hands, were raised toward her.

Tori was so close she could see the tremor of intent. In a fraction of a second he would fire, and the explosion would give them all away. If not the KGB, then the police would be alerted; a loud noise like that this late at night would be reported instantly by some concerned citizen.

Tori swung her steel truncheon into the man's left wrist, momentarily paralyzing his finger on the trigger. He kicked upward, caught her on the inside of her thigh.

She grunted, felt her balance going as her left leg crumpled. The Border Guard tracked her with the muzzle of the gun. He was taking no chances, aiming for her head.

Tori ducked, but slammed into the back of the wooden pew. The Border Guard reached up, his mouth in a rictus of pain, as he grabbed a handful of her blouse, pulled her toward him with his left hand.

That cost him a lot. Tori's first blow had fractured his wrist, but he was dedicated, and not about to give up.

Now Tori was too close to use the truncheon, and she let it go just before he smashed the side of his pistol into her rib cage. Breath hissed through Tori's clenched teeth as she collapsed onto her knees. The Border Guard pressed the muzzle of his pistol against her forehead.

"Da zvedanye, suka," he said, managing to grin through his agony. Good-bye, bitch.

Tori slammed her fists against his ears, grabbed his right wrist with one hand, the barrel of his pistol with another. He fought her every inch. The cords at the sides of his neck stood out as he beat against her with his powerless left hand.

Tori was straddled across his legs so he could not use them against her. Both she and the Border Guard were concentrated on the gun. Tori had the leverage, but he had the brute strength. They struggled silently, violently, force against force. It was a standoff, until Tori, employing one of the main principles of aikido, abruptly dropped her resistance to him. His aim came down with his unimpeded arm, past her face, past her body. She used a *kite* against the side of his neck, and his arm fell to his side. His eyes rolled up into his head.

She looked up. Now she had lost the third Border Guard.

"Put your pistol down," the Border Guard said to the cowled figure, who did as he was ordered.

"Kick it over here."

When Russell saw the Border Guard's eyes flick toward the gun, he stepped forward and across and, as he had been taught, chopped down straight and hard, thinking not of the man's flesh but of the space beyond.

The Border Guard went down as his shoulder blade cracked beneath the assault. He was scrabbling to lift his Kalishnikov into position when Russell hit the nerve at the inside of his elbow, and his arm went dead. Russell took the Kalishnikov out of his hand, swiped him across the side of the head with the stock end.

Tori winced slightly as she crouched, began to move out of the aisle of pews into the sanctuary where she had last caught a glimpse of Russell. She saw him now. He was standing above the body of the third Border Guard, and there was a robed priest with him. A disguised Bondasenko? Tori hoped so.

"Russell," she said as she came up to them, "have you seen Pokov?"

"No. What about the other two of his men?"

"Taken care of," Tori said. "Like this one." She felt gingerly at her side.

"Are you all right?" When she nodded, Russell stared at her for some time. "You really are a very scary human being."

"Mr. Slade—"

"Yes, yes," Russell said. "Tori, this is Valeri Bondasenko. Valeri, this is Tori Nunn."

"We have a lot to talk about," Tori said.

The robed figure nodded. "This way," he whispered.

"Not at this time, comrade. Maybe later." Lieutenant Pokov emerged from the shadows where he had been hidden. He had stayed so still that even Tori had not been aware of him. She cursed herself for her lapse. *Sensei* would have been very angry with her.

Lieutenant Pokov nodded his head. "A pleasure to make your acquaintance, Comrade Bondasenko. Or I should say traitor Bondasenko."

Russell was furious. "Tori, I told you we shouldn't have trusted that sonuvabitch, Nikolev."

"Ah, poor Nikolev." Lieutenant Pokov laughed. He could afford to be jovial now. "So misguided. Unfortunately, he was stupid enough to have told you the truth. Not that it will do you any good now. You're on your way to the Lubyanka, where Mars

Volkov will interview you. Comrade Volkov is notorious in the Lubyanka for his interviews. I don't envy any of you." He made a sharp motion with his gun. "That way is the exit, lady and gentlemen. Use it."

Pokov followed them down the aisle of pews. They passed the second man that Tori had dispatched. Pokov looked at her grimly. "I'll have something to say about this. I'll take a measure of their shortened lives out of you when Volkov is done with you."

Tori saw ahead of them the first man she had fought with. She could see his pistol lying on the floor where she had left it. She put her hand in her pocket.

"So you switched sides, Pokov," Russell said.

Pokov laughed. "I never changed sides is more accurate. Nikolev was a fool to try to cross Mars Volkov. No one does that and lives very long. I myself like life too much to play the fool."

During this exchange, Tori had come to the fallen Border Guard. Putting her consciousness in mind/no mind, feeling the void fill her with the elemental power of the universe, she bent down with her back to Pokov.

He saw her almost immediately. "What are you doing?" he shouted. "Get away from there!"

Tori turned. She had the Border Guard's pistol in her hand.

Pokov took one look at it and threw his head back, laughing. "Oh, good try. But it's empty. Do you think I would have left it lying around, otherwise?" His lip curled in contempt. "Stupid Americans, sending a woman to do a man's job. A man would know better."

"Oh, yeah?" Tori said, and pulled the trigger.

Pokov was slammed back against the end of a pew. His legs crumpled under him, and his expression of shock and rage transformed his face into a stylized mask.

"But it was empty," he whispered. "I know it was."

Tori walked up to him, held out a handful of bullets.

Pokov's eyes fluttered, his head hung as he slid to the floor of the church.

"*Da zvedanye*, Pokov," Tori said, throwing the pistol onto his unmoving chest.

Sergei, the man with the strawberry birthmark, pulled the cowl off his face. "By God, that was well done," he said. "I think it's safe enough now to—"

"No," Valeri said, striding toward them from the far end of

the sanctuary. "I am Valeri Denysovich Bondasenko." He clapped Sergei on the shoulder. "You have protected me from danger long enough, my friend."

Tori and Russell introduced themselves, and Valeri nodded to them. "Our terrible risk in bringing you here may prove our downfall. I have not been idle while you were here, valiantly defending me." He nodded toward the dead Border Guards. "Your courage is beyond reproach and very much appreciated, but I'm afraid it may be for nothing. These four did not come alone. There is a contingent of Border Guards setting themselves in a standard perimeter around the church."

"That bastard Pokov," Russell said. "He must have been in communication with Volkov."

"No doubt," Valeri said. "And now Mars Petrovich has pulled his net tightly around us."

"Perhaps too tightly, comrade," Sergei said. "Remember the tunnels that lead out of the crypts beneath the church."

Valeri nodded grimly. "But even so, Volkov's patrols are everywhere. We will have no chance at this hour on foot."

"Maybe that's not so important right now," Russell said. He recounted Captain Nikolev's warning about the dawn invasion of the Baltic states and the simultaneous assassination of the Soviet president.

Valeri closed his eyes. He seemed infinitely weary. "Yes, I suspected something of that nature. But not so soon."

"Nikolev said that White Star is the wild card in the equation. He said that if we could get to you, White Star's leader, you would be able to mobilize the organization to prevent the invasion and the coup." Russell stared at Valeri. "We know about the nuclear weapons Bernard Godwin has been selling you. It's time to put them to use."

Valeri shook his head. "Not selling, Mr. Slade. Mr. Godwin has been giving the devices to us. He is thought of as a great patriot here. He is one of White Star's spiritual leaders."

"Good Christ," Russell said.

"But all this does no good, I'm afraid," Valeri said. "We are rather cut off here. There is no transcontinental communication possible from the church. I was barely able to manage to get your local communiqué. That was what caused the delay in my responding. No. We've got to get out of here."

"We've got to get to Star Town," Tori broke in. "Mars Volkov has a woman named Irina and your computer. Is it true that the whole of White Star is in its hard disk?"

"Irina," Valeri said. "So Mars caught Irina going into my apartment. That must mean he suspects her loyalty is to me."

"So the computer could betray you," Tori said.

Valeri nodded. "Yes. The entire network is secreted in the software. But no one could possibly dig it out. It's a ghost in the machine." Then he stopped. All the color drained from his face. "My God," he said softly. "A ghost in the machine. I told Irina, and she is well versed in computers. She could— If Mars forced her— Dear God!" He glanced at his watch, then looked at Tori. "It's almost three in the morning. Yes, you're right. We must get to Star Town now."

"But how, comrade?" Sergei asked. "The tunnels will take us to the streets, but what then?"

And then Russell said, "We have a car." He almost laughed in his relief. "Pokov's car." He knelt down, went through Pokov's pockets, stood up with the key in his hand.

At that moment the front door to the church crashed in.

"KGB. Keep calm!"

"Quickly!" Valeri whispered. "This way!"

They ran back through the sanctuary, through doors that Valeri carefully closed and bolted behind them. He left them for a moment, while Sergei continued to lead them downward.

They were on the second flight of stairs going down to the crypts when Valeri rejoined them. "I smashed out the window in the back of the sacristy," he said. "Thinking we have escaped, they will never find us down here now."

In the crypt itself Valeri turned to the man with the strawberry birthmark. "Sergei, you must stay here with my daughter. I don't want her moved again so soon, and in any event, there won't be room in the car for everyone."

"I understand, comrade."

"Take good care of her."

"As if she were my own daughter."

The two men embraced.

"Godspeed, Valeri."

"I will come for you myself, Sergei. After dawn."

Then Valeri Denysovich Bondasenko was leading Tori and Russell into the tunnels, into the darkness and the light, on his final race to save his country from certain disaster.

Mars had a murderous look in his eyes. "Stay away from me," he said to Lara and Tatiana. "I'll deal with you later." He strode through the pool room. The women gaped at the

500

blood caked on him just as the guards outside had. At this time of the night, there was no one else in the building.

Mars stood by the pool. In his absence the Hero had awakened from his sleep, returned to the pool. Or perhaps, in this growing crisis, he had been awakened. Mars stared down at the Hero. "Here," he said. "A present for you." He swung the damaged Toshiba in a flat arc, let go of the cloth handles at the apex. The computer in its case flew into the water. The resultant splash slapped at Mars's shoes and trouser bottoms.

"You see, Odysseus, I don't need it anymore. And do you want to know why? But you must. You can read my mind, yes?" The murderous look in his eyes intensified. "I don't need the computer because I have the real thing." He gave off a feral grin. "My men found my archenemy, as you so aptly put it. Even as I say this, they are bringing Valeri Denysovich here to me for interrogation. How does that make you feel?"

"Sorry for you," the Hero said.

Mars clenched his jaw. His fists balled into white claws.

"That's right," Odysseus said. "Why fight it, comrade? Why not jump into the gladiator's arena and have it out with me, man to man. That's what you want, isn't it? But then again, it might not be what you think. It might not be man to man, but man to . . . well, what do you think, Volkov? You can't possibly know what I am or what I could do to you in here. So go about your dirty little business on dry land. Go on."

Mars bent over the edge of the pool. "You think you know it all, that you've got all the answers. Well, we'll see just how clever you are now, Odysseus!"

Mars stalked to where Irina was watching him. He reached out in a blur, grabbed a handful of hair, yanked it back so hard that she cried out as she fell to her knees.

"Volkov!"

Mars looked at Lara and Tatiana. "If either of you interferes, I'll kill you." Then he slapped Irina hard across the face.

"Volkov!"

"*Comrade* Volkov to you, Odysseus."

"Comrade Volkov," Odysseus said. "Stop it."

"Oh, no," Mars said. "It's gone too far for that." He yanked at Irina's hair again, bending her painfully backward. She whimpered. "I'm going to hurt her, Odysseus. I want you to know that in advance, because you're going to be the principal witness."

"She's just a woman, comrade. Leave her out of it."

"But I can't," Mars said reasonably. "She insinuated herself into my game. She got one whiff of it and she was excited beyond control. It was her decision. She agreed to play by my rules the moment she seduced me."

"She had no way of knowing."

"But she did, Odysseus. She seduced me, then she spied on Valeri Denysovich for me. She befriended Natasha Mayakova, and then she betrayed her. Did you know that? Betrayed her just like that. And then she betrayed me. No, she's as cold-blooded as any man I ever met. She accepted the violence, and now she must learn the lesson that violence begets violence. It's only fair, Odysseus. Live by the sword, die by the sword."

"It's revenge, comrade. Revenge, pure and simple."

"No!" Mars fairly shouted it. "I am speaking of justice here, not revenge."

"Your definition, Volkov. It's always your definition." Odysseus made a disgusted sound. "This is your world. It is my fate that I am stuck in a Rome ruled by a Caesar such as you. There is no justice here. We are governed by your whims. And isn't it ironic? Who really seeks to be the living god? Not me, comrade."

"Damn you and your circumlocutions," Mars said. "Who taught you to use language like a weapon?"

"I act only out of self-defense, comrade. Language is the only weapon you allow me."

"No, no," Mars said. "I have given you too much of what you want, Odysseus. I see now that I have been far too lenient with you. I have bent rules for you—even broken one or two, yes. I was like a father indulging his only child, I see that clearly now. And the result is painfully predictable. You are willful, spiteful, spoiled. But now it must end." His head snapped up. "Tatiana, come here."

Tatiana did as he commanded.

Arbat stuck her head out of the water, began to chatter frantically.

"Volkov," Odysseus said warily, "what are you up to?"

"This is the end for you, Odysseus. You *will* learn to behave in a proper way, to be respectful, to give full and honest answers to the questions put to you."

"Volkov—"

"Shut up!" Mars snapped. He raised the gun, aimed, pulled the trigger all in one motion. Tatiana tumbled silently backward into the pool. Irina screamed. The reverberations of the single shot echoed in the pool room.

Lara watched with wide eyes the corpse in the pool, sinking, then rising, rolling slightly with the lapping of the saltwater against the coping.

Arbat stopped her furious clicking. She swam slowly to Tatiana's corpse, poked at it over and over as if she could bring Tatiana back to life. Then she dived deep to the bottom of the pool.

"You bastard!" Odysseus said.

"You hate me now, don't you?" Mars said. "Why don't you come up here and stop me, then, as a real man would?"

"You're stupid, Volkov," Odysseus said. "Like all would-be gods, your mind is limited to the precepts of power. But I think you'll find that holding on to power is far more treacherous than gaining it."

Mars waggled the gun. "I don't believe you're in any position to offer me advice." His head swung around as he watched Lara walk purposefully across the room.

Odysseus, seeing where she was heading, shouted. "No! Lara, stay away from there!"

A slow smile spread across Mars's face. "I see that there are truly no secrets from you, Odysseus. I was right, in the end, to suspect these two women."

Lara had reached the far side of the room. She took out a set of keys, put one in the lock of a narrow wall cabinet.

"Somehow you worked your magic on them, didn't you? Very impressive. Both Tatiana and Lara were highly skilled KGB agents until they came under your curious spell."

Odysseus heard the past tense, shouted, "Volkov, no! It's enough now!"

"You must learn your lessons, my son," Mars said. "And they are by definition hard lessons. Your spitefulness has made them so."

Mars waited until Lara had opened the cabinet before he shot her twice in the back.

Lara's body was thrown aside as if by an invisible fist. She had been holding on to the top of the cabinet door, and it swung open to reveal the contents of the arsenal: a vertical line of loaded Kalishnikovs ready for any emergency. The well-oiled semiautomatic machine guns gleamed in the low light.

"Ah, God!"

Mars smiled down benevolently at the top of the Hero's bent

head. "Good," he said gently. "You are beginning to learn the true parameters of power." He reached out, almost as if he were a prelate about to bless a petitioning acolyte.

"But not quite yet," Mars said. He twined his hand in Irina's hair, jerked her head back once again.

Irina cried out, and Odysseus's head came up. His eyes were a dull black. "What is it you want, Volkov?"

"If you have to ask the question, you still have a ways to go." Mars held Irina down with one massive forearm, pressed the muzzle of his gun into her mouth. "Soon, Odysseus, you'll give me everything I want, won't you?"

"I'll give it to you now," the Hero said dully. "Only don't kill her."

"Oh, I have no intention of killing her, Odysseus. She's far too valuable for that. And, as you will see, I can be a benevolent Caesar. No. I am going to hurt her a little at a time. In between, I'm going to ask you questions, and each time you give me an answer that is incomplete or false, I will hurt her some more. You know, I don't think you can conceive of just how long this process can be drawn out."

"Don't do this!"

"Are you pleading now, Odysseus? Oh, you are a sorry excuse for a man. You're even worse than Valeri Denysovich."

"Is that so?"

Both Mars and the Hero turned at the same instant.

"By Christ," Mars said. "It is you, comrade."

Valeri emerged from the shadows. "I'm sorry it took me so long to get here, Mars Petrovich, but there were many complications to surmount."

Mars looked around. "Where is Pokov? Where are my men?"

"They couldn't make it, I'm afraid."

Mars let go of Irina, stood up facing Valeri. His face registered shock and confusion. "You're here by yourself? How did you get into this fortress past my guards?"

"There's a way," Valeri said. "It's been done often enough." He looked around at the carnage. "My God, what have you done to Lara and Tatiana?"

"How do you know them?"

"I know a great deal, comrade," Valeri said. "But I fear it's too late to begin explaining, and anyway, I doubt if you'd understand."

Mars looked from Valeri to the Hero and back again as understanding slowly flooded through him. "What an idiot I've been," he said at last. "Natasha wasn't only bringing Odysseus limited distribution KGB files you stole, she was ferrying White Star intelligence back and forth. The two of you are in this together. Odysseus has been helping you organize White Star."

"Almost right," Valeri said. "You're still the dull-witted oaf, I'm afraid. Don't bother trying. You'll never get it all."

During this exchange Irina had slowly crawled away from the arena the two antagonists had drawn for themselves. She could almost see their enmity crackling like lightning, it was so palpable. Ice-blue and indigo shadows filled the pool room; there was a ghastly sense of blood heat, as exposed as a white bone protruding through purple flesh.

She was sobbing silently. The terror that filled her seemed to leak out her eyes as tears, the pores of her skin as sweat. It racked her like a terrible ague, so that she shook uncontrollably.

Her mind was at once numb and on fire. She could not believe the depths of Mars's depravity. The thought that he had once made her so content, that she had happily contemplated becoming part of his family, made her sick to her stomach.

But there was so much more. As she watched with hollow eyes the harrowing confrontation between these two men who had once meant something to her, she saw how removed she was from the mentality of men. What drove them to such cruelty and violence? She could feel the sickness in their souls permeating the room like an inimical miasma, and she saw, horrified, how she had been infected by their hideously distorted lust for power, control, dominion over others.

She recognized at last how Mars and Valeri, each in his own way, had used her, twisted her around the force of his personality as if forging a blade out of a slab of steel. But she was not made of steel. No matter to them; they had tried, in their infinite masculine arrogance, to make her into steel.

And she saw the truth at last, that there was no difference between Mars and Valeri. In the end it did not matter what each wanted, what each stood for, because the two of them were so intent on getting what they wanted, they made certain that nothing and no one got in their way.

Irina saw them confronting one another, and this new truth said to her, Leave them alone. Do nothing. Let their violence burn itself out naturally. They will kill one another, and that will be the end of it.

Then she saw Mars raise his gun, fire. She saw Valeri stagger back, his right shoulder red with blood. It was too much.

"No!" she screamed.

Irina, weeping, could not understand what was happening inside her. She wanted to do nothing, to sit and watch these two men destroy each other. But she could not.

To her horror, she found herself next to the open arsenal cabinet. Now she was standing, reaching inside. She took down a Kalishnikov. Her finger curled around the trigger, and lowering the muzzle, she walked toward the two men.

Mars was aiming at Valeri. Dimly, she was aware of other figures in the shadows, and she thought with terror of Mars's Border Guards.

KGB. Keep calm.

"Stop it, Mars!" she said as she advanced.

"Shut up!" Mars snapped.

"Keep out of this, Irina," Valeri said.

Mars was about to pull the trigger again. Instead, Irina did.

The sound was deafening. Irina and Mars screamed at almost the same instant. Mars's body was blown forward by the force of the fusillade of bullets, and his body slid across the floor to come to rest at Valeri's feet.

Tears were streaming down Irina's face. She dropped the Kalishnikov, rubbed the palms of her hands down her thighs. She saw the blood leaking out of Mars's back, and she slipped to her knees, began to gag.

"Odysseus," she whispered softly. "Save me."

The Hero reached up over the edge of the pool, drew her slowly onto the coping, slid her into the pool next to him. Arbat broke from the pool bottom, came to nuzzle her bottle nose against Irina's side.

"Oh, Arbat!" Irina laughed, then immediately began to cry again.

"Are you all right?" Tori said, coming up to where Valeri knelt.

He was holding his shoulder, staring down at Mars. "I don't know," he said. "Something odd has happened. I've thought about this moment for a long time. I thought I would feel elated when it came. But you know, the funny thing is, I don't. I feel deflated, empty." He put his hand briefly on the top of Mars's bloody head. "Almost as if a part of myself has died."

"That was a damned stupid way to come in here," Russell said from the other side of him. "That sonuvabitch could have killed you with the first shot."

506

"It was the only way," Valeri said, wiping the sweat off his face. "If Mars saw you, he would have shot you both without a moment's hesitation. And it was far too risky to attempt to infiltrate this room. One hint of our presence and Mars would have had two precious hostages to defeat us with."

"Bullshit," Russell said. "We would have had time to—"

"You did not know Mars as I did," Valeri said. He took a deep breath. "And, in any case, he did not kill me with the first shot." He looked away from Mars for the first time, up into Russell's face. "He was the finest marksman, you know."

"Talk to me," the Hero said to Irina.

"I feel unclean." She put her head against his shoulder. "Hold me," she whispered, and when she felt his arms around her, said, "Mars was right, violence does beget violence. Everything he said was true. I seduced and I lied, and I loved it. Then, I was in so deep, I betrayed Natasha and Valeri. I didn't know what I was doing. I didn't know who Mars was when I told him. But it doesn't matter. That's just a rationalization. I should never have betrayed the trust Natasha put in me. She was my friend, and surely I had a hand in her torture. And now this. I've killed someone with my own hands. Now I am truly part of Mars's world."

"If that is really how you feel," Odysseus said, "I cannot help you."

Irina drew her head back. She stared into his fathomless eyes. "What do you mean? You must! I'm relying on you."

"No, Irina. It's time for you to rely on yourself. I can help, yes, that's true. But only you can save yourself from the violent world you fell so madly in love with. And only if you want to."

The tension came into her frame, and her blackness returned, the blackness she recognized as her fear of the endless Siberian winter, the bars over her moon, the country as her prison, and a voice inside her said, *Now you have nothing. You're lost, utterly lost.*

Irina could feel the tears welling hotly in her eyes, but this time she fought them back, just as she fought the voice inside her. She did not have to be lost, it was not preordained.

There were alternatives to being utterly lost, and now she found that she wanted more than anything to explore those alternatives.

They would not be in America, as she had dreamed, but it was a foolish dream, an adolescent's wanting to run away from

507

responsibility. And if there was anything she could learn from the Hero, it was a sense of responsibility.

She stared into the depths of Odysseus's opalescent eyes, and in the silence of their communication, told him that she was ready.

While Russell saw to Valeri's wound, Tori went to where Lara lay, checked to see if she was still alive. She wasn't. Then she walked to the edge of the pool, bent down, pulled Tatiana from the water. She rolled her over, saw that she was dead, too.

Such a waste of life, she thought sadly. Where will it end? That was a question she had been asking herself ever since she had watched Koi commit ritual suicide in an attempt to cleanse her spirit and her conscience of the blood staining it.

Tori could not forget that moment, as if it were fixed in time in her memory: the blue of the sky, the white of Koi's clothes, the red of the blood flowing. And the lights of Koi's mountains, burning for her. Silently, Tori said a prayer for Koi's spirit—and her own.

Slowly, almost hesitantly, she walked along the edge of the pool. Her legs seemed to have lost their strength. Here was the Hero, the Russian cosmonaut who had trained and lived with her brother Greg. The man who had last seen Greg alive. What strange fate that had brought her here!

And now that she was here, Tori found that she was almost afraid to approach him. She heard the water purling against the coping, she saw the ice-blue and indigo shadows moving in mysterious patterns across the face of the water. She heard the odd clicks of Arbat's language. And all these things lent an otherworldly cast to the pool, as if they were not inside a fortress in the heart of the USSR at all, but in another time, another place altogether.

Tori saw Arbat first, and she was so surprised she did not know what to say. The blue dolphin immediately broke away from where the Hero and Irina hung in the pool, ducked her head, swam up to where Tori stood.

In a rush, Arbat leaped fully out of the water. Her nose brushed Tori's cheek, and then her great sleek body was gone, in one enormous splash hidden beneath the churning water.

Tori stood very still. Her legs trembled and she looked toward the two humans in the pool. Irina swam over, introduced herself.

"I'm Tori Nunn," Tori said, sitting on the coping. "We've

come with Valeri to help White Star." She extended her hand. Irina took it.

For a moment the two women stared deep into each other's eyes. What transpired then? Was there a silent communication of words, of feelings, or of something far more elemental, something impossible to define? In any case, there was a sense of a shared emotion if not a shared destiny that leaped between the women when they touched.

"I'm sorry," Tori said, breaking the silence, "but I was stunned by what the dolphin did."

Irina smiled. "Arbat has very particular likes and dislikes. It's obvious she likes you a great deal." She turned. "Odysseus? Come meet Tori. She's one of the Americans who—" Irina stopped, frozen by the look on Odysseus's face. "Is something the matter?"

The Hero swam slowly into what light there was in the shadowy pool room. Arbat surfaced next to him, and he put his hand on her back.

Tori watched as the Hero emerged from the darkness. Her heart was pounding so hard she could scarcely breathe. She could see his gleaming, silvery skin first, as sleek as Arbat's. She saw the contours of his face, the utter hairlessness of him. And then she caught a glimpse of his opalescent eyes.

Tori opened her mouth, closed it with a snap. Opened it again. She stared into his angel eyes.

"Greg?"

"Tori," the Hero said. "God in Heaven."

Tori tumbled into the pool, clothes and all. She swam to where Odysseus floated with Arbat. Tears were streaming from her eyes.

"Don't," Odysseus said. "Oh, don't." He stroked her head.

"Greg."

Tori pulled him to her, embraced him, kissed his cheeks. She held him and held him. She did not want to let go, and for a long time she didn't.

When at last she unclasped him, she said, "But I thought you were dead. We all did. How is it—"

"The Russians," Gregory Nunn said. "Viktor Shevchenko and I were part of a secret experiment these bastards devised to see if exposure to measured amounts of cosmic radiation could counter the crippling effects of weightlessness. Then the EVA event happened, and Viktor was killed. I came home, but was in a coma for several months. When I regained consciousness, the Russians figured I was too valuable to give back to the Americans.

"I don't know how they convinced our people it was me who died in space, but they did. Then they set about calling me Viktor, I suppose in order to try to indoctrinate me to my new life in a Russian prison. Of course, I had one all to myself, but it was no less a prison for that."

"Tori," Russell said from the edge of the pool behind her, "the deadline."

She turned. "Russ, this is my brother Greg! It was the Russian cosmonaut who died in space, not him. The Russians have been holding him here."

"Hey, Jesus Christ." He squatted down. "What the hell have they done to you?"

"It's a long story."

"I'll bet," Russell said. His frown deepened. "Are you okay?"

"It's hard to say."

"Well, one thing's for sure, we've got to get you out of here. I can tell you there'll be a lot of people back home falling all over themselves to talk to you."

"Not so different from the Russians."

Russell cocked his head at Greg's cynical tone. "What am I missing here?"

"Time," Tori said to Russell, but she was looking past him to her brother.

Russell said, "Okay. Greg, believe me, I want to get the whole story, but right now—"

"Odysseus," Valeri interrupted, coming up behind Russell, "the KGB and the military have combined as we had suspected." His right shoulder was wrapped with surgical tape. "At dawn today the order will be given to invade the Baltic states of Latvia and Lithuania. At the same moment, the president will be assassinated by his own bodyguards."

"So soon," Greg said. "We're not yet altogether ready."

"Nevertheless, we're going to have to make do," Valeri said. He winced with pain. "We are going to have to deploy the MANDs."

"MANDs?" Russell said.

"Yes," Gregory Nunn said. "The Mobile Anti-personnel Nuclear Devices that Bernard Godwin has provided us with." He nodded at Valeri. "I agree. It's the only way to avert disaster." He swam to the edge of the pool. "Help me up."

Valeri and Russell bent down, lifted him from the pool. Valeri used only his left arm, but sucked in his breath sharply at the strain.

Greg looked at him inquiringly, and Valeri grinned. "Only a flesh wound," he said. "Not to worry."

"The bullet went clear through him," Russell said. "Only the muscle is damaged. I've stopped the bleeding, applied antibiotic cream, and I've wrapped him well. There's an excellent medical dispensary here. Still, he must see a surgeon."

"But not now," Valeri said.

During this exchange, Irina had climbed out of the pool. Now she went over to where the Hero's wheelchair sat. She brought it over and, as they sat him in it, she covered him with an oversized towel as she had seen Lara and Tatiana do. Then, as Tori emerged, dripping, Irina wrapped another towel around her, began to rub her shoulders to bring up the warmth.

Valeri wheeled Greg over to the communications area and, as Greg began to set up, he said, "Mars was almost right. But he never could have grasped the whole truth—or believed it.

"We have been building the concept of White Star for years. First, we had to fight state repression, then the people's fear of that repression. More recently, as pockets of nationalism in Georgia, Lithuania, the Ukraine, and other sectors of the Soviet Union sprang up through our encouragement, we've had to battle the divided nature of that nationalism. The Georgians cared only about Georgia, Ukrainians only about Ukrainians, and so on."

He paused, and they could all hear him breathing hard as he tried to block out the pain. The shock had dissipated, and the full brunt of the pain had set in. Of course, he had refused to take a painkiller.

"Then, eighteen months ago, Greg dropped into our laps like a star from heaven," he continued, gathering himself. "Greg was the Hero of the Odin-Galaktika II disaster. He was of Soviet descent, being incarcerated and interrogated almost daily by the KGB. He became a rallying point about which *all* the disparate nationalist elements could agree, a symbol to which every splinter group could relate. He was our Rosetta stone, our Shogun, bringing order out of chaos. And he became the leader of White Star."

They could hear Greg on the shortwave, talking in short bursts, moving the frequencies every twenty seconds in a preset pattern.

"From here," Valeri said, "the MANDs can be deployed quickly and efficiently."

"But even so," Russell said, "it's almost five in the morning. The invasion will begin clear across the country."

"Not if the orders are never implemented," Valeri said. "The MANDs are hidden here in Moscow." He smiled. "Actually, right around the corner from the church where you found me. They're in the basement of the Atomic Energy Administration on Staromonetny Street."

He nodded. "Odysseus—pardon me, Gregor—is seeing that our people get the MANDs immediately. With them, they can get to the generals in their villas in the Lenin Hills, the KGB leaders in the Lubyanka and Lefortovo. You see, our people are highly placed, and they need only go that far."

He bent down, retrieved the Kalishnikov that Irina had dropped. "Of course it won't be as straightforward as that. It never is. There will inevitably be complications, and before it's over, some of us may die. Which is why I must go. I must see that none of the generals slip our net. And then I must confront the president, to give him an account of this treachery first-hand."

"Isn't there anything we can do?" Russell asked.

Valeri smiled. "You and Miss Nunn have already done your part. Now you must stand aside and let us do ours. At this stage, it would not be helpful to anyone if news got out of American agents being involved in this crisis."

"What will happen here?" Tori said.

"I don't know. No one does," Valeri admitted. "But it is clear that some form of compromise between the Russians and the national minorities must be hammered out. A good degree of national autonomy is needed, but no one in White Star wants to cripple this country. We just want the repression and prejudice against us to end."

After Greg was finished on the shortwave, Russell took over to send a coded signal via the Berlin station to Mall Central. Irina took Tori into the shower and changing room, showed her where Tatiana and Lara kept their clothes.

Irina was in the shower, and Tori was just finishing dressing, when Greg wheeled himself in.

"It's good to see you, Tori. You can't know how good."

Tori knelt in front of him. "What's happened to you, Greg? Mom and Dad will be so frightened when they see you."

He looked into her eyes, said, "I don't think so."

512

"What do you mean?"

Greg reached out, gripped her shoulders. "They know, Tori."

"Mom and Dad know you're alive?" Her face was a mask of shock. "But how?"

Then something flashed in her mind. Russell saying, *How the devil is Bernard getting the funds to buy these nuclear weapons?* And, with fingers half paralyzed, she fumbled out the photo that Ariel had pressed into her hands at the point of death. *But there must be something more to this photo. What's so incriminating about it?* Russell had said. *Bernard could have gone to San Francisco for any one of a million reasons.*

Tori looked past Ariel in the foreground, the bronze sundial, the little girl playing in the park. She saw Bernard in the lower left-hand corner of the frame, and then, coming toward him, *coming to meet him,* the couple.

She peered through the gloom. Could it be? Did the photo show Tori's mother and father meeting Bernard Godwin in a San Francisco park? To discuss financing? Were Ellis and Laura Nunn financing White Star? Was it their money that Bernard used to buy the MANDs from the Japanese coalition?

And then it all clicked together.

Tori said with a bit of wonder in her voice, "Valeri contacted Bernard and told him about you, didn't he, Greg? And then Bernard went to Dad. He told him you were alive, that this was Dad's chance to help free the people of the Soviet Union."

She saw the truth in Greg's eyes. "Jesus Christ, Bernard wasn't content with roping me into his secret world, he had to drag Mom and Dad in after me."

"I don't think it was quite as simple as that," Greg said softly. "I think Dad and Mom decided on their own—"

"No, no," Tori said heatedly. "You don't know Bernard as I've come to. He coerced them—maybe not directly—Dad isn't so easily coercible. But even he has his weak spot. You. I've no doubt that Bernard used you to get Dad's and Mom's backing."

"I think you're giving too much power to Bernard, and not enough credit to Mom and Dad."

"Bernard's gone too far this time," she said grimly.

"But don't you see the good he's done? Bernard's opened up the door, and for the first time in decades a new light is shining in."

"But at what cost?" Tori said. "Greg, you don't know how much blood has been spilled because of him."

"I know how much blood has spilled here over the past eigh-

513

teen months, and how much more would have been spilled without his efforts—and yours.''

Tori knew he was right—but she also knew that Bernard had to be taught a lesson. His free reign above the law must be put to an end.

"Tori, at least talk to Dad before you make up your mind," Greg said.

"We'll both talk to him," Tori said. "I'm taking you home."

"No." In the electric silence Greg said, "I'm not going back to America. I can't leave here, not now. There's too much to do. I've made too many friends, bound myself with too many unbreakable ties."

"Greg, you can't mean it!"

"But I do." Seeing her stricken look, he said, "How can I explain it to you?" He thought a moment. "Did Dad ever tell you the story of the Zen Policeman?"

"Yes," Tori said so softly he had to bend close to hear her.

"Well, that's me, Tori. The Zen Policeman, locked away at the crossroads of an eerie corridor, in a strange structure, in an alien land. But I've come there for a reason—believe me I've had enough time to come to understand that—and it's a reason that's larger than I am as an individual."

"But what about our family? What about home?"

"My family will come see me, God willing. And as far as home is concerned, it's no longer here for me. I have another home. It's inside myself now."

Tori began to cry. "Greg, Greg. I've just found you. I don't want to lose you again."

"Ah, Tori. Who are you weeping for? Me? Or yourself?" He put his hand under her chin, lifted her head up. "Don't you see that you can be through living in my shadow?"

She tried to laugh through her tears. "But who'll help me with Mom and Dad? You know I can't cope with them without you."

"You don't mean that, Tori. You never needed me to intercede with Mom and Dad, you just thought you did. It was easier to want my relationship with them, than to fight for your own." He kissed her lightly. "This is *your* life, Tori. Have the courage to live it."

At that moment Russell stuck his head into the room. "What's taking you so long? I've gotten a reply from Bernard. He wants us back in the States right away."

Irina came out of the shower cubicle with a towel wrapped

around her. She looked from Greg to Tori's tear-streaked face. "Is everything all right?" she asked.

"It's just the good-byes," Tori said, wiping away her tears. "I hate long ones."

She took Russell's hand, stared once more into those angel eyes.

Greg said, "Give my regards to Diana's Garden," as Irina slipped an arm around his shoulders. And then, because he was anxious for her, "You'll talk to Dad. Promise me you will."

Tori said, "I'll give them both your love."

Just before she turned away, Greg said enigmatically, "Remember the Zen Policeman."

Tori saw the small smile on his face, and wondered at its meaning all during the long flight home.

HOME

LOS ANGELES/STAR TOWN

Tori returned to Los Angeles and Diana's Garden in the midst of a dreadful heat wave that had kept polluted air inverted over the sprawling city for more than a week. Children and people over the age of sixty-five or with breathing disorders were being warned to stay inside. It was a Los Angeles not that much different from the Tokyo they had so recently left.

Russell told her he was staying at the airport to wait for Bernard's flight in from the East Coast. Tori said that she was not going to stay. They sat facing one another for a time in the dimly lit interior of the 727. They both seemed in an emotional as well as a physical limbo. They had slept fitfully on the flight home, both still too tired to feel the full extent of their exhaustion.

At last Russell said, ''Just before we landed, we got a fax from Bernard sending us his heartiest congratulations.''

''Honestly, I don't know whether to laugh or cry.''

''Me neither.''

''I don't understand.'' Tori looked at him. ''After all that's happened, how can you wait for him here, as if it's business as usual?''

"I've still got a job to do."

Russell leaned over, poured himself coffee, stirred in sugar. "After Moscow, we know it isn't so cut and dried, is it?" He sipped some coffee. "Is Bernard guilty? And if so, of what? And is it anything we ourselves aren't guilty of as well? I'm no judge in these matters, Tori, and neither, I suspect, are you. The truth is buried too deeply under conflicting layers of altruism and obsession. In any case, I've got to work things out with Bernard during the debriefing, come to some sort of compromise, or I'll have to quit the Mall."

She smiled. "At least that's not the career man I used to know talking."

"That Russell Slade is dead." He frowned. "But you should be here when Bernard arrives. He'll be here any minute."

"Debriefing or no debriefing, Bernard can wait," Tori said, kissing him. "I can't. My family comes first now. Besides, I'm not ready yet to confront him. I need some time to get this all in perspective. If I don't know how I feel about him, I'm sure to make a shambles of the debriefing."

Russell said, "Sure," but something in his eyes gave her pause.

"What is it, Russ?"

"Listen," he said, holding on to her, "you're not going to pull one of your patented stunts and disappear over the horizon?"

"No," she said seriously. "I don't have reason to do that anymore."

Still, he would not let her go. "We have so much to say to each other."

She touched him on the cheek. "Are you afraid we won't have the time?"

Russell poured himself more coffee. "When I was in college, I had a recurring dream about coming to the end of a vast, flat, featureless plain across which I had been walking for years. In front of me was a sheer drop into blackness, and I would wake up, terrified because I did not want to take another step forward." He looked at her. "Now I think I'd prefer stepping over the edge than staying on that flat, featureless plain."

"Then we'll step over it together," Tori said. She threw her arms around him, kissed him good-bye. "We'll have as much time as we need, I promise you."

520

She went off the plane. There was a sickly, burnt smell in the brown air, as if all of Los Angeles was on fire. With her diplomatic credentials, she passed quickly through Customs and Immigration. She stopped to get some work done at the Mall facility at the airport. Russell was so mobile he had insisted that the Mall have stations at the airports in Washington, New York, Los Angeles, and San Francisco.

It was there that Tori ran into Bernard Godwin. They stood in silence, looking at one another for some time.

"Ah, the prodigal returns," Bernard said. Oddly, he seemed smaller than she remembered. But that patrician countenance had not changed. "Can I buy you a cup of coffee?"

"No."

"I'd like a chance to talk to you."

"Russell's waiting." Tori got her work back. She signed the receipt with Russell's name, thanked the agent.

Bernard started all over again. "You and Russell did one helluva job."

"For you," Tori said at length. "Only for you, Bernard."

"That's nonsense and you know it."

Tori said nothing.

"What's the matter? I gave you everything you wanted: reinstatement, a field command, Russell. I even gave you your brother back."

Bastard, Tori thought. He deserves to be cut off at the knees. And then she told him how Hitasura had used him to further the manufacture and distribution of the supercocaine. She saw the blood drain from Bernard's face by degrees. He put one hand out to steady himself. She did not make a move to help him.

When she was finished, she said, "It's important to remember that there's a price tag for everything, Bernard. Even freedom."

She left him there, shaken and mute. She had thought that telling him would make her feel better. She was wrong.

When Tori arrived at Diana's Garden, Laura Nunn was over at Universal, shooting something called *The Black Fox Dossier*. It was a spy film. She played the mother of the hero. Very fitting.

On the other hand, to Tori's utter astonishment, Ellis Nunn had taken the day off. He had spent the hour from six to seven in the morning making his essential overseas calls from his den in the huge house. Laura Nunn's limo had picked her up at five to take her to the studio for makeup.

521

Tori had arrived after her mother had left, but before anyone else was stirring. She had let herself into the house, had left whatever baggage she had in the enormous entrance hall, and had stolen up to bed. She had given her parents no notice of her coming but, as usual, her room was immaculate, ready for her. She collapsed gratefully onto her bed.

When she woke up, she looked out her window, saw her father strolling beside the pool. The sunlight, already red and dripping with heat, fell across his broad shoulders. In a moment he stopped, looked up toward Tori's bedroom window, and she saw him full on.

She was immediately struck by this fact: no matter how much time and energy he had spent trying to be American, he still had that classic Russian face. It was a beautifully sculptured face, rugged but somehow not harsh. His eyes, so similar to his children's, gave his countenance its splash of warmth and gentleness. Tori could imagine him striding purposefully down Gorky Street.

A half hour later, she joined Ellis Nunn in the dining room where a prodigious buffet breakfast had been laid out. He kissed her on both cheeks, in the traditional manner.

"Dobro pojalovatz," he said in Russian. Welcome home. "I'm damn glad you're in one piece." He gestured. "You must be starved. At least your mother thought so. She dragged Maria out of bed at an ungodly hour to prepare all this."

"Mom was gone when I arrived. She's on the set. I got all the hot news from Maria on my way downstairs."

"Mmm. Well, Maria must have seen your bags in the entrance and done this on her own. She always did have a soft spot for you."

That was when Tori trotted out the photograph the Mall people had made at their LAX airport facility.

Ellis Nunn took the revelation with admirable sangfroid. "Imagine," he said. "Bernard and me caught in the act." He bent over, peering more closely at the sixteen-by-twenty-inch blowup of Ariel Solares's photo. "There I am with your mother, coming to meet Bernard. By God, that's eerie to see on film."

"It's a good thing the picture was taken by one of Bernard's own agents."

Ellis Nunn nodded. "Yes. I suppose it is."

When it appeared that neither of them was hungry, they drifted outside. They began to walk the grounds, as Ellis Nunn loved to do, first by the pool, and then into the sun-dappled gardens. The scent of lime was everywhere.

Tori ducked her head. "Why didn't you ever tell me about La Lumière d'Or?" She was speaking of the American-owned French firm Koi had told her about—which she now knew was owned by her father—that was the conduit for the MANDs' hafnium.

"What was there to tell? I have subsidiaries in Italy, Spain, Hong Kong, as well as France. I never told you about those, either. It never occurred to me that you'd be in the least interested."

Tori snorted. "I think I'd have been interested in La Lumière d'Or's extracurricular activities."

"They were none of your business." He looked at her. "Oh, don't look like that. I'd say the same thing to your mother if she ever asked. Which she never has."

"But she was involved with the scheme that you and Bernard—"

"Bernard talked to her independently. As a woman of means, your mother has always made her own business decisions. She's good at it and, anyway, it saves wear and tear on the both of us."

"How exactly did Bernard rope you into paying for these MANDs? He told you about Greg, right?"

"Well, first of all, Bernard didn't rope your mother and me into anything. We both went into this with our eyes wide open. He outlined the risks."

Tori again heard Bernard Godwin's voice saying, *No matter what we become involved in, we would never be brought before a court of law.*

"Some risks," she said.

Ellis Nunn stopped, turned toward her. "I meant the risks to Greg and you, not to your mother or myself."

"Oh." Tori did not know what to say.

They continued their walk. They strolled beneath the pergola, losing themselves in the blooms and vines of high summer. Tori thought of her father's tales of the Georgian peasants toiling heroically in their fields.

"What was it like there?"

Tori knew he meant Russia. "It's not like home, Aunty Em."

He grunted, and she remembered belatedly how he used to admonish her for using her wit at inappropriate times.

523

"I found Moscow . . . strange," she said immediately. "It was not what I had expected."

"Did you like it?"

Tori suspected that her answer was important to him, so she thought about it for some time before she spoke. "I didn't hate it," she said slowly. "I felt uncomfortable there, but that may just have been the circumstances. But it also had an—I don't know—a haunting quality, I guess you could say."

"Yes," Ellis Nunn said, and Tori could see that he was remembering his childhood, and that that past was as clear to him as was this dawning day.

"You didn't fully answer my question about how Bernard got you and Mom involved."

"I know."

There was silence for a time. Ellis Nunn stopped them in the center of the pergola. The wisteria twined over their heads, creating a cool, green bower.

"How did Greg seem to you?"

"Changed," Tori said, and she saw her father wince. "It's only to be expected, after what he's been through."

"Which is what? Even Bernard had no idea what the Russians were doing with him or why they were keeping him captive."

"It seems that he and his Russian cosmonaut counterpart were part of a highly secret experiment involving controlled exposure to cosmic rays."

"Good God." Tori could see her father shaking. In a moment he said, "We must make a pact. We will never under any circumstances tell your mother this."

"But Greg told me you knew what he looked like."

"Either he was mistaken or he was misinformed."

"Then she won't be able to see him. His skin is silvery and slick like a dolphin's; he's hairless. And there may be other changes by the time you get to see him."

Ellis Nunn sat abruptly on the Roman-style stone bench in the center of the pergola. He stared at nothing. "Ah," he said softly. "What a world."

They remained like that for some time, father and daughter, near one another yet in other, more important ways, apart.

Tori knew that her heart should go out to her father, yet she felt nothing. He was still as closed off to her as he had ever been. She wondered what went on in his mind. Other than his quite obvious love for Greg, she could discover nothing.

Into her mind crept memories of Koi. The essence of that last afternoon with Koi glowed like a pearl in the viscera of her memory. Intense splashes of color, the flash of the blade, the first splash of blood, so shocking. The lights in the mountains glowing. Opening the door, letting the light in. Wasn't that something that Greg had said? Tori wondered how one person's death could open the door, let the light in.

And, yet, it was so. Koi's last moments had somehow changed Tori in the same way they had changed Koi herself. *I was also wearing white that afternoon,* Tori thought. *Her blood seeped onto me, into me. She was obsessed the way I was. But being with her allowed me to look into the mirror of my own soul, to see what for so long I had not wanted to see.*

I was addicted to violence, to the power wielding it gave me in a man's world. But in her I saw how utterly corrupting violence is. In the end Koi understood that about herself. So sad that she had to die; so sad that she could not change as I will make myself change.

Ellis Nunn shook himself. He became aware of Tori, watched for a time the look on her face. He opened his mouth as if to say something, then closed it.

Silence seeped in around them like the twining vines of the wisteria.

Laura Nunn arrived back in Diana's Garden just before midnight. She always seemed to have a knack of knowing where Tori was in the vast house, and so she swept into the library where Tori sat curled in a chair, reading Stanley Karnow's *Vietnam: A History*.

"Darling! It's so wonderful to have you home again!"

"Hello, Mother." Tori closed her book.

Laura Nunn frowned, arranged herself in the lotus position at the foot of Tori's chair. "Yoga keeps the body young and supple." She laughed a little at the stilted phrase, learned from her instructor.

Tori knew she was nervous. She sat up. She had never known her mother to be nervous.

Laura Nunn said, "I understand you saw Greg."

"Why didn't you tell me he was alive? Why did you let me go on grieving for him?"

"Oh, my darling, don't you think your father and I weren't grieving for the torture he was undergoing?"

"You're avoiding answering me."

"I've never been very good at handling inquisitions."

Tori moaned. "One question is not an inquisition, Mother."

"It's the tone I'm talking about, not the number."

"All right, I'm sorry." Tori knew she'd never get anywhere unless she acquiesced.

Laura Nunn nodded. "I was told not to."

"By whom?"

"Why, your father, of course."

Tori regarded her mother for some time before she said, "Was not telling me his idea?"

"Well, no," Laura Nunn said. "As I remember it, Bernard Godwin might have mentioned it."

"Do you know why?" One had to be patient, like dealing with a recalcitrant six-year-old.

"Of course I do," Laura Nunn said, angry. "He wanted to spare you." She nodded. "Yes, those were his words exactly. 'I want to spare Tori any unnecessary anxiety.' "

"I think I'm going to need a better explanation than that."

"You must ask your father, then."

Tori leaned forward. "I'm asking *you*."

"Don't do this to me, Tori. It's not my place—"

"You're my mother," Tori said heatedly. "It *is* your place."

Laura Nunn put her head in her hands, began to sob. Tori watched her, uncertain whether this scene was real, planned, or was simply another of her mother's ad-libbed "actor's exercises."

"I suppose you think I'm a foolish woman," Laura Nunn said when her sobbing subsided sufficiently. "Always involved in the latest fashions, always throwing lavish parties. No, don't bother to deny it. There's no point anymore." She wiped her eyes, sighed. "The truth is, I detest all that. The truth is, I'm a simple country girl who is, at heart, far too insecure to risk being herself."

She tossed her head, sniffled. "Anyway, I'm in the wrong city, the wrong profession for that. No one seems interested in finding out what's below the careful facade. In this town, when anyone bothers to scratch the surface, they do it to draw blood, not to discover what's underneath."

"Sort of like my profession," Tori said, seeing it for the first time.

Laura Nunn cocked her head thoughtfully. "Yes, now that you mention it, perhaps that's true. But only in a way." She reached out, put her hand gently, almost shyly, on her daughter's knee. "But you're so much more, Tori. I mean, you're the Zen Policeman, aren't you?"

Tori, her heart thudding heavily, could hear Greg saying, *Remember the Zen Policeman*, and his small smile that had stayed with her all the way home.

"What do you mean?"

"Well, I shouldn't tell you this, I suppose, but . . . Well, that's how your father thinks of you, as the Zen Policeman." She took Tori's hand in hers, squeezed it. "Oh, I know you think he's hard and uncaring. I know it hurts you to think that he loves Greg and not you. But that's so far from the truth it's laughable.

"The truth is that Greg was always the difficult one. He drove your father to distraction. He was a weak child, and always afraid, of the dark, of being alone, and especially of being in the water. I took to protecting him which, I'm afraid, angered your father further. 'A boy should look up to his father,' Ellis once told me sternly. 'Not his mother.'

"Anyway, Ellis fell madly in love with you from the moment I gave birth to you. You were such a happy baby. And you were strong and so very smart when he played with you. You so delighted him! You were going to fulfill his every dream.

"And then, inexplicably, you left him. You ran away—all the way to Japan, the other side of the world. You abandoned him, and he was utterly devastated."

Once again Tori heard Bernard Godwin's voice, saying, *Well, if life has taught me anything it's this: truth is a complex animal. Every time you think you've caught it by the tail, it turns around and bites you on the ass*.

"But my leaving wasn't inexplicable," Tori said.

"Oh, I know that, my dear. But your father couldn't—or wouldn't—understand. You were his universe, and you left him flat. That's all he could see."

"And he's been punishing me ever since?"

"No, no." Laura's eyes widened. "Oh, how could you ever think such a thing? Who do you think roused Maria out of bed this morning to make sure everything you liked to eat was ready for you when you awoke? He'd never admit it, of course.

"No, Ellis has been punishing himself. He's convinced he failed you in some way. Otherwise, he reasons, why would you have left so suddenly, so utterly."

She rose up, kissed Tori warmly on the lips. "We're so proud of what you do." She smiled a little. "Do you see now why he became involved with Bernard? It was only partially for Greg's sake, and for the sake of his own Soviet heritage.

"Bernard gave us no guarantees that what we would do would help Greg in any way. But your father saw a way to become, if only peripherally, a part of your life again. He never admitted that to me, but I can assure you, darling, that this was his main reason for accepting Bernard's offer."

Laura Nunn stroked Tori's hair, wiped away her daughter's tears, and smiled. "You know, in the beginning Bernard said he could give us no assurances that Greg would be protected. He said he had no agents whom he could trust enough, and do you know what your father said? 'Bernard, you're wrong. You have the Zen Policeman.' "

Tori found her father taking his laps in the pool. He had come home early from work, but had not sought her out. It was late in the afternoon of the following day. The light slanted in through the palms and the cropped Norfolk pines, illuminating the surface of the water, Ellis Nunn's powerful shoulder muscles as he worked up and down the length of the pool.

Tori, in a one-piece bathing suit, slipped silently into the water. She was immediately reminded of Greg, and felt a pang of mingled joy and sadness.

For a while she did nothing but parallel her father, and he, intent on his exercise, did not let up his pace, though surely he was aware of her presence.

When, finally, he broke off, he said, "It's nice having you in the pool with me again."

They hung in the water with the California sun burnishing their faces. The leaves rustled briefly as the ghost of a breeze came up.

"Dad," Tori began, "I'm sorry I left you."

Ellis Nunn turned away, but Tori swam in front of him. "You know, sooner or later, I had to leave." She searched his face. "Dad?" She took a deep breath. "It wasn't anything you did."

"Your mother's been talking to you," he said tightly.

"Don't be angry with her. It was time for me to know. I think she understood that."

"You shouldn't know these things."

She moved closer to him. "Why not?"

"You'll think I'm weak." He lifted his head up. The sunlight struck him. "I'm not weak, you know."

"I know, Dad." She watched him. "Don't you think it's important I understand who you are?"

He looked at her finally. "Why did you do it? Why did you run away?"

Tori was still for some time. "I left because I was stifling here. Everything was so unreal, the parties, the money, the people. It got so I was lost in it all—lost in the glitter of the forest. Don't you see, Dad, I had to go far enough away to find a space for myself that wasn't cluttered by all of this."

"You hated it here, didn't you?"

"No." Tori shook her head. "Don't think that. I was so lost, I couldn't possibly have known what it was I felt. Try to understand, Dad. Only time could allow me to do that."

Ellis Nunn looked into his daughter's angel eyes. "I'll never forget. You were such a beautiful baby. You used to love to crawl across me and, laughing, pound your tiny fists against my chest." So it was true, there were other things beside his childhood in Russia that he remembered with fondness. He sniffed, rubbed his nose. "We never let each other inside, did we? Why was that, do you think?"

"Maybe we were always too much alike. We each had expectations, and they were unfulfilled because they were unrealistic."

Ellis Nunn thought about that for some time, then he nodded. "You were always a smart girl," he said.

"That was your doing, Dad," Tori said.

Ellis Nunn reached out for his daughter, crushed her against him.

"Dobro pojalovatz, Papa," Tori said. Welcome home.

Gregory Nunn was sleeping on Arbat's back. Irina floated beside him. The worst was over. Valeri and his White Star Moscow contingent had managed to keep a semblance of order as they rounded up the conspirators.

One of Valeri's men had been killed by a KGB colonel in

Lefortovo before control had been effected by the firing of a MAND. That had gotten everyone's attention. Another had been wounded in the course of subduing a Red Army general. Valeri was now locked away with the premier, trying to hammer out the preliminary guidelines to a compromise.

Irina watched the play of light as it softly touched the Hero's face. She wanted very much to be with him, but he had been so exhausted, and he seemed so close to a state of grace that she did not want to wake him. But perhaps her thoughts betrayed her, because at that moment his eyes opened.

Irina felt the opalescent light from his gaze caress her like gentle sunlight.

"Did you sleep as well?" he asked.

"A little. Mostly, I was watching you sleep." She was so aware of him, it almost hurt. "Do you miss your sister?"

"Yes," he said. "But I miss other things more."

Irina nodded. "I understand."

"I know you do."

"I wonder," she said, "whether they will let me go with you."

"If I ask it, how can they refuse?"

"But I have no training."

"I will train you myself." He laughed. "I hope you aren't claustrophobic."

Irina said seriously, "How can you be so sure they will expend the time and money to send us back there?"

Gregory Nunn shrugged. "Human nature. It isn't a matter of speculation, you know. They can't help themselves. Once they assimilate what it was I encountered up there in space between the stars, they will have no other choice. Man's innate curiosity is well-documented."

In the pool, beside them, Arbat stirred. She rolled, gazing up at them with an eye like black ice. She gave a little call, which Greg echoed. She rolled back over.

Irina said, "What will we find up there?"

"Do you really want to know before we get there?"

"Yes."

There was silence for a time, and Irina, able now to differentiate the natures of silence, felt this one accumulating like golden weights upon a scale. She could discern in Greg's face a light like the sun rising in the desert: clear and radiant, an illumination from which nothing could be hidden. She felt her love for him and for the enigma he had discovered enfolding them both like the eternal cloak of the cosmos. A joy filled her, his joy as well as hers, and she knew what he would say before he said it.

"We will find time." Greg gave her his slow, enigmatic smile. "Time enough for the patience of angels."

ABOUT THE AUTHOR

Eric V. Lustbader is the author of the bestselling novels *White Ninja*, *French Kiss*, *Shan*, *Jian*, *The Miko*, *The Ninja*, and *Black Heart*. He lives in New York City and in Southampton, Long Island, with his wife, editor Victoria Schochet Lustbader.

ERIC
LUSTBADER